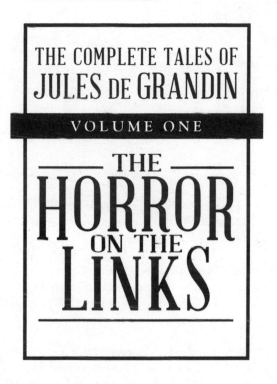

THE COMPLETE TALES OF
JULES DE GRANDIN

VOLUME ONE

THE
HORROR
ON THE
LINKS

SEABURY QUINN

EDITED BY GEORGE A. VANDERBURGH

Night Shade Books
New York

Night Shade books may be purchased in bulk at special discounts for sales promotion, corporate gifts, fund-raising, or educational purposes. Special editions can also be created to specifications. For details, contact the Special Sales Department, Night Shade Books, 307 West 36th Street, 11th Floor, New York, NY 10018 or info@skyhorsepublishing.com.

Night Shade Books® is a registered trademark of Skyhorse Publishing, Inc.®, a Delaware corporation.

Visit our website at www.nightshadebooks.com.

10 9 8 7 6 5 4 3 2 1

Library of Congress Cataloging-in-Publication Data is available on file.

Print ISBN: 978-1-59780-893-4
Ebook ISBN: 978-1-59780-909-2

Cover illustration by Donato Giancola
Cover design by Claudia Noble

Printed in the United States of America

TABLE OF CONTENTS

*Cover by Joseph Doolin
+Cover by C. Barker Petrie, Jr.
^Cover by Curtis C. Senf

THE COMPLETE TALES OF Jules de Grandin is dedicated to the memory of Robert E. Weinberg, who passed away in fall of 2016. Weinberg, who edited the six-volume paperback series of de Grandin stories in the 1970s, also supplied many original issues of *Weird Tales* magazine from his personal collection so that Seabury Quinn's work could be carefully scanned and transcribed digitally. Without his knowledge of the material and his editorial guidance, as well as his passion for Quinn's work over a long period of time (when admirers of the Jules de Grandin stories were often difficult to come by), this series would not have been possible, and we owe him our deepest gratitude and respect.

Introduction

by George A. Vanderburgh and Robert E. Weinberg

W EIRD TALES, THE SELF-DESCRIBED "Unique Magazine," and one of the most influential Golden Age pulp magazines in the first half of the twentieth century, was home to a number of now-well-recognized names, including Robert Bloch, August Derleth, Robert E. Howard, H. P. Lovecraft, Clark Ashton Smith, and Manly Wade Wellman.

But among such stiff competition was another writer, more popular at the time than all of the aforementioned authors, and paid at a higher rate because of it. Over the course of ninety-two stories and a serialized novel, his most endearing character captivated pulp magazine readers for nearly three decades, during which time he received more front cover illustrations accompanying his stories than any of his fellow contributors.

The writer's name was Seabury Quinn, and his character was the French occult detective Jules de Grandin.

Perhaps you've never heard of de Grandin, his indefatigable assistant Dr. Trowbridge, or the fictional town of Harrisonville, New Jersey. Perhaps you've never even heard of Seabury Quinn (or maybe only in passing, as a historical footnote in one of the many essays and reprinted collections of Quinn's now-more-revered contemporaries). Certainly, de Grandin was not the first occult detective—Algernon Blackwood's John Silence, Hodgson's Thomas Carnacki, and Sax Rohmer's Moris Klaw preceded him—nor was he the last, as Wellman's John Thunstone, Margery Lawrence's Miles Pennoyer, and Joseph Payne Brennan's Lucius Leffing all either overlapped with the end of de Grandin's run or followed him. And without doubt de Grandin shares more than a passing resemblance to both Sir Arthur Conan Doyle's Sherlock Holmes (especially with his Dr. Watson-like sidekick) and Agatha Christie's Hercule Poirot.

Indeed, even if you were to seek out a de Grandin story, your options over the years would have been limited. Unlike Lovecraft, Smith, Wellman, Bloch, and other *Weird Tales* contributors, the publication history of the Jules de Grandin tales is spotty at best. In 1966, Arkham House printed roughly 2,000 copies of *The Phantom-Fighter*, a selection of ten early works. In the late 1970s, Popular Library published six paperback volumes of approximately thirty-five assorted tales, but they are now long out of print. In 2001, the specialty press The Battered Silicon Dispatch Box released an oversized, three-volume hardcover set of every de Grandin story (the first time all the stories had been collected), and, while still in production, the set is unavailable to the general trade.

So, given how obscure Quinn and his character might seem today, it's justifiably hard to understand how popular these stories originally were, or how frequently new ones were written. But let the numbers tell the tale: from October 1925 (when the very first de Grandin story was released) to December 1933, a roughly eight-year span, de Grandin stories appeared in an incredible sixty-two of the ninety-six issues that *Weird Tales* published, totaling well-over three-quarters of a million words. Letter after letter to the magazine's editor demanded further adventures from the supernatural detective.

If Quinn loomed large in the mind of pulp readers during the magazine's hey-day, then why has his name fallen on deaf ears since? Aside from the relative unavailability of his work, the truth is that Quinn has been successfully marginalized over the years by many critics, who have often dismissed him as simply a hack writer. The de Grandin stories are routinely criticized as being of little worth, and dismissed as unimportant to the development of weird fiction. A common argument, propped up by suspiciously circular reasoning, concludes that Quinn was not the most popular writer for *Weird Tales*, just the most prolific.

These critics seem troubled that the same audience who read and appreciated the work of Lovecraft, Smith, and Howard could also enjoy the exploits of the French ghostbuster. And while it would be far from the truth to suggest that the literary merits of the de Grandin stories exceed those of some of his contemporaries' tales, Quinn was a much more skillful writer, and the adventures of his occult detective more enjoyable to read, than most critics are willing to acknowledge. In the second half of the twentieth century, as the literary value of some pulp-fiction writers began to be reconsidered, Quinn proved to be the perfect whipping boy for early advocates attempting to destigmatize weird fiction: He was the hack author who churned out formulaic prose for a quick paycheck. Anticipating charges that a literary reassessment of Lovecraft would require reevaluating the entire genre along with him, an arbitrary line was quickly drawn in the sand, and as the standard-bearer of pulp fiction's popularity, the creator of Jules de Grandin found himself on the wrong side of that line.

First and foremost, it must be understood that Quinn wrote to make money, and he was far from the archetypal "starving artist." At the same time that his Jules de Grandin stories were running in *Weird Tales*, he had a similar series of detective stories publishing in *Real Detective Tales*. Quinn was writing two continuing series at once throughout the 1920s, composing approximately twenty-five thousand words a month on a manual typewriter. Maintaining originality under such a grueling schedule would be difficult for any author, and even though the de Grandin stories follow a recognizable formula, Quinn still managed to produce one striking story after another. It should also be noted that the tendency to recycle plots and ideas for different markets was very similar to the writing practices of *Weird Tales*'s other prolific and popular writer, Robert E. Howard, who is often excused for these habits, rather than criticized for them.

Throughout his many adventures, the distinctive French detective changed little. His penchant for amusingly French exclamations was a constant through all ninety-three works, as was his taste for cigars and brandy after (and sometimes before) a hard day's work, and his crime-solving styles and methods remained remarkably consistent. From time to time, some new skill or bit of knowledge was revealed to the reader, but in most other respects the Jules de Grandin of "The Horror on the Links" was the same as the hero of the last story in the series, published twenty-five years later.

> He was a perfect example of the rare French blond type, rather under medium height, but with a military erectness of carriage that made him look several inches taller than he really was. His light-blue eyes were small and exceedingly deep-set, and would have been humorous had it not been for the curiously cold directness of their gaze. With his wide mouth, light mustache waxed at the ends in two perfectly horizontal points, and those twinkling, stock-taking eyes, he reminded me of an alert tomcat.

Thus is de Grandin described by Dr. Trowbridge in the duo's first meeting in 1925. His personal history is dribbled throughout the stories: de Grandin was born and raised in France, attended medical school, became a prominent surgeon, and in the Great War served first as a medical officer, then as a member of the intelligence service. After the war, he traveled the world in the service of French Intelligence. His age is never given, but it's generally assumed that the occult detective is in his early forties.

Samuel Trowbridge, on the other hand, is a typical conservative small-town doctor of the first half of the twentieth century (as described by Quinn, he is a cross between an honest brother of George Bernard Shaw and former Chief Justice of the United States Charles Evans Hughes). Bald and bewhiskered, most—if not all—of his life was spent in the same town. Trowbridge is old-fashioned and somewhat conservative, a member of the Knights Templar, a vestryman in the Episcopal Church, and a staunch Republican.

While the two men are dissimilar in many ways, they are also very much alike. Both are fine doctors and surgeons. Trowbridge might complain from time to time about de Grandin's wild adventures, but he always goes along with them; there is no thought, ever, of leaving de Grandin to fight his battles alone. More than any other trait, though, they are two men with one mission, and perhaps for that reason they remained friends for all of their ninety-three adventures and countless trials.

The majority of Quinn's de Grandin stories take place in or near Harrisonville, New Jersey, a fictional community that rivals (with its fiends, hauntings, ghouls, werewolves, vampires, voodoo, witchcraft, and zombies) Lovecraft's own Arkham, Massachusetts. For more recent examples of a supernatural-infested community, one need look no further than the modern version of pulp-fiction narratives . . . television. *Buffy the Vampire Slayer*'s Sunnydale, California, and *The Night Strangler*'s Seattle both reflect the structural needs of this type of supernatural narrative.

Early in the series, de Grandin is presented as Trowbridge's temporary house guest, having travelled to the United States to study both medicine and modern police techniques, but Quinn quickly realized that the series was due for a long run and recognized that too much globe-trotting would make the stories unwieldy. A familiar setting would be needed to keep the main focus of each tale on the events themselves. Harrisonville, a medium-sized town outside New York City, was completely imaginary, but served that purpose.

Most of the de Grandin stories feature beautiful girls in peril. Quinn discovered early on that Farnsworth Wright, *Weird Tales*'s editor from 1924 to 1940, believed nude women on the cover sold more copies, so when writing he was careful to always feature a scene that could translate to appropriately salacious artwork. Quinn also realized that his readers wanted adventures with love and romance as central themes, so even his most frightening tales were given happy endings (. . . of a sort).

And yet the de Grandin adventures are set apart from the stories they were published alongside by their often explicit and bloody content. Quinn predated the work of Clive Barker and the splatterpunk writers by approximately fifty years, but, using his medical background, he wrote some truly terrifying horror stories; tales like "The House of Horror" and "The House Where Time Stood Still" feature some of the most hideous descriptions of mutilated humans ever set down on paper. The victims of the mad doctor in "The House of Horror" in particular must rank near the top of the list of medical monstrosities in fiction.

Another element that set Quinn's occult detective apart from others was his pioneering use of modern science in the fight against ancient superstitions.

De Grandin fought vampires, werewolves, and even mummies in his many adventures, but oftentimes relied on the latest technology to save the day. The Frenchman put it best in a conversation with Dr. Trowbridge at the end of "The Blood-Flower":

> "And wasn't there some old legend to the effect that a werewolf could only be killed with a silver bullet?"
> "Ah, bah," he replied with a laugh. "What did those old legend-mongers know of the power of modern firearms? . . . When I did shoot that wolfman, my friend, I had something more powerful than superstition in my hand. *Morbleu*, but I did shoot a hole in him large enough for him to have walked through."

Quinn didn't completely abandon the use of holy water, ancient relics, and magical charms to defeat supernatural entities, but he made it clear that de Grandin understood that there was a place for modern technology as well as old folklore when it came to fighting monsters. Nor was de Grandin himself above using violence to fight his enemies. Oftentimes, the French occult investigator served as judge, jury and executioner when dealing with madmen, deranged doctors, and evil masterminds. There was little mercy in his stories for those who used dark forces.

While sex was heavily insinuated but rarely covered explicitly in the pulps, except in the most general of terms, Quinn again was willing to go where few other writers would dare. Sexual slavery, lesbianism, and even incest played roles in his writing over the years, challenging the moral values of the day.

In the end, there's no denying that the de Grandin stories are pulp fiction. Many characters are little more than assorted clichés bundled together. De Grandin is a model hero, a French expert on the occult, and never at a loss when battling the most evil of monsters. Dr. Trowbridge remains the steadfast companion, much in the Dr. Watson tradition, always doubting but inevitably following his friend's advice. Quinn wrote for the masses, and he didn't spend pages describing landscapes when there was always more action unfolding.

The Jules de Grandin stories were written as serial entertainment, with the legitimate expectation that they would not be read back to back. While all of the adventures are good fun, the best way to properly enjoy them is over an extended period of time. Plowing through one story after another will lessen their impact, and greatly cut down on the excitement and fun of reading them. One story a week, which would stretch out this entire five-volume series over two years, might be the perfect amount of time needed to fully enjoy these tales of the occult and the macabre. They might not be great literature, but they don't pretend to be. They're pulp adventures, and even after seventy-five years, the stories read well.

Additionally, though the specific aesthetic values of *Weird Tales* readers were vastly different than those of today's readers, one can see clearly see the continuing allure of these types of supernatural adventures, and the long shadow that they cast over twentieth and early twenty-first century popular culture. Sure, these stories are formulaic, but it is a recipe that continues to be popular to this day. The formula of the occult detective, the protector who stands between us and the monsters of the night, can be seen time and time again in the urban fantasy and paranormal romance categories of commercial fiction, and is prevalent in today's television and movies. Given the ubiquity and contemporary popularity of this type of narrative, it's actually not at all surprising that Seabury Quinn was the most popular contributor to *Weird Tales*.

We are proud to present the first of five volumes reprinting every Jules de Grandin story written by Seabury Quinn. Organized chronologically, as they originally appeared in *Weird Tales* magazine, this is the first time that the collected de Grandin stories have been made available in trade editions.

Each volume has been graced by tremendous artwork from renowned artist Donato Giancola, who has given Quinn's legendary character an irresistible combination of grace, cunning and timelessness. We couldn't have asked for a better way to introduce "the occult Hercule Poirot" to a new generation of readers.

Finally, if Seabury Quinn is watching from above, and closely scrutinizing the shelves of bookstores, he would undoubtedly be pleased as punch, and proud as all get-out, to find his creation, Dr. Jules de Grandin, rising once again in the minds of readers around the world, battling the forces of darkness . . . wherever, whoever, or whatever the nature of their evil might be.

When the Jaws of Darkness Open,
Only Jules de Grandin Stands in Satan's Way!

Robert E. Weinberg
Chicago, Illinois, USA

and

George A. Vanderburgh
Lake Eugenia, Ontario, Canada

23 September 2016

The Horror on the Links

I T MUST HAVE BEEN past midnight when the skirling of my bedside telephone awakened me, for I could see the moon well down toward the horizon as I looked through the window while reaching for the instrument.

"Dr. Trowbridge," an excited voice bored through the receiver, "this is Mrs. Maitland. Can you come over right away? Something dreadful has happened to Paul!"

"Eh?" I answered half asleep. "What's wrong?"

"We—we don't know," she replied jerkily. "He's unconscious. You know, he'd been to the dance at the country dub with Gladys Phillips, and we'd been in bed for hours when we heard someone banging on the door. Mr. Maitland went down, and when he opened the door Paul fell into the hall. Oh, Doctor, he's been hurt dreadfully. Won't you please come right over?"

Physicians' sleep is like a park—public property. With a sigh I climbed out of bed and into my clothes, teased my superannuated motor to life and set out for the Maitland house.

Young Maitland lay on his bed, eyes closed, teeth clenched, his face set in an expression of unutterable dread, even in his unconsciousness. Across his shoulders and on the backs of his arms I found several long incised wounds, as though the flesh had been raked by a sharp pronged instrument.

I sterilized and bandaged the cuts and applied restoratives, wondering what sort of encounter had produced such hurts.

"Help! Help! O, God, help!" the lad muttered thickly, like a person trying to call out in a nightmare. "Oh, oh, it's got me; it's"—his words drowned in a gurgling, inarticulate cry of fear and he sat bolt upright, staring round with vacant, fear-filmed eyes.

"Easy, easy on, young fellow," I soothed. "Lie back, now; take it easy, you're all right. You're home in bed."

He looked uncomprehendingly at me a moment, then fell to babbling inanely. "The ape-thing—the ape-thing! It's got me! Open the door; for God's sake, open the door!"

"Here," I ordered gaffly as I drove my hypodermic into his arm, "none o' that. You quiet down."

The opiate took effect almost immediately, and I left him with his parents while I returned to catch up the raveled ends of my torn sleep.

H EADLINES SHRIEKED AT ME from the front page of the paper lying beside my breakfast grapefruit:

SUPER FIEND SOUGHT IN
GIRL'S SLAYING

Body of Young Woman Found Near Sedgemore
Country Club Mystifies Police—Criminal
Pervert Blamed for Killing—Arrest Imminent

Almost entirely denuded of clothing, marred by a score of terrible wounds, her face battered nearly past recognition and her neck broken, the body of pretty Sarah Humphreys, nineteen, a waitress in the employ of the Sedgemore Country Club, was found lying in one of the bunkers of the dub's golf course this morning by John Burroughs, a greens keeper. Miss Humphreys, who had been employed at the clubhouse for three months, completed her duties shortly before midnight, and, according to statements of fellow workers, declared she was going to take a short cut across the links to the Andover Road, where she could get a late bus to the city. Her body, terribly mutilated, was found about twenty-five yards from the road on the golf course this morning.

Between the golf links and the Andover Road is a dense growth of trees, and it is thought the young woman was attacked while walking along the path through the woods to the road. Deputy Coroner Nesbett, who examined the body, gave his opinion that she had been dead about five hours when found. She had not been criminally assaulted.

Several suspicious characters have been seen in the neighborhood of the club's grounds recently, and the police are checking up on their movements. An early arrest is expected.

"There's two gintelmen to see ye, sor." Nora McGinnis, my household factotum, interrupted my perusal of the paper. "'Tis Sergeant Costello an' a

Frinchman, or Eyetalian, or sumpin. They do be wantin' ter ax ye questions about th' murther of th' pore little Humphreys gurl."

"Ask *me* about the murder?" I protested. "Why, the first I knew of it was when I looked at this paper, and I'm not through reading the account of the crime yet."

"That's all right, Dr. Trowbridge," Detective Sergeant Costello answered with a laugh as he entered the dining room. "We don't figure on arrestin' you, but there's some questions we'll be askin', if you don't mind. This is Professor de Grandin of the Paris police. He's been doin' some work for his department over here, an' when this murder broke he offered th' chief his help. We'll be needin' it, too, I'm thinkin'. Professor de Grandin, Dr. Trowbridge," he waved an introductory hand from one of us to the other.

The professor bowed stiffly from the hips in continental fashion, then extended his hand with a friendly smile. He was a perfect example of the rare French blond type, rather under medium height, but with a military erectness of carriage that made him seem several inches taller than he actually was. His light blue eyes were small and exceedingly deep-set, and would have been humorous had it not been for the curiously cold directness of their gaze. With his blond mustache waxed at the ends in two perfectly horizontal points and those twinkling, stocktaking eyes, he reminded me of an alert tomcat. Like a cat's, too, was his lithe, noiseless step as he crossed the room to shake hands.

"I fear Monsieur Costello gives you the misapprehension, doctor," he said in a pleasant voice, almost devoid of accent. "It is entirely true I am connected with the *Service de Sûreté*, but not as a vocation. My principal work is at the University of Paris and St. Lazaire Hospital; at present I combine the vocation of *savant* with the avocation of criminologist. You see—"

"Why," I interrupted as I grasped his slim, strong hand, "you're Professor Jules de Grandin, the author of *Accelerated Evolution?*"

A quick, infectious grin swept across his mouth and was reflected in his eyes. "You know me, *hein?* Good, it is that I am among friends! However, at the moment our inquiries lie in quite another field. You have a patient, one Monsieur Paul Maitland, yes? He was set upon last night in the Andover Road, no?"

"I have a patient named Paul Maitland," I admitted, "but I don't know where he received his injuries."

"Nor do we," he answered with a smile, "but we shall inquire. You will go with us while we question him, no?"

"Why, yes," I acquiesced. "I should be looking in on him this morning, anyhow."

"AND NOW, YOUNG MONSIEUR," Professor de Grandin began when introductions had been completed, "you will please tell us what happened last night to you. Yes?"

Paul looked uncomfortably from one of us to the other and swallowed nervously. "I don't like to think of it," he confessed, "much less talk about it; but here's the truth, believe it or not:

"I took Gladys home from the club about eleven o'clock, for she had developed a headache. After I'd said good night to her I decided to go home and turn in, and had gotten nearly here when I reached in my pocket for a cigarette. My case was gone, and I remembered laying it on a window ledge just before my last dance.

"The Mater gave me that case last birthday, and I didn't want to lose it, so, instead of telephoning the club and asking one of the fellows to slip it in his pocket, like a fool I decided to drive back for it.

"You know—at least Dr. Trowbridge and Sergeant Costello do—the Andover Road dips down in a little valley and curves over by the edge of the golf course between the eighth and ninth holes. I'd just reached that part of the road nearest the links when I heard a woman scream twice—it really wasn't two screams, more like one and a half, for her second cry was shut off almost before it started.

"I had a gun in my pocket, a little .22 automatic—good thing I did, too—so I yanked it out and drew up at the roadside, leaving my engine running. That was lucky, too, believe me.

"I ran into the woods, yelling at the top of my voice, and there I saw something dark, like a woman's body, lying across the path. I started toward it when there was a rustling in the trees overhead and—*plop!*—something dropped right down in front of me.

"Gentlemen, I don't know what it was, but I know it wasn't human. It wasn't quite as tall as I, but it looked about twice as wide, and its hands hung down. Clear down to the ground.

"I yelled, 'What the hell goes on here?' and pointed my gun at it, and it didn't answer, just started jumping up and down, bouncing with its feet and hands on the ground at once. I tell you, it gave me the horrors.

"'Snap out of it,' I yelled again, 'or I'll blow your head off.' Next moment—I was so nervous and excited I didn't know what I was doing—I let fly with my pistol, right in the thing's face.

"That came near bein' my last shot, too. Believe me or not, that thing, whatever it was, reached out, snatched the gun out of my hand, and broke it. Yes, sir, snapped that pistol in two with its bare hands as easily as I could break a match.

"Then it was on me. I felt one of its hands go clear over my shoulder from breast to back in a single clutch, and it pulled me toward it. Ugh! It was hairy, sir. Hairy as an ape!"

"*Morbleu!* Yes? And then?" de Grandin prompted eagerly.

"Then I lunged out with all my might and kicked it on the shins. It released its grip a second, and I beat it. Ran as I never had on the quarter-mile track, jumped into my car and took off down the road with everything wide open. But I got these gashes in my back and arms before I got to the roadster. He made three or four grabs for me, and every one of 'em took the flesh away where his nails raked me. By the time I got home I was almost crazy with fright and pain and loss of blood. I remember kicking at the door and yelling for the folks to open, and then I went out like a light."

The boy paused and regarded us seriously. "You think that I'm the biggest liar out of jail, most likely, but I've been telling you the absolute, straight truth, sirs."

Costello looked skeptical, but de Grandin nodded eagerly, affirmatively. "But certainly you speak the truth, *mon vieux*," he agreed. "Now, tell me, if you can, this *poilu*, this hairy one, how was he dressed?"

"Um," Paul wrinkled his brow. "I can't say surely, for it was dark in the woods and I was pretty rattled, but—I—think it was in evening clothes. Yes; I'd swear to it. I saw his white shirt bosom."

"Ah?" de Grandin murmured. "A hairy thing, a fellow who leaps up and down like a mad monkey or a jumping-jack and wears the evening clothes? It is to think, *mes amis.*"

"I'll say it is," Costello agreed. "It is to think what sort o' hooch they're servin' to th' youngsters nowadays—or mebbe they can't take it like us old vets o' th' first World War—"

"Dr. Trowbridge is wanted on the 'phone, please," a maid's announcement cut his ponderous irony. "You can take it on this one, if you wish, sir. It's connected with the main line."

"This is Mrs. Comstock, doctor," a voice informed me. "Your cook told us you were at Mrs. Maitland's. Can you come to my house when you leave there? Mr. Manly, my daughter's fiancé, was hurt last night."

"Hurt last night?" I repeated.

"Yes, out by the country club."

"Very well, I'll be right over," I promised, and held out my hand to Professor de Grandin. "Sorry I have to run away," I apologized, "but another man was hurt at the club last night."

"*Pardieu!*" His little round blue eyes bored into mine. "That club, it are a most unhealthy place, *n'est-ce-pas?* May I accompany you? This other man may tell us something that we ought to know."

YOUNG MANLY'S INJURY PROVED to be a gunshot wound inflicted by a small caliber weapon, and was located in the left shoulder. He was reticent concerning it, and neither de Grandin nor I felt inclined to press him insistently, for Mrs. Comstock hovered in the sick room from our entrance till the treatment was concluded.

"*Nom d'un petit porc!*" the little Frenchman muttered as we left the Comstock residence. "He is close-mouthed, that one. Almost, it would appear—*pah!* I talk the rot. Let us go to the morgue, *cher collègue*. You shall drive me there in your motor and tell me what it is you see. Oft times you gentlemen of general practice see things that we specialists cannot because we wear the blinders of our specialties, *n'est-ce-pas?*"

In the cold, uncharitable light of the city mortuary we viewed the remains of poor little Sarah Humphreys. As the newspaper had said, she was disfigured by a score or more of wounds, running, for the most part, down her shoulders and arms in a series of converging lines, and incised deeply enough to reveal the bone where skin and flesh had been shorn through in places. On throat and neck were five distinct livid patches, one some three inches in size, roughly square, the other four extending in parallel lines almost completely round her neck, terminating in deeply pitted scars, as though the talons of some predatory beast had sunk into her flesh. But the most terrifying item of the grisly sight was the poor girl's face. Repeated blows had hammered her once-pretty features to a purpled level, and bits of sand and fine gravel still bedded in the cuticle told how her countenance must have been ground into the earth with terrific force. Never, since my days as emergency hospital interne, had I seen so sickening an array of injuries on a single body.

"And what is it you see, my friend?" the Frenchman asked in a low, raucous whisper. "You look, you meditate. You do think—what?"

"It's terrible," I began, but he cut me off impatiently.

"But certainly. One does not look to see the beautiful in the morgue. I ask for what you see, not for your aesthetic impressions. *Parbleu!*"

"If you want to know what interests me most," I answered, "it is those wounds on her shoulder and arms. Except in degree, they're exactly like those which I treated on Paul Maitland last night."

"Ah-*ha?*" His small blue eyes were dancing with excitement, his cat's-whiskers mustache was bristling more fiercely than ever. "Name of a little blue man! We begin to make the progress. Now,"—he touched the livid patches on the dead girl's throat daintily with the tip of a well manicured nail—"these marks, do they tell you something?"

I shook my head. "Possibly the bruise left by some sort of garrote," I hazarded. "They are too long and thick for fingerprints; besides, there's no thumb mark."

"Ha-ha." His laugh was mirthless as that of an actor in a high school play. "No thumb mark, you say? My dear sir, had there been a thumb mark I should have been all at sea. These marks are the stigmata of the truth of young Monsieur

Maitland's story. When were you last at *le jardin des plantes*, the how do you say him?—zoölogical garden?"

"The zoo?" I echoed wonderingly.

"*Précisément*, the zoo, as you call him. Have you never noted how the quadrumana take hold of a thing? I tell you, *cher collègue*, it is not very much of an exaggeration to say the thumb is the difference between man and monkey. Man and the chimpanzee grasp objects with the fingers, using the thumb as a fulcrum. The gorilla, the orangutan, the gibbon are all fools, they know not how to use their thumbs. Now see"—again he indicated the bruises on the dead girl's throat—"this large square patch, it is the mark of the heel of the hand, these circling lines, they are the fingers, and these wounds, they are nail prints. Name of an old and very wicked tomcat! It was the truth young Maitland told. It was an ape that he met in the wood. An ape in evening clothes! What do you make of that, *hein?*"

"God knows," I answered helplessly.

"Assuredly," he nodded solemnly. "*Le bon Dieu* truly knows, but me, I am determined that I shall know, too." Abruptly he turned from the dead girl and propelled me gently toward the door by the elbow. "No more, no more now," he declared. "You have your mission of help to the sick to perform; I also have some work to do. If you will take me to police headquarters I shall be obliged to you, and, if the imposition is not too great, may I dwell at your house while I work upon this case? You consent? Good. Until tonight, then, *au 'voir.*"

I T WAS SOME TIME after eight o'clock that evening when he came to the house, laden with almost enough bundles to tax a motor truck. "Great Scott, professor," I exclaimed as he laid his parcels on a convenient chair and gave me a grin which sent the waxed points of his mustache shooting upward like a pair of miniature horns, "have you been buying out the town?"

"Almost," he answered as he dropped into an easy chair and lit an evil smelling French cigarette. "I have talked much with the grocer, the druggist, the garage man and the tobacconist, and at each place I made purchases. I am, for the time, a new resident of your so charming city of Harrisonville, eager to find out about my neighbors and my new home. I have talked like a garrulous old woman, I have milled over much wordy chaff, but from it I have sifted some good meal, *grâce à Dieu!*"

He fixed me with his curiously unwinking cat-stare as he asked: "You have a Monsieur Katmar as a neighbor, have you not?"

"Yes, I believe there's such a person here," I replied, "but I know very little about him."

"Tell me that little, if you will be so kind."

"H'm. He's lived here just about a year, and kept very much to himself. As far as I know he's made no friends and has been visited by no one but tradesmen.

I understand he's a scientist of some sort and took the old Means place out on the Andover Road so he could pursue his experiments in quiet."

"One sees," de Grandin tapped his cigarette case thoughtfully. "So much I have already gathered from my talks with the trades people. Now tell me, if you can, is this Monsieur All-Unknown a friend of the young Manly's—the gentleman whose wound from gunshot you dressed this morning?"

"Not that I know," I answered. "I've never seen them together. Manly's a queer, moody sort of chap, never has much to say to anyone. How Millicent Comstock came to fall in love with him I've no idea. He rides well and is highly thought of by her mother, but those are about the only qualifications he has as a husband that I've been able to see."

"He is very strong, that one?"

"I wouldn't know," I had to confess.

"Very well, then. Listen at me, if you please. You think de Grandin is a fool, *hein?* Perhaps yes; perhaps no. Today I do other things than talk. I go to the Comstock lady's house and reconnoiter. In an ash can I find a pair of patent leather dress shoes, very much scratched. I grease the palm of a servant and find out they belong to that Monsieur Manly. In the trash container I make further researches, and find a white-linen dress shirt with blood on it. It is torn about the cuffs and split at the shoulder, that shirt. It, too, I find, belonged to Monsieur Manly. Me, I am like the dealer in old clothes when I talk with Madame Comstock's servant. I buy that shirt and those shoes from him. Behold!"

From one of his parcels he drew forth a pair of dress shoes and a shirt and spread them for my inspection as if they were curios of priceless value. "In Paris we have ways of making the inanimate talk," he asserted as he thrust his hand into his pocket and drew out a bit of folded paper. "That shirt, those shoes, I put them through the degree of the third time, and how they talk to me. *Mordieu,* they gabble like a pair of spinsters over the teacups!" Opening the paper he disclosed three coarse dull-brown hairs, varying from a half inch to three inches in length.

I looked at them curiously. They might have been from a man's head, for they were too long and straight to be body-hairs, but their texture seemed too harsh for human growth. "U'm," I commented noncommittally.

"*Précisément,*" he grinned. "You cannot classify them, eh?"

"No," I admitted. "They're entirely too coarse to have come from Manly's head. Besides, they're almost black; his hair is a distinct brown."

"My friend," he leaned toward me and stared unwinkingly into my face, "I have seen hairs like that before. So have you, but you did not recognize them. They are from a gorilla."

"From a gor—man, you're raving!" I jerked back. "How could a gorilla's hair get on young Manly's shirt?"

"You have the wrong preposition," he corrected. "They were not on his shirt, but *in* it. Below the neck line, where a bullet had torn through the linen and wounded him. The hairs I found embedded in the dried blood. Look at this garment, if you please"—he held the shirt before me for inspection—"behold how it is split. It has been on a body much too big for it. I tell you, Monsieur Trowbridge, that shirt was worn by the thing—the monster—which killed that pitiful girl dead on the links last night, which attacked the young Maitland a few minutes later, and—which got paint from Madame Comstock's house on these shoes when it climbed into that house last night.

"You start, you stare? You say to yourself, 'This de Grandin he is crazy like the April-fish, him!' Attend me while I prove each step in the ladder:

"This morning, while you were examining young Monsieur Manly's wound, I was examining both him and his room. On his window sill I noted a few scratches—such scrapes as one who drags his legs and feet might make in clambering across the window ledge. I look out of the window, and on the white-painted side of the house I see fresh scratches in the paint. Also, I find scratch-marks on the painted iron pipe that carries water from the roof in rainy weather. That pipe runs down the corner of the house near Manly's window, but too far away for a man to reach it from the sill. But if a man has arms as long as my leg, what then? Ah, then he could have made the reach most easily. Yes.

"Now, when I buy those shoes, that shirt, from Madame Comstock's servant, I note both paint and scratches on the patent leather. Later I compare the paint on the shoes with that on the house-side. They are the same.

"Also I note the shirt, how he is blood-stained and all burst-out, as though the man who wore him suddenly expanded and burst through him. I find beast-hairs in the blood stains on the shirt. So, now, you see?"

"I'm hanged if I do," I denied.

He bent forward again, speaking with rapid earnestness: "The Comstock servant tells me more when I quiz him. He tells me, by example, that last night the young Manly was nervous, what you call ill at ease. He complained of head-ache, backache, he felt what he called rotten. Yes. He went to bed early, and his fiancée went to the country club dance without him. The old madame, she, too, went to bed early.

"Ha, but later in the night—at almost midnight—the young man went for a walk, because, he said, he could not sleep. That is what he told the servant this morning, but"—he paused impressively, then went on, spacing his words carefully—"the servant had been up all night with the toothache, and while he heard the young man come in sometime after midnight, *he did not hear him leave,* as he certainly would have done had he gone out the door.

"And now, consider this: A policeman of the motorcycle tells me he observed the young Manly coming from that Monsieur Kalmar's house, staggering like one drunk. He wonders, that policeman, if Monsieur Kalmar keeps so much to himself because he sells unlicenced liquor after the saloons are closed. What now, *cher collègue?* You say what?"

"Damn it!" I exploded. "You're piecing out the silliest nonsense story I ever heard, de Grandin. One of us is crazy as hell, and I don't think it's I!"

"Neither of us is crazy, *mon vieux*," he returned gravely, "but men have gone mad with knowing what I know, and madder yet with suspecting what I am beginning to suspect. Will you be good enough to drive me past the house of Monsieur Kalmar?"

A FEW MINUTES' RUN CARRIED us to the lonely dwelling occupied by the eccentric old man whose year's residence had been a twelve months' mystery. "He works late, that one," de Grandin commented as we drove by. "Observe, the light burns in his workshop."

Sure enough, from a window at the rear of the house a shaft of bright light cut the evening shadow, and, as we stopped the car and gazed, we could see Kalmar's bent form, swathed in a laboratory apron, passing and repassing the window. The little Frenchman looked long at the white-draped figure, as if he would imprint its image on his memory, then touched me on the elbow. "Let us go back," he ordered softly, "and as we go I shall tell you a story.

"Before the war that wrecked the world there came to Paris from Vienna one Doctor Beneckendorff. As a man he was intolerable, but as a *savant* without parallel. With my own eyes I saw him do things that in an age less tolerant of learning would have brought him to the stake as a wizard.

"But science is God's tool, my friend. It is not meant that man should play at being God. That man, he went too far. We had to put him in restraint."

"Yes?" I answered, not particularly interested in his narrative. "What did he do?"

"Ha, what did he not do, *pardieu?* Children of the poor were found missing at night. They were nowhere. The gendarmes' search narrowed to the laboratory of this Beneckendorff, and there they found not the poor missing infants, but a half-score ape-creatures, not wholly human nor completely simian, but partaking horribly of each, with fur and hand-like feet, but with the face of something that had once been of mankind. They were all dead, those poor ones, fortunately for them.

"He was adjudged mad as the June-beetle by the court, but ah, my friend, what a mentality, what a fine brain gone bad!

"We shut him up for the safety of the public, and for the safety of humanity we burned his notebooks and destroyed the serums with which he had injected the human babes to turn them into pseudo-apes."

"Impossible!" I scoffed.

"Incredible," he agreed, "but not, unfortunately, impossible—for him. His secret entered the madhouse with him; but in the turbulence of war he escaped."

"Good God," I cried. "You mean this monster-maker is loose on the world?"

He shrugged his shoulders with Gallic fatalism. "Perhaps. All trace of him has vanished, but there are reports he was later seen in the Congo Belgique."

"But—"

"No buts, my friend, if you will be so kind. To speculate is idle. We have arrived at an *impasse*, but presently we may find our way over, under or around it. One favor, if you will be good enough to grant it: When next you attend the young Manly, permit that I accompany you. I would have a few minutes' talk with Madame Comstock."

Cornelia Comstock was a lady of imposing physique and even more imposing manner. She browbeat fellow club members, society reporters, even solicitors for "causes," but to de Grandin she was merely a woman who had information he desired. Prefacing his inquiry with the sort of bow no one but a Frenchman can achieve, he began directly:

"Madame, do you, or did you ever, know one Doctor Beneckendorff?"

Mrs. Comstock gave him a look beside which the basilisk's most deadly glare would have been languishing. "My good man—" she began as if he were an overcharging taxi driver, but the Frenchman met her cold gaze with one equally frigid.

"You will be good enough to answer me," he told her. "Primarily I represent the Republic of France; but I also represent humanity. Once more, please, did you ever know a Doctor Beneckendorff?"

Her cold eyes lowered before his unwinking stare, and her thin lips twitched a little. "Yes," she answered in a voice not much more than a whisper.

"Ah. So. We make progress. When did you know him—in what circumstances? Believe me, you may speak in confidence before me and Dr. Trowbridge, but please speak frankly. The importance is great."

"I knew Otto Beneckendorff many years ago. He had just come to this country from Europe and was teaching biology at the university near which I lived as a girl. We—we were engaged."

"And your betrothal, for what reason was it broken, please?"

I could scarcely recognize Cornelia Comstock in the woman who regarded Jules de Grandin with wondering frightened eyes. She trembled as with a chill, and her hands played nervously with the cord of her tortoiseshell pince-nez as she replied: "He—he was impossible, sir. We had vivisectionists, even in those days—but this man seemed to torture poor, defenseless beasts for the love of it. I handed back his ring when he boasted of one of his experiments to me. He positively seemed to gloat over the memory of the poor brute's sufferings before it died."

"*Eh bien*, Madame," de Grandin shot me a quick glance, "your betrothal, then, was broken. He left you, one assumes, but did he leave in friendship?"

Cornelia Comstock looked as if she were upon the verge of fainting as she whispered, "No, sir. No! He left me with a dreadful threat. I recall his very words—how can I ever forget them? He said, 'I go, but I return. Nothing but death can cheat me, and when I come back I shall bring on you and yours a horror such as no man has known since the days before Adam.'"

"*Parbleu*," the little Frenchman almost danced in his excitement. "We have the key to the mystery, almost, Friend Trowbridge!" To Mrs. Comstock he added, "One more little, so small question, if you please, Madame: Your daughter is betrothed to one Monsieur Manly. Tell me, when and where did she meet this young man?"

"I introduced them," Mrs. Comstock's hauteur showed signs of return. "Mr. Manly came to my husband with letters of introduction from an old schoolmate of his—a fellow student at the university—in Capetown."

"Capetown, do you say, Madame? Capetown in South Africa? *Nom d'un petit bonhomme!* When was this, if you please?"

"About a year ago. Why—"

"And Monsieur Manly, he has lived with you how long?" his question shut off her offended protest half uttered.

"Mr. Manly is *stopping* with us," Comstock answered icily. "He is to marry my daughter next month. And, really, sir, I fail to see what interest the Republic of France, which you represent, and humanity, which you also claim to represent, can have in my private affairs. If—"

"This Capetown friend," the little Frenchman interrupted feverishly. "His name was what, and his business?"

"Really, I must decline—"

"*Tell me!*" He thrust forth both his slender hands as if to shake an answer from her. "It is that I must know. *Nom d'un fusil!* Tell me, at once!"

"We do not know his street and number," Mrs. Comstock seemed completely cowed, "but his name is Alexander Findlay, and he's a diamond factor."

"*Bien.*" The Frenchman struck his heels together and bowed as if hinged at the hips. "Thank you, Madame. You have been most kind and helpful."

IT WAS PAST MIDNIGHT when the 'phone began to ring insistently. "Western Union speaking," a girl's voice announced. "Cablegram for Dr. Jules de Grandin. Ready?"

"Yes," I answered, seizing pencil and pad from the bedside table, "Read it please."

"'No person named Alexander Findlay diamond factor known here no record of such person in last five years. Signed, Burlingame, Inspector of Police.'

"It's from Capetown, South Africa," she added as I finished jotting down her dictation.

"Very good," I answered. "Forward a typed confirmation, please."

"*Mille tonneres!*" de Grandin exclaimed as I read the message to him. "This makes the picture-puzzle complete, or very nearly so. Attend me, if you please."

He leaped across the room and extracted a black-leather notebook from his jacket pocket. "Behold," he consulted a notation, "this Monsieur Kalmar whom no one knows, he has lived here for ten months and twenty-six days—twenty-seven when tomorrow morning comes. This information I have from a realtor whom I interviewed in my rôle as compiler of a directory of scientists.

"The young Monsieur Manly, he has known the Comstocks for 'about a year.' He brought them letters from a schoolmate of Monsieur Comstock who proves to be unknown in Capetown. *Parbleu*, my friend, from now on Jules de Grandin turns night into day, if you will be so kind as to take him to a gun merchant from whom he may procure a Winchester rifle. Yes," he nodded solemnly, "it is so. *Vraiment.*"

TIME DRIFTED BY, DE Grandin going gun in hand each night to keep his lonely vigils, but no developments in the mystery of the Humphreys murder or the attack on Paul Maitland were reported. The date of Millicent Comstock's wedding approached, and the big house was filled to overflowing with boisterous young folks; still de Grandin kept up his lonely patron—and kept his own counsel.

THE NIGHT BEFORE THE wedding day he accosted me as he came down the stairs. "Trowbridge, my friend, you have been most patient with me. If you will come with me tonight I think that I may show you something."

"All right," I agreed. "I haven't the slightest notion what all this folderol's about, but I'm willing to be convinced."

A little after twelve we parked the car at a convenient corner and walked quickly to the Comstock place, taking shelter in the shadow of a hedge that marked the boundary of the lawn.

"Lord, what a lovely night!" I exclaimed. "I don't think I remember ever seeing brighter moonlight—"

"H'm'm'm'm!" His interruption was one of those peculiar nasal sounds, half grunt, half whinny, which none but the true Frenchman can produce. "Attend me, if you please, my friend: No man knows what part Tanit the Moon Goddess plays in our affairs, even today when her name is forgotten by all but dusty-dry antiquaries. This we do know, however; at the entrance of life our appearance is governed by the phases of the moon. You, as a physician with wide obstetrical experience, can confirm that. Also, when the time of exit approaches, the crisis of disease is often governed by the moon's phase. Why this should be we do not know, but that it is so we know all too well. Suppose, then, the cellular organization of a body be violently, unnaturally, changed, and nature's whole force be exerted toward a readjustment. May we not suppose that Tanit who affects childbirth and death, might have some force to apply in such a case?"

"I dare say," I conceded, "but I don't follow you. Just what is it you expect, or suspect, de Grandin?"

"Hélas, nothing," he answered. "I suspect nothing, I affirm nothing, I deny nothing. I am agnostic, but also hopeful. It may be that I make a great black *lutin* of my own shadow, but he who is prepared for the worst is most agreeably disappointed if the best occurs." Irrelevantly he added, "That light yonder, it shines from Mademoiselle Millicent's chamber, *n'est-ce-pas?*"

"Yes," I confirmed, wondering if I were on a fool's errand with an amiable lunatic for company.

The merrymaking in the house had quieted, and one by one the lights went out in the upper windows. I had an almost overwhelming desire to smoke, but dared not strike a match. The little Frenchman fidgeted nervously, fussing with the lock of his Winchester, ejecting and reinserting cartridges, playing a devil's tattoo on the barrel with his long white fingers.

A wrack of clouds had crept across the moon, but suddenly it swept away, and like a floodlight turned on the scene the bright, pearly moonlight deluged everything. "Ah," my companion murmured, "now we shall see what we shall see—perhaps."

As if his words had been a cue there echoed from the house a scream of such wild, frenzied terror as a lost soul might emit when summoned to eternal torment. "Ah-*ha?*" de Grandin exclaimed as he raised his rifle. "Will he come forth or—"

Lights flashed inside the house. The patter of terrified feet sounded among the babel of wondering, questioning voices, but the scream was not repeated.

"Come forth, accursèd one—come forth and face de Grandin!" I heard the small Frenchman mutter, then: "Behold, my friend, he comes—*le gorille!*"

From Millicent's window, horrible as a devil out of lowest hell, there came a hairy head set low upon a pair of shoulders at least four feet across. An arm which somehow reminded me of a giant snake slipped past the window casing, grasped the cast-iron downspout at the corner of the house, and drew a thickset, hairy body after it. A leg tipped with a handlike foot was thrown across the sill, and, like a spider from its lair, the monster leaped from the window and hung a moment to the iron pipe, its sable body silhouetted against the white wall of the house.

But what was that, that white-robed thing which hung pendant from the grasp of the beast's free arm? Like a beautiful white moth inert in the grasp of the spider, her fair hair unbound, her silken night robe rent into a motley of tatters, Millicent Comstock lay senseless in the creature's grasp.

"Shoot, man, shoot!" I screamed, but only a thin whisper came from my fear-stiffened lips.

"Silence, *imbécile!*" de Grandin ordered as he pressed his cheek against his gunstock. "Would you give warning of our ambuscade?"

Slowly, so slowly it seemed an hour was consumed in the process, the great primate descended the water-pipe, leaping the last fifteen feet of the descent and crouching on the moonlit lawn, its small red eyes glaring malignantly, as if it challenged the world for possession of its prey.

The bellow of de Grandin's rifle almost deafened me, and the smokeless powder's flash burned a gash in the night. He threw the loading mechanism feverishly, and fired a second time.

The monster staggered drunkenly against the house as the first shot sounded. At the second it dropped Millicent to the lawn and uttered a cry which was part roar, part snarl. Then, one of its great arms trailing helplessly, it leaped toward the rear of the house in a series of long, awkward bounds which reminded me, absurdly, of the bouncing of a huge inflated ball.

"Attend her, if you please, my friend," de Grandin ordered as we reached Millicent's inert form. "I shall make *Monsieur le Gorille* my personal business!"

I BENT ABOVE THE SENSELESS girl and put my ear to her breast. Faint but perceptible, I made out a heart-beat, and lifted her in my arms.

"Dr. Trowbridge!" Mrs. Comstock, followed by a throng of frightened guests, met me at the front door. "What's happened? Good heavens, Millicent!" Seizing her daughter's flaccid hand in both her own she burst into a flood of tears. "Oh, what's happened? What is it?"

"Help me get Millicent to bed, then get some smelling salts and brandy," I commanded, ignoring her questions.

A little later, with restoratives applied and electric pads at her feet and back, the girl showed signs of waking. "Get out—all of you!" I ordered. Hysterical women, especially patients' mothers, are rather less than useless when consciousness returns after profound shock.

"Oh—oh, the ape-thing! The dreadful ape-thing!" cried Millicent in a small, childish whimper. "It's got me—help—"

"It's all right, dear," I comforted. "You're safe, safe home in your own bed, with old Dr. Trowbridge standing by." It was not till several hours later that I realized her first waking exclamation had been almost identical to Paul Maitland's when he revived from his faint.

"Dr. Trowbridge," Mrs. Comstock whispered from the bedroom door. "We've looked all over, but there's no sign of Mr. Manly. Do—do you suppose anything could have happened to him?"

"I think it quite likely that something could—and did," I answered curtly, turning from her to smooth her daughter's fluttering hand.

"PAR LE BARBE D'UN *bouc vert!*" de Grandin exclaimed as, disheveled, but with a light of exhilaration in his eyes, he met me in the Comstock hall some two hours later. "Madame Comstock, you are to be congratulated. But for my so brave colleague Dr. Trowbridge and my own so very clever self your charming daughter would have shared the fate of the poor Sarah Humphreys.

"Trowbridge, *mon vieux*, I have not been quite frank with you. I have not told you all. But this thing, it was so incredible, so seemingly impossible, that you would not have believed. *Parbleu*, I do not quite believe it myself, even though I know that it is so!

"Let us recapitulate: When this *sacré* Beneckendorff was in the madhouse he raved continually that his confinement cheated him of his revenge—the revenge he had so long planned against one Madame Cornélie Comstock of America.

"We French are logical, not like you English and Americans. We write down and keep for reference even what a madman says. Why not? It may be useful someday, who knows?

"Now, Friend Trowbridge, some time ago I told you this Beneckendorff was reported in the Congo Belgique. Yes? But I did not tell you he were reported in charge of a young, half-grown gorilla. No. When this so unfortunate Mademoiselle Humphreys is killed in that so terrible manner I remember my own African experiences, and I say to me, 'Ah-ha, Jules de Grandin, it look as if *Monsieur le Gorille* has had a finger in this pie.' And thereupon I ask to know if any such have escape from a circus or zoo nearby. All answers are no.

"Then that Sergeant Costello, he bring me to this so splendid *savant*, Dr. Trowbridge, and with him I go to interview the young Monsieur Maitland who have encountered much strangeness where the young Humphreys girl met death.

"And what does the young Maitland tell me? He tells of something that have hair, that jump up and down like an enraged ape and that act like a gorilla, but wears man's evening clothes, *parbleu!* It is to think. No gorilla have escaped, yet what *seems* like a gorilla—in gentleman's evening clothes, *Mordieu!*—have been encountered on the golf links.

"Thereupon I search my memory. I remember that madman and the poor infants he has turned into half-ape things by administration of his so vile serums.

I say to me, 'If he can turn man-children into monkey-things, for why can he not turn ape-things into men-things. *Hein?*'

"Then I find one Dr. Kalmar who has lived here for a year, almost, and of whom no one knows anything. I search about, I make the inquiries, and learn one man has been seen coming to and from his place in secret. Also, in this same man's discarded shirt I find the hairs of a gorilla. *Morbleu!* I think some more, and what I think is not particularly pleasant.

"I reason: Suppose this serum which may make a man-thing of an ape-thing is not permanent in its effect? What then? If it is not renewed at stated intervals the man becomes an ape again. You follow? *Bien.*

"Now, the other day I learn something which gives me to think some more. This Beneckendorff, he raves against one Madame Comstock. You, Madame, admit you once knew him. He had loved you as he understood love. Now he hated you as only he could hate. Is it not against you he plans this devilish scheme? I think it quite possible.

"And so I send a cablegram—never mind to whom, Dr. Trowbridge knows that—and I got the answer I expect and fear. The man in whose shirt I find those hairs of the gorilla is no man at all, he is one terrible masquerade of a man. So. Now, I reason, 'Suppose this masquerading monkey-thing do not get his serum as expected, what will he do?' I fear to answer my own question, but I make myself do so: *Voilà*, I buy me a rifle.

"This gun has bullets of soft lead, and I make them even more effective by cutting a V-shaped notch in each of their heads. When they strike something they spread out and make a nobly deadly wound.

"Tonight what I have feared, but yet expected, comes to pass. *Ha*, but I am ready, me! I shoot, and each time I shoot my bullet tears a great hole in the ape-thing. He drops his prey and seeks the only shelter that his little ape-brain knows, the house of Dr. Kalmar. Yes.

"I follow all quickly, and reach the house almost as soon as he. He is maddened with the pain of my bullets, and in his rage he tears this so vile Kalmar into little bits, even as he has done to poor young Sarah Humphreys. And I, arriving with my gun, dispatch him with another shot. *C'est une affaire finie.*

"But before I come back here I recognize the corpse of this Dr. Kalmar. Who is he? Who but the escaped lunatic, the monster-maker, the entirely detestable Dr. Otto Beneckendorff? Before I leave I destroy the devil's brews with which he makes monkeys of men and men of monkeys. It is far better that their secret be forever lost.

"I think Mademoiselle Humphreys was unfortunate enough to meet this ape-man when he was on his way to Dr. Kalmar's, as he had been taught to come. As a man, perhaps, he did not know this Kalmar, or, as we know him,

Beneckendorff; but as a brute he knew no other man but Beneckendorff—his master, the man who brought him from Africa.

"When he came upon the poor girl on the golf links she screamed in terror, and at once his savageness became uppermost. Believe me, the gorilla is more savage than the bear, the lion or the tiger. Therefore, in his anger, he tear her to pieces. He also tried to tear the young Monsieur Maitland, but luckily for us he failed, and so we got the story which put us on his trail.

"*Voilà*, it is finished. Anon I shall report to the good Sergeant Costello and show him the bodies at the Kalmar house. Also I shall cable back to Paris. The Ministry of Health will be glad to know that Beneckendorff is no more."

"But, Monsieur de Grandin," Mrs. Comstock demanded, "who was this man—or ape—you killed?"

I held my breath as he fixed his cold stare on her, then sighed with relief as he answered. "I can not say, Madame."

"Well," Mrs. Comstock's natural disputatiousness came to the surface, "I think it's very *queer*—"

His laugh was positively Olympian. "*You* think it very queer, Madame? *Mort d'un rat mort*, as Balkis said of Solomon's magnificence, the half has not been told you!"

"WHEN THE POLICE LOOK for Monsieur Manly—*mon dieu*, what a name for an ape-thing!—they will be puzzled," he told me as we walked to my car. "I must warn Costello to enter his disappearance as a permanently unsolved case. No one will ever know the true facts but you, I and the Ministry of Health, Friend Trowbridge. The public would not believe, even if we told them."

The Tenants of Broussac

1

T HE RUE DES BATAILLES was justifying its name. From my table on the narrow sidewalk before the Café de Liberté I could view three distinct fights alternately, or simultaneously. Two cock-sparrows contended noisily for possession of a wisp of straw, a girl with unbelievably small feet and incredibly thick ankles addressed a flood of gamin abuse to an oily-haired youth who wore a dirty black-silk muffler in lieu of a collar. At the curb a spade-bearded patron, considerably the worse for *vin ordinaire*, haggled volubly with an unshaven taxi chauffeur over an item of five francs.

I had dropped my cigar end into my empty coffee cup, motioned the waiter for my *addition* and shoved back my chair, when a light but commanding tap fell on my shoulder.

"Now for it," I muttered, feeling sure some passing bravo, aching for a fight, had chosen me for his attentions. Turning suddenly, I looked straight into a pair of light blue eyes, round as a cat's, and just missing a humorous expression because of their challenging directness. Beneath the eyes was a straw-colored mustache, trimly waxed into a horizontal line and bristling so belligerently as to heighten its wearer's resemblance to a truculent tomcat. Below the feline mustache was a grin wider and friendlier than any I'd seen in Paris.

"*Par la barbe d'un bouc vert!*" swore my accoster. "If it is not truly my friend, the good Dr. Trowbridge, then I am first cousin to the Emperor of China."

"Why, de Grandin," I exclaimed, grasping his small sinewy hand, "fancy meeting you this way! I called at the *École de Médecine* the day after I arrived, but they told me you were off on one of your wild goose chases and only heaven knew when you'd be back."

He tweaked the points of his mustache alternately as he answered with another grin. "But of course! Those dull-witted ones would term my researches in the domain of inexact science a wild goose hunt. *Pardieu!* They have no vision beyond their test tubes and retorts, those ones."

"What is it this time?" I asked as we caught step. "A criminal investigation or a ghost-breaking expedition?"

"*Morbleu!*" he answered with a chuckle; "I think, perhaps, it is a little of both. Listen, my friend, do you know the country about Rouen?"

"Not I," I replied. "This is my first trip to France, and I've been here only three days."

"Ah, yes," he returned, "your ignorance of our geography is truly deplorable; but it can be remedied. Have you an inflexible program mapped out?"

"No. This is my first vacation in ten years—since 1915—and I've made no plans, except to get as far away from medicine as possible."

"Good!" he applauded. "I can promise you a complete change from your American practice, my friend, such a change as will banish all thoughts of patients, pills and prescriptions entirely from your head. Will you join me?"

"Hm, that depends," I temporized. "What sort of case are you working on?" Discretion was the better part of acceptance when talking with Jules de Grandin, I knew. Educated for the profession of medicine, one of the foremost anatomists and physiologists of his generation, and a shining light in the University of Paris faculty, this restless, energetic little scientist had chosen criminology and occult investigation as a recreation from his vocational work, and had gained almost as much fame in these activities as he had in the medical world. During the war he had been a prominent, though necessarily anonymous, member of the Allied Intelligence Service; since the Armistice he had penetrated nearly every quarter of the globe on special missions for the French Ministry of Justice. It behooved me to move cautiously when he invited me to share an exploit with him; the trail might lead to India, Greenland or Tierra del Fuego before the case was closed.

"*Eh bien,*" he laughed. "You are ever the old cautious one, Friend Trowbridge. Never will you commit yourself until you have seen blueprints and specifications of the enterprise. Very well, then, listen:

"Near Rouen stands the very ancient château of the de Broussac family. Parts of it were built as early as the eleventh century; none of it is less than two hundred years old. The family has dwindled steadily in wealth and importance until the last two generations have been reduced to living on the income derived from renting the château to wealthy foreigners.

"A common story, *n'est-ce-pas?* Very well, wait, comes now the uncommon part: Within the past year the Château Broussac has had no less than six tenants; no renter has remained in possession for more than two months, and each tenancy has terminated in a tragedy of some sort.

"Stories of this kind get about; houses acquire unsavory reputations, even as people do, and tenants are becoming hard to find for the château.

Monsieur Bergeret, the de Broussac family's *avoue*, has commissioned me to discover the reason for these interrupted tenancies; he desires me to build a dam against the flood of ill fortune which makes tenants scarce at the château and threatens to pauperize one of the oldest and most useless families of France."

"You say the tenancies were terminated by tragedies?" I asked, more to make conversation than from interest.

"But yes," he answered. "The cases, as I have their histories, are like this:

"Monsieur Alvarez, a wealthy Argentine cattle raiser, rented the château last April. He moved in with his family, his servants and entirely too many cases of champagne. He had lived there only about six weeks when, one night, such of the guests as retained enough soberness to walk to bed missed him at the goodnight round of drinks. He was also missing the following morning, and the following night. Next day a search was instituted, and a servant found his body in the chapel of the oldest part of the château. *Morbleu*, all the doctors in France could not reassemble him! Literally, my friend, he was strewn about the sanctuary; his limbs torn off, his head severed most untidily at the neck, every bone in his trunk smashed like crockery in a china store struck by lightning. He was like a doll pulled to pieces by a peevish child. *Voilà*, the Alvarez family decamped the premises and the Van Brundt family moved in.

"That Monsieur Van Brundt had amassed a fortune selling supplies to the *sale Boche* during the war. *Eh bien*, I could not wish him the end he had. Too much food, too much wine, too little care of his body he took. One night he rose from his bed and wandered in the château grounds. In the place where the ancient moat formerly was they found him, his thick body thin at last, and almost twice its natural length—squeezed out like a tube of *creme* from a lady's dressing table trodden under foot by an awkward servant. He was not a pretty sight, my friend.

"The other tenants, too, all left when some member of their families or suites met a terrifying fate. There was Simpson, the Englishman, whose crippled son fell from the battlements to the old courtyard, and Biddle, the American, whose wife now shrieks and drools in a madhouse, and Muset, the banker from Montreal, who woke one night from a doze in his study chair to see Death staring him in the eye.

"Now Monsieur Luke Bixby, from Oklahoma, resides at Broussac with his wife and daughter, and—I wait to hear of a misfortune in their midst.

"You will come with me? You will help me avert peril from a fellow countryman?"

"Oh, I suppose so," I agreed. One part of France appealed to me as strongly as another, and de Grandin was never a dull companion.

"Ah, good," he exclaimed, offering his hand in token of our compact. "Together, *mon vieux*, we shall prove such a team as the curse of Broussac shall find hard to contend with."

2

THE SUN WAS WELL down toward the horizon when our funny little train puffed officiously into Rouen the following day. The long European twilight had dissolved into darkness, and oblique shadows slanted from the trees in the nascent moonlight as our hired *moteur* entered the château park.

"Good evening, Monsieur Bixby," de Grandin greeted as we followed the servant into the great hallway. "I have taken the liberty to bring a compatriot of yours, Dr. Trowbridge, with me to aid in my researches." He shot me a meaning glance as he hurried on. "Your kindness in permitting me the facilities of the château library is greatly appreciated, I do assure you."

Bixby, a big, full-fleshed man with ruddy face and drooping mustache, smiled amiably. "Oh, that's all right, Monsoor," he answered. "There must be a couple o' million books stacked up in there, and I can't read a one of 'em. But I've got to pay rent on 'em, just the same, so I'm mighty glad you, or someone who savvies the lingo, can put 'em to use."

"And Madame Bixby, she is well, and the so charming *Mademoiselle*, she, too, is in good health, I trust?"

Our host looked worried. "To tell you the truth, she ain't," he replied. "Mother and I had reckoned a stay in one of these old houses here in France would be just the thing for her, but it seems like she ain't doin' so well as we'd hoped. Maybe we'd better try Switzerland for a spell; they say the mountain air there . . ."

De Grandin bent forward eagerly. "What is the nature of *Mademoiselle's* indisposition?" he asked. "Dr. Trowbridge is one of your America's most famous physicians, perhaps he . . ." He paused significantly.

"That so?" Bixby beamed on me. "I'd kind o' figured you was one of them doctors of philosophy we see so many of round here, 'stead of a regular doctor. Now, if you'd be so good as to look at Adrienne, Doc, I'd take it right kindly. Will you come this way? I'll see supper's ready by the time you get through with her."

He led us up a magnificent stairway of ancient carved oak, down a corridor paneled in priceless wainscot, and knocked gently at a high-arched door of age-blackened wood. "Adrienne, darlin'," he called in a huskily tender voice, "here's a doctor to see you—an American doctor, honey. Can you see him?"

"Yes," came the reply from beyond the door, and we entered a bedroom as large as a barrack, furnished with articles of antique design worth their weight in gold to any museum rich enough to buy them.

Fair-haired and violet-eyed, slender to the borderline of emaciation, and with too high flush on her cheeks, Bixby's daughter lay propped among a heap of real-lace pillows on the great carved bed, the white of her thin throat and arms only a shade warmer than the white of her silk nightdress.

Her father tiptoed from the room with clumsy care and I began my examination, observing her heart and lung action by auscultation and palpation, taking her pulse and estimating her temperature as accurately as possible without my clinical thermometer. Though she appeared suffering from fatigue, there was no evidence of functional or organic weakness in any of her organs.

"Hm," I muttered, looking as professionally wise as possible, "just how long have you felt ill, Miss Bixby?"

The girl burst into a storm of tears. "I'm not ill," she denied hotly. "I'm not—oh, why won't you all go away and leave me alone? I don't know what's the matter with me. I—I just want to be let alone!" She buried her face in a pillow and her narrow shoulders shook with sobs.

"Friend Trowbridge," de Grandin whispered, "a tonic—something simple, like a glass of sherry with meals—is indicated, I think. Meantime, let us repair to the so excellent supper which waits below."

We repaired. There was nothing else to do. His advice was sound, I knew, for all the physician's skill is powerless to cheer a young woman who craves the luxury of being miserable.

3

"FIND ANYTHING SERIOUS, DOC?" Bixby asked as de Grandin and I seated ourselves in the paneled dining hall of the château.

"No," I reassured him. "She seems a little run down, but there's certainly nothing wrong which can't be corrected by a light tonic, some judicious exercise and plenty of rest."

"Uh-huh?" he nodded, brightening. "I've been right smart worried over her, lately.

"You know, we wasn't always rich. Up to a couple o' years ago we was poor as church mice—land poor, in the bargain. Then, when they begun findin' oil all round our place, Mother kept at me till I started some drillin', too, and darned if we didn't bring in a gusher first crack outa the box.

"Adrienne used to teach school when we was ranchin' it—tryin' to, rather—an' she an' a young lawyer, name o' Ray Keefer, had it all fixed up to get married.

"Ray was a good, upstandin' boy, too. Had a considerable practice worked up over Bartlesville way, took his own company overseas durin' the war, an' would a' been ran for the legislature in a little while, like as not. But when we started takin' royalties on our leases at the rate of about three hundred dollars a week, Mother, she ups and says he warn't no fittin' match for our daughter.

"Then she and Adrienne had it hot an' heavy, with me stayin' outa the fuss an' bein' neutral, as far as possible. Mother was all for breakin' the engagement off short, Adrienne was set on gettin' married right away, an' they finally compromised by agreein' to call a truce for a year while Ray stayed home an' looked after his practice an' Adrienne come over here to Europe with Mother an' me to see the world an' 'have her mind broadened by travel,' as Mother says.

"She's been gettin' a letter from Ray at every stop we made since we left home, an' sendin' back answers just as regular, till we come here. Lately she ain't seemed to care nothin' about Ray, one way or the other. Don't answer his letters—half the time don't trouble to open 'em, even, an' goes around the place as if she was sleep-walkin'. Seems kind o' peaked an' run down, like, too. We've been right worried over her. You're sure it ain't consumption, or nothin' like that, Doc?" He looked anxiously at me again.

"Have no fear, Monsieur," de Grandin answered for me. "Dr. Trowbridge and I will give the young lady our greatest care; rest assured, we shall effect a complete cure. We . . ."

Two shots, following each other in quick succession, sounded from the grounds outside, cutting short his words. We rushed to the entrance, meeting a breathless gamekeeper in the corridor. "*Le serpent, le serpent!*" he exclaimed excitedly, rushing up to Bixby. "*Ohé, Monsieur, un serpent monstrueux, dans le jardin!*"

"What is it you say?" de Grandin demanded. "A serpent in the garden? Where, when; how big?"

The fellow spread his arms to their fullest reach, extending his fingers to increase the space compassed. "A great, a tremendous serpent, *Monsieur*," he panted. "Greater than the boa constrictor in the Paris menagerie—ten meters long, at the shortest!"

"*Pardieu*, a snake thirty feet long?" de Grandin breathed incredulously. "Come, *mon enfant*, take us to the spot where you saw this so great zoological wonder."

"Here, 'twas here I saw him, with my own two eyes," the man almost screamed in his excitement, pointing to a small copse of evergreens growing close beside the château wall. "See, it's here the shots I fired at him cut the bushes"—he pointed to several broken limbs where buckshot from his fowling piece had crashed through the shrubs.

"Here? *Mon Dieu!*" muttered de Grandin.

"Huh!" Bixby produced a plug of tobacco and bit off a generous mouthful. "If you don't lay off that brandy they sell down at the village you'll be seein' pink elephants roostin' in the trees pretty soon. A thirty-foot snake! In this country? Why, we don't grow 'em that big in Oklahoma! Come on, gentlemen, let's get to bed; this feller's snake didn't come out o' no hole in the wall, he came outa a bottle!"

4

M RS. BIXBY, A BUXOM woman with pale eyes and tinted hair, had small courtesy to waste on us next morning at breakfast. A physician from America who obviously did not enjoy an ultra fashionable practice at home, and an undersized foreigner with a passion for old books, bulked of small importance in her price-marked world. Bixby was taciturn with the embarrassed silence of a wife-ridden man before strangers, and de Grandin and I went into the library immediately following the meal without any attempt at making table talk.

My work consisted, for the most part, of lugging ancient volumes in scuffed bindings from the high shelves and piling them on the table before my colleague. After one or two attempts I gave over the effort to read them, since those not in archaic French were in monkish Latin, both of which were as unintelligible to me as Choctaw.

The little Frenchman, however, dived into the moldering tomes like a gourmet attacking a feast, making voluminous notes, nodding his head furiously as statement after statement in the books seemed to confirm some theory of his, or muttering an occasional approving "*Morbleu!*" or "*Pardieu!*"

"Friend Trowbridge," he looked up from the dusty book spread before him and fixed me with his unwinking stare, "is it not time you saw our fair patient? Go to her, my friend, and whether she approves or whether she objects, apply the stethoscope to her breast, and, while you do so, *examine her torso for bruises.*"

"Bruises?" I echoed.

"Precisely, exactly, quite so!" he shot back. "Bruises, I have said it. They may be of the significance, they may not, but if they are present I desire to know it. I have an hypothesis."

"Oh, very well," I agreed, and went to find my stethoscope.

Though she had not been present at breakfast, I scarcely expected to find Adrienne Bixby in bed, for it was nearly noon when I rapped at her door.

"S-s-s-sh, *Monsieur le Docteur,*" cautioned the maid who answered my summons. "Mademoiselle is still asleep. She is exhausted, the poor, pretty one."

"Who is it, Roxanne?" Adrienne demanded in a sleepy, querulous voice. "Tell them to go away."

I inserted my foot in the door and spoke softly to the maid. "*Mademoiselle* is more seriously ill than she realizes; it is necessary that I make an examination."

"Oh, good morning, doctor," the girl said as I pushed past the maid and approached the bed. Her eyes widened with concern as she saw the stethoscope dangling from my hand. "Is—is there anything the matter—seriously the matter with me?" she asked. "My heart? My lungs?"

"We don't know yet," I evaded. "Very often, you know, symptoms which seem of no importance prove of the greatest importance; then, again, we often find that signs which seem serious at first mean nothing at all. That's it, just lie back, it will be over in a moment."

I placed the instrument against her thin chest, and, as I listened to the accelerated beating of her healthy young heart, glanced quickly down along the line of her ribs beneath the low neckband of her night robe.

"Oh, oh, doctor, what is it?" the girl cried in alarm, for I had started back so violently that one of the earphones was shaken from my head. Around the young girl's body, over the ribs, was *an ascending livid spiral*, definitely marked, as though a heavy rope had been wound about her, then drawn taut.

"How did you get that bruise?" I demanded, tucking my stethoscope into my pocket.

A quick flush mantled her neck and cheeks, but her eyes were honest as she answered simply, "I don't know, doctor. It's something I can't explain. When we first came here to Broussac I was as well as could be; we'd only been here about three weeks when I began to feel all used up in the morning. I'd go to bed early and sleep late and spend most of the day lying around, but I never seemed to get enough rest. I began to notice these bruises about that time, too. First they were on my arm, about the wrist or above the elbow—several times all the way up. Lately they've been around my waist and body, sometimes on my shoulders, too, and every morning I feel tireder than the day before. Then—then"—she turned her face from me and tears welled in her eyes—"I don't seem to be interested in th-things the way I used to be. Oh, doctor, I wish I were dead! I'm no earthly good, and . . ."

"Now, now," I soothed. "I know what you mean when you say you've lost interest in 'things.' There'll be plenty of interest when you get back to Oklahoma again, young lady."

"Oh, doctor, are we going back, really? I asked Mother if we mightn't yesterday and she said Dad had leased this place for a year and we'd have to stay until the lease expired. Do you mean she's changed her mind?"

"M'm, well," I temporized, "perhaps you won't leave Broussac right away; but you remember that old saying about Mohammed and the mountain? Suppose we were to import a little bit of Oklahoma to France, what then?"

"No!" She shook her head vigorously and her eyes filled with tears again. "I don't want Ray to come here. This is an evil place, doctor. It makes people forget all they ever loved and cherished. If he came here he might forget me . . ." as the sentence dissolved in a fresh flood of tears.

"Well, well," I comforted, "we'll see if we can't get Mother to listen to medical advice."

"Mother never listened to anybody's advice," she sobbed as I closed the door softly and hurried downstairs to tell de Grandin my discovery.

5

"*C*ORDIEU!*" DE GRANDIN SWORE excitedly as I concluded my recitation. "A bruise? A bruise about her so white body, and before that on her arms? *Non d'un nom!* My friend, this plot, it acquires the thickness. What do you think?"

"M'm." I searched my memory for long-forgotten articles in the *Medical Times*. "I've read of these stigmata appearing on patients' bodies. They were usually connected with the presence of some wasting disease and an abnormal state of mind, such as extreme religious fervor, or . . ."

"Ah, bah!" he cut in. "Friend Trowbridge, you can not measure the wind with a yardstick nor weigh a thought on the scales. We deal with something not referable to clinical experiments in this case, or I am much mistaken."

"Why, how do you mean . . . ?" I began, but he turned away with an impatient shrug.

"I mean nothing, now," he answered. "The wise judge is he who gives no decision until he has heard all the testimony." Again, he commenced reading from the huge volume open before him, making notations on a slip of paper as his eyes traveled rapidly down the lines of faded type.

Mrs. Bixby did not join us at dinner that evening, and, as a consequence, the conversation was much less restrained. Coffee was served in the small corridor connecting the wide entrance hall with the library, and, under the influence of a hearty meal, three kinds of wine and several glasses of *liqueur*, our host expanded like a flower in the sun.

"They tell me Joan of Arc was burned to death in Ruin," he commented as he bit the end from a cigar and elevated one knee over the arm of his chair. "Queer way to treat a girl who'd done so much for 'em, seems to me. The guide told us she's been made a saint or somethin' since then, though."

"Yes," I assented idly, "having burned her body and anathematized her soul, the ecclesiastical authorities later decided the poor child's spirit was unjustly condemned. Too bad a little of their sense of justice wasn't felt by the court which tried her in Rouen."

De Grandin looked quizzically at me as he pulled his waxed mustaches alternately, for all the world like a tomcat combing his whiskers. "Throw not too many stones, my friend," he cautioned. "Nearly five hundred years have passed since the Maid of Orleans was burned as a heretic. Today your American courts convict high school-teachers for heresy far less grave than that charged against our Jeanne. We may yet see the bones of your so estimable Thomas Jefferson and Benjamin Franklin exhumed from their graves and publicly burned by your heretic-baiters of this today. No, no, my friend, it is not for us of today to sneer at the heretic-burners of yesterday. Torquemada's body lies in the tomb these many years, but his spirit still lives. *Mon Dieu!* What is it that I say? 'His spirit still lives'? *Sacré nom d'une souris!* That may be the answer!" And, as if propelled by a spring, he bounded from his seat and rushed madly down the corridor into the library.

"De Grandin, what's the matter?" I asked as I followed him into the book-lined room.

"*Non, non,* go away, take a walk, go to the devil!" he shot back, staring wildly around the room, his eager eyes searching feverishly for a particular volume. "You vex me, you annoy me, you harass me; I would be alone at this time. Get out!"

Puzzled and angered by his bruskness, I turned to leave, but he called over his shoulder as I reached the door: "Friend Trowbridge, please interview Monsieur Bixby's chef—and obtain from him a sack of flour. Bring it here to me in not less than an hour, please."

<h1 style="text-align:center">6</h1>

"FORGIVE MY RUDENESS, FRIEND Trowbridge," he apologized when I re-entered the library an hour or so later, a parcel of flour from Bixby's pantry under my arm. "I had a thought which required all my concentration at the time, and any disturbing influence—even your own always welcome presence—would have distracted my attention. I am sorry and ashamed I spoke so."

"Oh, never mind that," I replied. "Did you find what you were looking for?"

He nodded emphatically. "*Mais oui,*" he assured me. "All which I sought—and more. Now let us to work. First I would have you go with me into the garden where that gamekeeper saw the serpent last night."

"But he couldn't have seen such a snake," I protested as we left the library. "We all agreed the fellow was drunk."

"Surely, exactly; of course," he conceded, nodding vigorously. "Undoubtedly the man had drunk brandy. Do you recall, by any chance, the wise old Latin proverb, '*In vino veritas*'?"

"'In wine is truth'?" I translated tentatively. "How could the fact that the man was drunk when he imagined he saw a thirty-foot snake in a French garden make the snake exist when we know perfectly well such a thing could not be?"

"Oh la, la," he chuckled. "What a sober-sided one you are, *cher ami.* It was here the fellow declared *Monsieur le Serpent* emerged, was it not? See, here are the shot-marks on the shrubs."

He bent, parting the bushes carefully, and crawled toward the château's stone foundation. "Observe," he commanded in a whisper, "between these stones the cement has weathered away, the opening is great enough to permit passage of a sixty-foot serpent, did one desire to come this way. No?"

"True enough," I agreed, "but the driveway out there would give room for the great Atlantic sea serpent himself to crawl about. You don't contend he's making use of it, though, do you?"

He tapped his teeth thoughtfully with his forefinger, paying no attention to my sarcasm. "Let us go within," he suggested, brushing the leaf-mold carefully from his knees as he rose.

W E RE-ENTERED THE HOUSE and he led the way through one winding passage after another, unlocking a succession of nail-studded doors with the bunch of jangling iron keys he obtained from Bixby's butler.

"And here is the chapel," he announced when half an hour's steady walk brought us to a final age-stained door, "It was here they found that so unfortunate Monsieur Alvarez. A gloomy place in which to die, truly."

It was, indeed. The little sanctuary lay dungeon-deep, without windows or, apparently, any means of external ventilation. Its vaulted roof was composed of a series of equilateral arches whose stringers rose a scant six feet above the floor and rested on great blocks of flint carved in hideous designs of dragons' and griffins' heads. The low altar stood against the farther wall, its silver crucifix blackened with age and all but eaten away with erosion. Row on row, about the low upright walls, were lined the crypts containing the coffins of long dead de Broussacs, each closed with a marble slab engraved with the name and title of its occupant. A pall of cobwebs, almost as heavy as woven fabrics, festooned from vaulted ceiling to floor, intensifying the air of ghostly gloom which hung about the chamber like the acrid odor of ancient incense.

My companion set the flickering candle-lantern upon the floor beside the doorway and broke open the package of flour. "See, Friend Trowbridge, do as I do," he directed, dipping his hand into the flour and sprinkling the white powder lightly over the flagstone pavement of the chapel. "Back away toward the door," he commanded, "and on no account leave a footprint in the meal. We must have a fair, unsoiled page for our records."

Wonderingly, but willingly, I helped him spread a film of flour over the chapel floor from altar-step to doorway, then turned upon him with a question: "What do you expect to find in this meal, de Grandin? Surely not footprints. No one who did not have to would come to this ghastly place."

He nodded seriously at me as he picked up his lantern and the remains of the package of flour. "Partly right and partly wrong you are, my friend. One may come who must, one may come who wants. Tomorrow, perhaps, we shall know more than we do today."

7

I WAS IN THE MIDST of my toilet when he burst into my bedroom next morning, feline mustache bristling, his round eyes fairly snapping with excitement. "Come, *mon vieux*," he urged, tugging at my arm as a nervous terrier might have urged his master to go for a romp, "come and see; right away, quick, at once, immediately!"

We hastened through the château's modern wing, passed the doors blocking the corridors of the fifteenth century buildings and came at last to the eleventh century chapel. De Grandin paused before the oak-and-iron door like a showman about to raise the curtain from an exhibit as he lit the candle in his lantern, and I heard his small, even teeth clicking together in a chill of suppressed excitement. "Behold, *mon ami*," he commanded in a hoarse whisper more expressive of emotion than a shout, "behold what writings are on the page which we did prepare!"

I looked through the arched doorway, then turned to him, dumb with surprise.

Leading from the chapel entrance, and ending at the center of the floor, directly before the altar, was the unmistakable trail of little, naked feet. No woodcraft was needed to trace the walker's course. She had entered the sanctuary, marched straight and unswervingly to a spot about fifteen feet from the altar, but directly before it, then turned about slowly in a tiny circle, no more than two feet in diameter, for at that point the footprints were so superimposed on each other that all individual traces were lost.

But the other track which showed in the strewn flour was less easily explained. Beginning at a point directly opposite the place the footprints ceased, this other trail ran some three or four inches wide in a lazy zigzag, as though a single automobile wheel had been rolled in an uncertain course across the floor by someone staggeringly drunk. But no prints of feet followed the wheel-track. The thing had apparently traversed the floor of its own volition.

"See," de Grandin whispered, "flour-prints lead away from the door"—he pointed to a series of white prints, plainly describing bare heels and toes, leading up the passage from the chapel floor, diminishing in clearness with each step until they faded out some ten paces toward the modern part of the château. "And see," he repeated, drawing me inside the chapel to the wall where the other, inexplicable, track began, "a trail leads outward here, too."

Following his pointing finger with my eye I saw what I had not noticed before, a cleft in the chapel wall some five inches wide, evidently the result of crumbling cement and gradually sinking foundation stones. At the entrance of the fissure a tiny pile of flour showed, as though some object previously dusted with the powder had been forced through the crevice.

I blinked stupidly at him. "Wh-what is this track?" I asked in bewilderment.

"Ah, bah!" he exclaimed disgustedly. "The blindest man is he who shuts his own eyes, my friend. Did you never, as a boy, come upon the trail of a serpent in the dusty road?"

"A snake track"—my mind refused the evidence of my eyes—"but how can that be—here?"

"The gamekeeper *thought* he saw a serpent in the garden *exactly outside this chapel*," de Grandin replied in a low voice, "and it was where that besotted gamekeeper imagined he beheld a serpent that the body of Mijnheer Van Brundt was found crushed out of semblance to a human man. Tell me, Friend Trowbridge—you know something of zoology—what creature, besides the constrictor-snake, kills his prey by crushing each bone of his body till nothing but shapeless pulp remains? *Hein?*"

"Bu—but . . ." I began, when he cut me short.

"Go call on our patient," he commanded. "If she sleeps, do not awaken her, but *observe the drugget on her floor!*"

I HASTENED TO ADRIENNE BIXBY'S room, pushed unceremoniously past Roxanne, the maid, and tiptoed to the girl's bedside. She lay on her side, one cheek pillowed on her arm, sleeping the sleep of utter exhaustion. I bent over her a moment, listening to her even breathing, then, nodding to the maid, turned and walked softly from the room, my eyes glued to the dark-red plush carpet which covered the chamber floor.

Five minutes later I met the little Frenchman in the library, my excitement now as high as his own. "De Grandin," I whispered, involuntarily lowering my voice, "I looked at her carpet. The thing's made of red velvet and shows a spot of dust ten feet away. A trail of faint white footprints leads right up to her bed!"

8

"SACRÉ NOM D'UN PETIT *bonhomme!*" He reached for his green felt hat and turned toward the door. "The trail becomes clear; even my good, skeptical friend Trowbridge can follow it, I think. Come, *cher ami*, let us see what we can see."

He led me through the château park, between the rows of tall, trembling poplar trees, to a spot where black-boughed evergreens cast perpetual shade above a stonefenced area of a scant half acre. Rose bushes, long deteriorated from their cultivated state, ran riot over the ground, the whole enclosure had the gloomy aspect of a deserted cemetery. "Why," I asked, "what place is this, de Grandin? It's as different from the rest of the park as . . ."

"As death is from life, *n'est-ce-pas?*" he interjected. "Yes, so it is, truly. Observe." He parted a mass of intertwined brambles and pointed to a slab of stone, once white, but now brown and roughened with centuries of exposure. "Can you read the inscription?" he asked.

The letters, once deeply cut in the stone, were almost obliterated, but I made out:

CI GIT TOUJOURS RAIMOND
SEIGNEUR DE BROUSSAC

"What does it say?" he demanded.

"'Here lies Raimond, Lord of Broussac,'" I replied, translating as well as I could.

"*Non, non,*" he contradicted. "It does not say, '*Ci git,*' here lies; but '*Ci git toujours*'—here lies always, or forever. Eh, my friend, what do you make of that, if anything?"

"Dead men usually lie permanently," I countered.

"Ah, so? Have I not heard your countrymen sing:

John Brown's body lies a-moldering
in the grave,
But his soul goes marching on.

"What of the poor Seigneur de Broussac, is he to lie buried here *toujours*, or shall he, too, not rise once again?"

"I'm not familiar with French idioms," I defended. Perhaps the stonecutter merely intended to say the Seigneur de Broussac lies here for his last long sleep."

"*Cher* Trowbridge," de Grandin replied, speaking with slow impressiveness, "when a man's monument is carved the words are not chosen without due consideration. Who chose Raimond de Broussac's epitaph thought long upon its wording, and when he dictated those words his wish was father to his thought."

He stared thoughtfully at the crumbling stone a moment, repeating softly to himself, "And *Madame l'Abesse* said, 'Snake thou art, and . . .'" he shook his shoulders in an impatient shrug as though to throw off some oppressive train of thought. "*Eh bien*, but we waste time here, my friend; let us make an experiment." Turning on his heel he led the way to the stables.

"I would have some boards, a hammer and some sharp nails, if you please," he informed the hostler who greeted us at the barn door. "My friend, the very learned *Docteur* Trowbridge, from America, and I desire to test an idea."

WHEN THE SERVANT BROUGHT the desired materials, de Grandin sawed the boards into two lengths, one about eighteen inches, the other about three feet, and through these he drove the sharp-pointed horseshoe nails at intervals of about three-quarters of an inch, so that, when he finished, he had what resembled two large combs of which the boards were the backs and the needle-pointed nails the teeth. "Now," he announced, surveying his work critically, "I think we are prepared to give a little surprise party."

Taking up the hammer and two short pieces of boards in addition to his "combs," he led the way to the spot outside the château walls where the tipsy gamekeeper claimed to have seen the great snake. Here he attached the two strips of wood at right angles to the shorter of the pieces of board through which he had driven the nails, then, using the lateral lengths of wood as stakes, attached the comblike contrivance he had made firmly to the earth, its back resting levelly in the ground, its sharp spikes pointing upward before the crevice in the château foundations. Any animal larger than an earthworm desiring to make use of the crack in the wall as a passageway would have to jump or crawl over the sharp, lancelike points of the nails. "*Bien*," he commented, viewing his work with approval, "now to put your wise American maxim of 'Safety First' into practice."

We found our way to the ancient, gloomy chapel, and he wedged the longer of the nail-filled boards firmly between the jambs at the inner side of the doorway. "And now," he announced, as we turned once more toward the inhabited part of the house, "I have the splendid appetite for dinner, and for sleep, too, when bedtime arrives."

"What on earth does all this child's play mean, de Grandin?" I demanded, my curiosity getting the better of me.

He winked roguishly by way of answer, whistled a snatch of tune, then remarked, irrelevantly, "If you have the desire to gamble, *cher ami*, I will lay you a wager of five francs that our fair patient will be improved tomorrow morning."

9

HE WON THE BET. For the first time since we had been seen at Broussac, Adrienne Bixby was at the breakfast table the following day, and the healthy color in her cheeks and the clear sparkle of her lovely eyes told of a long, restful sleep.

Two more days passed, each seeing a marked improvement in her spirits and appearance. The purple semicircles beneath her eyes faded to a wholesome pink, her laughter rippled like the sound of a purling brook among the shadows of the château's gloomy halls.

"I gotta hand it to you, Doc," Bixby complimented me. "You've shore brought my little girl round in great, shape. Name your figger an' I'll pay the bill, an' never paid one with a better heart, neither."

"Dr. Trowbridge," Adrienne accosted me one morning as I was about to join de Grandin in the library. "Remember what you said about importing a little bit of Oklahoma to France the other day? Well, I've just received a letter—the dearest letter—from Ray. He's coming over—he'll be here day after tomorrow, I think, and no matter what Mother says or does, we're going to be married, right away. I've been Mrs. Bixby's daughter long enough; now I'm going to be Mr. Keefer's wife. If Mother makes Dad refuse to give us any money, it won't make the least little bit of difference. I taught school before Father got his money, and I know how to live as a poor man's wife. I'm going to have my man—my own man—and no one—*no one at all*—shall keep him away from me one day longer!"

"Good for you!" I applauded her rebellion. Without knowing young Keefer I was sure he must be a very desirable sort of person to have incurred the enmity of such a character as Bixby's wife.

B UT NEXT MORNING ADRIENNE was not at breakfast, and the downcast expression of her father's face told his disappointment more eloquently than any words he could have summoned. "Reckon the girl's had a little set-back, Doc," he muttered, averting his eyes. His wife looked me fairly between the brows, and though she said never a word I felt she considered me a pretty poor specimen of medical practitioner.

"*Mais non, Monsieur le Docteur,*" Roxanne demurred when I knocked at Adrienne's door, "you shall not waken her. The poor lamb is sleeping, she exhaust this morning, and she shall have her sleep. I, Roxanne, say so."

Nevertheless, I shook Adrienne gently, rousing her from a sleep which seemed more stupor than slumber. "Come, come, my dear," I scolded, "this won't do, you know. You've got to brace up. You don't want Ray to find you in this condition, do you? Remember, he's due at Broussac tomorrow."

"Is he?" she answered indifferently. "I don't care. Oh, doctor, I'm—so—tired." She was asleep again, almost at the last word.

I turned back the covers and lifted the collar of her robe. About her body, purple as the marks of a whiplash, lay the wide, circular bruise, fresher and more extensive than it had been the day I first noticed it.

"Death of my life!" de Grandin swore when I found him in the library and told him what I had seen. "That *sacré* bruise again? Oh, it is too much! Come and see what else I have found this cursed day!" Seizing my hand he half led, half dragged me outdoors, halting at the clump of evergreens where he had fixed his nail-studded board beside the château wall.

Ripped from its place and lying some ten feet away was the board, its nails turned upward in the morning sunlight and reminding me, somehow, of the malicious grin from a fleshless skull.

"Why, how did this happen?" I asked.

He pointed mutely to the moist earth in which the dwarf cedars grew, his hand shaking with excitement and rage. In the soft loam beside the place where the board had been fixed were the prints of two tiny, bare feet.

"What's it mean?" I demanded, exasperated at the way he withheld information from me, but his answer was no more enlightening than any of his former cryptic utterances.

"The battle is joined, my friend," he replied through set teeth. "Amuse yourself as you will—or can—this day. I go to Rouen right away, immediately, at once. There are weapons I must have for this fight besides those we now have. Eh, but it will be a fight to the death! Yes, *par la croix*, and we shall help Death reclaim his own too. *Pardieu!* Am I not Jules de Grandin? Am I to be made a monkey of by one who preys on women? *Morbleu*, we shall see!"

And with that he left me, striding toward the stables in search of a motor car, his little yellow mustache bristling with fury, his blue eyes snapping, French oaths pouring from him like spray from a garden-sprinkler.

10

IT WAS DARK BEFORE he returned, his green hat set at a rakish angle over his right ear, a long, closely wrapped brown paper parcel under his arm. "*Eh bien*," he confided to me with an elfish grin, "it required much argument to secure this. That old priest, he is a stubborn one and unbelieving, almost as skeptical as you, Friend Trowbridge."

"What on earth is it?" I demanded, looking curiously at the package. Except that it was too long, it might have been an umbrella, judging by its shape.

He winked mysteriously as he led the way to his room, where, having glanced about furtively, as though he apprehended some secret watcher, he laid the bundle on the bed and began cutting the strings securing its brown paper swaddling clothes with his pocket knife. Laying back the final layer of paper he uncovered a long sword, such a weapon as I had never beheld outside a museum. The blade was about three and a half feet in length, tapering from almost four inches and a half at the tip, where, it terminated in a beveled point. Unlike modern weapons, this one was furnished with two sharpened edges, almost keen enough to do duty for a knife, and, instead of the usual groove found on the sides of sword blades, its center presented a distinct ridge where the steep bevels met at an obtuse angle as they sloped from the edges. The handle, made of ivory or some smoothly polished bone, was long enough to permit a two-handed grip, and the hilt which crossed the blade at a right angle turned downward toward the point, its ends terminating in rather clumsily carved cherubs' heads. Along the blade, apparently carved, rather than etched, marched a procession of miscellaneous angels, demons and men at arms with a mythological monster, such as a griffin or dragon, thrown in for occasional good measure. Between the crudely carved figures I made out the letters of the motto: *Dei Gratia*—by the grace of God.

"Well?" I asked wonderingly as I viewed the ancient weapon.

"Well?" he repeated mockingly, then: "Had you as many blessings on your head as this old bit of carved metal has received, you would be a very holy man indeed, Friend Trowbridge. This sword, it was once strapped to the thigh of a saint—it matters not which one—who fought the battles of France when France needed all the champions, saintly or otherwise, she could summon. For centuries it has reposed in a very ancient church at Rouen, not, indeed, as a relic, but as a souvenir scarcely less venerated. When I told the *curé* I proposed borrowing it for a day or more I thought he would die of the apoplexy forthwith, but"—he gave his diminutive mustache a complacent tweak—"such was my power of persuasion that you see before you the very sword."

"But what under heaven will you do with the thing, now you've got it?" I demanded.

"Much—perhaps," he responded, picking up the weapon, which must have weighed at least twenty pounds, and balancing it in both hands as a wood-chopper holds his ax before attacking a log.

"*Nom d'un bouc!*" he glanced suddenly at his wristwatch and replaced the sword on his bed. "I do forget myself. Run, my friend, fly, fly like the swallow to Mademoiselle Adrienne's room and caution her to remain within—at all hazards. Bid her close her windows, too, for we know not what may be abroad or what can climb a wall this night. See that stubborn, pig-foolish maid of hers has instructions to lock her mistress' door on the inside and, should Mademoiselle rise in the night and desire to leave, on no account permit her to pass. You understand?"

"No, I'll be banged if I do," I replied. "What . . . ?"

"*Non, non!*" he almost shrieked. "Waste not time nor words, my friend. I desire that you should do as I say. Hurry, I implore; it is of the importance, I do assure you."

I DID AS HE REQUESTED, having less difficulty than I had expected concerning the windows, since Adrienne was already sunk in a heavy sleep and Roxanne possessed the French peasant's inborn hatred of fresh air.

"Good, very, very good," de Grandin commended when I rejoined him. "Now we shall wait until the second quarter of the night—then, ah, perhaps I show you something to think about in the after years, Friend Trowbridge."

He paced the floor like a caged animal for a quarter-hour, smoking one cigarette after another, then: "Let us go," he ordered curtly, picking up the giant sword and shouldering it as a soldier does his rifle. "*Aller au feu!*"

We tramped down the corridor toward the stairway, when he turned quickly, almost transfixing me with the sword blade, which projected two feet and more beyond his shoulder. "One more inspection, Friend Trowbridge," he urged. "Let us see how it goes with Mademoiselle Adrienne. *Eh bien*, do we not carry her colors into battle this night?"

"Never mind that monkey-business!" we heard a throaty feminine voice command as we approached Adrienne's room. "I've stood about all I intend to from you; tomorrow you pack your clothes, if you've any to pack, and get out of this house."

"Eh, what is this?" de Grandin demanded as we reached the chamber door and beheld Roxanne weeping bitterly, while Mrs. Bixby towered over her like a Cochin hen bullying a half-starved sparrow.

"I'll tell you what it is!" replied the irate mistress of the house. "I came to say goodnight to my daughter a few minutes ago and this—this hussy!—refused to open the door for me. I soon settled her, I can tell you. I told her to open that door and get out. When I went into the room I found every window locked tight—in this weather, too.

"Now I catch her hanging around the door after I'd ordered her to her room. Insubordination; rank insubordination, it is. She leaves this house bright and early tomorrow morning, I can tell you!"

"Oh, Monsieur Trow-breege, Monsieur de Grandin," sobbed the trembling girl, "I did but attempt to obey your orders, and—and she drove me from my duty. Oh, I am so soree!"

De Grandin's small teeth shut with a snap like a miniature steel trap. "And you forced this girl to unbar the door?" he asked, almost incredulously, gazing sternly at Mrs. Bixby.

"I certainly did," she bridled, "and I'd like to know what business is it of yours. If . . ."

He brushed by her, leaping into the bedroom with a bound which carried him nearly two yards beyond the doorsill.

We looked past him toward the bed. It was empty. Adrienne Bixby was gone.

"Why—why, where can she *be?*" Mrs. Bixby asked, her domineering manner temporarily stripped from her by surprise.

"I'll tell you where she is!" de Grandin, white to the lips, shouted at her. "She is where you have sent her, you meddling old ignoramus, you, you—oh, *mon Dieu*, if you were a man how I should enjoy cutting your heart out!"

"Say, see here . . ." she began, her bewilderment sunk in anger, but he cut her short with a roar.

"Silence, you! To your room, foolish, criminally foolish one, and pray *le bon Dieu* on your bare knees that the pig-ignorance of her mother shall not have cost your daughter her life this night! Come, Trowbridge, my friend, come away; the breath of this woman is a contamination, and we must hurry if we are to undo her fool's work. Pray God we are not too late!"

WE RUSHED DOWNSTAIRS, TRAVERSED the corridors leading to the older wing of the house, wound our way down and down beneath the level of the ancient moat till we stood before the entrance of the chapel.

"Ah," de Grandin breathed softly, lowering his sword point a moment as he dashed the sweat from his forehead with the back of his hand, "no sound, Friend Trowbridge. Whatever happens, whatever you may see, do not cry out; 'tis death to one we seek to save if you waken her!"

Raising his hand, he signed himself quickly with the cross, muttering an indistinct *in nomine*, while I gaped in amazement to see the cynical, scoffing little man of science shedding his agnosticism and reverting to a simple act of his childhood's faith.

Lifting the sword in both hands, he gave the chapel door a push with his foot, whispering to me, "Hold high the lanterns, Friend Trowbridge; we need light for our work."

The rays from my lamp streamed across the dark, vaulted chapel and I nearly let the lantern crash to the floor at what I beheld.

Standing before the ancient, tumbledown altar, her nude, white body gleaming in the semi-darkness like a lovely, slender statue of sun-stained marble, was Adrienne Bixby. Her long rippling hair, which had always reminded me of molten gold in the assayer's crucible, streamed over her shoulders to her waist; one arm was raised in a gesture of absolute abandon while her other hand caressed some object which swayed and undulated before her. Parted in a smile such as Circe, the enchantress, might have worn when she lured men to their ruin, her red lips were drawn back from her gleaming teeth, while she crooned a slow, sensuous melody the like of which I had never heard, nor wish to hear again.

My astounded eyes took this in at first glance, but it was my second look which sent the blood coursing through my arteries like river-water in zero weather. About her slender, virginal torso, ascending in a spiral from hips to shoulders, *was the spotted body of a gigantic snake*.

The monster's horrid, wedge-shaped head swung and swayed a scant half-inch before her face, and its darting, lambent tongue licked lightly at her parted lips.

But it was no ordinary serpent which held her, a laughing prisoner, in its coils. Its body shone with alternate spots of green and gold, almost as if the colors were laid on in luminous paint; its flickering tongue was red and glowing as a flame of fire, and in its head were eyes as large and blue as those of human kind, but set and terrible in their expression as only the eyes of a snake can be.

Scarcely audible, so low his whisper was, de Grandin hissed a challenge as he hurled himself into the chapel with one of his lithe, catlike leaps: "*Snake thou art, Raimond de Broussac, and snake thou shalt become! Garde à vous!*"

With a slow, sliding motion, the great serpent turned its head, gradually released its folds from the leering girl's body and slipped to the floor, coiled its length quickly, like a giant spring, and launched itself like a flash of green-and-gold lightning at de Grandin!

But quick as the monster's attack was, de Grandin was quicker. Like the shadow of a flying hawk, the little Frenchman slipped aside, and the reptile's darting head crashed against the granite wall with an impact like a wave slapping a ship's bow.

"One!" counted de Grandin in a mocking whisper, and swung his heavy sword, snipping a two-foot length from the serpent's tail as neatly as a seamstress snips a thread with her scissors. "*En garde, fils du diable!*"

Writhing, twisting, turning like a spring from which the tension has been loosed, the serpent gathered itself for another onslaught, its malign, human-seeming eyes glaring implacable hatred at de Grandin.

Not this time did the giant reptile launch a battering-ram blow at its adversary. Instead, it reared itself six feet and more in the air and drove its wicked, scale armored head downward with a succession of quick, shifting jabs, seeking to take de Grandin off his guard and enfold him in its crushing coils.

But like a veritable *chevaux-de-frise* of points, de Grandin's sword was right, left, and in between. Each time the monster's head drove at the little man, the blade engraved with ancient battle-cry stood in its path, menacing the hateful blue eyes and flashing, backward-curving fangs with its sharp, tapering end.

"Ha, ha!" de Grandin mocked; "to fight a man is a greater task than to bewitch a woman, *n'est-ce-pas, M'sieur le Serpent?*

"Ha! You have it!" Like a wheel of living flame, the sword circled through the air; there was a sharp, slapping impact, and the steel sheared clean and clear through the reptile's body, six inches below the head.

"*Sa, ha; sa, ha!*" de Grandin's face was set in a look of incomparable fury; his small mouth was squared beneath his bristling mustache like that of a snarling wildcat, and the sword rose and fell in a quick succession of strokes, separating the writhing body of the serpent into a dozen, twenty, half a hundred sections.

"*S-s-h*, no noise!" he cautioned as I opened my lips to speak. "First clothe the poor child's nakedness; her gown lies yonder on the floor."

I looked behind me and saw Adrienne's silk nightrobe lying in a crumpled ring against the altar's lowest step. Turning toward the girl, revulsion and curiosity fighting for mastery of my emotions, I saw she still retained the same fixed, carnal smile; her right hand still moved mechanically in the air as though caressing the head of the loathsome thing yet quivering in delayed death at her white feet.

"Why, de Grandin," I exclaimed in wonder, "why, she's *asleep!*"

"*S-s-h*, no sound!" he cautioned again, laying his finger on his lips. "Slip the robe over her head, my friend, and pick her up gently. She will not know."

I draped the silken garment about the unconscious girl, noticing as I did so, that a long, spiral bruise was already taking form on her tender flesh.

"Careful! Friend Trowbridge," de Grandin commanded, picking up the lantern and sword and leading the way from the chapel. "Carry her tenderly, the poor, sinned-against one. Do not waken her, I beseech you. *Pardieu*, if that scolding mother of hers does but open her shrewish lips within this poor lamb's hearing this night, I shall serve her as I did the serpent. *Mordieu*, may Satan burn me if I do not so!"

II

"TROWBRIDGE, TROWBRIDGE, MY FRIEND, come and see!" de Grandin's voice sounded in my ear.

I sat up, sleepily staring about me. Daylight had just begun; the gray of early morning still mingled with the first faint rose of the new day, and outside my window the blackbirds were singing.

"Eh, what's up?" I demanded, swinging my feet to the floor.

"Plenty, a very plenty, I do assure you," he answered, tugging delightedly first at one end of his mustache, then the other. "Arise, my friend, arise and pack your bags; we must go immediately, at once, right away."

He fairly pranced about the room while I shaved, washed, and made ready for the journey, meeting my bewildered demands for information only with renewed entreaties for haste. At last, as I accompanied him down the great stairway my kit bags banging against my knees:

"Behold!" he cried, pointing dramatically to the hall below. "Is it not superb?"

On a couch before the great empty fireplace of the château hall sat Adrienne Bixby, dressed and ready for a trip, her slender white hands securely held in a pair of bronzed ones, her fluffy golden head pillowed on a broad, home-spun-clad shoulder.

"Monsieur Trowbridge," de Grandin almost purred in his elation, "permit that I present to you Monsieur Ray Keefer, of Oklahoma, who is to make happy our so dear Mademoiselle Adrienne at once, right away, immediately. Come, *mes enfants*, we must go away," he beamed on the pair of lovers. "The American consul at Rouen, he will unite you in the bonds of matrimony, then—away for that joyous wedding trip, and may your happiness never be less than it is this day. I have left a note of explanation for Monsieur your father, Mademoiselle; let us hope he gives you his blessing. However, be that as it may, you have already the blessing of happiness."

A large motor was waiting outside, Roxanne seated beside the chauffeur, mounting guard over Adrienne's baggage.

"I did meet Monsieur Keefer as he entered the park this morning," de Grandin confided to me as the car gathered speed, "and I did compel him to wait while I rushed within and roused his sweetheart and Roxanne from their sleep. Ha, ha, what was it Madame the Scolding One did say to Roxanne last night, that she should pack her clothes and leave the house bright and early this morning? *Eh bien*, she has gone, *n'est-ce-pas?*"

Shepherded by de Grandin and me, the lovers entered the consulate, emerging a few minutes later with a certificate bearing the great seal of the United States of America and the information that they were man and wife.

De Grandin hunted feverishly in the gutters, finally discovered a tattered old boot, and shied it after them as, with the giggling Roxanne, they set out for Switzerland, Oklahoma and happiness.

"Name of a little green man!" he swore, furtively flicking a drop of moisture from his eyes. "I am so happy to see her safe in the care of the good young man who loves her that I could almost bring myself to kiss that so atrocious Madame Bixby!"

12

"NOW, DE GRANDIN," I threatened, as we seated ourselves in a compartment of the Paris express, "tell me all about it, or I'll choke the truth out of you!"

"*La, la,*" he exclaimed in mock terror, "he is a ferocious one, this *Americain!* Very well, then, *cher ami*, from the beginning:

"You will recall how I told you houses gather evil reputations, even as people do? They do more than that, my friend; they acquire character.

"Broussac is an old place; in it generations of men have been born and have lived, and met their deaths; and the record of their personalities—all they have dreamed and thought and loved and hated—is written fair upon the walls of the house for him who cares to read. These thoughts I had when first I went to Broussac to trace down the reason for these deaths which drove tenant after tenant from the château.

"But fortunately for me there was a more tangible record than the atmosphere of the house to read. There was the great library of the de Broussac family, with the records of those who were good, those who were not so good, and those who were not good at all written down. Among those records did I find this story:

"In the years before your America was discovered, there dwelt at Broussac one Sieur Raimond, a man beside whom the wickedest of the Roman emperors was a mild-mannered gentleman. What he desired he took, this one, and as most of his desires leaned toward his neighbors' women folk, he was busy at robbery, murder and rapine most of the time.

"*Eh bien*, he was a mighty man, this Sieur Raimond, but the Bishop of Rouen and the Pope at Rome were mightier. At last, the wicked gentleman came face-to-face with the reckoning of his sins, for where the civil authorities were fearful to act, the church stepped in and brought him to trial.

"Listen to this which I found among the chronicles at the château, my friend. Listen and marvel!" He drew a sheaf of papers from his portmanteau and began reading slowly, translating as he went along:

Now when the day for the wicked Sieur Raimond's execution was come, a great procession issued from the church where the company of faithful people were gone to give thanks that Earth was to be ridded of a monster.

Francois and Henri, the de Broussac's wicked accomplices in crime, had become reconciled to Mother Church, and so were accorded the mercy of strangling before burning, but the Sieur Raimond would have none of repentance, but walked to his place of execution with the smile of a devil on his false, well-favored face.

And as he marched between the men at arms toward the stake set up for his burning, behold, the Lady Abbess of the convent of Our Lady of Mercy, together with the gentlewomen who were her nuns, came forth to weep and pray for the souls of the condemned, even the soul of the unrepentant sinner, Raimond de Broussac.

And when the Sieur Raimond was come over against the place where the abbess stood with all her company, he halted between his guards and taunted her, saying, "What now, old hen, dost seek the chicks of thy brood who are missing?" (For it was a fact that three novices of the convent of Our Lady had been ravished away from their vows by this vile man and great was the scandal thereof everywhere.)

Then did the Lady Abbess pronounce these words to that wicked man, "Snake thou art, Raimond de Broussac, snake thou shalt become and snake thou must remain until some good man and true shall cleave thy foul body into as many pieces as the year hath weeks."

And I, who beheld and heard all, do declare upon the rood that when the flames were kindled about that wicked man and his sinful body had been burned to ashes, a small snake of the colors of green and gold was seen by all to emerge from the fire and, maugre the efforts of the men at arms to slay it, did escape to the forest of the château of Broussac.

"Eh? What think you of that, Friend Trowbridge?" he asked as he laid the papers beside him on the car-seat.

"Rather an interesting medieval legend," I answered, "but hardly convincing today."

"Truly," he conceded, "but as your English proverb has it, where there is much smoke there is apt to be a little flame. Other things I found in the records, my friend. For instance:

"The ashes of this Raimond de Broussac could not be buried in the château chapel among his ancestors and descendants, for the chapel is consecrated ground, and he died excommunicate. They buried him in what was then a pine forest hard by the house where he lived his evil life, and on the stone which they set over him they did declare that he lay there forever.

"But one year from the day of his execution, as the de Broussac chaplain was reciting his office in the chapel, he did see a green-and-gold snake, something thicker than a monk's girdle but not so long as a man's forearm, enter the chapel, and the snake attacked the holy man so fiercely that he was much put to it to defend himself.

"Another year went by, and a servant bearing off to refill the sanctuary lamp in the chapel did behold a similar snake, but now grown to the length of a man's arm, coiled above one of the tombs; and the snake also attacked that servant, and nearly slew him.

"From year to year the records go on. Often about Broussac was seen a snake, but each succeeding time it appeared larger than before.

"Too, there were strange stories current—stories of women of the locality who wandered off into the woods of Broussac, who displayed strange bruises upon their bodies, and who died eventually in a manner unexplained by any natural cause. One and all, *mon ami*, they were crushed to death.

"One was a member of the de Broussac family, a distant kinswoman of Sieur Raimond himself, who had determined to take the veil. As she knelt in prayer in the chapel one day, a great sleep fell upon her, and after that, for many days, she seemed distrait—her interest in everything, even her religious vocation, seemed to wane to nothing. But it was thought that she was very saintly, for those who watched her did observe that she went often to the chapel by night. One morning she was found, like the others, crushed to death, and on her face was the look not of the agony of dying but the evil smile of an abandoned woman. Even in death she wore it.

"These things I had already read when that gamekeeper brought us news of the great snake he had seen in the garden, and what I had noted down as idle legend appeared possible to me as a sober fact—if we could prove it.

"You recall how we spread flour on the chapel floor; you also recall the tracks we read in the flour next day.

"I remembered, too, how that poor Madame Biddle, who went mad in the château Broussac, did so when she wandered one day by chance into the chapel, and I remembered how she does continually cry out of a great snake which seems to *kiss* her. The doctor who first attended her, too, when her reason departed, told me of a bruise not to be explained, a spiral bruise about the lady's arm.

"*Pardieu!* I think I will test these legends some more, and I search and search until I find this wicked Sieur Raimond's grave. It was even as the chronicler wrote, for, to prove it, I made you go with me and read the inscription on the tombstone. *Morbleu!* Against my reason I am convinced, so I make and place them so that their sharp nails would scratch the belly of any snake—if he were really a snake—who tried to crawl over them. *Voilà*, next she was better. Then I knew for a certainty that she was under the influence of this Sieur Raimond snake, even as that poor intend-ing-nun lady who met so tragic a death in the days of long ago.

"Something else I learn, too. This demon snake, this relic of the accurst Raimond de Broussac, was like a natural snake. Material iron nails would keep him from the house his wickedness had so long held under a spell. If this was so, then a natural weapon could kill his body if one man was but brave enough to fight him. '*Cordieu*, I am that man!' says Jules de Grandin to Jules de Grandin.

"But in the meantime what do I see? *Hélas!* That wicked one has now so great an influence over poor Mademoiselle Adrienne that he can compel her, by his wicked will, to rise from her bed at night and go barefoot to the garden to tear away the barrier I have erected for her protection.

"*Nom d'un coq!* I am angered, I am furious. I decide this snake-devil have already lived too long; I shall do even as the Lady Abbess prescribes and slash his so loathly body into as many parts as the year has weeks.

"*Morbleu!* I go to Rouen and obtain that holy sword; I come back, thinking I shall catch that snake waiting alone in the chapel for his assignation, since I shall bar Mademoiselle's way to him. And then her so stupid mother must needs upset all my plans, and I have to fight that snake almost in silence—I can not shout and curse at him as I would, for if I raise my voice I may waken that then, perhaps she goes mad, even as did Madame Biddle.

"*Eh bien*, perhaps it is for the best. Had I said all the foul curses I had in mind as I slew that blue-eyed snake, all the priests, clergymen and rabbis in the world could scarce have shriven my soul of their weight."

The Isle of Missing Ships

T HE MEVROUW, SUMATRA-BOUND OUT of Amsterdam, had dropped the low
Holland coast an hour behind that day in 1925, when I recognized a familiar figure among the miscellany of Dutch colonials. The little man with the
erect, military carriage, trimly waxed mustache and direct, challenging blue
eyes was as conspicuous amid the throng of over-fleshed planters, traders and
petty administrators as a *fleur-de-lis* growing in the midst of a cabbage patch.

"For the Lord's sake, de Grandin! What are you doing here?" I demanded,
seizing him by the hand. "I thought you'd gone back to your microscopes and
test tubes when you cleared up the Broussac mystery."

He grinned at me like a blond brother of Mephistopheles as he linked his
arm in mine and caught step with me. "*Eh bien,*" he agreed with a nod, "so did I;
but those inconsiderate Messieurs Lloyd would not have it so. They must needs
send me an urgent message to investigate a suspicion they have at the other end
of the earth.

"I did not desire to go. The summer is come and the blackbirds are singing
in the trees at St. Cloud. Also, I have much work to do; but they tell me: 'You
shall name your own price and no questions shall be asked,' and, *hélas*, the franc
is very low on the exchange these days.

"I tell them, 'Ten pounds sterling for each day of my travels and all expenses.'
They agree. *Voilà.* I am here."

I looked at him in amazement. "Lloyds? Ten pounds sterling a day?" I
echoed. "What in the world—?"

"*La, la!*" he exclaimed. "It is a long story, Friend Trowbridge, and most like
a foolish one in the bargain, but, at any rate, the English money is sound. Listen"—he sank his voice to a confidential whisper—"you know those Messieurs
Lloyd, *hein?* They will insure against anything from the result of one of your

American political elections to the loss of a ship in the sea. That last business of theirs is also my business, for the time.

"Of late the English insurers have had many claims to pay—claims on ships which should have been good risks. There was the Dutch Indiaman *Van Damm*, a sound little iron ship of twelve thousand tons displacement. She sail out of Rotterdam for Sumatra, and start home heavy-laden with spices and silks, also with a king's ransom in pearls safely locked in her strong box. Where is she now?" He spread his hands and shrugged expressively. "No one knows. She was never heard of more, and the Lloyds had to make good her value to her owners.

"There was the French steamer *l'Orient*, also dissolved into air, and the British merchantman *Nightingale*, and six other sound ships gone—all gone, with none to say whither, and the estimable Messieurs Lloyd to pay insurance. All within one single year. *Parbleu*, it is too much! The English company pays its losses like a true sportsman, but it also begins to sniff the aroma of the dead fish. They would have me, Jules de Grandin, investigate this business of the monkey and tell them where the missing ships are gone.

"It may be for a year that I search; it may be for only a month, or, perhaps, I spend the time till my hair is as bald as yours, Friend Trowbridge, before I can report. No matter; I receive my ten pounds each day and all incidental expenses. Say now, are not those Messieurs Lloyd gambling more recklessly this time than ever before in their long career?"

"I think they are," I agreed.

"But," he replied with one of his elfish grins, "remember, Trowbridge, my friend, those Messieurs Lloyd were never known to lose money permanently on any transaction. *Morbleu!* Jules de Grandin, as the Americans say, you entertain the hatred for yourself!"

The *Mevrouw* churned and wallowed her broad-beamed way through the cool European ocean, into the summer seas, finally out upon the tropical waters of Polynesia. For five nights the smalt-blue heavens were ablaze with stars; on the sixth evening the air thickened at sunset. By ten o'clock the ship might have been draped in a pall of black velvet as a teapot is swathed in a cozy, so impenetrable was the darkness. Objects a dozen feet from the porthole lights were all but indistinguishable, at twenty feet they were invisible, and, save for the occasional phosphorescent glow of some tumbling sea denizen, the ocean itself was only an undefined part of the surrounding blackness.

"Eh, but I do not like this," de Grandin muttered as he lighted a rank Sumatra cigar from the ship steward's store and puffed vigorously to set the fire going: "this darkness, it is a time for evil doings, Friend Trowbridge."

He turned to a ship's officer who strode past us toward the bridge. "Is it that we shall have a storm, Monsieur?" he asked. "Does the darkness portend a typhoon?"

"No," returned the Dutchman. "Id iss folcanic dust. Some of dose folcano mountains are in eruption again and scatter steam and ash over a hundred miles. Tomorrow, perhaps, or de nex' day, ve are out of id an' into de zunzhine again."

"Ah," de Grandin bowed acknowledgment of the information, "and does this volcanic darkness frequently come at this latitude and longitude, Monsieur?"

"Ja," the other answered, "dese vaters are almost alvays cofered; de chimneys of hell poke up through de ocean hereabouts, *Mijnheer*."

"*Cordieu!*" de Grandin swore softly to himself. "I think he has spoken truth, Friend Trowbridge. Now if—*Grand Dieu*, see! What is that?"

Some distance off our port bow a brand of yellow fire burned a parabola against the black sky, burst into a shower of sparks high above the horizon and flung a constellation of colored fireballs into the air. A second flame followed the first, and a third winged upward in the wake of the second. "Rockets," de Grandin announced. "A ship is in distress over there, it would seem."

Bells clanged and jangled as the engine room telegraph sent orders from the bridge; there was a clanking of machinery as the screws churned in opposite directions and the steering mechanism brought the ship's head about toward the distress signals.

"I think we had best be prepared, my friend," de Grandin whispered as he reached upward to the rack above us and detached two kapok swimming jackets from their straps. "Come, slip this over your shoulders, and if you have anything in your cabin you would care to save, get it at once," he advised.

"You're crazy, man," I protested, pushing the life preserver away. "We aren't in any danger. Those lights were at least five miles away, and even if that other ship is fast on a reef our skipper would hear the breakers long before we were near enough to run aground."

"*Nom d'un nom!*" the little Frenchman swore in vexation. "Friend Trowbridge, you are one great zany. Have you no eyes in that so empty head of yours? Did you not observe how those rockets went up?"

"How they went up?" I repeated. "Of course I did; they were fired from the deck—perhaps the bridge—of some ship about five miles away."

"So?" he replied in a sarcastic whisper. "Five miles, you say? And you, a physician, do not know that the human eye sees only about five miles over a plane surface? How, then, if the distressed ship is five miles distant, could those flares have appeared to rise from *a greater height than our own deck*? Had they really a masthead, at that distance—they should have appeared to rise across the horizon. As it was, they first became visible at a considerable height."

"Nonsense," I rejoined; "whoever would be setting off rockets in midair in this part of the world?"

"Who, indeed?" he answered, gently forcing the swimming coat on me. "That question, *mon ami*, is precisely what those Messieurs Lloyd are paying me ten pounds a day to answer. Hark!"

Distinctly, directly in our path, sounded the muttering roar of waves breaking against rocks.

Clang! The ship's telegraph shrieked the order to reverse, to put about, to the engine room from the bridge.

Wheels and chains rattled, voices shouted hoarse orders through the dark, and the ship shivered from stem to stern as the engine struggled hysterically to break our course toward destruction.

Too late! Like a toy boat caught in a sudden wind squall, we lunged forward, gathering speed with each foot we traveled. There was a rending crash like all the crockery in the world being smashed at once, de Grandin and I fell headlong to the deck and shot along the smooth boards like a couple of ball players sliding for second base, and the stout little *Mevrouw* listed suddenly to port, sending us banging against the deck rail.

"Quick, quick, my friend!" de Grandin shouted. "Over the side and swim for it. I may be wrong, *prie-Dieu* I am, but I fear there will be devil's work here anon. Come!" He lifted himself to his feet, balanced on the rail a moment, then slipped into the purple water that swirled past the doomed ship's side a scant seven feet below us.

I followed, striking out easily toward the quiet water ahead, the kapok jacket keeping me afloat and the rushing water carrying me forward rapidly.

"By George, old fellow, you've been right this far," I congratulated my companion, but he shut me off with a sharp hiss.

"Still, you fool," he admonished savagely. "Keep your silly tongue quiet and kick with your feet. Kick, kick, I tell you! Make as great commotion in the water as possible—*nom de Dieu!* We are lost!"

Faintly luminous with the phosphorescence of tropical sea water, something seeming as large as a submarine boat shot upward from the depths below, headed as straight for my flailing legs as a sharpshooter's bullet for its target.

De Grandin grasped my shoulder and heaved me over in a clumsy back somersault, and at the same time thrust himself as deeply into the water as his swimming coat would permit. For a moment his fiery silhouette mingled with that of the great fish and he seemed striving to embrace the monster, then the larger form sank slowly away, while the little Frenchman rose puffing to the surface.

"*Mordieu!*" he commented, blowing the water from his mouth, "that was a near escape, my friend. One little second more and he would have had your leg in his belly. Lucky for us, I knew the pearl divers' trick of slittin' those fellows' gills with a knife, and luckier still I thought to bring along a knife to slit him with."

"What was it?" I asked, still bewildered by the performance I had just witnessed. "It looked big enough to be a whale."

He shook his head to clear the water from his eyes as he replied. "It was our friend, *Monsieur le Requin*—the shark. He is always hungry, that one, and such morsels as you would be a choice titbit for his table, my friend."

"A shark!" I answered incredulously. "But it couldn't have been a shark, de Grandin, they have to turn on their backs to bite, and that thing came straight at me."

"*Ah, bah!*" he shot back disgustedly. "What old wives' tale is that you quote? *Le requin* is no more compelled to take his food upside down than you are. I tell you, he would have swallowed your leg up to the elbow if I had not cut his sinful gizzard in two!"

"Good Lord!" I began splashing furiously. "Then we're apt to be devoured any moment!"

"Possibly," he returned calmly, "but not probably. If land is not too far away that fellow's brethren will be too busy eating him to pay attention to such small fry as us. *Grace à Dieu*, I think I feel the good land beneath our feet even now."

It was true. We were standing armpit-deep on a sloping, sandy beach with the long, gentle swell of the ocean kindly pushing us toward the shore. A dozen steps and we were safely beyond the tide-line, lying face down upon the warm sands and gulping down great mouthfuls of the heavy, sea-scented air. What de Grandin did there in the dark I do not know, but for my part I offered up such unspoken prayers of devout thanksgiving as I had never breathed before.

My devotions were cut short by a sputtering mixture of French profanity.

"What's up?" I demanded, then fell silent as de Grandin's hand closed on my wrist like a tightened tourniquet.

"Hark, my friend," he commanded. "Look across the water to the ship we left and say whether or no I was wise when I brought us away."

Out across the quiet lagoon inside the reef the form of the stranded *Mevrouw* loomed a half shade darker than the night, her lights, still burning, casting a fitful glow upon the crashing water at the reef and the quiet water beyond. Two, three, four, half a dozen shades gathered alongside her; dark figures, like ants swarming over the carcass of a dead rat, appeared against her lights a moment, and the stabbing flame of a pistol was followed a moment later by the reports of the shots wafted to us across the lagoon. Shouts, cries of terror, screams of women in abject fright followed one another in quick succession for a time, then silence, more ominous than any noise, settled over the water.

Half an hour, perhaps, de Grandin and I stood tense-muscled on the beach, staring toward the ship, waiting expectantly for some sign of renewed life. One by one her porthole lights blinked out; at last she lay in utter darkness.

"It is best we seek shelter in the bush, my friend," de Grandin announced matter-of-factly. "The farther out of sight we get the better will be our health."

"What in heaven's name does it all mean?" I demanded as I turned to follow him.

"Mean?" he echoed impatiently. "It means we have stumbled on as fine a nest of pirates as ever cheated the yardarm. When we reached this island, Friend Trowbridge, I fear we did but step from the soup kettle into the flame. *Mille tonneres*, what a fool you are, Jules de Grandin! You should have demanded fifty pounds sterling a day from those Messieurs Lloyd! Come, Friend Trowbridge, let us seek shelter. Right away, at once, immediately."

2

THE SLOPING BEACH GAVE way to a line of boulders a hundred yards inland, and these in turn marked the beginning of a steady rise in the land, its lower portion overgrown with bushes, loftier growth supplanting the underbrush as we stumbled upward over the rocks.

When we had traversed several hundred rods and knocked nearly all the skin from our legs against unexpectedly projecting stones, de Grandin called a halt in the midst of a copse of wide-leafed trees. "We may as well rest here as elsewhere," he suggested philosophically. "The pack will scarcely hunt again tonight."

I was too sleepy and exhausted to ask what he meant. The last hour's events had been as full of surprises to me as a traveling carnival is for a farmhand.

It might have been half an hour later, or only five minutes, judging by my feelings, that I was roused by the roar of a muffled explosion, followed at short intervals by two more detonations. "*Mordieu!*" I heard de Grandin exclaim. "Up, Friend Trowbridge. Rise and see!" He shook me roughly by the shoulder, and half dragged me to an opening in the trees. Out across the lagoon I saw the hulk of the *Mevrouw* falling apart and sliding into the water like a mud bank attacked by a summer flood, and round her the green waters boiled and seethed as though the entire reef had suddenly gone white hot. Across the lagoon, wave after swelling wave raced and tumbled, beating on the glittering sands of the beach in a furious surf.

"Why—" I began, but he answered my question before I could form it.

"Dynamite!" he exclaimed. "Last night, or early this morning, they looted her, now they dismantle the remains with high explosives; it would not do to let her stand there as a sign-post of warning for other craft. *Pardieu!* They have system, these ones. Captain Kidd and Blackbeard, they were but freshmen in crime's college, Friend Trowbridge. We deal with postgraduates here. Ah"—his small, womanishly slender hand caught me by the arm—"observe, if you please; what is that on the sands below?"

Following his pointing finger with my eyes, I made out, beyond a jutting ledge of rocks, the rising spiral of a column of wood smoke. "Why," I exclaimed delightedly "some of the people from the ship escaped, after all! They got to shore and built a fire. Come on, let's join them. Hello, down here; hello, hello! You . . ."

"Fool!" he cried in a suppressed shout, clapping his hand over my mouth. "Would you ruin us altogether, completely, entirely? *Le bon Dieu* grant your ass's bray was not heard, or, if heard, was disregarded!"

"But," I protested, "those people probably have food, de Grandin, and we haven't a single thing to eat. We ought to join them and plan our escape."

He looked at me as a school teacher might regard an unusually backward pupil. "They have food, no doubt," he admitted, "but what sort of food, can you answer me that? Suppose—*nom d'un moinçau, regardez-vous!*"

A s IF IN ANSWER to my hail, a pair of the most villainous-looking Papuans I had ever beheld came walking around the rocky screen beyond which the smoke rose, looked undecidedly toward the heights where we hid, then turned back whence they had come. A moment later they reappeared, each carrying a broad-bladed spear, and began climbing over the rocks in our direction.

"Shall we go to meet them?" I asked dubiously. Those spears looked none too reassuring to me.

"*Mais non!*" de Grandin answered decidedly. "They may be friendly; but I distrust everything on this accurst island. We would better seek shelter and observe."

"But they might give us something to eat," I urged. "The whole world is pretty well civilized now, it isn't as if we were back in Captain Cook's day."

"Nevertheless," he returned as he wriggled under a clump of bushes, "we shall watch first and ask questions later."

I crawled beside him and squatted, awaiting the savages' approach.

But I had forgotten that men who live in primitive surroundings have talents unknown to their civilized brethren. While they were still far enough away to make it impossible for us to hear the words they exchanged as they walked, the two Papuans halted, looked speculatively at the copse where we hid, and raised their spears menacingly.

"*Ciel!*" de Grandin muttered. "We are discovered." He seized the stalk of one of the sheltering plants and shook it gently.

The response was instant. A spear whizzed past my ear, missing my head by an uncomfortably small fraction of an inch, and the savages began clambering rapidly toward us, one with his spear poised for a throw, the other drawing a murderous knife from the girdle which constituted his sole article of clothing.

"*Parbleu!*" de Grandin whispered fiercely. "Play dead, my friend. Fall out from the bush and lie as though his spear had killed you." He gave me a sudden push which sent me reeling into the open.

I fell flat to the ground, acting the part of a dead man as realistically as possible and hoping desperately that the savages would not decide to throw a second spear to make sure of their kill.

Though my eyes were closed, I could feel them standing over me, and a queer, cold feeling tingled between my shoulder blades, where I momentarily expected a knife thrust.

Half opening one eye, I saw the brown, naked shins of one of the Papuans beside my head, and was wondering whether I could seize him by the ankles and drag him down before he could stab me, when the legs beside my face suddenly swayed drunkenly, like tree trunks in a storm, and a heavy weight fell crashing on my back.

STARTLED OUT OF MY sham death by the blow, I raised myself in time to see de Grandin in a death grapple with one of the savages. The other one lay across me, the spear he had flung at us a few minutes before protruding from his back directly beneath his left shoulder blade.

"A *moi*, Friend Trowbridge!" the little Frenchmen called. "Quick, or we are lost."

I tumbled the dead Papuan unceremoniously to the ground and grappled with de Grandin's antagonist just as he was about to strike his dirk into my companion's side.

"*Bien, très bien!*" the Frenchman panted as he thrust his knife forward, sinking the blade hilt-deep into the savage's left armpit. "Very good, indeed, Friend Trowbridge. I have not hurled the javelin since I was a boy at school, and I strongly misdoubted my ability to kill the one with a single throw from my ambush, but, happily, my hand has not lost its cunning. *Voilà*, we have a perfect score to our credit! Come, let us bury them."

"But was it necessary to kill the poor fellows?" I asked as I helped him scrape a grave with one of his victim's knives. "Mightn't we have made them understand we meant them no harm?"

"Friend Trowbridge," he answered between puffs of exertion as he dragged one of the naked bodies into the shallow trench we had dug, "never, I fear me, will you learn the sense of the goose. With fellows such as these, even as with the shark last night, we take necessary steps for our own protection first.

"This interment which we make now, think you it is for tenderness of these *canaille*? Ah, *non*. We bury them that their friends find them not if they come searching, and that the buzzards come not flapping this way to warn the others of what we have done. Good, they are buried. Take up that one's spear and come with me. I would investigate that fire which they have made."

We approached the heights overlooking the fire cautiously, taking care to remain unseen by any possible scout sent out by the main party of natives. It was more than an hour before we maneuvered to a safe observation post. As we crawled over the last ridge of rock obstructing our view I went deathly sick at my stomach and would have fallen down the steep hill, had not de Grandin thrown his arm about me.

Squatting around a blazing bonfire in a circle, like wolves about the stag they have run to earth, were perhaps two dozen naked savages, and, bound upright to a stake fixed in the sand, was a white man, lolling forward against the restraining cords with a horrible limpness. Before him stood two burly Papuans, the war clubs in their hands, red as blood at the tips, telling the devil's work they had just completed. It was blood on the clubs. The brown fiends had beaten their helpless captive's head in, and even now one of them was cutting the cords that held his body to the stake.

But beyond the dead man was a second stake, and, as I looked at this, every drop of blood in my body seemed turned to liquid fire, for, lashed to it, mercifully unconscious, but still alive, was a white woman whom I recognized as the wife of a Dutch planter going out from Holland to join her husband in Sumatra.

"Good God, man!" I cried. "That's a woman; a white woman. We can't let those devils kill *her!*"

"Softly, my friend," de Grandin cautioned, pressing me back, for I would have risen and charged pell-mell down the hill. "We are two, they are more than a score; what would it avail us, or that poor woman, were we to rush down and be killed?"

I TURNED ON HIM IN amazed fury. "You call yourself a Frenchman," I taunted, "yet you haven't chivalry enough to attempt a rescue? A fine Frenchman you are!"

"Chivalry is well—in its place," he admitted, "but no Frenchman is so foolish as to spend his life where there is nothing to be bought with it. Would it help her if we, too, were destroyed, or, which is worse, captured and eaten also? Do we, as physicians, seek to throw away our lives when we find a patient hopelessly sick with phthisis? But no, we live that we may fight the disease in others—that we may destroy the germs of the malady. So let it be in this case. Save that poor one we can not; but take vengeance on her slayers we can and will. I, Jules de Grandin, swear it. Ha, she has it!"

Even as he spoke one of the cannibal butchers struck the unconscious woman over the head with his club. A stain of red appeared against the pale yellow of her hair, and the poor creature shuddered convulsively, then hung passive and flaccid against her bonds once more.

"*Par le sang du diable*," de Grandin gritted between his teeth, "if it so be that the good God lets me live, I swear to make those *sales bouchers* die one hundred deaths apiece for every hair in that so pitiful woman's head!"

He turned away from the horrid sight below us and began to ascend the hill. "Come away, Friend Trowbridge," he urged. "It is not good that we should look upon a woman's body served as meat. *Pardieu*, almost I wish I had followed your so crazy advice and attempted a rescue; we should have killed some of them so! No matter, as it is, we shall kill all of them, or may those Messieurs Lloyd pay me not one penny."

3

F EELING SECURE AGAINST DISCOVERY by the savages, as they were too engrossed in their orgy to look for other victims, we made our way to the peak which towered like a truncated cone at the center of the island.

From our station at the summit we could see the ocean in all directions and get an accurate idea of our surroundings. Apparently, the islet was the merest point of land on the face of the sea—probably only the apex of a submarine volcano. It was roughly oval in shape, extending for a possible five miles in length by two-and-a-quarter miles at its greatest width, and rising out of the ocean with a mountainous steepness, the widest part of the beach at the water-line being not more than three or four hundred feet. On every side, and often in series of three or four, extended reefs and points of rock (no doubt the lesser peaks of the mountain whose un-submerged top constituted the island) so that no craft larger than a whaleboat could hope to come within half a mile of the land without having its bottom torn out by the hidden semi-submerged crags.

"*Nom d'un petit bonhomme!*" de Grandin commented. "This is an ideal place for its purpose, *c'est certain*. Ah, see!"—he drew me to a ridge of rock which ran like a rampart across the well-defined path by which we had ascended. Fastened to the stone by bolts were three sheet-iron troughs, each pointing skyward at an angle of some fifty degrees, and each much blackened by smoke stains. "Do you see?" he asked. "These are for firing rockets—observe the powder burns on them. And here"—his voice rose to an excited pitch and he fairly danced in eagerness—"see what is before us!"

U P THE PATH, ALMOST at the summit of the peak, and about twenty-five feet apart, stood two poles, each some twelve feet in height and fitted with a pulley and lanyard. As we neared them we saw that a lantern with a green globe rested at the base of the right-hand stake, while a red-globed lamp was secured to the rope of the left post "Ah, clever, clever," de Grandin muttered, staring from one pole to the other. "Observe, my friend. At night the lamps can be lit and hoisted to the tops of these masts then gently raised and lowered. Viewed at a distance against the black background of this mountain they will simulate a ship's lights to the life. The unfortunate mariner making for them will find his ship fast on these rocks while the lights are still a mile or more away, and—too well we know what happens then. Let us see what more there is, eh?"

Rounding the peak we found ourselves looking down upon the thatched beehive-roofs of a native village, before which a dozen long Papuan canoes were beached on the narrow strip of sand. "Ah," de Grandin inspected the cluster of huts, "it is there the butchers dwell, eh? That will be a good spot for us to avoid, my friend. Now to find the residence of what you Americans call the master mind. Do you see aught resembling a European dwelling, Friend Trowbridge?"

I searched the greenery below us, but nowhere could I descry a roof. "No," I answered after a second inspection, "there's nothing like a white man's house down there; but how do you know there's a white man here, anyway?"

"Ho, ho," he laughed, "how does the rat know the house contains a cat when he hears it mew? Think you those *sacré* eaters of men would know enough to set up such devil's machinery as this, or that they would take care to dynamite the wreck of a ship after looting it? No, no, my friend, this is white man's work, and very bad work it is, too. Let us explore."

Treading warily, we descended the smooth path leading to the rocket-troughs, looking sharply from left to right in search of anything resembling a white man's house. Several hundred feet down the mountain the path forked abruptly, one branch leading toward the Papuan village, the other running to a narrow strip of beach bordering an inlet between two precipitous rock walls. I stared and stared again, hardly able to believe my eyes, for, drawn up on the sand and made fast by a rope to a ringbolt in the rock was a trim little motor-boat, flat-bottomed for navigating the rock-strewn waters in safety, broad-beamed for mastering the heavy ocean swells, and fitted with a comfortable, roofed-over cabin. Forward, on the little deck above her sharp clipper bow, was an efficient looking Lewis gun mounted on a swivel, and a similar piece of ordnance poked its aggressive nose out of the engine cockpit at the stern.

"*Par la barbe d'un bouc vert*," de Grandin swore delightedly, "but this is marvelous, this is magnificent, this is superb! Come, Friend Trowbridge, let us take advantage of this miracle; let us leave this hell-hole of an island right away, immediately, at once. *Par—*" The exclamation died, half uttered, and he stared past me with the expression of a superstitious man suddenly face-to-face with a sheeted specter.

4

"Surely, Gentlemen," said a suave voice behind me, "you are not going to leave without permitting me to offer you some slight hospitality? That would be ungenerous."

I turned as though stung by a wasp and looked into the smiling eyes of a dark-skinned young man, perhaps thirty years of age. From the top of his spotless *topi* to the tips of his highly polished tan riding boots he was a perfect model of the well-dressed European in the tropics. Not a stain of dust or travel showed on his spruce white drill jacket or modishly cut riding breeches, and as he waved his silver-mounted riding crop in greeting, I saw his slender hands were carefully manicured, the nails cut rather long and stained a vivid pink before being polished to the brightness of mother-of-pearl.

De Grandin laid his hand upon the knife at his belt, before he could draw it, a couple of beetle-browed Malays in khaki jackets and *sarongs* stepped from the bushes bordering the path and leveled a pair of business-like Mauser rifles at us. "I wouldn't," the young man warned in a blasé drawl, "I really wouldn't, if I were you. These fellows are both dead shots and could put enough lead in you to sink you forty fathoms down before you could get the knife out of its sheath, much less into me. Do you mind, really?" He held out his hand for the weapon. "Thank you, that is much better"—he tossed the blade into the water of the inlet with a careless gesture—"really, you know, the most frightfully messy accidents are apt to happen with those things."

De Grandin and I eyed him in speechless amazement, but he continued as though our meeting were the most conventional thing imaginable.

"Mr. Trowbridge—pardon my assumption, but I heard your name called a moment ago—will you be good enough to favor me with an introduction to your friend?"

"I am Dr. Samuel Trowbridge, of Harrisonville, New Jersey," I replied, wondering, meanwhile, if I were in the midst of some crazy dream, "and this is Dr. Jules de Grandin, of Paris."

"So good of you," the other acknowledged with a smile. "I fear I must be less frank than you for the nonce and remain veiled in anonymity. However, one really must have some sort of designation, mustn't one? So suppose you know me for the present as Goonong Besar. Savage, unchristian-sounding sort of name, I'll admit, but more convenient than calling, 'hey, you!' or simply whistling when you wish to attract my attention. Eh, what? And now"—he made a slight bow—"if you will be so kind as to step into my humble burrow in the earth . . . Yes, that is it, the doorway right before you."

Still under the menacing aim of the Malays' rifles, de Grandin and I walked through the cleft in the rock, traversed a low, narrow passage, darker than a windowless cellar, made a sharp turn to the left, and halted abruptly, blinking our eyes in astonishment.

Before us, seeming to run into infinity, was a wide, long apartment paved with alternate squares of black and white marble, colonnaded down each side with double rows of white-marble pillars and topped with a vaulted ceiling of burnished copper plates. Down the center of the corridor, at intervals of about twenty feet, five silver oil lamps with globes of finely cut crystal hung from the polished ceiling, making the entire room almost as bright as equatorial noon.

"Not half bad, eh?" our host remarked as he viewed our astonishment with amusement. "This is only the vestibule, gentlemen; you really have no idea of the wonders of this house under the water. For instance, would either of you care to retrace your steps? See if you can find the door you came in."

We swung about, like soldiers at the command of execution, staring straight at the point where the entranceway should have been. A slab of marble, firm and solid as any composing the walls of the room, to all appearances, met our gaze; there was neither sign nor remote evidence of any door or doorway before us.

Goonong Besar chuckled delightedly and gave an order to one of his attendants in the harsh, guttural language of Malaya. "If you will look behind you, gentlemen," he resumed, again addressing us, "you will find another surprise."

We wheeled about and almost bumped into a pair of grinning Malay lads who stood at our elbows.

"These boys will show you to your rooms." Goonong Besar announced. "Kindly follow them. It will be useless to attempt conversation, for they understand no language but their native speech, and as for replying, unfortunately, they lack the benefits of a liberal education and can not write, while . . ." he shot a quick order to the youths, who immediately opened their mouths as though yawning. Both de Grandin and I gave vent to exclamations of horror. The boys mouths gaped emptily. Both had had their tongues cut off at the roots.

"You see," Goonong went on in the same musical, slightly bored voice, "these chaps can't be a bit of use to you as gossips, they really can't.

"I think I can furnish you with dinner clothes, Dr. de Grandin, but"—he smiled apologetically—"I'm afraid you, Dr. Trowbridge, are a little too—er—corpulent to be able to wear any garments made for me. So sorry! However, no doubt we can trick you out in a suit of whites Captain Van Thun—er, that is, I'm sure you can be accommodated from our stores. Yes.

"Now, if you will follow the guides, please"—he broke off on a slightly interrogative note and bowed with gentle courtesy toward each of us in turn—"you will excuse me for a short time, I'm sure."

Before we could answer, he signaled his two attendants, and the three of them stepped behind one of the marble columns. We heard a subdued click, as of two pieces of stone coming lightly together.

"But, Monsieur, this is incredible, this is monstrous!" de Grandin began, striding forward. "You shall explain, I demand—*Cordieu*, he is gone!"

He was. As though the wall had faded before his approach, or his own body had dissolved into ether, Goonong Besar had vanished. We were alone in the brilliantly lighted corridor with our tongueless attendants.

Nodding and grinning, the lads signaled us to follow them down the room. One of them ran a few paces ahead and parted a pair of silken curtains, disclosing a narrow doorway through which only one could go at a time. Obeying the lad's gestures, I stepped through the opening, followed by de Grandin and our dumb guides.

The lad who had held aside the curtains for us ran ahead a few paces and gave a strange, eerie cry. We looked sharply at him, wondering what the utterance portended, and from behind us sounded the thud of stone on stone. Turning, we saw the second Malay grinning broadly at us from the place where the doorway had been. I say "had been" advisedly, for, where the narrow arched door had pierced the thick wall a moment before, was now a solid row of upright marble slabs, no joint or crack showing which portion of the wall was solid stone and which cunningly disguised door.

"*Sang du diable!*" de Grandin muttered. "But I do not like this place. It reminds me of that grim fortress of the Inquisition at Toledo where the good fathers, dressed as demons, could appear and disappear at will through seeming solid walls and frighten the wits out of and the true faith into superstitious heretics."

I suppressed a shudder with difficulty. This underground house of secret doors was too reminiscent of other practises of the Spanish Inquisition besides the harmless mummery of the monks for my peace of mind.

"*Eh bien*," de Grandin shrugged, "now we are here we may as well make the best of it. Lead on, *Diablotins*"—he turned to our dark-skinned guides—"we follow."

We were standing in a long, straight passage, smoothwalled with panels of polished marble, and, like the larger apartment, tiled with alternate squares of black and white. No doorways led off the aisle, but other corridors crossed it at right angles at intervals of thirty to thirty-five feet. Like the larger room, the passage was lighted by oil lamps swung from the ceiling.

Following our guides, we turned to the right down a passageway the exact duplicate of the first, entered a third corridor, and, after walking a considerable distance, made another turn and stopped before a narrow curtained archway. Through this we entered a large square room, windowless, but well lighted by lamps and furnished with two bedsteads of bamboo having strong China matting on them in lieu of springs or mattress. A low bamboo dressing table, fitted with a mirror of polished metal, and several reed chairs constituted the residue of the furniture.

One of the boys signed to us to remove our clothes, while the other ran out, returning almost immediately dragging two sheet-iron bath tubs after him. Placing these in the center of the room he left us again, and reappeared in a few minutes with a wheeled contrivance something like a child's express wagon in which stood six large earthen jars, four containing warm water, the other two cold.

We stepped into the tubs and the lads proceeded to rub us down with an oily liquid, strongly perfumed with sandalwood and very soothing to feel. When this had been well worked into our skins the lads poured the contents of the warm-water jars over us, splashing us thoroughly from hair to feet, then sluiced us off with a five-gallon douche of almost ice-cold water. Towels of coarse native linen were unfolded, and in less than five minutes we were as thoroughly cleansed, dried and invigorated as any patron of a Turkish bath at home.

I felt rather dubious when my personal attendant produced a clumsy native razor and motioned me to be seated in one of the cane chairs, but the lad proved a skillful barber, light and deft of touch and absolutely speechless—a great improvement upon the loquacious American tonsorialist, I thought.

Dinner clothes and a suit of carefully laundered white drill, all scented with the pungent, pleasing odor of clove husks, were brought in on wicker trays, and as we put the finishing touches on our toilet one of the lads produced a small casket of polished cedar in which reposed a layer of long, black cigars, the sort which retail for a dollar apiece in Havana.

"NOM D'UN PETIT BONHOMME!" de Grandin exploded as he exhaled a lungful of the fragrant smoke; "this is marvelous; it is magnificent; it is superb—but I like it not, Friend Trowbridge."

"Bosh," I responded, puffing in placid content, "you're afraid of your shadow, de Grandin! Why, man, this is wonderful—think where we were this morning, shipwrecked, pursued by man-eaters, with starvation as the least of our perils, and look at us now, both dressed in clean clothes, with every attention and convenience we could have at home, and safe, man, safe."

"Safe?" he answered dubiously. "'Safe,' do you say? Did you apprehend, my friend, how our host, that so mysterious Monsieur Goonong, almost spoke of Captain Van Thun when the question of clothing you came up?"

"Why, now you speak of it, I do remember how he seemed about to say something about Captain Something-or-Other, and apparently thought better of it," I agreed. "But what's that to do with us?"

The little Frenchman came close to me and sank his voice to a scarcely audible whisper: "Captain Franz Van Thun," he breathed, "was master of the Dutch Indiaman *Van Damm*, which sailed from Rotterdam to Sumatra, and was lost, as far as known, *with all on board*, on her homeward voyage."

"But—" I protest.

"*She-s-sh!*" he cut me off. "Those servant boys are beckoning: come, we are wanted elsewhere."

I looked up at the two mutes, and shuddered at sight of the leering grins on their faces.

5

THE LADS LED US through another bewildering series of corridors till our sense of location was completely obfuscated, finally paused, one on each side of an archway, and, bowing deeply, signaled us to enter.

We strode into a long, marble-tiled room which, unlike every other apartment in the queer house, was not brilliantly lighted. The room's sole illumination was furnished by the glow of fourteen wax candles set in two seven-branched silver candelabra which stood at opposite ends of a polished mahogany table of purest Sheraton design, its waxed surface giving back reflections of crystal, and silver dinner service fit for the table of a king.

"Ah, gentlemen," Goonong Besar, arrayed in immaculate evening clothes, greeted us from the farther end of the room. "I hope you have brought good appetites with you. I'm fairly ravenous, for my part. Will you join me?"

The same Malay servitors who had accompanied him at our meeting stood behind him now, their semi-military khaki jackets and sarongs exchanged for costumes of freshly ironed white linen and their rifles replaced by a pair of large-caliber Luger pistols which each wore conspicuously tucked in his scarlet silk cummerbund.

"Sorry I can't offer you a cocktail," our host apologized as we seated ourselves, "but ice is not among the improvements available in my modest little menage, unfortunately. However, we find the sea caves do quite well as refrigerators and I think you'll find this chilled wine really acceptable as a substitute. Ah"—he looked diffidently from one of us to the other, finally fixing his gaze on me—"will you be good enough to ask the blessing, Dr. Trowbridge? You look as if you might be experienced in that line."

Startled, but greatly reassured by the request, I bowed my head and repeated the customary formula, almost springing from my chair with amazement as I opened my eyes at the prayer's end. While de Grandin and I had bent above the table during grace, the servants had pulled back the rich *batik* with which the wall facing us was draped, revealing a series of heavy plate glass panels against which the ocean's green waters pressed. We are looking directly on to the sea bottom.

"Jolly clever idea, what?" Goonong Besar inquired smiling at our surprised faces. "Thought it all up myself; like to see the little finny fellows swim past, you know. Had a beastly hard time getting workmen to do the job for me, too; but all sorts of unbelievable persons trickle into these islands from time to time—architects gone *ga-ga* with drink, skilled artisans in all the trades and what-not—I finally managed to collect the men I wanted."

"But, Monsieur, the expense," de Grandin protested with typical Gallic logic, "it must have been prodigious!"

"Oh, no," the young man answered negligently. "I had to feed the beggars, of course, but most of 'em were habituated to native food, and that's not very expensive."

"But their salaries," de Grandin persisted; "why Monsieur, this house is a work of genius, a marvel of engineering; even drink-ruined architects and engineers capable of producing such a place as this would demand fabulous fees for their services—and the laborers, the men who cut and polished the marble here, they must have been numerous as an army; their wages would be ruinous."

"Most of the marble was salvaged from deserted Dutch colonial palaces," Goonong Besar replied. "You know, Holland built a mighty empire in these islands a century or so ago, and her planters lived in palaces fit for kings. When the empire crumbled the planters left, and he who cared to might help himself to their houses, wholly or in part. As for wages"—he waved a jeweled hand carelessly—"I am rich, but the wages made no great inroads on my fortune. Do you remember your medieval history, Dr. de Grandin?"

"Eh? But certainly," the Frenchman responded, "but . . ."

"Don't you recall, then, the precaution the nobles, ecclesiastical as well as temporal, took to insure the secrecy of their castle or cathedral plans?" He paused, smiling quizzically at de Grandin.

"*Parbleu!* But you would not; you could not, you would not dare!" the Frenchman almost shouted, half rising from his chair and staring at our host as though a mad dog sat in his place.

"Nonsense, of course I would—and did," the other replied good-humoredly. "Why not? The men were bits of human flotsam, not worth salvaging. And who was to know? Dead men are notoriously uncommunicative, you know. Proverbially so, in fact."

"But, you tell this to me?" de Grandin looked at him incredulously.

Our host's face went perfectly expressionless as he stared directly at de Grandin for a period while one might count five slowly, then his dark, rather sullen face lighted with a smile. "May I offer you some more wine, my dear doctor?" he asked.

I LOOKED ALTERNATELY AT MY companions in wonderment. Goonong Besar had made some sinister implication which de Grandin had been quick to comprehend, I knew, and their subsequent conversation concerning dead men telling no tales contained a thinly veiled threat; but try as I would I could not find the key to their enigmatic talk. "Medieval castles and cathedrals? Dead men tell no tales?" I repeated to myself. What did it all mean?

Goonong Besar broke in on my thought: "May I offer you a bit more of this white meat, Dr. Trowbridge?" he asked courteously. "Really, we find this white meat" (the words were ever, so slightly emphasized) "most delicious. So tender and well flavored, you know. Do you like it?"

"Very much, thank you," I replied. "It's quite different from anything I've ever tasted. In a way it reminds me of delicate young pork, yet it's different, too. Is it peculiar to the islands, Mr. Goonong?"

"Well—er"—he smiled slightly as he cut a thin slice of the delicious roast and placed it on my plate—"I wouldn't say it is peculiar to our islands, though we have an unusual way of preparing it in this house. The natives hereabouts refer to the animal from which it comes as 'long pig'—really a disgusting sort of beast while living; but quite satisfactory when killed and properly cooked. May I serve you again, Dr. de Grandin?" He turned toward the Frenchman with a smile.

I sat suddenly upright in utter, dumfounded amazement as I beheld Grandin's face. He was leaning forward in his chair, his fierce little blue eyes very round and almost protruding from his head, his weather-tanned cheeks gone the color of putty as he stared at our host like a subject regarding a professional hypnotist. "*Dieu, grand Dieu!*" he ejaculated in a choking whisper. "'Long pig,' did you say? *Sang de St. Denis!* And I have eaten it!"

"My dear chap, are you ill?" I cried, leaping from my chair and hastening to his side. "Has your dinner disagreed with you?"

"*Non, non!*" he waved me away, still speaking that choking whisper. "Sit down, Friend Trowbridge, sit down; but *par l'amour de Dieu*, I beseech you, eat no more of that accurst meat, at least not tonight."

"Oh, my dear sir!" Goonong Besar protested mildly. "You have spoiled Dr. Trowbridge's appetite, and he was enjoying this delicious white meat so much, too. This is really too bad, you know. Really, it is!"

He frowned at the silver meat platter before him a moment, then signaled one of his attendants to take it away, adding a quick command in Malayan as he did so.

"Perhaps a little entertainment will help us forget this unfortunate *contretemps*," he suggested. "I have sent for Miriam. You will like her, I fancy. I have great hopes for her; she has the makings of a really accomplished *artiste*, I think."

The servant who had taken away the meat returned and whispered something in our host's ear. As he listened, Goonong Besar's thin, well-bred face took on such an expression of fury as I had never before seen displayed by a human being. "What?" he shouted, forgetting, apparently, that the Malay did not understand English. "I'll see about this—we'll soon see who says 'must' and 'shall' in this house."

He turned to us with a perfunctory bow as he rose. "Excuse me, please," he begged. "A slight misunderstanding has arisen, and I must straighten it out. I shan't keep you waiting long, I hope; but if you wish anything while I am gone, Hussein"—he indicated the Malay who stood statue-still behind his chair— "will attend your wants. He speaks no English, but you can make him understand by signs, I think."

"Quick, de Grandin, tell me before he comes back," I besought as Goonong, accompanied by one of the Malays, left the room.

"Eh?" replied the Frenchman, looking up from an absorbed contemplation of the tableware before him. "What is it you would know, my friend?"

"What was all that word-juggling about medieval builders and dead men telling no tales?" I demanded.

"Oh, that?" he answered with a look of relief. "Why, do you not know that when a great lord of the Middle Ages commissioned an architect to build a castle for him it was almost tantamount to a death sentence? The architect, the master builders, even the principal workmen, were usually done to death when the building was finished in order that they might not divulge its secret passages and hidden defenses to an enemy, or duplicate the design for some rival noble."

"Why—why, then, Goonong Besar meant he killed the men who built this submarine house for him!" I ejaculated, horror-stricken.

"Precisely," de Grandin answered, "but, bad as that may be, we have a more personal interest in the matter. Did you notice him when I showed surprise he should confess his guilt to us?"

"Good heavens, yes!" I answered. "He meant—"

"That, though still breathing, we are, to all intents dead men," de Grandin supplied.

"And that talk of 'white meat,' and 'long pig'?" I asked.

He drew a shuddering breath, as though the marble-lined cavern had suddenly gone icy-cold. "Trowbridge my friend," he answered in a low, earnest whisper, "you must know this thing; but you must control yourself, too. Not by word or sign must you betray your knowledge. Throughout these devil-ridden islands, wherever the brown fiends who are their natives eat men, they refer to the cannibal feast as a meal of long pig. That so unfortunate man we saw dead at the stake this morning, and that pitiful Dutch woman we saw clubbed to death—they, my friend, were 'long pigs.' That was the *white meat* this devil out of lowest hell set before us this night. That is the food we have eaten at this accurst table!"

"My God!" I half rose from my chair, then sank back, overcome with nausea. "Did we—do you suppose—was it *her* flesh—?"

"*S-s-sh!*" he warned sharply. "Silence, my friend; control yourself. Do not let him see you know. He is coming!"

As though de Grandin's words had been a theatrical cue for his entrance, Goonong Besar stepped through the silken portieres at the doorway beyond the table, a pleased smile on his swarthy face. "So sorry to keep you waiting," he apologized. "The trouble is all adjusted now, and we can proceed with our entertainment. Miriam is a little diffident before strangers, but I—er—persuaded her to oblige us." He turned toward the door through which he had entered and waved his hand to someone behind the curtains.

Three Malays, one a woman bent with age and hideously wrinkled, the other two vacant-faced youths, came through the doorway at his gesture. The woman, bearing a section of bamboo fitted with drumheads of rawhide at each end, led the way, the first boy rested his hand on her shoulder, and the second lad, in turn, held tightly to his companion's jacket. A second glance told us the reason for this procedure. The woman, though aged almost to the point of paralysis, possessed a single malignant, blood-shot eye; both boys were sightless, their scarred and sunken eyelids telling mutely of eyeballs gouged from their faces by unskilled hands which had torn the surrounding tissues as they ripped the optics from the quivering flesh.

"*Ha-room; ha-room!*" cried the old crone in a cracked treble, and the two blind boys seated themselves cross-legged on the marble floor. One of them raised a reed pipe to his lips, the other rested a sort of zither upon his knees, and each began trying his instrument tentatively, producing a sound approximating the complaints of a tomcat suffering with cholera morbus.

"*Ha-room; ha-room!*" the hag cried again, and commenced beating a quick rhythm on her drum, using her fingertips and the heels of her hands alternately for drumsticks. "*Tauk-auk-a—tauk-auk-a—tauk-auk-a!*" the drum-beats boomed hollowly, the first stroke heavily accented, the second and third following in such quick succession that they seemed almost indivisible parts of one continuous thrumming.

Now the pipe and zither took up the tribal tune, and a surge of fantastic music swirled and eddied through the marble-walled apartment. It was unlike anything I had ever heard, a repetitious, insistent, whining of tortured instruments, an air that pleaded with the hearers' evil nature to overthrow restraint and give the beast within him freedom, a harmony that drugged the senses like opium or the extract of the cola-nut. The music raced and soared, faster, shriller and higher, the painted-silk curtains swung apart and a girl glided out upon the tessellated pavement.

S HE WAS YOUNG — SIXTEEN, OR seventeen at the most—and the sinuous, lithe grace of her movements was as much due to healthy and perfectly co-ordinated muscles as to training. The customary *sarong* of the islands encased her nether limbs, but, instead of the native woman's jacket, her *sarong* was carried up beyond the gold six-inch wide belt about her waist and tightly wrapped about her bosom so that it formed a single comprehensive garment covering her from armpits to ankles. Save for a chaplet of blazing cabochon rubies about her slender throat, her neck and shoulders were bare, but ornaments in the form of flexible golden snakes with emerald eyes twined up each arm from elbow to shoulder, and bangles of pure, soft gold, hung with triple rows of tiny hawk-bells, circled her wrists. Other bangles, products of the finest goldsmiths of India, jangled about her white ankles above the pearl-encrusted slippers of amethyst velvet, while the diamond aigrette fastened comb-fashion in her sleekly parted black hair was worth a king's ransom. Fit to ransom a monarch, too, was the superb blue-white diamond of her nose-stud, fixed in her left nostril, and the rope of pearls which circled her waist and hung swaying to the very hem of her sarong of Philippine pineapple gauze was fit to buy the Peacock Throne of the Grand Mogul himself.

Despite the lavishly applied cosmetics, the antimony which darkened her eyelids to the color of purple grape skins, the cochineal which dyed her lips and cheeks a brilliant scarlet and the powdered charcoal which traced her eyebrows in continuous, fluted line across her forehead, she was beautiful with the rich, ripe beauty of the women who inspired Solomon of old to indite his *Song of Songs*. None but the Jewish race, or perhaps the Arabian, could have produced a woman with the passionate, alluring beauty of Miriam, the dancer in the house beneath the sea.

Back and forth across the checkered floor the girl wove her dance, tracing patterns intricate as lace from Canary or the looms of spiders over the marble with the soft soles of her velvet slippers, the chiming bells at her wrists and ankles keeping time to the calling, luring tune of the old hag and her blind musicians with the consummate art of a Spanish castanet dancer following the music with her hand cymbals.

At last the dance was done.

Shaking like a leaf with the intoxication of her own rhythmic movements, Miriam flung herself full length face downward, before Goonong Besar, and lay upon the marble floor in utter, abject self-abasement.

What he said to her we did not understand, for the words were in harsh Malayan, but he must have given her permission to go, for she rose from her prostration like a dog expecting punishment when its master relents, and ran from the room, bracelets and anklets ringing time to her panic flight, pearls clicking together as they swayed with the motion of her *sarong*.

The old crone rose, too, and led her blind companions from the room, and we three sat staring at each other under the winking candles' light with the two impassive Malay guards standing motionless behind their master's chair.

"Do you think she is beautiful?" Goonong Besar asked as he lighted a cigarette and blew a cloud of smoke toward the copper ceiling.

"Beautiful?" de Grandin gasped, "*Mon Dieu*, Monsieur, she is wonderful, she is magnificent, she is superb. Death of my life, but she is divine! Never have I seen such a dancer; never such, such—*nom de Dieu*, I am speechless as the fish! In all the languages I know there are no words to describe her!"

"And you, Dr. Trowbridge, what do you think of my little Miriam?" Goonong addressed me.

"She is very lovely," I acknowledged, feeling the words foolishly inadequate.

"Ha, ha," he laughed good-naturedly. "Spoken with true Yankee conservatism, by Jove.

"And that, gentlemen," he continued, "leads us to an interesting little proposition I have to make you. But first you will smoke? You'll find these cigars really good. I import them from Havana." He passed the polished cedar humidor across the table and held a match for us to light our selections of the expensive tobacco.

"Now, then," he commenced, inhaling a deep lungful of smoke, "first a little family history, then my business proposition. Are you ready, gentlemen?"

De Grandin and I nodded, wondering mutely what the next chapter in this novel of incredible surprises would be.

6

"When we met so auspiciously this afternoon," our host began in his pleasant voice, "I requested that you call me Goonong Besar. That, however, is what we might call, for want of a better term, merely my *nom de l'ile*. Actually gentlemen, I am the Almost Honorable James Abingdon Richardson.

"*Parbleu*, Monsieur," de Grandin demanded, "how is it you mean that, 'the Almost Honorable'?"

The young man blew a cloud of fragrant smoke toward the room's copper ceiling and watched it float upward a moment before he replied: "My father was an English missionary, my mother a native princess. She was not of the Malay blood, but of the dominant Arab strain, and was known as Laila, Pearl of the Islands.

"My father had alienated himself from his family when he and an elder sister deserted the Church of England and, embracing a dissenting creed, came to Malay to spread the gospel of repentance or damnation among the heathen in their blindness."

He drew thoughtfully at his cigar and smiled rather bitterly as he resumed: "He was a fine figure of a man, that father of mine, six feet tall, blue-eyed and curly-haired, with a deep, compelling voice and the fire of fanaticism burning in his heart. The natives, Arab and Malay alike, took to his fiery gospel as the desert dwellers of Arabia once listened to the preaching of Mohammed, the camel driver. My grandfather, a pirate prince with a marble palace and a thousand slaves of his own, was one of the converts, and came to the mission bringing his ten-year-old daughter, Laila, with him. He left her at the mission school to learn the gentle teachings of the Prophet of Nazareth. She stayed there four years."

Again our host paused, puffing silently at his cigar, seemingly attempting to marshal his thoughts. "I believe I said my father was a dissenting clergyman? Yes, so I did, to be sure. Had he been a member of the established church things might have been different. The established English clergy are bad enough, with their fox hunting and general worldliness, but they're usually sportsmen. When she was a scant fifteen years old—women of the East mature more rapidly than your Western women, you know—Laila, the Pearl of the Islands, came back to her father's palace of marble and cedar, bearing a little boy baby in her arms. The charitable Christian sister of the missionary had driven her out of the mission settlement when she learned that she (the sister) was about to have a little nephew whose birth was not pre-sanctified by a wedding ring.

"The old pirate prince was furious. He would have put his daughter and her half-caste child to death and swooped down on the mission with fire and dagger, but my mother had learned much of Christian charity during her stay at the school. She was sure, if she went to my father with as many pearls as her hands could hold, and with a dowry of rubies strung round her neck, he would receive her as his wife—er—make an honest woman of her, as the saying goes.

"However, one thing and another prevented her return to the mission for three years, and when we finally got there we found my reverend sire had taken an English lady to wife.

"Oh, he took the jewels my mother brought—no fear of his refusing—and in return for them he permitted us to live in the settlement as native hangers-on. She, a princess, and the daughter of generations of princesses, scrubbed floors and baked bread in the house presided over by my father's wife and I, my father's first-born son, duly christened with his name, fetched and carried for my father's younger sons.

"They were hard, those days at the mission school. The white boys who were my half-brothers overlooked no chance to remind me of mother's shame and my own disgrace. Humility and patience under affliction were the lessons my mother and I had ground into us day by day while we remained there.

"Then, when I was a lad of ten years or so, my father's cousin, Viscount Abingdon, broke his neck at a fox hunt, and, as he died without issue, my father became a member of England's landed gentry, and went back home to take over the title and the entails. He borrowed on his expectancy before he left and offered my mother money to have me educated as a clerk in some trader's store, but my mother, for all her years of servitude, was still a princess of royal blood. Also she remembered enough Scripture to quote, 'Thy money perish with thee.' So she spat in his face and went back to the palace of her father, telling him that her husband was dead.

"I was sent to school in England—oh, yes, I'm a public school man, Winchester, you know—and I was down from my first term at Cambridge when the war broke out in 1914.

"Why should I have fought for England? What had England or the English ever done for me? It was the call of the blood—the English blood—perhaps. At any rate I joined up and was gazetted to a London regiment. Everything was death or glory those days, you know. 'For King and Country,' and all that sort of tosh. Racial lines were wiped out, and every man, whatever his color or creed, was for the common cause. Rot!

"I came into the officers' mess one night after a hard day's drill, and was presented to a young man from one of the guards regiments. 'Lieutenant Richardson,' my captain said, 'this is Lieutenant Richardson. Queer coincidence, you chaps are both James Abingdon Richardson. Ought to be great pals on that account, what?'

"The other Lieutenant Richardson looked me over from head to foot, then repeated distinctly, so everyone in the room could hear and understand. 'James, my boots need polishing. Attend to it.' It was the same order he had given me at the mission school a hundred times when we were lads together. He was Lieutenant the Honorable James Abingdon Richardson, *legitimate* eldest son of Viscount Abingdon. I was . . ."

He broke off, staring straight before him a moment, then: "There was a devil of a row. Officers weren't supposed to beat other officers into insensibility in company mess, you know. I was dismissed from the service, and came back to the islands.

"My grandfather was dead; so was my mother. I was monarch of all I surveyed—if I was willing not to look too far—and since my return I have consecrated my life to repaying my debt to my father on such of his race as crossed my path.

"The hunting has been fairly good, too. White men are such fools! Ship after ship has run aground on the rocks here, sometimes in answer to my signal rockets, sometimes mistaking the red and green lamps on the hill up yonder for ships' lights.

"It's been profitable. Nearly every ship so far has contained enough loot to make the game distinctly worth the trouble. I must admit your ship was somewhat of a disappointment in respect of monetary returns, but then I have had the pleasure of your company; that's something.

"I keep a crew of Papuans around to do the dirty work, and let 'em eat a few prisoners now and then by way of reward—don't mind an occasional helping of 'long pig' myself, as a matter of fact, provided it's a white one.

"But"—he smiled unpleasantly—"conditions aren't ideal, yet. I still have to install electricity in the house and rig up a wireless apparatus—I could catch more game that way—and then there's the question of women. Remember how Holy Writ says, 'It is not good for man to dwell alone'? I've found it out, already.

"Old Umera, the woman who played the drum tonight, and the slave girl, Miriam, are the only women in the establishment, thus far, but I intend to remedy that soon. I shall send to one of the larger islands and buy several of the most beautiful maidens available within the next few months, and live as befits a prince—a pirate prince, even as my grandfather was.

"Now, white men"—his suave manner dropped from him like a mask let down, and implacable hatred glared from his dark eyes—"this is my proposition to you. Before I establish my seraglio it is necessary that I possess suitable furniture. I can not spare any of my faithful retainers for the purpose of attending my women, but you two come into my hands providentially. Both of you are surgeons—you shall perform the necessary operations on each other. It is a matter of indifference to me which of you operates first—you may draw straws for the privilege if you wish—but it is my will that you do this thing, and my will is law on this island."

Both de Grandin and I looked at him in speechless horror, but he took no notice of amazement. "You may think you will refuse," he told us, "but you will not. Captain Van Thun, of the Dutch steamer *Van Damm*, and his first mate were offered the same chance and refused it. They chose to interview a little pet I keep about the premises as an alternative: But when the time for the interview came both would gladly have reconsidered their decision. This house is the one place in the world where a white man must keep his word, willy-nilly. Both of them were obliged to carry out their bargain to the letter—and I can not say the prestige of the pure Caucasian breed was strengthened by the way they did it.

"Now, I will give you gentlemen a greater opportunity for deliberation than I gave the Dutchmen. You shall first be allowed to see my pet, then decide whether you will accept my offer or not. But I warn you beforehand, whatever decision you make must be adhered to.

"Come." He turned to the two armed Malays who stood behind his chair and barked an order. Instantly de Grandin and I were covered by their pistols, and the scowling faces behind the firearms' sights told us we might expect no quarter if the order to fire were given.

"Come," Goonong Besar—or Richardson—repeated imperiously, "walk ahead, you two, and remember, the first attempt either of you makes to escape will mean a bullet through his brain."

WE MARCHED DOWN A series of identical corridors as bewildering as the labyrinth of Crete, mysterious stone doors thudding shut behind us from time to time, other doors swinging open in the solid walls as our guards pressed cunningly concealed springs in the walls or floor. Finally we brought up on a sort of colonnaded porch, a tiled footpath bordered with a low stone parapet from which a row of carved stone columns rose to a concave ceiling of natural stone. Below the balcony's balustrade stretched a long, narrow pool of dead-motionless water between abrupt vertical walls of rock, and, some two hundred feet away, through the arch of a natural cave, the starlit tropical sky showed like a little patch of freedom before our straining eyes. The haze which had thickened the air the previous night must have cleared away, for rays of the bright, full moon painted a "path to Spain" over the waters at the cavern's mouth, and sent sufficient light as far back as our balcony to enable us to distinguish an occasional tiny ripple on the glassy surface below us.

"Here, pretty, pretty!" our captor called, leaning forward between two columns. "Come up and see the brave white men who may come to play with you. Here, pretty pet; come up, come up!"

We stared into the purple waters like lost souls gazing on the hell prepared for them, but no motion agitated the depths.

"Sulky brute!" the half-caste exclaimed, and snatched a pistol from the girdle of one of his attendants. "Come up," he repeated harshly. "Damn you, come when I call!" He tossed the weapon into the pool below.

De Grandin and I uttered a gasp of horror in unison, and I felt his nails bite into my arm as his strong slender fingers gripped me convulsively.

AS THOUGH THE PISTOL had been superheated and capable of setting the water in the cave boiling by its touch, the deep, blue-black pool beneath us suddenly woke to life. Ripples—living, groping ripples—appeared on the pool's smooth face and long, twisting arms, sinuous as snakes, thick as fire-hose, seemed waving just under the surface, flicking into the air now and again and displaying tentacles roughened with great, wart-like protuberances. Something like a monster bubble, transparent-gray like a jelly-fish, yet, oddly, spotted like an unclean reptile, almost as big around as the umbrellas used by teamsters on their wagons in summer-time, and, like an umbrella, ribbed at regular intervals, rose from the darker water, and a pair of monstrous, hideous white eyes, large as dinner plates, with black pupils large as saucers, stared greedily, unwinkingly, at us.

"*Nom de Dieu de nom de Dieu!*" de Grandin breathed. "The sea-devil; the giant octopus!"

"Quite so," Goonong Besar agreed affably, "the giant octopus. What he grasps he holds forever, and he grasps all he can reach. A full-grown elephant thrown into that water would have no more chance of escape than a minnow— or, for unpleasant example, than you gentlemen would. Now, perhaps you realize why Captain Van Thun and his first officer wished they had chosen to enter my—er—employ, albeit in a somewhat extraordinary capacity. I did not afford them a chance of viewing the alternative beforehand, as I have you, however. Now that you have had your chance, I am sure you will take the matter under serious advisement before you refuse.

"There is no hurry; you will be given all tonight and tomorrow to arrive at a decision. I shall expect your answer, at dinner tomorrow. Good gentlemen, my boys will show you to your room. Good night, and—er—may I wish you pleasant dreams?"

With a mocking laugh he stepped quickly back into the shadows, we heard the sound we had come to recognize as the closing of one of the hidden stone doors, and found ourselves alone upon the balcony over-looking the den of the giant octopus.

"*Bon Dieu!*" de Grandin cried despairingly, "Trowbridge, my friend, they make a mistake, those people who insist the devil dwells in hell. *Parbleu!* What is that?"

The noise which startled him was the shuffling of bare brown feet. The tongueless youths who acted as our *valets de chambre* were coming reluctantly toward us down the passageway, their eyes rolling in fearful glances toward the balustrade beyond which the devil of the sea lurked in his watery lair.

"*En bien*," the Frenchman shrugged, "it is the two devilkins again. Lead on, *mes enfants*; any place is better than this threshold of hell."

7

"**A**ND NOW," HE ANNOUNCED as he dropped into one of the bedroom's wicker chairs and lighted a cigarette, "we are in what you Americans would call a tight fix, Friend Trowbridge. To accede to that half-caste hellion's proposition would be to dishonor ourselves forever—that is unthinkable. But to be eaten up by that so infernal octopus, that, too, is unthinkable. *Morbleu*, had I known then what I know now I should have demanded one thousand pounds a day from those Messieurs Lloyd and then refused their offer. As your so splendid soldiers were wont to say during the war, we are, of a surety, S.O.L., my friend."

Beneath the bamboo bedstead across the room a slight rustling sounded. I looked apathetically toward the bed, indifferent to any fresh horror which might appear; but, wretched as I was, I was not prepared for the apparition which emerged.

Stripped of her gorgeous raiment of pineapple gauze, a *sarong* and jacket of the cheapest native cotton inadequately covering her glorious body, an ivory-wood button replacing her diamond nose-stud, her feet bare and no article of jewelry adorning her, Miriam, the dancer, crept forth and flung herself to her knees before de Grandin.

"Oh, Monsieur," she begged in a voice choked with tears, "have pity on me, I implore you. Be merciful to me, as you would have another in your place be pitiful to your sister, were she in mine."

"*Morbleu*, child, is it of me you ask pity?" de Grandin demanded. "How can I, who can not even choose my own death, show compassion to you?"

"Kill me," she answered fiercely. "Kill me now, while yet there is time. See, I have brought you this"—from the folds of her scanty sarong she drew a native kris, a wavy-bladed short sword with a razor edge and needle point.

"Stab me with it," she besought, "then, if you wish, use it on your friend and yourself; there is no other hope. Look about you, do not you see there is no way of dying in this prison room? Once on a time the mirror was of glass, but a captive white man broke it and almost succeeded in cutting his wrists with the pieces until he died. Since then Goonong Besar has had a metal mirror in this room."

"*Pardieu*, you are right, child!" de Grandin agreed as he glanced at the dressing table over which the metal mirror hung. "But why do you seek death? Are you, too, destined for the octopus?"

She shuddered. "Some day, perhaps, but while I retain my beauty there is small fear of that. Every day old Umera, the one-eyed she-devil, teaches me to dance, and when I do not please her (and she is very hard to please) she beats me with bamboo rods on the soles of my feet till I can scarcely bear to walk. And Goonong Besar makes me dance for him every night till I am ready to drop, and if I do not smile upon him as I dance, or if I grow weary too soon, so that my feet lag before he gives me permission to stop, he beats me.

"Every time a ship is caught in his trap he saves some of the officers and makes me dance before them, and I know they are to be fed to the fish-devil, yet I must smile upon them, or he will beat me till my feet bleed, and the old woman will beat me when he is weary of it.

"My father was French, Monsieur, though I, myself, was born in England of a Spanish mother. We lost all our money in the war, for my father kept a goldsmith's shop in Rheims, and the *sale boche* stole everything he had. We came to the islands after the war, and my father made money as a trader. We were returning home on the Dutch ship *Van Damm* when Goonong Besar caught her in his trap.

"Me he kept to be taught to dance the dances of the islands and to be tortured—see, he has put a ring in my nose, like a native woman's." She lifted a trembling hand to the wooden peg which kept the hole pierced in her nose from growing together when she was not wearing her jeweled stud. "My father—oh, God of Israel!—he fed to the devil-fish before my eyes and told me he would serve me the same way if I proved not submissive to his will in all things.

"And so, Monsieur," she ended simply, "I would that you cause me to die and be out of my unhappiness."

As the girl talked, de Grandin's face registered every emotion from amazement to horror and compassion. As she completed her narrative he looked thoughtful. "Wait, wait, my pretty one," he besought, as she would have forced the *kris* into his hand. "I must think. *Pardieu!* Jules de Grandin, you silly fool, you must think now as never before." He sank his face in his hands and bowed his chin nearly to his knees.

"Tell me, my little cabbage," he demanded suddenly, "do they let you out of this accurst house by daylight, *hein?*"

"Oh, yes," she responded. "I may go or come as I will when I am not practicing my dances or being beaten. I may go anywhere on the island I wish, for no one, not even the cannibals who live on the shore, would dare lay his little finger on me for fear of the master. I belong to Goonong Besar, and he would feed anyone who touched his property to the great fish-devil."

"And why have you never sought to die by your own hand?" de Grandin asked suspiciously.

"Jews do not commit suicide," she answered proudly. "To die by another's hand is not forbidden—Jephthah's daughter so died—but to go from life with your hands reddened with your own blood is against the law of my fathers."

"Ah, yes, I understand," he agreed with a short nod. "You children of Jacob shame us so-called Christians in the way you keep your precepts, child. *Eh bien,* 'tis fortunate for all us you have a strong conscience, my beautiful.

"Attend me: In your walks about this never-enough-to-be-execrated island have you observed, near the spot where the masts which carry the false ship's lights stand, certain plants growing, plants with shining leaves and a fruit like the unripe apple which grows in France—a low bush with fruit of pale green?"

The girl wrinkled her white forehead thoughtfully, then nodded twice. "Yes," she replied, "I have seen such a plant."

"*Très bien,*" he nodded approvingly, "the way from this evil place seems to open before us, *mes amis.* At least, we have the sporting chance. Now listen, and listen well, my little half-orange, for upon your obedience rests our chance of freedom.

"Tomorrow, when you have a chance to leave this vestibule of hell, go you to the place where those fruits like apples grow and gather as many of them as you can carry in your *sarong*. Bring these fruits of the *Cocculus indicus* to the house and mash them to a pulp in some jar which you must procure. At the dinner hour, pour the contents of that jar into the water where dwells the devil-fish. Do not fail us, my little pigeon, for upon your faithful performance of your trust our lives, and yours, depend, *pardieu!* If you do but carry out your orders we shall feed that Monsieur Octopus such a meal as he will have small belly for, *parbleu!*

"When you have poured all the crushed fruit into the water, secret yourself in the shadows near by and wait till we come. You can swim? Good. When we do leap into the water, do you leap also, and altogether we shall swim to that boat I was about to borrow when we met this so excellent Monsieur Goonong-Besar-James-Abingdon-Richardson-Devil. *Cordieu,* I think that Jules de Grandin is not such a fool as I thought he was!

"Good night, fairest one, and may the God of your people, and the gentle Mary, too, guard you this night, and all the nights of your life."

8

"GOOD EVENING, GENTLEMEN," GOONONG Besar greeted as we entered the dining room next evening; "have you decided upon our little proposition?"

"But certainly," de Grandin assured him. "If we must choose between a few minutes' conversation with the octopus and a lifetime, or even half an hour's sight of your neither-black-nor-white face, we cast our vote for the fish. He, at least, does what he does from nature; he is no vile parody of his kind. Let us go to the fish-house *tout vite, Monsieur.* The sooner we get this business completed, the sooner we shall be rid of you!"

Goonong Besar's pale countenance went absolutely livid with fury. "You insignificant little fool," he cried, "I'll teach you to insult me! *Ha-room!*" he sent the call echoing through the marble-lined cave. "You'll not be so brave when you feel those tentacles strangling the life out of your puny body and that beak tearing your flesh off your bones before the water has a chance to drown you."

He poured a string of burning orders at his two guards, who seized their rifles and thrust them at us. "Off, off to the grotto!" he shrieked, beside himself with rage. "Don't think you can escape the devil-fish by resisting my men. They won't shoot to kill; they'll only cripple you and drag you to the pool. Will you walk, or shall we shoot you first and pull you there?"

"Monsieur," de Grandin drew himself proudly erect, "a gentleman of France fears no death a Malay *batard* can offer. Lead on!"

Biting his pale lips till the blood ran to keep from screaming with fury, Goonong Besar signaled his guards, and we took up our way toward the sea monster's lair.

"*La bon Dieu* grant *la belle juive* has done her work thoroughly," de Grandin whispered as we came out upon the balcony. "I like not this part of our little playlet, my friend. Should our plan have failed, *adieu*." He gave my hand a hasty pressure.

"Who goes first?" Goonong Besar asked as we halted by the balustrade.

"*Pardieu*, you do!" de Grandin shouted, and before anyone was aware of his intention he dashed one of his small hard fists squarely into the astonished half-caste's face, seized him about the waist and flung him bodily into the black, menacing water below.

"In, Friend Trowbridge!" he called, leaping upon the parapet. "Dive and swim—it is our only chance!"

I waited no second bidding, but jumped as far outward as possible, striking out vigorously toward the far end of the cave, striving to keep my head as near water level as possible, yet draw an occasional breath.

Horror swam beside me. Each stroke I took I expected one of the monster's slimy tentacles to seize me and drag me under; but no great, gray bubble rose from the black depths, no questing arms reached toward me. For all we could observe to the contrary, the pool was as harmless as any of the thousands of rocky caves which dot the volcanic coast of Malaya.

Bullets whipped and tore the water around us, striking rocky walls and singing off in vicious ricochets; but the light was poor, and the Malay marksmen emptied their pieces with no effect.

"*Triomphe!*" de Grandin announced, blowing the water from his mouth in a great, gusty sigh of relief as we gained the shingle outside the cave. "Miriam, my beautiful one, are you with us?"

"Yes," responded a voice from the darkness. "I did as you bade me, Monsieur, and the great fish-devil sank almost as soon as he thrust his snake-arms into the fruit as it floated on the water. But when I saw he was dead I did not dare wait; but swam out here to abide your coming."

"It is good," de Grandin commended. "One of those bullets might easily have hit you. They are execrable marksmen, those Malays, but accidents do occur.

"Now, Monsieur," he addressed the limp bundle he towed behind him in the water, "I have a little business proposition to make to *you*. Will you accompany us, and be delivered to the Dutch or British to be hanged for the damned pirate you are, or will you fight me for your so miserable life here and now?"

"I cannot fight you now," Goonong Besar answered, "you broke my arm with your cowardly jiu jitsu when you took advantage of me and attacked me without warning."

"Ah, so?" de Grandin replied, helping his captive to the beach. "That is unfortunate, for—*Mordieu*, scoundrel, would you do so!"

The Eurasian had suddenly drawn a dagger from his coat and lunged viciously at de Grandin's breast.

With the agility of a cat the Frenchman evaded the thrust, seized his antagonist's wrist, and twisted the knife from his grasp. His foot shot out, he drove his fist savagely into Goonong's throat, and the half-caste sprawled helplessly on the sand.

"Attend Mademoiselle!" de Grandin called to me. "It is not well for her to see what I must do here."

There was the sound of a scuffle, then a horrible gargling noise, and the beating of hands and feet upon the sands.

"*Fini!*" de Grandin remarked nonchalantly, dipping his hands in the water and cleansing them of some dark stains.

"You . . . ?" I began.

"*Mais certainement*," he replied matter-of-factly. "I slit his throat. What would you have? He was a mad dog; why should he continue to live?"

Walking hurriedly along the beach, we came to the little power-boat moored in the inlet and set her going.

"Where to?" I asked as de Grandin swung the trim little craft around a rocky promontory.

"Do you forget, *cher* Trowbridge, that we have a score to settle with those cannibals?" he asked.

We settled it. Running the launch close inshore, de Grandin shouted defiance to the Papuans till they came tumbling out of their cone-shaped huts like angry bees from their hives.

"*Sa ha, messieurs*," de Grandin called, "we give you food of another sort this night. Eat it, *sacré canaille*; eat it!" The Lewis machine-gun barked and sputtered, and a chorus of cries and groans rose from the beach.

"I T IS WELL," HE announced as he resumed the wheel. "They eat no more white women, those ones. Indeed, did I still believe the teachings of my youth, I should say they were even now partaking of the devil's hospitality with their late master."

"But see here," I demanded as we chugged our way toward the open water, "what was it you told Miriam to put in the water where the octopus was, de Grandin?"

He chuckled. "Had you studied as much biology as I, Friend Trowbridge, you would recognize that glorious plant, the *Cocculus indicus*, when you saw it. All over the Polynesian islands the lazy natives, who desire to obtain food with the minimum of labor, mash up the berry of that plant and spread it in the water where the fish swim. A little of it will render the fish insensible, a little more will kill him as dead as the late lamented Goonong Besar. I noticed that plant growing on the island, and when our lovely Jewess told me she could go and come at will I said to me, 'By the George, why not have her poison that great devil-fish and swim to freedom?' *Voilà tout!*"

A PASSING DUTCH STEAMER PICKED us up two days later.
    The passengers and crew gaped widely at Miriam's imperial beauty, and wider still at de Grandin's account of our exploits. "*Pardieu!*" he confided to me one night as we walked the deck, "I fear those Dutchmen misbelieve me, Friend Trowbridge. Perhaps I shall have to slit their ears to teach them to respect the word of a Frenchman."

I T WAS SIX MONTHS later that a Western Union messenger entered my consulting room at Harrisonville and handed me a blue-and-white envelope. "Sign here," he ordered.
    I tore the envelope open, and this is what I read:

Miriam made big sensation in Folies Bérgères tonight. Felicitations.— de Grandin

The Vengeance of India

A LL DAY THE MARCH wind had been muttering and growling like a peevish giant with a toothache. As darkness fell it began to raise its voice; by nine o'clock it was shrieking and screaming like a billion banshees suffering with *cholera morbus*. I huddled over the coke fire burning in my study grate and tried to concentrate on my book, to forget the wailing of the wind and the misfortunes of the day, but made very poor work of it.

Mingling with the wind's skirling there suddenly sounded the raucous bellow of an automobile siren, followed, a moment later, by a hammering and clattering at the front door as if whoever stood outside would beat the panels in by main force.

"If ye plaze, sor," Nora, my maid of all work, announced, poking her nose around the half-opened study door, "there's a gintilman ter see ye—an Eyetalian man, I think he is." Nora disapproves strongly of "furriners" in general and Italians in particular, and when they come, as they frequently do, to summon me from the house on a stormy night, her disapproval is hidden neither from my callers nor me.

Tonight, however, I greeted the interruption with something like relief. Action of any sort, even traveling a dozen miles to set an Italian laborer's broken limb without much hope of compensation, would provide a welcome distraction from the pall of gloom which enveloped me. "Bring him in," I ordered.

"*Parbleu!*" exclaimed a voice behind her. "He is already in! Did you think, my friend, that I would travel all this way on such a night to have your servant debate entrance with me?"

I leaped from my chair with a whoop of delight and seized both my visitor's slender hands in mine. "De Grandin!" I exclaimed delightedly. "Jules de Grandin! What in the world are you doing here? I thought you'd be in your laboratory at the Sorbonne by now."

"But no," he denied, handing his sopping cap and raincoat to Nora and seating himself across the fire from me, "there is little rest for the wicked in this world, my friend, and for Jules de Grandin there is none at all. Hardly had we finished with that villainous Goonong Besar than I was dispatched, post-haste, to Brazil, and when my work was finished there I must needs be called to tell of my experiments before your association of physicians in New York. *Eh bien*, but I fear me I shall not see my peaceful laboratory for some time, my friend."

"Oh, so you were in Brazil?" I answered thoughtfully.

"Trowbridge, my friend!" he put out both hands impulsively. "The mention of that country distresses you. Tell me, can I be of help?"

"H'm, I'm afraid not," I replied sadly. "It's an odd coincidence, your coming from there today, though. You see, a patient of mine, a Brazilian lady, died today, and I've no more idea what killed her than an African Bushman has about the nebular hypothesis."

"*Oh, la, la!*" he chuckled. "Friend Trowbridge, to see you is worth traveling twice around the world. Forty years a physician, and he worries over a faulty diagnosis! My dear fellow, do you not know the only truthful certificate a physician ever gives for the cause of death is when he writes down 'unknown'?"

"I suppose so," I agreed, "but this case is out of the ordinary, de Grandin. These people, the Drigos, have lived here only a few weeks, and virtually nothing is known of them, except that they seem to have plenty of money. This morning, about eleven o'clock, I was called to attend their only child, a daughter about eighteen years of age, and found her in a sort of stupor. Not a faint, nor yet a condition of profound depression, simply sleepy, like any young woman who was up late the previous night. There was no history of unusual activity on her part; she had gone to bed at her usual hour the night before, and was apparently in good health within an hour of the time I was called. I could see no reason for my services, to tell you the truth, for her condition did not appear at all serious, yet, before I could reassure her parents and leave the house, she went to sleep and slept her life away. *Died in what appeared a healthy, natural sleep in less than ten minutes!*"

"A-a-ah?" he answered on a rising note. "You interest me, my friend. It is, perhaps, some new, acute form of sleeping sickness we have here. Come, can you make some excuse to go to the people's house? I would make inquiries from them. Perchance we shall learn something for the benefit of science."

I was about to demur when the tinkle of my telephone cut in. "Dr. Trowbridge," called the party at the other end, "this is Johnston, the undertaker, speaking. Can you come over to Drigo's to sign the death certificate, or shall I bring it to your house tomorrow? I can't get any information from these folks. They don't even know what she died of."

"Neither do I," I muttered to myself, but aloud I said, "Why, yes, Mr. Johnston, I'll come right over. There's a friend of mine, another doctor, here; I'll bring him along."

"Good enough," he responded. "If I have to argue with these dagoes much longer I'll need you and your friend, too, to patch up my nerves."

R OBED IN A GOWN of priceless old lace, a white net mantilla drawn over her smoothly parted black hair, Ramalha Drigo lay at rest in an elaborate open-couch casket of mahogany, her slender, oleander-white hands piously crossed upon her virginal bosom, a rosary of carved ebony, terminating in a silver crucifix, intertwined in her waxen fingers.

"*Bon Dieu*," de Grandin breathed as he bent over the girl's composed oval face, "she was beautiful, this poor one! *Hélas* that she should die this early!"

I murmured an assent as I took the form Mr. Johnston proffered me and wrote "unknown" in the space reserved for cause of death and "about one-half hour" in the place allotted for duration of last illness.

"Gosh, Doc, he's a queer one, that foreign friend of yours," the undertaker commented, attracting my attention with a nudge and nodding toward de Grandin. The little Frenchman was bending over the casket, his blond, waxed mustache twitching like the whiskers of an alert tomcat, his slender, womanish hands patting the girl's arms and breast questioningly, as though they sought the clue to her mysterious death beneath the folds of her robe.

"He's queer, all right," I agreed, "but I've never seen him do anything without good reason. Why—"

A faltering step in the hall cut short my remark as Mr. Drigo entered the parlor. "Good evening, Dr. Trowbridge," he greeted with a courteous bow. "Dr. de Grandin"—as I presented the Frenchman—"I am honored to make your acquaintance."

De Grandin nodded an absent-minded acknowledgment of the courtesy and turned away, addressing Mr. Johnston in a whisper. "You are an embalmer, my friend?" he asked, almost eagerly, it seemed to me.

"Yes," answered the other, wonderingly. "I've had a license to practice for ten years."

"And it is customary that you embalm the dead in this country, yes?" de Grandin insisted.

"Yes, sir; but sometimes—"

"And when embalmment is not made, it is the exception, rather than the rule?"

"Decidedly, but—"

"You would embalm as a matter of course, unless expressly ordered to the contrary, then?"

"Yes," Johnston admitted.

"Ah, then, was it Monsieur Drigo who forbade that you embalm his daughter?"

The undertaker started as though pricked with a needle. "How did you know?" he demanded.

The ghost of one of his impish smiles flickered across de Grandin's face, to be replaced instantly with a look more suited to the occasion. "In France, my friend," he confided, "the science of embalming, as practised in America, is still a rarity. But in Paris we have a young man, a Canadian, who preserves the dead even as you do here, and from him I have learn many things. I have, for example, learned that you inject the preserving fluids in either the brachial, the carotid, the axillary or the femoral artery. Très bien, if you have embalmed this poor child here, you have used one of those arteries, n'est-ce-pas? The chances are that an American embalmer would not utilize the femoral artery to embalm a woman's body, so I feel to see if you have bandaged the arm or breast of that poor dead child where you have inserted your fluid-tube in one of those other arteries. I find no bandage; I feel her cheeks, they are firm as life; therefore, I decide embalmment have not been done, and, knowing your custom here, I ask to know who have ordered the contrary. Voilà, it are not magic which make me know, but the ordinary sense of the horse."

He linked his arm in mine. "Come, Friend Trowbridge," he announced, "there is no more we can do here. Let us leave this sad house to its sorrow. Tomorrow, or the next day, perhaps, you will have more of these so mysterious cases, and we can study them together. Meanwhile, let us leave what we can not help."

The three of us, Johnston, de Grandin and I, were about to pass from the house when the Frenchman paused, gazing intently at a life-sized half-length portrait in oils hanging on the hall wall. "Monsieur Drigo," he asked, "forgive my unseemly curiosity, but that gentleman, who was he?"

Something like terror appeared in the other's face as he answered, "My grandfather, sir."

"Ah, but Monsieur," de Grandin objected, "that gentleman, he wears the British uniform, is it not so?"

"Yes," Drigo replied. "My mother's father was a British officer, her mother was a Portuguese lady."

"Thank you," de Grandin replied with a bow as he followed me through the front door.

THEY BURIED RAMALHA DRIGO in the little graveyard of the Catholic chapel the following day. It was a dreary ceremony, no one but the old priest, the Drigo family, de Grandin and I were in attendance, and the wailing March wind seemed echoing our own somber thoughts as it soughed through the branches of the leafless Lombardy poplars.

"It is old, that cemetery?" de Grandin hazarded as we drove from the church to my house following the brief committal service.

"Very old," I assented. "St. Benedict's is one of the earliest Roman Catholic parishes in New Jersey, and the cemetery is one of the few in this neighborhood dating back to Colonial days."

"And have you noticed any strange colored men in the neighborhood lately?" he asked irrelevantly.

"Strange colored men?" I echoed. "What in the world are you driving at, de Grandin? First you ask me if the cemetery is old, then you go off at a tangent, and want to know if there are any strange Negroes in the neighborhood. You—"

"Tell me, my friend," he interrupted, "how did the poor dead lady spend her time? Did she walk much in the country, or go from home much in the night?"

"For heaven's sake!" I looked at him in wonderment, and almost ran the car into the roadside ditch. "Have you lost your senses completely, or are you trying to see how foolish you can be? I never heard such rambling questions!"

"Nor have you ever heard that the longest way round is usually the shortest way home, apparently," he added. "Believe me, my friend, I do not ask aimless questions. But no, that is not my method. Come, if you will set me down I shall walk through the village and attempt to collect some information. My regards to your amiable cook, if you please, and request that she will prepare some of her so excellent apple pie for dinner. I shall be home by meal time, never fear."

H E WAS AS GOOD as his word. It lacked twenty minutes of the dinner hour when he hurried into the house, his cheeks reddened from brisk walking in the chilly March air. But something in his manner, his nervously quick movements, his air of suppressed excitement, told me he was on the track of some fresh mystery.

"Well, what is it?" I asked as we adjourned to the library after dinner. "Have you heard anything of the strange colored men you were so anxious about this afternoon?" I could not forbear a malicious grin as I reminded him of his senseless question.

"But of course," he returned evenly as he lighted a French cigarette and blew a cloud of acrid smoke toward the ceiling. "Am I not Jules de Grandin, and does not Jules de Grandin get the information he seeks? At all times? Most certainly."

He laughed outright at the amazed look with which I greeted his egotistical sally. "*La la*, Friend Trowbridge," he exclaimed, "you are so droll! Always you Americans and English would have the world believe you have yourselves in perfect control, yet I can play upon you as a harpist plays upon his strings.

When will you learn that my honest, well-merited self-respect is not empty boastfulness?"

He cast aside his bantering manner and leaned forward very suddenly. "What do you know of St. Benedict's cemetery?" he demanded.

"Eh, St. Benedict's—?" I countered, at a loss to answer.

"Precisely, exactly," he affirmed. "Do you, for example, know that the entire ground near the old chapel is underlaid with ancient tombs—vaulted, brick-lined passageways?"

"No," I replied. "Never heard such a thing."

"Ah, so?" he answered sarcastically. "All your life you have lived here, yet you know naught of this curiosity. Truly, I have said not half enough in praise of Jules de Grandin, I fear. And, since you know nothing of the tombs, I take it you did not know that when the Drigo family became affiliated with St. Benedict's congregation they bought the freehold to a pew, and, along with it, the license to bury their dead in one of the old tombs. Eh, you did not know that?"

"Of course not," I returned. "I'm a physician, not a detective, de Grandin. Why should I pry into my patients' private affairs?"

"U'm, why, indeed?" he replied. Then, with an abrupt change of subject: "Have you heard Beinhauer's new hypothesis concerning catabolism? No?" And with that he launched on a long and highly technical explanation of the Austrian's theory of destructive metabolism, nor could all my efforts drag him back to a single word concerning his discoveries of the afternoon.

"PRETTY BAD BUSINESS, DOWN to th' graveyard, ain't it, Doc?" asked the postman as I passed him on my way to my morning calls the following day.

"What's that?" I asked, startled. "What's happened?"

He smiled with the conscious superiority of one who has interesting gossip to retail. "That Drigo girl"—he jerked an indicative thumb in the general direction of the Drigo home,—"th' one that died th' other day. Some grave robbers musta dug her up last night, 'cause th' sexton of St. Benedict's found her veil layin' on th' ground this mornin'. They're goin' to open her grave this afternoon to see if her body's still there, I hear. 'Tain't likely they'll find nothin', though; them body-snatchers don't usually leave nothin' layin' around when they get through."

"Good heavens!" I exclaimed. "Grave robbery?"

"Yep; that's what they say."

I hurried on my way, my thoughts racing faster than the wheels of my motor. It was all too likely. Gossip of the mysterious cause of the girl's death was bound to have got about, and her lovely body would have proved an irresistibly attractive bait for some anatomist with a passion for morbid research. At my first stop I called the house and told de Grandin.

"*Cordieu!* Is it so!" he shouted in answer. "I have won my bet, then!"

"You—what?" I replied incredulously.

"Last night, when I had learned what I had learned, I wagered with myself that she would not remain grave-bound," he replied. "Now I have won. This afternoon I go to witness the exhumation; but it is little more than a waste of time. She will not be there. On that I bet myself ten francs."

"What the devil—" I began, but a sharp click told me he had hung up. Three minutes later, when I reestablished communication with the office, Nora told me that the "furrin gintilman" had "gone down th' road as if th' Little Good Paypul wuz aftther 'im."

B Y FOUR O'CLOCK THAT afternoon the entire village was buzzing with the gruesome news of the rifling of Ramalha Drigo's grave. Father Lamphier, the aged parish priest of St. Benedict's, wrung his hands in an agony of vicarious suffering for the girl's distracted parents; Arthur Lesterton, the county prosecutor, vowed legal vengeance on the miscreants; Duffey, the police chief, gave an interview to a reporter from our one and only evening paper declaring that the police had several suspects under surveillance and expected to make an early arrest. Indignation was at fever heat; everybody made endless impracticable suggestions, nobody did anything. In all the town there seemed only two calm people: Ricardo Drigo, Ramalha's father, and Jules de Grandin.

Drigo thanked me courteously when I expressed sympathy for his misfortune, and said quietly, "It is fate, Doctor. It can not be escaped." De Grandin nodded his head sapiently once or twice, and said nothing at all. But the glitter of his little blue eyes and the occasional nervous twitching of his slender white hands told me he was seething inwardly.

We ate dinner in silence, I with no appetite at all, de Grandin with a gusto which seemed to me, in the circumstances, hardly decent.

Each of us took a book in the library after dinner, and several hours passed in gloomy quiet.

Suddenly: "The time approaches, Trowbridge, my friend," de Grandin exclaimed, shutting his book with a snap and rising from his chair.

"Eh?" I answered wonderingly.

"We go; we observe; perhaps we find that answer to this *sacré* riddle tonight," he replied.

"Go? Observe?" I echoed stupidly.

"But certainly. Have I been going hither and elsewhere all this time to sit idly by when the opportunity to act has come? Your coat, my friend, and your hat! We go to that St. Benedict's cemetery. Right away, at once, immediately. This night, perhaps, I show you that which you have never seen before."

S T. BENEDICT'S CHURCHYARD LAY stark and ghastly in the night-light as I parked my car beside the dilapidated fence separating the little God's Acre from the road. Discolored tombstones reared themselves from the dead winter grass like bones long dried upon some ancient battlefield, patches of hoar-frost showed leprous against the sod, and, mingling with the moaning of the night wind in the poplar boughs, the shrill, eery cry of a screech-owl came to us like the lament of an earth-bound spirit.

"Have a care, my friend," de Grandin warned in a low breath as he clambered over the fence and made his way between the graves, "the ground is treacherous here. One false step, and *pouf!* your leg is broken against some of these mementoes of mortality."

I followed him as quickly as I could till his upraised hand signaled a halt. "It is here we shall see what we shall see, if, indeed, we see it at all," he promised, sinking to the moss at the foot of a great pine tree. "Observe that monument yonder? *Bien,* it is to it we must give our particular attention this night."

I recognized the gravestone he indicated as standing in the Drigos' burial plot. It was one of the cemetery's oldest monuments, a low, table-like box of stone consisting of a flat horizontal slab about the size of a grave's ground dimensions, supported by four upright pieces of marble, the name and vital dates of the family which first owned the plot being engraved on the tomb's top. I recalled having heard the grave space originally belonged to the Bouvier family, but the last of the line had gone to his eternal rest long before I was born.

Fixing my eyes steadily on the old monument, I wondered what my companion meant by his assertion, wondered again, and turned to look over my shoulder toward the road where the clatter of a passing vehicle sounded on the macadam.

Somewhere in the town a tower clock began telling midnight. *Bong, bong, bong,* the sixteen-note chime sounded the full hour, followed by the deep resonant *boom* of the bell as it began its twelve strokes. One—two—three—

"*Regardez!*" de Grandin's slim fingers bit into my arm as he hissed the command. A shiver, not due to the raw March air, raced up my spine and through my scalp, raising the short hairs above my greatcoat collar as a current of electricity might have done.

Beyond the Bouvier tomb, like a column of mist, too strong to be dissipated by the wind, yet almost too impalpable to be seen, a slender white form was rising, taking shape—*coming toward us.*

"Good God!" I cried in a choking voice, shrinking against de Grandin with the involuntary, unreasoning fear of the living for the dead. "What is it?"

"*Zut!*" he shook off my restraining clutch as an adult might brush aside a child in time of emergency. "*Attendez, mon ami!*" With a catlike leap he cleared the intervening graves and planted himself square in the path of the advancing wraith. *Click!* His pocket electric flash shot a beam of dazzling light straight into the specter's face. I went sick with horror as I recognized the drawn features and staring, death-glazed eyes of—

"Ramalha Drigo, look at me,—I command it!" De Grandin's voice sounded shrill and rasping with the intensity of purpose which was behind it. Coming abreast of him, I saw his little blue eyes were fairly starting from his face as he bent an unwinking stare on the dead face before him. The waxed ends of his small, blond mustache started upward, like the horns of an inverted crescent, as his lips drew themselves about his words. "Look—at—me—Ramalha Drigo,—I—command—it!"

Something like a tremor passed through the dead girl's flaccid cheeks. For an instant her film-coated eye flickered with a look of lifelike intelligence. Then the face went limp with the flaccidity of death once more, the lids half dropped before the staring eyes, and her whole body crumpled like a wax figure suddenly exposed to a blast of heat.

"Catch her, Trowbridge, my friend!" de Grandin ordered excitedly. "Bear her to her father's house and put her to bed. I come as soon as possible; meantime I have work to do."

Thrusting the flashlight into his pocket he jerked out a small whistle and blew three quick, shrilling blasts. "À *moi, sergent; à moi, mes enfants!*" he called as the whistle fell clinking and bouncing to the gravestone beneath his feet.

As I carried the light, crumpled body of Ramalha Drigo toward the cemetery gate I heard the crash of booted feet against the graveyard shrubs mingling with hoarsely shouted commands and the savage, eager baying of police dogs straining at the leash. A hulking shape brushed past me at a run, and I made out the form of a state trooper rushing toward de Grandin, swinging a riot stick as he ran.

Something cold as clay touched my face. It was one of Ramalha's little hands lying against my cheek as her arm had bent between her body and my shoulder when I caught her as she fell. Shifting her weight to one arm I took the poor dead hand in my free hand and lowered it to her side, then froze like a statue in my tracks. Faint, so faint it could scarcely be recognized, but perceptible, nevertheless, a feeble pulse was beating in her wrist.

"Good Lord!" I almost shouted to the unheeding night. "Merciful heaven, the child is alive!"

Rushing as I had not rushed since my cub days as an ambulance surgeon, I carried her to my waiting car, bundled the motor rug about her and drove to her father's house at a pace which took account of no speed limit save my engine's greatest capacity.

Kicking at the door, I roused the Drigo family from their beds, carried the senseless girl upstairs and placed her between woolen blankets with every available water-bottle and hot-pack in the house at her feet and spine.

Ten, fifteen minutes I watched beside her, administering a hypodermic injection of strychnine each five minutes. Gradually, like the shadow of the dawn breaking against a winter horizon, the faint flush of circulating blood appeared in her pallid lips and cheeks.

Standing at my elbow, Ricardo Drigo watched first apathetically, then wonderingly, finally in a fever of incredulous hope and fear. As a faint respiration fluttered in the girl's breast, he fell to his knees beside the bed, burying his face in his hands and sobbing aloud in hysterical joy. "Oh, Lord of heaven," he prayed between sobs, "reward, I beseech you, this Dr. de Grandin, for surely he is not as other men!"

"*Tiens*, my friend, you do speak truth!" agreed a complacent voice from the doorway behind us. "Of a certainty Jules de Grandin is a very remarkable fellow; but if you seek some necromancer, you would better look elsewhere. This de Grandin, he is a scientist; no more. *Cordieu!* Is that not enough!"

"PAR LA BARBE D'UN *corbeau*, M*onsieur*, but this port is exquisite!" de Grandin assured Drigo three hours later as he passed his tumbler across the table for replenishment. "And these so divine cigars"—he raised both hands in mute admiration,—"*parbleu*, I could smoke three of them at once and mourn because my mouth would not accommodate a fourth!

"But I see our good friend Trowbridge grows restless. He would have the whole story, from the beginning. Very well, then, to begin:

"As I told Friend Trowbridge, I had but come from Rio when I arrived in New York the other day. While I was in that so superb city of Brazil I became acquainted with more than one *delegado* of police, and from them I heard many strange things. For example"—he fixed his penetrating gaze on Drigo for a moment—"I heard the mystery of a Portuguese gentleman who came to Brazil from East Africa and took a beautiful house in the Praia Botafogo, only to relinquish it before his furniture was fairly settled in it. Before this gentleman lived in Africa he had dwelt in India. He was born there, in fact.

"Why he left that so beautiful city of Rio, the police did not know; but they had a story from one of their detectives that that gentleman came suddenly face to face with a Hindoo sailor from one of the ships in the harbor while he and his daughter were shopping in the Ouvidor. The Hindoo, it was said, had but looked at the daughter and laughed in the father's face; but it was enough. He departed from Rio the next day, that gentleman; both he and his family and all his servants. To the United States he went, though none knew to what part, or why.

"*Eh bien*, it was one of the fragments of mystery which we of the Service de Sûreté do constantly encounter—a little incident of life without beginning or end, without ancestry or posterity. Never mind, I stored it in my brain for future reference. Sooner or later all things we remember come to have a use, *n'est-ce-pas?*

"When next I see my dear friend Trowbridge he is looking very long in the face. One of his patients, a Brazilian lady, have died that very day, and he can not account for her death. But his story sounds interesting, and I think, perhaps—maybe, I find out something of some new disease, so I ask him to let me investigate.

"When we come to the house where this dead lady lay I am struck with— with *something* about her look, and I remember most American dead are embalmed almost instantly for their burial. I touch her face, it has not the hardness of flesh preserved with formaldehyde. Then I feel for the wounds where the embalmer would have cut; but I find none. One thing more I find. While her face were cold, it were not cold as the surrounding air. 'How does this come?' asks Jules de Grandin of Jules de Grandin; but answer there was none at all.

"As my dear Trowbridge and I leave that house of death I see the portrait of a gentleman who much resembled our host, but who wore a uniform such as the British army once wore. Yet not quite. There was a difference there, but what it was I can not say then.

"I ask Monsieur Drigo who the painted gentleman was, and he say, 'He are my grandfather.'

"That night I do much thinking; finally I believe I have the thread of this mystery in my hands. I put together my knowledge and this is what I have:

"The uniform that painted gentleman wore are not of the British army, but of the British India Company. So. Now, he was a man in early middle life, this painted gentleman who wear the insignia of an artilleryman on his uniform, and, judging by his grandson's apparent age, he should have lived about the time of the American Civil War. Very good, what was happening in India, where this painted gentleman lived, then? I think some more; then, 'Ah,' Jules de Grandin tell Jules de Grandin, 'Jules de Grandin, you are one great stupid head; it was in 1857 that the Sepoy troops revolted against the English in India.'

"Yes? And what then? For once in history those English did act with sense. They meted to those Indian rebels with such measure as the rebels gave to them. For the atrocities of Nana Sahib they took logical vengeance by tying those rebels to the mouths of cannon and—*pouf!* it was soon over when the cannoneers fired their guns.

"So far, so good. What then? Those Indians are a vengeful race. They harbor hatred through many generations. This much I know. Something else I know, too. In India they sometimes, for money, will hypnotize a man—or, perchance, a woman—and bury him, to all appearances dead, in the earth for so long a time that corn planted above his grave will take root and grow several inches high. I have seen that with my own two eyes. Also I remember how one Colonel Ainsworth, an English gentleman who commanded some of the cannon from which those mutineers were blown to death, had apparently died in his English home in 1875, *but came to life in the family vault ten days later.*

"Almost he went crazy from that experience, though he was at length rescued. Two years later he suffered the same terrible fate. He was buried for dead, and came back to life again. And each time, before he had his seeming death, he had encountered a Hindoo in the road. At last he could stand the strain no more; but shot himself really dead rather than face the terror of a third living burial.

"Now, the people who wrote down the strange case of Colonel Ainsworth did but note that he had met Hindoos before he seemingly died; but, apparently, they attached no importance to these meetings. I do otherwise; for when I search my memory I find that of the officers who commanded the British guns at the Sepoys' executions, nearly all died violent or sudden deaths. How do we know how many of them were buried alive, but not rescued as Colonel Ainsworth was? Eh? Also I remember from the records that many of the descendants of those officers had died mysteriously or suddenly, sometimes both.

"'*Morbleu*,' I tell myself, 'Jules de Grandin, I think maybe—perhaps we have discover something!'

"I bet with myself, therefore, that this poor dead lady will not rest easy in her grave. Dead she may be, *cher* Trowbridge has so certified; but if she were not first dead in fact—the Brazilians do not believe in embalming their dead, and the embalmer's instruments not therefore have made certain that she is dead altogether. Very well, then; wait and see.

"Next day my friend Trowbridge tell me her grave was robbed. I go to watch them open it, and find the tombs in that cemetery are old passages underground. She is not in her grave, I see that; but she might be somewhere in the cemetery, nevertheless. I learn, by asking what my friend Trowbridge would call silly questions, that the grave space where this lady was buried once belonged to a family called Bouvier. Old Monsieur Bouvier, who live and die many years ago, had a morbid fear of being buried alive, so he had a special tomb constructed in such manner that if he come to life underground he can slide back a panel of stone as you would open a door, and walk home to his family. This old tomb is still standing above the spot where this unfortunate dead lady have been buried. 'Maybe,' I tell myself, 'maybe something have happen in that cemetery while no one was watching.'

"Already I have made inquiries and find that two strange Negroes have been in town since some days before this poor lady died. But though they lived in the Negro quarter they had nothing to do with the other colored people. Query: Were they Negroes or were they not Negroes, and if not, what were they? Hindoo, perhaps? I think yes.

"What then? The girl's mantilla has been found above ground; her body has not been found below. Perhaps they play cat-and-mouse with her, sending her forth from her grave at night like a very vampire, perhaps to injure her father or others whom she had loved in life. I decide I will see.

"I seek out that Monsieur Lesterton, who is the *juge d'instruction*—how do you say? county prosecutor?—and tell him all.

"He is a lawyer in a million, that one. Instead of saying, 'Talk to the Marines about it,' he nod his head and tell me I may have as many gendarmes as I wish to help me with my plan.

"Tonight I go with friend Trowbridge and watch beside that old Monsieur Bouvier's tomb. Presently that poor girl who is found fast in the death which is not death comes forth, walking over her own grave.

"Jules de Grandin is no fool. He, too, can hypnotize, and what a man can do he can undo, likewise, if he be clever. I order her to wake up. I flash my light in her eyes and I bring her to consciousness, then to natural sleep, as she was before the Hindoos' power make her appear dead. I turn her over to Friend Trowbridge to make all well while I and the gendarmes search for those men who are the masters of death.

"We find them hidden in an old tomb, far underground. One of them I have the felicity of killing when he would resist arrest. The other is shot by a trooper when he would fly, but ere his life ran out with his blood he tells me he and his companion have followed Monsieur Drigo from India to Africa and from Africa to America. Two days before she 'died' Mademoiselle Ramalha is met by these men as she walks in the country. They hypnotize her and order her to 'die' in forty-eight hours—to die and be buried, then come forth from her grave each night at midnight and visit her father's house. *Voilà*, that fellow, he too, died; but not before I had the truth."

"But how did you make him confess, de Grandin?" I asked. "Surely his conscience did not trouble him, and if he knew he was dying he had nothing to fear from you."

"Eh, did he not?" de Grandin answered with an elfish grin. "Ah, but he did! The pig is unclean to those people. If they do but so much as touch a *porc* they do lose their caste. I did promise that fellow that if he did not tell me all, and tell the truth, right away, immediately, at once, I would see he was buried in the same coffin with a pig's carcass and that his grave should be wet with the blood of a slaughtered swine every full moon. *Pardieu*, you should have seen him make haste to tell me all before he died!"

He turned toward Drigo; "Mademoiselle Ramalha has little to fear in the future, *Monsieur*," he promised. "The agents of vengeance have failed, and I do not think they will make another attempt upon her.

"Meanwhile, Friend Trowbridge, the morning breaks and the shadows flee away. Let us bid Monsieur Drigo good-night and hasten home.

"*Cordieu!*" he chuckled as we climbed into my waiting motor, "had I stayed beside Monsieur Drigo's wine a half-hour longer I should not have been able to leave at all. As it is, Trowbridge, my friend, I see two of you sitting beside me!"

The Dead Hand

J ULES DE GRANDIN PASSED his coffee cup across the breakfast table for its third replenishment. "It seems, my friend," he told me with a serio-comic grimace, "as if I exercise some sort of malign influence upon your patients. Here I have been your guest but two short weeks and you all but lose Mademoiselle Drigo and the so excellent Madame Richards is dead altogether."

"I'd hardly blame you for Mrs. Richards' death," I comforted as I refilled his cup. "She'd suffered from mitral stenosis for the past two years, and the last time I examined her I was able to detect a diastolic murmur without my stethoscope. No, her trouble dated back some time before your advent, de Grandin."

"You relieve my conscience," he replied. "And now you go to offer your condolences to the family? May I accompany you? Always, I have found, there is opportunity for those who will to learn something."

"N OM D'UN NOM, BUT it is the good Sergeant Costello!" he exclaimed as a heavy-set man closed the door of the Richards mansion and strode across the wide veranda. "*Eh bien*, my friend, do not you remember me?" He stretched both slender, well kept hands to the big Irishman. "Surely, you have not forgotten—"

"I'll say I ain't," the big detective denied with a welcoming grin. "You sure showed us some tricks in the Kalmar case, sir. Belike you'd like to give us a lift with this one?" He jerked a thumb toward the house he had just quit. "It's a bughouse in there, Dr. de Grandin."

"Ha, do you say so?" de Grandin's small eyes lit up expectantly. "You interest me. Assuredly you shall have such help as I can provide. Come let us enter; together we shall shake the facts from this mystery of yours as a mother shakes the stolen cookies from her *enfant's* blouse, by blue!"

W ILLIS RICHARDS, FINANCIAL NABOB of our small sub-metropolitan community, stood on the hearth rug of his library, a living testimonial to the truth of the axiom that death makes all men equals. For all his mop of white hair, his authoritative manner and imposing embonpoint, he was only a bereft and bewildered old man, unable to realize that in his wife's death he had encountered something not to be remedied by his signature on a five-figured check.

"Well, Sergeant," he asked with a pitiful attempt at his usual brusque manner, as he recognized Costello at de Grandin's elbow, "have you found out anything?"

"No, sir," the policeman confessed, "but here's Dr. de Grandin of Paris, France, and he can help us out if anyone can. He's done some mighty fine work for us before, and—"

"A French detective!" Richards scoffed. "D'ye need to get a foreigner to help you find some stolen property? Why—"

"Monsieur!" de Grandin's angry protest brought the irate financier's expostulation to an abrupt halt, "you do forget yourself. I am Jules de Grandin, occasionally connected with the *Service de Sûreté*, but more interested in the solution of my cases than in material reward."

"Oh," Mr. Richards' disgust deepened, "an amateur, eh? Costello, I'm ashamed of you, bringing a dabbler into my private affairs. By George, I'll telephone the Blynn Agency and take the whole case out o' your hands!"

"One moment, Mr. Richards," I broke in, relying on my position as family physician to lend strength to my statement. "This gentleman is Dr. Jules de Grandin of the Sorbonne, one of Europe's foremost criminologists and one of the world's greatest scientists. Criminal investigation is a phase of his work, just as military service was a phase of George Washington's; but you can no more compare him with professional detectives than you can compare Washington with professional soldiers."

Mr. Richards looked from de Grandin to me, then back again. "I'm sorry," he confessed, extending his hand to the little Frenchman, "and I shall be very grateful for any help that you can give me, sir."

"To be entirely frank," he motioned us to seats and began pacing the floor restlessly, "Mrs. Richards' death was not quite so natural as Dr. Trowbridge believes. Though it's true she had been suffering from heart disease for some time, it was not heart disease alone that caused her death. She was scared to death. Literally.

"I returned from New York, where I'd been attending a banquet of my alumni association, about two o'clock day before yesterday morning. I let myself in with my latch key and went directly to my room, which adjoined my wife's. I was beginning to undress when I heard her call, and ran into her bedroom just in time to see her fall to the floor, clutching at her throat and trying to say something about a hand."

"Ah?" de Grandin regarded our host with his sharp cat-stare. "And then, Monsieur?"

"And then I saw—well, fancied I saw—something drift across the room, about level with my shoulders, and go out the window. I ran over to my wife, but when I reached her she was dead."

The little Frenchman made small deprecating sounds while he looked at his well cared for nails, but otherwise he made no comment.

Richards gave him an annoyed look as he continued. "It was not till this morning that I discovered all my wife's jewels and about twenty thousand dollars worth of unregistered securities had disappeared from the wall safe in her room.

"Of course," he concluded, "I didn't really see anything in the air when I ran from my room. That's palpably absurd."

"Quite obviously," I agreed.

"Sure," Costello nodded.

"Not at all," de Grandin denied, shaking his head vigorously. "It is entirely possible your eyes did not deceive you, Monsieur. Tell us, what was it you saw?"

Mr. Richards' annoyance deepened to exasperation. "It looked like a hand," he snapped. "A hand with four or five inches of wrist attached to it, *and no body*. D'ye mean to tell me I saw anything like that?"

"*Quod erat demonstrandum*," the Frenchman replied softly.

"What say?" demanded Richards testily.

"I said this is a truly remarkable case, Monsieur."

"Well, d'ye want to take a look at my wife's room?" Mr. Richards turned to lead the way upstairs, but again de Grandin shook his head.

"Not at all, Monsieur. The good Sergeant Costello has already seen it, he can tell me all I need to know. Me, I shall look elsewhere for the confirmation of a possible theory."

Mr. Richards' white thatch fairly bristled. "I'll give you forty-eight hours to accomplish something—you and Costello. Then I'll call up the Blynn Agency and see what real detectives can do for me."

"You are more than generous in your allowance, Monsieur," de Grandin replied icily.

To me, as we left the house, he confided, "I should greatly enjoy pulling that one's fat nose, Friend Trowbridge."

"CAN YOU COME OVER to my house at once, Doctor?" a voice hailed me as de Grandin and I entered my office.

"Why, what's the matter, Mr. Kinnan?" I asked as I recognized the visitor.

"Huh! What isn't the matter, Doctor? My wife's been in hysterics since this morning, and I'm not sure I shouldn't ask you to commit me to the asylum."

"*Pardieu*, Monsieur," de Grandin exclaimed, "this statement, he is vastly interesting, but not particularly enlightening. You will explain yourself, *n'est-ce-pas?*"

"Explain? What d'ye mean? How am I going to explain a thing I know's impossible? At twenty minutes after five this morning my wife and I saw something that wasn't there, and saw it take the Lafayette cup, to boot!"

"*Sacré nom d'un petit porc!*" de Grandin swore. "What is it that you say? You saw a thing that was not there and saw it take a cup of Monsieur le Marquis de Lafayette? *Non, non, non!* Not you, but I am of the deranged mind. Friend Trowbridge, look to me. I hear remarks this gentleman has not made!"

In spite of his own trouble Kinnan laughed at the little Frenchman's tragic face. "I'll be more explicit," he promised. "The baby was fretful the entire early part of last evening, and we didn't get to sleep till well after midnight. Along about five this morning he woke up on another rampage, and my wife and I went to the nursery to see what we could do. Our maid had gone to New York for the night, and as usual there wasn't a drop of milk ready for the youngster, so I started to pasteurize some for him in the dining room chafing dish. I can place the time exactly, for the library clock has been running erratically of late and only yesterday I'd gotten it so it ran just ten minutes fast. Well, that clock had just struck half-past five when—like an echo of the gong—there came a crash at the window, and the pane was shattered, right before our eyes."

"U'm?" observed de Grandin noncommittally.

"Right before our eyes, gentlemen. By a hammer."

"Ah?" de Grandin's interest in the narrative seemed something less than breathless.

"And whether you believe me or not, that hammer was held in a hand—a woman's hand—and that was all! No arm, no body; just a hand—a hand that smashed that windowpane with a hammer and floated through the air as if it were attached to an invisible body, right across the room to the cabinet where the Lafayette cup was. It unlatched the cabinet door, took the cup out and floated out the window with it. How's that for a pipe-dream? The only trouble with it is it's true!"

"Ah? Ah-ha-ha?" de Grandin exclaimed on a rising accent.

"Oh, I don't expect you to believe me. I'd say anyone who told me such a wild tale was a candidate for the bughouse, but—"

"*Au contraire*, Monsieur," de Grandin denied, "I do believe you. For why? Because, *mordieu*, that same hand-without-body was seen at Monsieur Richards' house the night his wife died."

"Eh? The devil!" This time it was Kinnan who looked skeptical. "You say someone else saw that hand. Wh—why, they couldn't!"

"Of course not," agreed Jules de Grandin evenly. "Nevertheless, they did, and there is reason to suspect it made away with jewellery and securities. Now tell me, if you please, this Lafayette cup, what was it?"

"It's a silver wine goblet that belonged to my great, great-grandfather, sir. Intrinsically I don't suppose it worth more than thirty or forty dollars, but it's valuable to us as an heirloom because Lafayette drank out of it while he was on his second visit to this country. I've been offered up to a thousand dollars for it by collectors."

De Grandin beat his fingertips together in a nervous tattoo. "This are a most unusual burglar we have here, *mes amis*. He has a hand, but no body; he enters sick ladies' bedrooms and frightens them to death; he breaks honest men's windows with a hammer and steals away the cup of Monsieur le Marquis de Lafayette while they heat milk for their babies. *Cordieu*, he will bear investigation, this one!"

"You don't believe me," Kinnan declared, half truculently, half shamefacedly.

"Have I not said I do?" the Frenchman answered almost angrily. "When you have seen such things as I have seen, Monsieur—*parbleu*, when you have seen one half as much!—you will learn to believe many things that fools declare impossible.

"This hammer"—he rose, almost glaring at Kinnan, so intense with his stare—"Where is he? I would see him, if you please."

"It's over at the house," our visitor replied, "lying right where it fell when the hand dropped it. Neither Dorothy nor I would touch it for a farm."

"Tremendous, gigantic, magnificent!" de Grandin ejaculated, nodding vigorously as he shot out each adjective. "Come, my friends, let us hasten, let us fly. Trowbridge, my old friend, you shall attend the so excellent Madame Kinnan while I go upon the trail of this bodiless burglar, and it shall be a matter of remarkableness if I do not find him. *Morbleu, Monsieur le Fantôme*, when you slay poor Madame Richards with fright, that is one thing; when you steal Monsieur Kinnan's cup of Monsieur le Marquis de Lafayette, that is also one thing, but when you think to thumb your invisible nose at Jules de Grandin—*parbleu*, that is entirely something else! We shall see who makes a monkey out of whom, and that without unnecessary delay."

The hammer proved to be an ordinary one, with nickel head and imitation ebony handle, such as could be bought at any hardware store, but de Grandin pounced on it like a famished tomcat on a mouse.

"But this is wonderful, this is superb!" he almost cooed as he swathed the implement in several layers of paper and stowed it tenderly in the pocket of his great coat.

"Trowbridge, my friend," he threw me one of his quick, enigmatic smiles, "do you attend the good Madame Kinnan. I have important duties to perform elsewhere. If possible I shall return for dinner, and if I do I pray that you will have your amiable cook prepare for me one of her so delicious apple tarts. If I should be delayed"—his little blue eyes twinkled for a moment with frosty laughter—"I shall eat that tart for my breakfast tomorrow, like a good Yon-kee."

DINNER WAS LONG SINCE over, and the requested apple tart had been reposing on the pantry shelf for several hours when de Grandin popped from a taxicab like a jack-in-the-box from its case and rushed up the front steps, the waxed ends of his little blond mustache twitching like the whiskers of an excited cat. "Quick, quick, Friend Trowbridge," he commanded as he laid a bulky paper parcel on the office desk, "to the telephone! Call that Monsieur Richards, that rich man who so generously allowed me forty-eight hours to recover his lost treasures, and that Monsieur Kinnan, whose so precious cup of the Marquis de Lafayette was stolen—call them both and bid them come here right away, at once, immediately!

"*Mordieu!*" He strode across the office with a step that was half run, half jig, "This Jules de Grandin, he is the sly, clever one. Never is the task imposed too great for him. No, of a certainty!"

"What the devil's biting you?" I asked as I rang up the Richards house.

"*Non, non,*" he waved my question aside, lit a cigarette, and flung it away almost unpuffed. "Wait, I entreat you; only wait until those others come, then you shall hear about my monstrous cleverness!"

The Richards limousine, like its owner impressive in both size and upholstery, was panting before my door in half an hour, and Kinnan drove up in his modest sedan almost at the same time. Sergeant Costello, looking mystified, but concealing his wonder with the inborn reticence of the professional policeman, came into the office close on Kinnan's heels.

"What's all this nonsense, Trowbridge?" Mr. Richards asked. "Why couldn't you come over to my house instead of dragging me out this hour o' night?"

"Tut, tut, Monsieur," de Grandin cut him short, running the admonitions so close together that they sounded like the exhaust of a miniature motor boat. "Tut, tut, Monsieur, is it not worth a short trip in the cold to have these back?" From a brown-paper parcel he produced a purple velvet case which he snapped open dramatically, disclosing an array of scintillating gems.

"These, one assumes, were once the property of Madame your wife?"

"Great Scott!" gasped Richards, reaching for the jewels. "Why, you got 'em!"

"But naturally, Monsieur." The Frenchman deftly drew the jewellery out of Richard's reach. "And also I have these." From another parcel he drew a sheaf of engraved stock certificates. "You said twenty thousand dollars' worth, I believe? *Bien.* There are here just twenty-one thousand dollar certificates, according to my count.

"Monsieur Kinnan," he bowed to the other visitor, "permit that I restore to you the cup of Monsieur le Marquis de Lafayette." The Lafayette cup was duly extracted from another package and handed to its owner.

"And now," de Grandin lifted an oblong pasteboard box of the sort used for shoes and held it toward us as a prestidigitator might hold the hat from which he was about to extract a rabbit, "I will ask you to give me the close attention. *Regardez, s'il vous plaît.* Is it not this you gentlemen saw in your respective houses?"

As he withdrew the box lid we beheld lying on a bed of crumpled tissue paper what appeared to be the perfectly modeled reproduction of a beautiful hand and wrist. The thumb and fingers, tipped with long, almond-shaped nails, were exquisitely slender and graceful, and the narrow palm, where it showed above the curling digits, was pink and soft-looking as the underside of a La France rose petal. Only the smear of collodion across the severed wrist told us we gazed on something which once pulsed with life instead of a marvelously exact reproduction.

"Is this not it?" he repeated, glancing from the lovely hand to Richards and Kinnan in turn.

Each nodded a mute confirmation, but each forbore to speak, as though the sight of the eerie, lifeless thing before him had put a seal of silence on his lips.

"*Très bon.*" He nodded vigorously. "Now, attend me, if you please: when Monsieur Kinnan told me of the hammer which broke his window, I decided the road by which to trace this bodiless burglar was mapped out on that hammer's handle. *Pourquoi?* Because this hand which frightens sick ladies to death and breaks windowpanes is one of three things. First"—he ticked off on his fingers—"it may be some mechanical device. In that case I shall find no traces. But then again it may be the ghost hand of someone who once lived, in which case, again, it is one of two things: a ghost hand, *per se*, or the reanimated flesh of one who is dead. Or, perchance, it is the hand of someone who can make the rest of him invisible.

"Now, then, if it is a ghost hand, either true ghost or living-dead flesh, it is like other hands, it has ridges and valleys and loops and whorls, which can be traced and recognized by fingerprint experts. Or, if a man can, by some process all unknown to us, make all of him except his hand invisible, why, then, his hand, too, must leave fingerprints. *Hein?*

"'Now, Jules de Grandin,' I say to me, 'is it not highly probable that one who steals jewels and stocks and bonds and the cup of Monsieur le Marquis de Lafayette, has stolen things before, perhaps been apprehended and fingerprinted?'

"'*Parbleu*, it may be even as you say, Jules de Grandin,' I reply to me.

"Thereupon I take that hammer from Monsieur Kinnan's house and go with him to police headquarters. '*Monsieur le Préfet*,' I say to the commissioner, 'I would that you permit your identification experts to examine this hammer, and tell me, of their kindness, whose fingerprints appear thereon.'

"*Bien*. He is an amiable gentleman, the commissioner, and he gives the order as requested. In due time comes the report. The handle of that hammer bears the manual autograph of one Katherine O'Brien, otherwise known to the police as Catherine Levoy, and also as Catherine Dunstan. The police have a *dossier* for her. She was in turn a shoplifter, a decoy woman for some badger-game gentlemen, a forger and the partner of one Professor Mysterio, a theatrical hypnotist. Indeed, they tell me, she was married to this professor à *l'Italienne*, and with him she travelled the country, sometimes giving exhibitions, sometimes indulging in crime, as, for instance, burglary and pocket-picking.

"Now, about a year ago, while she and the professor were exhibiting themselves at Coney Island, this lady died. Her partner gave her a remarkable funeral; but the ceremonies were marred by one untoward incident—while her body lay in the mortuary some miscreant climbed through the window and removed one of her hands. In the dead of night he severed from the lovely body of that wicked woman the hand that had so often made away with others' property. He made away with it, nor could the efforts of the police trace him, or it, to his place of hiding.

"Meanwhile, this Professor Mysterio, he who was the woman's partner, has retired from the stage and lives here in New Jersey on the fortune he has amassed.

"'New Jersey, New Jersey,' I say to me when I hear this. 'Why, this is New Jersey!'

"So the good Sergeant Costello and I make a survey. We find that this *ci-devant* professor lives out on the Andover Road where he does nothing for a livelihood but smoke a pipe and drink whisky. 'Come, let us take him in,' the Sergeant says to me.

"Now, while we ride out to the professor's house I do much thinking. Hypnotism is thought, and thought is a thing—a thing which does not die. If this deceased woman had been habituated to obeying mental commands of this Professor Mysterio—had been accustomed to obey those orders with all parts of her body as soon as they were given—had she not formed a habit-pattern of obedience? Trowbridge, my friend, you are a physician, you have seen men die. You know that the suddenly killed man falls in an attitude which had been characteristic in life, is it not so?"

I nodded agreement.

"Very well, then. I ask me if it is not possible that the hand this professor had commanded so many times in life can not be made to do his bidding after death? *Mon Dieu*, the idea is novel, but not impossible for that reason! Did not that so superb Monsieur Poe hint at some such thing in his story of the dying man who remained alive because he was hypnotized? Assuredly.

"So, when we get to the professor's house Costello points his pistol at the gentleman and says, 'I make you arrested,' and meanwhile I search the place.

"In it I find Monsieur Richards' jewellery and certificates, also the cup of Monsieur le Marquis de Lafayette. I also find much else, including this hand of a dead woman which is not itself dead. *Dieu de Dieu!* When I go to take it from its case it attack me like a living thing, and Costello have to promise he will punch Professor Mysterio in the nose before he order it to be quiet. And it obeyed his voice! *Mordieu*, when I see that I have the flesh of geese all over me!"

"Rot!" Richards flung the comment like a missile. "I don't know what sort o' hocus-pocus made that hand move, but if you expect me to believe any such nonsense as this stuff you've been telling you've got the wrong pig by the ear. I shouldn't be surprised if you and this Professor What's-His-Name were in cahoots, and you got cold feet and left him holding the bag!"

I stared aghast at the man. De Grandin's vanity was as colossal as his ability, and though he was as gentle as a woman in ordinary circumstances, like a woman he was capable of sudden flares of vixenish temper in which his regard for human life became no greater than his concern for a troublesome fly.

The little Frenchman turned to me, his face as pale as a dead man's, the muscles of his jaws working. "Friend Trowbridge you will act for me, of course?" he asked in a low, husky voice. "You will—ha!"

With the ejaculation he dodged suddenly, almost falling to the floor in his haste to avoid the flashing white object that dashed at his face.

Nor was his dodge a split-second too soon. Like the lid of a boiling kettle, the top of the shoe box had lifted, and the slim quiescent hand that lay within leaped through the opening and hurtled across intervening space like a quarrel from a crossbow. All delicate, firm-muscled fingers outspread, it swooped like a hawk, missed de Grandin by the barest fraction of in inch, and fastened itself, snapping like a strong springed steel trap, in the puffy flesh of Willis Richards' neck.

"Ah—*ulp!*" The startled financier gasped as he stumbled backward, tearing futilely at the eldritch thing which sank its long and pointed nails into his purpling skin. "Ah—God, it's choking me!"

Costello rushed to him and strove with all his strength to drag the clutching hand away. He might as well have tried to wrench apart the clasp of a chrome-steel handcuff.

"*Non, non,*" De Grandin shouted, "not that way, Sergeant. It is useless!"

Leaping to my instrument case he jerked out an autopsy knife and dashed his shoulder against the burly detective, almost sending him sprawling. Next instant, with the speed and precision of an expert surgeon, he was dissecting the deadly white fingers fastened in Richards' dewlap.

"*C'est complete,*" he announced matter-of-factly as he finished his grisly task. "A restorative, if you please, Friend Trowbridge, and an antiseptic dressing for his wounds. The nails may not have been sterile."

Wheeling, he seized the telephone and dialed police headquarters. "*Allo, Monsieur le Geôlier,*" he greeted when his call was put through. "You have one Professor Mysterio in confinement there, yes? But certainly, he is booked upon the suspicion—the what you call him? open charge? How is he, what is it he does?"

A pause, then: "Ah, you say so? I thought as much. Many thanks, Monsieur."

He put the telephone back in its cradle, and faced us again. "My friends," he announced, "the professor is no more. Two minutes ago he was heard to cry out in a loud, distinct voice, 'Katie, kill the Frenchman; I command you. Kill him!' When they rushed to his cell they found him hanging from the grating of the door by his waist-belt. The fall had snapped his neck, and he was dead as a herring.

"*Eh bien,*" he shook himself like a spaniel emerging from the water, "it was a lucky thing for me I saw that box lid lift itself when the dead hand obeyed its dying master's last command. None of you would have thought of the knife, I fear, before the thing had strangled my life away. As it is, I acted none too soon for Monsieur Richards' good."

Still red in the face, but regaining his self-possession under my ministrations, Mr. Richards sat up in his chair. "If you'll give me my property I'll be getting out o' this hell-house," he announced gruffly, reaching for the jewels and securities de Grandin had placed on the desk.

"Assuredly, Monsieur," the Frenchman agreed. "But first you will comply with the law, *n'est-ce-pas?* You have offered a reward of five thousand dollars for your property's return. Make out two checks, if you will be so kind, one for half the amount to Sergeant Costello, the other half for me."

"I'm hanged if I do," Richards demurred. "Why should a man have to buy back his own stuff?"

Sergeant Costello rose ponderously to his feet and gathered the parcels containing Mr. Richards' belongings into his capacious hands. "Law's law," he announced decisively. "There'll be no bonds or jools returned till that reward is paid, sir."

"All right, all right," Richards agreed, reaching for his checkbook. "I'll pay it, but it's the damndest hold-up I've ever had pulled on me."

"H'm," growled Costello as the door banged to behind the banker, "if I ever catch that bird parkin' by a fireplug or exceedin' the speed limit, he'll see a hold-up that *is* a hold-up. I'll give him every summons in me book an' holler for a fresh pad."

"*Tenez*, my friends, think of the swine no more," de Grandin ordered. "In France, had a man so insulted me, I should have called him out and run him through the body. But that one? *Pouf!* Gold is his life's blood. I hurt him far more by forcing the reward from him than if I had punctured his fat skin a dozen times.

"Meanwhile, Friend Trowbridge"—his small blue eyes snapped with the heat-lightning of his sudden smile—"there waits in the pantry that delicious apple tart prepared by your so amiable cook. Sergeant, Monsieur Kinnan, will you not join us? A wedge of apple tart and a cold mug of beer—*morbleu*, it makes a feast fit for an emperor!"

The House of Horror

"MORBLEU, FRIEND TROWBRIDGE, HAVE a care," Jules de Grandin warned as my lurching motor car almost ran into the brimming ditch beside the rain-soaked road.

I wrenched the steering wheel viciously and swore softly under my breath as I leaned forward, striving vainly to pierce the curtains of rain which shut us in.

"No use, old fellow," I confessed, turning to my companion, "We're lost; that's all there is to it."

"Ha," he laughed shortly, "do you just begin to discover that fact, my friend? *Parbleu*, I have known it this last half-hour."

Throttling my engine down, I crept along the concrete roadway, peering through my streaming windshield and storm curtains for some familiar landmark, but nothing but blackness, wet and impenetrable, met my eyes.

Two hours before, that stormy evening in 192–, answering an insistent 'phone call, de Grandin and I had left the security of my warm office to administer a dose of toxin anti-toxin to an Italian laborer's child who lay, choking with diphtheria, in a hut at the workmen's settlement where the new branch of the railroad was being put through. The cold, driving rain and the Stygian darkness of the night had misled me when I made the detour around the railway cut, and for the past hour and a half I had been feeling my way over unfamiliar roads as futilely as a lost child wandering in the woods.

"*Grace à Dieu*," de Grandin exclaimed, seizing my arm with both his small, strong hands, "a light! See, there it shines in the night. Come, let us go to it. Even the meanest hovel is preferable to this so villainous rain."

I peeped through a joint in the curtains and saw a faint, intermittent light flickering through the driving rain some two hundred yards away.

"All right," I acquiesced, climbing from the car, "we've lost so much time already we probably couldn't do anything for the Vivianti child, and maybe these people can put us on the right road, anyway."

Plunging through puddles like miniature lakes, soaked by the wind-driven rain, barking our shins again and again on invisible obstacles, we made for the light, finally drawing up to a large, square house of red brick fronted by an imposing white-pillared porch. Light streamed out through the fanlight over the white door and from the two tall windows flanking the portal.

"*Parbleu*, a house of circumstance, this," de Grandin commented, mounting the porch and banging lustily at the polished brass knocker.

I wrinkled my forehead in thought while he rattled the knocker a second time. "Strange, I can't remember this place," I muttered. "I thought I knew every building within thirty miles, but this is a new one . . ."

"Ah bah!" de Grandin interrupted. "Always you must be casting a wet blanket on the parade, Friend Trowbridge. First you insist on losing us in the midst of a *sacré* rainstorm, then when I, Jules de Grandin, find us a shelter from the weather, you must needs waste time in wondering why it is you know not the place. *Morbleu*, you will refuse shelter because you have never been presented to the master of the house, if I do not watch you, I fear."

"But I ought to know the place, de Grandin," I protested. "It's certainly imposing enough to . . ."

My defense was cut short by the sharp click of a lock, and the wide, white door swung inward before us.

We strode over the threshold, removing our dripping hats as we did so, and turned to address the person who opened the door.

"Why . . ." I began, and stared about me in open-mouthed surprise.

"Name of a little blue man!" said Jules de Grandin, and added his incredulous stare to mine.

A S FAR AS WE could see, we were alone in the mansion's imposing hall. Straight before us, perhaps for forty feet, ran a corridor of parquetry flooring, covered here and there by rich-hued Oriental rugs. White-paneled walls, adorned with oil paintings of imposing-looking individuals, rose for eighteen feet or so to a beautifully frescoed ceiling, and a graceful curving staircase swept upward from the farther end of the room. Candles in cut glass sconces lighted the high-ceilinged apartment, the hospitable glow from a log fire burning under the high white marble mantel lent an air of homely coziness to the place, but of anything living, human or animal, there was no faintest trace or sign.

Click! Behind us, the heavy outer door swung to silently on well-oiled hinges and the automatic lock latched firmly.

"Death of my life!" de Grandin murmured, reaching for the door's silver-plated knob and giving it a vigorous twist. "*Par la moustache du diable*, Friend Trowbridge, it is locked! Truly, perhaps it had been better if we had remained outside in the rain!"

"Not at all, I assure you, my dear sir," a rich mellow voice answered him from the curve of the stairs. "Your arrival was nothing less than providential, gentlemen."

Coming toward us, walking heavily with the aid of a stout cane, was an unusually handsome man attired in pajamas and dressing gown, a sort of nightcap of flowered silk on his white head, slippers of softest morocco on his feet.

"You are a physician, sir?" he asked, glancing inquiringly at the medicine case in my hand.

"Yes," I answered. "I am Dr. Samuel Trowbridge, from Harrisonville, and this is Dr. Jules de Grandin, of Paris, who is my guest."

"Ah," replied our host, "I am very, very glad to welcome you to Marston Hall, gentlemen. It so happens that one—er—my daughter, is quite ill, and I have been unable to obtain medical aid for her on account of my infirmities and the lack of a telephone. If I may trespass on your charity to attend my poor child, I shall be delighted to have you as my guests for the night. If you will lay aside your coats"—he paused expectantly. "Ah, thank you"—as we hung our dripping garments over a chair—"you will come this way, please?"

We followed him up the broad stairs and down an upper corridor to a tastefully furnished chamber where a young girl—fifteen years of age, perhaps—lay propped up with a pile of diminutive pillows.

"Anabel, Anabel, my love, here are two doctors to see you," the old gentleman called softly.

The girl moved her fair head with a weary, peevish motion and whimpered softly in her sleep, but gave no further recognition of our presence.

"And what have been her symptoms, if you please, *Monsieur?*" de Grandin asked as he rolled back the cuffs of his jacket and prepared to make an examination.

"Sleep," replied our host, "just sleep. Some time ago she suffered from influenza; lately she has been given to fits of protracted slumber from which I can not waken her. I fear she may have contracted sleeping sickness, sir. I am told it sometimes follows influenza."

"H'm." De Grandin passed his small, pliable hands rapidly over the girl's cheeks in the region of the ears, felt rapidly along her neck over the jugular vein, then raised a puzzled glance to me. "Have you some laudanum and aconite in your bag, Friend Trowbridge?" he asked.

"There's some morphine," I answered, "and aconite; but no laudanum."

"No matter," he waved his hand impatiently, bustling over to the medicine case and extracting two small phials from it. "No matter, this will do as well. Some water, if you please, *Monsieur*," he turned to the father, a medicine bottle in each hand.

"But, de Grandin"—I began, when a sudden kick from one of his slender, heavily-shod feet nearly broke my shin—"de Grandin, do you think that's the proper medication?" I finished lamely.

"Oh, *mais oui*, undoubtedly," he replied. "Nothing else would do in this case. Water, if you please, *Monsieur*," he repeated, again addressing the father.

I STARED AT HIM IN ill-disguised amazement as he extracted a pellet from each of the bottles and quickly ground them to powder while the old gentleman filled a tumbler with water from the porcelain pitcher which stood on the chintz-draped wash-stand in the corner of the chamber. He was as familiar with the arrangement of my medicine case as I was, I knew, and knew that my phials were arranged by numbers instead of being labeled. Deliberately, I saw, he had passed over the morphine and aconite, and had chosen two bottles of plain, unmedicated sugar of milk pills. What his object was I had no idea, but I watched him measure out four teaspoonfuls of water, dissolve the powder in it, and pour the sham medication down the unconscious girl's throat.

"Good," he proclaimed as he washed the glass with meticulous care. "She will rest easily until the morning, *Monsieur*. When daylight comes we shall decide on further treatment. Will you now permit that we retire?" He bowed politely to the master of the house, who returned his courtesy and led us to a comfortably furnished room farther down the corridor.

"SEE HERE, DE GRANDIN," I demanded when our host had wished us a pleasant good-night and closed the door upon us, "what was your idea in giving that child an impotent dose like that . . . ?"

"S-s-sh!" he cut me short with a fierce whisper. "That young girl, *mon ami*, is no more suffering from encephalitis than you or I. There is no characteristic swelling of the face or neck, no diagnostic hardening of the jugular vein. Her temperature was a bit subnormal, it is true—but upon her breath I detected the odor of chloral hydrate. For some reason, good I hope, but bad I fear, she is drugged, and I thought it best to play the fool and pretend I believed the man's statements. *Pardieu*, the fool who knows himself no fool has an immense advantage over the fool who believes him one, my friend."

"But . . ."

"But me no buts, Friend Trowbridge; remember how the door of this house opened with none to touch it, recall how it closed behind us in the same way, and observe this, if you will." Stepping softly, he crossed the room, pulled aside the chintz curtains at the window and tapped lightly on the frame which held the thick plate glass panes. "*Regardez vous*," he ordered, tapping the frame a second time.

Like every other window I had seen in the house, this one was of the casement type, small panes of heavy glass being sunk into latticelike frames. Under de Grandin's directions I tapped the latter, and found them not painted wood, as I had supposed, but stoutly welded and bolted metal. Also, to my surprise, I found the turnbuckles for opening the casement were only dummies, the metal frames being actually securely bolted to the stone sills. To all intents, we were as firmly incarcerated as though serving a sentence in the state penitentiary.

"The door . . ." I began, but he shook his head.

Obeying his gesture, I crossed the room and turned the handle lightly. It twisted under the pressure of my fingers, but, though we had heard no warning click of lock or bolt, the door itself was as firmly fastened as though nailed shut.

"Wh—why," I asked stupidly, "what's it all mean, de Grandin?"

"*Je ne sais quoi,*" he answered with a shrug, "but one thing I know: I like not this house, Friend Trowbridge. I . . ."

Above the hissing of the rain against the windows and the howl of the sea-wind about the gables, there suddenly rose a scream, wire-edged with inarticulate terror, freighted with utter, transcendental anguish of body and soul.

"*Cordieu!*" He threw up his head like a hound hearing the call of the pack from far away. "Did you hear it, too, Friend Trowbridge?"

"Of course," I answered, every nerve in my body trembling in horripilation with the echo of the hopeless wail.

"Pardieu," he repeated, "I like this house less than ever, now! Come, let us move this dresser before our door. It is safer that we sleep behind barricades this night, I think."

We blocked the door, and I was soon sound asleep.

"TROWBRIDGE, TROWBRIDGE, MY FRIEND"—DE Grandin drove a sharp elbow into my ribs—"wake up, I beseech you. Name of a green goat, you lie like one dead, save for your so abominable snoring!"

"Eh?" I answered sleepily, thrusting myself deeper beneath the voluminous bedclothes. Despite the unusual occurrences of the night I was tired to the point of exhaustion, and fairly drunk with sleep.

"Up; arise, my friend," he ordered, shaking me excitedly. "The coast is clear, I think, and it is high time we did some exploring."

"Rats!" I scoffed, disinclined to leave my comfortable couch. "What's the use of wandering about a strange house to gratify a few unfounded suspicions? The girl might have been given a dose of chloral hydrate, but the chances are her father thought he was helping her when he gave it. As for these trick devices for opening and locking doors, the old man apparently lives here alone and has installed these mechanical aids to lessen his work. He has to hobble around with a cane, you know."

"Ah!" my companion assented sarcastically. "And that scream we heard, did he install that as an aid to his infirmities, also?"

"Perhaps the girl woke up with a nightmare," I hazarded, but he made an impatient gesture.

"Perhaps the moon is composed of green cheese, also," he replied. "Up, up and dress; my friend. This house should be investigated while yet there is time. Attend me: But five minutes ago, through this very window, I did observe *Monsieur* our host, attired in a raincoat, depart from his own front door, and without his cane. *Parbleu*, he did skip, as agilely as any boy, I assure you. Even now he is almost at the spot where we abandoned your automobile. What he intends doing there I know not. What I intend doing I know full well. Do you accompany me or not?"

"Oh, I suppose so," I agreed, crawling from the bed and slipping into my clothes. "How are you going to get past that locked door?"

He flashed me one of his sudden smiles, shooting the points of his little blond mustache upward like the horns of an inverted crescent. "Observe," he ordered, displaying a short length of thin wire. "In the days when a woman's hair was still her crowning glory, what mighty deeds a lady could encompass with a hairpin! *Pardieu*, there was one little *grisette* in Paris who showed me some tricks in the days before the war! Regard me, if you please."

Deftly he thrust the pliable loop of wire into the key's hole, twisting it tentatively back and forth, at length pulling it out and regarding it carefully. "*Très bien*," he muttered as he reached into an inside pocket, bringing out a heavier bit of wire.

"See," he displayed the finer wire, "with this I take an impression of that lock's tumblers, now"—quickly he bent the heavier wire to conform to the waved outline of the lighter loop—"*voilà*, I have a key!"

And he had. The lock gave readily to the pressure of his improvised key, and we stood in the long, dark hall, staring about us half curiously, half fearfully.

"This way, if you please," de Grandin ordered; "first we will look in upon *la jeunesse*, to see how it goes with her."

We walked on tiptoe down the corridor, entered the chamber where the girl lay, and approached the bed.

SHE WAS LYING WITH her hands folded upon her breast in the manner of those composed for their final rest, her wide, periwinkle-blue eyes staring sightlessly before her, the short, tightly curled ringlets of her blonde, bobbed hair surrounding her drawn, pallid face like a golden nimbus encircling the ivory features of a saint in some carved ikon.

My companion approached the bed softly, placing one hand on the girl's wrist with professional precision. "Temperature low, pulse weak," he murmured, checking off her symptoms. "Complexion pale to the point of lividity—ha, now for the eyes; sleeping, her pupils should have been contracted, while they should now be dilate—*Dieu de Dieu!* Trowbridge, my friend, come here.

"Look," he commanded, pointing to the apathetic girl's face. "Those eyes—*grand Dieu*, those eyes! It is sacrilege, nothing less."

I looked into the girl's face, then started back with a half-suppressed cry of horror. Asleep, as she had been when we first saw her, the child had been pretty to the point of loveliness. Her features were small and regular, clean-cut as those of a face in a cameo, the tendrils of her light-yellow hair had lent her a dainty, ethereal charm comparable to that of a Dresden china shepherdess. It had needed but the raising of her delicate, long-lashed eyelids to give her face the animation of some laughing sprite playing truant from fairyland.

Her lids were raised now, but the eyes they unveiled were no clear, joyous windows of a tranquil soul. Rather, they were the peepholes of a spirit in torment. The irises were a lovely shade of blue, it is true, but the optics themselves were things of horror. Rolling grotesquely to right and left, they peered futilely in opposite directions, lending to her sweet, pale face the half-ludicrous, wholly hideous expression of a bloating frog.

"Good heavens!" I exclaimed, turning from the deformed girl with a feeling of disgust akin to nausea; "What a terrible affliction!"

De Grandin made no reply, but bent over the girl's still form, gazing intently at her malformed eyes. "It is not natural," he announced. "The muscles have been tampered with, and tampered with by someone who is a master hand at surgery. Will you get me your syringe and some strychnine, Friend Trowbridge? This poor one is still unconscious."

I HASTENED TO OUR BEDROOM and returned with the hypodermic and stimulant, then stood beside him, watching eagerly, as he administered a strong injection.

The girl's narrow chest fluttered as the powerful drug took effect, and the pale lids dropped for a second over her repulsive eyes. Then, with a sob which was half moan, she attempted to raise herself on her elbow, fell back again, and, with apparent effort, gasped, "The mirror, let me have the mirror! Oh, tell me it isn't true; tell me it was a trick of some sort. Oh, the horrible thing I saw in the glass couldn't have been I. Was it?"

"*Tiens, ma petite,*" de Grandin replied, "but you speak in riddles. What is it you would know?"

"He—he"—the girl faltered weakly, forcing her trembling lips to frame the words—"that horrible old man showed me a mirror a little while ago and said the face in it was mine. Oh, it was horrible, horrible!"

"Eh? What is this?" de Grandin demanded on a rising note. "'He'? 'Horrible old man'? Are you not his daughter? Is he not your father?"

"No," the girl gasped, so low her denial was scarcely audible. "I was driving home from Mackettsdale last—oh, I forget when it was, but it was at night— and my tires punctured. I—I think there must have been glass on the road, for the shoes were cut to ribbons. I saw the light in this house and came to ask for help. An old man—oh, I thought he was so nice and kind!—let me in and said he was all alone here and about to eat dinner, and asked me to join him. I ate some—some—oh, I don't remember what it was—and the next thing I knew he was standing by my bed, holding a mirror up to me and telling me it was my face I saw in the glass. Oh, please, *please*, tell me it was some terrible trick he played on me. I'm not truly hideous, am I?"

"*Morbleu!*" de Grandin muttered softly, tugging at the ends of his mustache. "What is all this?"

To the girl he said: "But of course not. You are like a flower, *Mademoiselle*. A little flower that dances in the wind. You . . ."

"And my eyes, they aren't—they aren't"—she interrupted with piteous eagerness—"please tell me they aren't . . ."

"*Mais non, ma chère,*" he assured her. "Your eyes are like the *pervenche* that mirrors the sky in springtime. They are . . ."

"Let—let me see the mirror, please," she interrupted in an anxious whisper. "I'd like to see for myself, if you—oh, I feel all weak inside . . ." She lapsed back against the pillow, her lids mercifully veiling the hideously distorted eyes and restoring her face to tranquil beauty.

"*Cordieu!*" de Grandin breathed. "The chloral re-asserted itself none too soon for Jules de Grandin's comfort, Friend Trowbridge. Sooner would I have gone to the rack than have shown that pitiful child her face in a mirror."

"But what's it all mean?" I asked. "She says she came here, and . . ."

"And the rest remains for us to find out, I think," he replied evenly. "Come, we lose time, and to lose time is to be caught, my friend."

D E GRANDIN LED THE way down the hall, peering eagerly into each door we passed in search of the owner's chamber, but before his quest was satisfied he stopped abruptly at the head of the stairs. "Observe, Friend Trowbridge," he ordered, pointing a carefully manicured forefinger to a pair of buttons, one white, one black, set in the wall. "Unless I am more mistaken than I think I am, we have here the key to the situation—or at least to the front door."

He pushed vigorously at the white button, then ran to the curve of the stairs to note the result.

Sure enough, the heavy door swung open on its hinges of cast bronze, letting gusts of rain drive into the lower hall.

"*Pardieu*," he ejaculated, "we have here the open sesame; let us see if we possess the closing secret as well! Press the black button, Trowbridge, my friend, while I watch."

I did his bidding, and a delighted exclamation told me the door had closed.

"Now what?" I asked, joining him on the stairway.

"U'm," he pulled first one, then the other end of his diminutive mustache meditatively; "the house possesses its attractions, Friend Trowbridge, but I believe it would be well if we went out to observe what our friend, *le vieillard horrible*, does. I like not to have one who shows young girls their disfigured faces in mirrors near our conveyance."

Slipping into our raincoats we opened the door, taking care to place a wad of paper on the sill to prevent its closing tightly enough to latch, and scurried out into the storm.

As we left the shelter of the porch a shaft of indistinct light shone through the rain, as my car was swung from the highway and headed toward a depression to the left of the house.

"*Parbleu*, he is a thief, this one!" de Grandin exclaimed excitedly. "*Holà, Monsieur!*" He ran forward, swinging his arms like a pair of semaphores. "What sort of business is it you make with our *moteur?*"

The wailing of the storm tore the words from his lips and hurled them away, but the little Frenchman was not to be thwarted. "*Pardieu*," he gasped, bending his head against the wind-driven rain, "I will stop the scoundrel if—*nom d'un coq*, he has done it!"

Even as he spoke the old man flung open the car's forward door and leaped, allowing the machine to go crashing down a low, steep embankment into a lake of slimy swamp-mud.

For a moment the vandal stood contemplating his work, then burst into a peal of wild laughter more malignant than any profanity.

"*Parbleu*, robber, Apache! You shall laugh from the other side of your mouth!" de Grandin promised, as he made for the old man.

But the other seemed oblivious of our presence. Still chuckling at his work, he turned toward the house, stopped short as a sudden heavy gust of wind shook the trees along the roadway, then started forward with a yell of terror as a great branch, torn bodily from a towering oak tree came crashing toward the earth.

He might as well have attempted to dodge a meteorite. Like an arrow from the bow of divine justice, the great timber hurtled down, pinning his frail body to the ground like a worm beneath a laborer's brogan.

"Trowbridge, my friend," de Grandin announced matter-of-factly, "observe the evil effects of stealing motor cars."

W E LIFTED THE HEAVY bough from the prostrate man and turned him over on his back. De Grandin on one side, I on the other, we made a hasty examination, arriving at the same finding simultaneously. His spinal column was snapped like a pipestem.

"You have some last statement to make, *Monsieur?*" de Grandin asked curtly. "If so, you had best be about it, your time is short."

"Y—yes," the stricken man replied weakly. "I—I meant to kill you, for you might have hit upon my secret. As it is, you may publish it to the world, that all may know what it meant to offend a Marston. In my room you will find the documents. My—my pets—are—in—the—cellar. She—was—to—have—been—one—of—them."

The pauses between his words became longer and longer, his voice grew weaker with each labored syllable. As he whispered the last sentence painfully there was a gurgling sound, and a tiny stream of blood welled up at the corner of his mouth. His narrow chest rose and fell once with a convulsive movement, then his jaw dropped limply. He was dead.

"Oh ho," de Grandin remarked, "it is a hemorrhage which finished him. A broken rib piercing his lung. U'm? I should have guessed it. Come, my friend, let us carry him to the house, then see what it was he meant by that talk of documents and pets. A pest upon the fellow for dying with his riddle half explained! Did he not know that Jules de Grandin can not resist the challenge of a riddle? *Parbleu*, we will solve this mystery, *Monsieur le Mort*, if we have to hold an autopsy to do so!"

"Oh, for heaven's sake, hush, de Grandin," I besought, shocked at his heartlessness. "The man is dead."

"Ah bah!" he returned scornfully. "Dead or not, did he not steal your motor car?"

W E LAID OUR GRUESOME burden on the hall couch and mounted the stairs to the second floor. With de Grandin in the lead we found the dead man's room and began a systematic search for the papers he had mentioned, almost with his last breath. After some time my companion unearthed a thick, leather-bound portfolio from the lower drawer of a beautiful old mahogany highboy, and spread its wide leaves open on the white-counterpaned bed.

"Ah," he drew forth several papers and held them to the light, "we begin to make the progress, Friend Trowbridge. What is this?"

He held out a newspaper clipping cracked from long folding and yellowed with age. It read:

ACTRESS JILTS SURGEON'S CRIPPLED
SON ON EVE OF WEDDING

Declaring she could not stand the sight of his deformity, and that she had engaged herself to him only in a moment of thoughtless pity, Dora Lee, well-known variety actress, last night repudiated her promise to marry John Biersfield Marston, Jr., hopelessly crippled son of Dr. John Biersfield Marston, the well-known surgeon and expert osteologist. Neither the abandoned bridegroom nor his father could be seen by reporters from the *Planet* last night.

"Very good," de Grandin nodded, "we need go no farther with that account. A young woman, it would seem, once broke her promise to marry a cripple, and, judging from this paper's date, that was in 1896. Here is another, what do you make of it?"

The clipping he handed me read as follows:

SURGEON'S SON A SUICIDE

Still sitting in the wheel-chair from which he has not moved during his waking hours since he was hopelessly crippled while playing polo in England ten years ago, John Biersfield Marston, son of the famous surgeon of the same name, was found in his bedroom this morning by his valet. A rubber hose was connected with a gas jet, the other end being held in the young man's mouth.

Young Marston was jilted by Dora Lee, well-known vaudeville actress, on the day before the date set for their wedding, one month ago. He is reported to have been extremely low-spirited since his desertion by his fiancée.

Dr. Marston, the bereaved father, when seen by reporters from the *Planet* this morning, declared the actress was responsible for his son's death and announced his intention of holding her accountable. When asked if legal proceedings were contemplated, he declined further information.

"So?" de Grandin nodded shortly. "Now this one, if you please." The third clipping was brief to the point of curtness:

WELL-KNOWN SURGEON RETIRES

Dr. John Biersfield Marston, widely known throughout this section of the country as an expert in operations concerning the bones, has announced his intention of retiring from practice. His house has been sold, and he will move from the city.

"The record is clear so far," de Grandin asserted, studying the first clipping with raised eyebrows, "but—*morbleu*, my friend, look, look at this picture. This Dora Lee, of whom does she remind you? Eh?"

I took the clipping again and looked intently at the illustration of the article announcing young Marston's broken engagement. The woman in the picture was young and inclined to be overdressed in the voluminous, fluffy mode of the days before the Spanish-American War.

"U'm, no one whom I know . . ." I began, but halted abruptly as a sudden likeness struck me. Despite the towering pompadour arrangement of her blonde hair and the unbecoming straw sailor hat above the coiffure, the woman in the picture bore a certain resemblance to the disfigured girl we had seen a half-hour before.

The Frenchman saw recognition dawn in my face, and nodded agreement. "But of course," he said. "Now, the question is, is this young girl whose eyes are so out of alignment a relative of this Dora Lee, or is the resemblance a coincidence, and if so, what lies behind it? *Hein?*"

"I don't know," I admitted, "but there must be some connection . . ."

"Connection? Of course there is a connection," de Grandin affirmed, rummaging deeper in the portfolio. "A-a-ah! What is this? *Nom d'un nom*, Friend Trowbridge, I think I smell the daylight! Look!"

He held a full page story from one of the sensational New York dailies before him, his eyes glued to the flowing type and crude, coarse-screened halftones of half a dozen young women which composed the article.

"What Has Become of the Missing Girls?" I read in boldfaced type across the top of the page.

"*Are sinister, unseen hands reaching out from the darkness to seize our girls from palace and hovel, shop, stage and office?*" the article asked rhetorically. "*Where are Ellen Munro and Dorothy Sawyer and Phyllis Bouchet and three other lovely, light-haired girls who have walked into oblivion during the past year?*"

I read to the end the sensational account of the girls' disappearances. The cases seemed fairly similar; each of the vanished young women had failed to return to her home and had never been accounted for in any manner, and in no instance, according to the newspaper, had there been any assignable reason for voluntary departure.

"*Parbleu*, but he was stupid, even for a journalist!" de Grandin asserted as I completed my inspection of the story. "Why, I wager even my good Friend Trowbridge has already noticed one important fact which this writer has treated as though it were as commonplace as the nose on his face."

"Sorry to disappoint you, old chap," I answered, "but looks to me as though the reporter had covered the case from every possible angle."

"Ah? So?" he replied sarcastically. "*Morbleu*, we shall have to consult the oculist in your behalf when we return home, my friend. Look, look I beseech you, upon the pictures of these so totally absent and unaccounted for young women, *cher ami*, and tell me if you do not observe a certain likeness among them, not only a resemblance to each other, but to that Mademoiselle Lee who jilted the son of Dr. Marston? Can you see it, now I have pointed it out?"

"No—wh—why, yes—yes, of course!" I responded, running my eye over the pictures accompanying the story. "By the Lord Harry, de Grandin, you're right; you might almost say there is a family resemblance between these girls! You've put your fingers on it, I do believe."

"*Hélas*, no!" he answered with a shrug. "I have put my finger on nothing as yet, my friend. I reach, I grope, I feel about me like a blind man tormented by a crowd of naughty little boys, but nothing do the poor fingers of my mind encounter. *Pah!* Jules de Grandin, you are one great fool! Think, think, stupid one!"

He seated himself on the edge of the bed, cupping his face in his hands and leaning forward till his elbows rested on his knees.

Suddenly he sprang erect, one of his elfish smiles passing across his small, regular features. "*Nom d'un chatrouge*, my friend, I have it—I have it!" he announced. "The pets—the pets that old stealer of motor cars spoke of! They are in the basement! *Pardieu*, we will see those pets, *cher* Trowbridge; with our four collective eyes we will see them. Did not that so execrable stealer declare she was to have been one of them? Now, in the name of Satan and brimstone, whom could he have meant by 'she' if not that unfortunate child with eyes like *la grenouille*? Eh?"

"Why . . ." I began, but he waved me forward.

"Come, come; let us go," he urged. "I am impatient, I am restless, I am not to be restrained. We shall investigate and see for ourselves what sort of pets are kept by one who shows young girls their deformed faces in mirrors and—*Parbleu!*—steals motor cars from my friends."

Hurrying down the main stairway, we hunted about for the cellar entrance, finally located the door and, holding above our heads a pair of candles from the hall, began descending a flight of rickety steps into a pitch-black basement, rock-walled and, judging by its damp, moldy odor, unfloored save by the bare, moist earth beneath the house.

"*Parbleu*, the dungeons of the château at Carcassonne are more cheerful than this," de Grandin commented as he paused at the stairs' foot, holding his candle aloft to, make a better inspection of the dismal place.

I suppressed a shudder of mingled chill and apprehension as I stared at the blank stone walls, unpierced by windows or other openings of any sort, and made ready to retrace my steps. "Nothing here," I announced. "You can see that with half an eye. The place is as empty as . . ."

"Perhaps, Friend Trowbridge," he agreed, "but Jules de Grandin does not look with half an eye. He uses both eyes, and uses them more than once if his first glance does not prove sufficient. Behold that bit of wood on the earth yonder. What do you make of it?"

"U'm—a piece of flooring, maybe," I hazarded.

"Maybe yes, maybe no," he answered. "Let us see."

Crossing the cellar, he bent above the planks, then turned to me with a satisfied smile. "Flooring does not ordinarily have ringbolts in it, my friend," he remarked bending to seize the iron ring which was made fast to the boards by a stout staple.

"Ha!" As he heaved upward the planks came away from the black earth, disclosing a board-lined well about three feet square and of uncertain depth. An almost vertical ladder of two-by-four timbers led downward from the trap-door to the well's impenetrable blackness.

"*Allons*, we descend," he commented, turning about and setting his foot on the topmost rung of the ladder.

"Don't be a fool," I advised. "You don't know what's down there."

"True"—his head was level with the floor as he answered—"but I shall know, with luck, in a few moments. Do you come?"

I sighed with vexation as I prepared to follow him.

A T THE LADDER'S FOOT he paused, raising his candle and looking about inquiringly. Directly before us was a passageway through the earth, ceiled with heavy planks and shored up with timbers like the lateral workings of a primitive mine.

"Ah, the plot shows complications," he murmured, stepping briskly into the dark tunnel. "Do you come, Friend Trowbridge?"

I followed, wondering what manner of thing might be at the end of the black, musty passage, but nothing but fungus-grown timbers and walls of moist, black earth met my questing gaze.

De Grandin preceded me by some paces, and, I suppose, we had gone fifteen feet through the passage when a gasp of mingled surprise and horror from my companion brought me beside him in two long strides. Fastened with nails to the timbers at each side of the tunnel were a number of white, glistening objects, objects which, because of their very familiarity, denied their identity to my wondering eyes. There was no mistaking the things; even a layman could not have failed to recognize them for what they were. I, as a physician, knew them even better. To the right of the passage hung fourteen perfectly articulated skeletons of human legs, complete from foot to ilium, gleaming white and ghostly in the flickering light of the candles.

"Good heavens!" I exclaimed.

"*Sang du diable!*" Jules de Grandin commented. "Behold what is there, my friend," he pointed to the opposite wall. Fourteen bony arms, complete from hand to shoulder-joint, hung pendulously from the tunnel's upright timbers.

"*Pardieu*," de Grandin muttered, "I have known men who collected stuffed birds and dried insects; I have known those who stored away Egyptian mummies—even the skulls of men long dead—but never before have I seen a collection of arms and legs! *Parbleu*, he was *caduc*—mad as a hatter, this one, or I am much mistaken."

"So these were his pets?" I answered. "Yes, the man was undoubtedly mad to keep such a collection, and in a place like this. Poor fellow . . ."

"*Nom d'un canon!*" de Grandin broke in; "what was that?"

From the darkness before us there came a queer, inarticulate sound, such as a man might make attempting to speak with a mouth half-filled with food, and, as though the noise had wakened an echo slumbering in the cavern, the sound was repeated, multiplied again and again till it resembled the babbling of half a dozen overgrown infants—or an equal number of full grown imbeciles.

"Onward!" Responding to the challenge of the unknown like a warrior obeying the trumpet's call to charge, de Grandin dashed toward the strange noise, swung about, flashing his candle this side and that, then:

"*Nom de Dieu de nom de Dieu!*" he almost shrieked. "Look, Friend Trowbridge, look and say that you see what I see, or have I, too, gone mad?"

Lined up against the wall was a series of seven small wooden boxes, each with a door composed of upright slats before it, similar in construction to the coops in which country folk pen brooding hens—and no larger. In each of the hutches huddled an object, the like of which I had never before seen, even in the terrors of nightmare.

The things had the torsos of human beings, though hideously shrunken from starvation and encrusted with scales of filth, but there all resemblances to mankind ceased. From shoulders and waist there twisted flaccid tentacles of unsupported flesh, the upper ones terminating in flat, paddle-like flippers which had some remote resemblance to hands, the lower ones ending in almost shapeless stubs which resembled feet, only in that each had a fringe of five shriveled, unsupported protuberances of withered flesh.

On scrawny necks were balanced caricatures of faces, flat, noseless chinless countenances with horrible crossed or divergent eyes, mouths widened almost beyond resemblance to buccal orifices and—horror of horrors!—elongated, split tongues protruding several inches from the lips and wagging impotently in vain efforts to form words.

"Satan, thou art outdone!" de Grandin cried as he held his candle before a scrap of paper decorating one of the cages after the manner of a sign before an animal's den at the zoo. "Observe!" he ordered, pointing a shaking finger at the notice.

I looked, then recoiled, sick with horror. The paper bore the picture and name of Ellen Munro, one of the girls mentioned as missing in the newspaper article we had found in the dead man's bedroom.

Beneath the photograph was scribbled in an irregular hand: "*Paid 1-25-97.*"

Sick at heart we walked down the line of pens. Each was labeled with the picture of a young and pretty girl with the notation, "*Paid,*" followed by a date. Every girl named as missing in the newspaper was represented in the cages.

Last of all, in a coop somewhat smaller than the rest, we found a body more terribly mutilated than any. This was marked with the photograph and name of Dora Lee. Beneath her name was the date of her "payment," written in bold red figures.

"*Parbleu*, what are we to do, my friend?" de Grandin asked in an hysterical whisper. "We can not return these poor ones to the world, that would be the worst form of cruelty; yet—yet I shrink from the act of mercy I know they would ask me to perform if they could speak."

"Let's go up," I begged. "We must think this thing over, de Grandin, and if I stay here any longer I shall faint."

"*Bien,*" be agreed, and turned to follow me from the cavern of horrors.

"It is to consider," he began as we reached the upper hall once more. "If we give those so pitiful ones the stroke of mercy we are murderers before the law, yet what service could we render them by bringing them once more into the world? Our choice is a hard one, my friend."

I nodded.

"*Morbleu*, but he was clever, that one," the Frenchman continued, half to me, half to himself. "What a surgeon! Fourteen instances of Wyeth's amputation of the hip and as many more of the shoulder—and every patient lived, lived to suffer the tortures of that hell-hole down there! But it is marvelous! None but a madman could have done it.

"Bethink you, Friend Trowbridge. Think how the mighty man of medicine brooded over the suicide of his crippled son, meditating hatred and vengeance for the heartless woman who had jilted him. Then—snap! went his great mentality, and from hating one woman he fell to hating all, to plot vengeance against the many for the sin of the one. And, *cordieu*, what a vengeance! How he must have laid plans to secure his victims; how he must have worked to prepare that hell-under-the-earth to house those poor, broken bodies which were his handiwork, and how he must have drawn upon the great surgical skill which was his, even in his madness, to transform those once lovely ones into the visions of horror we have just beheld! Horror of horrors! To remove the bones and let the girls still live!"

He rose, pacing impatiently across the hall. "What to do? What to do?" he demanded, striking his open hands against his forehead.

I followed his nervous steps with my eyes, but my brain was too numbed by the hideous things I had just seen to be able to respond to his question.

I looked hopelessly past him at the angle of the wall by the great fireplace, rubbed my eyes and looked again. Slowly, but surely, the wall was declining from the perpendicular.

"De Grandin," I shouted, glad of some new phenomenon to command my thoughts, "the wall—the wall's leaning!"

"Eh, the wall?" be queried. "*Pardieu*, yes! It is the rain; the foundations are undermined. Quick, quick, my friend! To the cellars, or those unfortunate ones are undone!"

We scrambled down the stairs leading to the basement, but already the earth floor was sopping with water. The well leading to the madman's sub-cellar was more than half full of bubbling, earthy ooze.

"Mary, have pity!" de Grandin exclaimed. "Like rats in a trap, they did die. God rest their tired souls"—he shrugged his shoulders as he turned to retrace his steps—"it is better so. Now, Friend Trowbridge, do you hasten aloft and bring down that young girl from the room above. We must run for it if we do not wish to be crushed under the falling timbers of this house of abominations!"

T HE STORM HAD SPENT itself and a red, springtime sun was peeping over the horizon as de Grandin and I trudged up my front steps with the mutilated girl stumbling wearily between us. We had managed to flag a car when we got out.

"Put her to bed, my excellent one," de Grandin ordered Nora, my housekeeper, who came to meet us enveloped in righteous indignation and an outing flannel nightgown. "*Parbleu*, she has had many troubles!"

In the study, a glass of steaming whisky and hot water in one hand, a vile-smelling French cigarette in the other, he faced me across the desk. "How was it you knew not that house, my friend?" he demanded.

I grinned sheepishly. "I took the wrong turning at the detour," I explained, "and got on the Yerbyville Road. It's just recently been hard-surfaced, and I haven't used it for years because it was always impassable. Thinking we were on the Andover Pike all the while, I never connected the place with the old Olmsted Mansion I'd seen hundreds of times from the road."

"Ah, yes," he agreed, nodding thoughtfully, "a little turn from the right way, and—*pouf!*—what a distance we have to retrace."

"Now, about the girl upstairs," I began, but he waved the question aside.

"The mad one had but begun his devil's work on her," he replied. "I, Jules de Grandin, will operate on her eyes and make them as straight as before, nor will I accept one penny for my work. Meantime, we must find her kindred and notify them she is safe and in good hands.

"And now"—he handed me his empty tumbler—"a little more whisky, if you please, Friend Trowbridge."

Ancient Fires

"TIENS, FRIEND TROWBRIDGE, THIS is interesting." Jules de Grandin passed the classified page of the *Times* across the breakfast table and indicated one of the small advertisements with the polished nail of his well-groomed forefinger. "Regard this *avis*, if you please, and say if I am not the man."

Fixing my reading glasses firmly on my nose, I perused the notice he pointed out:

> WANTED—A man of more than ordinary courage to undertake confidential and possibly dangerous mission. Great physical strength not essential, but indomitable bravery and absolute fearlessness in the face of seemingly supernatural manifestations are. This is a remarkable work and will require the services of a remarkable man. A fee up to $10,000 will be paid for the successful prosecution of the case.
>
> X.L. Selfridge, Attorney, Jennifer Building.

De Grandin's round blue eyes shone with elated anticipation as I put down the paper and regarded him across the cloth. "*Morbleu*, is it not an apple from the tree of Divine Providence?" he demanded, twisting the ends of his diminutive blond mustache ferociously. "A remarkable man for a remarkable work, do they say? *Cordieu*, but Jules de Grandin is that man, nor do I in any wise imply perhaps! You will drive me down to that so generous *soliciteur*, Friend Trowbridge, and we shall together collect from him this ten thousand dollars, or may I never hear the blackbirds whistle in the trees of St. Cloud again."

"Sounds like some bootlegger advertising for a first lieutenant," I discouraged, but he would not be gainsaid.

"We shall go, we shall most certainly go to see this remarkable lawyer who offers a remarkable fee to a remarkable man," he, insisted, rising and dragging me from the table. "*Morbleu*, my friend, excitement is good, and gold is good, too; but gold and excitement together—*la, la*, they are a combination worthy of any man's love! Come, we shall go right away, at once, immediately."

We went. Half an hour later we were seated across a flat-topped mahogany desk, staring at a thin, undersized little man with an oversized bald head and small, sharp, bird-like black eyes.

"This seems incredibly good, gentlemen," the little lawyer assured us when he had finished examining the credentials de Grandin showed. "I had hoped to get some ex-service man—some youngster who hadn't gotten his fill of adventure in the great war, perhaps—or possibly some student of psychic phenomena—but—my dear sir!"—he beamed on my friend—"to secure a man of your standing is more than I had dared hope. Indeed, I did not suspect such characters existed outside book covers."

"*Parbleu, Monsieur l'Avoué,*" de Grandin replied with one of his impish smiles, "I have been in what you Americans call some tight places, but never have I been shut up in a book. Now, if you will be so good as to tell us something of this so remarkable mission you wish undertaken—" He paused, voice and eyebrows raised interrogatively.

"To be sure"—the attorney passed a box of cigars across the desk—"you'll probably consider this a silly sort of case for a man of your talents but—well, to get down to brass tacks, I've a client who wants to sell a house."

"Ah?" de Grandin murmured noncommittally. "And we are to become indomitably fearless real estate brokers, perhaps?"

"Not quite," the lawyer laughed, "nothing quite as simple as that. You see, Redgables is one of the finest properties in the entire lake region. It lies in the very heart of the mountains, with a commanding view, contains nearly three thousand acres of good land, and, in fact, possesses nearly every requisite of an ideal country estate or a summer hotel or sanatarium. Normally, it's worth between three and four hundred thousand dollars; but, unfortunately, it possesses one drawback—a drawback which makes its market value practically nil. It's haunted."

"Eh, do you say so?" De Grandin sat up very straight in his chair and fixed his unwinking stare on the attorney. "*Parbleu*, it will be a redoubtable ghost whom Jules de Grandin can not eject for a fee of two hundred thousand francs! Say on, my friend; I burn with curiosity."

"The house was built some seventy-five years ago when that part of New York State was little better than a wilderness," the attorney resumed. "John Aglinberry, son of Sir Rufus Aglinberry, and the great-uncle of my client, was the builder. He came to this country under something of a cloud—pretty well estranged from his family—and built that English manor house in the midst of our hills as a refuge from all mankind, it seems.

"As a young man he'd served with the British army in India, and got mixed up in rather a nasty scandal. Went *ghazi*—fell in love with a native girl and threatened to marry her. There was a devil of a row. His folks used influence to have him dismissed from the service and cut off his allowance to force him back to England. After that they must have made life pretty uncomfortable for him, for when he inherited a pile of money, from a spinster aunt, he packed up and came to America, building that beautiful house out there in the woods and living like a hermit the rest of his life.

"The girl's family didn't take matters much easier than Aglinberry's, it seems. Something mysterious happened to her before he left India—I imagine he'd have stayed there in spite of hell and high water, if she'd lived.

"Somehow, the Aglinberry fortune petered out. John Aglinberry's younger brothers both came to this country and settled in New York, working at one thing and another till he died. They inherited the property share and share alike under our law; but it never did them any good. Neither of them was ever able to live in it, and they never could sell it. Something—mind you, I'm not saying it was a ghost—but something damned unpleasant, nevertheless, has run off every tenant who's ever attempted to occupy that place.

"My client is young John Aglinberry, great-nephew of the builder, and last of the family. He hasn't a cent to bless himself with, except the potential value of Redgables.

"That's the situation, gentlemen; a young man, heir to a baronetcy, if he wished to go to England to claim it, poorer than a church mouse, with a half-million dollar property eating itself up in taxes and no way to convert it into a dime in cash till he can find someone to demonstrate that the place isn't devil-ridden. Do you understand why we're willing to pay a ten thousand dollar fee—contingent on the success of re-establishing Redgables' good name?"

"*Tiens, Monsieur*," de Grandin exclaimed, grinding the fire from his half-smoked cigar, "we do waste the time. I am all impatience to try conclusions with this property-destroying ghost who keeps your so deserving client out of the negotiation of his land and me from a ten thousand dollar fee. *Morbleu*, this is a case after my own heart! When shall we start for this so charming estate which is to pay me ten thousand dollars for ridding it of its specter tenants?"

JOHN AGLINBERRY, CHIEFLY DISTINGUISHED by a wide, friendly grin, met us at the railway station which lay some five miles from Redgables, and extended a warm handclasp in greeting. "It's mighty good of you gentlemen to come up here and give me a lift," he exclaimed as he shepherded us along the platform and helped stow our traps into the unkempt tonneau of a Ford which might have seen better days, though not recently. "Mr. Selfridge 'phoned me yesterday morning, and I hustled up here to do what I could to make you comfortable. I doubt you'd have been able to get any of the village folks to drive you over to the place—they're as frightened of it as they would be of a mad dog."

"But, *Monsieur*," de Grandin expostulated, "do you mean to say you have been in that house by yourself this morning?"

"Uh-huh, and last night, too," our host replied. "Came up here on the afternoon train yesterday and tidied things up a bit."

"And you saw nothing, felt nothing, heard nothing?" de Grandin persisted.

"Of course not," the young man answered impatiently. "There isn't anything to see, or feel, or hear, either, if you except the usual noises that go with a country place in springtime. There's nothing wrong with the property, gentlemen. Just a lot of silly gossip which has made one of the finest potential summer resorts in the county a drug on the market. That's why Mr. Selfridge and I are so anxious to get the statement of gentlemen of your caliber behind us. One word from you will outweigh all the silly talk these yokels can blab in the next ten years."

De Grandin cast me a quick smile. "He acknowledges our importance, my friend," he whispered. "Truly, we shall have to walk fast to live up to such a reputation."

Further conversation was cut short by our arrival at the gates of our future home. The elder Aglinberry had spared no expense to reproduce a bit of England in the Adirondacks. Tall posts of stone flanked the high iron gate which pierced the ivy-mantled wall surrounding the park, and a wide graveled driveway, bordered on each side by a wall of cedars, led to the house, which was a two-story Tudor structure with shingles of natural red cedar from which the place derived its name. Inside, the house bore out the promise of its exterior. The hall was wide and stone-paved, wainscoted with panels of walnut and with a beamed ceiling of adz-hewn cedar logs and slabs. A field-stone fireplace, almost as large as the average suburban cottage's garage, pierced the north wall, and the curving stairs were built with wide treads and balustraded with hand-carved walnut. A single oil painting, that of the elder John Aglinberry, relieved the darkness of the wall facing the stairway.

"But, *Monsieur*, this is remarkable," de Grandin asserted as he gazed upon the portrait. "From the resemblance you bear your late kinsman you might easily be taken for his son—yes *pardieu*, were you dressed in the archaic clothes of his period, you might be himself!"

"I've noticed the resemblance, too," young Aglinberry smiled. "Poor old Uncle John, gloomy-looking cove, wasn't he! Anyone would think all his friends were dead and he was making plans to visit the village undertaker himself."

The Frenchman shook his head reprovingly at the younger man's facetiousness. "Poor gentleman," he murmured, "he had cause to look sad. When you, too, have experienced the sacrifice of love, you may look saddened, my friend."

We spent the remainder of the afternoon surveying the house and surrounding grounds. Dinner was cooked on a portable camp outfit over blazing logs in the hall fireplace, and about nine o'clock all three of us mounted the stairs to bed. "Remember," de Grandin warned, "if you hear or see the slightest intimation of anything which is not as it should be, you are to ring the bell beside your bed, my friend. Dr. Trowbridge and I shall sleep like the cat, with one eye open, and claws alert."

"Not a chance," our host scoffed. "I slept here last night and never saw or heard anything more supernatural than a stray rat, and mighty few of those."

I MIGHT HAVE SLEPT HALF an hour or twice that long when a gentle nudge brought me wide awake and sitting bolt upright in bed. "Trowbridge, Friend Trowbridge," de Grandin's voice came through the darkness from across the room, "rise and follow; I think I hear Monsieur Aglinberry's alarm bell!"

I slipped a bathrobe over my pyjamas and took the loaded automatic and flashlight from under my pillow. "All right," I whispered, "I'm ready."

We stole down the hall toward our host's room, and de Grandin paused beside the door. Clearly we made out the sound of an untroubled sleeper's heavy breathing. "Guess you've been hearing things, de Grandin," I chuckled in a low voice, but he held up one slender hand in warning.

"P-s-st, be still!" he commanded. "Do not you hear it, too, my friend? Hark!"

I listened with bated breath, but no sound save the occasional ghostly creak of a floor-board came to my ears, then—

Faint, so faint it might have been mistaken for the echo of an imagined sound, had it not been for its insistence, I heard the light, far-away-sounding tinkle-tinkle of bells. "Tink-a-*tink*, a-*tink*-a-tink; tink-a-*tink*, a-*tink*-a-tink" they sounded, scarcely louder than the swishing of silk, every third and fifth beat accentuated in an endless "circular" rhythm; but their music did not emanate from the room beyond the door. Rather, it seemed to me, the tiny, fairylike ringing came up the stairway from the hall below.

My companion seemed struck by the same thought, for he crept past me toward the stairhead, his soft-soled slippers making no more noise against the hardwood floor than the beating of a moth's wings against the night air.

Close behind him I slipped, my gun and flashlight held in instant readiness, but at sight of his eager, strained face as he paused at the top of the stair I forgot my weapons and stole forward to peep over his shoulder.

A shutter must have come unfastened at one of the small, high windows in the hall, for a patch of dim moonlight, scarcely more than three feet in diameter, lay upon the floor directly beneath the portrait of the elder Aglinberry, and against the circle of luminance a thin, almost impalpable wreath of smoke seemed drifting before a draft of air from the fireplace. I looked again. No, it was not smoke, it was something with a defined outline. It was—it was a wisp of muslin, air-light and almost colorless in its sheerness, but cloth, nevertheless. And now, as I gazed unbelievingly, something else seemed slowly taking form in the moonlight. A pair of narrow, high-arched feet and tapering, slender ankles, unclothed except for a double loop of bell-studded chains, were mincing and gyrating on flexible toes, while, fainter than the feet, but still perceptible, the outline of a body as fair as any that ever swayed to the tempo of music showed against the black background of the darkened hall like a figure dimly suggested in an impressionistic painting. Round and round, in a dazing but incredibly graceful dance the vision whirled, the hem of the muslin skirt standing outward with the motion of the pirouetting feet, the tiny, golden bells on the chain anklets sending out their faerie music.

"*Morbleu!*" de Grandin whispered softly to himself. "Do you see it, also, Friend Trowbridge?"

"I—" I began in a muted voice, but stopped abruptly, for a puff of passing breeze must have closed the shutter, cutting off the moonbeam as a theatrical spotlight is shut off by a stage electrician. The illusion vanished instantly. There was no elfin, dancing form before the painted likeness of old John Aglinberry, no sound of clinking anklets in the old house. We were just a pair of sleep-disheveled men in bathrobes and pyjamas standing at a stairhead and staring foolishly into the darkness of a deserted hallway.

"I thought I saw—" I began again, but again I was interrupted, this time by the unmistakable clatter of the hand-bell in Aglinberry's room.

We raced down the corridor to him and flung open the door. "Monsieur Aglinberry!" de Grandin gasped, "did it—did anything come into your room? Dr. Trowbridge and I—"

The young man sat up in bed, grinning sheepishly at us in the double beam of our flashlights. "I must be getting a case of nerves," he confessed. "Never had the jumps like this before. Just a moment ago I fancied I felt something touch my lips—like the tip of a bat's wing, it was, soft as velvet, and so light I could scarcely feel it; but it woke me up, and I grabbed the bell and began ringing, like a fool. Funny, too"—he glanced toward the window—"it couldn't have been a bat, for I took particular pains to nail mosquito netting over that window this morning. It's—why, it's *torn!*"

Sure enough, the length of strong netting which our host had thoughtfully tacked across the windows of both our room and his as a precaution against early spring insects, was rent from top to bottom as though by a knife. "H'm," he muttered, "it *might* have been a bat, at that."

"To be sure," de Grandin agreed, nodding so vigorously that he resembled a Chinese mandarin, "it might, as you say, *Monsieur*, have been a bat. But I think you would sleep more safely if you closed the window." Crossing the room he drew the casement to and shot the forged iron bolt into place. "*Bon soir*, my friend"—he bowed formally at the doorway—"a good night, and be sure you leave your window closed."

"WOULD YOU GENTLEMEN LIKE to look at the property down by the lake?" Aglinberry asked as we finished our breakfast of bacon and eggs, coffee and fried potatoes the following morning.

"Assuredly," de Grandin replied as he donned topcoat and cap, slipping his ever-ready automatic pistol into his pocket, "a soldier's first caution should be to familiarize himself with the terrain over which he is to fight."

We marched down a wide, curving drive bordered by pollarded willows, toward the smooth sheet of water flashing in the early morning sunlight.

"We have one of the finest stands of native hardwood to be found anywhere in this part of the country," Aglinberry began, waving his stick toward an imposing grove to our right. "Just the timber alone is worth—well, of all the copper-riveted nerve!" he broke off angrily, hastening his pace and waving his cane belligerently. "See there? Some fool camper has started a fire in those woods. Hi, there, you! Hi, there; what're you doing?"

Hurrying through the trees we came upon a little clearing where a decrepit, weather-blistered van was drawn up beside a small spring, two moth-eaten-appearing horses tethered to a nearby tree and several incredibly dirty children wrestling and fighting on the short grass. A man in greasy corduroys lay full length on the ground, a black slouch hat pulled over his eyes, while another lounged in the doorway of the van. Two women in faded shawls and headkerchiefs and an amazing amount of pinchbeck jewelry were busily engaged, one in hewing down underbrush to replenish the camp fire, the other stirring some sort of savory mess in a large, smoke-blackened kettle which swung over the blazing sticks.

"What the devil do you mean by building a fire here?" Aglinberry demanded angrily as we came to a halt. "Don't you know you're likely to start a blaze in these woods? Go down to the lake if you want to camp; there's no danger of burning things up there."

The women looked at him in sullen silence, their fierce black eyes smoldering angrily under their straight black brows; but the man lying beside the fire was not minded to be hustled from his comfortable couch.

"Too mucha stone by da lake," he informed Aglinberry lazily, raising the hat from his face, but making no other move toward obeying the summons to quit. "Too mucha stone an' sand. I lika dissa grass to lay on. I stay here. See?"

"By George, we'll see about that!" replied our irate host. "You'll stay here, will you? Like hell you will!" Stepping quickly to the fire, he shouldered the crouching woman out of his path and scattered the blazing sticks from under the kettle with a vigorous kick of his heavy boot, stamping the flame from the brands and kicking earth over the embers. "Stay here, will you?" he repeated. "We'll see about that. Pull your freight, and pull it in a hurry, or I'll have the whole gang of you arrested for trespass."

The reclining gipsy leaped to his feet as though propelled by a spring. "You tella me pulla da freight? You keek my fire out? You? Ha, I show you somet'ing!" His dirty hand flew to the girdle about his greasy trousers, and a knife's evil flash showed in the sunlight. "You t'ink you make da fool of Nikolai Brondovitch? I show you!"

Slowly, with a rolling tread which reminded me of a tiger preparing to leap, he advanced toward Aglinberry, his little, porcine eyes snapping vindictively, his bushy eyebrows bent into an almost straight line with the ferocity of his scowl.

"Eh, bien, Monsieur le Bohémien," Jules de Grandin remarked pleasantly, "were I in your shoes—and very dirty shoes they are, too—I would consider what I did before I did it." The gipsy turned a murderous scowl on him and stopped short in his tracks, his narrow eyes contracting to mere slits with apprehension. The Frenchman had slipped his pistol from his pocket and was pointing its uncompromising black muzzle straight at the center of the Romany's checked shirt.

"Meester," the fellow pleaded, sheathing his knife hurriedly and forcing his swarthy features into the semblance of a smile, "I maka da joke. I not mean to hurt your frand. I poor man, trying to make honest living by selling horses. I not mean to scare your frand. We taka da camp offa hees lan' right away."

"Pardieu, my friend, I think you will," de Grandin agreed, nodding approvingly. "You will take your so filthy wagon, your horses, your women and your brats from off this property. You leave at once, immediately, right away!" He waved his blue steel pistol with an authoritative gesture. "Come; I have already waited too long; try not my patience, I beseech you."

Muttering imprecations in their unintelligible tongue and showering us with looks as malignant as articulate curses, the gipsies broke camp, under our watchful supervision, and we followed them down the grass grown drive toward the lake front. We watched them off the land, then proceeded with our inspection of the estate.

REDGABLES WAS AN EXTENSIVE property and we spent the better part of the day exploring its farther corners. By nightfall all three of us were glad to smoke a sociable pipe and turn in shortly after dinner.

I was lying on my back, staring straight upward to the high ceiling of our chamber and wondering if the vision of the night before had been some trick of our imaginations, when de Grandin's sharp, strident whisper cut through the darkness and brought me suddenly wide-awake. "Trowbridge," he murmured, "I hear a sound. Someone is attempting entrance!"

I lay breathless a moment, straining my ears for any corroboration of his statement, but only the soughing of the wind through the evergreens outside and the occasional rasp of a bough against the house rewarded my vigil. "Rats!" I scoffed. "Who'd try to break into a house with such a reputation as this one's? Why, Mr. Selfridge told us even the tramps avoided the place as if it were a plague-spot."

"Nevertheless," he insisted as he drew on his boots and pulled a topcoat over his pyjamas, "I believe we have uninvited guests, and I shall endeavor to mend their manners, if such they be."

There was nothing to do but follow him. Downstairs, tiptoe, our flashlights held ready and our pistols prepared for emergency, we stole through the great, dark hall, undid the chain-fastener of the heavy front door, and walked softly around the angle of the house.

At de Grandin's direction, we kept to the shadow of the tall, black-branched pine trees which grew near the house, watching the moonlit walls of the building for any evidence of a housebreaker.

"It is there the young Aglinberry sleeps," de Grandin observed in a low voice as he indicated a partly opened casement on the second floor, its small panes shining like nacre in the rays of the full moon. "I observe he has not obeyed our injunctions to close his sash in the night-time. *Morbleu*, that which we did see last night might have been harmless, my friend, but, again, it might have been—ah, my friend, look; *look!*"

Stealthily, silently as a shadow, a stooped form stole around the corner of the wall, paused huddled in a spot of darkness where the moonbeams failed to reach, then slowly straightened up, crept into the light, and began mounting the rough rubblestone side of the house, for all the world like some great, uncanny lizard from the preadamite days. Clinging to the protuberances of the rocks with clawlike hands, feeling for toeholds in the interstices where cement had weathered away, the thing slowly ascended, nearer and yet nearer Aglinberry's unlatched window.

"*Dieu de Dieu*," de Grandin muttered, "if it be a phantom, our friend Aglinberry is in misfortune, for 'twas he himself who left his window unfastened. If it be not a ghost—*parbleu*, it had better have said its paternosters, for when he puts his head in that window, I fire!" I saw the glint of moonlight, on the blue steel of his pistol barrel as he trained it on the climbing thing.

Inch by inch the creature—man or devil—crept up the wall, reached its talon hands across the stone sill, began drawing itself through the casement. I held my breath, expecting the roar of de Grandin's pistol each second, but a sudden gasp of astonishment beside me drew my attention from the creeping thing to my companion.

"Look, Friend Trowbridge, *regardez, s'il vous plait!*" he bade me in a tremulous whisper, nodding speechlessly toward the window into which the marauder was disappearing like a great, black serpent into its lair. I turned my gaze toward the window again and blinked my eyes in unbelief.

An odd luminescence, as if the moon's rays had been focused by a lens, appeared behind the window opening. It was like a mirror of dull silver, or a light faintly reflected from a distance. Tiny bits of impalpable dust, like filings from a silversmith's rasp, seemed floating in the air, whirling, dancing lightly in the converging moon rays, circling about each other like dust-motes seen in a sun-shaft through a darkened room, driving together, *taking form*. Literally out of moonlight, a visible, discernible something was being made. Spots of shadow appeared against the phosphorescent gleam, alternate high-lights and shadows became apparent, limning the outlines of a human face, a slender, oval face with smoothly-parted hair sleekly drawn across a high, broad forehead; a face of proud-mouthed, narrow-nosed beauty such as the highest-caste women of the Rajputs have.

A moment it seemed suspended there, more like the penumbra of a shadow than an actual entity, then seemed to surge forward, to lose its sharpness of outline, and blend, mysteriously, with the darkness of the night-prowler's form, as though a splash of mercury were suddenly thrown upon a slab of carbon.

A moment the illusion of light-on-darkness held, then a scream of wire-edged terror, mingled with mortal pain, shuddered through the quiet night as a lightning flash rips across a thunder cloud. The climber loosed both hands from the window sill, clawed frantically at the empty air above him, then hurtled like a plummet to the earth, almost at our feet.

Our flashlights shot their beams simultaneously on the fallen man's face as we reached his side, revealing the features of Nikolai Brondovitch, the gipsy Aglinberry had ordered off the place that morning.

But it was a different face from that the Romany had displayed when threatening Aglinberry or attempting to conciliate de Grandin. The eyes were starting from their sockets, the mouth hung open with an imbecile, hang-jawed flaccidity. And on the gipsy's lean, corded throat was a knotted swelling, as though a powerful clamp had seized and crushed the flesh together, shutting off breath and blood in a single mighty grasp. Both de Grandin and I recognized the thing before us for what it was—trust a physician to recognize it! Death is unique, and nothing in the world counterfeits it. The scoundrel had died before his body touched the ground.

"*Nom d'un nom!*" de Grandin murmured wonderingly, "And did you also see it, Friend Trowbridge?"

"I saw something," I answered, shuddering at the recollection.

"And what did you see?" his words came quickly, like an eager lawyer cross-examining a reluctant witness.

"It—it looked like a woman's face," I faltered, "but—"

"*Nom de Dieu*, yes," he agreed, almost hysterically, "a woman's face—a face with no body beneath it! *Parbleu*, my friend, I think this adventure is worthy of our steel. Come, let us see the young Aglinberry."

We hurried into the house and up the stairs, hammering on our host's door, calling his name in frenzied shouts.

"Eh, what's up?" his cheery voice responded, and next moment he unfastened the door and looked at us, a sleepy grin mantling his youthful face. "What's the idea of you chaps breaking a fellow's door down at this time o' night?" he wanted to know. "Having bad dreams?"

"*Mon—Monsieur!*" de Grandin stammered, his customary aplomb deserting him. "Do you mean—have you been *sleeping?*"

"Sleeping?" the other echoed. "What do you think I went to bed for? What's the matter, have you caught the family ghost?" He grinned at us again.

"And you have heard nothing, seen nothing—you do not know an entrance to your room was almost forced?" de Grandin asked incredulously.

"An entrance to my room?" the other frowned in annoyance, looking quizzically from one of us to the other. "Say, you gentlemen had better go back to bed. I don't know whether I'm lacking in a sense of humor or what my trouble is, but I don't quite get the joke of waking a man up in the middle of the night to tell him that sort of cock-and-bull story."

"*Nom d'un chou-fleur!*" De Grandin looked at me and shook his head wonderingly. "He has slept through it all, Friend Trowbridge!"

Aglinberry bristled with anger. "What're you fellows trying to do, string me?" he demanded hotly.

"Your hat, your coat, your boots, *Monsieur!*" de Grandin exclaimed in reply. "Come outside with us; come and see the vile wretch who would have slaughtered you like a pig in the shambles. Come and behold, and we shall tell you how he died."

BY MUTUAL CONSENT WE decided to withhold certain details of the gipsy's death from the coroner's jury next day, and a verdict to the effect that the miscreant had come to his death while attempting to "break and enter the dwelling house of one John Aglinberry in the night-time, forcibly, feloniously aud against the form of the statute in such case made and provided" was duly returned.

The gipsy was buried in the Potter's Field and we returned to our vigil in the haunted house.

Aglinberry was almost offensively incredulous concerning the manner of the gipsy's death. "Nonsense!" he exclaimed when we insisted we had seen a mysterious, faintly luminous face at the window before the would-be house-breaker hurtled to his death. "You fellows are so fed up on ghost-lore that you've let this place's reputation make you see things—things which weren't there."

"*Monsieur,*" de Grandin assured him with injured dignity, "it is that you speak out of the conceit of boundless ignorance. When you have seen one-half—*pardieu*, one-quarter or one-eighth—the things I have seen, you will learn not to sneer at whatever you fail to understand. As that so magnificent Monsieur Shakespeare did say, 'There are more things in heaven and earth than are dreamt of in your philosophy.'"

"Probably," our host interrupted, smothering a yawn, "but I'm content to let 'em stay there. Meantime, I'm going to bed. Goodnight." And up the stairs he marched, leaving us to share the warmth of the crackling pitch-pine fire.

De Grandin shook his head pityingly after the retreating youngster. "He is the perfect type of that Monsieur Babbitt," he confided. "Worldly, materialistic, entirely devoid of imagination. *Parbleu*, we have them in France, too! Did they not make mock of Pasteur, *le grand*, when he announced his discoveries to a skeptical world? Most assuredly. Like the poor, the materialist we have always with us.—Ha! what is that! Do you hear it, Trowbridge, my friend?"

Faintly, so faintly it was like the half-heard echo of an echo, the fine, musical jangle of tiny bells wafted to us through the still, cold air of the dark old house.

"In there, 'twas in the library it sounded!" the Frenchman insisted in an excited whisper as he leaped to his feet and strode across the hall. "Your light, Friend Trowbridge; quick, your light!"

I threw the beam of my electric torch about the high-walled, sombre old reading room, but nothing more ghostly than the tall walnut book cases, empty of books and laden only with dust these many years, met our eyes. Still the soft, alluring chime sounded somewhere in the shadows, vague and indefinite as the cobwebbed darkness about us, but insistent as a trumpet call heard across uncounted miles of night.

"*Morbleu*, but this is strange!" de Grandin asserted, circling the room with quick, nervous steps. "Trowbridge, Trowbridge, my friend, as we live, those bells are calling us, calling—ah, *cordieu*, they are here!"

He had halted before a carved panel under one of the old bookcases and was on his hands and knees, examining each figure of the conventionalized flowers and fruits which adorned its surface. With quick, questing fingers he felt the carvings, like a cracksman feeling out the combination of a safe. "*Nom d'un fromage*, I have it!" he called in lilting triumph as he bore suddenly down upon a bunch of carved grapes and the panel swung suddenly inward upon invisible hinges. "Trowbridge, *mon ami, regardez vous!*"

Peering into the shallow opening left by the heavy, carved plank, we beheld a package carefully wrapped in linen, dust-covered and yellowed with age.

"Candles, if you please, Friend Trowbridge," de Grandin commanded as he bore our find in triumph to the hall. "We shall see what secret of the years these bells have led us to." He sank into his armchair and began unwinding the linen bands.

"Ah? And what is this?" He unreeled the last of the bandages and displayed a small roll of red morocco leather, a compact little case such as an elder generation of men carried with them for supplying needles, buttons, thread and other aids to the womanless traveler. Inside the wallet was a length of tough, age-tanned parchment, and attached to it by a loop of silk was a single tiny hawk-bell of gold, scarcely larger than a bead, but capable of giving off a clear, penetrating tinkle as the parchment shook in de Grandin's impatient hands.

I looked over his shoulder in fascinated interest, but drew back with disappointment as I saw the vellum was covered with closely-written scrawls somewhat resembling shorthand.

"U'm!" de Grandin regarded the writing a moment, then tapped his even, white teeth with a meditative forefinger. "This will require much study, Friend Trowbridge." he murmured. "Many languages have I studied, and my brain is like a room where many people speak together—out of the babel I can distinguish but few words unless I bear my attention on some one talk. This"—he tapped the crinkling parchment—"is Hindustani, if I mistake not; but to translate it will require more time than these candles will burn. Nevertheless, we shall try."

He hurried to our bedroom, returning in a moment with a pad of paper and a fresh supply of candles. "I shall work here for a time," he announced, reseating himself before the fire. "It will be long before I am prepared for bed, and it may be well for you to seek repose. I shall make but poor company these next few hours."

I accepted the dismissal with an answering grin and, taking my candle, mounted the stairs to bed.

"EH BIEN, MY FRIEND, you do sleep like the dead—the righteous dead who have no fear of purgatory!" de Grandin's voice roused me the following morning.

The bright spring sunshine was beating into our chamber through the open casement, and a puff of keen breeze fluttered the trailing bed-clothes, but my friend's face rivaled the brilliance of the breaking day. "*Triomphe!*" he exclaimed, brandishing a sheaf of papers above his blond head. "It is finished, it is complete, it is done altogether entirely. Attend me, my friend, listen with care, for you are not like to hear such a tale soon again:

> Lord of my life and master of my heart: This day is the fulfilment of the fate overhanging the wretched woman who has unworthily been honored by your regard, for this night I was bidden by my father to choose whether I would be married by the priests to the god Khandoka, and become a temple bayadere—and my lord well knows what the life of such an one is—or go to the shrine of Omkar, God of Destruction, to become *kurban*. I have chosen to make the leap, my lord, for there is no other way for Amari.
>
> We have sinned, thou against thy people and I against mine, in that we did dare defy *varna* and love, when such a love is forbidden between the races. *Varna* forbids it, the commands of thy people and mine forbid it, and yet we loved. Now our brief dream of *kailas* is broken as the mists of morning break and fly before the scarlet lances of the sun, and thou returnest to thy people; Amari goes to her fate.
>
> By the leap I assure my sinful spirit of a resting place in *kailas*, for to the *kurban* all sins are forgiven, even unto that of taking the life of a Brahmin or giving herself in love to one of another race; but she who retreats from the leap commits a sin with each step so great that a thousand reincarnations can not atone for it.
>
> In this life the walls of *varna* stand between us, but, perchance, there may come a life when Amari inhabits the body of a woman of the sahib's race, or my lord and master may be clothed in the flesh of one of Amari's people. These things it is not given Amari to know, but this she knows full well: Throughout the seven cycles of time which shall endure through all the worlds and through all eternity, when worlds and the gods themselves shall have shuddered into dust, Amari's heart is ever and always inclined to the sahib, and the walls of death or the force of life shall not keep her from him. Farewell, master of Amari's breath, perchance we shall meet again upon some other star, and our waking spirits may remember the dream of this unhappy life. But ever, and always, Amari loves thee, sahib John."

"Yes?" I asked as he finished reading. "And then?"

"*Parbleu*, my friend, there was no then!" he answered. "Listen, you do not know India. I do. In that so depraved country they do consider that the woman who goes to the bloody shrine of the god Omkar and hurls herself down from a cliff upon his bloody altar attains to sainthood. It was that which this poor one meant when she did speak of 'the leap' in her farewell note to her white lover. *Kurban* is the word in their so detestable language for human sacrifice, and when she speaks of attaining *kailas* she refers to their heathenish word for heaven.

When she says *varna* stood between them she did mean caste. *Cordieu*—you English, you Americans! Always you drive yourselves crazy with thoughts of what should and what should not be done, *Nom d'un coq!* Why did not this Monsieur Aglinberry the elder take this Hindoo woman to wife, if he loved her, and thumb his nose at her brown-skinned relatives and his fair-eyed English kin as well? 'Tis what a Frenchman would have done in like case. But no, he must needs allow the woman he loved to hurl herself over a cliff for the edification of a crowd of monkey-faced heathen who are undoubtedly stewing in hell at this moment, while he ran overseas to America and built him a mansion in the wilderness. A mansion, *pardieu!* A mansion without the light of love in its rooms or the footfalls of little children on its floors. *Nom de Dieu de nom de Dieu*, a mansion of melancholy memories, it is! À *bas* such a people! They deserve *la prohibition*, nothing better!" He walked back and forth across the room in a fury of disgust, snapping his fingers and scowling ferociously.

"All right," I agreed, laughing in spite of myself, "we'll grant all you say; but where does that get us as regards Redgables? If the ghost of this Hindoo girl haunts this house, how are we going to lay it?"

"How should I know?" he returned peevishly. "If the ancient fires of this dead woman's love burn on the cold hearth of this *sacré* house, who am I to put them out? Oh, it is too pitiful, too pitiful; that such a love as theirs should have been sacrificed on the altar of *varna*—caste!"

"Hullo, hullo, up there!" came a cheery hail from the hall below. "You chaps up yet? Breakfast is ready, and we've got callers. Come down."

"Breakfast!" de Grandin snorted disgustedly. "He talks of breakfast, in a house where the ghost of murdered love dwells! But"—he turned an impish grin on me—"I hope he has compounded some of those so delicious flap-the-jacks for us, even so."

"DR. DE GRANDIN, THIS is Dr. Wiltsie," Aglinberry introduced as we descended to the hall. "Dr. Trowbridge, Dr. Wiltsie. Wiltsie is superintendent of a sanatarium for the feeble-minded over there"—he waved his arm in a vague gesture—"and when he heard Dr. de Grandin was in the neighborhood, he came over for a consultation. It seems—oh, you tell him your troubles, Wiltsie."

Dr. Wiltsie was a pleasant-looking young man with a slightly bald head and large-lensed, horn-rimmed spectacles. He smiled agreeably as he hastened to comply with Aglinberry's suggestion. "Fact is, doctor," he began as de Grandin piled his plate high with "flap-the-jacks," "we've got a dam' peculiar case over at Thornwood. It's a young girl who's been in our charge for the past twelve years—ever since she was ten years old. The poor child suffered a terrible fright when she was about six, according to the history we have of her case—horses of the carriage in which she and her mother were riding ran away, threw 'em both out, killed the mother and—well, when they picked the youngster up she was just one of God's little ones. No more reason than a two-months-old baby.

"Her family's rich enough, but she has no near relatives, so she's been in our care at Thornwood, as I said, for the past twelve years. She's always been good as gold, scarcely any trouble at all, sitting on the bed or the floor and playing with her fingers or toes, like an infant, most of the time; but lately she's been acting up like the devil. Fact. Tried to brain the nurse with a cup three nights ago, and made a break at one of the matrons yesterday morning. From a simple, sweet-tempered little idiot she's turned into a regular hell-cat. Now, if she'd been suffering from ordinary dementia, I'd—"

"Very good, very good, my friend," de Grandin replied as he handed his plate to Aglinberry for further replenishment. "I shall be delighted to look at your patient this morning. *Parbleu*, a madhouse will be a pleasant contrast to this never enough to be execrated place!"

"He likes my house," Aglinberry commented to Dr. Wiltsie with a sardonic grin as we rose and prepared to go to the sanatarium.

THORNWOOD SANATARIUM WAS A beautiful, remodeled private country home, and differed in no wise from the near-by estates except that the park about the house was enclosed in a high stone wall topped with a chevaux-de-frise of barbed wire.

"How's Mary Ann, Miss Underwood?" Wiltsie asked as we entered the spacious central hall and paused at the door of the executive office.

"Worse, doctor," replied the competent-looking young woman in nurse's uniform at the desk. "I've sent Mattingly up to her twice this morning, but the dosage has to be increased each time, and the medicine doesn't seem to hold as well."

"H'm," Wiltsie muttered noncommittally, then turned to us with an anxious look. "Will you come to see the patient, gentlemen? You, too, Aglinberry, if you wish. I imagine this'll be a new experience for you."

Upstairs, we peered through the small aperture in the door barring the demented girl's room. If we had not been warned of her condition, I might easily have taken the young woman asleep on the neat, white cot for a person in perfect health. There was neither the emaciation nor the obesity commonly seen in cases of dementia, no drawing of the face, not even a flaccidity of the mouth as the girl lay asleep.

Her abundant dark hair had been clipped short as a discouragement to the vermin which seem naturally to gravitate to the insane in spite of their keepers' greatest care, and she was clothed in a simple muslin nightdress, cut modestly at the neck and without sleeves. One cheek, pale from confinement, but otherwise flawless, lay pillowed on her bent arm, and it seemed to me the poor girl smiled in her sleep with the wistfulness of a tired and not entirely happy child. Long, curling lashes fringed the ivory lids which veiled her eyes, and the curving brows above them were as delicately pencilled and sharply defined as though drawn on her white skin with a camel's hair brush.

"*La pauvre enfant!*" de Grandin murmured compassionately, and at the sound of his voice the girl awoke.

Gone instantly was the reposeful beauty from her face. Her lips stretched into a square like the mouth of one of those old Greek tragic masks, her large, brown eyes glared fiercely, and from her gaping red mouth issued such a torrent of abuse as might have brought a blush to the face of the foulest fishwife in Billingsgate.

Wiltsie's face showed a dull flush as he turned to us. "I'm dashed if I can understand it," he admitted "She goes on this way for hours on end, now."

"Eh, is it so?" de Grandin responded. "And what, may I ask, have you been doing for this condition? It appears more like delirium than like dementia, my friend."

"Well, we've been administering small doses of brandy and strychnine, but they don't seem to have the desired effect, and the doses have to be increased constantly."

"Ah!"—de Grandin's smile was slightly satirical—"and has it never occurred to you to employ hypnotics? Hyoscine by example?"

"By George, it didn't!" Wiltsie confessed. "Of course, hyoscine would act as a cerebral sedative, but we'd never thought of using it."

"Very well, I suggest you employ a hypodermic injection of hyoscine hypobromide," de Grandin dismissed the case with an indifferent shrug of his shoulders, but Aglinberry, moved by that curiosity which is akin to fascination felt by the normal person regarding the insane, looked past him at the raving girl inside the cell.

An instant change came over her. From a cursing, blaspheming maniac, the girl became a quiet, sorrowful-looking child, and on her suddenly calmed face was such a look of longing as I have seen children undergoing strict diet give some particularly toothsome and forbidden dainty.

Young Aglinberry suppressed a shudder with difficulty. "Poor, child," he muttered, "poor, poor little girl, to be so lovely and so hopeless!"

"*Oui, Monsieur,*" de Grandin agreed moodily as we went down the stairs, "you do well to pity her, for the intelligence—the very soul of her—has been dead these many years; only her body remains alive, and—*pitié de Dieu*—what a life it is! Ah, if only some means could be found to graft the healthy intelligence animating a sick body into that so healthy body of hers, what an economy!" He lapsed into moody silence, which remained unbroken during our drive back to Redgables.

THE SUN HAD GONE down in a blaze of red against the western sky, and the pale new moon was swimming easily through a tumbling surf of a bank of foaming cirrus clouds when the deep-throated, belling bay of a hound came echoing to us from the grounds outside the old house. "*Grand Dieu!*" de Grandin leaped nervously from his chair. "What is that? Do they hunt in this country while the mating season is but blossoming into flower among the wild things?"

"No, they don't," Aglinberry answered testily. "Someone has let his dogs out on my land. Come on let's chase 'em off. I won't have 'em poaching on the game here like that."

We trailed out of the hall and walked quickly toward the sound of the baying, which rose fuller and fuller from the region of the lake. As we neared the dogs, the sound of human voices became audible. "That you, Mr. Aglinberry?" a man called, and the flash of an electric torch showed briefly among the new-leafed thickets by the waterfront.

"Yes," our host answered shortly. "Who the devil are you, and what are you doing here?"

"We're from Thornwood, sir," the man answered, and we saw the gleam of his white hospital uniform under his dark topcoat. "The crazy girl, Mary Ann, got away about an hour ago, and we're trailing her with the hounds. She went completely off her head after you left this morning, and fought so they couldn't give her the hypo without strapping her. After the injection she quieted down, but when the matron went to her room with dinner she suddenly woke up, threw the woman against the wall so hard she almost cracked her ribs, and got clean away. She can't have gotten far, though, running over this broken country in her bare feet."

"Oh, hell!" Aglinberry stormed, striking a bush beside the path a vicious slash with his stick. "It's bad enough to have my place overrun with gipsies and gossiped about by all the country yaps in the county, but when lunatics get to making a hangout of it, it's too much!

"Hope you find her," he flung back over his shoulder as he turned toward the house. "And for the Lord's sake, if you do get her, keep her at Thornwood. I don't want her chasing all over *this* place!"

"*Monsieur*—" de Grandin began, but Aglinberry cut him short.

"Yes, I know what you'll say," he broke in, "you want to tell me a ghost-woman will protect me from the lunatics, just as she did from the gipsy, don't you?"

"No, my friend," de Grandin began with surprising mildness, "I do not think you need protection from the poor mad one, but—" He broke off with his sentence half spoken as he stared intently at an object hurrying toward us across a small clearing.

"Good God!" Aglinberry exclaimed. "It's she! The crazy girl!"

Seemingly gone mad himself, he rushed toward the white-robed figure in the clearing, brandishing his heavy stick. "I'll handle her," he called back, "I don't care how violent she is; I'll handle her!"

In another moment he was half-way across the cleared space, his thick walking stick poised for a blow which would render the maniac unconscious.

Any medical student with the most elementary knowledge of insanity could have told him a lunatic is not to be cowed by violence. As though the oaken cudgel had been a wisp of straw, the maniac rushed toward him, then stopped a scant dozen feet away and held out her tapering arms.

"John," she called softly, a puzzling, exotic thickness in her pronunciation. "John, *sahib*, it is I!"

Aglinberry's face was like that of a man suddenly roused from sound slumber. Astonishment, incredulity, joy like that of a culprit reprieved as the hangman knots the noose about his neck, shone on his features. The threatening club fell with a soft thud to the turf, and he gathered the madwoman's slender body to his breast, covering her upturned face with kisses.

"Amari, my Amari; Amari, my beloved!" he crooned in a soft, sobbing voice. "Oh, my love, my precious, precious love. I have found you; I have found you at last!"

The girl laughed lightly, and in her laughter there was no hint or taint of madness, "Not Amari, Mary Ann in this life, John," she told him, "but yours, John *sahib*, whether we stand beside the Ganges or the Hudson, beloved through all the ages."

"Ah, got her, sir?" The hospital attendants, a pair of bloodhounds tugging at the leash before them, broke through the thicket at the clearing's farther side. "That's right, sir; hold her tight till we slip the straitjacket on her."

Aglinberry thrust the girl behind him and faced the men. "You can't have her," he announced uncompromisingly. "She's mine."

"Wha—what?" the attendant stammered, then turned toward the underbrush and called to some invisible companion. "Hey, Bill, come 'ere; there's two of 'em!"

"You can't have her," Aglinberry repeated as two more attendants reinforced the first pair. "She's going to stay with me—always."

"Now, look here, sir," the leader of the party argued, "that girl's a dangerous lunatic; she nearly killed a matron this evenin', an' she's been regularly committed to Thornwood Sanatarium. We've tracked her here, an' we're goin' to take her back."

"Over the dead corpse of Jules de Grandin," the Frenchman interrupted as he pressed forward. "*Parbleu*, me, I am in authority here. I shall be responsible for her conduct."

The man hesitated a moment, then shrugged his shoulders. "It's your funeral if anything happens on account o' this," he warned. "Tomorrow Dr. Wiltsie will start legal proceedings to get her back. You can't win."

"Ha, can I not?" the little Frenchman's teeth gleamed in the moonlight. "My friend, you do not know Jules de Grandin. There is no lunacy commission in the world to which I can not prove her sanity. I do pronounce her cured, and the opinion of Jules de Grandin of the Sorbonne is not to be lightly sneezed upon, I do assure you!"

To Aglinberry he said: "Pick her up, my friend; pick her up and bear her to the house, lest the stones bruise her tender feet. Dr. Trowbridge and I will follow and protect you. *Parbleu*"—he glared defiantly about him—"me, I say nothing shall separate you again. Lead on!"

"FOR HEAVEN'S SAKE, DE Grandin," I besought as we followed Aglinberry and the girl toward the house, "what does this all mean?"

"*Morbleu*," he nodded solemnly at me, "it means we have won ten thousand dollars, Friend Trowbridge. No more will the ghost of that so pitiful Hindoo woman haunt this house. We have earned our fee."

"Yes, but—" I pointed mutely toward our host as he strode through the moonlight with the girl in his arms.

"Ah—that?" he laughed a silent, contented laugh. "That, my friend, is a demonstration that the ancient fires of love die not, no matter how much we heap them with the ashes of hate and death.

"The soul of Amari, the sacrificed Hindoo girl, has come to rest in the body of the lunatic, Mary Ann, just as the soul of John Aglinberry the elder was reborn into the body of his namesake and double, John Aglinberry the younger. Did not the deceased Indian girl promise that she would some day come back to her forbidden lover in another shape? *Parbleu*, but she has fulfilled her vow! Always have the other members of Aglinberry's family been unable to live in this house, because they were of the clan who had helped separate the elder lovers.

"Now, this young man, knowing nothing of his uncle's intimate affairs, but bearing in his veins the blood of the older Aglinberry, and on his face the likeness of the uncle, too, must have borne within his breast the soul of the disappointed man who ate out his heart in sorrow and loneliness in this house which he had builded in the American woods. And the spirit of Amari, the Hindoo, who has kept safe the house from alien blood and from the members of her soulmate's family who would have robbed him of his inheritance, did find near at hand the healthy body of a lunatic whose soul—or intelligence, if you please—had long since sped, and entered thereinto to dwell on earth again. Did you not see sanity and longing looking out of her eyes when she beheld him in the madhouse this morning, my friend? Sanity? But yes, it was recognition, I tell you!

"Her violence? 'Twas but the clean spirit of the woman fighting for mastery of a body long untenanted by an intelligence. Were you to attempt to play a long-disused musical instrument, Trowbridge, my friend, you could make but poor work of it first, but eventually you would be able to produce harmony. So it is in this case. The spirit sought to use a long-disused brain, and at first, the music she could make was nothing but noise. Now, however, she has seen the mastery of her instrument, and henceforth the body of Mary Ann will function as that of a healthy young woman. I, Jules de Grandin, will demonstrate her sanity to the world, and you, my friend, shall help me. Together we shall win, together we shall make certain that these lovers thwarted in one life, shall complete this cycle in happiness.

"*Eh bien*," he twisted the end of his blond mustache and set his hand at a rakish angle on the side of head, "it is possible that somewhere in space there waits for me the spirit of a woman whom I have loved and left in another life. I wonder, when she comes, if I, like the lucky young Aglinberry yonder, shall 'wake, and remember, and understand'?"

The Great God Pan

"**B**UT OF COURSE, MY friend," Jules de Grandin conceded as he hitched his pack higher on his shoulders and leaned forward against the grade of the wooded hill, "I grant you American roads are better than those of France; but look to what inconvenience these same good roads put us. Everything in America is arranged for the convenience of the motorist—the man who covers great distances swiftly. Your roads are the direct result of motorized transportation for the millions, and, consequently, you and I must tramp half the night and very likely sleep under the stars, because there is no inn to offer shelter.

"Now in France, where roads were laid out for stage-coaches hundreds of years before your Monsieur Ford was dreamed of, there is an abundance of resting places for the pedestrian. Here—" He spread his hands in an eloquent gesture of deprecation.

"Oh, well," I comforted, "we started out on a hiking trip, you know, and we've had mighty fine weather so far. A night in the open won't do us any harm. That cleared place at the top of the hill looks like a good spot to make camp."

"Eh, yes, I suppose so," he acquiesced as he breasted the crown of the hill and paused for breath. "*Parbleu*," he gazed about him, "I fear we trespass, Friend Trowbridge! This is no natural glade, it has been cleared for human habitation. Behold!" He waved his arm in a commanding gesture.

"By George, you're right!" I agreed in disappointment as I surveyed the clearing.

"The trees—beech, birch and poplar—had been cut away for the space of an acre or more, and the stumps removed, the cleared land afterward being sown with grass as smooth and well cared for as a private estate's lawn. Twenty yards ahead a path of flat, smooth stones was laid in the sod, running from a dense thicket of dwarf pine and rhododendron across the sward to a clump of tall, symmetrical cedars standing almost in the center of the clearing. Through the dark, bearded boughs of the evergreens we caught the fitful gleam of lights as the soft summer-evening breeze swayed the branches."

"Too bad," I murmured; "guess we'll have to push on a little farther for our bivouac."

"*Mille cochons, non!*" de Grandin denied. "Not I. *Parbleu*, but my feet faint from exhaustion, and my knees cry out for the caress of Mother Earth with a piety they have not known these many years! Come, let us go to the proprietor of that mansion and say, '*Monsieur*, here are two worthy gentleman tramps who crave the boon of a night's lodging and a meal, also a bath and a cup of wine, if that so entirely detestable Monsieur Volstead has allowed you to retain any.' He will not refuse us, my friend. *Morbleu*, a man with the charity of a Senegalese idol would not turn us away in the circumstances! I shall ask him with tears in my voice—*pardieu*, I shall weep like a lady in the cinema; I shall wring my hands and entreat him! Never fear, my friend, we shall lodge in yonder house this night, or Jules de Grandin goes supperless to a bed of pine-needles."

"Humph, I hope your optimism is justified," I grunted as I followed him across the close-cropped lawn to the stone path and marched toward the lights in the cedars.

We had progressed a hundred feet or so along the path when a sudden squealing cry, followed by a crashing in the thicket at the clearing edge, stopped us in our tracks. Something fluttering and white, gleaming like a ghost in the faint starlight, broke through the bushes, and a soft slapping noise, as though someone were beating his hands lightly and quickly together, sounded as the figure approached us.

"Oh, sirs, run, run for your lives, it—it's *Pan!*" the girl called in a frightened voice as she came abreast of us. "Run, run, if you want to live; *he's* there, I tell you! I saw his face among the leaves!"

One of de Grandin's small, slender hands rose with an involuntary gesture to stroke his little blond mustache as he surveyed our admonisher. She was tall and built with a stately, statuesque beauty which was doubly enhanced by the simple white linen garment which fell in straight lines from her lovely bare shoulders to her round, bare ankles. The robe was bound about the waist with a corded girdle which crossed above her breast, and was entirely sleeveless, though cut rather high at the neck, exposing only a few inches of white throat. Her feet, narrow and high-arched, and almost as white as the linen of her robe, were innocent of any covering, and I realized that the slapping sound I had heard was the impact of her bare soles on the stones of the path as she ran.

"*Tiens, Mademoiselle*," de Grandin declared with a bow, "you are as lovely as Pallas Athene herself. Who is it has dared frighten you? *Cordieu*, I shall do myself the honor of twisting his unmannerly nose!"

"No, no!" the girl besought in a trembling voice. "Do not go back, sir, *please!* I tell you Pan—the Great God Pan, Himself—is in those bushes. I went to bathe in the fountain a few minutes ago, and as I came from the water I—I saw his face grinning at me between the rhododendron bushes! It was only for a second, and I was so frightened I did not look again, but—oh, let us go to the house! Hurry, hurry, or we may see him in good earnest, and—" She broke off with a shudder and turned from us, walking hurriedly, but with consummate grace, toward the knot of cedars before us.

"*Sacré nom!*" de Grandin murmured as he fell in behind her. "Is it that we have arrived at a home for the feeble-minded, Friend Trowbridge, or is this beautiful one a goddess from the days of old? *Nom d'un coq*, she speaks the English like an American, but her costume, her so divine beauty, they are things of the days when Pygmalion hewed living flesh from out the lifeless marble!"

THE MURMUR OF FEMININE voices, singing softly in unison, came to us as we made our way through the row of cedar trees and approached the house. The building was almost square, as well as we could determine in the uncertain light, constructed of some sort of white or light-colored stone, and fronted by a wide portico with tall pillars topped with Doric capitals. The girl ran lightly up the three wide steps leading to the porch, her bare feet making no sound on the stone treads, and we followed her, wondering what sort of folk dwelt in this bit of classic Greece seemingly dropped from some other star in the midst of the New Jersey woods.

"*Morbleu!*" de Grandin exclaimed softly in wonderment as we paused at the wide, doorless entrance. Inside the house, or temple, was a large apartment, almost fifty feet square, paved with alternate slabs of white and grey-green stone. In the center stood a square column of black stone, some three feet in height, topped by an urn of some semi-transparent substance in which a light glowed dimly. The place was illuminated by a series of flaring torches hung in rings let into the walls, their uncertain, flickering light showing us a circle of ten young women, dressed in the same simple classic costume as that worn by the girl we had met outside, kneeling about the central urn, their faces bowed modestly toward the floor, white arms raised above their heads, hands bent inward toward the center of the room. As we stood at gaze the girl who had preceded us hurried soundlessly across the checkered pavement and sank to her knees, inclining her shapely head and raising her arms in the same position of mute adoration assumed by the others.

"Name of a sacred pig!" de Grandin whispered. "We have here the votaries, but the hierophant, where is he?"

"There, I think," I answered, nodding toward the lighted urn in the pavement's center.

"*Parbleu*, yes," my companion assented, "and a worthy one for such a class, *n'est-ce-pas?*"

Standing beside the central altar, if such it could be called, was a short, pudgy little man, clothed in a short *chiton* of purple cloth bordered about neck, sleeves and bottom with a zig-zag design of gold braid. His bald head, gleaming in the torchlight, was crowned with a wreath of wild laurel, and a garland of roses hung about his fat, creased neck like an overgrown Hawaiian *lei*. Clasped in the crook of his left elbow was a zither, or some similar musical instrument, while a little stick, ending in a series of curved teeth, something like the fingers of a Japanese back-scratcher, was clasped in his dimpled right hand.

"Come, my children," the comic little man exclaimed in a soft, unctuous voice, "let us to our evening worship. Beauty is love, love beauty; that is all ye know and all ye need to know. Come, Chloë, Thisbe, Daphne, Clytie, let us see how well you know the devotion of beauty!"

He waved his stick like a monarch gesturing with his scepter, and drew its claw-tipped end across the strings of his zither, striking a chord, whereat the kneeling girls began singing, or, rather, humming, a lilting, swinging tune vaguely reminiscent of Mendelssohn's *Spring Song*, and four of their number leaped nimbly to their feet, ran lightly to the center of the room, joined hands in a circle and began a dance of light, lithe grace.

Faster and faster their white feet whirled in the convolutions of the dance, their graceful arms weaving patterns of living beauty as they swung in time to the measures of the song. They formed momentary tableaux of sculptural loveliness, only to break apart instantly into quadruple examples of individual posturing such as would have set an artist mad with delight.

The music ceased on a long-drawn, quavering note, the four dancers ran quickly back to their positions in the circle, and dropped again to their knees, extending their arms above their heads and bending their supple hands inward.

"It is well," the fat little man pronounced oracularly. "The day is done; let us to our rest."

The girls rose with a subdued rustling of white garments and separated into whispering, laughing groups, while the little man posed more pompously than ever beside the lighted urn.

"*Tiens*, Friend Trowbridge," de Grandin whispered with a chuckle, "do you behold how this bantam would make a peacock of himself? He is vain, this one. Surely, we shall spend the night here!

"*Monsieur*," he emerged from the shadow of the doorway and advanced toward the absurd figure posturing beside the urn, "we are two weary travelers, lost in the midst of these woods, without the faintest notion of the direction of the nearest inn. Will you not, of your so splendid generosity, permit that we spend the night beneath your roof?"

"Eh, what's that?" the other exclaimed with a start as he beheld the little Frenchman for the first time. "What d'ye want? Spend the night here? No, no; I can't have that. Get my school talked about. Couldn't possibly have it. Never have any men in this place."

"Ah, but *Monsieur*," de Grandin replied smoothly, "you do forget that you are already here. If it were but a question of having male guests at this so wonderful school of the arts, is not the reputation of the establishment already ruined? Surely a gentleman with so much of the appeal to beauty as *Monsieur* unquestionably possesses would cause much gossip if he were not so well known for his discretion. And, *Monsieur's* discretion being already so firmly established, who would dare accuse him of anything save great-heartedness if he did permit two wanderers—and medical men in the bargain—to remain overnight in his house? Permit me, *Monsieur*; I am Dr. Jules de Grandin, of the Sorbonne, and this is Dr. Samuel Trowbridge, of Harrisonburg, New Jersey, both entirely at your good service, *Monsieur*."

The little fellow's fat face creased in a network of wrinkles as he regarded de Grandin with a self-satisfied smirk. "Ah, you appreciate the pure beauty of our school?" he remarked with almost pathetic eagerness. "I am Professor Judson—Professor Herman Judson, sir—of the School of the Worship of Beauty. These—ah—young ladies whom you have seen here tonight are a few of my pupils. We believe that the old ideals—the old thought—of ancient Greece is a living, motivating thing today, just as it was in centuries gone by. We assert sir, that the religion of beauty which actuated the Greeks is still a living, vital thing. We believe that the old gods are not dead; but come to those who woo them with the ancient rite of song and the dance. In fine, sir, we are pagans—apostles of the religion of neo-paganism!"

He drew himself up to his full height, which could not have exceeded five feet six inches, and glared defiantly at de Grandin, as though expecting a shocked protest at his announcement.

The Frenchman's smile became wider and blander than ever. "Capital, *Monsieur*," he congratulated. "Anyone with the eye of a blind man could see that you are the very personality to head such an incontestably sensible school of thought. The expertness with which your pupils perform their dances shows that they have a teacher worthy of all your claims. We do felicitate you most heartily, *Monsieur*. Meantime"—he slipped the pack from his shoulders and lowered it to the pavement—"you will undoubtlessly permit that we shall pass the night here? No?"

"We-ell," the professor's doubt gave way slowly, "you seem to be more appreciative than the average modern barbarian. Yes, you may remain here overnight; but you must be off in the morning—early in the morning, mind you. Never do to have the neighbors seeing strange men coming from this place. Understand?"

"Perfectly, *Monsieur*," de Grandin answered with a bow. "And, if we might make so bold, may we trespass on your hospitality for a bite—the merest morsel of food?"

"U'm, pay for it?" the other demanded dubiously.

"But assuredly," de Grandin replied, producing a roll of bills. "It would cause us the greatest anguish, I do assure you, if it were ever said that we accepted the hospitality of the great Professor 'Erman Judson without making adequate return."

"Very well," the professor assented, and hurried through a door at the farther end of the apartment, returning in a few minutes with a tray of cold roast veal, warm, ripe apples, a loaf of white bread and a jug of more than legally strong, sour wine.

"Ah," de Grandin boasted as he washed down a sandwich with a draft of the acid liquor, "did I not tell you we should spend the night here, Friend Trowbridge?"

"You certainly made good your promise," I agreed as I shoved the remains of my meal from me, undid my pack and prepared to pillow my head on my rolled-up jacket. "See you in the morning, old fellow."

"Very good," he agreed. "Meantime, I go out of doors to smoke a last cigarette before I join you in sleep."

I MIGHT HAVE SLEPT AN hour, perhaps a little more, when a sharp, insistent poke in my ribs woke me sufficiently to understand the words whispered fiercely in my ear. "Trowbridge, Trowbridge, my friend," Jules de Grandin breathed so low I could scarcely make out the syllables. "This house, it is not all as it should be, I fear me."

"Eh, what's that?" I demanded sleepily, sitting up and blinking half comprehendingly at his dim outline in the semidarkness of the big room.

"S-s-sh, not so loud," he cautioned, then leaned nearer, speaking rapidly: "Do you know from whence your English word 'panic' comes, my friend?"

"What?" I demanded in disgust. "Did you wake me up to discuss etymology—after a day's hiking? Good Lord, man—"

"Be still!" he ordered sharply; then, inconsistently, "Answer me, if you please; whence comes that word?"

"Hanged if I know," I replied, "and I'm hanged if I care a whoop, either. It can come from the Cannibal Islands, for all I—"

"Quiet!" he commanded, then hurried on: "In the old days when such things were, my friend, Pan, the god of Nature, was very real to the people.

They believed, firmly, that whoso saw Pan after nightfall, that one died instantly. Therefore, when a person is seized with a blind, unreasoning fear; even to this day, we say he has a panic. Of what consequence is this? Remember, my friend, the young lady whom we did meet as we approached this house told us she had seen Pan's face grinning at her from out the bushes as she bathed. Is it not so?"

"I guess so," I answered, putting my head back on my improvised pillow and preparing to sleep while he talked.

But he shook my shoulder with a sharp, imperative gesture. "Listen, my friend," he besought, "when I did go out of doors to smoke my cigarette, I met one of those beautiful young women who frequent this temple of the new heathenism, and engaged her in conversation. From her I learned much, and some of it sounds not good to my ears. For instance, I learn that this Professor Herman Judson is a much misunderstood man. Oh, but yes. The lawyers, they have misunderstood him many times. Once they misunderstood him so that he was placed in the state's prison for deceiving gullible women with fortune-telling tricks. Again he was misunderstood so that he went to the Bastille for attempting to secure some money which a certain deceased lady's heirs believed should have gone to them—which *did* go to them eventually."

"Well, what of it?" I growled. "That's no affair of ours. We're not a committee on the morals of dancing masters, are we?"

"Eh, are we not so?" he replied. "I am not entirely sure of that, my friend. I fear we, too, are about to misunderstand this Professor Judson. Some other things I find out from that young lady with the Irish nose and the Greek costume. This professor he has founded this school of dancing and paganism, taking for his pupils only young women who have no parents or other near relations, but much money. He is not minded to be misunderstood by heirs-at-law. What think you of that, *hein?*"

"I think he's got more sense than we gave him credit for," I replied.

"Undoubtlessly," he agreed, "very much more; for also I discovered that *Monsieur le Professeur* has had his school regularly incorporated, and has secured from each of his pupils a last will and testament in which she does leave the bulk of her estate to the corporation."

"Well," I challenged, giving up hope of getting my sleep till he had talked himself out, "what of it? The man may be sincere in his attempt to found some sort of aesthete cult, and he'll need money, for the project."

"True, quite true," he conceded, nodding his head like a China mandarin, "but attend me, Friend Trowbridge; while we walked beneath the stars I did make an occasion to take that young lady's hand in mine, and—"

"You old rake!" I cut in, grinning, but he shut me off with a snort of impatience.

"— and that was but a ruse to feel her pulse," he continued. "*Parbleu*, my friend, her heart did race like the engine of a *moteur*! Not with emotion for me—never think it, for I did talk to her like a father or uncle, well, perhaps more like a cousin—but because it is of an abnormal quickness. Had I a stethoscope with me I could have told more, but as it is I would wager a hundred dollars that she suffers a chronic myocarditis, and the prognosis of that ailment is always grave, my friend. Think you a moment—what would happen if that young girl with a defective heart should see what she took to be the face of the great god Pan peering at her from the leaves, as the lady we first saw declared she did? Remember, these children believe in the deities of old, my friend."

"By George!" I sat bolt upright. "Do you mean—you don't mean that—"

"No, my friend, as yet I mean nothing," he replied evenly, "but it would be well if we emulated the cat, and slept with one eye and both ears open this night. Perhaps"—he shrugged his shoulders impatiently—"who knows what we may see in this house where the dead gods are worshiped with song and the dance?"

A MARBLE PAVEMENT IS A poor substitute for a bed, even when the sleeper is thoroughly fatigued from a long day's tramp, and I slept fitfully, troubled by all manner of unpleasant dreams. The forms of lithe, classically draped young girls dancing about a fire-filled urn alternated with visions of goat-legged, grinning satyrs in my sleep as I rolled from side to side on my hard bed; but the sudden peal of devilish laughter, quavering sardonically, almost like the bleating of a goat, was the figment of no dream. I sat suddenly up, wide-awake, as a feminine scream, keen-edged with the terror of death, rent the tomblike stillness of the early morning, and ten white-draped forms came rushing in the disorder of abject fright into the room about us.

Torches were being lighted, one from another, and we beheld the girls, their tresses unloosed from the classic fillets which customarily bound them, their robes hastily adjusted, huddled fearfully in a circle about the glowing urn, while outside, in the moonless night, the echo of that fearful scream seemed wandering blindly among the evergreens.

"Professor, Professor!" one of the girls cried, wringing her hands in an agony of apprehension. "Professor, where are you? Chloë's missing, Professor!"

"Eh, what is it that you say?" de Grandin demanded, springing up and gazing questioningly about him. "What is this? One of your number missing! And the professor, too? *Parbleu*; me, I shall investigate this! Do you attend the young ladies, Friend Trowbridge. I, Jules de Grandin, shall try conclusions with whatever god or devil accosts the missing one!"

"Wait a minute," I cautioned. "The professor will be here in a moment. You can't go out there now; you haven't any gun."

"Ha, have I not?" he replied sarcastically, drawing the heavy, blue-steel pistol from his jacket pocket. "Friend Trowbridge, there are entirely too many people of ill repute who desire nothing more than the death of Jules de Grandin to make it safe for me to be without a weapon at any time. Me, I go to investigate."

"Never mind, sir," the smooth, oily voice of Professor Judson sounded from the door at the rear of the room as he marched with short-legged dignity toward the altar. "Everything is all right, I assure you.

"My children," he turned to the frightened girls, "Chloë has been frightened at the thought of Pan's presence. It is true that the great god of all Nature hovers ever near his worshipers, especially at the dark of the moon, but there is nothing to fear.

"Chloë will soon be all right. Meantime, let us propitiate Pan by prayer and sacrifice. Thetis, bring hither a goat!" He turned his small, deep-set eyes on the young girl we had met as we entered the grounds, and waved a pudgy hand commandingly.

The girl went white to the lips, but with a submissive bow she hurried from the room, returning in a moment leading a half-grown black goat by a string, a long, sharp butcher-knife and a wide, shallow dish under her free arm.

She led the animal to the altar where the professor stood, gave the leading string into his hand and presented the sacrificial knife, then knelt before him, holding the dish beneath the terrified goat's head, ready to catch the blood when the professor should have cut the creature's throat.

It was as if some beady, madness-compelling fume had suddenly wafted into the room. For a single breathless moment the other girls looked at their preceptor and his kneeling acolyte with a gaze of fear and disgust, their tender feminine instincts rebelling at the thought of the warm blood soon to flow, then, as a progressive, contagious shudder seemed to run through them, one after another, they leaped wildly upward with frantic, frenzied bounds as though the stones beneath their naked feet were suddenly turned white-hot, beating their hands together, waving their arms convulsively above their heads, bending forward till their long, unbound hair cascaded before their faces and swept the floor at their feet, then leaping upward again with rolling, staring eyes and wantonly waving arms. With a maniac shriek one of them seized the bodice of her robe and rent it asunder, exposing her breasts, another tore her gown from hem to hips in half a dozen places, so that streamers of tattered linen draped like ribbons about her rounded limbs as she sprang and crouched and sprang again in the abandon of her voluptuous dance.

And all the while, as madness seemed to feed on madness, growing wilder and more depraved each instant, they chanted in a shrill, hysterical chorus:

Upon thy worshipers now gaze,
    Pan, Pan, Io Pan,

To thee be sacrifice and praise,
　　Pan, Pan, to Pan.
Give us the boon of the seeing eye,
That we may behold ere yet we die
The ecstasies of thy mystery,
　　Pan, Pan, *Pan!*

Repeated insistently, with maniacal fervor, the name "Pan" beat against the air like the rhythm of a tom-tom. Its shouted repetition seemed to catch the tempo of my heart-beats; despite myself I felt an urging, strong as an addict's craving for his drug, to join in the lunatic dance, to leap and shout and tear the encumbering clothing from my body as I did so.

The professor changed his grip from the goat's tether to its hind legs. He swung the bleating animal shoulder-high, so that as it held its head back its throat curved above the dish held by the girl, who twitched her shoulders and swayed her body jerkily in time to the pagan hymn as she knelt at his feet.

"Oh, Pan, great goat-god, personification of all Nature's forces, immortal symbol of the ecstasy of passion, to Thee we make the sacrifice; to Thee we spill the blood of this victim," the professor cried, his eyes gleaming brilliantly in the reflection of the torches and the altar fire. "Behold, goat of thy worshiper's flock, we—"

"*Zut!* Enough of this; *cordieu*, too much!" de Grandin's furious voice cut through the clamor as a fire-bell stills the noise of street traffic. "Hold your hand, accursed of heaven, or by the head of St. Denis, I scatter your brains in yonder dish!" His heavy pistol pointed unwaveringly at the professor's bald head till the terrified man unloosed his hold upon the squirming goat.

"To your rooms, my little ones," de Grandin commanded, his round, blazing eyes traveling from one trembling girl to another. "Be not deceived, God is not mocked. Evil communications corrupt good manners—*parbleu, Monsieur*, I do refer to you and no one else—" he glowered at the professor. "And you, Mademoiselle," he called to the kneeling girl, "do you put down that dish and have nothing to do with this sacrifice of blood. Do as I say. I, Jules de Grandin, command it!

"Now, *Monsieur le Professeur*," he waved his pistol to enforce his order, "do you come with me and explore these grounds. If we find your great god Pan I shall shoot his evil eyes from out his so hideous head. If we do not find him, *morbleu*, it were better for you that we find him, I damn think!"

"Get outa my house!" Professor Judson's mantle of culture ripped away, revealing the coarse fibre beneath it; "I'll not have any dam' Frenchman comin' around here an'—"

"Softly, *Monsieur*, softly; you will please remember there are ladies present," de Grandin admonished, motioning toward the door with his pistol. "Will you come with me, or must I so dispose of you that you can not ran away until I return? I could most easily shoot through one of your fat legs."

Professor Judson left the altar of Pan and accompanied de Grandin into the night. I do not know what took place out under the stars, but when the Frenchman returned some ten minutes later, he carried the inert form of the eleventh young woman in his arms, and the professor was not with him.

"Quickly, Friend Trowbridge," he commanded as he laid the girl on the pavement, "give me some of the wine left from our supper. It will help this poor one, I think. Meantime"—he swung his fierce, unwinking gaze about the clustering circle of girls—"do you young ladies assume garments more fitted for this day and age, and prepare to evacuate this house of hell in the morning. Dr. Trowbridge and I shall remain here until the day, and tomorrow we notify the police that this place is permanently closed forever."

I T WAS A GRIM, hard task we had bringing the unconscious girl out of her swoon, but patience and the indomitable determination of Jules de Grandin finally induced a return of consciousness.

"Oh, oh, I saw Pan—Pan looked at me from the leaves!" the poor child sobbed hysterically as she opened her eyes.

"Non, non, ma chère," de Grandin assured her. "'Twas but a papier-mâché mask which the so odious one placed in the branches of the bush to terrify you. Behold, I will bring it to you that you may touch it, and know it for the harmless thing it is!"

He darted to the doorway of the temple, returning instantly with the hideous mask of a long, leering face, grinning mouth stretched from pointed ear to pointed ear, short horns rising from the temples and upward-slanting eyes glaring in fiendish malignancy. "It is ugly, I grant you," he admitted, flinging the thing upon the pavement and grinding it beneath his heavily booted heel, "but see, the foot of one who fears them not is mightier than all the gods of heathendom. Is it not so?"

The girl smiled faintly and nodded.

D E GRANDIN WAS OUT of the house at sunup, and returned before nine o'clock with a fleet of motor cars hastily commandeered from a roadhouse garage which he discovered a couple of miles down the road. "Remember, Mesdemoiselles," he admonished as the cars swung away from the portico of the temple with the erstwhile pupils of the School of Neopaganism, "those wills and testaments, they must be revoked forthwith. The detestable one, he has the present copies, but any will which you wish to make will revoke those he holds. Leave your money to found a vocal school for Thomas cats, or for a gymnasium for teaching young frogs to leap, but bequeath it to some other cause than this temple of false gods, I do implore you."

"Ready, sport?" the driver of the car reserved for us demanded, lighting a cigarette and flipping the match toward the temple steps with a disdainful gesture.

"In one moment, my excellent one," de Grandin answered as he turned from me and hurried into the house. "Await me, Friend Trowbridge," he called over his shoulder; "I have an important mission to perform."

"WHAT THE DICKENS DID you run back into that place for when the chauffeur was all ready to drive us away?" I demanded as we bowled over the smooth road toward the railway station.

He turned his unwinking cat's stare on me a moment, then his little blue eyes sparkled with a gleam of elfin laughter. "*Pardieu*, my friend," he chuckled, "that Professor Judson, I found a trunkful of his clothes in the room he occupied, and paused to burn them all. Death of my life, I did rout him from the premises in that Greek costume he wore last night, and when he returns he will find naught but glowing embers of his modern garments! What a figure he will cut, walking into a haberdasher's clothed like Monsieur Nero, and asking for a suit of clothes. *La, la*, could we but take a motion picture of him, our eternal fortunes would be made!"

The Grinning Mummy

"I S THAT YOU, DE Grandin!" I called as the front door's slam was followed by the sound of quick footsteps on the polished boards of the hall floor.

"No!" an irate voice responded as my friend, Professor Frank Butterbaugh, strode into my study. "'Pologize for comin' in without knockin', Trowbridge," he offered in excuse, "but I'm too confounded mad to pay 'tention to the amenities right now. Look at this, will you? Look at this dam', impertinent—" he broke off, choking with choler, and gave the paper another bellicose flourish. "Of all the unqualified, unmitigated—"

"What is it?" I queried, reaching for the offending document.

"What is it?" he echoed. "It's an outrage, a disgraceful outrage, that's what it is. Listen to this." Snatching at the wide black ribbon looped about his neck, he dragged a pair of gold-and-tortoise-shell pince-nez from the pocket of his white waistcoat, thrust them on his high-bridged nose with a savage, chopping motion, and read in a voice crackling with indignation:

Dr. Frank Butterbaugh,
The Beeches,
Harrisonville, New Jersey.

Dear Dr. Butterbaugh:

The tombstone you ordered for your lot in Rosedale Cemetery has been prepared in accordance with your directions, and is now ready for delivery. We shall be obliged if you will indicate when you will meet our representative at the cemetery and direct where you wish the monument placed.

In accordance with your order, the stone has been inscribed

DR. FRANCIS BUTTERBAUGH
August 23, 1852—October 18, 1926

Cave Iram Deorum
Very truly yours,
ELGRACE MONUMENT WORKS.

"Well—" I began, but he shouted me down.

"'Well', the devil!" he rasped. "It isn't well. I got that note in today's afternoon delivery, and came into town hot-foot to give the Elgrace people boiling hell for writing me such balderdash. Found they'd shut up shop for the day, so got John Elgrace on the 'phone at his house and made the wires sizzle with the dressing-down I gave him, and he had the brass-bound, copper-riveted gall to tell me he'd acted on my orders. My *orders*, d'ye understand? Claimed to have my written authority for preparing a monument for my family plot, and—"

"And he didn't?" I cut in incredulously. "You mean this letter is the first inkling you've had of a tombstone—"

"Sulfur and brimstone, yes!" the professor yelled. "D'ye think I wouldn't have remembered if I'd ordered a headstone for my own grave?—that's what it amounts to, for my name's on the thing. And what the triple-horned devil would I have had today's date cut on it for? Today's October eighteenth, in case you've forgotten it. And why in blazing Tophet should I have anything as silly as '*Cave Iram Deorum*' on my tombstone, even if I had a rush of bone to the head and ordered the dam' thing?"

"Wait a moment, professor," I asked. "I'm a little rusty on my Latin, '*Cave Iram Deorum*'—let's see, that means—"

"It means 'Beware the Wrath of the Gods,' if that is what you're after," he shot back, "but that's of no importance. What I'd like to know is who the devil dared order a tombstone in my name—"

"*Pardonnez-moi, Monsieur*, perhaps it is that someone makes *la mauvasse plaisanterie*—how do you say it? the practical joke?—upon you." Jules de Grandin, very debonair in faultless dinner clothes, a white gardenia in his lapel and a slender ebony walking stick in his hand, stood smiling at us from the study doorway. "Trowbridge, *mon cher*," he turned to me, "I did let myself in without knocking, in order to save the excellent Nora the trouble of opening the door, and I could not well escape overhearing this gentleman's extraordinary statement. Will you not tell me more, *Monsieur?*" He regarded the professor with his round, childishly wide, blue eyes.

"More, more?" Professor Butterbaugh barked. "That's all there is; there isn't any more. Some fool with a perverted sense of humor has forged my name to an order for a tombstone. By Set and Ahriman, I'll be hanged if the Elgrace people get a red-headed cent out of *me* for it! Let 'em find out who ordered it and charge it to him!"

"Pardon, *Monsieur*, I did hear you refer to the malignant deities of Egypt and Persia; is it that you—"

"Oh, excuse me," I broke in, coming to a tardy recognition of my social obligations. "Professor Butterbaugh, this is Dr. Jules de Grandin, of the University of Paris. Dr. de Grandin, this is Professor Frank Butterbaugh, who headed—"

"*Parbleu*, yes!" de Grandin interrupted, crossing the room hurriedly, and seizing Butterbaugh's hand in both of his. "No need for further introductions, Friend Trowbridge. Who has not heard of that peerless savant, that archeologist second only to the great Boussard? The very great honor is entirely mine, *Monsieur*."

Professor Butterbaugh grinned a trifle sheepishly at the Frenchman's enthusiastic greeting, fidgeted with the monument company's letter and his glasses a moment, then reached for his hat and gloves. "Must be movin'," he ejaculated in his queer, disjointed way. "Got to get home before Alice gives me double-jointed fits. Keepin' dinner waitin', you know. Glad to've met you," he held out his hand almost diffidently to de Grandin, "mighty glad. Hope you an' Trowbridge can come over tomorrow. Got an unusual sort o' mummy I'm figurin' on startin' to unwrap tonight. Like to have you medics there when I expose the body."

"Ah?" de Grandin assented, helping himself to a cigarette. "This mummy, then, it is different—?"

"You bet it is," Butterbaugh assured him colloquially. "Don't believe there's another like it in the country. I've only seen one other of the kind—the one supposed to be Ra-nefer, in the British Museum, you know. It has no funerary statue, just linen and bitumen molded to conform to the body's contours. Had the devil's own time gettin' it out of Egypt, too. Arabs went on strike half a dozen times while we were diggin', Egyptian government tried to collar the body, an', to top the whole business, a gang o' swell-headed young Copts sent me a batch o' black-hand letters, threatenin' all sorts o' penalties unless I returned the thing to its tomb. Huh, catch me givin' up a relic literally worth its weight in gold to a crew o' half-baked Johnnies like that!"

"But, *Monsieur le Professeur*," de Grandin urged, his diminutive blond mustache bristling with excitement, "this letter, this tombstone order, it may have some relation—"

"Not a chance!" Butterbaugh scoffed. "Egypt's half-way 'round the world from here, and I've no more chance of runnin' foul o' those chaps in this town than I have of bein' bitten by a crocodile; but"—his lips tightened stubbornly and a faint flush deepened the sun-tanned hue of his face—"but if all the Egyptian secret societies from Ghizeh to Beni Hassan were camped on my front lawn, I'd start unwrappin' that mummy tonight. Yes, by Jingo, an' finish the job, too; no matter how much they howled!"

He glowered at us a moment as though he expected us to forbid him, jammed his knockabout hat over his ears, slapped his thigh pugnaciously with his motoring gloves and strode from the study, his back as stiffly straight as though a ramrod had been thrust down the collar of his Norfolk jacket.

"SOMETHING TERRIBLE HAS HAPPENED!"

"Eh, what's that?" I muttered stupidly into the transmitter of my bed-side telephone, still too immersed in sleep to understand the import of the message coming over the wire.

"This is Alice Butterbaugh, Dr. Trowbridge," the fluttering voice repeated. "Alice Butterbaugh, Professor Butterbaugh's niece. Something dreadful has happened. Uncle Frank's dead!"

"Dead?" I echoed, swinging my feet to the floor. "Why, he was over to my house this evening, and—"

"Yes, I know," she interrupted. "He told me he stopped to show you that mysterious letter he got from the Elgrace company. He was well enough then, doctor, but—but—I think—*he was murdered!* Can you come right over?"

"Of course," I promised, hanging up the receiver and hustling into my clothes.

"De Grandin," I called, opening his door on my way to the bathroom to wash the lingering sleep from my eyes with a dash of cold water, "de Grandin, Professor Butterbaugh is dead—murdered, his niece thinks."

"*Mille tonneres!*" The Frenchman was out of his bed like a jack-in-the-box popping from its case. "The half of one little minute, Friend Trowbridge"—his silk pajamas were torn from his slender white body and he struggled furiously into a white crape union suit—"do you but wait until I have applied the water to my face, the brush to my hair and the wax to my mustache—*nom d'un cochon!* where is that wax?" He had drawn on socks, trousers and boots, as he talked, and was already before the washstand, a bath sponge, dripping with cold water, in one hand, a face towel in the other.

"Fly, my friend, hasten to the telephone and advise the good Sergeant Costello what has occurred," he admonished. "I would that he meets us at the professor's house. *Pardieu,* if some scoundrel has taken the life of that so great scholar, I, Jules de Grandin, will track him down and deliver him to justice— yes, though he takes refuge beneath the throne of Satan himself!"

Ten minutes later we were riding furiously toward the sinking moon over the smooth macadam road which led to The Beeches.

HER PRETTY YELLOW HAIR in attractive disorder, an orchid negligée drawn over her filmy nightdress—and French-heeled satin mules of the same color on her little white feet, Alice Butterbaugh met us in the wide reception hall of The Beeches, a very much frightened and entirely inarticulate butler at her elbow.

"Oh, Dr. Trowbridge," she sobbed, seizing my arm in both her small hands, "I'm so glad you got here! I—" She started back, folding the negligée across her diaphanous nightrobe as she became aware of de Grandin's presence. "This is Dr. Jules de Grandin, my dear," I introduced. "He is a member of the faculty of the University of Paris, and has been stopping with me for a while. He will be of great assistance in case it develops your uncle met with foul play."

"How do you do, Dr. de Grandin?" Alice acknowledged, extending her hand. "I am sure you will be able to help us in our trouble."

"*Mademoiselle*," de Grandin bowed his sleek blond head as he pressed his lips to her fingers, "*commandez-moi: j' suis prêt.*

"And now"—his air of gallantry fell from him like a cloak as he straightened his shoulders—"will you be good enough to take us to the scene and tell us all?"

"I'd gone to bed," the girl began as she led the way toward her uncle's library. "Uncle Frank was terribly excited all afternoon after he received that letter, and when he came back from Harrisonville he was still boiling inwardly. I could hardly get him to eat any dinner. Just as soon as dinner was over he went to the library where he has been keeping the latest addition to his collection of mummies, and told me he was going to begin unpacking it.

"I went to bed about half-past eleven and called good-night to him through the library door as I passed. I went to sleep almost immediately, but something—I don't know what, but I'm sure it was not a noise of any kind—woke me up a few minutes after two. I lay there trying to get back to sleep until nearly three, then decided to go to the bathroom for a bromide tablet. As I walked down the passage I noticed a light shining out of the library door into the lower hall, so I knew the door must be open.

"Uncle never left the door unclosed when he was working, for he hated to have the servants look in at him, and they would stand in the passage and stare if they thought he doing anything with his mummies—it seemed to fascinate them. Knowing Uncle's habits, I thought he had gone to bed without shutting off the light, and went down to turn it out. When I got here I found—" She paused beside the door with averted eyes and motioned toward the room beyond.

Professor Butterbaugh lay on his back, staring with sightless, dead eyes at the glowing globes of the electric chandelier, his body straight and stiff, legs extended, arms lying at his sides, as though he had fallen backward from an upright position and remained immovable since his fall. Despite the post-mortem flaccidity of his features, his countenance retained something of the expression it must have worn when death touched him, and, gazing at his face, it seemed to me he looked more startled than frightened or angry. Nowhere was there evidence of any sort of struggle; not so much as a paper was disturbed on the big, flat-topped desk beside which the dead scientist lay, and the only witness testifying to tragedy was the still, inert remnant of what had been one of the world's foremost Egyptologists some three or four hours before.

"Beg pardon, Miss Alice," the pale-faced man-servant, trousers and coat pulled over his night-clothes, tip-toed toward the professor's niece, "there's a gentleman outside, a Sergeant Costello, from the police department—"

"The police!" the girl's pallid face went paler still. "Wh—what are the police doing here—who told them?"

"I—I don't know, Miss," the serving man stammered.

"I did notify the good sergeant, *Mademoiselle*," de Grandin announced, looking up from beside the professor's body.

"Send him to me at once, immediately, right away," he ordered the butler, and walked quickly to the door to greet the burly, red-headed Irishman.

"*Holà*, my friend," he called as the detective crossed the hall, "we have here a wicked business to investigate. Some miscreant has struck down your famous fellow townsman from the back, and—"

"H'm, from th' back, is it?" Costello replied, looking meditatively at Butterbaugh's supine form. "An' how d'ye make that out, Dr. de Grandin? Seems to me there's no marks o' violence on th' body at all, an' th' pore gentleman died from natural causes. Apoplexy, it was, belike. He was a peppery-tempered old divil, God rest his soul!"

"Apoplexy, yes," de Grandin agreed with a mirthless smile, "since apoplexy is only a general name for the condition more definitely called cerebral hemorrhage. Behold the cause of this apoplexy, my friend." Stooping, he raised the professor's head, pointing to the occipital region. Against the dead man's smoothly brushed iron-gray hair lay a stain of blood, scarcely larger than a twenty-five cent piece, and so meager in its moisture that the Turkish rug on which the head had rested showed hardly any discoloration. Parting the hair, de Grandin showed a small, smooth-edged wound about the caliber of an ordinary lead-pencil, a bit of whitish substance welling up to the very edge of the opening and all but stopping any blood-flow from inside the head.

"Gun?" Costello bent to examine the puncture.

"I do not think so," the Frenchman replied. "Had a shot been fired from a pistol at close range or a rifle from a distance the bullet would probably have gone out of the head, yet there is only one wound here. Had a firearm of low power, unable to drive the missile through the head, been used, the bone would have shattered at the point of entrance, yet here we have a clean-cut wound. No, my friend, this injury is the result of some hand-weapon. Besides, Mademoiselle Butterbaugh was in the house, as were also the servants, yet none recalls having heard a shot fired.

"*Mademoiselle*," he rose from his examination of the body, "you did mention that your uncle was unwrapping a certain mummy tonight. This mummy, where is it, if you please?"

"I—I don't know," the girl faltered. "I thought it was in here, but—"

"But it is not," de Grandin supplied dryly. "Come, *mes amis*, let us search for this missing cadaver. There are times when the dead can tell us more than the living."

We crossed the library, passed between a pair of heavy brocade curtains, and entered a smaller room walled with smooth plaster, its only furniture being a series of glass cases containing small specimens of Egyptiana and a rank of upright mummy cases standing straight and sentinel-like against the farther wall. "Howly mither!" Costello exclaimed, his native brogue cutting through his acquired American accent, as he pointed one hand toward one of the mummy cases, signing himself piously with the cross with the other.

The center figure in the rank of mummies stood in a case somewhat taller than its fellows, and, unlike the others, was not hidden from view by a coffin lid, for the cover from its case had fallen to the floor, disclosing the mummy to our gaze. The body had been almost entirely denuded of its bandages, the face, arms and lower portion of the legs having been freed, so that, had it been a living man instead of a corpse, neither walking nor the use of the arms would have been impeded by the linen bands which remained in place. This much I saw at a glance, but the cause of Costello's outcry was not plain until I had looked a second time. Then I added my amazed gasp to the big Irishman's exclamation, for in the right hand of the dead thing was firmly grasped a rod of polished wood tipped by a hawk's head executed in metal, the bird's beak being some three inches in length, curved and sharp as the hooked needles used by upholsterers to sew heavy fabrics. Upon the metal point of the beak was a faintly perceptible smear of blood, and a drop of the grisly liquid had fallen to the floor, making a tiny, dark-red stain at the mummy's desiccated feet.

And on the mummy's face, drawn by the embalming process into a sort of sardonic grin, was another reddish smear, as, though the dead thing had bent its lips to the wound inflicted by the instrument clutched in its dead hand.

"*Pardieu*, Friend Trowbridge, I think we need look no farther for the weapon which took Monsieur Butterbaugh's life," de Grandin commented, twisting the end of his mustache with a nervous gesture.

"Wuz this th' mummy th' professor wuz workin' on?" Costello demanded, turning to the butler, who had followed us to the door of the specimen room.

"Oh, my Gawd!" the servant exclaimed with a shudder as he beheld the armed and sneering cadaver standing in its case, one mummified foot slightly advanced, as though the thing were about to step into the room in search of fresh victims.

"Never mind th' bawlin'," Costello ordered; "answer me question. Wuz this th' mummy Professor Butterbaugh wuz unwrappin, when—when it happened to him?"

"I don't know, sir," the servant quavered. "I never saw the thing before, an', s'welp me Gawd, I never want to see it again. But I think it must be the one Dr. Butterbaugh had in mind, for there are five mummies there now, and this mornin', when I came in to open the blinds, there were only four standin' against the walls and one was layin' on the floor over by the door."

"Humph, guess this is th' one, then," Costello replied. "Go outside there an' git th' other servants. Tell 'em I want to question 'em, an' *don't tell what you've seen here.*"

De Grandin walked quickly to the grinning mummy and examined the pointed instrument in its hand minutely. "*Très bien,*" he murmured to himself, giving the relic room a final appraising glance.

"Aren't you going to look into those other mummy cases?" I asked as he turned to leave.

"Not I," he denied. "Let Sergeant Costello busy himself with them. Me, I have other matters of more importance to attend to. Come, let us examine the servants."

The cook, a large and very frightened Negress, a diminutive and likewise badly frightened colored boy who tended the garden and acted as chauffeur, two white maids, both safely past the heyday of youth, and the butler composed the domestic staff of The Beeches. Costello marshaled them in line and began a series of searching questions, but de Grandin, after a single look at the crowd, approached the sergeant and excused himself, saying we would talk the matter over the following morning.

"Thank you, sor," Costello acknowledged: "I take it kindly of ye to see that I got th' first look-in on this case before anny of th' newspaper boys had a chanst to spoil it. I'll be comin' over to your house tomorrow an' we'll go over all th' evidence together, so we will."

"*Très excellent,*" de Grandin agreed. "Good night, Sergeant. I am not sure, but I think we shall soon have these murderers beneath the lock and key of your so efficiently strong jail."

"Murderers?" Costello echoed. "Ye think there wuz more 'n one of 'em, then, sor?"

"*Parbleu,* yes; I know it," de Grandin responded. "Good night, *mon vieux.*"

"WELL, DR. DE GRANDIN," Sergeant Costello announced as he entered my office the following afternoon, "we've got about as far as we can with th' case."

"Ah," de Grandin smiled pleasantly as he pushed a box of cigars across the table, "and what have you discovered, *cher Sergent?*"

"Well, sor," the Irishman grinned deprecatingly, "I can't rightly say we've found out much of annythin', precisely. F'r instance, we've found that somebody forged Professor Butterbaugh's signature to th' letter to th' Elgrace Monument Works. We put it under a lens at headquarters today, an' you can see where th' name's been traced as plain as daylight."

"Yes," de Grandin encouraged. "And have you any theory as to who forged that letter, or who killed the professor?"

"No, sor, we haven't," the detective confessed. "Between you an' me, sor, that Miss Alice may know more about th' business than she lets on. I wouldn't say she wuz exactly glad to see me when I come last night, an', an'—well, she hasn't been anny too helpful. This mornin', when I wuz puttin' th' servants through their paces agin, to see if there wuz anny discrepancies between th' stories they told last night an' what they might be sayin' this time, she ups an' says, says she, 'Officer,' she says, 'you've been over all that before,' she says, 'an' I'll not have my servants hu-milly-ated,' she says, 'by havin' you ask 'em every few hours which one of 'em killed me uncle.'

"So I ups an' says, 'All right, Miss. I don't suppose *you* have anny suspicions concernin' who killed him?' An' she says, 'Certainly *not!*' just like that. An' that wuz that, sor.

"Now, don't you be gittin' me wrong, Dr. de Grandin an' Dr. Trowbridge. Miss Butterbaugh is a high-toned lady, an' all that, an' I'm not makin' anny wise cracks about her bein' guilty, or even havin' guilty knowledge: but—"

The sharp staccato of my office 'phone cut his statement in half. "Hello?" I called tentatively, as I lifted the receiver.

"Sergeant Costello; I want to speak to Sergeant Costello," an excited voice demanded. "This is Schultz speaking."

"All right," I replied, passing the instrument to the sergeant.

"Hello?" Costello growled, "Yes, Schultz, this is Costello, what's—*what?* When? Oh, it did, did it? Yes, you bet your sweet life I'll be right over, an' you'd best git busy and cook up a sweet young alibi by th' time I git there, too, young felly me lad!

"Gentlemen," he turned a blank face to us, "that wuz Schultz, th' uniformed man I'd left on duty at Th' Beeches. He tells me that mummy—th' one with th' little pickax in its hand—has disappeared from th' house, right before his eyes."

"*Tout les démons!*" de Grandin cried, springing from his chair. "I expected this. Come, my friends; let us hasten, let us speed, let us fly! *Parbleu,* but the trail may not yet have grown cold!"

"I WAS MAKING MY ROUNDS, as you told me, sir," Patrolman Schultz explained to Sergeant Costello. "I'd been through the house and looked in on that queer-lookin' mummy in the little room, and seen everything was in order, then

I went out to the garage. Julius, the chauffeur, was telling me that he was going to quit his job as soon as the police investigation was done, 'cause he wouldn't dare live here after what's happened, and I was wondering if he was suffering from a guilty conscience, or what, so I stopped to talk to him and see what he'd say. I couldn't a' been outside more than fifteen minutes, all told, and I came right back in the house; but that mummy was clean gone when I got back."

"Oh, it wuz, wuz it?" Costello answered sarcastically. "I don't suppose you heard it hollerin' for help while it wuz bein' kidnaped, or annythin' like that while you wuz out Sherlock Holmesin' th' chauffeur, did you? O' course not! You wuz too busy, playin' Ol' King Brady to pay attention to your regular duties. Well, now, young felly, let me tell you somethin'. We'll find that missin' mummy, an' we'll find him toot sweet, as Dr. de Grandin would say, or badge number six hundred an' eighty-seven will be turned in at headquarters tonight, d'ye git me?"

He turned on his heel and walked toward the house, leaving the crestfallen young patrolman staring helplessly after him.

We were about to follow him when the rattle of a Ford delivery wagon on the gravel driveway drew our attention. A young man in white apron and jacket jumped from the machine and approached the service porch, a basket of groceries on his arm.

"Sorry to keep your order waitin'," he told the cook as he handed her the hamper and a duplicate sales slip for her signature, "but I liked to got kilt comin' up th' road about twenty minutes ago. I was drivin' out th' pike slow an' easy when a big touring car shot outa th' lane an' crowded me into the ditch. If I hadn't had my foot on th' gas an' been able to skedaddle outa th' way before they ran me down I'd most likely a' been killed, an' maybe th' cake-eater an' Sheba in th' other car, as well."

"Where was it you had this so close escape?" de Grandin asked, approaching the youth with an ingratiating smile.

"Down th' road a piece," the other replied, nothing loth to dilate on his adventure. "You know, there's a lane that skirts th' edge of Professor Butterbaugh's place an' runs out to th' pike near Twin Pines. There's a tall hedge growin' on each side of th' lane where it comes out on th' pike, an' these folks musta been throwin' a neckin' party or sumpin up there, for they was runnin' in low—kind o' sneakin' along—not makin' a bit o' noise till they was within a few feet of th' main road, then they stepped on her for fair, an' come out into th' highway runnin' like a scairt dawg."

"Indeed?" de Grandin raised sympathetic eyebrows. "And did you notice the people in this car? They should be arrested for such actions."

"I'll say I noticed 'em," the grocery boy answered with an emphatic nod. "The sheik who was drivin' was one o' them lounge-lizards with patent leather hair, an' th' Jane was little an' dark, with big eyes an' a sort o' sneery look. She was holdin' sumpin in her lap; looked like it might o' been another girl's head, or sumpin. Anyways, it was all covered up with cloth. An' they didn't even excuse theirselves for crowdin' me into the ditch—just went on down th' road toward Morristown like greased lightnin'."

De Grandin's little mustache was twitching with eagerness, like the whiskers of a tomcat before a rat-hole, but his voice was casual as he asked, "And did you notice the number of this car which so nearly wrecked you, *mon petit?*"

"Whassat?" the other replied suspiciously.

"Did you make note of their license plate?"

"You betcha," the lad produced a brown-paper-backed note-book, obviously intended for emergency orders from his patrons, and thumbed through its dog-eared leaves. "Yep, here it is—Y 453-677-5344. New Jersey plate."

"Ah, my excellent one, my incomparable little cabbage!" de Grandin restrained himself from kissing the white-aproned youth with the utmost difficulty. "My Napoleon among *épiciers*—behold, I shall make restitution for the fright these miscreants have given you!" From his trousers pocket he produced a billfold and extracted a five-dollar note, which he pressed into the delivery boy's hand. "Take it, my wise one," he urged, quite unnecessarily—"Take it and buy a plaything for one of your numerous sweethearts. *Pardieu*, such a well-favored youth must play the devil with the maidens' hearts, *n'est-ce-pas?*" He thrust a playful finger into the astonished youngster's ribs. "Sure," the other responded, pocketing the bill and backing away rather hastily. "Sure, I gotta jane; d'ye think I'm a dead one?"

"*Nom d'un coq*, quite otherwise; you do possess the eye of Argus and the sagacity of Solon, *mon brave*," de Grandin assured him, then, to me:

"Come, Trowbridge, my friend, let us fly with all celerity to the lane of which this so charming urchin has told us. Let us discover what we can see!"

We ran across the wide lawn to the tall, rank-growing privet hedge which marked the margin of the Butterbaugh place, slipped through the shrubbery, and began walking slowly, down the unpaved roadway.

"*Nom de Dieu*, we have it!" the Frenchman exclaimed, pointing dramatically to the soft sand at out feet. "Behold, Friend Trowbridge, where a car, even as described by the youthful Solomon, has been driven up this path and turned about at this point. Also, observe how two pairs of feet, one shod in wide-soled shoes, the other in slippers with the French heels, have walked from that car to the hedge, and—here, do you not see it?—back again, *and with wider steps and deeper impressions in the earth. Parbleu*, my friend, our noses are to the earth. Anon we shall bring the quarry into view!"

Slipping through the hedge, he ran at top speed to the house, entered one of the open French windows and called excitedly for Costello.

"Quick, *mon vieux*," he urged when the sergeant came in answer to his repeated hails, "we must delay the expedition. I would that you broadcast by telephone an alarm to all towns and villages in the direction of Morristown to have a touring car bearing the New Jersey license Y 453-677-5344 stopped at all costs. It must be delayed, it must be held, it must be impeded until I arrive!"

Costello regarded him in open-mouthed wonder, but proceeded to telephone headquarters to post a general lookout for the wanted car.

"An' now, Dr. de Grandin, sor," he whispered, "if you'd be good enough to lend me a bit of a hand in questionin' these here servants, I believe we could git somethin' outa them. They're beginnin' to weaken."

"Ah, bah," de Grandin replied. "Waste not your breath on these innocent ones, my friend. We shall be within reaching distance of these criminals when that car has been apprehended. In truth, they did fit the description to a perfection."

"Description?" echoed the sergeant. "What description? Has someone been spillin' th' beans to you, sor?"

"Ha, yes, someone has talked to me, in silence," de Grandin replied. "There were at least two people in the library with Professor Butterbaugh when he was killed, and one of them, at least, had straight hair, smoothed down with some sort of unguent—hair, moreover, which had been cut about two weeks ago. This person must have been somewhat shorter than the professor, and must have stood immediately before him when he was struck down from behind—"

Sergeant Costello looked at him a moment in speechless wonder, then an ingratiating grin spread over his face. He rose, facing de Grandin with upraised forefinger, like an adult telling a fable to a dubious youngster. "An' th' wolf said to Little Red Riding Hood, 'Where are ye goin', me pret-ty child,'" he interrupted. "I've seen ye do a lot o' things which I'd a' thought wuz magic if I hadn't seen 'em with me own two eyes, Dr. de Grandin," he confessed, "but when ye go into a trance like that an' begin fortune-tellin' about how many people wuz present when th' professor was kilt, an' how long it had been since one of 'em had his hair cut, I'm havin' to remind ye that it's been many a year since I believed in fairy-tales, sor."

"Fairy-tales, do you say?" de Grandin returned good-naturedly. "*Parbleu*, my friend, do not you know that the most improbable of the tales of the fairies is sober logic itself beside the seemingly impossible miracles which science performs each day? *Nom d'un porc*, a hundred years ago men were hanged as wizards for knowing not one-tenth as much as Jules de Grandin has forgotten these twenty years!

"Amuse yourself, *cher Sergent*. Question the servants to your heart's content; but be ready to accompany me the minute that missing car is reported caught, I do entreat you."

"It's th' Templeton police department speakin', Dr. de Grandin," Costello announced some three-quarters of an hour later as he looked up from the telephone. "Will ye be talkin' to 'em, sor? Sure, I haven't th' ghost of an idea what it is you're wantin' with th' young lad and lady that wuz ridin' in th' car ye wanted held up."

"*Allo, allo!*" de Grandin barked into the telephone as he snatched the receiver from the sergeant's hand. "This is Jules de Grandin speaking, *Monsieur le Chef*. You have the occupants of that car in custody? *Bien*, you do delight me! Charge? *Parbleu*, I had forgotten that you require a specific charge on which to hold persons in custody in this country. Tell me, *Monsieur*, you have searched that car, no?" A pause, during which he drummed nervously, on the telephone table with the tips of his slender white fingers, then:

"Ah, so? *Très bien*, I and Sergeant Costello, of the Harrisonville police, come on the wings of the wind to relieve you of your prisoners. Responsibility? But of course. Hold them, my friend. Place them under the double lock, with gendarmes at door and window, and I shall indubitably indemnify you against all responsibility. Only, I beseech you, hold them in safety until we arrive."

He turned to us, his small blue eyes sparkling with excitement. "Come, my friends, come away; let us make haste to that commandant of police at Templeton. He has there the birds for our cage!"

We jumped into my waiting car and turned toward Templeton, Costello sitting in the tonneau, a black cigar at a rakish angle in his mouth, an expression of doubt on his face; de Grandin beside me, drumming on the leather upholstery of the seat and humming excitedly to himself.

"What's it all about, de Grandin?" I asked as, responding to his urging, I pressed my foot on the accelerator and drove the machine several miles beyond the legal speed.

"Mean? Mean?" he answered, turning a twitching face and dancing eyes on me. "Possess yourself in patience, my friend. Restrain your curiosity for only a few little minutes. Curb your inquisitiveness only so long as it takes this abominably slow *moteur* to convey us to that police chief at Templeton. Then—*parbleu!*—you shall know. Yes, *par la barbe du prophète*, you and the good Costello, too, shall know all—all!" He threw back his head and burst into a snatch of marching song:

Elle rit, C'est tout l' mal qu'elle sait faire,
Madelon, Madelon, Madelon!

"We've got 'em locked in there," the Templeton police chief told us when I brought my panting motor to a halt before the little town's near graystone municipal building. "Far's I can see, there's no charge you can hold 'em on, legally, and there's apt to be some trouble over this business.

"Sure, we found a mummy in the car"—in response to de Grandin's eager question—"but I don't know any law against transporting a mummy through the streets. Go in and talk to 'em, if you want to, but make it snappy, and remember; if there's any comeback about a false arrest or anything like that, it's strictly your funeral."

"*Parbleu, Monsieur le Chef*," de Grandin replied with a smile, "it is like to be a double funeral, with the State of New Jersey officiating, unless Jules de Grandin is more mistaken than he thinks he is!"

T WO PEOPLE, A YOUNG man of twenty-five or twenty-six and a young woman of about the same age, sat on the polished oak benches of the municipal council room which the Templeton police chief had turned into an improvised dungeon for their detention. The man was dressed with that precise attention to detail which characterizes the better-class foreigner, while the woman's mod-ish traveling costume was more reminiscent of the Rue de la Paix than of the dressmakers of America. Both were dark-skinned with the clear olive complex-ion of the South, black-eyed, and patrician of feature. And despite their air of hauteur, they were plainly ill at ease.

"This is an outrage!" the man burst forth in a perfectly accentless voice which proclaimed more plainly than faulty speech that the words he used were not of his mother tongue. "This is an outrage, sir. What right have you to hold us here against our will?"

De Grandin fixed him with a level stare, rigid and uncompromising as a pointed bayonet. "And the murder of a respected citizen of this country, *Mon-sieur*," he asked, "is that, perhaps, not also an outrage?"

"What do you mean—?" the man began, but the Frenchman cut him off curtly.

"You and your companion did enter the house of Professor Francis Butter-baugh last night, or more definitely, early this morning," he replied, "and one of you did engage him in conversation while the other took the scepter of Isis from the wrappings of the mummy and struck him with it—from behind. Do not lie to me, my Egyptian friend; your tongue may be false—*cordieu*, are you not a nation of liars?—but the hairs of your head tell the truth. *Parbleu*, you did not think that your victim would throw out his arm at the moment you murdered him and seize evidence which would put the rope of justice about your necks. You did not apprehend that I, Jules de Grandin, would be at hand to deliver you to the public executioner, *hein?*"

The prisoners stared at him in astonished silence. Then: "You have no proof that we were near Butterbaugh's house last night," the man answered, moving a step toward a sheeted object which lay on one of the council benches.

De Grandin smiled unpleasantly. "No proof, do you say?" he returned. "*Pardieu*, I have all the proof needed to put you both to a shameful death. I have—Trowbridge, Costello, stop him!"

He flung himself at the prisoner, who had rounded the end of the bench and reached suddenly toward the thing under the sheet, drawn forth a tiny, wriggling object, and pressed it quickly to his wrist.

"Too late," the man observed, holding out his hand to the woman beside him and sinking to the bench beside the sheeted object. "Dr. Jules de Grandin is too late!"

The young woman hesitated the fraction of a second as her fingers met those of her companion, then, with widening eyes, thrust her hand into the low-cut bosom of her dress, drew herself up very straight, and, as a slight shiver ran through her frame, dropped to the bench beside the man.

"*Dieu et le diable!*" de Grandin swore furiously. "You have cheated me! I—back, Friend Trowbridge, back, *Sergent*; there is death on the floor!"

He cannoned into me, sending me stumbling toward the row of council seats, poised himself on tiptoe, and leaped lithely into the air, coming down with both feet close together, grinding his heels savagely on the floor. Beneath the edge of his boot sole I made out the sharp-pointed, thrashing end of some small, cylindrical object.

"Five thousand years of life, in death, and now eternal death beneath the feet of Jules de Grandin." he announced, stepping back and revealing a short, black thing, scarcely thicker through its crushed body than an angle worm, and no longer than a man's hand.

"What is it, sor?" Costello queried, looking at the still-writhing thing disclosed by the Frenchman's lifted foot.

"I blame you not for failing to recognize him, *cher Sergent*," the other replied; "the good St. Patrick did drive him and all his family from your native land some fifteen hundred years ago."

To me he said: "Friend Trowbridge, before you lies what remains of such a snake as did kill Cleopatra, no less. To discourage robbers from the graves of their great ones, I have heard, the Egyptians did sometimes secrete the comatose bodies of serpents among the wrappings of their mummies. I have often heard such tales, but never before have I seen evidence of their truth. Like the toad, and the frog, who are found within fossil rocks, the snake has the ability to live indefinitely in suspended animation. When these miscreants did expose this viper to the air he was revived, and I make no doubt they allowed him to live against just such a contingency as this.

"Do you desire more proof? Is not their double suicide a confession sufficient of guilt?" He turned questioning eyes from Costello to me, then glared at the prisoners shivering on the bench beside the sheeted object.

"What's this?" Costello demanded, striding to the seat where the man and woman sat and snatching the sheet from the form beside them.

"Howly St. Judas, 'tis th' grinnin' mummy itself!" he exclaimed as he bared the sardonically smiling features of the thing we had seen in Professor Butterbaugh's relic room the night of his murder.

"But of course," de Grandin replied, "what else! Did I not surmise an much when that young grocery man told us of the fleeing couple in the motor car? And did I not have you send out the alarm for the detention of that same car? And did I not particularly question the police chief of this city concerning the presence of a mummy in the motor when he did inform me that he had apprehended our fugitives? Most assuredly. Me, I am Jules de Grandin. I do not make mistakes."

He directed a quizzical gaze at the prisoners. "Your time grows short," he stated. "Will you confess now, or must I assure you that I shall cut your hearts from out your dead bodies and feed them to carrion crows? Remember, I am a medical man, and my request that I be allowed to perform an autopsy on you will unquestionably be honored. You will confess; or—" he waved an eloquent hand, the gesture expressing unpleasant possibilities.

The man twisted his thin lips in a mirthless grin. "You may as well know," he replied, "but we must be assured our ashes will be taken to Egypt for burial before I tell you anything."

The Frenchman raised his hand. "You have my assurance of that if you tell all, and my equal assurance that you shall be dissected as subjects of anatomical study if you do not," he promised. "Come, begin. Time presses and there is much to tell. Make haste."

"IT DOES NOT MATTER who we are, you can find our names and residences from our papers," the prisoner began. "As to what we are, you have perhaps heard of the movement to revive the secret worship of the old gods of Egypt among those who trace their ancestry to the ancient rulers of the earth?"

De Grandin nodded shortly.

"We are members of that movement," the man continued, "We Copts possess the blood of Ramses, mighty ruler of the world of Tut-ankh-amen and Ra-nefer; our race was old and glorious when Babylon was a swamp and you Franks were only naked savages. Pagan Greek and pagan Roman, Christian Frank and Moslem Arab—all have swarmed in upon us, forcing their religions down our throats at the sword's point, but our hearts have remained constant to the gods we worshiped in the days of our greatness. For centuries a faithful few have done honor to Osiris and Isis, to Horus and Nut and Anubis and mighty, ram-headed Ra, father of gods and fashioner of men; but only in recent years, with the weakening of the Moslems' hated power, have we dared extend our organization. Today we have a complete hierarchy. I am a vowed servant of Osiris, my sister here is a dedicated priestess of Isis.

"That the barbarians of Europe and America should delve among the tombs of our illustrious dead and drag their sacred relics forth for fools to gape at has long been intolerable to us—as the violation of the tombs of Napoleon or Washington would be to French or Americans—but for years we have been forced to suffer these insults in silence. Before this robber, Butterbaugh, desecrated the tomb of Ankh-ma-amen"—he motioned toward the uncovered, grinning mummy on the bench beside him—"our priesthood had passed sentence of death on all who despoiled our burying places in future. The Englishman, Carnarvon, died by our orders; other tomb-robbers met their just deserts at our hands. Now you know why Butterbaugh was executed.

"We gave the thieving savage fair warning of our intent before he took the stolen body out of Egypt, but the English police—may Set burn them!—prevented our carrying out our sentence there, so we followed him to America. We had obtained a specimen of his signature in Cairo; it was easy to forge his name to the order for his tombstone.

"Last night my sister and I waited outside his house until his servants had gone to bed. We watched the thief gloating over the body of our sacred dead, saw him unwind the sacerdotal wrappings from it, and while he was still at his ghoulish work we entered an open window and read him the death sentence pronounced on him by the council of our priests. The grave-robber ordered us from his house—threatened us with arrest and would have assaulted me, but my sister, who stood behind him, struck him dead with a single blow of the holy scepter of Isis which he had taken from the cerements of the body outraged by his profane hands.

"We restored the body of Ankh-ma-amen to its case and were about to take it to our car, that we might carry it back to its tomb in Egypt, when we heard someone moving about upstairs and had to make our escape. We put the scepter of Isis in the hand of our ancestor, for it was to avenge his desecrated tomb that we put Butterbaugh to death. A smear of the robber's blood was on my sister's hand, and she wiped it off on Ankh-ma-amen's lips. It was poetic justice; our outraged countryman drank the blood of his ravisher!

"Today we returned and took our dead from the polluting atmosphere of Butterbaugh's house—while your stupid police looked on and saw nothing.

"How you discovered us we do not know, but may the lightnings of Osiris blast you; may Apepi, the serpent, crush your bones and the pestilence of Typhon wither your flesh! May—"

A convulsive shudder ran through him, he half rose from the bench, then slid forward limply, his hands clutching futilely at the withered hands of the mummy which grinned sardonically into his face.

I glanced hastily toward the girl, who had sat silent during her brother's narrative. Her jaw had dropped, her head sagged forward on her breast, and her eyes stared straight before her with the inane, fixed stare of the newly dead.

De Grandin studied the three bodies before us a long moment, then turned to Costello. "You will make what report is necessary, my friend?" he asked.

"Sure, I will, sor," the detective assented, "an' I got to hand it to ye for cleanin' up th' mystery so neat, too; but, beggin' your pardon, how d'ye intend makin' good on your promise to ship these here dead corpses back home?"

De Grandin smiled quickly. "Did you not hear him demand my promise to ship his *ashes* to Egypt?" he asked. "When the official formalities are concluded, we shall have them cremated."

"E XCUSE ME FOR BOTHERIN' you, Dr. Jules de Grandin," Costello apologized as we concluded dinner at my house that evening, "but I ain't eddycated like you an' Dr. Trowbridge here, an' there's a lot o' things that's plain as ABC to you gentlemen that don't seem to mean nothin' at all to me. Would you mind tellin' me how you figured this here case out so easy, an'"—his florid face went a shade redder—"an' excuse me for tryin' to git funny with you this after- noon when you wuz tellin' th' kind o' hair th' gink we must find had?"

"Yes, de Grandin," I urged, "tell us; I'm as much in the dark as Servant Costello."

"Glory be," the Irishman exclaimed fervently, "then I'm not the only dumb- bell in th' party!"

De Grandin turned his quick, elfish smile on each of us in turn, then knocked the ashes from his cigar into his coffee cup.

"All men have two eyes—unless they have one," he began, "and all see the same things; but not all do know what it is that they see.

"When we did go to that Professor Butterbaugh's house after he had been murdered, I did first observe the size, appearance and location of the wound whereof he died; next I did look very carefully about to see what autograph his murderers had left. Believe me, my friends, all criminals leave their visiting cards, if only the police can read them.

"*Très bien*, I did find that in the professor's right hand were clutched four or five short, black hairs—straight, glossy hairs, with traces of pomade still upon them.

"Now, at the *Faculté de Médicine Légal*, to which I have the honor to belong, we have spent much time in the study of such things. We know, for example, that in case of sudden death, especially where there has been injury done the nervous system, the body undergoes an instantaneous rigidity, making the dead hand grasp and firmly hold any object within its reach. Thus we have found sol- diers, shot on the field of battle, firmly holding their rifles; suicides clutching the pistols with which they have ended their lives, or, occasionally, drowned bodies grasping grass, weeds or gravel. Also we have learned that fragments of clothing, hair or other foreign substances clutched in a dead man's hand—unless they be from his own attire or person—indicate the presence of some other person at the instant of death, and hence point to murder rather than suicide.

"Again, we have paid much attention to the evidence borne by the location of wounds. Friend Trowbridge,"—he turned to me—"will you be so good as to take up that spoon, stand behind me, and make as though you would dash out my brains with it!"

Wonderingly, I picked up a spoon, placed myself behind him, and struck him quickly, though lightly, on the head.

"*Bon, très bon!*" he exclaimed. "Make careful note where your blow did fall, my friend.—Now, *Sergent*, will you do likewise?"

Costello obeyed, and I could not repress a start of surprise. The blow struck by Costello came into contact with the Frenchman's sleek light hair less than an inch from where my spoon had struck.

"You see?" de Grandin grinned delightedly. "Almost always it is so. Wounds of the head from axes, hammers and the like are almost invariably found on the left parietal area if the assailant is in front, if he stands behind his victim the injury will usually be found on the right side of the occiput—where both of you unconsciously struck me.

"Very well. When I did examine Professor Butterbaugh's death wound I knew he was struck down from behind.

"Excellent, so far. But if he was killed from the back, how came those hairs grasped in his hand? He could not have reached behind to seize his murderer, the hairs would not have been so clutched had the murderer first confronted him, then rushed behind to strike the fatal blow, and that wound could not possibly have been given by one standing before him. *Voilà*, there were two persons, at least, present when the professor died.

"The weapon used we found in the hand of that mummy which did grin like the cats of Cheshire, and on his lips we found a smear of blood. That, coupled with the professor's experiences in Egypt, the so mysterious tombstone which he had not ordered, and which said, 'Beware the Wrath of the Gods,' and the fact that no robbery had been attempted—all convinced me it was a killing of revenge.

"*C'est beau!* I did examine those hairs under the microscope while my good Trowbridge slept that night. Their color and texture excluded the possibility of their belonging to the professor or to any of his servants, they could not have come from the mummy's head, for he was shaven-pated, and the condition of their ends—which was slightly rounded—showed they had been cut by a barber some two weeks hence.

"I say to me: 'Suppose some person have come from Egypt to kill this Professor Butterbaugh; suppose he have come on the sea some three or four weeks; suppose, again, he are a wealthy, fastidious man, what would be one of the first things he would do when he came to shore?'

"I answer: '*Parbleu*, he would undoubtlessly have his hair cut!'

"'Correct,' I reply. 'And could he arrange to kill the professor and order a tombstone in two weeks?'

"'He could,' I respond.

"Very well. I have argued so far with myself and decided we must look for two people, one of them, at least, with brunette hair which have been cut some two weeks ago, both of them, probably, dark-skinned, because they are probably Egyptian, but not black, because the hair say he belong to a white man.

"Where shall we find these murderers in a nation of one hundred million people of many different complexions?

"'I do not know; but I shall try,' I promise me, and then—*cordieu!*—and then we meet that so charming lad from the grocery shop who tells us of the couple in the speeding car and of the young woman who holds some wrapped-up thing in her lap.

"The mummy is missing, these people speed, there are wheel tracks and footprints of a most suspicious kind in the lane by the professor's house—Friend Trowbridge and I have seen them—*parbleu*, why are not these two runaways the persons we seek?

"We did seek them, my friends, and we did find them; and though that ancient snake did cheat your executioner, we did exact their lives in payment for that of Professor Butterbaugh."

He smiled contentedly as he resumed his seat and poured a thimbleful of glowing crème de menthe over the crushed ice in his liqueur glass.

"Justice, my friends," he pronounced, "she is hard to evade. When she are accompanied by Jules de Grandin—*grand Dieu*, she are invincible!"

The Man Who Cast No Shadow

I

"BUT NO, MY FRIEND," Jules de Grandin shook his sleek blond head decidedly and grinned across the breakfast table at me, "we will go to this so kind Madame Norman's tea, of a certainty. Yes."

"But hang it all," I replied, giving Mrs. Norman's note an irritable shove with my coffee spoon, "I don't want to go to a confounded tea party! I'm too old and too sensible to dress up in a tall hat and a long coat and listen to the vaporings of a flock of silly flappers. I—"

"*Mordieu*, hear the savage!" de Grandin chuckled delightedly. "Always does he find excuses for not giving pleasure to others, and always does he frame those excuses to make him more important in his own eyes. Enough of this, Friend Trowbridge; let us go to the kind Madame Norman's party. Always there is something of interest to be seen if one but knows where to look for it."

"H'm, maybe," I replied grudgingly, "but you've better sight than I think you have if you can find anything worth seeing at an afternoon reception."

The reception was in full blast when we arrived at the Norman mansion in Tuscarora Avenue that afternoon in 192–. The air was heavy with the commingled odors of half a hundred different perfumes and the scent of hot poured jasmine tea, while the clatter of cup on saucer, laughter and buzzing conversation filled the wide hall and dining room. In the long double parlors the rugs had been rolled back and young men in frock coats glided over the polished parquetry in company with girls in provocatively short skirts to the belching melody of a saxophone and the drumming rhythm of a piano.

"*Pardieu*," de Grandin murmured as he viewed the dancers a moment, "your American youth take their pleasures with seriousness, Friend Trowbridge. Behold their faces. Never a smile, never a laugh. They might be recruits on their first parade for all the joy they show—ah!" He broke off abruptly, gazing with startled, almost horrified, eyes after a couple whirling in the mazes of a foxtrot at the farther end of the room. "*Nom d'un fromage,*" he murmured softly to himself, "this matter will bear investigating, I think!"

"Eh, what's that?" I asked, piloting him toward our hostess.

"Nothing; nothing, I do assure you," he answered as we greeted Mrs. Norman and passed toward the dining room. But I noticed his round, blue eyes strayed more than once toward the parlors as we drank our tea and exchanged amiable nothings with a pair of elderly ladies.

"Pardon," de Grandin bowed stiffly from the hips to his conversational partner and turned toward the rear drawing room, "there is a gentleman here I desire to meet, if you do not mind—that tall, distinguished one, with the young girl in pink."

"Oh, I guess you mean Count Czerny," a young man laden with an ice in one hand and a glass of non-Volstead punch in the other paused on his way from the dining room. "He's a rare bird, all right. I knew him back in '13 when the Balkan Allies were polishing off the Turks. Queer-lookin' duck, ain't he? First-class fightin' man, though. Why, I saw him lead a bayonet charge right into the Turkish lines one day, and when he'd shot his pistol empty he went at the enemy with his teeth! Yes, sir, he grabbed a Turk with both hands and bit his throat out, hanged if he didn't."

"Czerny," de Grandin repeated musingly. "He is a Pole, perhaps?"

His informant laughed a bit shamefacedly. "Can't say," he confessed. "The Serbs weren't asking embarrassing questions about volunteers' nationalities those days, and it wasn't considered healthful for any of us to do so, either. I got the impression he was a Hungarian refugee from Austrian vengeance; but that's only hearsay. Come along, I'll introduce you, if you wish."

I saw de Grandin clasp hands with the foreigner and stand talking with him for a time, and, in spite of myself I could not forbear a smile at the contrast they made.

The Frenchman was a bare five feet four inches in height, slender as a girl, and, like a girl, possessed of almost laughably small hands and feet. His light hair and fair skin, coupled with his trimly waxed diminutive blond mustache and round, unwinking blue eyes, gave him a curiously misleading appearance of mildness. His companion was at least six feet tall, swarthy-skinned and black-haired, with bristling black mustaches and fierce, slate-gray eyes set beneath beetling black brows. His large nose was like the predatory beak of some bird of prey, and the tilt of his long, pointed jaw bore out the uncompromising ferocity of the rest of his visage. Across his left cheek, extending upward over the temple and into his hair, was a knife-, or saber-scar, a streak of white showing the trail of the steel in his scalp, and shining like silver inlaid in onyx against the blue-black of his smoothly pomaded locks.

What they said was, of course, beyond reach of my ears, but I saw de Grandin's quick, impish smile flicker across his keen face more than once, to be answered by a slow, languorous smile on the other's dark countenance.

At length the count bowed formally to my friend and whirled away with a wisp of a girl, while de Grandin returned to me. At the door he paused a moment, inclining his shoulders in a salute as a couple of debutantes brushed past him. Something—I know not what—drew my attention to the tall foreigner a moment, and a sudden chill rippled up my spine at what I saw. Above the georgette-clad shoulder of his dancing partner the count's slate-gray eyes were fixed on de Grandin's trim back, and in them I read all the cold, malevolent fury with which a caged tiger regards its keeper as he passes the bars.

"What on earth did you say to that fellow?" I asked as the little Frenchman rejoined me. "He looked as if he would like to murder you."

"Ha?" he gave a questioning, single-syllabled laugh. "Did he so? Obey the noble Washington's injunction, and avoid foreign entanglements, Friend Trowbridge; it is better so, I think."

"But look here," I began, nettled by his manner, "what—"

"*Non, non,*" he interrupted, "you must be advised by me, my friend. I think it would be better if we dismissed the incident from our minds. But stay—perhaps you had better meet that gentleman, after all. I will have the good Madame Norman introduce you."

More puzzled than ever, I followed him to our hostess and waited while he requested her to present me to the count.

In a lull in the dancing she complied with his request, and the foreigner acknowledged the introduction with a brief handclasp and an almost churlish nod, then turned his back on me, continuing an animated conversation with the large-eyed young woman in an abbreviated party frock.

"And did you shake his hand?" de Grandin asked as we descended the Norman's steps to my waiting car.

"Yes, of course," I replied.

"Ah? Tell me, my friend, did you notice anything—ah—peculiar, in his grip?"

"H'm." I wrinkled my brow a moment in concentrated thought. "Yes, I believe I did."

"So? What was it?"

"Hanged if I can say, exactly," I admitted, "but—well, it seemed—this sounds absurd, I know—but it seemed as though his hand had two backs—no palm at all—if that means anything to you."

"It means much, my friend; it means a very great deal," he answered with such a solemn nod that I burst into a fit of laughter. "Believe me, it means much more than you suspect."

It must have been some two weeks later that I chanced to remark to de Grandin, "I saw your friend, Count Czerny, in New York yesterday."

"Indeed?" he answered with what seemed like more than necessary interest. "And how did he impress you at the time?"

"Oh, I just happened to pass him on Fifth Avenue," I replied. "I'd been up to see an acquaintance in Fifty-ninth Street and was turning into the avenue when I saw him driving away from the Plaza. He was with some ladies."

"No doubt," de Grandin responded dryly. "Did you notice him particularly?"

"Can't say that I did, especially," I answered, "but it seems to me he looked older than the day we met him at Mrs. Norman's."

"Yes?" the Frenchman leaned forward eagerly. "Older, do you say? *Parbleu*, this is of interest; I suspected as much!"

"Why—" I began, but he turned away with an impatient shrug. "Pah!" he exclaimed petulantly. "Friend Trowbridge, I fear Jules de Grandin is a fool, he entertains all sorts of strange notions."

I had known the little Frenchman long enough to realize that he was as full of moods as a prima donna, but his erratic, unrelated remarks were getting on my nerves. "See here, de Grandin," I began testily, "what's all this nonsense—"

The sudden shrill clatter of my office telephone bell cut me short. "Dr. Trowbridge," an agitated voice asked over the wire, "can you come right over, please? This is Mrs. Norman speaking."

"Yes, of course," I answered, reaching for my medicine case; "what is it—who's ill?"

"It's—it's Guy Eckhart, he's been taken with a fainting fit, and we don't seem to be able to rouse him."

"Very well," I promised, "Dr. de Grandin and I will be right over.

"Come on, de Grandin," I called as I shoved my hat down over my ears and shrugged into my overcoat, "one of Mrs. Norman's house guests has been taken ill; I told her we were coming."

"*Mais oui*," he agreed, hurrying into his outdoors clothes. "Is it a man or a woman, this sick one?"

"It's a man," I replied, "Guy Eckhart."

"A man," he echoed incredulously. "A man, do you say? No, no, my friend, that is not likely."

"Likely or not," I rejoined sharply, "Mrs. Norman says he's been seized with a fainting fit, and I give the lady credit for knowing what she's talking about."

"*Eh bien*," he drummed nervously on the cushions of the automobile seat, "perhaps Jules de Grandin really is a fool. After all, it is not impossible."

"It certainly isn't," I agreed fervently to myself as I set the car in motion.

Young Eckhart had recovered consciousness when we arrived, but looked like a man just emerging from a lingering fever. Attempts to get a statement from him met with no response, for he replied slowly, almost incoherently, and seemed to have no idea concerning the cause of his illness.

Mrs. Norman was little more specific. "My son Ferdinand found him lying on the floor of his bath with the shower going and the window wide open, just before dinner," she explained. "He was totally unconscious, and remained so till just a few minutes ago."

"Ha, is it so?" de Grandin murmured half heedlessly, as he made a rapid inspection of the patient.

"Friend Trowbridge," he called me to the window, "what do you make of these objective symptoms: a soft, frequent pulse, a fluttering heart, suffused eyes, a hot, dry skin and a flushed, hectic face?"

"Sounds like an arterial hemorrhage," I answered promptly, "but there's been no trace of blood on the boy's floor, nor any evidence of a stain on his clothing. Sure you've checked the signs over?"

"Absolutely," he replied with a vigorous double nod. Then to the young man: "Now, *mon enfant*, we shall inspect you, if you please."

Quickly he examined the boy's face, scalp, throat, wrists and calves, finding no evidence of even a pinprick, let alone a wound capable of causing syncope.

"*Mon Dieu*, this is strange," he muttered; "of a surety, it has the queerness of the devil! Perhaps the bleeding is internal, but—ah, *regardez vous*, Friend Trowbridge!"

He had turned down the collar of the youngster's pajama jacket, more in idle routine than in hope of discovering anything tangible, but the livid spot to which he pointed seemed the key to our mystery's outer door. Against the smooth, white flesh of the young man's left breast there showed a red, angry patch, such as might have resulted from a vacuum cup being held some time against the skin, and in the center of the discoloration was a double row of tiny punctures scarcely larger than needlepricks, arranged in horizontal divergent arcs, like a pair of parentheses laid sidewise.

"You see?" he asked simply, as though the queer, blood-infused spot explained everything.

"But he couldn't have bled much through that," I protested. "Why, the man seems almost drained dry, and these wounds wouldn't have yielded more than a cubic centimeter of blood, at most."

He nodded gravely. "Blood is not entirely colloidal, my friend," he responded. "It will penetrate the tissues to some extent, especially if sufficient force is applied."

"But it would have required a powerful suction—" I replied, when his rejoinder cut me short:

"Ha, you have said it, my friend. Suction—that is the word!"

"But what could have sucked a man's blood like this?" I was in a near-stupor of mystification.

"What, indeed?" he replied gravely. "That is for us to find out. Meantime, we are here as physicians. A quarter-grain morphine injection is—indicated here, I think. You will administer the dose; I have no license in America."

W HEN I RETURNED FROM my round of afternoon calls next day I found de Grandin seated on my front steps in close conference with Indian John.

Indian John was a town character of doubtful lineage who performed odd jobs of snow shoveling, furnace tending and grass cutting, according to season, and interspersed his manual labors with brief incursions into the mercantile field when he peddled fresh vegetables from door to door. He also peddled neighborhood gossip and retailed local lore to all who would listen, his claim to being a hundred years old giving him the standing of an indisputable authority in all matters antedating living memory.

"*Pardieu,* but you have told me much, *mon vieux,*" de Grandin declared as I came up the porch steps. He handed the old rascal a handful of silver and rose to accompany me into the house.

"Friend Trowbridge," he accused as we finished dinner that night, "you had not told me that this town grew up on the site of an early Swedish settlement."

"Never knew you wanted to know," I defended with a grin.

"You know the ancient Swedish church, perhaps," he persisted.

"Yes, that's old Christ Church," I answered. "It's down in the east end of town; don't suppose it has a hundred communicants today. Our population has made some big changes, both in complexion and creed, since the days when the Dutch and Swedes fought for possession of New Jersey."

"You will drive me to that church, right away, at once, immediately?" he demanded eagerly.

"I guess so," I agreed. "What's the matter now; Indian John been telling you a lot of fairy-tales?"

"Perhaps," he replied, regarding me with one of his steady, unwinking stares. "Not all fairy-tales are pleasant, you know. Do you recall those of *Chaperon Rouge*—how do you say it, Red Riding Hood?—and Bluebeard?"

"Huh!" I scoffed; "they're both as true as any of John's stories, I'll bet."

"Undoubtlessly," he agreed with a quick nod. "The story of Bluebeard, for instance, is unfortunately a very true tale indeed. But come, let us hasten; I would see that church tonight, if I may."

C HRIST CHURCH, THE OLD Swedish place of worship, was a combined demonstration of how firmly adz-hewn pine and walnut can resist the ravages of time and how nearly three hundred years of weather can demolish any structure erected by man. Its rough-painted walls and short, firm-based spire shone ghostly and pallid in the early spring moonlight, and the cluster of broken and weather-worn tombstones which staggered up from its unkempt burying ground were like soiled white chicks seeking shelter from a soiled white hen.

Dismounting from a car at the wicket gate of the churchyard, we made our way over the level graves, I in a maze of wonderment, de Grandin with an eagerness almost childish. Occasionally he flashed the beam from his electric torch on some monument of an early settler, bent to decipher the worn inscription, then turned away with a sigh of disappointment.

I paused to light a cigar, but dropped my half-burned match in astonishment as my companion gave vent to a cry of excited pleasure. "*Triomphe!*" he exclaimed delightedly. "Come and behold, Friend Trowbridge. Thus far your lying friend, the Indian man, has told the truth. *Regardez!*"

He was standing beside an old, weather-gnawed tombstone, once marble, perhaps, but appearing more like brown sandstone under the ray of his flashlight. Across its upper end was deeply cut the one word:

SARAH

While below the name appeared a verse of half-obliterated doggerel:

Let nonne difturb her deathleffe fleepe
Abote ye tombe wilde garlick keepe
For if fhee wake much woe will boaft
Prayfe Faither, Sonne & Holie Goaft.

"Did you bring me out here to study the orthographical eccentricities of the early settlers?" I demanded in disgust.

"Ah bah!" he returned. "Let us consult the *ecclesiastique*. He, perhaps, will ask no fool's questions."

"No, you'll do that," I answered tartly as we knocked at the rectory door.

"Pardon, Monsieur," de Grandin apologized as the white-haired old minister appeared in answer to our summons, "we do not wish to disturb you thus, but there is a matter of great import on which we would consult you. I would that you tell us what you can, if anything, concerning a certain grave in your churchyard. A grave marked 'Sarah' if you please."

"Why"—the elderly cleric was plainly taken aback—"I don't think there is anything I can tell you about it, sir. There is some mention in the early parish records, I believe, of a woman believed to have been a murderess being buried in that grave, but it seems the poor creature was more sinned against than sinning. Several children in the neighborhood died mysteriously—some epidemic the ignorant physicians failed to understand, no doubt—and Sarah, whatever the poor woman's surname may have been, was accused of killing them by witchcraft. At any rate, one of the bereft mothers took vengeance into her own hands, and strangled poor Sarah with a noose of well-rope. The witch-craft belief must have been quite prevalent, too, for there is some nonsense verse on the tombstone concerning her 'deathless sleep' and an allusion to her waking from it; also some mention of wild garlic being planted about her."

He laughed somewhat ruefully. "I wish they hadn't said that," he added, "for, do you know, there are garlic shoots growing about that grave to this very day. Old Christian, our sexton, declares that he can't get rid of it, no matter how much he grubs it up. It spreads to the surrounding lawn, too," he added sadly.

"*Cordieu!*" de Grandin gasped. "This is of the importance, sir!"

The old man smiled gently at the little Frenchman's impetuosity.

"It's an odd thing," he commented, "there was another gentleman asking about that same tomb a few weeks ago; a—pardon the expression—a foreigner."

"So?" de Grandin's little waxed mustache twitched like the whiskers of a nervous tomcat. "A foreigner, do you say? A tall, rawboned, fleshless living skel-eton of a man with a scar on his face and a white streak in his hair?"

"I wouldn't be quite so severe in my description," the other answered with a smile. "He certainly was a thin gentleman, and I believe he had a scar on his face, too, though I can't be certain of that, he was so very wrinkled. No, his hair was entirely white, there was no white streak in it, sir. In fact, I should have said he was very advanced in age, judging from his hair and face and the manner in which he walked. He seemed very weak and feeble. It was really quite pitiable."

"*Sacré nom d'un fromage vert!*" de Grandin almost snarled. "Pitiable, do you say, Monsieur? *Pardieu*, it is damnable, nothing less!"

He bowed to the clergyman and turned to me. "Come, Friend Trowbridge, come away," he cried. "We must go to Madame Norman's at once, right away, immediately."

"What's behind all this mystery?" I demanded as we left the parsonage door.

He elevated his slender shoulders in an eloquent shrug. "I only wish I knew," he replied. "Someone is working the devil's business, of that I am sure; but what the game is, or what the next move will be, only the good God can tell, my friend."

I turned the car through Tunlaw Street to effect a short-cut, and as we drove past an Italian green grocer's, de Grandin seized my arm. "Stop a moment, Friend Trowbridge," he asked, "I would make a purchase at this shop.

"We desire some fresh garlic," he informed the proprietor as we entered the little store, "a considerable amount, if you have it."

The Italian spread his hands in a deprecating gesture. "We have it not, *Signor*," he declared. "It was only yesterday morning that we sold our entire supply." His little black eyes snapped happily at the memory of an unexpected bargain.

"Eh, what is this?" de Grandin demanded. "Do you say you sold your supply? How is that?"

"I know not," the other replied. "Yesterday morning a rich gentleman came to my shop in an automobile, and called me from my store. He desired all the garlic I had in stock—at my own price, *Signor*, and at once. I was to deliver it to his address in Rupleysville the same day."

"Ah?" de Grandin's face assumed the expression of a cross-word fiend as he begins to see the solution of his puzzle. "And this liberal purchaser, what did he look like?"

The Italian showed his white, even teeth in a wide grin. "It was funny," he confessed. "He did not look like one of our people, nor like one who would eat much garlic. He was old, very old and thin, with a much-wrinkled face and white hair, he—"

"*Nom d'un chat!*" the Frenchman cried, then burst into a flood of torrential Italian.

The shopkeeper listened at first with suspicion, then incredulity, finally in abject terror. "No, no," he exclaimed. "No, *Signor*; *santissima Madonna*, you do make the joke!"

"Do I so?" de Grandin replied. "Wait and see, foolish one."

"*Santo Dio* forbid!" The other crossed himself piously, then bent his thumb across his palm, circling it with his second and third fingers and extending the fore and little fingers in the form of a pair of horns.

The Frenchman turned toward the waiting car with a grunt of inarticulate disgust.

"What now?" I asked as we got under way once more; "what did that man make the sign of the evil eye for, de Grandin?"

"Later, my friend; I will tell you later," he answered. "You would but laugh if I told you what I suspect. He is of the Latin blood, and can appreciate my fears." Nor would he utter another word till we reached the Norman house.

"Dr. Trowbridge—Dr. de Grandin!" Mrs. Norman met us in the hall; "you must have heard my prayers; I've been phoning your office for the last hour, and they said you were out and couldn't be reached."

"What's up?" I asked.

"It's Mr. Eckhart again. He's been seized with another fainting fit. He seemed so well this afternoon, and I sent a big dinner up to him at eight o'clock, but when the maid went in, she found him unconscious, and she declares she saw something in his room—"

"Ha?" de Grandin interrupted. "Where is she, this servant? I would speak with her."

"Wait a moment," Mrs. Norman answered; "I'll send for her."

The girl, an ungainly young Southern Negress, came into the front hall, sullen dissatisfaction written large upon her black face.

"Now, then," de Grandin bent his steady, unwinking gaze on her, "what is it you say about seeing someone in the young Monsieur Eckhart's room, *hein?*"

"Ah, did see sumpin', too," the girl replied stubbornly. "Ah don' care who says Ah didn't see nothin', Ah says Ah did. Ah'd just toted a tray o' vittles up to Mistuh Eckhart's room, an' when Ah opened de do', dere wuz a woman—dere wuz a woman—yas, sar, a skinny, black-eyed white woman-a-bendin' ober 'um an'—an'—"

"And what, if you please?" de Grandin asked breathlessly.

"A-bitin' 'um!" the girl replied defiantly. "Ah don' car whut Mis' Norman says, she wuz a-bitin' 'um. Ah seen her. Ah knows whut she wuz. Ah done hyeah tell erbout dat ol' Sarah woman what come up out 'er grave wid a long rope erbout her neck and go 'round bitin' folks. Yas, sar; an' she wuz a-bitin' 'um, too. Ah seen her!"

"Nonsense," Mrs. Norman commented in an annoyed whisper over de Grandin's shoulder.

"*Grand Dieu,* is it so?" de Grandin exclaimed, and turning abruptly, leaped up the stairs toward the sick man's room, two steps at a time.

"See, see, Friend Trowbridge," he ordered fiercely when I joined him at the patient's bedside. "Behold, it is the mark!" Turning back Eckhart's pajama collar, he displayed two incised horizontal arcs on the young man's flesh. There was no room for dispute, they were undoubtedly the marks of human teeth, and from the fresh wounds the blood was flowing freely.

As quickly as possible we staunched the flow and applied restoratives to the patient, both of us working in silence, for my brain was too much in a whirl to permit the formation of intelligent questions, while de Grandin remained dumb as an oyster.

"Now," he ordered as we completed our ministrations, "we must get back to that cemetery, Friend Trowbridge, and once there, we must do the thing which must be done!"

"What the devil's that?" I asked as we left the sickroom.

"*Non, non,* you shall see," he promised as we entered my car and drove down the street.

"Quick, the crank-handle," he demanded as we descended from the car at the cemetery gate, "it will make a serviceable hammer." He was prying a hemlock paling from the graveyard fence as he spoke.

We crossed the unkempt cemetery lawn again and finally paused beside the tombstone of the unknown Sarah.

"Attend me, Friend Trowbridge," de Grandin commanded, "hold the searchlight, if you please." He pressed his pocket flash into my hand. "Now—" He knelt beside the grave, pointing the stick he had wrenched from the fence straight downward into the turf. With the crank of my motor he began hammering the wood into the earth.

Farther and farther the rough stake sank into the sod, de Grandin's blows falling faster and faster as the wood drove home. Finally, when there was less than six inches of the wicket projecting from the grave's top, he raised the iron high over his head and drove downward with all his might.

The short hair at the back of my neck suddenly started upward, and little thrills of horripilation chased each other up my spine as the wood sank suddenly, as though driven from clay into sand, and a low hopeless moan, like the wailing of a frozen wind through an ice-cave, wafted up to us from the depths of the grave.

"Good God, what's that?" I asked, aghast.

For answer he leaned forward, seized the stake in both hands and drew suddenly up on it. At his second tug the wood came away. "See," he ordered curtly, flashing the pocket lamp on the tip of the stave. For the distance of a foot or so from its pointed end the wood was stained a deep, dull red. It was wet with blood.

"And now forever," he hissed between his teeth, driving the wood into the grave once more, and sinking it a full foot below the surface of the grass by thrusting the crank-handle into the earth. "Come, Friend Trowbridge, we have done a good work this night. I doubt not the young Eckhart will soon recover from his malady."

H IS ASSUMPTION WAS JUSTIFIED. Eckhart's condition improved steadily. Within a week, save for a slight pallor, he was, to all appearances, as well as ever.

The pressure of the usual early crop of influenza and pneumonia kept me busily on my rounds, and I gradually gave up hope of getting any information from de Grandin, for a shrug of the shoulders was all the answer he vouchsafed to my questions. I relegated Eckhart's inexplicable hemorrhages and the blood-stained stake to the limbo of never-to-be-solved mysteries. But—

2

" G OOD MORNIN', GENTLEMEN," DETECTIVE Sergeant Costello greeted as he followed Nora, my household factotum, into the breakfast room, "it's sorry

I am to be disturbin' your meal, but there's a little case puzzlin' th' department that I'd like to talk over with Dr. de Grandin, if you don't mind."

He looked expectantly at the little Frenchman as he finished speaking, his lips parted to launch open a detailed description of the case.

"*Parbleu*," de Grandin laughed, "it is fortunate for me that I have completed my breakfast, *cher Sergent*, for a riddle of crime detection is to me like a red rag to a bullfrog—I must needs snap at it, whether I have been fed or no. Speak on, my friend, I beseech you; I am like Balaam's ass, all ears."

The big Irishman seated himself on the extreme edge of one of my Heppelwhite chairs and gazed deprecatingly at the derby he held firmly between his knees. "It's like this," he began. "'Tis one o' them mysterious disappearance cases, gentlemen, an' whilst I'm thinkin' th' young lady knows exactly where she's at an' why she's there, I hate to tell her folks about it.

"All th' high-hat folks ain't like you two gentlemen, askin' your pardon, sors— they mostly seems to think that a harness bull's unyform is sumpin' like a livery— like a shofur's or a footman's or sumpin', an' that a plainclothes man is just a sort o' inferior servant. They don't give th' police credit for no brains, y'see, an' when one o' their darters gits giddy an' runs off th' reservation, if we tells 'em th' gurrl's run away of her own free will an' accord they say we're a lot o' lazy, good-fer-nothin' bums who are tryin' to dodge our laygitimate jooties by castin' mud on th' young ladies' char-ac-ters, d'ye see? So, when this Miss Esther Norman disappears in broad daylight leastwise, in th' twilight—o' th' day before her dance, we suspects right away that th' gurrl's gone her own ways into th' best o' intentions, y'see; but we dasn't tell her folks as much, or they'll be hollerin' to th' commissioner fer to git a bran' new set o' detectives down to headquarters, so they will.

"Now, mind ye, I'm not sayin' th' young lady mightn't o' been kidnaped, y'understand, gentlemen, but I do be sayin' 'tis most unlikely. I've been on th' force, man an' boy, in unyform and in plain clothes fer th' last twenty-five years, an' th' number of laygitimate kidnapin's o' young women over ten years of age I've seen can be counted on th' little finger o' me left hand, an' I ain't got none there at all, at all."

He held the member up for our inspection, revealing the fact that the little finger had been amputated close to the knuckle.

D E GRANDIN, ELBOWS ON the table, pointed chin cupped in his hands, was puffing furiously at a vile-smelling French cigarette, alternately sucking down great drafts of its acrid smoke and expelling clouds of fumes in double jets from his narrow, aristocratic nostrils.

"What is it you say?" he demanded, removing the cigarette from his lips. "Is it the so lovely Mademoiselle Esther, daughter of that kind Madame Tuscarora Avenue Norman, who is missing?"

"Yes, sor," Costello answered, "'tis th' same young lady's flew the coop, accordin' to my way o' thinkin'."

"*Mordieu!*" The Frenchman gave the ends of his blond mustache a savage twist. "You intrigue me, my friend. Say on, how did it happen, and when?"

"'Twas about midnight last night th' alarm came into headquarters," the detective replied. "Accordin' to th' facts as we have 'em, th' young lady went downtown in th' Norman car to do some errands. We've checked her movements up, an' here they are."

He drew a black-leather memorandum book from his pocket and consulted it.

"At 2:45 or thereabouts, she left th' house, arrivin' at th' Ocean Trust Company at 2:55, five minutes before th' instytootion closed for th' day. She drew out three hundred an' thirty dollars an' sixty-five cents, an' left th' bank, goin' to Madame Gerard's, where she tried on a party dress for th' dance which was bein' given at her house that night.

"She left Madame Gerard's at 4:02, leavin' orders for th' dress to be delivered to her house immeejately, an' dismissed her sho-fur at th' corner o' Dean an' Tunlaw Streets, sayin' she was goin' to deliver some vegytables an' what-not to a pore family she an' some o' her friends was keepin' till their oldman gits let out o' jail—'twas meself an' Clancey, me buddy, that put him there when we caught him red-handed in a job o' housebreakin', too.

"Well, to return to th' young lady, she stopped at Pete Bacigalupo's store in Tunlaw Street an' bought a basket o' fruit an' canned things, at 4:30, an'—" He clamped his long-suffering derby between his knees and spread his hands emptily before us.

"Yes, 'and'—?" de Grandin prompted, dropping the glowing end of his cigarette into his coffee cup.

"An' that's all," responded the Irishman. "She just walked off, an' no one ain't seen her since, sor."

"But—*cordieu!*—such things do not occur, my friend," de Grandin protested. "Somewhere you have overlooked a factor in this puzzle. You say no one saw her later? Have you nothing whatever to add to the tale?"

"Well"—the detective grinned at him—"there are one or two little incidents, but they ain't of any importance in th' case, as far as I can see. Just as she left Pete's store an old gink tried to 'make' her, but she give him th' air, an' he went off an' didn't bother her no more.

"I'd a' liked to seen th' old boy, at that. Day before yesterday there was an old felly hangin' 'round by the silk mills, annoyin' th' gurrls as they come off from work. Clancey, me mate, saw 'im an' started to take 'im up, an' darned if th' old rummy wasn't strong as a bull. D'ye know, he broke clean away from Clancey an' darn near broke his arm, in th' bargain? Belike 'twas th' same man accosted Miss Norman outside Pete's store."

"Ah?" de Grandin's slender, white fingers began beating a devil's tattoo on the tablecloth. "And who was it saw this old man annoy the lady, *hein?*"

Costello grinned widely, "'Twas Pete Bacigalupo himself, sor," be answered. "Pete swore be recognized th' old geezer as havin' come to his store a month or so ago in an autymobile an bought up all his entire stock o' garlic. Huh! Th' fool said he wouldn't a gone after th' felly' for a hundred dollars—said he had th' pink-eye, or th' evil eye, or some such thing. That sure do burn me up!"

"*Dieu et le diable!*" de Grandin leaped up, oversetting his chair in his mad haste. "And we sit here like three *poissons d'avril*—like poor fish—while he works his devilish will on her! Quick, Sergeant! Quick, Friend Trowbridge! Your hats, your coats; the motor! Oh, make haste, my friends, fly, fly, I implore you; even now it may be too late!"

As though all the fiends of pandemonium were at his heels he raced from the breakfast room, up the stairs, three steps at a stride, and down the upper hall toward his bedroom. Nor did he cease his shouted demands for haste throughout his wild flight.

"Cuckoo?" The sergeant tapped his forehead significantly.

I shook my head as I hastened to the hall for my driving clothes. "No," I answered, shrugging into my topcoat, "he's got a reason for everything he does; but you and I can't always see it, Sergeant."

"You said a mouthful that time, doc," he agreed, pulling his hat down over his ears. "He's the darndest, craziest Frog I ever seen, but, at that, he's got more sense than nine men out o' ten."

"To Rupleysville, Friend Trowbridge," de Grandin shouted as he leaped into the seat beside me. "Make haste, I do implore you. Oh, Jules de Grandin, your grandfather was an imbecile and all your ancestors were idiots, but you are the greatest zany in the family. Why, oh, why, do you require a sunstroke before you can see the light, foolish one?"

I swung the machine down the pike at highest legal speed, but the little Frenchman kept urging greater haste. "*Sang de Dieu, sang de Saint Denis, sang du diable!*" he wailed despairingly. "Can you not make this abominable car go faster, Friend Trowbridge? Oh, ah, *hélas*, if we are too late! I shall hate myself, I shall loathe myself—*pardieu*, I shall become a Carmelite friar and eat fish and abstain from swearing!"

WE TOOK SCARCELY TWENTY minutes to cover the ten-mile stretch to the aggregation of tumbledown houses which was Rupleysville, but my companion was almost frothing at the mouth when I drew up before the local apology for a hotel.

"Tell me, Monsieur," de Grandin cried as he thrust the hostelry's door open with his foot and brandished his slender ebony cane before the astonished proprietor's eyes, "tell me of *un vieillard*—an old, old man with snow-white hair and an evil face, who has lately come to this so detestable place. I would know where to find him, right away, immediately, at once!"

"Say," the boniface demanded truculently, "where d'ye git that stuff? Who are you to be askin'—"

"That'll do"—Costello shouldered his way past de Grandin and displayed his badge—"you answer this gentleman's questions, an' answer 'em quick an' accurate, or I'll run you in, see?"

The innkeeper's defiant attitude melted before the detective's show of authority like frost before the sunrise. "Guess you must mean Mr. Zerny," he replied sullenly. "He come here about a month ago an' rented the Hazeltown house, down the road about a mile. Comes up to town for provisions every day or two, and stops in here sometimes for a—" He halted abruptly, his face suffused with a dull flush.

"Yeah?" Costello replied. "Go on an' say it; we all know what he stops here for. Now listen, buddy"—he stabbed the air two inches before the man's face with a blunt forefinger—"I don't know whether this here Zerny felly's got a tellyphone or not, but if he has, you just lay off tellin' 'im we're comin'; git me? If anyone's tipped him off when we git to his place I'm comin' back here and plaster more padlocks on this place o' yours than Sousa's got medals on his blouse. Savvy?"

"Come away, *Sergent*; come away, Friend Trowbridge," de Grandin besought almost tearfully. "Bandy not words with the *cancre*; we have work to do!"

Down the road we raced in the direction indicated by the hotelkeeper, till the picket fence and broken shutters of the Hazelton house showed among a rank copse of second-growth pines at the bend of the highway.

The shrewd wind of early spring was moaning and soughing among the black boughs of the pine trees as we ran toward the house, and though it was bright with sunshine on the road, there was chill and shadow about us as we climbed the sagging steps of the old building's ruined piazza and paused breathlessly before the paintless front door.

"Shall I knock?" Costello asked dubiously, involuntarily sinking his voice to a whisper.

"But no," de Grandin answered in a low voice, "what we have to do here must be done quietly, my friends."

He leaned forward and tried the doorknob with a light, tentative touch. The door gave under his hand, swinging inward on protesting hinges, and we tiptoed into a dark, dust-carpeted hall. A shaft of sunlight, slanting downward from a chink in one of the window shutters, showed innumerable dust-motes flying lazily in the air, and laid a bright oval of light against the warped floorboards.

"Huh, empty as a pork-butcher's in Jerusalem," Costello commented disgustedly, looking about the unfurnished rooms, but de Grandin seized him by the elbow with one hand while he pointed toward the floor with the ferrule of his slender ebony walking stick.

"Empty, perhaps," he conceded in a low, vibrant whisper, "but not recently, *mon ami*." Where the sunbeam splashed on the uneven floor there showed distinctly the mark of a booted foot, two marks—a trail of them leading toward the rear of the house.

"Right y'are," the detective agreed. "Someone's left his track here, an' no mistake."

"Ha!" de Grandin bent forward till it seemed the tip of his high-bridged nose would impinge on the tracks. "Gentlemen," he rose and pointed forward into the gloom with a dramatic flourish of his cane, "they are here! Let us go!"

Through the gloomy hall we followed the trail by the aid of Costello's flashlight, stepping carefully to avoid creaking boards as much as possible. At length the marks stopped abruptly in the center of what had formerly been the kitchen. A disturbance in the dust told where the walker had doubled on his tracks in a short circle, and a ringbolt in the floor gave notice that we stood above a trap-door of some sort.

"Careful, Friend Costello," de Grandin warned, "have ready your flashlight when I fling back the trap. Ready? *Un—deux—trois!*"

He bent, seized the rusty ringbolt and heaved the trap-door back so violently that it flew back with a thundering crash on the floor beyond.

The cavern had originally been a cellar for the storage of food, it seemed, and was brick-walled and earth-floored, without window or ventilation opening of any sort. A dank, musty odor assaulted our nostrils as we leaned forward, but further impressions were blotted out by the sight directly beneath us.

White as a figurine of carven alabaster, the slender, bare body of a girl lay in sharp reverse silhouette against the darkness of the cavern floor, her ankles crossed and firmly lashed to a stake in the earth, one hand doubled behind her back in the position of a wrestler's hammerlock grip, and made firm to a peg in the floor, while the left arm was extended straight outward, its wrist pinioned to another stake. Her luxuriant fair hair had been knotted together at the ends, then staked to the ground, so that her head was drawn far back, exposing her rounded throat to its fullest extent, and on the earth beneath her left breast and beside her throat stood two porcelain bowls.

Crouched over her was the relic of a man, an old, old, hideously wrinkled witch-husband, with matted white hair and beard. In one hand he held a long, gleaming, double-edged dirk while with the other he caressed the girl's smooth throat with gloating strokes of his skeleton fingers.

"Howly Mither!" Costello's County Galway brogue broke through his American accent at the horrid sight below us.

"My God!" I exclaimed, all the breath in my lungs suddenly seeming to freeze in my throat.

"*Bonjour, Monsieur le Vampire!*" Jules de Grandin greeted nonchalantly, leaping to the earth beside the pinioned girl and waving his walking stick airily. "By the horns of the devil, but you have led us a merry chase, Baron Lajos Czuczron of Transylvania!"

The crouching creature emitted a bellow of fury and leaped toward de Grandin, brandishing his knife.

The Frenchman gave ground with a quick, catlike leap and grasped his slender cane in both hands near the top. Next instant he had ripped the lower part of the stick away, displaying a fine, three-edged blade set in the cane's handle, and swung his point toward the frothing-mouthed thing which mouthed and gibbered like a beast at bay. "A-ah?" he cried with a mocking, upward-lilting accent. "You did not expect this, eh, Friend Blood-drinker? I give you the party-of-surprise, *n'est-ce-pas?* The centuries have been long, *mon vieux*; but the reckoning has come at last. Say, now will you die by the steel, or by starvation?"

The aged monster fairly champed his gleaming teeth in fury. His eyes seemed larger, rounder, to gleam like the eyes of a dog in the firelight, as he launched himself toward the little Frenchman.

"*Sa-ha!*" the Frenchman sank backward on one foot then straightened suddenly forward, stiffening his sword-arm and plunging his point directly into the charging beastman's distended, red mouth. A scream of mingled rage and pain filled the cavern with deafening shrillness and the monster half turned, as though on an invisible pivot, clawed with horrid impotence at the wire-fine blade of de Grandin's rapier, then sank slowly to the earth, his death cry stilled to a sickening gurgle as his throat filled with blood.

"*Fini!*" de Grandin commented laconically, drawing on his handkerchief and wiping his blade with meticulou care, then cutting the unconscious girl's bonds with hi pocket-knife. "Drop down your overcoat, Friend Trowbridge," he added, "that we may cover the poor child's nudity until we can piece out a wardrobe for her.

"Now, then"—as he raised her to meet the hands Costello and I extended into the pit—"if we clothe her in the motor rug, your jacket, *Sergent*, Friend Trowbridge's topcoat and my shoes, she will be safe from the chill. *Parbleu*, I have seen women refugees from the Boche who could not boast so complete a toilette!"

With Esther Norman, hastily clothed in her patchwork assortment of garments, wedged in the front seat between de Grandin and me, we began our triumphant journey home.

"An' would ye mind tellin' me how ye knew where to look for th' young lady, Dr. de Grandin, sor?" Detective Sergeant Costello asked respectfully, leaning forward from the rear seat of the car.

"Wait, wait, my friend," de Grandin replied with a smile. "When our duties are all performed I shall tell you such a tale as shall make your two eyes to pop outward like a snail's. First, however, you must go with us to restore this *pauvre enfant* to her mother's arms; then to the headquarters to report the death of that *sale bête*. Friend Trowbridge will stay with the young lady for so long as he deems necessary, and I shall remain with him to help. Then, this evening—with your consent, Friend Trowbridge—you will dine with us, *Sergent*, and I shall tell you all, everything, in total. Death of my life, what a tale it is! *Parbleu*, but you shall call me a liar many times before it is finished!"

J ULES DE GRANDIN PLACED his demitasse on the tabouret and refilled his liqueur glass. "My friends," he began, turning his quick, elfish smile first on Costello, then on me, "I have promised you a remarkable tale. Very well, then, to begin."

He flicked a wholly imaginary fleck of dust from his dinner jacket sleeve and crossed his slender, womanishly small feet on the hearth rug.

"Do you recall, Friend Trowbridge, how we went, you and I, to the tea given by the good Madame Norman? Yes? Perhaps, then, you will recall how at the entrance of the ballroom I stopped with a look of astonishment on my face. Very good. At that moment I saw that which made me disbelieve the evidence of my own two eyes. As the gentleman we later met as Count Czerny danced past a mirror on the wall I beheld—*parbleu*! what do you suppose?—the reflection only of his dancing partner! It was as if the man had been non-existent, and the young lady had danced past the mirror by herself.

"Now, such a thing was not likely, I admit; you, *Sergent*, and you, too, Friend Trowbridge, will say it was not possible; but such is not the case. In certain circumstances it is possible for that which we see with our eyes to cast no shadow in a mirror. Let that point wait a moment; we have other evidence to consider first.

"When the young man told us of the count's prowess in battle, of his incomparable ferocity, I began to believe that which I had at first disbelieved, and when he told us the count was a Hungarian, I began to believe more than ever.

"I met the count, as you will remember, and I took his hand in mine. *Parbleu*, it was like a hand with no palm—it had hairs on both sides of it! You, too, Friend Trowbridge, remarked on that phenomenon.

"While I talked with him I managed to maneuver him before a mirror. *Morbleu*, the man was as if he had not been; I could see my own face smiling at me where I knew I should have seen the reflection of his shoulder!

"Now, attend me; The *Sûreté General*—what you call the Police Headquarters—of Paris is not like your English and American bureaus. All facts, no matter however seemingly absurd, which come to that office are carefully noted down for future reference. Among other histories I have read in the archives of that office was that of one Baron Lajos Czuczron of Transylvania, whose actions had once been watched by our secret agents.

"This man was rich and favored beyond the common run of Hungarian petty nobles, but he was far from beloved by his peasantry. He was known as cruel, wicked and implacable, and no one could be found who had ever one kind word to say for him.

"Half the countryside suspected him of being a *loup-garou*, or werewolf, the others credited a local legend that a woman of his family had once in the olden days taken a demon to husband and that he was the offspring of that unholy union. According to the story, the progeny of this wicked woman lived like an ordinary man for one hundred years, then died on the stroke of the century *unless his vitality was renewed by drinking the blood of a slaughtered virgin!*

"Absurd? Possibly. An English intelligence office would have said 'bally nonsense' if one of its agents had sent in such a report. An American bureau would have labeled the report as being the sauce-of-the apple; but consider this fact: In six hundred years there was no single record of a Baron Czuczron having died. Barons grew old—old to the point of death—but always there came along a new baron, a man in the prime of life, not a youth, to take the old baron's place, nor could any say when the old baron had died or where his body had been laid.

"Now, I had been told that a man under a curse—the werewolf, the vampire, or any other thing in man's shape, who lives more than his allotted time by virtue of wickedness—can not cast a shadow in a mirror; also that those accursed ones have hair in the palms of their hands. *Eh bien*, with this foreknowledge, I engaged this man who called himself Count Czerny in conversation concerning Transylvania. *Parbleu*, the fellow denied all knowledge of the country. He denied it with more force than was necessary. 'You are a liar, *Monsieur le Comte*,' I tell him, but I say it to myself. Even yet, however, I do not think what I think later.

"Then came the case of the young Eckhart. He loses blood, he can not say how or why, but Friend Trowbridge and I find a queer mark on his body. I think to me, 'if, perhaps, a vampire—a member of that accursed tribe who leave their graves by night and suck the blood of the living—were here, that would account for this young man's condition. But where would such a being come from? It is not likely.'

"Then I meet that old man, the one you call Indian John. He tells me much of the history of this town in the early days, and he tells me something more. He tells of a man, an old, old man, who has paid him much money to go to a certain grave—the grave of a reputed witch—in the old cemetery and dig from about it a growth of wild garlic. Garlic, I know, is a plant intolerable to the vampire. He can not abide it. If it is planted on his grave he can not pass it.

"I ask myself, 'Who would want such a thing to be, and why? But I have no answer; only, I know, if a vampire have been confined to that grave by planted garlic, then liberated when that garlic is taken away, it would account for the young Eckhart's strange sickness.

"*Tiens*, Friend Trowbridge and I visit that grave, and on its tombstone we read a verse which makes me believe the tenant of that grave may be a vampire. We interview the good minister of the church and learn that another man, an old, old man, have also inquired about that strange grave. 'Who have done this? I ask me; but even yet I have no definite answer to my question.

"As we rush to the Norman house to see young Eckhart I stop at an Italian green grocer's and ask for fresh garlic, for I think perhaps we can use it to protect the young Eckhart if it really is a vampire which is troubling him. *Parbleu*, some man, an old, old man, have what you Americans call 'cornered' the available supply of garlic. '*Cordieu*,' I tell me, 'this old man, he constantly crosses our trail! Also he is a very great nuisance.'

"The Italian tell me the garlic was sent to a house in Rupleysville, so I have an idea where this interfering ol' rascal may abide. But at that moment I have greater need to see our friend Eckhart than to ask further question of the Italian. Before I go, however, I tell that shopkeeper that his garlic customer has the evil eye. *Parbleu*, Monsieur Garlic-Buyer you will have no more dealings with that Italian! He knows what he knows.

"When we arrive at the Norman house we find young Eckhart in great trouble, and a black serving maid tells of a strange-looking woman who bit him. Also, we find toothmarks on his breast. 'The vampire woman, Sarah, is, in very truth, at large,' I tell me, and so I hasten to the cemetery to make her fast to her grave with a wooden stake, for, once he is staked down, the vampire can no longer roam. He is finished.

"Friend Trowbridge will testify he saw blood on the stake driven into a grave dug nearly three hundred years ago. Is it not so, *mon ami?*"

I nodded assent, and he took up his narrative:

"Why this old man should wish to liberate the vampire woman, I know not; certain it is, one of that grisly guild, or one closely associated with it, as this 'Count Czerny' undoubtedly was, can tell when another of the company is in the vicinity, and I doubt not he did this deed for pure malice and deviltry.

"However that may be, Friend Trowbridge tells me he have seen the count, and that he seems to have aged greatly. The man who visited the clergyman and the man who bought the garlic was also much older than the count as we knew him. 'Ah ha, he is coming to the end of his century,' I tell me; 'now look out for devilment, Jules de Grandin. Certainly, it is sure to come.'

"And then, my Sergeant, come you with your tale of Mademoiselle Norman's disappearance, and I, too, think perhaps she has run away from home voluntarily, of her own free will, until you say the Italian shopkeeper recognized the old man who accosted her as one who has the evil eye. Now what old man, save the one who bought the garlic and who lives at Rupleysville, would that Italian accuse of the evil eye? *Pardieu*, has he not already told you the same man once bought his garlic? But yes. The case is complete.

"The girl has disappeared, an old, old man has accosted her; an old, old man who was so strong he could overcome a policeman; the count is nearing his century mark when he must die like other men unless he can secure the blood of a virgin to revivify him. I am more than certain that the count and baron are one and the same and that they both dwell at Rupleysville. *Voilà*, we go to Rupleysville, and we arrive there not one little minute too soon. *N'est-ce-pas, mes amis?*"

"Sure," Costello agreed, rising and holding out his hand in farewell, "you've got th' goods, doc. No mistake about it."

To me, as I helped him with his coat in the hall, the detective confided, "An' he only had one shot o' licker all evenin'! Gosh, doc, if one drink could fix me up like that I wouldn't care how much prohibition we had!"

The Blood-Flower

"ALLO," JULES DE GRANDIN seized the receiver from the office telephone before the echo of the tinkling bell had ceased, "who is it, please? But of course, Mademoiselle, you may speak with Dr. Trowbridge." He passed the instrument to me and busied himself with a third unsuccessful attempt to ignite the evil-smelling French cigarette with which he insisted on fumigating the room.

"Yes?" I queried, placing the receiver to my ear.

"This is Miss Ostrander, Dr. Trowbridge," a well modulated voice informed me. "Mrs. Evander's nurse, you know."

"Yes?" I repeated, a little sharply, annoyed at being called by an ordinary case after an onerous day. "What is it?"

"I—I don't quite know, sir." She laughed the short, semi-hysterical laugh of an embarrassed woman. "She's acting very queerly. She—she's—oh, my, there it goes again, sir! Please come over right away; I'm afraid she's becoming delirious!" And with that she hung up, leaving me in a state of astounded impatience.

"Confound the woman!" I scolded as I prepared to slip into my overcoat. "Why couldn't she have hung on thirty seconds more and told me what the matter was?"

"Eh, what is it, my friend?" de Grandin gave up his attempt to make the cigarette burn and regarded me with one of his fixed, unwinking stares. "You are puzzled, you are in trouble; can I assist you?"

"Perhaps," I replied. "There's a patient of mine, a Mrs. Evander, who's been suffering from a threatened leukemia—I've administered Fowler's solution and arsenic trioxide and given her bed-rest treatment for the past week. It looked as if we had the situation pretty well in hand, but . . ." I repeated Miss Ostrander's message.

"Ah?" he murmured, musingly. "'There it goes again,' she did say? What, I wonder, was 'it'; a cough, a convulsion, or—who can say? Let us hasten, my friend. *Parbleu*, she does intrigue me, that Mademoiselle Ostrander with her so cryptic 'There it goes again!'"

Lights were gleaming through the storm from the windows of the Evander house as we came to a stop before its wide veranda. A servant, half-clothed and badly frightened, let us in and ushered us on tiptoe to the upper story chamber where the mistress of the establishment lay sick.

"What's wrong?" I demanded as I entered the sickroom, de Grandin at my heels.

A glance at the patient reassured me. She lay back on a little pile of infant pillows, her pretty blonde hair trickling in stray rivulets of gold from the confines of her lace sleeping cap, her hand, almost as white as the linen itself, spread restfully on the Madeira counterpane.

"Humph!" I exclaimed, turning angrily to Miss Ostrander. "Is this what you called me out in the rain to see?"

The nurse raised a forefinger quickly to her lips and motioned toward the hall with her eyes. "Doctor," she said in a whisper when we stood outside the sickroom door, "I know you'll think me silly, but—but it was positively ghastly!"

"*Tiens*, Mademoiselle," de Grandin cut in, "I pray you be more explicit: First you tell Friend Trowbridge that something—we know not what—goes again, now you do inform us that something is ghastly. *Pardieu*, you have my sheep—*non, non*, how do you say?—my goat!"

In spite of herself the girl laughed at the tragic face he turned to her, but she recovered her gravity quickly.

"Last night," she went on, still in a whisper, "and the night before, just at twelve, a dog howled somewhere in the neighborhood. I couldn't place the sound, but it was one of those long, quavering howls, almost human. Positively you might have mistaken it for the cry of a little child in pain, at first."

De Grandin tweaked first one, then the other end of his trimly waxed blond mustache. "And it was the sleepless dog's lament which went again, and which was so ghastly, Mademoiselle?" he inquired solicitously.

"No!" the nurse exploded with suppressed vehemence and heightened color. "It was Mrs. Evander, sir. Night before last, when the beast began baying, she stirred in her sleep—turned restlessly for a moment, then went back to sleep. When it howled the second time, a little nearer the house, she half sat up, and made a queer little growling noise in her throat. Then she slept. Last night the animal was howling louder and longer, and Mrs. Evander seemed more restless and made odd noises more distinctly. I thought the dog was annoying her, or that she might be having a nightmare, so I got her a drink of water; but when I tried to give it to her, *she snarled at me!*"

"*Eh bien*, but this is of interest," de Grandin commented. "She did snarl at you, you say?"

"Yes, sir. She didn't wake up when I touched her on the shoulder; just turned her head toward me and showed her teeth and growled. Growled like a bad-tempered dog."

"Yes? And then?"

"Tonight the dog began howling a few minutes earlier, five or ten minutes before midnight, perhaps, and it seemed to me his voice was much stronger. Mrs. Evander had the same reaction she had the other two nights at first, but suddenly she sat bolt-upright in bed, rolled her head from side to side, and drew back her lips and growled, then she began snapping at the air, like a dog annoyed by a fly. I did my best to quiet her, but I didn't like to go too near—I was afraid, really—and all at once the dog began howling again, right in the next yard, it seemed, and Mrs. Evander threw back her bedclothes, knelt up in bed and answered him!"

"Answered him?" I echoed in stupefaction.

"Yes, doctor, she threw back her head and howled—long quavering howls, just like his. At first they were low, but they grew louder and higher till the servants heard them, and James, the butler, came to the door to see what the matter was. Poor fellow, he was nearly scared out of his wits when he saw her."

"And then . . . ?" I began.

"Then I called you. Right while I was talking to you, the dog began baying again, and Mrs. Evander answered him. That was what I meant"—she turned to de Grandin—"when I said 'There it goes again.' I had to hang up before I could explain to you, Dr. Trowbridge, for she had started to crawl out of bed toward the window, and I had to run and stop her."

"But why didn't you tell me this yesterday, or this afternoon when I was here?" I demanded.

"I didn't like to, sir. It all seemed so crazy, so utterly impossible, especially in the daytime, that I was afraid you'd think I'd been asleep on duty and dreamed it all; but now that James has seen it, too . . ."

Outside in the rain-drenched night there suddenly rose a wail, long-drawn, pulsating, doleful as the cry of an abandoned soul. "O-o-o—o-o-o-o—o-o-o—o-o-o-o!" it rose and fell, quavered and almost died away, then resurged with increased force. "O-o-o—o-o-o-o—o-o-o—o-o-o-o!"

"Hear it?" the nurse cried, her voice thin-edged with excitement and fear.

Again, "O-o-o—o-o-o-o—o-o-o—o-o-o-o!" like the echo of the howls outside came an answering cry from the sickroom beyond the door.

Miss Ostrander dashed into the room, de Grandin and I close behind her.

The dainty white counterpane had been thrown back. Mrs. Evander, clad only in her Georgette nightrobe and bed cap, had crossed the floor to the window and flung up the sash. Already, the wind-whipped rain was beating in upon her as she leaned across the sill, one pink sole toward us, one little white foot on the window-ledge, preparatory to jumping.

"*Mon Dieu*, seize her!" de Grandin shrieked, and, matching command with performance leaped across the room, grasped her shoulders in his small, strong hands, and bore her backward as she flexed the muscles of her legs to hurl herself into the yard below.

For a moment she fought like a tigress, snarling, scratching, even snapping at us with her teeth, but Miss Ostrander and I overbore her and thrust her into bed, drawing the covers over her and holding them down like a strait-jacket against her furious struggles.

De Grandin leaned across the window-sill, peering out into the stormy darkness. "Aroint thee, accursed of God!" I heard him shout into the wind as he drew the sash down, snapped the catch fast and turned again to the room.

"Ah?" he approached the struggling patient and bent over her, staring intently. "A grain and a half of morphine in her arm, if you please, Friend Trowbridge. The dose is heavy for a non-addict, but"—he shrugged his shoulders—"it is *necessaire* that she sleep, this poor one. So! That is better.

"Mademoiselle," he regarded Miss Ostrander with his wide-eyed stare, "I do not think she will be thus disturbed in the day, but I most strongly urge that hereafter you administer a dose of one-half grain of codeine dissolved in eighty parts of water each night not later than half-past ten. Dr. Trowbridge will write the prescription.

"Friend Trowbridge," he interrupted himself, "where, if at all, is Madame's husband, Monsieur Evander?"

"He's gone to Atlanta on a business trip," Miss Ostrander supplied. "We expect him back tomorrow."

"Tomorrow? *Zut*, that is too bad!" de Grandin exclaimed. "*Eh bien*, with you Americans it is always the business. Business before happiness; *cordieu*, business before the safety of those you love!

"Mademoiselle, you will please keep in touch with Dr. Trowbridge and me at all times, and when that Monsieur Evander does return from his business trip, please tell him that we desire to see him soon—at once, right away, immediately.

"Come, Friend Trowbridge—*bonne nuit*, Mademoiselle."

"I SAY, DR. TROWBRIDGE," NILES Evander flung angrily into my consulting room, "what's the idea of keeping my wife doped like this? Here I just got back from a trip to the South last night and rushed out to the house to see her before she went to sleep, and that dam' nurse said she'd given her a sleepin' powder and couldn't waken her. I don't like it, I tell you, and I won't have it! I told the nurse that if she gave her any dope tonight she was through, and that goes for you, too!" He glared defiantly at me.

De Grandin, sunk in the depths of a great chair with a copy of de Gobineau's melancholy *Lovers of Kandahar*, glanced up sharply, then consulted the watch strapped to his wrist. "It is a quarter of eleven," he announced apropos of nothing, laying down the elegant blue-and-gold volume and rising from his seat.

Evander turned on him, eyes ablaze. "You're Dr. de Grandin," he accused. "I've heard of you from the nurse. It was you who persuaded Trowbridge to dope my wife—buttin' in on a case that didn't concern you. I know all about you," he went on furiously as the Frenchman gave him a cold stare. "You're some sort of charlatan from Paris, a dabbler in criminology and spiritualism and that sort of rot. Well, sir, I want to warn you to keep your hands off my wife. American doctors and American methods are good enough for me!"

"Your patriotism is most admirable, Monsieur," de Grandin murmured with a suspicious mildness. "If you . . ."

The jangle of the telephone bell cut through his words. "Yes?" he asked sharply, raising the receiver, but keeping his cold eyes fixed on Evander's face. "Yes, Mademoiselle Ostrander, this is—*grand Dieu!* What? How long? Eh, do you say so? *Dix million diables!* But of course, we come, we hasten—*morbleu*, but we shall fly.

"Gentlemen," he hung up the receiver, then turned to us, inclining his shoulders ceremoniously to each of us in turn, his gaze as expressionless as the eyes of a graven image, "that was Mademoiselle Ostrander on the 'phone. Madame Evander is gone—disappeared."

"Gone? Disappeared?" Evander echoed stupidly, looking helplessly from de Grandin to me and back again. He slumped down in the nearest chair, gazing straight before him unseeing. "Great God!" he murmured.

"Precisely, Monsieur," de Grandin agreed in an even, emotionless voice. "That is exactly what I said. Meantime"—he gave me a significant glance— "let us go, *cher* Trowbridge. I doubt not that Mademoiselle Ostrander will have much of interest to relate.

"Monsieur"—his eyes and voice again became cold, hard, stonily expressionless—"if you can so far discommode yourself as to travel in the company of one whose nationality and methods you disapprove, I suggest you accompany us."

Niles Evander rose like a sleep-walker and followed us to my waiting car.

T HE PREVIOUS DAY'S RAIN had turned to snow with a shifting of the wind to the northeast, and we made slow progress through the suburban roads. It was nearly midnight when we trooped up the steps to the Evander porch and pushed vigorously at the bell-button.

"Yes, sir," Miss Ostrander replied to my question, "Mr. Evander came home last night and positively forbade my giving Mrs. Evander any more codeine. I told him you wanted to see him right away, and that Dr. de Grandin had ordered the narcotic, but he said . . ."

"Forbear, if you please, Mademoiselle," de Grandin interrupted. "Monsieur Evander has already been at pain to say as much—and more—to us in person. Now, when did Madame disappear, if you please?"

"I'd already given her her medicine last night," the nurse took up her story at the point of interruption, "so there was no need of calling you to tell you of Mr. Evander's orders. I thought perhaps I could avoid any unpleasantness by pretending to obey him and giving her the codeine on the sly this evening, but about nine o'clock he came into the sickroom and snatched up the box of powders and put them in his pocket. Then he said he was going to drive over to have it out with you. I tried to telephone you about it, but the storm had put the wires out of commission, and I've been trying to get a message through ever since."

"And the dog, Mademoiselle, the animal who did howl outside the window, has he been active?"

"Yes! Last night he screamed and howled so I was frightened. Positively, it seemed as though he were trying to jump up from the ground to the window. Mrs. Evander slept through it all, though, thanks to the drug."

"And tonight?" de Grandin prompted.

"Tonight!" The nurse shuddered. "The howling began about half-past nine, just a few minutes after Mr. Evander left for the city. Mrs. Evander was terrible. She seemed like a woman possessed. I fought and struggled with her, but nothing I could do had the slightest effect. She was savage as a maniac. I called James to help me hold her in bed once, and then, for a while, she lay quietly, for the thing outside seemed to have left.

"Sometime later the howling began again, louder and more furious, and Mrs. Evander was twice as hard to manage. She fought and bit so that I was beginning to lose control of her, and I screamed for James again. He must have been somewhere downstairs, though, for he didn't hear my call. I ran out into the hall and leaned over the balustrade to call again, and when I ran back—I wasn't out there more than a minute—the window was up and Mrs. Evander was gone."

"And didn't you do anything?—didn't you look for her?" Evander cut in passionately.

"Yes, sir. James and I ran outside and called and searched all through the grounds, but we couldn't find a trace of her. The wind is blowing so and the snow falling so rapidly, any tracks she might have made would have been wiped out almost immediately."

De Grandin took his little pointed chin between the thumb and forefinger of his right hand and bowed his head in silent meditation. "Horns of the devil!" I heard him mutter to himself. "This is queer—those cries, that delirium, that attempted flight, now this disappearance, *Pardieu*, the trail seems clear. But why? *Mille cochons*, why?"

"See here," Evander broke in frantically, "can't you do something? Call the police, call the neighbors, call . . ."

"Monsieur," de Grandin interrupted in a frigid voice, "may I inquire your vocation?"

"Eh?" Evander was taken aback. "Why—er—I'm an engineer."

"Precisely, exactly. Dr. Trowbridge and I are medical men. We do not attempt to build bridges or sink tunnels. We should make sorry work of it. You, Monsieur have already once tried your hand at medicine by forbidding the administration of a drug we considered necessary. Your results were most deplorable. Kindly permit us to follow our profession in our own way. The thing we most of all do not desire in this case is the police force. Later, perhaps. Now, it would be more than ruinous."

"But . . ."

"There are no buts, Monsieur. It is my belief that your wife, Madame Evander, is in no immediate danger. However, Dr. Trowbridge and I shall institute such search as may be practicable, and do you meantime keep in such communication with us as the storm will permit." He bowed formally. "A very good night to you, Monsieur."

Miss Ostrander looked at him questioningly. "Shall I go with you, doctor?" she asked.

"*Mais non*," he replied. "You will please remain here, *ma nourice*, and attend the homecoming of Madame Evander."

"Then you think she will return?"

"Most doubtlessly. Unless I am more badly mistaken than I think I am, she will be back to you before another day."

"Say," Evander, almost beside himself burst out, "what makes you so cocksure she'll be back? Good Lord, man, do you realize she's out in this howling blizzard with only her nightclothes on?"

"Perfectly. But I do declare she will return."

"But you've nothing to base your absurd. . . ."

"Monsieur!" de Grandin's sharp, whiplike reply cut in. "Me, I am Jules de Grandin. When I say she will return, I mean she will return. I do not make mistakes."

"WHERE SHALL WE BEGIN the search?" I asked as we entered my car.

He settled himself snugly in the cushions and lighted a cigarette. "We need not search, *cher ami*," he replied. "She will return of her own free will and accord."

"But, man," I argued, "Evander was right; she's out in this storm with nothing put a Georgette nightdress on."

"I doubt it," he answered casually.

"You doubt it? Why . . . ?"

"Unless the almost unmistakable signs fail, my friend, this Madame Evander, thanks to her husband's pig-ignorance, is this moment clothed in fur."

"Fur?" I echoed.

"Perfectly. Come, my friend, tread upon the gas. Let us snatch what sleep we can tonight—*eh bien*, tomorrow is another day."

HE WAS UP AND waiting for me as I entered the office next morning. "Tell me, Friend Trowbridge," he demanded, "this Madame Evander's leukemia, upon what did you base your diagnosis?"

"Well," I replied, referring to my clinical cards, "a physical examination showed the axillary glands slightly enlarged, the red corpuscles reduced to little more than a million to the count, the white cells stood at about four hundred thousand, and the patient complained of weakness, drowsiness and a general feeling of malaise."

"U'm?" he commented noncommitally. "That could easily be so. Yes; such signs would undoubtlessly be shown. Now . . ." The telephone bell broke off his remarks half uttered.

"Ah?" his little blue eyes snapped triumphantly, as he listened to the voice on the wire. "I did think so. But yes; right away, at once, immediately.

"Trowbridge, my old one, she has returned. That was Mademoiselle Ostrander informing me of Madame Evander's reappearance. Let us hasten. There is much I would do this day."

"AFTER YOU WENT LAST night," Miss Ostrander told us, "I lay down on the chaise longue in the bedroom and tried to sleep. I suppose I must have napped by fits and starts, but it seemed to me I could hear the faint howling of dogs, sometimes mingled with yelps and cries, all through the night. This morning, just after six o'clock, I got up to prepare myself a piece of toast and a cup of tea before the servants were stirring, and as I came downstairs I found Mrs. Evander lying on the rug in the front hall."

She paused a moment, and her color mounted slightly as she went on. "She was lying on that gray wolfskin rug before the fireplace, sir, and was quite nude. Her sleeping cap and nightgown were crumpled up on the floor beside her."

"Ah?" de Grandin commented. "And . . . ?"

"I got her to her feet and helped her upstairs, where I dressed her for bed and tucked her in. She didn't seem to show any evil effects from being out in the storm. Indeed, she seems much better this morning, and is sleeping so soundly I could hardly wake her for breakfast, and when I did, she wouldn't eat. Just went back to sleep."

"Ah?" de Grandin repeated. "And you bathed her, Mademoiselle, before she was put to bed?"

The girl looked slightly startled. "No sir, not entirely; but I did wash her hands. They were discolored, especially about the fingertips, with some red substance, almost as if she had been scratching something, and gotten blood under her nails."

"*Parbleu!*" the Frenchman exploded. "I did know it, Friend Trowbridge. Jules de Grandin, he is never mistaken.

"Mademoiselle," he turned feverishly to the nurse, "did you, by any happy chance, save the water in which you laved Madame Evander's hands?"

"Why, no, I didn't, but—oh I see—yes, I think perhaps some of the stain may be on the washcloth and the orange stick I cleaned her nails with. I really had quite a time cleaning them, too."

"*Bien, très bien!*" he ejaculated. "Let us have these cloths, these sticks, at once, please. Trowbridge, do you withdraw some blood from Madame's arm for a test, then we must hasten to the laboratory. *Cordieu*, I burn with impatience!"

An hour later we faced each other in the office. "I can't understand it," I confessed. "By all the canons of the profession, Mrs. Evander ought to be dead after last night's experience, but there's no doubt she's better. Her pulse was firmer, her temperature right, and her blood count practically normal today."

"Me, I understand perfectly, up to a point," he replied. "Beyond that, all is dark as the cave of Erebus. Behold, I have tested the stains from Madame's fingers. They are—what do you think?"

"Blood?" I hazarded.

"*Parbleu*, yes, but not of humanity. *Mais non*, they are blood of a dog, my friend."

"Of a dog?"

"Perfectly. I, myself, did greatly fear they might prove human, but *grace à Dieu*, they are not. Now, if you will excuse, I go to make certain investigations, and will meet you at the *maison* Evander this evening. Come prepared to be surprised, my friend. *Parbleu*, I shall be surprised if I do not astonish myself!"

F OUR OF US, DE Grandin, Miss Ostrander, Niles Evander and I, sat in the dimly lighted room, looking alternately toward the bed where the mistress of the house lay in a drugged sleep, into the still-burning fire of coals in the fireplace grate, and at each other's faces. Three of us were puzzled almost to the point of hysteria, and de Grandin seemed on pins and needles with excitement and expectation. Occasionally he would rise and walk to the bed with that quick soundless tread of his which always made me think of a cat. Again he would dart into the hall, nervously light a cigarette, draw a few quick puffs from it, then glide noiselessly into the sickroom once more. None of us spoke above a whisper and our conversation was limited to inconsequential things. Throughout our group there was the tense expectancy and solemn, taut-nerved air of medical witnesses in the prison death chamber awaiting the advent of the condemned.

Subconsciously, I think, we all realized what we waited for, but my nerves nearly snapped when it came.

With the suddenness of a shot, unheralded by any preliminary, the wild, vibrating howl of a beast sounded beneath the sickroom window, its sharp, poignant wail seeming to split the frigid, moonlit air of the night.

"O-o-o—o-o-o-o—o-o-o—o-o-o-o!" it rose against the winter stillness, diminished to a moan of heart-rending melancholy, then suddenly crescendoed upward, from a moan to a wail, from a wail to a howl, despairing, passionate, longing as the lament of a damned spirit, wild and fierce as the rallying call of the fiends of hell.

"Oh!" Miss Ostrander exclaimed involuntarily.

"Let be!" Jules de Grandin ordered tensely, his whisper seeming to carry more because of its sharpness than from any actual sound it made.

"O-o-o—o-o-o-o—o-o-o—o-o-o-o!" again the cry shuddered through the air, again it rose to a pitch of intolerable shrillness and evil, then died away, and, as we sat stone-still in the shadowy chamber, a new sound, a sinister, scraping sound, intensified by the ice-hard coldness of the night, came to us. Someone, some *thing*, was swarming up the rose-trellis outside the house!

Scrape, scratch, scrape, the alternate hand- and foot-holds sounded on the cross-bars of the lattice. A pair of hands, long, slender, corded hands, like hands of a cadaver long dead, and armed with talons, blood-stained and hooked, grasped the window-ledge, and a face—God of Mercy, such a face!—was silhouetted against the background of the night.

Not human, nor yet wholly bestial it was, but partook grotesquely of both, so that it was at once a foul caricature of each. The forehead was low and narrow, and sloped back to a thatch of short, nondescript-colored hair resembling an animal's fur. The nose was elongated out of all semblance to a human feature and resembled the pointed snout of some animal of the canine tribe except that it curved sharply down at the tip like the beak of some unclean bird of prey. Thin, cruel lips were drawn sneeringly back from a double row of tusk-like teeth which gleamed horridly in the dim reflection of the open fire, and a pair of round, baleful eyes, green as the luminescence from a rotting carcass in a midnight swamp, glared at us across the windowsill. On each of us in turn the basilisk glance dwelt momentarily, then fastened itself on the sleeping sick woman like a falcon's talons on a dove.

Miss Ostrander gave a single choking sob and slid forward from her chair unconscious. Evander and I sat stupefied with horror, unable to do more than gaze in terror-stricken silence at the apparition, but Jules de Grandin was out of his seat and across the room with a single bound of feline grace and ferocity.

"Aroint thee, accursed of God!" he screamed, showering a barrage of blows from a slender wand on the creature's face. "Back, spawn of Satan! To thy kennel, hound of hell! I, Jules de Grandin, command it!"

The suddenness of his attack took the thing by surprise. For a moment it snarled and cowered under the hailstorm of blows from de Grandin's stick, then, as suddenly as it had come into view, it loosed its hold on the windowsill and dropped from sight.

"*Sang de Dieu, sang du diable; sang des tous les saints de ciel!*" de Grandin roared, hurling himself out the window in the wake of the fleeing monster. "I have you, vile wretch. *Pardieu, Monsieur Loup-garou*, but I shall surely crush you!"

Rushing to the window, I saw the tall, skeleton-thin form of the enormity leaping across the moonlit snow with great, space-devouring bounds, and after it, brandishing his wand, ran Jules de Grandin, shouting triumphant invectives in mingled French and English.

By the shadow of a copse of evergreens the thing made a stand. Wheeling in its tracks, it bent nearly double, extending its cadaverous claws like a wrestler searching for a hold, and baring its glistening tusks in a snarl of fury.

De Grandin never slackened pace. Charging full tilt upon the waiting monstrosity, he reached his free hand into his jacket pocket. There was a gleam of blue metal in the moonlight. Then eight quick, pitiless spurts of flame stabbed through the shadow where the monster lurked, eight whiplike crackling reports echoed and re-echoed in the midnight stillness—and the voice of Jules de Grandin:

"Trowbridge, *mon vieux, ohé*, Friend Trowbridge, bring a light quickly! I would that you see what I see!"

Weltering in a patch of blood-stained snow at de Grandin's feet we found an elderly man, ruddy-faced, gray-haired, and, doubtless, in life, of a dignified, even benign aspect. Now, however, he lay in the snow as naked as the day his mother first saw him, and eight gaping gunshot wounds told where de Grandin's missiles had found their mark. The winter cold was already stiffening his limbs and setting his face in a mask of death.

"Good heavens," Evander ejaculated as he bent over the lifeless form, "it's Uncle Friedrich—my wife's uncle! He disappeared just before I went south."

"*Eh bien*," de Grandin regarded the body with no more emotion than if it had been an effigy molded in snow, "we shall know where to find your uncle henceforth, Monsieur. Will some of you pick him up? Me—*pardieu* I would no more touch him than I would handle a hyena!"

"Now, Monsieur," de Grandin faced Evander across the living room table, "your statement that the gentleman at whose happy dispatch I so fortunately officiated was your wife's uncle, and that he disappeared before your southern trip, does interest me. Say on, tell me all concerning this Uncle Friedrich of your wife's. When did he disappear, and what led up to his disappearance? Omit nothing, I pray you, for trifles which you may consider of no account may be of the greatest importance. Proceed Monsieur. I listen."

Evander squirmed uncomfortably in his chair like a small boy undergoing catechism. "He wasn't really her uncle," he responded. "Her father and he were schoolmates in Germany—Heidelberg—years ago. Mr. Hoffmeister—Uncle Friedrich—immigrated to this country shortly after my father-in-law came back, and they were in business together for years. Mr. Hoffmeister lived with my wife's people—all the children called him Uncle Friedrich—and was just like one of the family.

"My mother-in-law died a few years ago, and her husband died shortly after, and Mr. Hoffmeister disposed of his share of the business and went to Germany on a long visit. He was caught there in the war and didn't return to America until '21. Since that time he lived with us."

Evander paused a moment, as though debating mentally whether he should proceed, then smiled in a half shamefaced manner. "To tell you the truth," he continued, "I wasn't very keen on having him here. There were times when I didn't like the way he looked at my wife a dam' bit."

"Eh," de Grandin asked, "how was that, Monsieur?"

"Well, I can't quite put a handle to it in words, but more than once I'd glance up and see him with his eyes fastened on Edith in a most peculiar way. It would have angered me in a young man, but in an old man, it both angered and disgusted me. I was on the point of asking him to leave when he disappeared and saved me the trouble."

"Yes?" de Grandin encouraged. "And his disappearance, what of that?"

"The old fellow was always an enthusiastic amateur botanist," Evander replied, "and he brought a great many specimens for his herbarium back from Europe with him. Off and on he's been messing around with plants since his return, and about a month ago he received a tin of dried flowers from Kerovitch, Rumania, and they seemed to set him almost wild."

"Kerovitch? *Mordieu!*" de Grandin exclaimed. "Say on, Monsieur; I burn with curiosity. Describe these flowers in detail, if you please."

"H'm," Evander took his chin in his hand and studied in silence a moment. "There wasn't anything especially remarkable about them that I could see. There were a dozen of them, all told, perhaps, and they resembled our ox-eyed daisies a good deal, except that their petals were red instead of yellow. Had a queer sort of odor, too. Even though they were dried, they exuded a sort of sick-ly-sweet smell, yet not quite sweet either. It was a sort of mixture of perfume and stench, if that means anything to you.

"*Pardieu*, it means much!" de Grandin assured him. "And their sap, where it had dried, did it not resemble that of the milkweed plant?"

"Yes! How did you know?"

"No matter. Proceed, if you please. Your Uncle Friedrich did take these so accursed flowers out and . . ."

"And tried an experiment with them," Evander supplied. "He put them in a bowl of water, and they freshened up as though they had not been plucked an hour."

"Yes—and his disappearance—name of a little green man!—his disappearance?"

"That happened just before I went south. All three of us went to the theater one evening, and Uncle Friedrich wore one of the red flowers in his buttonhole. My wife wore a spray of them in her corsage. He tried to get me to put one of the things in my coat, too, but I hated their smell so much I wouldn't do it."

"Lucky you!" de Grandin murmured so low the narrator failed to hear him.

Uncle Friedrich was very restless and queer all evening," Evander proceeded, "but the old fellow had been getting rather childish lately, so we didn't pay any particular attention to his actions. Next morning he was gone."

"And did you make inquiry?"

"No, he often went away on little trips without warning us beforehand, and, besides, I was glad enough to see him get out. I didn't try to find him. It was just after this that my wife's health became bad, but I had to make this trip for our firm, so I called in Dr. Trowbridge, and there you are."

"Yes, *parbleu*, here we are, indeed!" de Grandin nodded emphatically. "Listen carefully, my friends; what I am about to say is the truth:

"When first I came to visit Madame Evander with Friend Trowbridge, and heard the strange story Mademoiselle Ostrander told, I was amazed. 'Why,' I ask me, 'does this lady answer the howling of a dog beneath her window?' *Parbleu*, it was most curious!

"Then while we three—Friend Trowbridge, Mademoiselle Ostrander and I—did talk of Madame's so strange malady, I did hear the call of that dog beneath the window with my own two ears, and did observe Madame Evander's reaction to it.

"Out the window I did put my head, and in the storm I saw no dog at all, but what I thought might be a human man—a tall, thin man. Yet a dog had howled beneath that window and had been answered by Madame but a moment before. Me, I do not like that.

"I call upon that man, if such he be, to be gone. Also I do request Mademoiselle Ostrander to place her patient under an opiate each night, that the howls beneath her window may not awaken Madame Evander.

"*Eh bien*, thus far, thus good. But you do come along, Monsieur, and countermand my order. While Madame is not under the drug that unholy thing beneath her window does howl once more, and Madame disappears. Yes.

"Now, there was no ordinary medical diagnosis for such a case as this, so I search my memory and my knowledge for an extraordinary one. What do I find in that storehouse of my mind?

"In parts of Europe, my friends—believe me, I know whereof I speak!—there are known such things as werewolves, or wolf-men. In France we know them as *les loups-garoux*; in Wales they call them the bug-wolves, or bogie-wolves; in the days of old the Greeks did know them under the style of *lukanthropos*. Yes.

"What he is no one knows well. Sometimes he is said to be a wolf—a magical wolf—who can become a man. Sometimes, more often, he is said to be a man who can, or must, become a wolf. No one knows accurately. But this we know: The man who is also a wolf is ten times more terrible than the wolf who is only a wolf. At night he quests and kills his prey, which is most often his fellow man, but sometimes his ancient enemy, the dog. By day he hides his villainy under the guise of a man's form. Sometimes he changes entirely to a wolf's shape, sometimes he becomes a fearful mixture of man and beast, but always he is a devil incarnate. If he be killed while in the wolf shape, he at once reverts to human form, so by that sign we know we have slain a werewolf and not a true wolf. Certainly.

"Now, some werewolves become such by the aid of Satan; some become so as the result of a curse; a few are so through accident. In Transylvania, that devil-ridden land, the very soil does seem to favor the transformation of man into beast. There are springs from which the water, once drunk, will make its drinker into a savage beast, and there are flowers—*cordieu*, have I not seen them?—which, if worn by a man at night during the full of the moon, will do the same. Among the most potent of these blooms of hell is *la fleur de sang*, or blood-flower, which is exactly the accursed weed you have described to us, Monsieur Evander—the flower your Uncle Friedrich and your lady did wear to the theater that night of the full moon. When you mentioned the village of Kerovitch, I did see it all at once, immediately, for that place is on the Rumanian side of the

Transylvanian Alps, and there the blood-flowers are found in greater numbers than anywhere else in the world. The very mountain soil does seem cursed with lycanthropy.

"Very well. I did not know of the flower when first I came into this case, but I did suspect something evil had cast a spell on Madame. She did exhibit all the symptoms of a lycanthrope about to be transformed, and beneath her window there did howl what was undoubtedly a wolf-thing.

"'He has put his cursed sign upon her and does even now seek her for his mate,' I tell me after I order him away in the name of the good God.

"When Madame disappeared I was not surprised. When she returned after a night in the snow, I was less surprised. But the blood on her hands did perturb me. Was it human? Was she an all-unconscious murderess, or was it, happily, the blood of animals? I did not know. I analyzed it and discovered it were dog's blood. 'Very well,' I tell me. 'Let us see where a dog has been mauled in that vicinity.'

"This afternoon I made guarded inquiries. I find many dogs have been strangely killed in this neighborhood of late. No dog, no matter how big, was safe out of doors after nightfall.

"Also I meet a man, an *ivrogne*—what you call a drunkard—one who patronizes the leggers-of-the-boot not with wisdom, but with too great frequency. He is no more so. He have made the oath to remain sober. *Pourquoi?* Because three nights ago, as he passed through the park he were set upon by a horror so terrible that he thought he was in alcoholic delirium. It were like a man, yet not like a man. It had a long nose, and terrible eyes, and great, flashing teeth, and it did seek to kill and devour him. My friends, in his way, that former drunkard did describe the thing which tried to enter this house tonight. It were the same.

"Fortunately for the poor drunken man, he were carrying a walking cane of ash wood, and when he raised it to defend himself, the terror did shrink from him. 'Ah ha,' I tell me when I hear that, 'now we know it were truly *le loup-garou*,' for it is notorious that the wood of the ash tree is as intolerable to the werewolf as the bloom of the garlic is unpleasant to the vampire.

"What do I do? I go to the woods and cut a bundle of ash switches. Then I come here. Tonight the wolf-thing come crying for the mate who ranged the snows with him last night. He is lonely, he is mad for another of his kind. Tonight, perhaps, they will attack nobler game than dogs. Very well, I am ready.

"When Madame Evander, being drugged, did not answer his call, he was emboldened to enter the house. *Pardieu*, he did not know Jules de Grandin awaited him! Had I not been here it might well have gone hard with Mademoiselle Ostrander. As it was"—he spread his slender hands—"there is one less man-monster in the world this night."

Evander stared at him in round-eyed wonder. "I can't believe it," he muttered, "but you've proved your case. Poor Uncle Friedrich! The curse of the blood-flower." He broke off, an expression of mingled horror and despair on his face. "My wife!" he gasped. "Will she become a thing like that? Will . . . ?"

"Monsieur," de Grandin interrupted gently, "she *has* become one. Only the drug holds her bound in human form at this minute."

"Oh," Evander cried, tears of grief streaming down his face, "save her! For the love of heaven, save her! Can't you do anything to bring her back to me?"

"You do not approve my methods," de Grandin reminded him.

Evander was like a pleading child. "I apologize," he whimpered. "I'll give you anything you ask if you'll only save her. I'm not rich, but I think I can raise fifty thousand dollars. I'll give it to you if you'll cure her!"

The Frenchman twisted his little blond mustache furiously. "The fee you name is attractive, Monsieur," he remarked.

"I'll pay it; I'll pay it!" Evander burst out hysterically. Then, unable to control himself, he put his folded arms on the table, sank his head upon them, and shook with sobs.

"Very well," de Grandin agreed, casting me the flicker of a wink. "Tomorrow night I shall undertake your lady's case. Tomorrow night we attempt the cure. *Au revoir*, Monsieur. Come away, Friend Trowbridge, we must rest well before tomorrow night."

D E GRANDIN WAS SILENT to the point of moodiness all next morning. Toward noon he put on his outdoor clothing and left without luncheon, saying he would meet me at Evander's that night.

He was there when I arrived and greeted me, saying that the main business would start soon.

"Meantime, Trowbridge, *mon vieux*, I beg you will assist me in the kitchen. There is much to do and little time in which to do it."

Opening a large valise he produced a bundle of slender sticks which he began splitting into strips like basket-withes, explaining that they were from a mountain ash tree. When some twenty-five of these had been prepared, he selected a number of bottles from the bottom of the satchel, and, taking a large aluminum kettle, began scouring it with a clean cloth.

"Attend me carefully, Friend Trowbridge," he commanded; "do you keep close tally as I compound the draft, for much depends on the formula being correct. To begin."

Arranging a pair of apothecary's scales and a graduate glass before him on the table, he handed me this memorandum:

℞
3 pints pure spring water
2 drachms sulfur
½ oz. castorium
6 drachms opium
3 drachms asafoetida
½ oz. hypericum
¾ oz. aromatic ammonia
½ oz. gum camphor

As he busied himself with scales and graduate I checked the amounts he poured into the kettle. "*Voilà*," he announced, "we are prepared!"

Quickly he thrust the ash withes into a pailful of boiling water and proceeded to bind together a three-stranded hyssop of ash, poplar and birch twigs.

"And now, my friend, if you will assist me, we shall proceed," he asserted, thrusting a large wash pan into my hands and preparing to follow me into the dining room with the kettle of liquor he had prepared, his little brush-broom thrust under his arm.

We moved the dining room furniture against the walls, and de Grandin put the kettle of liquid in the dishpan I had brought in, piling a number of light wood chips about it, and starting a small fire. As the liquid in the kettle began bubbling and seething over the flame, he knelt and began tracing a circle about seven feet in diameter with a bit of white chalk. Inside the first circle he drew a second ring some three feet in diameter, and within this traced a star composed  of two interlaced triangles. At the very center he marked down an odd-looking figure composed of a circle surmounted by a crescent and supported by a cross. "This is the Druid's foot, or pentagram," he explained, indicating the star. "The powers of evil are powerless to pass it, either from without or within. This," he pointed to the central figure, "is the sign of Mercury. It is also the sign of the Holy Angels, my friend, and the *bon Dieu* knows we shall need their kind offices this night. Compare, Friend Trowbridge, if you please, the chart I have drawn with the exemplar which I did most carefully prepare from the occult books today. I would have the testimony of both of us that I have left nothing undone."

Into my hand he thrust the following chart:

Quickly, working like one possessed, he arranged seven small silver lamps about the outer circle where the seven little rings on the chart indicated, ignited their wicks, snapped off the electric light and, rushing into the kitchen, returned with the boiled ash withes dangling from his hand.

Fast as he had worked, there was not a moment to spare, for Miss Ostrander's hysterical call, "Dr. de Grandin, oh, Dr. de Grandin!" came down the stairs as he returned from the kitchen.

O N THE BED Mrs. Evander lay writhing like a person in convulsions. As we approached, she turned her face toward us, and I stopped in my tracks, speechless with the spectacle before me.

It was as if the young woman's pretty face were twisted into a grimace, only the muscles, instead of resuming their wonted positions again, seemed to stretch steadily out of place. Her mouth widened gradually till it was nearly twice its normal size, her nose seemed lengthening, becoming more pointed, and crooking sharply at the end. Her eyes, of sweet cornflower blue, were widening, becoming at once round and prominent, and changing to a wicked, phosphorescent green. I stared and stared, unable to believe the evidence of my eyes, and as I looked she raised her hands from beneath the covers, and I went sick with the horror of it. The dainty, flower-like pink-and-white hands with their well-manicured nails were transformed into a pair of withered, corded talons armed with long, hornlike, curved claws, saber-sharp and hooked like the nails of some predatory bird. Before my eyes a sweet, gently bred woman was being transfigured into a foul hell-hag, a loathsome, hideous parody of herself.

"Quickly, Friend Trowbridge, seize her, bind her!" de Grandin called, thrusting a handful of the limber withes into my grasp and hurling himself upon the monstrous thing which lay in Edith Evander's place.

The hag fought like a true member of the wolf pack. Howling, clawing, growling and snarling, she opposed tooth and nail to our efforts, but at last we lashed her wrists and ankles firmly with the wooden cords and bore her struggling frantically, down the stairs and placed her within the mystic circle de Grandin had drawn on the dining room floor.

"Inside, Friend Trowbridge, quickly!" the Frenchman ordered as he dipped the hyssop into the boiling liquid in the kettle and leaped over the chalk marks. "Mademoiselle Ostrander, Monsieur Evander, for your lives, leave the house!"

Reluctantly the husband and nurse left us and de Grandin began showering the contorting, howling thing on the floor with liquid from the boiling kettle.

Swinging his hyssop in the form of a cross above the hideous changeling's head, he uttered some invocation so rapidly that I failed to catch the words, then, striking the wolf-woman's feet, hands, heart and head in turn with his bundle of twigs, he drew forth a small black book and began reading in a firm, clear voice: "*Out of the deep have I called unto Thee, O Lord; Lord hear my voice. . . .*"

And at the end he finished with a great shout: "*I know that my redeemer liveth . . . I am the resurrection and the life, saith the Lord: he that believeth in me, though he were dead, yet shall he live!*"

As the words sounded through the room it seemed to me that a great cloud of shadow, like a billow of black vapor, rose from the dark corners of the apartment, eddied toward the circle of lamps, swaying their flames lambently, then suddenly gave back, evaporated and disappeared with a noise like steam escaping from a boiling kettle.

"Behold, Trowbridge, my friend," de Grandin ordered, pointing to the still figure which lay over the sign of Mercury at his feet.

I bent forward, stifling my repugnance, then sighed with mingled relief and surprise. Calm as a sleeping child, Edith Evander, freed from all the hideous stigmata of the wolf-people, lay before us, her slender hands, still bound in the wooden ropes, crossed on her breast, her sweet, delicate features as though they had never been disfigured by the curse of the blood-flower.

Loosing the bonds from her wrists and feet the Frenchman picked the sleeping woman up in his arms and bore her to her bedroom above stairs.

"Do you summon her husband and the nurse, my friend," he called from the turn in the stairway. "She will have need of both anon."

"WH—WHY, SHE'S HERSELF AGAIN!" Evander exclaimed joyfully as he leaned solicitously above his wife's bed.

"But of course!" de Grandin agreed. "The spell of evil was strong upon her, Monsieur, but the charm of good was mightier. She is released from her bondage for all time."

"I'll have your fee ready tomorrow," Evander promised diffidently. "I could not arrange the mortgages today—it was rather short notice, you know."

Laughter twinkled in de Grandin's little blue eyes like the reflection of moonlight on flowing water. "My friend," he replied, "I did make the good joke on you last night. *Parbleu*, to hear you agree to anything, and to announce that you did trust to my methods, as well, was payment enough for me. I want not your money. If you would repay Jules de Grandin for his services, continue to love and cherish your wife as you did last night when you feared you were about to lose her. Me, *morbleu!* but I shall make the eyes of my *confrères* pop with jealousy when I tell them what I have accomplished this night. *Sang d'un poisson*, I am one very clever man, Monsieur!"

"IT'S ALL A MYSTERY to me, de Grandin," I confessed as we drove home, "but I'm hanged if I can understand how it was that the man was transformed into a monster almost as soon as he wore those flowers, and the woman resisted the influence of the things for a week or more."

"Yes," he agreed, "that is strange. Myself, I think it was because werewolfism is an outward and visible sign of the power of evil, and the man was already steeped in sin, while the woman was pure in heart. She had what we might call a higher immunity from the virus of the blood-flower."

"And wasn't there some old legend to the effect that a werewolf could only be killed with a silver bullet?"

"Ah bah," he replied with a laugh. "What did thost old legend-mongers know of the power of modern fire arms? *Parbleu*, had the good St. George possessed a military rifle of today, he might have slain the dragon without approaching nearer than a mile! When I did shoot that wolfman, my friend, I had something more powerful than superstition in my hand. *Morbleu*, but I did shoot a hole in him large enough for him to have walked through!"

"That reminds me," I added, "how are we going to explain his body to the police?"

"Explain?" he echoed with a chuckle. "*Nom d'un bouc*, we shall not explain: I, myself, did dispose of him this very afternoon. He lies buried beneath the roots of an ash tree, with a stake of ash through his heart to hold him to the earth. His sinful body will rise again no more to plague us, I do assure you. He was known to have a habit of disappearing. Very good. This time there will be no reappearance. We are through, finished, done with him for good."

We drove another mile or so in silence, then my companion nudged me sharply in the ribs. "This curing of werewolf ladies, my friend," he confided, "it is dry work. Are you sure there is a full bottle of brandy in the cellar?"

The Veiled Prophetess

"**B**UT, MADAME, WHAT YOU say is incredible," Jules de Grandin was saying to a fashionably dressed young woman as I returned to the consulting room from my morning round of calls.

"It may be incredible," the visitor admitted, "but it's so, just the same. I tell you she was there."

"Ah, Trowbridge, *mon cher*," de Grandin leaped up as he beheld me in the doorway, "this is Madame Penneman. She has a remarkable story to tell.

"*Madame*," he bowed ceremoniously to our caller, "will you have the goodness to relate your case to Dr. Trowbridge? He will be interested."

The young lady crossed her slender, gray-silk clad legs, adjusted her abbreviated black-satin dress in a manner to cover at least a portion of her patellæ, and regarded me with the fixed, dreamy stare of a pupil reciting a lesson learned by rote.

"My name is Naomi Penneman," she began; "my husband is Benjamin Penneman, of the chocolate importing firm of Penneman & Brixton. We have been married six months, and came to live in Harrisonville when we returned from our honeymoon trip, three months ago. We have the Barton place in Tunlaw Street."

"Yes?" I murmured.

"I heard of Dr. de Grandin through Mrs. Norman—she said he did a wonderful piece of work in rescuing her daughter Esther from some horrible old man—so I brought my case to you. I wouldn't dare go to the police with it."

"U'm?" I murmured. "Just what—"

"It's about my husband," she went on, without giving me time to form my query. "There's a woman—or something—trying to take him away from me!"

"Well—er—my, dear young lady, don't you think you would better have consulted a lawyer?" I objected. "Physicians sometimes undertake to patch up leaky hearts, but they are scarcely in the business of repairing outraged affections, you know."

"*Mais non*, Friend Trowbridge," de Grandin denied with a delighted chuckle, "you do misapprehend *Madame's* statement. Me, I think perhaps she speaks advisedly when she does say 'a woman *or something*' designs to alienate her husband.

"Proceed, *Madame*, if you please."

"I graduated from Barnard in '24," Mrs. Penneman took up her statement, "and married Ben last year. We went on a ninety-day cruise for our wedding tour, and moved here as soon as we came back.

"Our class had a reunion at the Allenton Thursday of Christmas week, and some of the girls were crazy about Madame Naîra, the Veiled Prophetess, a fortune-teller up in East Eighty-second Street. Thy talked about her so much the rest of us decided to pay her a call.

"I was afraid to go by myself, so I teased Ben, my husband, into going with me, and—and he's been acting queer ever since."

"Queer?" I echoed. "How?"

"Well"—she made a vague sort of gesture with one of her small, well-manicured hands and flushed slightly—"you know, Doctor, when two people have been married only six months the star-dust oughtn't to be rubbed off the wings of romance, ought it? Yet Ben's been cooler and cooler to me, commencing almost immediately after we went to see that horrid woman."

"You mean—"

"Oh, it's hard to put into words. Just little things, you know; none of them important in themselves, but pretty big in the aggregate. He forgets to kiss me good-bye in the morning, stays over in New York late at night—sometimes without calling me up to let me know he won't be home—and breaks engagements to take me places without warning. Then, when I expostulate, he pleads business."

"But my dear madame," I protested, "this is certainly no case for us. Not every man has the capacity for retaining romance after marriage. Mighty few of them have, I imagine. And it may easily be exactly as your husband says: His business may require his presence in New York at nights. Be reasonable, my dear; when you were first married, he might have strained a point to be home while dinner was still hot, and let his partners handle matters, but you're really old married folks now, you know, and he has to make a living for you both. You'd best let me give you a bromide—this thing may have gotten on your nerves—and go home and forget your silly suspicions."

"And will the bromide keep her—or it—out of my house—out of my bedroom—at night?" Mrs. Penneman asked.

"Eh, what's that?" I demanded.

"That's what made me call on Dr. de Grandin," she replied. "It was bad enough when Ben took to neglecting me, but on the second of last month, while we were in bed, *I saw a woman in our room.*"

"A woman—in your bedroom?" I asked. The story seemed more sordid than I had at first supposed.

"Well, if it wasn't a woman it was something in the shape of one," she replied. "I'd been pretty much upset by Ben's actions, and had reproached him pretty severely the Sunday before when he didn't show up to take me from the Ambersons' reception, and he'd promised to reform.

"He did, too. For four nights, from Monday to Thursday, he'd been home to dinner on time, and Thursday night—the second—we'd been to the theater over in New York. We went to a night club after the play and came back on the owl train. It must have been one o'clock before we got home. I was awfully tired and went to bed just as soon as I could get my clothes off; but Ben was in bed first, and was sound asleep when I got into mine.

"I was just dropping off when I happened to remember he hadn't kissed me good night—we'd rather gotten out of the habit during the last few weeks.

"I turned my covers back and was in the act of getting out of bed to lean over Ben and kiss him, when I noticed he was moaning, or talking in his sleep. Just as I put my feet to the floor, I heard him say, 'Second, Second!' twice, just like that, and put his hands out, as if he were pushing something away from him.

"Then I saw her. All at once she was standing by the door of our room, smiling at him like—like a cat smiling at a bird, if you can imagine such a thing—and walking toward him with her arms outstretched.

"I thought I was dreaming, but I wasn't. I tell you, I saw her. She walked across the rug and stood beside him, looking down with that queer, catty smile of hers, and took both his hands in hers. He sat up in bed, and looked at her like—as he used to look at me when we were first married!

"I was spellbound for a moment, then I said, 'Dream or no dream, she shan't have him!' and leaped to my feet. The woman loosed one of her hands from Ben's and pointed her finger at me, smiling that same awful, calm smile all the time.

"'Woman,' she said, 'get you gone. This man is mine, bound to me forever. He has put you away and wedded me. Be off!' That's just what she said, speaking in a sort of throaty voice—and then she went away."

"How do you mean, 'went away'?" I asked. "Did she vanish?"

"I don't know," Mrs. Penneman answered. "I couldn't say whether she actually vanished or faded out like a motion picture or went through the door. She just wasn't there when I looked again."

"And your husband?"

"He fell right back on the pillows and went to sleep. I had to shake him in order to wake him up."

"Shamming?"

"No-o, I don't think so. He really seemed asleep, and he didn't seem to know anything about the woman when I asked him."

"U'm?" I gave de Grandin a quick look, but there was no gleam of agreement in his round blue eyes as they encountered mine.

"Proceed, *Madame*, if you please," he urged with a nod at our caller.

"She's been back three times since then," Mrs. Penneman said, "and each time she has warned me to leave. The last time—night before last—she threatened me. Said she would wither me if I did not go."

"Tell me, *Madame*," de Grandin broke in, "is there any condition precedent to this strange visitant's appearance?"

"I—I don't believe I understand," the girl replied.

"Any particular conduct on your husband's part which would seem to herald her approach? Does he show any signs? Or, perhaps, do you have any feelings of apprehension or presentiment before she comes?"

"No-o," Mrs. Penneman answered thoughtfully, "no, I can't say that—wait a moment!—yes! Every time she's come it's been after a period of reformation on Ben's part, after he's been attentive to me for several days. As long as he's indifferent to me she stays away, but each time he begins to be his old, dear self, she makes her appearance, always very late at night or early in the morning, and always with the same command for me to leave.

"One thing more, Doctor. The last time she told me to go—the time she threatened me—I noticed Ben's seal ring on her finger."

"Eh, what is that?" de Grandin snapped. "His ring? How?"

"He lost his ring when we went to visit Madame Naîra. I'm sure he did, though he declares he didn't. It was a class ring with the seal of the university on it and his class numerals imposed on the seal."

"And how came he to lose it, if you please?"

"He was clowning," the girl answered. "Ben was always acting like a comedian in the old days, and he was showing off when we went to the Veiled Prophetess' that day. Really, I think the place rather impressed him and he was like a little boy whistling his way past the graveyard when he acted like a buffoon. The place was awfully weird, with a lot of Eastern bric-à-brac in the reception room where we waited for the Prophetess to see us. Ben went all around, examining everything, and seemed especially taken with the statue of a woman with a cat's head. The thing was almost life-size, and shaped something like a mummy—it gave me the creeps, really. Ben put his hat—he was wearing a derby that day—on its head, and then slipped his seal ring on its finger. Just then the door to the Prophetess' consulting room opened, and Ben snatched his hat off the thing's head in a hurry, but I'm sure he didn't get his ring back. We were ushered into the fortune-teller's place immediately, and went out by another door, and we were so full of the stuff she'd told us that neither of us missed the ring till we were on the train coming home.

"Ben 'phoned her place next day, but they said no such ring had been found. He didn't like to confess he'd put it on the statue's finger, so he told them he must have dropped it on the floor."

"Ah?" de Grandin drew a pad of paper and a pencil toward him and scribbled a note. "And what did she tell you, this Madame Veiled Prophetess Naîra, if you please, *Madame?*"

"Oh"—the girl spread her hands—"the usual patter the fortune-tellers have. Recited my history fairly accurately, told me I'd been to Egypt—nothing wonderful in that; I was wearing a scarab Ben bought me in Cairo—and ended up with some nonsense about my having to make a big sacrifice in the near future that others might have happiness and destiny be fulfilled."

She paused, a rosy flush suffusing her face. "That frightened us a little," she confessed, "because, when she said that, we both thought maybe she meant I was going to die when—well, you see—"

"Perfectly, *Madame*," de Grandin nodded with quick understanding. "Mankind is perpetuated by woman's going into the Valley of the Shadow of Death to fetch up new lives. Fear not, dear lady, I do assure you the Prophetess meant something quite otherwise."

"And you will help me?" she begged. "Dr. de Grandin, I—I am going to do what you said about the Valley of the Shadow this spring, and I want my husband. He is my man, my mate, and no one—*no thing*—shall take him from me. Can you make her go away? Please?"

"I shall try, *Madame*," the little Frenchman answered gently. "I can not say I quite understand everything—yet—but I shall make your case my study. *Parbleu*, but I shall sleep not until I have reached a working hypothesis!"

"Oh, thank you; thank you!" the young matron exclaimed. "I feel ever so much easier already."

"But of course," de Grandin acquiesced, bending a smile of singular sweetness on her, "that is as it should be, *ma chère*." He raised her fingers to his lips before escorting her from the room.

"And now, Friend Trowbridge, what do you think of our case?" he demanded when the front door had closed behind our caller.

"Since you ask me," I answered with brutal frankness, "I don't know who's the crazier, Mrs. Penneman or you; but I think you are, for you should know better. You know as well as I that illusions and hallucinations are apt to occur at any time during the puerperal period. This is a clear case of mild manic-depressive insanity. Because of her condition this poor child has construed her husband's absorption in his business as neglect. She's a psychic type, reacting readily to external stimuli, and in her state of depression she thinks his love has failed. That's preyed on her mind till she's on the borderline of insanity, and you were very unkind to humor her in her delusions."

He rested his elbows on the desk, cupping his little pointed chin in his hands, and puffed furiously on his cigarette till its acrid, unpleasant smoke surrounded his sleek blond head in a gray nimbus. "O, *la, la*, hear him!" he chuckled. "Suppose, Trowbridge, *mon vieux*, I were to say I do not consider *la belle* Penneman mad at all. Not even one little bit. What then?"

"Humph!" I returned. "I dare say you'd have agreed with her if she'd said that statue her husband put his ring on had come to life?"

"Perhaps," he returned with an irritating grin. "Before we are through with this case, my friend, we may see stranger things than that."

Two DAYS LATER HE announced matter-of-factly, "Today, Friend Trowbridge, we go to interview this Madame Naîra, the Prophetess of the Veil."

"We?" I responded. "Perhaps you do, but I'll have nothing to do with the matter."

"*Pardieu*, but you will!" he replied with a laugh. "This case, my friend, promises as much adventure as any you and I have had together. Come, a spice of the unusual will be a tonic for you after an uneventful season of house-to-house calls."

"Oh, all right," I agreed grudgingly. "I'll go along, but I want you to know I don't countenance any of this foolishness. What Mrs. Penneman needs is a nerve specialist, not this clowning we're going through."

Madame Naîra's atelier in East Eighty-second Street spoke volumes for the public's credulity. It was one of the old-fashioned brownstone front residences of two generations ago, located within a pebble's toss of Central Park, and worth its square footage in gold coin. Outside it was as like its neighbors in the block as one pea is like its fellows in the pod. Within it was a perfect example of good taste and expensive furnishings. A butler bearing all the hall-marks of having served in at least a duke's household, staidly resplendent in correct cutaway coat and striped trousers, admitted us and took the cards de Grandin handed him, inspecting them with minute care, accepted the Prophetess' fee (payable strictly in advance) and ushered us into a large and luxuriously furnished parlor.

"See here," I began as we seated ourselves in a pair of richly upholstered chairs, "if you expect to—"

A violent grimace on the Frenchman's face warned me to silence. Next moment he rose, remarking, "What a beautiful room we have here, my friend," and sauntered about, admiring the handsome pictures on the walls. Passing my chair he seated himself on its arm and slapped me jovially on the back, then bent close and whispered fiercely in my ear: "No talk, Friend Trowbridge; already I have discovered dictographs concealed behind nearly every picture, and I know not if they have periscope peepholes, to enable them to watch us as well. Caution! I had a friend at the French consulate make the appointment for us in his name, and I am Alphonse Charres, while you have assumed the role of William Tindell, an attorney. Remember."

Humming a snatch of tune he began a second circuit of the room.

Before he had completed his trip a slender, dark-skinned young man in flowing blue linen robes and a huge turban of red and yellow silk appeared almost as if by magic in the drawing room doorway, beckoning us with a thin bamboo cane which he bore like a badge of office.

Casting me the flicker of a wink de Grandin fell in step behind him and followed up the stairs.

The ground floor drawing room where we had first cooled our heels was a perfect example of Occidental elegance in furniture and appointments. The room into which we were now shown was a riot of Oriental extravagance. Rugs of hues and patterns as gorgeous as the plumage of paradise birds were strewn over the floor, in some cases three deep, the plaster walls were painted in glaring reproductions of Egyptian temple scenes, and fitted here and there with niches in which stood statues of plaster, stone or metal, many of them enameled in brilliant colors.

The only article of furniture in the apartment was a long crescent-shaped bench or settee of some dark wood thickly encrusted with mother-of-pearl inlays, which stood almost in the center of the room and faced what appeared to be the entrance to another chamber.

This entrance was constructed in the form of a temple gateway, or, it seemed to me, the door to a mausoleum. Plaster blocks, made to imitate stone, had been laid like a wall about it, and on each side of the opening there rose straight, thick columns topped with lotus capitals, while a slab of flat stone reached between them, forming the pediment of the doorway. On this was engraved the Egyptian symbol of the solar disk, vulture wings spreading from right and left of it. To the left of the door crouched a terra cotta androsphinx, while on the right stood a queer-looking statue representing a woman swathed in mummy bands about her lower body, naked from the waist upward, and having the head of a lioness set upon her shoulders. One hand she held against her rather prominent bosom, grasping an instrument something like an undersized tennis racket, only, instead of strings, the open oval of the racket was fitted with transverse horizontal bars on which rows of little bells hung. The other hand was extended as though bestowing a blessing, the long, tapering fingers widely separated.

I did not like the thing's looks. Involuntarily, even though I knew it to be only a lifeless piece of plaster and papier-mâché, I shuddered as I looked at it, and felt easier when my gaze rested elsewhere.

Straight before us the entrance to the next room opened between the pillars of the temple door. The doorway was fitted with two gates of iron grillwork, heavily gilded; behind the arabesqued iron hung curtains of royal purple silk.

At a sign from the usher we seated ourselves on the inlaid bench and faced the closed iron lattice.

"*Assez!*" de Grandin exclaimed in an irritable voice, "When you have done inspecting us, *Madame*, kindly have the goodness to admit us. We have urgent business elsewhere." To me he whispered: "They do peer at us through the meshes of the curtain! *Mordieu*, are we beasts at the menagerie to be stared at thus?"

As though in answer to his protest the lights in the room began to grow dimmer, a deep-toned gong sounded somewhere beyond the iron gates, and the grilled doors swung back, disclosing a darkened room beyond.

"Enter!" a deep, sepulchral voice bade us, and we stepped across the threshold of Madame Naîra's consultation room.

THE PLACE WAS PITCH-DARK, for the purple curtain fell behind us, shutting out all light from the room we had left. I stood stock-still, attempting vainly to pierce the enveloping darkness with my gaze, and it seemed as though an icy wind were blowing on my face, a chilling wind, like the draft from a long-disused tunnel. Subtly, too, the odor of sandalwood and acrid tang of frankincense was wafted to my nostrils, and in the darkness before me the faint, phosphorescent glow of a cold green-blue light became visible.

Slowly the luminosity spread, gradually taking form. Through the dark it shone, cold and hard as a far-distant star viewed on a frosty night, assuming the shape of an ancient coffin. Now the effulgence gained in strength till we could make out an upright figure in the mummy case; the figure of a woman, garbed in a straight-hanging robe of silk tissue thickly sewn with silver sequins. Her hands were crossed above her breast and her face was bowed upon them so that all we could observe at first was the whiteness of her arms and shoulders and the blackness of her hair, piled coil on coil in a high coronal. As the light increased we saw her bare feet rested on the center of a horizontal crescent moon, the horns of which extended upward on each side of her.

The breeze which blew through the dark increased its force. We could hear the flutter of the silken curtain behind us as the Prophetess raised her head and stepped majestically from her coffin, advancing toward us with a lithe, silent movement which somehow reminded me of the tread of a great, graceful leopardess.

By now the increasing light enabled us to see the woman's face was hidden in a sequin-spangled veil of the same material as her robe, and that her brows were bound with a diadem of blue-green enamel fashioned in the form of a pair of backward-bent hawk wings and bearing the circular symbol of the sun at its center.

"*Morbleu*," I heard de Grandin murmur, "are we at the circus, perhaps?"

Seemingly unaware of our presence, the veiled woman glided noiselessly across the room till she stood a scant two yards from us, extended one of her white, jewel-decked arms and motioned us to be seated. Simultaneously a crystal sphere suddenly appeared in the dark before her, glowing with cold inward fire like a monster opal, and she sank to rest in a carved chair, her long, sinuous hands hovering and darting in fantastic gestures about and above the crystal. On each fore- and little finger there gleamed a green-jeweled ring, so that her writhing hands looked for all the world like a pair of green-eyed serpents weaving a saraband in the purple dark.

"I see," she intoned in a rich contralto voice, "I see a man who vaunts his learning; a man who dares pit his puny strength against the powers which were old when Kronos himself was young. I warn that man to meddle not with what does not concern him. I warn him not to interfere in behalf of the wife who has been put away, or cross the path of one who draws her strength from the ancient goddess of Bubastis.

"Away with you, rash upstart"—one of her long, jeweled hands suddenly rose and pointed through the shadows at de Grandin—"back to your test-tubes and your retorts, your puny science and punier learning. Go give your aid to the sick and the ailing, but espouse not the cause of the woman who has been cursed by Bast, or your life shall pay the forfeit!"

Like the closing of an eyelid the light in the crystal and the paler light about the mummy case went out, leaving the room in total blackness. There came a greater gust of air than any we had yet felt, and with it an overpowering, cloying sweetness which stifled our breath and made our eyes smart like fumes from burning pepper.

"Seize her, Friend Trowbridge!" I heard de Grandin cry, then fall to coughing and gasping as the sharp, penetrating fumes attacked his mucous membranes. Something more potent than the darkness blotted out my sight, bringing hot tears to my eyes and smothering the answering hail I would have given. About me the gloom seemed filled with tiny shimmering star-points of wicked, dancing light. I reached blindly for the spot where the veiled woman had sat, encountered only empty space, and fell forward on my face, wrenched and racked with a fit of uncontrollable coughing.

Somewhere, far, far away, a light was shining, and in the greater distance a voice was calling my name, thinly, ineffectually, like a voice heard dimly in a dream. I sat up, rubbing my stinging eyes, and stared about me. The light which danced and flickered overhead was a city street lamp, and the voice ringing faintly in my ears was the voice of Jules de Grandin. We were sitting, the pair of us, on the curb of East Eighty-second Street, the arc-light laughing down at us through the cold, frosty air of the winter evening. Neither of us had hat or overcoat, and de Grandin's thin, white face was already pinched with cold.

"*Nom d'un colimaçon; nom d'un coq; nom de Dieu de nom de Dieu!*" he chattered through rattling teeth. "They have made of us one pair of fools, Friend Trowbridge. They have taken us as the fisherman takes the fish of April. Jules de Grandin, you are no more worthy to regard yourself in the mirror!"

"Whew!" I breathed, clearing my lungs of the fumes which still hung in them. "That was as sharp a trick as I ever saw, de Grandin. There must have been enough chloroform mixed with that incense to have put a dozen men away!" I got unsteadily to my feet and looked about me. We were a good two blocks from the house where Madame Naîra had hoodwinked us so neatly, though how we came there was more than I knew.

"*Parbleu*, yes," he agreed, rising and buttoning his jacket over his breast. "We were unconscious before we could so much as call the name of that Monsieur Jacques Robinson! Meantime, I famish with the cold. Can we not obtain suitable clothing?"

"H'm," I answered, "it is too late for any of the regular shops to be open, but we might get something to tide us over at one of the secondhand places in Third Avenue."

"Ha, is it so?" he replied. "By all means, then, let us do so at once, right away, immediately. *Mordieu*, me, I am likely to become a snow man at any minute. *Allons!*"

A Hebrew gentleman who dealt in cast-off garments eyed us suspiciously when we entered his musty emporium of relics, but the sight of our money quickly quieted any misgivings he might have entertained, and within half an hour, togged out in garments which almost sent their vendor into fits at their beauty and general excellence, we were seated in a taxicab proceeding toward the railway station.

"WELL," I TEASED AS we concluded our dinner that night, "you saw your Veiled Prophetess. Are you satisfied?"

"Satisfied!" He gave me a glare beside which the fabled basilisk's worst would have been a melting love-glance. "*Pardieu*, we shall see who shall make *un sacré singe* out of whom before we are through! That woman—that adventuress! She did warn me not to meddle in what was not my affair. *Nom d'un veau noir*, and is not a five-hundred-franc overcoat, to say nothing whatever of a hundred-franc hat, which she stole from me—are they, perhaps, not my affair? *Morbleu*, I shall say they are, my friend! *Mais oui*, I shall make that fortune-teller of the veil eat her words. *Cordieu*, but she shall eat them to the last crumb, nor will they prove a palatable meal for her, either!"

"You've got to admit she drew first blood, anyhow," I replied with a laugh.

"That is true," he agreed, nodding gravely, "but attend me, my friend, he bleeds best who bleeds last, I do assure you."

He was moody as a bear with a sore head all evening, and morose to the point of surliness the next day. Toward noon he took his hat and coat and left the house abruptly. "I shall return when I come back," he told me as he hastened down the steps.

It was long after dinner time when he put in an appearance, but his face wore its usual complacent expression, and, though his eyes twinkled now and again with elfish laughter, I could not get him to tell me of his adventures during the day.

EARLY NEXT MORNING HE left the house on another mysterious errand, and the same thing occurred each day during the week. The following Monday he suddenly insisted on my accompanying him to New York, and, at his direction, we took a taxicab from the Hudson Terminal and drove northward to Columbus Circle, turning in at the entrance of Central Park.

"Ah ha, my friend," he replied when I urged him to explain our errand, "you shall see what you shall see, and it shall be worth seeing."

Presently, as we proceeded toward Cleopatra's Needle, he gave me a sharp nudge in the ribs. "Observe that *moteur* yonder, my friend," he commanded, "that one of the color of pea soup. Regard the driver and his companion, if you please."

Our taxi leaped ahead at his sudden command to the driver, and we passed a long, low sport-model roadster driven by a young man in a heavy raccoon ulster. There was nothing remarkable about the fellow, except that he seemed more than commonly pleased with himself, but I was forced to admit that it was worth our trip to the city to view his companion. She was dark, dark with that mysterious, compelling beauty not possessed by one woman in a thousand. Despite the chill of the winter wind her cheeks showed not a touch of color, but were pale with the rich, creamy tint of old parchment, which made her vivid red lips seem all the more brilliant. Her head was small and finely poised, and fitted with a cap of some tawny-hued fur which nestled snugly to her blue black hair with the tightness of a turban. Her eyes were long and narrow and of that peculiar shade of hazel which defies exact classification, being sometimes topaz-brown, sometimes sea-green. Her lips were full, passionate and brightly rouged, and her long, oval face and prominent cheekbones gave her a decidedly Oriental appearance. Patrician she looked, even royal, and mysterious as night-veiled Isis herself. A collar of tawny fur frothed about her slender bare throat, and her shoulders were covered by a coat of some smooth, mustard-colored pelage which glistened in the morning sunlight like the back of a seal just emerged from the water.

"By George, she's a beauty," I admitted, "but—"

"Yes?" de Grandin elevated his brows interrogatively. "You did say 'but,' my friend?"

"I was thinking I wouldn't care to have her enmity," I replied. "Her claws seem a bit too near the surface, and I'll warrant they're sharp, too."

"*Eh bien*, you should know, *mon vieux*," he replied with a chuckle. "You have felt them."

"What—you mean—?"

"Nothing less. The lady is none other than our friend, Madame Naîra, the Veiled Prophetess."

"And the man—?"

"Is Benjamin Penneman, the husband of our client, Madame Penneman."

"Oh, so he *is* running about with Madame Naîra?" I replied. "His poor little wife."

"We'll have him back, and on his knees, to boot, or Jules de Grandin is a greater fool than Madame Naîra made of him the other night," he cut in. "Attend me, Friend Trowbridge. After our so humiliating fiasco at the house of the Prophetess that night, I was like a caged beast who sees her young slain before her eyes. Only desire for revenge actuated me, and I could not think clearly for my madness. Then I calmed myself. 'Jules de Grandin, you great zany,' I said to me, 'if you are to overcome the enemy, you must think, and to think you must have the clear brain. Control yourself.'

"And so I did. I went to New York and proceeded to play detective on the trail of this unfaithful husband. Where he went I went. When he stopped I stopped. *Parbleu*, but he led me a merry chase! He is active, that one.

"At last, however, my patience reaped its deserved reward. I did see him go to that accursed house in Eighty-second Street and come out with that woman. Again and again I did follow him, and always my trail led to the same burrow. '*Triomphe!*' I told me. 'We have at last established this lady's identity.' Today I did but bring you to see her that you might recognize her face without its veil. Tonight we begin our work of turning her temporary victory into crushing defeat."

"How are you going to pay her off?" I asked. "Name her as corespondent in a divorce suit?"

"*Non, non, non!*" he grinned at me. "All in good time, my friend. I have first planned my work; you shall now observe me as I work my plan. This very night I do begin." Nor could I get any further information from him.

F OR THREE CONSECUTIVE NIGHTS de Grandin watched our telephone as a cat mounts vigil over a rat-hole. On the fourth night, as we were preparing to go upstairs to bed, the bell rang, and he snatched the receiver from the hook before the little clapper had ceased to vibrate against the gongs.

"*Allo, allo!*" he called excitedly through the mouthpiece. "But yes; most certainly. Immediately, at once, right away!

"Trowbridge, my friend, come with me. Come and see the game we have caught in our trap. Death of my life, but that Madame Penneman is one clever woman!"

Waving away my questions, he hustled me into hat and coat and fairly dragged me to the automobile, urging more and more speed as we bowled along the road to the Penneman house.

Disdaining to knock, he burst the front door open and hurried up the stairs, turning unerringly down the upper hall and pushing open the first door to the right.

An amazing scene greeted us. The room was a tastefully furnished bed-chamber, pieces of mahogany, well chosen rugs and shaded lamps giving it the air of intimacy such apartments have at their best. Against the farther wall, opposite the dressing table, stood a pair of twin beds, and on the nearer one lay the pajama-clad form of the young man we had seen driving in the park a few days before. Obviously, he was asleep, and, quite as obviously his sleep was troubled, for he tossed and moaned restlessly, turning his head from side to side on the pillow, and once or twice attempting to rise to a sitting posture.

In the niche beside the windows, beside the telephone table, crouched Mrs. Penneman, clad in a negligée of orchid silk, her frightened eyes turning now on her sleeping husband, now on something which occupied the center of the room.

I followed her gaze as it swerved from the man on the bed and gasped in astonishment, then rubbed my eyes in wonder and gasped again. A circle of holly leaves, some six feet in diameter, lay upon the rug, and within it, half nebulous, like a ghost, but plainly visible, cowered the form of Madame Naîra, the Veiled Prophetess. She was clad as we had first seen her, in a diaphanous one-piece garment of midnight blue silk encrusted with tiny bright metal plates, and on her head was the crown of Egypt's royalty. But the veil was gone from her face, and if ever I beheld loathsome, inhuman hatred on human countenance, it sat upon the beautiful features of the fortune-teller. Her green eyes were no longer narrow, but opened to their greatest compass, round and flashing with fury, and her red mouth was squared like the grimacing of an old Greek tragic mask or those hideous carved heads made by the natives of Fiji. Now she extended her hands, long, slender and red-nailed, and now she beat her breasts with clenched fists. Again she opened her vivid lips and emitted gurgling sounds like the moanings of an enraged cat, or hissed with a sibilant, spitting noise, as though she were in very truth a cat and no woman at all.

"*Très bien, Madame,*" de Grandin bowed to Mrs. Penneman, "I see you have caught the marauder."

He turned nonchalantly to the hissing fury inside the circle of holly leaves. "I believe you did warn me not to pit my strength—my puny strength—against one who drew her power from the goddess of Bubastis?" he asked mockingly. "You have some further warnings to give, *n'est-ce-pas,* Madame?"

"Let me go; let me go!" she begged, stretching her hands out to him supplicatingly.

"Eh, what is this? You do beg deliverance of me?" he replied in mock misunderstanding. "Were you not about to forfeit my so worthless life if I continued to espouse the cause of the wife who had been put away? *Eh bien,* Madame Cat, you purr a different tune tonight, it would seem."

"Benjamin, Benjamin," the prisoned woman screamed. "Help me, my husband, my lover! See, by the ring I hold you with, I implore your aid!"

The man on the bed stirred uneasily and moaned in his sleep, but did not wake or rise.

"I fear my puny science has bested you, Madame Cat," de Grandin put in. "Your husband-lover is bound in a spell which I did conjure up from a bottle, and not all your magic can overcome it. Seek no help from him. I, Jules de Grandin, rule here!"

With that his cloak of sarcasm fell from him, and he faced her with a visage as savage and implacable as her own. "You—you would come into honest women's houses and take their men!" he fairly spat at her. "You would thrust your unclean magic between a man and the mother-to-be of his child! You—*mordieu*—you would steal the hat and coat of Jules de Grandin! Look not for mercy from me. Till cock-crow I shall hold you here, and then—" He elevated his shoulders in an expressive shrug.

"No, no; not that!" she begged, and her voice sank from a wail to a whimper. "See, I will give back his ring. I will release him from my charm—only let me go; let me go!"

"I make no promises to such as you," he responded, but the self-satisfied twinkle in his little blue eyes, and the half-checked gesture of his right hand as it rose to caress his trimly waxed blond mustache betrayed him.

The woman redoubled her entreaties. She sank to her knees and lowered her forehead to the floor. "Master!" she exclaimed. "I am your slave, your conquest. You have won. Show me mercy, and I will swear by the head of Bast, my mother, never to trouble this man or this woman again!"

"*Tiens,*" this time his hand would not be denied. It rose automatically to his mustache and tweaked the waxed end viciously. "Give back the ring, then, and go in peace. And make sure that you send us those hats and those overcoats which you did so unwisely steal from us."

She tossed a heavy gold seal ring across the intervening hedge of holly, and de Grandin bent forward, retrieving the trinket, before he displaced one of the green twigs with the toe of his boot.

There was a noise like steam escaping from an overheated teakettle, and the woman on the floor seemed suddenly to elongate, to draw out into a vapory nothingness, and vanish like a puff of smoke before a freshening breeze.

"Here, *Madame*," de Grandin bowed gallantly, French fashion, from the hips, as he extended the seal to Mrs. Penneman. "Do you place this upon your husband's finger and bid him be more careful in future. He will wake anon, and have no memory of the thralldom in which he has been held. Blame him not. He signed himself into slavery to a thing which was old—and very wicked— when time was still a youth."

Mrs. Penneman bent above her husband and slipped the golden circlet on the little finger of his left hand, then leaned forward and kissed him on the mouth. "My boy, my poor, sweet boy," she murmured, as gently as a mother might croon above her babe.

"Isn't he wonderful?" she asked de Grandin.

"Undoubtlessly, *Madame*," the Frenchman agreed with a quick bow. "Did he not have the rare judgment to pick you for a helpmeet? But me, I think I am a little wonderful, too." He twisted first one, then the other end of his mustache till the waxed points stood out from his lips like the whiskers of a belligerent tomcat.

"Of course you are—you're a darling!" she agreed enthusiastically, and before he was aware of her intention, she put her hands upon his shoulders and kissed him soundly first on one cheek, then the other, finally upon the lips.

"*Pardieu*, Friend Trowbridge, I think it is high time we did leave these reunited lovers together!" he exclaimed, his little eyes dancing like sunlight reflected on running water. "Come, my friend, let us go. *Allez-vous-en!*

"*Bonne, nuit, Madame!*"

"For the love of heaven, de Grandin." I demanded as we drove home, "what have I been seeing, or have I dreamed it all? Was that really Madame Naîra in the Pennemans' bedroom, and if it were—?"

"Ha!" he gave a short, delighted laugh. "Did I not tell you you should see what you should see, and that it would be worth seeing?"

"Never mind the showmanship," I cut in. "Just explain all this crazy business—if you can."

"*Eh bien*, that can also be arranged," he replied. "Listen, my friend. The average man will tell you there are no such things as witches, and he will, perhaps, be right in the main, but he will also be wrong. From the very birth of time there have been forces—evil forces, *parbleu!*—which the generality of men wisely forbore to understand or to know, but which a few sought out and allied themselves with for their own wicked advantage.

"These gods of ancient times, now—what were they but such forces? Nothing. Zeus, Apollo, Osiris, Ptah, Isis, Bast—such things are but names; they describe certain vaguely understood, but nonetheless potent forces. *Pardieu*, there is, no God but God, my friend; the rest are—who knows what?

"Now, when your countrymen hanged each other in Salem town in the winter of 1692, they undoubtlessly killed many innocent persons, but their basic idea was right. There were then, there have always been, and there still are certain servants of that evil entity, or combination of entities, which we call Satan.

"This Madame Naîra, she was one. *Cordieu*, she was a very great one, indeed.

"In some way, I know not how, she had become adept in using certain principles of evil for her ends, and set up in business as a fortune-teller in the world's richest city. Before our time there were thousands such in Thebes, Babylon, Ilium and Rome. Always these evil ones follow the course of the river of gold."

"And you mean to tell me Penneman actually married her when he put his ring on that statue's hand?" I asked, incredulously.

"*Mais non*, he did not wed her, for true marriage is a spiritual linking of the souls, my friend, but he did put himself in her power, for when he had gone she took the ring he left and kept it, and having such an intimately personal possession of his, she also acquired a powerful hold on its owner.

"The first clue I had to the true state of affairs was when Madame Penneman related the incident of the strange woman's appearance in her chamber. Already she had told of the incident of the missing ring, and when she declared her husband exclaimed, 'Second, Second!' in his sleep as the sorceress bent above him, at once I knew that what he said was not 'Second,' but 'Sechet,' which is another name for Bast, the cat-headed goddess.

"'Very good,' I tell me, 'we have here a votary of that cruel half woman, half cat, which reigned in olden times along the banks of the Nile. We shall see how we can defeat her.'

"I then undertook to ascertain what the young Penneman did while he neglected his wife. *Parbleu*, his time and money were lavished like water on that veiled woman for whose smile he forsook her he had sworn to love and cherish!"

"Then there really was a liaison between him and Madame Naîra?" I asked.

"Yes—yes, and no," he replied ambiguously. "For the touch of her lower lip he would have walked barefoot over miles of broken glass, yet he knew not what he did while doing it. His state was something akin to that of one under hypnosis—conscious of his acts and deeds while doing them, entirely unaware of them afterward. A sort of externally induced amnesia, it was.

"These things puzzled me much, but still I was unwilling to concede the woman possessed more than ordinary powers. 'We shall see this Veiled Prophetess,' I tell me. 'Friend Trowbridge and I shall interview her under assumed names, and prove to ourselves that she is but a charlatan.'

"*Eh bien*, we did see much. We did see the loss of our hats and overcoats!"

"But if Madame Naîra knew at once who you were and that you were fighting her, how was it she could not avoid the trap—and, by the way, what was that trap?" I demanded.

"I can not say," he responded. "Perhaps there are limitations on her powers of divination. It may well be that she could read my thoughts even to my name, when we were face to face, yet could not project herself through space to observe what I planned while away from her. Were not those other witches of olden times unable to say when the officers of the law were descending on them, and so were taken to perish at the stake?

"As for the trap we set, my friend, it was simple. That was not the Veiled Prophetess herself you did behold in Madame Penneman's room, but her simulacrum—her projection. It is possible for those people, by taking thought, to project their likenesses at great distances, but always they must be where there is sympathetic atmosphere. This the witch woman already had, because she had bound Benjamin Penneman in her spell. At will she could assume the likeness of herself in his room, or anywhere he happened to be, while her living body lay, as though locked in sleep, miles away. That explains how it is she vanished so mysteriously after warning Madame Penneman on her previous visits.

"But, *grâce à Dieu*, for all ill there is a remedy, if we can but find it. I bethought me. 'Is it not likely,' I ask me, 'that the things which charm away those other evil people, the werewolves and the vampires, will also prevent the free movement of the projection of a witch?'

"'*Morbleu*, but it is most probable,' I reply to me, and so I set about my work.

"First I did give to Madame Penneman a harmless drug—a hypnotic—to mix with the food and drink of her husband. That will induce a seemingly natural sleep, and hold him fast away from the wicked Madame Naîra. Very good. The first night the plan did work well, the second and third, also.

"Heretofore this woman have come in her spiritual likeness to charm her lover back when he have returned to his wife. I make sure she will do so again, and I have prepared a barrier which I think she can not pass. It is made of the wicks of blessed candles and on it are strung many leaves and twigs of holly— holly, the Christmas bloom, the touch of which is intolerable to evil spirits and over which they can not pass.

"When the projection of Madame Naîra comes to Penneman's house to-night, Madame Penneman does surround it suddenly with the ring of holly. Then she calls me. Had it been the real Naîra in the flesh, she could have stepped over the holly, but her projection, being spirit—and evil spirit, at that—was powerless to move. Also, my friend, I well knew that if I did but keep that spiritual seeming of the real Naîra away from her body until the crowing of the cock it might have great difficulty in returning to its habitation, and would, perhaps, be forced to wander forever through space. The flesh of Madame Naîra would, as we say, die, for there would be no spirit to animate it.

"Therefore, I was in position to bargain with her, to force her to give back the ring she stole by trick from the young Penneman and to quit the house and the lives of those young people forevermore."

"But why didn't you keep her in the holly circle, if what you say is true?" I asked. "Surely, she would be better dead."

"What!" he demanded. "And leave her evil spirit, freed from the bonds of flesh, to walk the earth by night? Not I, my friend. In the flesh she had certain restrictions; dying a natural death she shall probably return to that unpleasant place from whence she came; but had I torn her from her body by force, she would have still held the young Penneman beneath her spell, and that would have meant death, or worse, for him. No, my friend, I did act for the best, I assure you.

"Br-r-r-r!" he shivered and pulled a comic face as I brought the car to a stop before my door. "I do still shake like a little wet dog from that experience when she stole my coat, Friend Trowbridge," he announced. "Come, a long drink of your so excellent sherry before we go to bed! It will start the blood to flowing through my frozen veins once more."

The Curse of Everard Maundy

"MORT D'UN CHAT! I do not like this!" Jules de Grandin slammed the evening paper down upon the table and stared ferociously at me through the lamplight.

"What's up now?" I asked, wondering vaguely what the cause of his latest grievance was. "Some reporter say something personal about you?"

"*Parbleu, non*, he would better try," the little Frenchman replied, his round blue eyes flashing ominously. "Me, I would pull his nose and tweak his ears. But it is not of the reporter's insolence I speak, my friend; I do not like these suicides; there are too many of them."

"Of course there are," I conceded soothingly, "one suicide is that much too many; people have no right to—"

"Ah bah!" he cut in. "You do misapprehend me, *mon vieux*. Excuse me one moment, if you please." He rose hurriedly from his chair and left the room. A moment later I heard him rummaging about in the cellar.

In a few minutes he returned, the week's supply of discarded newspapers salvaged from the dust bin in his arms.

"Now, attend me," he ordered as he spread the sheets out before him and began scanning the columns hastily. "Here is an item from Monday's *Journal*:

TWO MOTORISTS DIE WHILE DRIVING CARS

The impulse to end their lives apparently attacked two automobile drivers on the Albemarle turnpike near Lonesome Swamp, two miles out of Harrisonville, last night. Carl Planz, thirty-one years old, of Martins Falls, took his own life by shooting himself in the head with a shotgun while seated in his automobile, which he had parked at the roadside where the pike passes nearest the swamp. His remains were identified by two letters, one addressed to his wife, the other to his father, Joseph

Planz, with whom he was associated in the real estate business at Martins Falls. A check for three hundred dollars and several other papers found in his pockets completed identification. The letters, which merely declared his intention to kill himself, failed to establish any motive for the act.

Almost at the same time, and within a hundred yards of the spot where Planz's body was found by State Trooper Henry Anderson this morning, the body of Henry William Nixon, of New Rochelle, N.Y., was discovered partly sitting, partly lying on the rear seat of his automobile, an empty bottle of windshield cleaner lying on the floor beside him. It is thought this liquid, which contained a small amount of cyanide of potassium, was used to inflict death. Police Surgeon Stevens, who examined both bodies, declared that the men had been dead approximately the same length of time when brought to the station house.

"What think you of that, my friend, hein?" de Grandin demanded, looking up from the paper with one of his direct, challenging stares.

"Why—er—" I began, but he interrupted.

"Hear this," he commanded, taking up a second paper, "this is from the *News* of Tuesday:

Mother and Daughters Die in Death Pact

Police and heartbroken relatives are today trying to trace a motive for the triple suicide of Mrs. Ruby Westerfelt and her daughters, Joan and Elizabeth, who perished by leaping from the eighth floor of the Hotel Dolores, Newark, late yesterday afternoon. The women registered at the hotel under assumed names, went immediately to the room assigned them, and ten minutes later Miss Gladys Walsh, who occupied a room on the fourth floor, was startled to see a dark form hurtle past her window. A moment later a second body flashed past on its downward flight, and as Miss Walsh, horrified, rushed toward the window, a loud crash sounded outside. Looking out, Miss Walsh saw the body of a third woman partly impaled on the spikes of a balcony rail.

Miss Walsh sought to aid the woman. As she leaned from her window and reached out with a trembling arm she was greeted by a scream: "Don't try! I won't be saved; I must go with Mother and Sister!" A moment later the woman had managed to free herself from the restraining iron spikes and fell to the cement area-way four floors below.

"And here is still another account, this one from tonight's paper," he continued, unfolding the sheet which had caused his original protest:

HIGH SCHOOL CO-ED TAKES LIFE IN ATTIC

The family and friends of Edna May McCarty, fifteen-year-old co-ed of Harrisonville High School, are at a loss to assign a cause for her suicide early this morning. The girl had no love affairs, as far as is known, and had not failed in her examinations. On the contrary, she had passed the school's latest test with flying colors. Her mother told investigating police officials that overstudy might have temporarily unbalanced the child's mind. Miss McCarty's body was found suspended from the rafters of her father's attic by her mother this morning when the young woman did not respond to a call for breakfast and could not be found in her room on the second floor of the house. A clothes line, used to hang clothes which were dried inside the house in rainy weather, was used to form the fatal noose.

"Now then, my friend," de Grandin reseated himself and lighted a vile-smelling French cigarette, puffing furiously, till the smoke surrounded his sleek, blond head like a mephitic nimbus, "what have you to say to those reports? Am I not right! Are there not too many—*mordieu* entirely too many!—suicides in our city?"

"All of them weren't committed here," I objected practically, "and besides, there couldn't very well be any connection between them. Mrs. Westerfelt and her daughters carried out a suicide pact, it appears, but they certainly could have had no understanding with the two men and the young girl—"

"Perhaps, maybe, possibly," he agreed, nodding his head so vigorously that a little column of ash detached itself from his cigarette and dropped unnoticed on the bosom of his stiffly starched evening shirt. "You may be right, Friend Trowbridge, but then, as is so often the case, you may be entirely wrong. One thing I know: I, Jules de Grandin, shall investigate these cases myself personally. *Cordieu*, they do interest me! I shall ascertain what is the what here."

"Go ahead," I encouraged. "The investigation will keep you out of mischief," and I returned to the second chapter of Haggard's *The Wanderer's Necklace*, a book which I have read at least half a dozen times, yet find as fascinating at each rereading as when I first perused its pages.

T HE MATTER OF THE six suicides still bothered him next morning. "Trowbridge, my friend," he asked abruptly as he disposed of his second helping of coffee and passed his cup for replenishment, "why is it that people destroy themselves?"

"Oh," I answered evasively, "different reasons, I suppose. Some are crossed in love, some meet financial reverses and some do it while temporarily deranged."

"Yes," he agreed thoughtfully, "yet every self-murderer has a real or fancied reason for quitting the world, and there is apparently no reason why any of these six poor ones who hurled themselves into outer darkness during the past week should have done so. All, apparently, were well provided for, none of them, as far as is known, had any reason to regret the past or fear the future; yet"—he shrugged his narrow shoulders significantly—"*voilà*, they are gone!

"Another thing: At the *Faculté de Médicine Légal* and the *Sûreté* in Paris we keep most careful statistics, not only on the number, but on the manner of suicides. I do not think your Frenchman differs radically from your American when it comes to taking his life, so the figures for one nation may well be a sign-post for the other. These self-inflicted deaths, they are not right. They do not follow the rules. Men prefer to hang, slash or shoot themselves; women favor drowning, poison or gas; yet here we have one of the men taking poison, one of the women hanging herself, and three of them jumping to death. *Nom d'un canard*, I am not satisfied with it!"

"H'm, neither are the unfortunate parties who killed themselves, if the theologians are to be believed," I returned.

"You speak right," he returned, then muttered dreamily to himself: "Destruction—destruction of body and imperilment of soul—*mordieu*, it is strange, it is not righteous!" He disposed of his coffee at a gulp and leaped from his chair. "I go!" he declared dramatically turning toward the door.

"Where?"

"Where? Where should I go, if not to secure the history of these so puzzling cases? I shall not rest nor sleep nor eat until I have the string of the mystery's skein in my hands." He paused at the door, a quick, elfin smile playing across his usually stern features. "And should I return before my work is complete," he suggested, "I pray you, have the excellent Nora prepare another of her so magnificent apple pies for dinner."

Forty seconds later the front door clicked shut, and from the dining room's oriel window I saw his neat little figure, trimly encased in blue chinchilla and gray worsted, pass quickly down the sidewalk, his ebony cane hammering a rapid tattoo on the stones as it kept time to the thoughts racing through his active brain.

"I AM DESOLATED THAT MY capacity is exhausted," he announced that evening as he finished his third portion of deep-dish apple pie smothered in pungent rum sauce and regarded his empty plate sadly. "*Eh bien*, perhaps it is as well. Did I eat more I might not be able to think clearly, and clear thought is what I shall need this night, my friend. Come; we must be going."

"Going where?" I demanded.

"To hear the reverend and estimable Monsieur Maundy deliver his sermon."

"Who? Everard Maundy?"

"But of course, who else?"

"But—but," I stammered, looking at him incredulously, "why should we go to the tabernacle to hear this man? I can't say I'm particularly impressed with his system, and—aren't you a Catholic, de Grandin?"

"Who can say?" he replied as he lighted a cigarette and stared thoughtfully at his coffee cup. "My father was a Huguenot of the Huguenots; a several times great-grandsire of his cut his way to freedom through the Paris streets on the fateful night of August 24, 1572. My mother was convent-bred, and as pious as anyone with a sense of humor and the gift of thinking for herself could well be. One of my uncles he for whom I am named—was like a blood brother to Darwin the magnificent, and Huxley the scarcely less magnificent, also. Me, I am"—he elevated his eyebrows and shoulders at once and pursed his lips comically—"what should a man with such a heritage be, my friend? But come, we delay, we tarry, we lose time. Let us hasten. I have a fancy to hear what this Monsieur Maundy has to say, and to observe him. See, I have here tickets for the fourth row of the hall."

Very much puzzled, but never doubting that something more than the idle wish to hear a sensational evangelist urged the little Frenchman toward the tabernacle, I rose and accompanied him.

"*Parbleu*, what a day!" he sighed as I turned my car toward the downtown section. "From coroner's office to undertakers' I have run; and from undertakers' to hospitals. I have interviewed everyone who could shed the smallest light on these strange deaths, yet I seem no further advanced than when I began. What I have found out serves only to whet my curiosity; what I have not discovered—" He spread his hands in a world-embracing gesture and lapsed into silence.

The Jachin Tabernacle, where the Rev. Everard Maundy was holding his series of non-sectarian revival meetings, was crowded to overflowing when we arrived, but our tickets passed us through the jostling crowd of half-skeptical, half-believing people who thronged the lobby, and we were soon ensconced in seats where every word the preacher uttered could be heard with ease.

Before the introductory hymn had been finished, de Grandin mumbled a wholly unintelligible excuse in my ear and disappeared up the aisle, and I settled myself in my seat to enjoy the service as best I might.

The Rev. Mr. Maundy was a tall, hatchet-faced man in early middle life, a little inclined to rant and make use of worked-over platitudes, but obviously sincere in the message he had for his congregation. From the half-cynical attitude of a regularly enrolled church member who looks on revivals with a certain disdain, I found myself taking keener and keener interest in the story of regeneration the preacher had to tell, my attention compelled not so much by his words as by the earnestness of his manner and the wonderful stage presence the man possessed. When the ushers had taken up the collection and the final hymn was sung, I was surprised to find we had been two hours in the tabernacle.

If anyone had asked me, I should have said half an hour would have been nearer the time consumed by the service.

"Eh, my friend, did you find it interesting?" de Grandin asked as he joined me in the lobby and linked his arm in mine.

"Yes, very," I admitted, then, somewhat sulkily: "I thought you wanted to hear him, too—it was your idea that we came here—what made you run away?"

"I am sorry," he replied with a chuckle which belied his words, "but it was *necessaire* that I fry other fish while you listened to the reverend gentleman's discourse. Will you drive me home?"

The March wind cut shrewdly through my overcoat after the superheated atmosphere of the tabernacle, and I felt myself shivering involuntarily more than once as we drove through the quiet streets. Strangely, too, I felt rather sleepy and ill at ease. By the time we reached the wide, tree-bordered avenue before my house I was conscious of a distinctly unpleasant sensation, a constantly-growing feeling of malaise, a sort of baseless, irritating uneasiness. Thoughts of years long forgotten seemed summoned to my memory without rime or reason. An incident of an unfair advantage I had taken of a younger boy while at public school, recollections of petty, useless lies and bits of naughtiness committed when I could not have been more than three came flooding back on my consciousness, finally an episode of my early youth which I had forgotten some forty years.

My father had brought a little stray kitten into the house, and I, with the tiny lad's unconscious cruelty, had fallen to teasing the wretched bundle of bedraggled fur, finally tossing it nearly to the ceiling to test the tale I had so often heard that a cat always lands on its feet. My experiment was the exception which demonstrated the rule, it seemed, for the poor, half-starved feline hit the hardwood floor squarely on its back, struggled feebly a moment, then yielded up its entire ninefold expectancy of life.

Long after the smart of the whipping I received in consequence had been forgotten, the memory of that unintentional murder had plagued my boyish conscience, and many were the times I had awakened at dead of night, weeping bitter repentance out upon my pillow.

Now, some forty years later, the thought of that kitten's death came back as clearly as the night the unkempt little thing thrashed out its life upon our kitchen floor. Strive as I would, I could not drive the memory from me, and it seemed as though the unwitting crime of my childhood was assuming an enormity out of all proportion to its true importance.

I shook my head and passed my hand across my brow, as a sleeper suddenly wakened does to drive away the lingering memory of an unpleasant dream, but the kitten's ghost, like Banquo's, would not down.

"What is it, Friend Trowbridge?" de Grandin asked as he eyed me shrewdly.

"Oh, nothing," I replied as I parked the car before our door and leaped to the curb, "I was just thinking."

"Ah?" he responded on a rising accent. "And of what do you think, my friend? Something unpleasant?"

"Oh, no; nothing important enough to dignify by that term," I answered shortly, and led the way to the house, keeping well ahead of him, lest he push his inquiries farther.

In this, however, I did him wrong. Tactful women and Jules de Grandin have the talent of feeling without being told when conversation is unwelcome, and besides wishing me a pleasant good-night, he spoke not a word until we had gone upstairs to bed. As I was opening my door, he called down the hall, "Should you want me, remember, you have but to call."

"Humph!" I muttered ungraciously as I shut the door. "Want him? What the devil should I want him for?" And so I pulled off my clothes and climbed into bed, the thought of the murdered kitten still with me and annoying me more by its persistence than by the faint sting of remorse it evoked.

How long I had slept I do not know, but I do know I was wide awake in a single second, sitting up in bed and staring through the darkened chamber with eyes which strove desperately to pierce the gloom.

Somewhere—whether far or near I could not tell—a cat had raised its voice in a long-drawn, wailing cry, kept silence a moment, then given tongue again with increased volume.

There are few sounds more eery to hear in the dead of night than the cry of a prowling feline, and this one was of a particularly sad, almost reproachful tone.

"Confound the beast!" I exclaimed angrily, and lay back on my pillow, striving vainly to recapture my broken sleep.

Again the wail sounded, indefinite as to location, but louder, more prolonged, even, it seemed, fiercer in its timbre than when I first heard it in my sleep.

I glanced toward the window with the vague thought of hurling a book or boot or other handy missile at the disturber, then held my breath in sudden affright. Staring through the aperture between the scrim curtains was the biggest, most ferocious-looking tomcat I had ever seen. Its eyes, seemingly as large as butter dishes, glared at me with the green phosphorescence of its tribe, and with an added demoniacal glow the like of which I had never seen. Its red mouth, opened to full compass in a venomous, soundless "spit," seemed almost as large as that of a lion, and the wicked, pointed ears above its rounded face were laid back against its head, as though it were crouching for combat.

"Get out! Scat!" I called feebly, but making no move toward the thing.

"S-s-s-sssh!" a hiss of incomparable fury answered me, and the creature put one heavy, padded paw tentatively over the window-sill, still regarding me with its unchanging, hateful stare.

"Get!" I repeated, and stopped abruptly. Before my eyes the great beast was *growing*, increasing in size till its chest and shoulders completely blocked the window. Should it attack me I would be as helpless in its claws as a Hindoo under the paws of a Bengal tiger.

Slowly, stealthily, its cushioned feet making no sound as it set them down daintily, the monstrous creature advanced into the room, crouched on its haunches and regarded me steadily, wickedly, malevolently.

I rose a little higher on my elbow. The great brute twitched the tip of its sable tail warningly, half lifted one of its forepaws from the floor, and set it down again, never shifting its sulfurous eyes from my face.

Inch by inch I moved my farther foot from the bed, felt the floor beneath it, and pivoted slowly in a sitting position until my other foot was free of the bedclothes. Apparently the cat did not notice my strategy, for it made no menacing move till I flexed my muscles for a leap, suddenly flung myself from the bedstead, and leaped toward the door.

With a snarl, white teeth flashing, green eyes glaring, ears laid back, the beast moved between me and the exit, and began slowly advancing on me, hate and menace in every line of its giant body.

I gave ground before it, retreating step by step and striving desperately to hold its eyes with mine, as I had heard hunters sometimes do when suddenly confronted by wild animals.

Back, back I crept, the ogreish visitant keeping pace with my retreat, never suffering me to increase the distance between us.

I felt the cold draft of the window on my back; the pressure of the sill against me; behind me, from the waist up, was the open night, before me the slowly advancing monster.

It was a thirty-foot drop to a cemented roadway, but death on the pavement was preferable to the slashing claws and grinding teeth of the terrible thing creeping toward me.

I threw one leg over the sill, watching constantly, lest the cat-thing leap on me before I could cheat it by dashing myself to the ground—

"Trowbridge, *mon Dieu*, Trowbridge, my friend! What is it you would do?" The frenzied hail of Jules de Grandin cut through the dark and a flood of light from the hallway swept into the room as he flung the door violently open and raced across the room, seizing my arm in both hands and dragging me from the window.

"Look out, de Grandin!" I screamed. "The cat! It'll get you!"

"Cat?" he echoed, looking about him uncomprehendingly. "Do you say 'cat', my friend? A cat will get me? *Mort d'un chou*, the cat which can make a mouse of Jules de Grandin is not yet whelped! Where is it, this cat of yours?"

"There! Th—" I began, then stopped, rubbing my eyes. The room was empty. Save for de Grandin and me there was nothing animate in the place.

"But it *was* here," I insisted. "I tell you, I saw it; a great, black cat, as big as a lion. It came in the window and crouched right over there, and was driving me to jump to the ground when you came—"

"*Nom d'un porc!* Do you say so?" he exclaimed, seizing my arm again and shaking me. "Tell me of this cat, my friend. I would learn more of this puss-puss who comes into Friend Trowbridge's house, grows great as a lion and drives him to his death on the stones below. Ha, I think maybe the trail of these mysterious deaths is not altogether lost! Tell me more, *mon ami*; I would know all—all!"

"OF COURSE, IT WAS just a bad dream," I concluded as I finished the recital of my midnight visitation, "but it seemed terribly real to me while it lasted."

"I doubt it not," he agreed with a quick, nervous nod. "And on our way from the tabernacle tonight, my friend, I noticed you were much *distrait*. Were you, perhaps, feeling ill at the time?"

"Not at all," I replied. "The truth is, I was remembering something which occurred when I was a lad four or five years old; something which had to do with a kitten I killed," and I told him the whole wretched business.

"U'm?" he commented when I had done. "You are a good man, Trowbridge, my friend. In all your life, since you attained to years of discretion, I do not believe you have done a wicked or ignoble act."

"Oh, I wouldn't say that," I returned, "we all—"

"*Parbleu*, I have said it. That kitten incident, now, is probably the single tiny skeleton in the entire closet of your existence, yet sustained thought upon it will magnify it even as the cat of your dream grew from cat's to lion's size. *Pardieu*, my friend, I am not so sure you did dream of that abomination in the shape of a cat which visited you. Suppose—" he broke off, staring intently before him, twisting first one, then the other end of his trimly waxed mustache.

"Suppose what?" I prompted.

"*Non*, we will suppose nothing tonight," be replied. "You will please go to sleep once more, my friend, and I shall remain in the room to frighten away any more dream-demons which may come to plague you. Come, let us sleep. Here I do remain." He leaped into the wide bed beside me and pulled the down comforter snugly up about his pointed chin.

" . . . . AND I'D LIKE VERY much to have you come right over to see her, if you will," Mrs. Weaver finished. "I can't imagine whatever made her attempt such a thing—she's never shown any signs of it before."

I hung up the telephone receiver and turned to de Grandin. "Here's another suicide, or almost-suicide, for you," I told him half teasingly. "The daughter of one of my patients attempted her life by hanging in the bathroom this morning."

"*Par la tête bleu*, do you tell me so?" he exclaimed eagerly. "I go with you, *cher ami*. I see this young woman; I examine her. Perhaps I shall find some key to the riddle there. *Parbleu*, me, I itch, I burn, I am all on fire with this mystery! Certainly, there must be an answer to it; but it remains hidden like a peasant's pig when the tax collector arrives."

"WELL, YOUNG LADY, WHAT'S this I hear about you?" I demanded severely as we entered Grace Weaver's bedroom a few minutes later. "What on earth have you to die for?"

"I—I don't know what made me want to do it, Doctor," the girl replied with a wan smile. "I hadn't thought of it before—ever. But I just got to—oh, you know, sort of brooding over things last night, and when I went into the bathroom this morning, something—something inside my head, like those ringing noises you hear when you have a head-cold, you know—seemed to be whispering, 'Go on, kill yourself; you've nothing to live for. Go on, do it!' So I just stood on the scales and took the cord from my bathrobe and tied it over the transom, then knotted the other end about my neck. Then I kicked the scales away and"—she gave another faint smile—"I'm glad I hadn't locked the door before I did it," she admitted.

De Grandin had been staring unwinkingly at her with his curiously level glance throughout her recital. As she concluded he bent forward and asked: "This voice which you heard bidding you commit an unpardonable sin, Mademoiselle, did you, perhaps, recognize it?"

The girl shuddered. "No!" she replied, but a sudden paling of her face about the lips gave the lie to her word.

"*Pardonnez-moi*, Mademoiselle," the Frenchman returned. "I think you do not tell the truth. Now, whose voice was it, if you please?"

A sullen, stubborn look spread over the girl's features, to be replaced a moment later by the muscular spasm which preludes weeping. "It—it sounded like Fanny's," she cried, and turning her face to the pillow, fell to sobbing bitterly.

"And Fanny, who is she?" de Grandin began, but Mrs. Weaver motioned him to silence with an imploring gesture.

I prescribed a mild bromide and left the patient, wondering what mad impulse could have led a girl in the first flush of young womanhood, happily situated in the home of parents who idolized her, engaged to a fine young man, and without bodily or spiritual ill of any sort, to attempt her life. Outside, de

Grandin seized the mother's arm and whispered fiercely: "Who is this Fanny, Madame Weaver? Believe me, I ask not from idle curiosity, but because I seek vital information!"

"Fanny Briggs was Grace's chum two years ago," Mrs. Weaver answered. "My husband and I never quite approved of her, for she was several years older than Grace, and had such pronounced modern ideas that we didn't think her a suitable companion for our daughter, but you know how girls are with their 'crushes.' The more we objected to her going with Fanny, the more she used to seek her company, and we were both at our wits' ends when the Briggs girl was drowned while swimming at Asbury Park. I hate to say it, but it was almost a positive relief to us when the news came. Grace was almost broken-hearted about it at first, but she met Charley this summer, and I haven't heard her mention Fanny's name since her engagement until just now."

"Ah?" de Grandin tweaked the tip of his mustache meditatively. "And perhaps Mademoiselle Grace was somewhere to be reminded of Mademoiselle Fanny last night?"

"No," Mrs. Weaver replied, "she went with a crowd of young folks to hear Maundy preach. There was a big party of them at the tabernacle—I'm afraid they went more to make fun than in a religious frame of mind, but he made quite an impression on Grace, she told us."

"*Feu de Dieu!*" de Grandin exploded, twisting his mustache furiously. "Do you tell me so, *Madame?* This is of the interest. *Madame,* I salute you," he bowed formally to Mrs. Weaver, then seized me by the arm and fairly dragged me away.

"Trowbridge, my friend," he informed me as we descended the steps of the Weaver portico, "this business, it has *l'odeur du poisson*—how is it you say?—the fishy smell."

"What do you mean?" I asked.

"*Parbleu*, what should I mean except that we go to interview this Monsieur Everard Maundy immediately, right away, at once? *Mordieu*, I damn think I have the tail of this mystery in my hand, and may the blight of prohibition fall upon France if I do not twist it!"

THE REV. EVERARD MAUNDY's rooms in the Tremont Hotel were not hard to locate, for a constant stream of visitors went to and from them.

"Have you an appointment with Mr. Maundy?" the secretary asked as we were ushered into the anteroom.

"Not we," de Grandin denied, "but if you will be so kind as to tell him that Dr. Jules de Grandin, of the Paris *Sûreté*, desires to speak with him for five small minutes, I shall be in your debt."

The young man looked doubtful, but de Grandin's steady, catlike stare never wavered, and he finally rose and took our message to his employer.

In a few minutes he returned and admitted us to the big room where the evangelist received his callers behind a wide, flat-topped desk.

"Ah, Mr. de Grandin," the exhorter began with a professionally bland smile as we entered, "you are from France, are you not, sir? What can I do to help you toward the light?"

"*Cordieu*, Monsieur," de Grandin barked, for once forgetting his courtesy and ignoring the preacher's outstretched hand, "you can do much. You can explain these so unexplainable suicides which have taken place during the past week—the time you have preached here. That is the light we do desire to see."

Maundy's face went mask-like and expressionless. "Suicides? Suicides?" he echoed. "What should I know of—"

The Frenchman shrugged his narrow shoulders impatiently. "We do fence with words, Monsieur," he interrupted testily. "Behold the facts: Messieurs Planz and Nixon, young men with no reason for such desperate deeds, did kill themselves by violence; Madame Westerfelt and her two daughters, who were happy in their home, as everyone thought, did hurl themselves from an hotel window; a little schoolgirl hanged herself; last night my good friend Trowbridge, who never understandingly harmed man or beast, and whose life is dedicated to the healing of the sick, did almost take his life; and this very morning a young girl, wealthy, beloved, with every reason to be happy, did almost succeed in dispatching herself.

"Now, Monsieur *le prédicateur*, the only thing this miscellaneous assortment of persons had in common is the fact that *each of them did hear you preach the night before, or the same night, he attempted self-destruction*. That is the light we seek. Explain us the mystery, if you please."

Maundy's lean, rugged face had undergone a strange transformation while the little Frenchman spoke. Gone was his smug, professional smirk, gone the forced and meaningless expression of benignity, and in their place a look of such anguish and horror as might rest on the face of one who hears his sentence of damnation read.

"Don't—don't!" he besought, covering his writhing face with his hands and bowing his head upon his desk while his shoulders shook with deep, soul-racking sobs. "Oh, miserable me! My sin has found me out!"

For a moment he wrestled in spiritual anguish, then raised his stricken countenance and regarded us with tear-dimmed eyes. "I am the greatest sinner in the world," he announced sorrowfully. "There is no hope for me on earth or yet in heaven!"

De Grandin tweaked the ends of his mustache alternately as he gazed curiously at the man before us. "Monsieur," he replied at length. "I think you do exaggerate. There are surely greater sinners than you. But if you would shrive you of the sin which gnaws your heart, I pray you shed what light you can upon these deaths, for there may be more to follow, and who knows that I shall not be able to stop them if you will but tell me all?"

"*Mea culpa!*" Maundy exclaimed, and struck his chest with his clenched fists like a Hebrew prophet of old. "In my younger days, gentlemen, before I dedicated myself to the salvaging of souls, I was a scoffer. What I could not feel or weigh or measure, I disbelieved. I mocked at all religion and sneered at all the things which others held sacred.

"One night I went to a Spiritualistic seance, intent on scoffing, and forced my young wife to accompany me. The medium was an old colored woman, wrinkled, half-blind, and unbelievably ignorant, but she had something—some secret power—which was denied the rest of us. Even I, atheist and derider of the truth that I was, could see that.

"As the old woman called on the spirits of the departed, I laughed out loud, and told her it was a fake. The negress came out of her trance and turned her deepset, burning old eyes on me. 'White man,' she said, 'yuh is gwine ter feel mighty sorry fo' dem words. Ah tells you de speerits can heah whut yuh says, an dey will take deir revenge on you an' yours—yas, an' on dem as foller yuh—till yuh wishes yo' tongue had been cut out befo' yuh said dem words dis yere night.'

"I tried to laugh at her—to curse her for a sniveling old faker—but there was something so terrible in her wrinkled old face that the words froze on my lips, and I hurried away.

"The next night my wife—my young, lovely bride—drowned herself in the river, and I have been a marked man ever since. Wherever I go it is the same. God has seen fit to open my eyes to the light of Truth and give me words to place His message before His people, and many who come to sneer at me go away believers; but wherever throngs gather to hear me bear my testimony there are always these tragedies. Tell me, gentlemen"—he threw out his hands in a gesture of surrender—"must I forever cease to preach the message of the Lord to His people? I have told myself that these self-murders would have occurred whether I came to town or not, but—is this a judgment which pursues me forever?"

Jules de Grandin regarded him thoughtfully. "Monsieur," he murmured, "I fear you make the mistakes we are all too prone to make. You do saddle *le bon Dieu* with all the sins with which the face of man is blackened. What if this were no judgment of heaven, but a curse of a very different sort, *hein?*"

"You mean the devil might be driving to overthrow the effects of my work?" the other asked, a light of hope breaking over his haggard face.

"U'm, perhaps; let us take that for our working hypothesis," de Grandin replied. "At present we may not say whether it be devil or devilkin which dogs your footsteps; but at the least we are greatly indebted to you for what you have told. Go my friend; continue to preach the Truth as you conceive the Truth to be, and may the God of all peoples uphold your hands. Me, I have other work to do, but it may be scarcely less important." He bowed formally and, turning on his heel, strode quickly from the room.

"THAT'S THE MOST FANTASTIC story I ever heard!" I declared as we entered the hotel elevator. "The idea! As if an ignorant old negress could put a curse on—"

"*Zut!*" de Grandin shut me off. "You are a most excellent physician in the State of New Jersey, Friend Trowbridge, but have you ever been in Martinique, or Haiti, or in the jungles of the Congo Belgique?"

"Of course not," I admitted, "but—"

"I have. I have seen things so strange among the *Voudois* people that you would wish to have me committed to a madhouse did I but relate them to you. However, as that Monsieur Kipling says, 'that is another story.' At the present we are pledged to the solving of another mystery. Let us go to your house. I would think, I would consider all this business-of-the-monkey. *Pardieu*, it has as many angles as a diamond cut in Amsterdam!"

"TELL ME, FRIEND TROWBRIDGE," he demanded as we concluded our evening meal, "have you perhaps among your patients some young man who has met with a great sorrow recently; someone who has sustained a loss of wife or child or parents?"

I looked at him in amazement, but the serious expression on his little heart-shaped face told me he was in earnest, not making some ill-timed jest at my expense.

"Why, yes," I responded. "There is young Alvin Spence. His wife died in childbirth last June, and the poor chap has been half beside himself ever since. Thank God I was out of town at the time and didn't have the responsibility of the case."

"Thank God, indeed," de Grandin nodded gravely. "It is not easy for us, though we do ply our trade among the dying, to tell those who remain behind of their bereavement. But this Monsieur Spence; will you call on him this evening? Will you give him a ticket to the lecture of Monsieur Maundy?"

"No!" I blazed, half rising from my chair. "I've known that boy since he was a little toddler—knew his dead wife from childhood, too; and if you're figuring on making him the subject of some experiment—"

"Softly, my friend," he besought. "There is a terrible Thing loose among us. Remember the noble martyrs of science, those so magnificent men who risked their lives that yellow fever and malaria should be no more. Was not their work a holy one? Certainly. I do but wish that this young man may attend the lecture tonight, and on my honor, I shall guard him until all danger of attempted self-murder is passed. You will do what I say?"

He was so earnest in his plea that, though I felt like an accessory before the fact in a murder, I agreed.

Meantime, his little blue eyes snapping and sparkling with the zest of the chase, de Grandin had busied himself with the telephone directory, looking up a number of addresses, culling through them, discarding some, adding others, until he had obtained a list of some five or six. "Now, *mon vieux*," he begged as I made ready to visit Alvin Spence on my treacherous errand, "I would that you convey me to the rectory of St. Benedict's Church. The priest in charge there is Irish, and the Irish have the gift of seeing things which you colder-blooded Saxons may not. I must have a confab with this good Father O'Brien before I can permit that you interview the young Monsieur Spence. *Mordieu*, me, I am a scientist; no murderer!"

I drove him past the rectory and parked my motor at the curb, waiting impatiently while he thundered at the door with the handle of his ebony walking stick. His knock was answered by a little old man in clerical garb and a face as round and ruddy as a winter apple.

De Grandin spoke hurriedly to him in a low voice, waving his hands, shaking his head, shrugging his shoulders, as was his wont when the earnestness of his argument bore him before it. The priest's round face showed first incredulity, then mild skepticism, finally absorbed interest. In a moment the pair of them had vanished inside the house, leaving me to cool my heels in the bitter March air.

"You were long enough," I grumbled as he emerged from the rectory.

"*Pardieu*, yes, just long enough," he agreed. "I did accomplish my purpose, and no visit is either too long or too short when you can say that. Now to the house of the good Monsieur Spence, if you will. *Mordieu*, but we shall see what we shall see this night!"

Six hours later de Grandin and I crouched shivering at the roadside where the winding, serpentine Albemarle Pike dips into the hollow beside the Lonesome Swamp. The wind which had been trenchant as a shrew's tongue earlier in the evening had died away, and a hard, dull bitterness of cold hung over the hills and hollows of the rolling countryside. From the wide salt marshes where the bay's tide crept up to mingle with the swamp's brackish waters twice a day there came great sheets of brumous, impenetrable vapor which shrouded the landscape and distorted commonplace objects into hideous, gigantic monstrosities.

"*Mort d'un petit bonhomme*, my friend," de Grandin commented between chattering teeth, "I do not like this place; it has an evil air. There are spots where the very earth does breathe of unholy deeds, and by the sacred name of a rooster, this is one such. Look you at this accursed fog. Is it not as if the specters of those drowned at sea were marching up the shore this night?"

"Umph!" I replied, sinking my neck lower in the collar of my ulster and silently cursing myself for a fool.

A moment's silence, then: "You are sure Monsieur Spence must come this way? There is no other road by which he can reach his home?"

"Of course not," I answered shortly. "He lives out in the new Weiss development with his mother and sister—you were there this evening—and this is the only direct motor route to the subdivision from the city."

"Ah, that is well," he replied, hitching the collar of his greatcoat higher about his ears. "You will recognize his car—surely?"

"I'll try to," I promised, "but you can't be sure of anything on a night like this. I'd not guarantee to pick out my own—there's somebody pulling up beside the road now," I interrupted myself as a roadster came to an abrupt halt and stood panting, its headlights forming vague, luminous spots in the haze.

"Mais oui," he agreed, "and no one stops at this spot for any good until It has been conquered. Come, let us investigate." He started forward, body bent, head advanced, like a motion picture conception of an Indian on the warpath.

Half a hundred stealthy steps brought us abreast of the parked car. Its occupant was sitting back on the driving seat, his hands resting listlessly on the steering wheel, his eyes upturned, as though he saw a vision in the trailing wisps of fog before him. I needed no second glance to recognize Alvin Spence, though the rapt look upon his white, set face transfigured it almost beyond recognition. He was like a poet beholding the beatific vision of his mistress or a medieval eremite gazing through the opened portals of Paradise.

"A-a-ah!" de Grandin's whisper cut like a wire-edged knife through the silence of the fog-bound air, "do you behold it, Friend Trowbridge?"

"Wha—" I whispered back, but broke the syllable half uttered. Thin, tenuous, scarcely to be distinguished from the lazily drifting festoons of the fog itself, there was a *something* in midair before the car where Alvin Spence sat with his yearning soul looking from his eyes. I seemed to see clear through the thing, yet its outlines were plainly perceptible, and as I looked and looked again, I recognized the unmistakable features of Dorothy Spence, the young man's dead wife. Her body—if the tenuous, ethereal mass of static vapor could be called such—was bare of clothing, and seemed imbued with a voluptuous grace and allure the living woman had never possessed, but her face was that of the young woman who had lain in Rosedale Cemetery for three-quarters of a year. If ever living man beheld the simulacrum of the dead, we three gazed on the wraith of Dorothy Spence that moment.

"Dorothy—my beloved, my dear, my dear!" the man half whispered, half sobbed, stretching forth his hands to the spirit-woman, then falling back on the seat as the vision seemed to elude his grasp when a sudden puff of breeze stirred the fog.

We could not catch the answer he received, close as we stood, but we could see the pale, curving lips frame the single word "Come!" and saw the transparent arms stretched out to beckon him forward.

The man half rose from his seat, then sank back, set his face in sudden resolution and plunged his hand into the pocket of his overcoat.

Beside me de Grandin had been fumbling with something in his inside pocket. As Alvin Spence drew forth his hand and the dull gleam of a polished revolver shone in the light from his dashboard lamp, the Frenchman leaped forward like a panther. "Stop him, Friend Trowbridge!" he called shrilly, and to the hovering vision:

"*Avaunt*, accursed one! Begone, thou exile from heaven! Away, snake-spawn!"

As he shouted he drew a tiny pellet from his inner pocket and hurled it point-blank through the vaporous body of the specter.

Even as I seized Spence's hand and fought with him for possession of the pistol, I saw the transformation from the tail of my eye. As de Grandin's missile tore through its unsubstantial substance, the vision-woman seemed to shrink in upon herself, to become suddenly more compact, thinner, scrawny. Her rounded bosom flattened to mere folds of leatherlike skin stretched drum-tight above staring ribs, her slender graceful hands were horrid, claw-tipped talons, and the yearning, enticing face of Dorothy Spence became a mask of hideous, implacable hate, great-eyed, thin-lipped, beak-nosed—such a face as the demons of hell might show after a million million years of burning in the infernal fires. A screech like the keening of all the owls in the world together split the fog-wrapped stillness of the night, and the monstrous thing before us seemed suddenly to shrivel, shrink to a mere spot of baleful, phosphorescent fire, and disappear like a snuffed-out candle's flame.

Spence saw it, too. The pistol dropped from his nerveless fingers to the car's floor with a soft thud, and his arm went limp in my grasp as he fell forward in a dead faint.

"*Parbleu*," de Grandin swore softly as he climbed into the unconscious lad's car. "Let us drive forward, Friend Trowbridge. We will take him home and administer a soporific. He must sleep, this poor one, or the memory of what we have shown him will rob him of his reason."

So we carried Alvin Spence to his home, administered a hypnotic and left him in the care of his wondering mother with instructions to repeat the dose if he should wake.

I T WAS A MILE or more to the nearest bus station, and we set out at a brisk walk, our heels hitting sharply against the frosty concrete of the road.

"What in the world was it, de Grandin?" I asked as we marched in step down the darkened highway. "It was the most horrible—"

"*Parbleu*," he interrupted, "someone comes this way in a monstrous hurry!"

His remark was no exaggeration. Driven as though pursued by all the furies from pandemonium, came a light motor car with plain black sides and a curving top. "Look out!" the driver warned as he recognized me and came to a bumping halt. "Look out, Dr. Trowbridge, it's walking! It got out and walked!"

De Grandin regarded him with an expression of comic bewilderment. "Now what is it that walks, *mon brave*?" he demanded. "*Mordieu*, you chatter like a monkey with a handful of hot chestnuts! What is it that walks, and why must we look out for it, *hein*?"

"Sile Gregory," the young man answered. "He died this mornin' an' Mr. Johnson took him to th' parlors to fix 'im up, an' sent me and Joe Williams out with him this evenin'. I was just drivin' up to th' house, an' Joe hopped out to give me a lift with th' casket, an' old Silas *got up an' walked away!* An' Mr. Johnson embalmed 'im this mornin' I tell you!"

"*Nom d'un chou-fleur!*" de Grandin shot back. "And where did this so remarkable demonstration take place, *mon vieux*? Also, what of the excellent Williams, your partner?"

"I don't know, an' I don't care," the other replied. "When a dead corpse I saw embalmed this mornin' gets outa its casket an' walks, I ain't gonna wait for nobody. Jump up here, if you want to go with me; I ain't gonna stay here no longer!"

"*Bien*," de Grandin acquiesced. "Go your way, my excellent one. Should we encounter your truant corpse, we will direct him to his waiting *bière*."

The young man waited no second invitation, but started his car down the road at a speed which would bring him into certain trouble if observed by a state trooper.

"Now, what the devil do you make of that?" I asked. "I know Johnson, the funeral director, well, and I always thought he had a pretty levelheaded crowd of boys about his place, but if that lad hasn't been drinking some powerful liquor, I'll be—"

"Not necessarily, my friend," de Grandin interrupted. "I think it not at all impossible that he tells but the sober truth. It may well be that the dead do walk this road tonight."

I shivered with something other than the night's chill as he made the matter-of-fact assertion, but forbore pressing him for an explanation. There are times when ignorance is a happier portion than knowledge.

We had marched perhaps another quarter-mile in silence when de Grandin suddenly plucked my sleeve. "Have you noticed nothing, my friend?" he asked.

"What d'ye mean?" I demanded sharply, for my nerves were worn tender by the night's events.

"I am not certain, but it seems to me we are followed."

"Followed? Nonsense! *Who* would be following us?" I returned, unconsciously stressing the personal pronoun, for I had almost said, "What would follow us," and the implication raised by the impersonal form sent tiny shivers racing along my back and neck.

De Grandin cast me a quick, appraising glance, and I saw the ends of his spiked mustache lift suddenly as his lips framed a sardonic smile, but instead of answering he swung round on his heel and faced the shadows behind us.

"*Holà, Monsieur le Cadavre!*" he called sharply. "Here we are, and—*sang du diable!*—here we shall stand."

I looked at him in open-mouthed amazement, but his gaze was turned steadfastly on something half seen in the mist which lay along the road.

Next instant my heart seemed pounding through my ribs and my breath came hot and choking in my throat, for a tall, gangling man suddenly emerged from the fog and made for us at a shambling gait.

He was clothed in a long, old-fashioned double-breasted frock coat and stiffly starched shirt topped by a standing collar and white, ministerial tie. His hair was neatly, though somewhat unnaturally, arranged in a central part above a face the color and smoothness of wax, and little flecks of talcum powder still clung here and there to his eyebrows. No mistaking it! Johnson, artist that he was, had arrayed the dead farmer in the manner of all his kind for their last public appearance before relatives and friends. One look told me the horrible, incredible truth. It was the body of old Silas Gregory which stumbled toward us through the fog. Dressed, greased and powdered for its last, long rest, the thing came toward us with faltering, uncertain strides, and I noticed, with the sudden ability for minute inventory fear sometimes lends our senses, that his old, sunburned skin showed more than one brand where the formaldehyde embalming fluid had burned it.

In one long, thin hand the horrible thing grasped the helve of a farmyard ax; the other hand lay stiffly folded across the midriff as the embalmer had placed it when his professional ministrations were finished that morning.

"My God!" I cried, shrinking back toward the roadside. But de Grandin ran forward to meet the charging horror with a cry which was almost like a welcome.

"Stand clear, Friend Trowbridge," he warned, "we will fight this to a finish, I and It!" His little, round eyes were flashing with the zest of combat, his mouth was set in a straight, uncompromising line beneath the sharply waxed ends of his diminutive mustache, and his shoulders hunched forward like those of a practised wrestler before he comes to grips with his opponent.

With a quick, whipping motion, he ripped the razor-sharp blade of his sword-cane from its ebony sheath and swung the flashing steel in a whirring circle about his head, then sank to a defensive posture, one foot advanced, one retracted, the leg bent at the knee, the triple-edged sword dancing before him like the darting tongue of an angry serpent.

The dead thing never faltered in its stride. Three feet or so from Jules de Grandin it swung the heavy, rust-encrusted ax above its shoulder and brought it downward, its dull, lack-luster eyes staring straight before it with an impassivity more terrible than any glare of hate.

"*Sa ha!*" de Grandin's blade flickered forward like a streak of storm lightning, and fleshed itself to the hilt in the corpse's shoulder.

He might as well have struck his steel into a bag of meal.

The ax descended with a crushing, devastating blow.

De Grandin leaped nimbly aside, disengaging his blade and swinging it again before him, but an expression of surprise—almost of consternation—was on his face.

I felt my mouth go dry with excitement, and a queer, weak feeling hit me at the pit of the stomach. The Frenchman had driven his sword home with the skill of a practised fencer and the precision of a skilled anatomist. His blade had pierced the dead man's body at the junction of the short head of the biceps and the great pectoral muscle, at the coracoid process, inflicting a wound which should have paralyzed the arm—yet the terrible ax rose for a second blow as though de Grandin's steel had struck wide of the mark.

"Ah?" de Grandin nodded understandingly as he leaped backward, avoiding the ax-blade by the breadth of a hair. "*Bien. À la fin!*"

His defensive tactics changed instantly. Flickeringly his sword lashed forward, then came down and back with a sharp, whipping motion. The keen edge of the angular blade bit deeply into the corpse's wrist, laying bare the bone. Still the ax rose and fell and rose again.

Slash after slash de Grandin gave, his slicing cuts falling with almost mathematical precision in the same spot, shearing deeper and deeper into his dreadful opponent's wrist. At last, with a short, clucking exclamation, he drew his blade sharply back for the last time, severing the ax-hand from the arm.

The dead thing collapsed like a deflated balloon at his feet as hand and ax fell together to the cement roadway.

Quick as a mink, de Grandin. thrust his left hand within his coat, drew forth a pellet similar to that with which he had transformed the counterfeit of Dorothy Spence, and hurled it straight into the upturned ghastly-calm face of the mutilated body before him.

The dead lips did not part, for the embalmer's sutures had closed them forever that morning, but the body writhed upward from the road, and a groan which was a muted scream came from its flat chest. It twisted back and forth a moment, like a mortally stricken serpent in its death agony, then lay still.

Seizing the corpse by its graveclothes, de Grandin dragged it through the line of roadside hazel bushes to the rim of the swamp, and busied himself cutting long, straight withes from the brushwood, then disappeared again behind the tangled branches. At last:

"It is finished," he remarked, stepping back to the road. "Let us go."

"Wha—what did you do?" I faltered.

"I did the needful, my friend. *Morbleu*, we had an evil, a very evil thing imprisoned in that dead man, and I took such precautions as were necessary to fix it in its prison. A stake through the heart, a severed head, and the whole firmly thrust into the ooze of the swamp—*voilà*. It will be long before other innocent ones are induced to destroy themselves by *that*."

"But—" I began.

"*Non, non*," he replied, half laughing. "*En avant, mon ami!* I would that we return home as quickly as possible. Much work creates much appetite, and I make small doubt that I shall consume the remainder of that so delicious apple pie which I could not eat at dinner."

J ULES DE GRANDIN REGARDED the empty plate before him with a look of comic tragedy. "May endless benisons rest upon your amiable cook, Friend Trowbridge," he pronounced, "but may the curse of heaven forever pursue the villain who manufactures the woefully inadequate pans in which she bakes her pies."

"Hang the pies, and the plate-makers, too!" I burst out. "You promised to explain all this hocus-pocus, and I've been patient long enough. Stop sitting there like a glutton, wailing for more pie, and tell me about it."

"Oh, the mystery?" he replied, stifling a yawn and lighting a cigarette. "That is simple, my friend, but these so delicious pies—however, I do digress:

"When first I saw the accounts of so many strange suicides within one little week I was interested, but not greatly puzzled. People have slain themselves since the beginning of time, and yet"—he shrugged his shoulders deprecatingly—"what is it that makes the hound scent his quarry, the war-horse sniff the battle afar off? Who can tell?

"I said to me: 'There is undoubtlessly more to these deaths than the newspapers have said. I shall investigate.'

"From the coroner's to the undertakers', and from the undertakers' to the physicians', yes, *Parbleu!* and to the family residences, as well, I did go, gleaning here a bit and there a bit of information which seemed to mean nothing, but which might mean much did I but have other information to add to it.

"One thing I ascertained early: In each instance the suicides had been to hear this Reverend Maundy the night before or the same night they did away with themselves. This was perhaps insignificant; perhaps it meant much. I determined to hear this Monsieur Maundy with my own two ears; but I would not hear him too close by.

"Forgive me, my friend, for I did make of you the guinea-pig for my laboratory experiment. You I left in a forward seat while the reverend gentleman preached; me, I stayed in the rear of the hall and used my eyes as well as my ears.

"What happened that night? Why, my good, kind Friend Trowbridge, who in all his life had done no greater wrong than thoughtlessly to kill a little, so harmless kitten, did almost *seemingly* commit suicide. But I was not asleep by the switch, my friend. Not Jules de Grandin! All the way home I saw you were *distrait*, and I did fear something would happen, and I did therefore watch beside your door with my eye and ear alternately glued to the keyhole. *Parbleu*, I entered the chamber not one little second too soon, either!

"'This is truly strange,' I tell me. 'My friend hears this preacher and nearly destroys himself. Six others have heard him, and have quite killed themselves. If Friend Trowbridge were haunted by the ghost of a dead kitten, why should not those others, who also undoubtlessly possessed distressing memories, have been hounded to their graves by them?'

"'There is no reason why they should not,' I tell me.

"Next morning comes the summons to attend the young Mademoiselle Weaver. She, too, have heard the preacher; she, too, have attempted her life. And what does she tell us? That she fancied the voice of her dead friend urged her to kill herself.

"'Ah, ha!' I say to me. 'This whatever-it-is which causes so much suicide may appeal by fear, or perhaps by love, or by whatever will most strongly affect the person who dies by his own hand. We must see this Monsieur Maundy. It is perhaps possible he can tell us much.'

"As yet I can see no light—I am still in darkness—but far ahead I already see the gleam of a promise of information. When we see Monsieur Everard Maundy and he tells us of his experience at that séance so many years ago—*parbleu*, I see it all, or almost all.

"Now, what was it acted as agent for that aged sorceress' curse?"

He elevated one shoulder and looked questioningly at me.

"How should I know?" I answered.

"Correct," he nodded, "how, indeed? Beyond doubt it were a spirit of some sort; what sort we do not know. Perhaps it were the spirit of some unfortunate who had destroyed himself and was earthbound as a consequence. There are such. And, as misery loves company in the proverb, so do these wretched ones seek to lure others to join them in their unhappy state. Or, maybe, it were an Elemental."

"A *what?*" I demanded.

"An Elemental—a Neutrarian."

"What the deuce is that?"

For answer he left the table and entered the library, returning with a small red-leather bound volume in his hand. "You have read the works of Monsieur Rossetti?" he asked.

"Yes."

"You recall his poem, *Eden Bowers*, perhaps?"

"H'm; yes, I've read it, but I never could make anything of it."

"Quite likely," he agreed, "its meaning is most obscure, but I shall enlighten you. *Attendez-moi!*"

Thumbing through the thin pages he began reading at random:

It was Lilith, the wife of Adam,
Not a drop of her blood was human,
But she was made like a soft, sweet woman . . .
Lilith stood on the skirts of Eden.
She was the first that thence was driven,
With her was hell and with Eve was heaven
What bright babes had Lilith and Adam,
Shapes that coiled in the woods and waters,
Glittering sons and radiant daughters . . .

"You see, my friend?"

"No, I'm hanged if I do."

"Very well, then, according to the rabbinical lore, before Eve was created, Adam, our first father, had a demon wife named Lilith. And by her he had many children, not human, nor yet wholly demon.

"For her sins Lilith was expelled from Eden's bowers, and Adam was given Eve to wife. With Lilith was driven out all her progeny by Adam, and Lilith and her half-man, half-demon brood declared war on Adam and Eve and their descendants forever. These descendants of Lilith and Adam have ever since roamed the earth and air, incorporeal, having no bodies like men, yet having always a hatred for flesh and blood. Because they were the first, or elder race, they are sometimes called Elementals in the ancient lore; sometimes they are called Neutrarians, because they are neither wholly men nor wholly devils. Me, I do not take odds in the controversy; I care not what they are called, but I know what I have seen. I think it is highly possible those ancient Hebrews, misinterpreting the manifestations they observed, accounted for them by their so fantastic legends. We are told these Neutrarians or Elementals are immaterial beings. Absurd? Not necessarily. What is matter—material. Electricity, perhaps—a great system of law and order throughout the universe and all the millions of worlds extending throughout infinity.

"Very good, so far; but when we have said matter is electricity, what are we to say if asked, 'What is electricity?' Me, I think it a modification of the ether.

"'Very good,' you say; 'but what is ether?'

"*Parbleu*, I do not know. The matter—or material—of the universe is little, if anything, more than electrons, flowing about in all directions. For here, now there, the electrons balance and form what we call solids—rocks and trees and men and women. But may they not coalesce at a different rate of speed, or vibration, to form beings which are real, with ambitions and loves and hates similar to ours, yet for the most part invisible to us, as is the air? Why not? No man can truthfully say, 'I have seen the air,' yet no one is so great a fool as to doubt its existence for that reason."

"Yes, but we can see the effects of air," I objected. "Air in motion, for instance, becomes wind, and—"

"*Mort d'un crapaud!*" he burst out. "And have we not observed the effects of these Elementals—these Neutrarians, or whatsoever their name may be? How of the six suicides; how of that which tempted the young Mademoiselle Weaver and the young Monsieur Spence to self-murder? How of the cat which entered your room? Did we see no effects there, *hein?*"

"But the thing we saw with young Spence, and the cat, were visible," I objected.

"But of course. When you fancied you saw the cat, you were influenced from within, even as Mademoiselle Weaver was when she heard the voice of her dead friend. What we saw with the young Spence was the shadow of his desire—the intensified love and longing for his dead wife, plus the evil entity which urged him to unpardonable sin."

"Oh, all right," I conceded. "Go on with your theory."

He stared thoughtfully at the glowing tip of his cigarette a moment, then: "It has been observed, my friend, that he who goes to a Spiritualistic seance may come away with some evil spirit attached to him—whether it be a spirit which once inhabited human form or an Elemental, it is no matter; the evil ones swarm about the lowered lights of the Spiritualistic meeting as flies congregate at the honey-pot in summer. It appears such a one fastened to Everard Maundy. His wife was its first victim, afterward those who heard him preach were attacked.

"Consider the scene at the tabernacle when Monsieur Maundy preaches: Emotion, emotion—all is emotion; reason is lulled to sleep by the power of his words; and the minds of his hearer's are not on their guard against the entrance of evil spirits; they are too intent on what he is saying. Their consciousness is absent. *Pouf!* The evil one fastens firmly on some unwary person, explores his innermost mind, finds out his weakest point of defense. With you, it was the kitten; with young Mademoiselle Weaver, her dead friend; with Monsieur Spence, his lost wife. Even love can be turned to evil purposes by such an one.

"These things I did consider most carefully, and then I did enlist the services of young Monsieur Spence. You saw what you saw on the lonely road this night. Appearing to him in the form of his dead beloved, this wicked one had all but persuaded him to destroy himself when we intervened.

"*Très bien*. We triumphed then; the night before I had prevented your death. The evil one was angry with me; also it was frightened. If I continued, I would rob it of much prey, so it sought to do me harm. Me, I am ever on guard, for knowledge is power. It could not lead me to my death, and, being spirit, it could not directly attack me. It had to recourse to its last resort. While the young undertaker's assistant was about to deliver the body of the old Monsieur Gregory, the spirit seized the corpse and animated it, then pursued me.

"Ha, almost I thought, it had done for me at one time, for I forgot it was no living thing I fought, and attacked it as if it could be killed. But when I found my sword could not kill that which was already dead, I did cut off its so abominable hand. I am very clever, my friend. The evil spirit reaped small profits from fighting with me."

He made the boastful admission in all seriousness, entirely unaware of its sound, for to him it was but a straightforward statement of undisputed fact. I grinned in spite of myself, then curiosity got the better of amusement. "What were those little pellets you threw at the spirit when it was luring young Spence to commit suicide, and later at the corpse of Silas Gregory?" I asked.

"Ah"—his elfish smile flickered across his lips then disappeared as quickly as it came—"it is better you do not ask me that, *mon cher*. Let it suffice when I tell you I convinced the good *Père* O'Brien that he should let me have what no layman is supposed to touch, that I might use the ammunition of heaven against the forces of hell."

"But how do we know this Elemental, or whatever it was, won't come back again?" I persisted.

"Little fear," he encouraged. "The resort to the dead man's body was its last desperate chance. Having elected to fight me physically, it must stand or fall by the result of the fight. Once inside the body, it could not quickly extricate itself. Half an hour, at least, must elapse before it could withdraw, and before that time had passed I had fixed it there for all time. The stake through the heart and the severed head makes that body as harmless as any other, and the wicked spirit which animated it must remain with the flesh it sought to pervert to its own evil ends henceforth and forever."

"But—"

"*Ah bah!*" He dropped his cigarette end into his empty coffee cup and yawned frankly. "We dally too much, my friend. This night's work has made me heavy with sleep. Let us take a tiny sip of cognac so the pie may not give us unhappy dreams and then to bed. Tomorrow is another day, and who knows what new task lies before us?"

Creeping Shadows

"**M**ON *DIEU!* IS IT that we are arrest'?" Jules de Grandin half rose from the dinner table in mock consternation as the vigorous ringing of the front door bell was followed by a heavy tramp in the hall, and Nora, my household factotum, ushered Detective Sergeant Costello and two uniformed policemen into the dining room.

"Not a bit of it," Costello negatived with a grin as he seated himself on the extreme forward edge of the chair I indicated and motioned the two patrolmen to seats beside him. "Not a bit of it, Dr. de Grandin, sor; but we're after askin' a favor of you, if you don't mind. This is Officer Callaghan"—he indicated the burly, red-headed policeman at his right—"an' this is Officer Schippert. Both good boys, sor, an' worthy to be believed, for I know 'em of old."

"I doubt it not," de Grandin acknowledged the introduction with one of his quick smiles, "those whom you vouch for are surely not to be despised, *mon vieux*. But this favor you would have of me, what of it?"

Detective Sergeant Costello, clasped his black derby hat in a viselike grip between his knees and stared into its interior as though he expected to find inspiration there. "We're after wantin' some information in th' Craven case, if ye don't mind, sor," he replied.

"Eh, the Craven case?" de Grandin echoed. "*Parbleu*, old friend, I fear you have come to the wrong bureau of information. I know nothing of the matter except such tags of gossip as I have heard, and that is little enough. Was it not that this Monsieur Craven, who lived alone by himself, was discovered dead in his front yard after having lain there in that condition for several days, and that there was evidence of neither struggle nor robbery? Am I right?"

"M'm," Costello mumbled. "They didn't tell ye nothin' about his head bein' cut off, then?"

An expression of almost tragic astonishment swept over the little Frenchman's face. "What is it that you say—he was beheaded?" he exclaimed incredulously. "*Mordieu*, why was I not informed of this? I had been told there was no evidence of struggle! Is it then that lonely gentlemen in America suffer the loss of their heads without struggling? Tell on, my friend. I burn, I am consumed with curiosity. What more of this so remarkable case where a man dies by decapitation and there is no sign of foul play? *Nom d'un raisin*, I am very wise, *cher sergent*, but it seems I have yet much to learn!"

"Well, sor," Costello began half apologetically, "I don't know why ye never heard about Craven's head bein' missin', unless th' coroner's office hustled th' body off too soon for th' folks to git wise. But that ain't th' strangest part of th' case; not by a dam' sight—askin' your pardon for th' expression, sor. Ye see, these boys here"—he indicated the officers, who nodded solemn confirmation of his remark before he uttered it—"these boys here have th' beat which goes past th' Craven house, an' they both of 'em swear they seen him in his front yard th' mornin' of th' very day he was found dead, *an' supposed to have been dead for several days when found!*

"Now, Dr. de Grandin, I'm just a police officer, an' Callaghan an' Schippert's just a pair o' harness bulls. We ain't had no eddycation, all th' doctors at the coroner's office ought to know what they're talkin' about when they say th' putrefactive state of his body showed Craven had been dead several days; but just th' same—" He paused, casting a glance at his two blue-uniformed confreres.

"*Nom d'un bouc*, go on, man; go on!" de Grandin urged. "I starve for further details, and you withhold your story like a naughty little boy teasing a dog with a bit of meat! Proceed, I beseech you."

"Well, sor, as I was sayin'," the detective resumed, "I ain't settin' up to be no medical doctor, nor nothin' like that; but I'll take me Bible oath, Mister Craven hadn't been dead no several days when they found him layin' in his garden. 'Twas early in th' mornin' of th' very day they found 'im I was walkin' past his house after bein' out most all night on a case, an' I seen him standin' in his front yard with me own two eyes, as plain as I see you this minute, sor. Callaghan an' Schippert, who was comin' off night duty, come past th' house not more 'n a' hour afterward, an' they seen 'im standin' among th' flowers, too."

"Eh, you are sure of this?" de Grandin demanded, his little blue eyes snapping with interest.

"Positive," Costello returned. "Meself, I might a' seen a ghost, an' Callaghan might a' done th' same, for we're Irish, sor, an' th' hidden people show 'emselves to us when they don't bid th' time o' day to th' rest o' yez; but Schippert here, if he seen a banshee settin' on a murderer's grave, combin' her hair with th' shinbone of a dead gipsy, he'd never give th' old gurrl a tumble unless her screechin' annoyed th' neighbors, an' then he'd tell her to shut up an' move on, or he'd run her in for disturbin' th' peace. So if Schippert says he seen Mr. Craven walkin' in his front garden half an hour after sun-up, why, Mr. Craven it were, sor, an' no ghost at all. I'll swear to that."

"*Morbleu*, and did you not tell the coroner as much at the inquisition?" de Grandin asked, producing a cigarette from his waistcoat pocket like a presti-digitator exhuming a rabbit from his trick hat, but forgetting to light it in his excitement. "Did you not inform *Monsieur le Coroneur* of this?"

"No, sor; we wasn't invited to th' inquest. I reported what I'd seen to head-quarters when I heard they'd found Mr. Craven's body, an' Callaghan an' Schip-pert done th' same at their precinct, but all they said to us was, 'Applesauce.' An' that was that, sor. Y'see, when we all three swore we'd seen th' man himself th' same mornin', an' th' doctors all swore he must a' been dead almost a week before he was found, they thought we was all cuckoo, an' paid us no more mind."

"*Nom d'un porc!* Did they so?" de Grandin barked. "They did tell you, my friend, that you spoke the sauce of the apple; you, who have assisted Jules de Grandin in more cases than one? *Mordieu*, it is the insult! I shall go to these *canaille*; I shall tell them to their foolish faces that they possess not the brain of a guinea-pig! I, Jules de Grandin, shall inform them—"

"Aisy, sor; go aisy, if ye please," Costello besought. "'Twould do us more harm than good should ye cause hard feelin's agin us at th' coroner's office; but ye can be a big help to us in another way, if ye will."

"*Morbleu*, speak on, my friend, enlighten me," de Grandin agreed. "If there be a mystery to this case, and a mystery there surely is, have no fear that Jules de Grandin will sleep or eat or drink till it shall be explained!" He poured himself another cup of coffee and imbibed it in two huge gulps. "Lead on, *mon brave*. What is it that you would have me do?"

"Well, sor," the Irishman grinned with delight at de Grandin's enthusiastic acceptance of his suggestion, "we knew as how you'd had all sorts an' kinds o' experience with dead folks, an' we're wonderin' if mebbe, you would go over to th' Craven house with us an' take a look round th' premises, sorter. Mebbe you'd be able to find out sumpin' that would make th' goin' aisier for us, for they're razzin' us sumpin' awful about sayin' we seen Mr. Craven several days after th' doctor says he was kilt, so they are. All th' same, no matter what they say at th' coroner's office," he added stubbornly, "a man that's well enough to be walkin' around his own front yard at half-past four in th' mornin' ain't goin' to be dead several days when he's found in th' same yard a few minutes after four o'clock th' same afternoon. That's what I say, an' Callaghan an' Schippert here says th' same."

"Sure do," Officers Callaghan and Schippert nodded solemn agreement.

"*Parbleu, mes amis*," de Grandin agreed as he rose from the table. I consider your logic irrefutable.

"Come, Trowbridge, my friend," he beckoned to me, "let us go to this house where men who died several days before—with their heads off, *parbleu!*—promenade their front yards." He held the door of my motor's tonneau courteously for the three officers, then vaulted nimbly to the front seat beside me. "Trowbridge, my old one," he whispered as I set the car in motion, "I damn think we shall have the beautiful adventure this night. Hasten, I would that it begins at once, right away."

T HE CRAVEN COTTAGE STOOD in the center of a quarter-acre tract, a low hedge cutting it off from the old military road on which it faced, an eight-foot brick wall surrounding its other three sides. Though the front grounds were planted in a run-down garden, there were no trees near the house, consequently we had an unobstructed view of the yard in the brilliant May moonlight.

"It was right here they found him," Officer Schippert volunteered, directing our attention to a bed of phlox which still bore the impression of some heavy weight. "He was standin' almost alongside, this here flower bed when I seen him that mornin', an' he must a' fallen where he stood. I can't understand what— ouch! What th' devil's that?" He drew his hand suddenly back from the mass of flowering plants, grasping his fore-finger in pain.

"Stick yerself, Schip," Callaghan asked casually. "I didn't know them things had thorns on 'em."

"I'll say I stuck myself," Officer Schippert replied, displaying a long, pointed sliver of wood adhering to the skin of his finger. "This thing was layin' right amongst them flowers, an'—oh, my God! Callaghan, Costello, I'm goin' blind; I'm dyin'!" With an exclamation which was half grunt, half choke, he slid forward to the earth, his stalwart body crushing the flowers which had bent beneath the weight of Craven's headless corpse some forty-eight hours earlier.

"Howly Mither!" Sergeant Costello exclaimed as he bent over the prostrate figure of the policeman. "Dr. de Grandin, he *is* dead! See here, sor; his heart's stopped beatin'!"

De Grandin and I leaned forward, making a hasty inspection. Costello's diagnosis was all too true. The sturdy patrolman, vibrant with life two minutes before, was lifeless as the man whose body lay in the city morgue, "apparently dead for several days when found," according to medical testimony.

Costello and I picked our fallen comrade up and bore him into the empty house of death, and while I struck a match and applied it to a gas jet, de Grandin opened the dead policeman's blouse and made a closer examination.

"Look here, Dr. de Grandin," the sergeant announced, looking up from the dead man's face with the dry-eyed sorrow of a man whose daily duty it is to take desperate risks, "there's something devilish about this business. Look at his face! He's turnin' spotty, a' ready! Why, you'd think he was dead a couple o' days, an' we only just carried him in here a minute ago."

De Grandin bent closer, examining the dead man's face, chest and arms attentively. "*Pardieu*, it may easily be so!" he murmured to himself, then aloud to Costello: "You are right, my friend. Do you and the good Callaghan go to the police bureau for an ambulance. Dr. Trowbridge and I will wait until they come for the—for your comrade. Meantime—" He broke off, gazing, abstractedly about the combination living-dining room in which we stood, noting the odd ornaments on the mantel-shelf, the neatly arranged blue plates in the china closet, the general air of stiff, masculine house-keeping which permeated the apartment.

"*Parbleu*, Trowbridge, my friend," he commented as the policemen tiptoed out, "I think this matter will require much thinking over. Me, I do not like the way this poor one died, and I have less liking for the intelligence that Monsieur Craven's head was missing."

"But Craven must have been cut down by some fiend." I interposed, "while poor Schippert—well, how *did* he die, de Grandin?"

"Who can say?" he queried in his turn, tapping his teeth thoughtfully with the polished nail of his forefinger.

"Now, Jules de Grandin, great *tête de chou* that you are, what have you to say to this?" he apostrophized himself as he inspected the splinter of wood which had scratched the dead policeman's hand. "That is what it is, undoubtlessly," he continued his monologue, "yes, *pardieu*, we do all know that, but why? Such things do not happen without reason, foolish one." He turned to the chest of drawers beneath the kitchen dresser and began ransacking it as methodically as though he were a burglar intent on looting the place.

"Ah? What have we here?" he demanded as a heavy package, securely wrapped in muslin, came to light. "Perhaps it is a plate—" He bore the parcel to the unpainted kitchen table and began undoing the nautical knots with which its wrappings were fastened. "*Morbleu*," he laid back the last layer of cloth, "it *is* a plate, Friend Trowbridge. And such a plate! Men have died for less—*cordieu*, I think men have died for *this*, unless I am more mistaken than I think."

Under the flickering gaslight there lay a disk of yellow metal some thirteen or fourteen inches in diameter, its outer edge decorated with a row of small, oblong ornaments, like a border of dominoes, an inner circle, three inches or so smaller than the plate's perimeter, serving as a frame for the bas-relief figure of a dancing man crowned with a feather headdress and brandishing a two-headed spear in one hand and a hook-ended war-club in the other.

"It is gold, my friend," he breathed almost reverently. "Solid, virgin gold, hammered by hand a thousand years ago, if a day. Pure Mayan it is, from Chichen-Itzá or Uxmal, and worth its weight in diamonds."

"Um'm, perhaps," I agreed doubtfully, "but nothing you've said means anything to me."

"No matter," he retorted shortly. "Let us see—ah, what have we here?" In a corner of the small open fireplace, innocent of any trace of ash or cinder, lay a tiny wisp of charred paper. Darting forward he retrieved the bit of refuse and spread it before him on the table.

"Um'm?" he muttered non-committally, staring at the relic as though he expected it to speak.

The paper had been burned to a crisp and had curled up on itself with the action of the flame, but the metallic content of the ink in which its message had been scribbled had bleached to a dark, leaden gray, several shades lighter than the carbonized surface of the note itself.

"*Regardez vous*, my friend," he commanded, taking a pair of laboratory tweezers from his dinner-coat pocket and straightening the paper slightly with a careful pressure. "Can not you descry words on this so black background?"

"No—yes!" I replied, looking over his shoulder and straining my eyes to the utmost.

"*Bien*, we shall read it together," he responded. "Now to begin:"

"*ar al*," we spelled out laboriously, as he turned the charred note gingerly to and fro beneath the lambent light. "*red ils av ot Murphy. Lay low an . . .*" the rest of the message was lost in the multitude of heat-wrinkles on the paper's blackened surface.

"*Mordieu*, but this is too bad!" he exclaimed when our united efforts to decipher further words proved fruitless. "There is no date, no signature, no anything. *Hélas*, we stand no nearer an answer to our puzzle than at first!"

He lighted one of his evil-smelling French cigarettes and took several lung-filling, thoughtful puffs, then threw the half-smoked tube into the fireplace and began re-wrapping the golden plate. "My friend," he informed me, his little blue eyes twinkling with sardonic laughter, "I lie. A moment since I did declare we were still at sea, but now I think we are, like Columbus, in sight of land. Moreover, again like Columbus, I think it is the coast of Central America which we do sight. Behold, we have established the motive for Monsieur Craven's murder, and we know how it was accomplished. There now remains only to ascertain who this Monsieur Murphy was and who inscribed this note of warning to the late Monsieur Craven."

"Well," I exclaimed impatiently, "I'm glad you've found out why and how Craven was killed. All I've seen here tonight is a policeman's tragic death and a silly-looking plate from Uxbridge, or some other absurd place."

He produced another cigarette and felt thoughtfully through his pockets for a match. "Those who know not what they see oft times see nothing, my friend," he returned with a sarcastic smile. "Come, let us go out into the air. This place—pah!—it has the reek of death on it."

We waited at the front gate until Costello and Callaghan arrived with the police ambulance. As the litter-bearers passed us on their grisly errand, de Grandin leaned from my car and whispered to Costello. "Tomorrow night, *cher sergent*. Perhaps we shall come to the end of the riddle then, and apprehend those who slew your friend, as well."

"Can ye, now, doctor?" the Irishman returned eagerly. "By gorry, I'll be present with bells—an' a couple o' guns—on if ye can trace th' murderin' devil for me."

"*Très bien*," de Grandin assented. "Meet us at Dr. Trowbridge's house about eight o'clock; if you please."

"Now, what's it all mean?" I demanded as I turned the car toward home. "You're as mysterious as a magician at the county fair. Come, out with it!"

"Listen, my friend," he bade. "The wise man who thinks he knows whereof he speaks retains silence until his thought becomes a certainty. Me, I have wisdom. Much experience has given it to me. Let us say no more of this matter until we have ascertained light on certain things which are yet most dark. Yes."

"But—"

"*Je suis le roi de ces montagnes . . .*"

He sang in high good humor, nor could all my threats or entreaties make him say one word more concerning the mystery of Craven's death, or Schippert's, or the queer, golden plate we found in the deserted house.

"BON SOIR, SERGENT," DE Grandin greeted as Costello entered the study shortly after nine o'clock the following evening. "We have awaited you with impatience."

"Have ye, now?" the Irishman replied. "Sure, it's too bad entirely that I've delayed th' party, but I've had th' devil's own time gettin' here this night. All sorts o' things have been poppin' up, sor."

"*Eh bien*, perhaps we shall pop up something more before the night is ended," the Frenchman returned. "Come, let us hasten; we have much to do before we seek our beds."

"All right," Costello, agreed as he prepared to follow, "where are we goin', if I may ask?"

"Ah, too many questions spoil the party of surprise, my friend," de Grandin answered with a laugh as he led the way to the car.

"Do you know the Rugby Road, Friend Trowbridge?" he asked as he climbed into the front seat beside me.

"Uh, yes," I replied without enthusiasm. The neighborhood he mentioned was in a suburb at the extreme east end of town, not at all noted for its odor of sanctity. Frankly, I had not much stomach for driving out there after dark, even with Sergeant Costello for company, but de Grandin gave me no time for temporizing.

"*Bien,*" he replied enthusiastically. "You will drive us with all celerity, if you please, and pause when I give the signal. Come, my friend; haste, I pray you. Not only may we save another life—we may apprehend those assassins who did Craven and the poor Schippert to death."

"All right," I agreed grudgingly, "but I'm not very keen on it."

Half an hour's run brought us to the winding, tree-shaded trail known as Rugby Road, a thoroughfare of broken pavements, tumbledown houses and wide spaces of open, uncultivated fields. At a signal from my companion I brought up before the straggling picket fence of a deserted-looking cottage, and the three of us swarmed out and advanced along the grass-choked path leading to the ruinous front stoop.

"I'm thinkin' we've had our ride for our pains, sor," Costello asserted as de Grandin's third imperative knock brought no response from beyond the weather-scarred door.

"Not we," the Frenchman denied, increasing both tempo and volume of his raps. "There is someone here, of a certainty, and here we shall stand until we receive an answer."

His persistence was rewarded, for a shuffling step finally sounded beyond the panels, and a cautious voice demanded haltingly, "Who's there?"

"*Parbleu,* friend, you are over long in honoring the presence of those who come to aid you!" de Grandin complained with testy irrelevancy. "Have the kindness to open the door."

"Who's there?" the voice repeated, this time with something like a tremor in it.

"*Nom d'un homard!*" the Frenchman ejaculated. "What does it matter what names we bear? We are come to help you escape 'the red devils'—those same demons who did away with Murphy and Craven. Quick, open, for the time is short!"

The man inside appeared to be considering de Grandin's statement, for there was a brief period of silence, then the sound of bolts withdrawing and a chain-lock being undone. "Quick—step fast!" the voice admonished as the door swung inward a scant ten inches without disclosing the person behind it. Next moment we stood in a dimly lighted hallway, surveying a perspiring little man in tattered pajamas and badly worn carpet slippers. He was an odd-looking bit of humanity, undersized, thin almost to the point of emaciation, with small, deep-sunken eyes set close together, a head almost denuded of hair and a mouth at once weak and vicious. I conceived an instant dislike for him, nor was my regard heightened by his greeting.

"What do you know about 'the red devils'?" he demanded truculently, regarding us with something more than suspicion. "If you're in cahoots with 'em—" he placed his hand against the soiled front of his jacket, displaying the outline of a revolver strapped to his waist.

"*Ah bah*, Deacons," de Grandin advised, "be not an utter fool. Were we part of their company, you know how much safety the possession of that toy would afford. Murphy was an excellent shot, so was Craven, but"—he waved an expressive hand—"what good were all their weapons?"

"None, by God!" the other answered with a shudder. "But what's a little pip squeak like you goin' to be able to do to help me?"

"*Morbleu*—a pip squeak—*I?*" The diminutive Frenchman bristled like a bantam game-cock, then interrupted himself to ask, "Why do you barricade yourself like this? Think you to escape in that way?"

"What d'ye want me to do?" the other replied sullenly. "Go out an' let 'em fill me full o'—"

"*Tiens*, the chances are nine to one that they will get you in any case," de Grandin cut in cheerfully. "We have come to offer you the tenth chance; my friend. Now attend me carefully: Have you a cellar beneath this detestable ruin of a house, and has it a floor of earth?"

"Huh? Yes," the other replied, looking at the Frenchman as though he expected him to proclaim himself Emperor of China with his next breath. "What of it?"

"*Parbleu*, much of it, stupid one! Quick, make haste, repair instantly to the cellar and bring me a panful of earth. Be swift, the night is too hot for us to remain long baking in this hell-hole of yours."

"Lookee here—" the other began, but de Grandin shut him off.

"Do as I bid!" he thundered, his little eyes blazing fiercely. "At once, right away, immediately, or we leave you to your fate. *Cordieu*, am I not Jules de Grandin? I will be obeyed!"

With surprising meekness our host descended to the cellar and struggled up the rickety stairs in a few minutes, a dishpan full of clayey soil from the unpaved floor in his hands.

"*Bien!*" De Grandin carried the earth to the kitchen sink and proceeded to moisten it with water from the tap, then began kneading it gently with his long, tapering fingers.

"Do you seat yourself between me and the light, my friend," he commanded, looking up from his work to address Deacons. "I would have a clear-cut view of your profile."

"Sa-a-ay—" the other began protestingly.

"Here, now, you, do what Dr. de Grandin tells ye, or I'll mash ye to a pulp," Costello cut in, evidently feeling he had already taken too little part in the proceedings. "Turn your ugly mug, now, like he tells ye, or I'll be turnin' it for ye, an' turnin' it so far ye'll have to walk backwards to see where ye're goin', too."

Under Costello's chaperonage Deacons sat sullenly while de Grandin deftly punched and pounded the mass of soggy clay into a rough simulacrum of his nondescript profile. "*Parbleu*, Trowbridge, my friend," he remarked with a grin, "when I was a lad studying at the *Beaux Arts* and learning I should never make an artist, little did I think I should one day apply such little skill as I absorbed in modeling such a *cochon* as that"—he indicated Deacons with a disdainful nod—"in earth scooped from his own cellar floor! *Eh bien*, he who tracks a mystery does many strange things before he reaches his trail's end, *n'est-ce-pas?*

"Now, then," he gave the clay a final scrape with his thumb, "let us consider the two of you. Be so good as to stand beside my masterpiece, *Monsieur*," he waved an inviting hand to his model and strode across the room to get a longer perspective on his work.

Deacons complied, still muttering complainingly about "fellers that comes to a man's house an' orders 'im about like he was a bloomin' servant."

The Frenchman regarded his handiwork through narrowed eyelids, turning his head first one side, then the other. Finally he gave a short grunt of satisfaction. "*Ma foi*," he looked from Costello to me, then back to Deacons and the bust. "I think I have bettered the work of *le bon Dieu*. Surely my creation from earth does flatter His. Is it not so, my friends?"

"Sure, it is," Costello commended, "but if it ain't askin' too much, I'd like to know what's th' idea o' all th' monkey business?"

De Grandin wiped the clay from his hands on the none-too-clean towel which hung from a nail in the kitchen door. "We are about to demonstrate the superiority of Aryan culture to the heathen in his blindness," he replied.

"Are we, now?" Costello answered. "Sure, that's fine. When do we start?"

"Now, immediately, right away. Deacons"—he turned curtly to our host— "Do you smoke a pipe? Habitually? *Bien*. You will put your pipe in that image's mouth, if you please. Careful, I do not wish my work spoiled by your clumsiness. Good." He regarded the image a thoughtful moment, then drawled to himself. "And—now—ah, *pardieu*, the very thing!" Seizing a roll of clothesline from the corner of the room he made it fast to a leg of the table on which the statuette rested, then began dragging it slowly toward him.

"Once more I would have your so generous criticism, *Sergent*," he requested of Costello. "Will you stand in the doorway, there, and observe the statue as it passes the light? Does its outline resemble the profile of our handsome friend yonder?"

"It does," the Policeman asserted after a careful inspection through half-closed eyes. "If I seen it at fifty foot or so in a bad light I'd think it were th' man himself, mebbe."

"Good, fine, excellent," de Grandin replied. "Those are the precise conditions under which I propose exhibiting my work to the audience I doubt not waits to examine it. *Parbleu*, we must hope their sense of artistic appreciation is not too highly developed. Trowbridge, *mon vieux*, will you assist me with the table? I would have it in the next room, please."

When we had placed the table some five feet from the living room window which overlooked the cottage's shabby side yard, de Grandin turned to Costello and me, his face tense with excitement. "Let us steal to the back door, my friends," he directed, "and you, *Sergent*, do you have your pistol ready, for it may be that we shall have quick and straight shooting to do before we age many minutes.

"Deacons," he turned at the doorway, speaking with a sharp, rasping note of command in his voice, "do you seat yourself on the floor, out of sight from the window, and draw the table toward you slowly with that rope when you hear my command. Slowly, my friend, mind you; about the pace a man might walk if he were in no hurry. Much depends upon your exact compliance with my orders. Now—"

Tiptoeing to the window, he seized the sliding blind, ran it up to its full height, then unbarred the shutters, flinging them wide, and dodged nimbly back from the window's opening.

"*Sergent*—Trowbridge!" he whispered tensely. "Attention; let us go, *allons!* Be ready," he flung the command to Deacons over his shoulder as he slipped from the room, "begin drawing in the rope when you hear the back door open!"

Silently as a trio of ghosts we stole out into the moonless, humid night, skirted the line of the house wall, and crouched in the shadow of a dilapidated rain-barrel.

"D'ye think anyone will—" Costello began in a hoarse whisper, but:

"S-s-sh!" de Grandin shut him off. "Observe, my friends; look yonder!"

A clump of scrub maple and poplar grew some forty feet from the house, and as we obeyed the Frenchman's imperative nod, a portion of the dense shadow thrown by the trees appeared to detach itself from the surrounding gloom and drift slowly toward the lighted window across which the crudely modeled bust of Deacons was being pulled.

"Careful, my friends; no noise!" de Grandin warned, so low the syllables were barely audible above the murmuring night noises. The drifting shadow was joined by another, the two merging into one almost imperceptible blot of blackness.

Nearer, still nearer the creeping patch of gloom approached, then, with the suddenness of a wind-driven cloud altering shape, the ebon blotch changed from horizontal to vertical, two distinct shapes—squat, crooked-legged human shapes—became visible against the darkness of the night's background, and a wild, eery, bloodcurdling yell rent the heavy, grass-scented air.

Two undersized, screaming shapes ran wildly toward the dimly lit window, but Detective Sergeant Costello was quicker than they. "I've got ye, ye murderin' devils!," he roared, leaping from his ambush and flourishing his revolver. "Stick up your paws, or I'll make, a fly-net out o' th' pair of yez!"

"Down—down, fool!" de Grandin shrieked despairingly, as he strove futilely to drag the big Irishman back into the shadow.

He gave up the attempt and leaped forward with lithe, catlike grace, interposing himself between the detective and the shadowy forms. Something shone dimly in the night's starless air, two flashes of intense orange flame spurted through the darkness, and the twin roar of a French army pistol crashed and reverberated against the house wall.

The racing shadows halted abruptly in their course, seemed to lean together an instant, to merge like a mass of vapor jostled by the wind, then slumped suddenly downward and lay still.

"Blessed St. Patrick!" Costello murmured, turning the prostrate forms over, inspecting the gaping wounds torn by de Grandin's soft-nosed bullets with a sort of pathetic awe. "That's what I call some shootin', Dr. de Grandin, sor. I knew ye was a clever little devil—askin' your pardon—but—"

"Parbleu, my friend, when shooting is necessary, I shoot," de Grandin replied complacently. "But we have other things of more importance to observe, if you please. Turn your flashlight here, if you will."

Sharply silhouetted against the circle of brilliance cast by the electric torch were two slender, thorn-like splinters of wood, their hard, pointed tips buried to a depth of a quarter-inch in the clapboard's crumbling surface.

"It was such as these which killed Craven and Comrade Schippert," the Frenchman explained shortly. "Had I not fired when I did, these"—he pointed gingerly to the thorns—"would have been in you, my friend, and you, I doubt not, would have been in heaven. Morbleu, as it was, I did despair of drawing you back before they had pierced you with their darts, and le bon Dieu knows I shot not a moment too soon!"

"But—howly Mither!—what th' devil is it, annyway, sor?" th' big detective demanded in a fever of mystification.

De Grandin blew methodically down the barrel of his pistol to clear the smoke fumes away before restoring the weapon to his shoulder holster. "They are darts, my friend. Arrows from blowguns—arrows of sure and certain death, for with them every hit is a fatal one. In South and Central America the Indians use them in blowguns for certain classes of hunting, and sometimes in war, and when they blow one of them into a jaguar, fierce and tenacious of life as the great cat is, he dies before he can fall from his tree to the earth. Beside the venom in which these darts are steeped the poison of the cobra or the rattle-snake is harmless as water.

"But come"—he turned again toward the house—"let us go in. Me, I think I have all this sad and sordid story by heart, but there is certain information I would get from the excellent Deacons, before we write the last chapter."

"Now, Monsieur," de Grandin leveled his unwinking, steel-hard stare at the little man cowering in the cottage's shabby living room, "you have spent much time in Central America, I take it. You and your compatriots, Murphy and Craven, were grave-robbers, n'est-ce-pas?"

"Huh? What's that?" Costello interrupted incredulously. "Grave-robbers, did ye say, sor? Stiff-stealers?"

"Non, non," the Frenchman returned with a quick smile, then turned a stern face toward Deacons. "Not stealers of corpses, my friend, but stealers of treasure. Morbleu, do I not know their ilk? But of course. My friends, I was with de Lesseps when he strove to consummate the wedding of the Atlantic with the Pacific at Panama. I was for a time with the French engineers when Diaz drove the railway across the Isthmus of Tehuantepec, and in that time I learned much of gentry such as these. In all Central America there is great store of gold and silver and turquoise buried in the graveyards and ruined cities of the native peoples whom the pig-ignorant Spaniards destroyed in their greed for gold and power. Today brave men of science do risk their lives that these priceless relics of a forgotten people may be brought to light, and fellows such as Deacons and his two dead partners hang about the head-quarters of exploring parties waiting for them to map the course to the ancient ruins, then rush in and steal each scrap of gold on which they can lay their so unclean hands. They are vandals more vile than the Spaniards who went before them, for they steal not only from the dead, but from the treasure-house of science as well."

"We didn't do nothin' worse than th' highbrows did," Deacons defended sullenly. "You never heard of us tryin' to alibi ourselves by claimin' to be workin' for some university, 'stead o' bein' just plain thieves. Them scientists are just as bad as we was, on'y they was *gentlemen*, an' could git away with their second-story work."

"About ten years ago," de Grandin went on as if Deacons had not spoken, "this fellow, together with Craven, Murphy and three others, stumbled on the ruins of an old Mayan city in Yucatan. Only the good God knows how they found it, but find it they did, and with it they found a perfect El Dorado of golden relics.

"The local Indians—poor, ignorant, oppressed wretches—had lost all knowledge of their once so splendid ancestors, and retained nothing of the ancient

Mayan culture but a few perverted legends and a deep, idolatrous veneration for the ruins of their vanished forebears' sacred cities. When they beheld Deacons and his companions pawing over the bodies in the tombs, kicking the skeletons about as though they were but rubbish, and snatching frantically at anything and everything with the glint of gold upon it—*cordieu*, how many priceless pieces of copal and obsidian these so ignorant ignoramuses must have thrown away!—they swooped down on the camp and the robbers had to shoot their way to freedom. Three of them were slain, but three of them escaped and won through to the coast. They made their way back to this country with their booty and—"

"Say"—Deacons looked at the Frenchman as a bird might regard a serpent—"how'd you find all this out?"

"*Parbleu*, my friend," the other smiled tolerantly, "Jules de Grandin is not to be fooled by such as you!

"*Sergent*"—he turned again to Costello—"while you and Callaghan did seek the ambulance to bear away the body of poor Schippert last night, Friend Trowbridge and I investigated the house where Monsieur Craven died. It was not hard for us to see the place was one occupied by a man much used to living alone and being his own servant in all ways—a sailor, perhaps, or a man much accustomed to the out-o-the-way places of the world. That was the first domino with which we had to begin building.

"Now, when we came to examine his *table de cuisine* we did find an ancient Mayan plate engraved with an effigy of a priest in full sacrificial regalia. This plate was the only thing of its kind among the dead man's effects and was carefully wrapped in a cotton rag. Evidently he had retained it as a souvenir. Those who knew not the goldsmithing trade in ancient Central America might easily have mistaken the plate for a piece of Oriental brass; but I, who know many things, realized it was of solid, unalloyed gold intrinsically worth from five to seven thousand dollars, perhaps, but priceless from the anthropologist's standpoint.

"'Now,' I ask me, 'what would a man like this Monsieur Craven, comfortably off, but not rich, be doing with such a relic among his things unless he himself had brought it from Yucatan?'

"'Nothing,' I say to me.

"'Quite right,' I reply. 'Jules de Grandin, you do not make mistakes.'

"Also there was the coroner's report that this Monsieur Deadman had been dead for several days when he was found, and your piece of intelligence that his head have disappeared. Also, again, we know from you and the other officers that he had *not* been dead several days, but only several hours when discovered. What is the answer to that?

"*Hélas*, we found it out only through your poor friend's death! Officer Schippert had pricked himself on what he thought was a thorn—so much like thorns do these accursed darts look that the police and coroner's attachés might have seen that one a thousand times, yet never recognized it for what it was. But our poor friend was wounded by it, and almost at once he died.

"Now, what was such a dart as this doing in the Craven yard? Why did the Poor Schippert have to scratch himself on a thing which should not have been in existence in that latitude and longitude? It is to seek the answer.

"We carried Schippert into the house, and what do we see? Almost at once he had begun to become *livide*—discolored. Yes. I have seen men shot with such arrows while I worked under the tropic sun, I had handled those splinters of death, and had seen the corpses assume the appearance of the long dead almost as I watched them. When I saw the appearance of the poor Schippert, and beheld the dart by which he died, I say to me, 'This is the answer. This is why the physicians at the coroner's office declare that my friend, the good Costello, speaks words of foolishness when he insists Craven was not long dead when found.' Yes.

"Also, you have told me of the missing head. I know from experience and hearsay that those Indians do take the heads of their enemies as your Apaches once took the scalps of theirs, and preserve them as trophies. Everything points one way.

"You see, we have these parts of our puzzle"—he checked the facts off on his fingers—"a man who brought a golden plate from Yucatan is found dead in his front yard. He is undoubtlessly the victim of an Indian blowgun dart, for his appearance and the dart which we have found too late to save the poor Schippert, all say so. Very good. No one knew anything about him, but he was apparently of those fortunate ones who can live in some comfort without working. From this I reason he might once have possessed other Indian gold which he has sold.

"Now, while I think of these things, I notice a piece of burned paper in his fireplace, and on it I read these fragments of words:
ar al red ils av ot Murphy. Lay low an . . .
"What does it mean?"
"I think some more, and decide what was written originally was:
Dear Pal: The red devils have got Murphy. Lay low and. . .
"Who are these 'red devils'? Because an Indian dart have killed both Craven and Schippert, must we not assume they are Indians? I think so. Most likely they were natives of Yucatan who had shipped as sailors on some tramp steamer and come to this land to wreak vengeance on those who despoiled their sacred cities and burying places. I have observed instances of such before. In Paris we have known of it, for there is no sort of crime with which the face of man is blackened which has not been at least once investigated by the *Service de Sûreté*.

"Now, from all this, it was most apparent the writer of this burned note had been warning Craven that one Murphy had been translated to another—though probably not a better—world, and that Craven must lie low, or he would doubtless share the same fate. So much is plain; *but who was Murphy, and who had written the warning?*

"I decided to shoot at the only target in sight. Next day I interviewed Dr. Symington, of the New York Museum of Natural History, asking him if he remembered Mayan relics being bought from a man named Craven or Murphy, or from anyone who mentioned any of those names in his conversation.

"A desperate chance, you say? But certainly. Yet it was by taking desperate chances that we turned back the *sale boche*; it was by taking desperate chances that the peerless Wright brothers learned to fly; it was by taking a desperate chance that I, Jules de Grandin, triumphed!

"Friend Symington had heard such names. Eight years ago one Michael Murphy had sold the Museum a small piece of Mayan jewelry, a little statuette of hammered rose-gold. He had boasted of exploits in Central America when he obtained this statue, told how he, together with Arthur Craven and Charles Deacons, had a fortune in bullion within their grasp, only to lose it when the outraged Indians attacked their camp and killed three of their companions. And that he spoke truth there was small doubt, for so greatly did he fear the Indian vengeance that he refused an offer of five thousand dollars and expenses to guide a party from the Museum to the place where he found the Indian gold.

"Very good. We have got the answer to our questions: 'Whom have the "red devils" gotten?' and 'Who wrote the warning letter to Craven?'

"But where is this Charles Deacons? In the directory of this city there are three of him listed, but only one of him is labeled as retired, and it was to him I looked for further light. I assume the Deacons I seek lives, as Craven did, on the proceeds of his thefts. I further assume he goes in deadly fear of the Indians' flying vengeance by day and by night. I find his address here, and"—he waved his hand in a gesture of finality—"here we come. *Voilà!*"

I started to put a question, but Costello was before me.

"How did ye know th' murderin' heathens would be here tonight, Dr. de Grandin?" he demanded.

"*Eh bien*, by elimination, of course," the Frenchman replied in high good humor. "Three men were sought by the Indians. Two of them had already been disposed of, therefore, unless Deacons had already fallen to their flying death, they still remained in the vicinity, awaiting a chance to execute him. We found him alive, hence we knew they had still one-third of their task to perform. So I did bait our trap with Deacons' dummy, for well I knew they would shoot their poisoned darts at him the moment they saw his shadow pass the lighted open window. *Morbleu*, my friend, how near your own foolish courage came to making you, instead, their victim!"

"Thanks to you, sor, I'm still alive an kickin'," Costello acknowledged. "Shall I be ringin' th' morgue wagon for th' fellies ye shot, sor?"

"I care not," de Grandin responded indifferently, "dispose of them as you will."

"Well, say"—Deacons suddenly seemed to emerge from his trance, and advanced, toward de Grandin, his lean hand extended—"I cert'ny got to thank you for pullin' me out of a mighty tight hole, sir."

De Grandin took no notice of the proffered hand. "*Pardieu, Monsieur*," he responded coldly, "it was from no concern for you that I undertook this night's work. Those Indians had slain a friend of my friend, Sergeant Costello. I came not to save you, but to execute the murderers. You were but the stinking goat with which our tiger-trap was baited."

The White Lady of the Orphanage

"**D**R. TROWBRIDGE? DR. DE Grandin?" our visitor looked questioningly from one of us to the other.

"I'm Trowbridge," I answered, "and this is Dr. de Grandin. What can we do for you?"

The gentle-faced, white-haired little man bowed rather nervously to each of us in turn, acknowledging the introduction. "My name is Gervaise, Howard Gervaise," he replied. "I'm superintendent of the Springville Orphans' Home."

I indicated a chair at the end of the study table and awaited further information.

"I was advised to consult you gentlemen by Mr. Willis Richards, of your city," he continued. "Mr. Richards told me you accomplished some really remarkable results for him at the time his jewelry was stolen, and suggested that you could do more to clear up our present trouble than anyone else. He is president of our board of trustees, you know," he added in explanation.

"U'm?" Jules de Grandin murmured noncommittally as he set fire to a fresh cigarette with the glowing butt of another. "I recall that Monsieur Richards. He figured in the affair of the disembodied hand, Friend Trowbridge, you remember. *Parbleu*, I also recall that he paid the reward for his jewels' return with very bad grace. You come poorly introduced, my friend"—he fixed his uncompromising cat-stare on our caller—"however, say on. We listen."

Mr. Gervaise seemed to shrink in upon himself more than ever. It took small imaginative powers to vision him utterly cowed before the domineering manner of Willis Richards, our local nabob. "The fact is, gentlemen," he began with a soft, deprecating cough, "we are greatly troubled at the orphanage. Something mysterious—most mysterious—is taking place there. Unless we can arrive at some solution we shall be obliged to call in the police, and that would be most unfortunate. Publicity is to be dreaded in this case, yet we are at a total loss to explain the mystery."

"U'm," de Grandin inspected the tip of his cigarette carefully, as though it were something entirely novel, "most mysteries cease to be mysterious, once they are explained, *Monsieur*. You will be good enough to proceed?"

"Ah—" Mr. Gervaise glanced about the study as though to take inspiration from the surroundings, then coughed apologetically again. "Ah—the fact is, gentlemen, that several of our little charges have—ah—mysteriously disappeared. During the past six months we have missed no less than five of the home's inmates, two boys and three girls and only day before yesterday a sixth one disappeared—vanished into air, if you can credit my statement."

"Ah?" Jules de Grandin sat forward a little in his chair, regarding the caller narrowly. "They have disappeared, vanished, you do say? Perhaps they have decamped?"

"No-o," Gervaise denied, "I don't think that's possible, sir. Our home is only a semi-public institution, you know, being supported entirely by voluntary gifts and benefits of wealthy patrons, and we do not open our doors to orphan children as a class. There are certain restrictions imposed. For this reason, we never entertain a greater number than we are able to care for in a fitting manner, and conditions at Springville are rather different from those obtaining in most institutions of a similar character. The children are well fed, well clothed and excellently housed, and—as far as anyone in their unfortunate situation can be—are perfectly contented and happy. During my tenure of office, more than ten years, we have never had a runaway; and that makes these disappearances all the harder to explain. In each case the surrounding facts have been essentially the same, too. The child was accounted for at night before the signal was given to extinguish the lights, and—and next morning he just wasn't there. That's all there is to say. There is nothing further I can tell you."

"You have searched?" de Grandin asked.

"Naturally. The most careful and painstaking investigations have been made in every case. It was not possible to pursue the little ones with hue and cry, of course, but the home has been to considerable expense in hiring private investigators to obtain some information of the missing children, all without result. There is no question of kidnaping, either, for, in every case, the child was known to be safely inside not only the grounds, but in the dormitories, on the night preceding the disappearance. Several reputable witnesses vouch for that in each instance.

"U'm?" de Grandin commented once more. "You say you have been at considerable expense in the matter, *Monsieur*?"

"Yes."

"Good. Very good. You will please be at some more considerable expense. Dr. Trowbridge and I are *gens d'affaires*—businessmen—as well as scientists, *Monsieur*, and while we shall esteem it an honor to serve the fatherless and motherless orphans of your home, we must receive an adequate consideration from Monsieur Richards. We shall undertake the matter of ascertaining the whereabouts of your missing charges at five hundred dollars apiece. Do you agree?"

"But that would be three thousand dollars—" the visitor began.

"Perfectly," de Grandin interrupted. "The police will undertake the case for nothing."

"But we can not have the police, as I have just explained—"

"You can not have us for less," the Frenchman cut in. "This Monsieur Richards, I know him of old. He desires not the publicity of a search by the gendarmes, and, though he loves me not, he has confidence in my ability, otherwise he would not have sent you. Go to him and say Jules de Grandin will act for him for no less fee than that I have mentioned. Meantime, will you smoke?"

He passed a box of my cigars to the caller, held a lighted match for him, and refused to listen to another word concerning the business which had brought Gervaise on the twenty-mile jaunt from Springville.

"TROWBRIDGE, MON VIEUX," HE informed me the following morning at breakfast, "I assure you it pays handsomely to be firm with these captains of industry, such as Monsieur Richards. Before you had arisen, my friend, that man of wealth was haggling with me over the telephone as though we were a pair of dealers in second-hand furniture. Morbleu, it was like an auction. Bid by bid he raised his offer for our services until he met my figure. Today his attorneys prepare a formal document, agreeing to pay us five hundred dollars for the explanation of the disappearance of each of those six little orphans. A good morning's business, n'est-ce-pas?"

"De Grandin," I told him, "you're wasting your talents in this work. You should have gone into Wall Street."

"Eh bien," he twisted the tips of his little blond mustache complacently, "I think I do very well as it is. When I return to la belle France next mouth I shall take with me upward of fifty thousand dollars—more than a million francs—as a result of my work here. That sum is not to be sneezed upon, my friend. And what is of even more value to me, I take with me the gratitude of many of your countrymen whose burdens I have been able to lighten. Mordieu, yes, this trip has been of great use to me, my old one."

"And—" I began.

"And tomorrow we shall visit this home of the orphans where Monsieur Gervaise nurses his totally inexplicable mystery. Parbleu, that mystery shall be explained, or Jules de Grandin is seven thousand francs poorer!"

"All arrangements have been made," he confided as we drove over to Springville the following morning. "It would never do for us to announce ourselves as investigators, my friend, so what surer disguise can we assume than that of being ourselves? You and I, are we not physicians? But certainly. Very well. As physicians we shall appear at the home, and as physicians we shall proceed to inspect all the little ones—separately and alone—for are we not to give them the Schick test for diphtheria immunity! Most assuredly."

"And then—?" I began, but he cut my question in two with a quick gesture and a smile.

"And then, my friend, we shall be guided by circumstances, and if there are no circumstances, *cordieu*, but we shall make them! *Allons*, there is much to do before we handle Monsieur Richards' check."

HOWEVER DARK THE MYSTERY overhanging the Springville Orphans' Home might have been, nothing indicating it was apparent as de Grandin and I drove through the imposing stone gateway to the spacious grounds. Wide, smoothly kept lawns, dotted here and there with beds of brightly blooming flowers, clean, tastefully arranged buildings of red brick in the Georgian style, and a general air of prosperity, happiness and peace greeted us as we brought our car to a halt before the main building of the home. Within, the youngsters were at chapel, and their clear young voices rose pure and sweet as bird-songs in springtime to the accompaniment of a mellow-toned organ:

There's a home for little children
    Above the bright blue sky,
Where Jesus reigns in glory,
    A home of peace and joy;
No earthly home is like it,
    Nor can with it compare . . .

We tiptoed into the spacious assembly room, dimly lit through tall, painted windows, and waited at the rear of the hall till the morning exercises were concluded. Right and left de Grandin shot his keen, stock-taking glance, inspecting the rows of neatly clothed little ones in the pews, attractive young female attendants, and the mild-faced, gray-haired lady of matronly appearance who presided at the organ. "*Mordieu*, Friend Trowbridge," he muttered in my ear, "truly, this is mysterious. Why should any of the *pauvres orphelins* voluntarily quit such a place as this?"

"S-s-sh!" I cut him off. His habit of talking in and out of season, whether at a funeral, a wedding or other religious service, had annoyed me more than once. As usual, he took the rebuke in good part and favored me with an elfish grin, then fell to studying an elongated figure representing a female saint in one of the stained-glass windows, winking at the beatified lady in a highly irreverent manner.

"Good morning, gentlemen," Mr. Gervaise greeted us as the home's inmates filed past us, two by two. "Everything is arranged for your inspection. The children will be brought to you in my office as soon as you are ready for them. Mrs. Martin"—he turned with a smile to the white-haired organist who had joined us—"these are Dr. de Grandin and Dr. Trowbridge. They are going to inspect the children for diphtheria immunity this morning."

To us he added: "Mrs. Martin is our matron. Next to myself she has entire charge of the home. We call her 'Mother Martin,' and all our little ones love her as though she were really their own mother."

"How do you do?" the matron acknowledged the introduction, favoring us with a smile of singular sweetness and extending her hand to each of us in turn.

"*Madame*," de Grandin took her smooth, white hand in his, American fashion, then bowed above it, raising it to his lips, "your little charges are indeed more than fortunate to bask in the sunshine of your ministrations!" It seemed to me he held the lady's hand longer than necessity required, but like all his countrymen my little friend was more than ordinarily susceptible to the influence of a pretty woman, young or elderly.

"And now, *Monsieur*, if you please—" He resigned Mother Martin's plump hand regretfully and turned to the superintendent, his slim, black brows arched expectantly.

"Of course," Gervaise replied. "This way, if you please."

"It would be better if we examined the little ones separately and without any of the attendants being present," de Grandin remarked in a businesslike tone, placing his medicine case on the desk and unfolding a white jacket.

"But surely you can not hope to glean any information from the children!" the superintendent protested. "I thought you were simply going to make a pretense of examining them as a blind. Mrs. Martin and I have questioned every one of them most carefully, and I assure you there is absolutely nothing to be gained by going over that ground again. Besides, some of them have become rather nervous, and we don't want to have their little heads filled with disagreeable notions, you know. I think it would be much better if Mother Martin or I were present while the children are examined. It would give them greater confidence, you know—"

"*Monsieur*"—de Grandin spoke in the level, toneless voice he assumed before one of his wild outbursts of anger—"you will please do exactly as I command. Otherwise—" He paused significantly and began removing the clinical smock.

"Oh, by no means, my dear sir," the superintendent hastened to assure him. "No, no; I wouldn't for the world have you think I was trying to put difficulties in your way. Oh, no; I only thought—"

"*Monsieur*," the little Frenchman repeated, "from this time onward, until we dismiss the case, I shall do the thinking. You will kindly have the children brought to me, one at a time."

To see the spruce little scientist among the children was a revelation to me. Always tart of speech to the verge of bitterness, with a keen, mordant wit which cut like a razor or scratched like a briar, de Grandin seemed the last one to glean information from children naturally timid in the presence of a doctor. But his smile grew brighter and brighter and his humor better and better as child after child entered the office, answered a few seemingly idle questions and passed from the room. At length a little girl, some four or five years old, came in, the hem of her blue pinafore twisted between her plump baby fingers in embarrassment.

"Ah," de Grandin breathed, "here is one from whom we shall obtain something of value, my friend, or I much miss my guess.

"*Holà, ma petite tête de chou!*" he exclaimed, snapping his fingers at the tot. "Come hither and tell Dr. de Grandin all about it!"

His "little cabbage-head" gave him an answering smile, but one of somewhat doubtful quality. "Dr. Grandin not hurt Betsy?" she asked, half confidently, half fearsomely.

"*Parbleu*, not I, my pigeon," he replied as he lifted her to the desk. "*Regardez-vous!*" from the pocket of his jacket he produced a little box of bonbons and thrust them into her chubby hand. "Eat them, my little onion," he commanded. "*Tête du diable*, but they are an excellent medicine for loosening the tongue!"

Nothing loth, the little girl began munching the sweetmeats, regarding her new friend with wide, wondering eyes. "They said you would hurt me—cut my tongue out with a knife if I talked to you," she informed him, then paused to pop another chocolate button into her mouth.

"*Mort d'un chat*, did they, indeed?" he demanded. "And who was the vile, detestable one who so slandered Jules de Grandin? I shall—s-s-sh!" he interrupted himself, turning and crossing the office in three long, catlike leaps. At the entrance he paused a moment, then grasped the handle and jerked the door suddenly open.

On the sill, looking decidedly surprised, stood Mr. Gervaise.

"Ah, *Monsieur*," de Grandin's voice held an ugly, rasping note as he glared directly into the superintendent's eyes, "you are perhaps seeking for something? Yes?"

"Er—yes," Gervaise coughed softly, dropping his gaze before the Frenchman's blazing stare. "Er—that is—you see, I left my pencil here this morning, and I didn't think you'd mind if I came to get it. I was just going to rap when—"

"When I saved you the labor, *n'est-ce-pas?*" the other interrupted. "Very good, my friend. Here"—hastening to the desk he grabbed a handful of miscellaneous pencils, pens and other writing implements, including a stick of marking chalk—"take these, and get gone, in the name of the good God." He thrust the utensils into the astonished superintendent's hands, then turned to me, the gleam in his little blue eyes and the heightened color in his usually pale cheeks showing his barely suppressed rage. "Trowbridge, *mon vieux*," he almost hissed, "I fear I shall have to impress you into service as a guard. Stand at the outer door, my friend, and should anyone come seeking pens, pencils, paintbrushes or printing presses, have the goodness to boot him away. Me, I do not relish having people looking for pencils through the keyhole of the door while I interrogate the children!"

Thereafter I remained on guard outside the office while child after child filed into the room, talked briefly with de Grandin, and left by the farther door.

"WELL, DID YOU FIND out anything worth while?" I asked when the examination was finally ended.

"U'm," he responded, stroking his mustache thoughtfully, "yes and no. With children of a tender age, as you know, the line of demarcation between recollection and imagination is none too clearly drawn. The older ones could tell me nothing; the younger ones relate a tale of a 'white lady' who visited the dormitory on each night a little one disappeared, but what does that mean? Some attendant making a nightly round? Perhaps a window curtain blown by the evening breeze? Maybe it had no surer foundation than some childish whim, seized and enlarged upon by the other little ones. There is little we can go on at this time, I fear.

"Meanwhile," his manner brightened, "I think I hear the sound of the dinner gong. *Parbleu*, I am as hungry as a carp and empty as a kettledrum. Let us hasten to the refectory."

Dinner was a silent meal. Superintendent Gervaise seemed ill at ease under de Grandin's sarcastic stare, and the other attendants who shared the table with us took their cue from their chief and conversation languished before the second course was served. Nevertheless, de Grandin seemed to enjoy everything set before him to the uttermost, and made strenuous efforts to entertain Mrs. Martin, who sat immediately to his right.

"But *Madame*," he insisted when the lady refused a serving of the excellent beef which constituted the roast course, "surely you will not reject this so excellent roast! Remember, it is the best food possible for humanity, for not only does it contain the nourishment we need, but great quantities of iron are to be found in it, as well. Come, permit that I help you to that which is at once food and tonic!"

"No, thank you," the matron replied, looking at the juicy roast with a glance almost of repugnance. "I am a vegetarian."

"How terrible!" de Grandin commiserated, as though she had confessed some overwhelming calamity.

"Yes, Mother Martin's been subsisting entirely on vegetables for the last six months," one of the nurses, a plump, red-cheeked girl, volunteered. "She used to eat as much meat as any of us, but all of a sudden she turned against, it, and—oh, Mrs. Martin!"

The matron had risen from her chair, leaning half-way across the table, and the expression on her countenance was enough to justify the girl's exclamation. Her face had gone pale—absolutely livid—her lips were drawn back against her teeth like those of a snarling animal, and her eyes seemed to protrude from their sockets as they blazed into the startled girl's. It seemed to me that not only rage, but something like loathing and fear were expressed in her blazing orbs as she spoke in a low, passionate voice: "Miss Bosworth, what I used to do and what I do now are entirely my own business. Please do not meddle with my affairs!"

For a moment silence reigned at the table, but the Frenchman saved the situation by remarking, "*Tiens, Madame*, the fervor of the convert is ever greater than that of those to the manner born. The Buddhist, who eats no meat from his birth, is not half so strong in defense of his diet as the lately converted European vegetarian!"

To me, as we left the dining hall, he confided, "A charming meal, most interesting and instructive. Now, my friend, I would that you drive me home at once, immediately. I wish to borrow a dog from Sergeant Costello."

"What!" I responded incredulously. "You want to borrow a—"

"Perfectly. A dog. A police dog, if you please. I think we shall have use for the animal this night."

"Oh, all right," I agreed. The workings of his agile mind were beyond me, and I knew it would be useless to question him.

SHORTLY AFTER SUNDOWN WE returned to the Springville home, a large and by no means amiable police dog, lent us by the local constabulary, sharing the car with us.

"You will engage Monsieur Gervaise in conversation, if you please," my companion commanded as we stopped before the younger children's dormitory. "While you do so, I shall assist this so excellent brute into the hall where the little ones sleep and tether him in such manner that he can not reach any of his little room-mates, yet can easily dispute passage with anyone attempting to enter the apartment. Tomorrow morning we shall be here early enough to remove him before any of the attendants who may enter the dormitory on legitimate business can be bitten. As for others—" He shrugged his shoulders and prepared to lead the lumbering brute into the sleeping quarters.

His program worked perfectly. Mr. Gervaise was nothing loth to talk with me about the case, and I gathered that he had taken de Grandin's evident dislike much to heart. Again and again he assured me, almost with tears in his eyes, that he had not the least intention of eavesdropping when he was discovered at the office door, but that he had really come in search of a pencil. It seemed he used a special indelible lead in making out his reports, and had discovered that the only one he possessed was in the office after we had taken possession. His protestations were so earnest that I left him convinced de Grandin had done him an injustice.

Next morning I was at a loss what to think. Arriving at the orphanage well before daylight, de Grandin and I let ourselves into the little children's dormitory, mounted the stairs to the second floor where the youngsters slept, and released the vicious dog which the Frenchman had tethered by a stout nail driven into the floor and a ten-foot length of stout steel chain. Inquiry among the building's attendants elicited the information that no one had visited the sleeping apartment after we left, as there had been no occasion for anyone connected with the home to do so. Yet on the floor beside the dog there lay a ragged square of white linen, such as might have been ripped from a night-robe or a suit of pajamas, reduced almost to a pulp by the savage brute's worrying, and—when Superintendent Gervaise entered the office to greet us, he was wearing his right arm in a sling.

"You are injured, *Monsieur?*" de Grandin asked with mock solicitude, noting the superintendent's bandaged hand with dancing eyes.

"Yes," the other replied, coughing apologetically, "yes, sir. I—I cut myself rather badly last night on a pane of broken glass in my quarters. The window must have been broken by a shutter being blown against it, and—"

"Quite so," the Frenchman agreed amiably. "They bite terrifically, these broken window-panes, is it not so?"

"Bite?" Gervaise echoed, regarding the other with a surprised, somewhat frightened expression. "I hardly understand you—oh, yes, I see," he smiled rather feebly. "You mean cut."

"*Monsieur,*" de Grandin assured him solemnly as he rose to leave, "I did mean exactly what I said; no more, and certainly no less."

"Now what?" I queried as we left the office and the gaping superintendent behind us.

"*Non, non,*" he responded irritably. "I know not what to think, my friend. One thing, he points this way, another, he points elsewhere. Me, I am like a mariner in the midst of a fog. Go you to the car, Friend Trowbridge, and chaperone our so estimable ally. I shall pay a visit to the laundry, meantime."

None too pleased with my assignment, I re-entered my car and made myself as agreeable as possible to the dog, devoutly hoping that the hearty breakfast de Grandin had provided him had taken the edge off his appetite. I had no wish to have him stay his hunger on one of my limbs. The animal proved docile enough, however, and besides opening his mouth once or twice in prodigious yawns which gave me an unpleasantly close view of his excellent dentition, did nothing to cause me alarm.

When de Grandin returned he was fuming with impatience and anger. "*Sacré nom d'un grillon!*" he swore. "It is beyond me. Undoubtlessly this Monsieur Gervaise is a liar, it was surely no glass which caused the wound in his arm last night; yet there is no suit of torn pajamas belonging to him in the laundry."

"Perhaps he didn't send them to be washed," I ventured with a grin. "If I'd been somewhere I was not supposed to be last night and found someone had posted a man-eating dog in my path, I'd not be in a hurry to send my torn clothing to the laundry where it might betray me."

"*Tiens*, you reason excellently, my friend," he complimented, "but can you explain how it is that there is no torn night-clothing of Monsieur Gervaise at the washrooms today, yet two ladies' night-robes—one of Mère Martin's, one of Mademoiselle Bosworth's—display exactly such rents as might have been made by having this bit of cloth torn from them?" He exhibited the relic we had found beside the dog that morning and stared gloomily at it.

"H'm, it looks as if you hadn't any facts which will stand the acid test just yet," I replied flippantly; but the seriousness with which he received my commonplace rejoinder startled me.

"*Morbleu*, the acid test, do you say?" he exclaimed. "*Dieu de Dieu de Dieu de Dieu*, it may easily be so! Why did I not think of it before? Perhaps. Possibly. Who knows! It may be so!"

"What in the world—" I began, but he cut me short with a frantic gesture.

"*Non, non*, my friend, not now," he implored. "Me, I must think. I must make this empty head of mine do the work for which it is so poorly adapted. Let us see, let us consider, let us ratiocinate!

"*Parbleu*, I have it!" He drew his hands downward from his forehead with a quick, impatient motion and turned to me. "Drive me to the nearest pharmacy, my friend. If we do not find what we wish there, we must search elsewhere, and elsewhere, until we discover it. *Mordieu*, Trowbridge, my friend, I thank you for mentioning that acid test! Many a wholesome truth is contained in words of idle jest, I do assure you."

FIVE MILES OUT OF Springville a gang of workmen were resurfacing the highway, and we were forced to detour over a back road. Half an hour's slow driving along this brought us to a tiny Italian settlement where a number of laborers originally engaged on the Lackawanna's right of way had bought up the swampy, low-lying lands along the creek and converted them into model track gardens. At the head of the single street composing the hamlet was a neatly whitewashed plank building bearing the sign *Farmacia Italiana*, together with a crudely painted representation of the Italian royal coat of arms.

"Here, my friend," de Grandin commanded, plucking me by the sleeve. "Let us stop here a moment and inquire of the estimable gentleman who conducts this establishment that which we would know."

"But what—?" I began, then stopped, noting the futility of my question. Jules de Grandin had already leaped from the car and entered the little drug store.

Without preamble he addressed a flood of fluent Italian to the druggist, receiving monosyllabic replies which gradually expanded both in verbosity and volume, accompanied by much waving of hands and lifting of shoulders and eyebrows. What they said I had no means of knowing, since I understood no word of Italian, but I heard the word *acido* repeated several times by each of them during the three minutes' heated conversation.

When de Grandin finally turned to leave the store, with a grateful bow to the proprietor, he wore an expression as near complete mystification and surprise as I had ever seen him display. His little eyes were rounded with mingled thought and amazement, and his narrow red lips were pursed beneath the line of his slim blond moustache as though he were about to emit a low, soundless whistle.

"Well?" I demanded—as we regained the car. "Did you find out what you were after?"

"Eh?" he answered absently. "Did I find—Trowbridge, my friend, I know not what I found out, but this I know: Those who lighted the witch-fires in olden days were not such fools as we believe them. *Parbleu*, at this moment they are grinning at us from their graves, or I am much mistaken. Tonight, my friend, be ready to accompany me back to that orphans' home where the devil nods approval to those who perform his business so skillfully."

THAT EVENING HE WAS like one in a muse, eating sparingly and seemingly without realizing what food he took, answering my questions absent-mindedly or not at all, even forgetting to light his customary cigarette between dinner and dessert. "*Nom d'un champignon*," he muttered, staring abstractedly into his coffee cup, "it must be that it is so; but who would believe it?"

I sighed in vexation. His habit of musing aloud but refusing to tell the trend of his thoughts while he arranged the factors of a case upon his mental chessboard was one which always annoyed me, but nothing I had been able to do had swerved him from his custom of withholding all information until he reached the climax of the mystery. "*Non, non*," he replied when I pressed him to take me into his confidence, "the less I speak, the less danger I run of showing myself to be one great fool, my friend. Let me reason this business in my own way, I beseech you." And there the matter rested.

Toward midnight he rose impatiently and motioned toward the door. "Let us go," he suggested. "It will be an hour or more before we reach our destination, and that should be the proper time for us to see what I fear we shall behold, Friend Trowbridge."

We drove across country to Springville through the early autumn night in silence, turned in at the orphanage gates and parked before the administration building, where Superintendent Gervaise maintained his living quarters.

"*Monsieur*," de Grandin called softly as he rapped gently on the superintendent's door, "it is I, Jules de Grandin. For all the wrong I have done you I humbly apologize, and now I would that you give me assistance."

Blinking with mingled sleep and surprise, the little, gray-haired official let us into his rooms and smiled rather fatuously at us. "What is it you'd like me to do for you, Dr. de Grandin?" he asked.

"I would that you guide us to the sleeping apartments of *Mère* Martin. Are they in this building?"

"No," Gervaise replied wonderingly. "Mother Martin has a cottage of her own over at the south end of the grounds. She likes the privacy of a separate house, and we—"

"*Précisément*," the Frenchman agreed, nodding vigorously. "I well understand her love of privacy, I fear. Come, let us go. You will show us the way?"

Mother Martin's cottage stood by the southern wall of the orphanage compound. It was a neat little building of the semi-bungalow type, constructed of red brick, and furnished with a low, wide porch of white-painted wood. Only the chirping of a cricket in the long grass and the long-drawn, melancholy call of a crow in the near-by poplars broke the silence of the starlit night as we walked noiselessly up the brick path leading to the cottage door. Gervaise was about to raise the polished brass knocker which adorned the white panels when de Grandin grasped his arm, enjoining silence.

Quietly as a shadow the little Frenchman crept from one of the wide, shutterless front windows to the other, looking intently into the darkened interior of the house, then, with upraised finger warning us to caution, he tiptoed from the porch and began making a circuit of the house, pausing to peer through each window as he passed it.

At the rear of the cottage was a one-story addition which evidently housed the kitchen, and here the blinds were tightly drawn, though beneath their lower edges there crept a faint, narrow band of lamplight.

"Ah—*bien!*" the Frenchman breathed, flattening his aquiline nose against the window-pane as though he would look through the shrouding curtain by virtue of the very intensity of his gaze.

A moment we stood there in the darkness, de Grandin's little waxed moustache twitching at the ends like the whiskers of an alert tomcat, Gervaise and I in total bewilderment, when the Frenchman's next move filled us with mingled astonishment and alarm. Reaching into an inner pocket, he produced a small, diamond-set glass-cutter, moistened it with the tip of his tongue and applied it to the window, drawing it slowly downward, then horizontally, then upward again to meet the commencement of the first down-stroke, thus describing an equilateral triangle on the pane. Before the cutter's circuit was entirely completed, he drew what appeared to be a square of thick paper from another pocket, hastily tore it apart and placed it face downward against the glass. It was only when the operation was complete that I realized how it was accomplished. The "plaster" he applied to the window was nothing more nor less than a square of fly-paper, and its sticky surface prevented any telltale tinkle from sounding as he finished cutting the triangle from the window-pane and carefully lifted it out by means of the gummed paper.

Once he had completed his opening he drew forth a small, sharp-bladed penknife, and working very deliberately, lest the slightest sound betray him, proceeded to slit a peep-hole through the opaque window-blind.

For a moment he stood there, gazing through his spy-hole, the expression on his narrow face changing from one of concentrated interest to almost incredulous horror, finally to fierce, implacable rage.

"À moi, Trowbridge, à moi, Gervaise!" he shouted in a voice which was almost a shriek as he thrust his shoulder unceremoniously against the pane, bursting it into a dozen pieces, and leaped into the lighted room beyond.

I scrambled after him as best I could, and the astounded superintendent followed me, mouthing mild protests against our burglarious entry of Mrs. Martin's house.

One glance at the scene before me took all thought of our trespass from my mind.

Wheeled about to face us, her back to a fiercely glowing coal-burning kitchen range, stood the once placid Mother Martin, enveloped from throat to knees in a commodious apron. But all semblance of her placidity was gone as she regarded the trembling little Frenchman who extended an accusing finger at her. Across her florid, smooth-skinned face had come such a look of fiendish rage as no flight of my imagination could have painted. Her lips, seemingly shrunk to half their natural thickness, were drawn back in animal fury against her teeth, and her blue eyes seemed forced forward from her face with the pressure of hatred within her. At the corners of her twisting mouth were little flecks of white foam, and her jaw thrust forward like that of an infuriated ape. Never in my life, on any face, either bestial or human, had I seen such an expression. It was a revolting parody of humanity on which I looked, a thing so horrible, so incomparably cruel and devilish, I would have looked away if I could, yet felt my eyes compelled to turn again to the evil visage as a fascinated bird's gaze may be held by the glitter in the serpent's film-covered eye.

But horrid as the sight of the woman's transfigured features was, a greater horror showed behind her, for, protruding half its length from the fire-grate of the blazing range was something no medical man could mistake after even a split-second's inspection. It was the unfleshed radius and ulna bones of a child's forearm, the wrist process still intact where the flesh and periosteum had not been entirely removed in dissection. On the tile-topped kitchen table beside the stove stood a wide-mouthed glass bowl filled with some liquid about the shade of new vinegar, and in this there lay a score of small, glittering white objects—a child's teeth. Neatly dressed, wound with cord like a roast, and, like a roast, placed in a wide, shallow pan, ready for cooking, was a piece of pale, veal-like meat.

The horror of it fairly nauseated me. The thing in woman's form before us was a cannibal, and the meat she had been preparing to bake was—my mind refused to form the words, even in the silence of my inner consciousness.

"You—*you*," the woman cried in a queer, throaty voice, so low it was scarcely audible, yet so intense in its vibrations that I was reminded of the rumbling of an infuriated cat's cry. "How—did—you—find—?"

"*Eh bien, Madame*," de Grandin returned, struggling to speak with his customary cynical flippancy, but failing in the attempt, "how I did find out is of small moment. What I found, I think you will agree, is of the great import."

For an instant I thought the she-fiend would launch herself at him, but her intention lay elsewhere. Before any of us was aware of her move she had seized the glass vessel from the table, lifted it to her lips and all but emptied its contents down her throat in two frantic swallows. Next instant, frothing, writhing, contorting herself horribly, she lay on the tiled floor at our feet, her lips thickening and swelling with brownish blisters as the poison she had drunk regurgitated from her esophagus and welled up between her tightly set teeth.

"Good heavens!" I cried, bending forward instinctively to aid her, but the Frenchman drew me back. "Let be, Friend Trowbridge," he remarked. "It is useless. She has taken enough hydrochloric acid to kill three men, and those movements of hers are only mechanical. Already she is unconscious, and in another five minutes she will have opportunity to explain her so strange life to One far wiser than we.

"Meantime," he assumed the cold, matter-of-fact manner of a morgue attendant performing his duties, "let us gather up these relics of the poor one"—he indicated the partially cremated arm-bones and the meat in the shining aluminum pan—"and preserve them for decent interment. I—"

A choking, gasping sound behind us turned our attention to the orphanage superintendent. Following more slowly through the window in de Grandin's wake he had not at first grasped the significance of the horrors we had seen. The spectacle of the woman's suicide had unnerved him, but when de Grandin pointed to the relics in the stove and on the table, the full meaning of our discovery had fallen on him. With an inarticulate cry he had dropped to the floor in a dead faint.

"*Pardieu*," the Frenchman exclaimed, crossing to the water-tap and filling a tumbler, "I think we had best bestow our services on the living before we undertake the care of the dead, Friend Trowbridge."

As he re-crossed the kitchen to minister to the unconscious superintendent there came an odd, muffled noise from the room beyond. "*Qui vive?*" he challenged sharply, placing the glass of water on the dresser and darting through the door, his right hand dropping into his jacket pocket where the ready pistol lay. I followed at his heels, and, as he stood hesitating at the threshold, felt along the wall, found the electric switch and pressed it, flooding the room with light. On the couch beneath the window, bound hand and foot with strips torn from a silk scarf and gagged with another length of silk wound about her face, lay little Betsy, the child who had informed us she feared being hurt when we made our pretended inspection of the home's inmates the previous day.

"*Morbleu*," de Grandin muttered as he liberated the little one from her bonds, "another?"

"Mother Martin came for Betsy and tied her up," the child informed us as she raised herself to a sitting posture. "She told Betsy she would send her to heaven with her papa and mamma, but Betsy must be good and not make a fuss when her hands and feet were tied."

She smiled vaguely at de Grandin. "Why doesn't Mother Martin come for Betsy?" she demanded. "She said she would come and send me to heaven in a few minutes, but I waited and waited, and she didn't come, and the cloth over my face kept tickling my nose, and—"

"Mother Martin has gone away on business, *ma petite*," the Frenchman interrupted. "She said she could not send you to your papa and mama, but if you are a very good little girl you may go to them some day. Meantime"—he fished in his jacket pocket, finally produced a packet of chocolates—"here is the best substitute I can find for heaven at this time, *chérie*."

"WELL, OLD CHAP, I'LL certainly have to admit you went right to the heart of the matter," I congratulated as we drove homeward through the paling dawn, "but I can't for the life of me figure out how you did it."

His answering smile was a trifle wan. The horrors we had witnessed at the matron's cottage had been almost too great a strain for even his iron nerve. "Partly it was luck," he confessed wearily, "and partly it was thought.

"When first we arrived at the home for orphans I had nothing to guide me, but I was convinced that the little ones had not wandered off voluntarily. The environment seemed too good to make any such hypothesis possible.

Everywhere I looked I saw evidences of loving care, and faces which could be trusted. But somewhere, I felt, as an old wound feels the coming changes of the weather, there was something evil, some evil force working against the welfare of those poor ones. Where could it be, and by whom was it exerted? 'This is for us to find out,' I tell me as I look over the attendants who were visible in the chapel.

"Gervaise, he is an old woman in trousers. Never would he hurt a living thing, no, not even a fly, unless it bit him first.

"*Mère* Martin, she was of a saintly appearance, but when I was presented to her I learn something which sets my brain to thinking. On the softness of her white hands are stains and callouses. Why? I hold her hand longer than convention required, and all the time I ask me, 'What have she done to put these hardnesses on her hands?'

"To this I had no answer, so I bethought me perhaps my nose could tell what my sense of touch could not. When I raised her hand to my lips I made a most careful examination of it, and also I did smell. Trowbridge, my friend, I made sure those disfigurements were due to HCl—what you call hydrochloric acid in English.

"'*Morbleu*, but this is extraordinary,' I tell me. 'Why should one who has no need to handle acid have those burns on her skin?'

"'That are for you to answer in good time,' I reply to me. And then I temporarily forget the lady and her hands, because I am sure that Monsieur Gervaise desires to know what we say to the young children. *Eh bien*, I did do him an injustice there, but the wisest of us makes mistakes, my friend, and he gave me much reason for suspicion.

"When the little Betsy was answering my questions she tells me that she has seen a 'white lady,' tall and with flowing robes, like an angel, come into the dormitory where she and her companions slept on many occasions, and I have ascertained from previous questions that no one enters those sleeping quarters after the lights are out unless there is specific need for a visit. What was I to think? Had the little one dreamed it, or has she seen, this so mysterious 'white lady' on her midnight visits? It is hard to say where recollection stops and romance begins in children's tales, my friend, as you well know, but the little Betsy was most sure the 'white lady' had come only on those nights when her little companions vanished.

"Here we had something from which to reason, though the morsel of fact was small. However, when I talk further with the child, she informed me it was *Mère* Martin who had warned her against us, saying we would surely cut her tongue with a knife if she talked to us. This, again, was worthy of thought. But Monsieur Gervaise had been smelling at the door while we were interrogating the children, and he had also disapproved of our seeing them alone. My suspicion of him would not die easily, my friend; I was stubborn, and refused to let my mind take me where it would.

"So, as you know, when we had posted the four-footed sentry inside the children's door, I made sure we would catch a fish in our trap, and next morning I was convinced we had, for did not Gervaise wear his arm in a sling! Truly, he did.

"But at the laundry they showed me no torn pajamas of his, while I found the gowns of both Mademoiselle Bosworth and Madame Martin torn as if the dog had bitten them. More mystery. Which way should I turn, if at all?

"I find that Gervaise's window really had been broken, but that meant nothing; he might have done it himself in order to construct an alibi. Of the reason for Mademoiselle Bosworth's torn robe I could glean no trace; but behind my brain, at the very back of my head, something was whispering at me; something I could not hear, but which I knew was of importance.

"Then, as we drove away from the home, you mentioned the acid test. My friend, those words of yours let loose the memory which cried aloud to me, but which I could not clearly understand. Of a suddenness I did recall the scene at luncheon, how Mademoiselle Bosworth declared Mère Martin ate no meat for six months, and how angry Madame Martin was at the mention of it. *Parbleu*, for six months the little ones had been disappearing—for six months Madame Martin had eaten no meat, yet she were plump and well-nourished. She had the look of a meat-eater!"

"Still," I protested, "I don't see how that put you on the track."

"No?" he replied. "Remember, my friend, how we stopped to interview the druggist. Why think you we did that?"

"Hanged if I know," I confessed.

"Of course not," he agreed with a nod. "But I know. 'Suppose,' I say to me, 'someone have eaten the flesh of these poor disappeared children? What would that one do with the bones?'

"'He would undoubtlessly bury or burn them,' I reply.

"'Very good, but more likely he would burn them, since buried bones, may be dug up, and burned bones are only ashes; but what of the teeth? They would resist fire such as can be had in the ordinary stove, yet surely they might betray the murderer.'

"'But of course,' I admit, 'but why should not the murderer reduce those teeth with acid, hydrochloric acid, for instance?'

"'Ah-ha,' I tell me, 'that are the answer. Already you have one whose hands are acid-stained without adequate explanation, also one who eats no meat at table. Find out, now, who have bought acid from some neighboring drug store, and perhaps you will have the answer to your question.'

"The Italian gentleman who keeps the pharmacy tells me that a lady of very kindly mien comes to him frequently and buys hydrochloric acid, which she calls muriatic acid, showing she are not a chemist, but knows only the commercial term for the stuff. She is a tall, large lady with white hair and kind blue eyes.

"'It are *Mère* Martin!' I tell me. 'She are the "white lady" of the orphanage!'

"Then I consult my memory some more, and decide we shall investigate this night.

"Listen, my friend: In the Paris *Sûreté* we have the history of many remarkable cases, not only from France, but other lands as well. In the year 1849 a miscreant named Swiatek was hauled before the Austrian courts on a charge of cannibalism, and in the same year there was another somewhat similar case where a young English lady—a girl of much refinement and careful education and nurture—was the defendant. Neither of these was naturally fierce or bloodthirsty, yet their crimes were undoubted. In the case of the beggar we have a transcription of his confession. He did say in part: When first driven by dire hunger to eat of human flesh he became, as the first horrid morsel passed his lips, as it were a ravening wolf. He did rend and tear the flesh and growl in his throat like a brute beast the while. From that time forth he could stomach no other meat, nor could he abide the sight or smell of it. Beef, pork or mutton filled him with revulsion. And had not Madame Martin exhibited much the same symptoms at table? Truly.

"Things of a strange nature sometimes occur, my friend. The mind of man is something of which we know but little, no matter how learnedly we prate. Why does one man love to watch a snake creep, while another goes into ecstasies of terror at sight of a reptile? Why do some people hate the sight of a cat, while others fear a tiny, harmless mouse as though he were the devil's brother-in-law? None can say, yet these things are. So I think it is with crime.

"This Madame Martin was not naturally cruel. Though she killed and ate her charges, you will recall how she bound the little Betsy with silk, and did it in such a way as not to injure her, or even to make her uncomfortable. That meant mercy? By no means, my friend. Myself, I have seen peasant women in my own land weep upon and fondle the rabbit they were about to kill for *déjeuner*. They did love and pity the poor little beast which was to die, but *que voulez vous?* One must eat.

"Some thought like this, I doubt not, was in Madame Martin's mind as she committed murder. Somewhere in her nature was a thing we can not understand; a thing which made her crave the flesh of her kind for food, and she answered the call of that craving even as the taker of drugs is helpless against his vice.

"*Tiens*, I am convinced that if we searched her house we should have the explanation of the children's disappearance, and you yourself witnessed what we saw. It was well she took the poison when she did. Death, or incarceration in a madhouse, would have been her portion had she lived, and"—he shrugged his shoulders—"the world is better off without her."

"U'm, I see how you worked it, out," I replied, "but will Mr. Richards be satisfied? We've accounted for one of the children, because we found part of her skeleton in the fire, but can we swear the rest disappeared in the same manner? Richards will want a statistical table of facts before he parts with three thousand dollars, I imagine."

"*Parbleu*, will he, indeed?" de Grandin answered, something like his usual elfish grin spreading across his face. "What think you would be the result were we to notify the authorities of the true facts, leading up to Madame Martin's suicide? Would not the newspapers make much of it. *Cordieu*, I shall say they would, and the home for orphans over which Monsieur Richards presides so pompously would receive what you call 'the black eye.' *Morbleu*, my friend, the very black eye, indeed! No, no; me, I think Monsieur Richards will gladly pay us the reward, nor haggle over terms.

"Meanwhile, we are at home once more. Come, let us drink the cognac."

"Drink cognac?" I answered. "Why, in heaven's name?"

"*Parbleu*, we shall imbibe a toast to the magnificent three thousand dollars Monsieur Richards pays us tomorrow morning!"

The Poltergeist

"AND SO, DR. DE Grandin," our visitor concluded, "this is really a case for your remarkable powers."

Jules de Grandin selected a fresh cigarette from his engine-turned silver case, tapped its end thoughtfully against his well-manicured thumb-nail and regarded the caller with one of his disconcertingly unwinking stares. "Am I to understand that all other attempts to effect a cure have failed, *Monsieur?*" he asked at length.

"Utterly. We've tried everything in reason, and out of it," Captain Loudon replied. "We've had some of the best neurologists in consultation, we've employed faith-healers, spiritualistic mediums, even had her given 'absent treatment,' all to no avail. All the physicians, all the cultists and quacks have failed us; now—"

"Now, I do not think I care to be numbered among those quacks, *Monsieur*," the Frenchman returned coldly, expelling a double column of smoke from his nostrils. "Had you called me into consultation with an accredited physician—"

"But that's just it," the captain interrupted. "Every physician we've had has been confident he could work a cure, but they've all failed. Julia is a lovely girl—I don't say it because she's my daughter, I state it as a fact—and was to have been married this fall, and now this—this disorder has taken complete possession of her and it's wrecking her life. Robert—Lieutenant Proudfit, her fiancé—and I are almost beside ourselves, and as for my daughter, I fear her mind will give way and she'll destroy herself unless *somebody* can do *something!*"

"Ah?" the little Frenchman arched the narrow black brows which were such a vivid contrast to his blond hair and moustache. "Why did not you say so before, *Monsieur le Capitaine?* It is not merely the curing of one nervous young lady that you would have me undertake, but the fruition of a romance I should bring about? *Bien*, good, very well; I accept. If you will also retain my good friend Dr. Trowbridge, so that there shall be a locally licensed and respected physician in the case, my powers which you have been kind enough to call remarkable are entirely at your disposal."

"Splendid!" Captain Loudon agreed, rising. "Then it's all arranged. I can expect you to—"

"One moment, if you please," de Grandin interrupted, raising his slender, womanishly small hand for silence. "Suppose we make a *précis* of the case before we go further." He drew a pad of note-paper and a pencil toward him as he continued:

"Your daughter, Mademoiselle Julie, how old is she *!*"

"Twenty-nine."

"A most charming age," the little Frenchman commented, scribbling a note. "And she is your only child?"

"Yes."

"Now, these manifestations of the *outré*, these so unusual happenings, they began to take place about six months ago?"

"Just about; I can't place the time exactly."

"No matter. They have assumed various mystifying forms? She has refused food, she has had visions, she shouts, she sings uncontrollably, she speaks in a voice which is strange to her—at times she goes into a deathlike trance and from her throat issue strange voices, voices of men, or other women, even of little children?"

"Yes."

"And other apparently inexplicable things occur. Chairs, books, tables, even such heavy pieces of furniture as a piano, move from their accustomed places when she is near, and bits of jewelry and other small objects are hurled through the air?"

"Yes, and worse than that, I've seen pins and needles fly from her work-basket and bury themselves in her cheeks and arms," the captain interrupted, "and lately she's been persecuted by scars—scars from some invisible source. Great weals, like the claw-marks from some beast, have appeared on her arms and face, right while I looked on, and I've been wakened at night by her screams, and when I rush into her room I find the marks of long, thin fingers on her throat. It's maddening, sir; terrifying. I'd say it was a case of demoniacal possession, if I didn't disbelieve all that sort of supernaturalism."

"U'm," de Grandin looked up from the pad on which he had been industriously scribbling. "There is nothing in the world, or out of it, which is supernatural, my friend; the wisest man today can not say where the powers and possibilities of nature begin or end. We say, 'Thus and so is beyond the bounds of our experience,' but does that therefore put it beyond the bounds of nature? I think not. Myself, I have seen such things as no man can hear me relate without calling me a liar, and my good, unimaginative friend Trowbridge has witnessed such wonders as no writer of fiction would dare set down on paper, yet I do declare we have never yet seen that which I would call supernatural.

"But come, let us go, let us hasten to your house, *Monsieur*; I would interview Mademoiselle Julie and see for myself some of these so remarkable afflictions of hers.

"Remember," he turned his fixed, unwinking stare on our patron as we paused for our outdoor things in the hall, "remember, if you please, *Monsieur*, I am not like those quacks, or even those other physicians who have failed you. I do not say I can work a cure. I can but promise to try. Good, we shall see what we shall see. Let us go."

R OBERT BEAUREGARD LOUDON WAS a retired navy captain, a widower with more than sufficient means to gratify his rather epicurean tastes, and possessed one of the finest houses in the fashionable new west side suburb. The furnishings spoke of something more than wealth as we surveyed them; they proclaimed that vague, but nevertheless tangible thing known as "background" which is only to be had from generations of ancestors to the manor born. Original pieces of mahogany by Sheraton and Chippendale and the Brothers Adam, family portraits from the brush of Benjamin West, silver in the best tradition of the early eighteenth century smiths, even the dignifiedly aloof, elderly colored butler, announced that our patient's father was in every way an officer and a gentleman in the best sense of the term.

"If you will give Hezekiah your things," Captain Loudon indicated the solemn old Negro with a nod, "I'll go up and tell my daughter you're here. I know she will be glad to—"

A clanking, banging noise, like a tin can bumping over the cobbles at the tail of some luckless terrier, interrupted his remarks, and we turned in amazement toward the wide, curving staircase at the further end of the long central hall. The noise grew louder, almost deafening, then ceased as abruptly as it began, and a young girl rounded the curve of the staircase, coming slowly toward us.

She was more than middle height, slender and supple as a willow withe, and carried herself with the bearing of a young princess. A lovely though almost unfashionably long gown of white satin and chiffon draped its uneven hem almost to her ankles, and about her slender bare shoulders and over her arms hung a richly embroidered shawl of Chinese silk. One hand rested lightly on the mahogany rail of the balustrade, as though partly for support, partly for guidance, as she slowly descended the red-carpeted steps. This much we saw at first glance, but our second look remained riveted on her sweet, pale face.

Almost unbeautifully long it was, pale with the rich, creamy pallor which is some women's birthright and not the result of poor health, and her vivid, scarlet lips showed in contrast to her ivory cheeks like a rose fallen in the snow.

Brows as delicate as those of a French doll, narrow, curving brows which needed no plucking to accentuate their patrician lines, dipped sharply together above the bridge of her small nose, and lashes which even at the distance we stood from her showed their vivid blackness veiled her eyes. At first I thought her gaze was on the steps before her, and that she made each forward movement with slow care lest she fall from weakness or nervous exhaustion, but a second's scrutiny of her face, told me the truth. The girl walked with lowered lids. Whether in natural sleep or in some supernatural trance, she was descending the stairs with tightly closed eyes.

"*La pauvre petite*," de Grandin exclaimed under his breath, his gaze fixed on her. "*Grand Dieu*, Friend Trowbridge, but she is beautiful! Why did I not come here before?"

Out of the empty air, apparently some six feet above the girl's proudly poised head, a burst of mocking, maniacal laughter answered him, and from the thick-piled carpet suddenly rose again the clang-bang racket we had heard before she came into view.

"*Hélas!*" De Grandin turned a pitying glance on the girl's father, then: "*Nom de Dieu!*" he cried, ducking his head suddenly and looking over his shoulder with rounded eyes. Against the wall of the apartment, some twenty feet distant, there hung a stand of arms, one or two swords, a spear and several bolos, trophies of the captain's service in the Philippines. As though seized by an invisible hand, one of the bolos had detached itself from the wall, hurtled whistling through the air and embedded itself nearly an inch deep in the white wainscoting behind the little Frenchman, missing his cheek by the barest fraction of a centimeter as it flew whirring past.

The clanking tumult beneath the girl's feet subsided as quickly as it commenced, she took an uncertain step forward and opened her eyes. They were unusually long, purple rather than blue in color, and held such an expression of changeless melancholy as I had never seen in one so young. It was the look of one foredoomed to inescapable death by an incurable disease.

"Why"—she began with the bewildered look of one suddenly roused from sleep—"why—Father! What am I doing here? I was in my room, lying down, when I thought I heard Robert's voice. I tried to get up, but 'It' held me down, and I think I fell asleep. I—"

"Daughter," Captain Loudon spoke gently, the sobs very near the surface, for all his iron self-control, "these gentlemen are Dr. de Grandin and Dr. Trowbridge. They've come to—"

"Oh," the girl made an impatient gesture which yet seemed somewhat languid, as though even remonstrance were useless, "more doctors! Why did you bring them, Father? You know they'll be just like all the rest. Nothing can help me—nothing seems any good!"

"*Pardonnez-moi, Mademoiselle*," de Grandin bent forward in a formal, European bow, heels together, elbows stiffly at sides, "but I think you will find us most different from the rest. To begin, we come to cure you and give you back to the man you love; and in the second place, I have a personal interest in this case."

"A personal interest?" she inquired, acknowledging his bow with a negligent nod.

"*Morbleu*, but I have. Did not the—the thing which troubles you, hurl a bolo-knife at me? *Sacré nom*, no *fantôme*, no *lutin* shall throw knives at Jules de Grandin, then boast of the exploit to his ghostly fellows. *Nom d'un petit Chinois*, I think we shall show them something before we are finished!"

"Now, MADEMOISELLE, WE MUST ask your pardon for these questions," he began when he had reached the drawing room. "To you it is an old and much-told tale, but we are ignorant of your case, save for such information as your father has imparted. Tell us, if you please, when did these so strange manifestations begin?" The girl regarded him silently a moment, her brooding, plum-colored eyes staring almost resentfully into his agate-blue ones.

"It was about six months ago," she began in a lifeless monotone, like a child reciting a rote-learned but distasteful lesson. "I had come home from a dance in New York with Lieutenant Proudfit, and it must have been about three o'clock in the morning, for we had not left New York until midnight, and our train was delayed by a heavy sleet-storm. Lieutenant Proudfit was stopping overnight with us, for we are—we were—engaged, and I had said good-night to him and gone to my room when it seemed I heard something fluttering and tapping at my window, like a bird attracted by the light, or—I don't know what made me think so, but I got the impression, somehow—a bat beating its wings against the panes.

"I remember being startled by the noise, at first, then I was overcome with pity for the poor thing, for it was bitter cold outside and the sleet was driving down like whiplashes with the force of the east wind. I went over to the window and opened it to see what was outside. I"—she hesitated a moment, then went forward with her narrative—"I was partly undressed by this time, and the cold wind blowing through the open window cut like a knife, but I looked out into the storm to see if I could find the bird, or whatever it was."

"Ah?" de Grandin's little eyes were sparkling with suppressed excitement, but there was neither humor nor warmth in their flash. Rather, they were like two tiny pools of clear, adamant-hard ice reflecting a cloudless winter sky and bright, cold winter sunshine. "Proceed, if you please," he commanded, his voice utterly toneless. "You did open your window to the tapping which was outside. And what did you next?"

"I looked out and said, 'Come in, you poor creature!'" the girl replied. "Even though I thought it was a bat at the pane, my reason told me it couldn't be, for bats aren't about in the dead of winter, and if it had been one, much as I hate the things, I couldn't have slept with the thought of its being outside in my mind."

"Ah!" de Grandin repeated, his voice raised slightly in interrogation. "And so you did invite what was outside to come in?" Level as his tone was, there was a certain pointedness in the way he spoke the words, almost as though they were uttered in faintly shocked protest.

"Of course," she returned. "I know it was silly for me to speak to a bird that way, as if it could understand, but, you know, we often address animals in that way. At any rate, I might have saved myself the chilling I got, for there was nothing there. I waited several minutes till the cold wind almost set my teeth to chattering, but nothing was visible outside, and there were no further flutterings at the window."

"Probably not," the Frenchman commented dryly. "What then, please?"

"Why, nothing—right away. It seemed as though the room had become permanently chilled, though, for even after I'd closed the window the air was icy cold, and I had to wrap my dressing gown about me while I made ready for bed. Then—" She stopped with an involuntary shudder.

"Yes, and then?" he prompted, regarding her narrowly while his lean white fingers tapped a devil's tattoo on his chair arm.

"Then the first strange thing happened. As I was slipping my gown off, I distinctly felt a hand grasp me about the upper arm—a long, thin, deathly cold hand!"

She looked up defiantly, as though expecting some skeptical protest, but: "Yes," he nodded shortly. "And after that?"

The girl regarded him with a sort of wonder. "You believe me—believe I actually felt something grasp me?" she asked incredulously.

"Have you not said so, *Mademoiselle?*" he returned a thought irritably. "Proceed, please."

"But every other doctor I've talked to has tried to tell me I didn't—couldn't have actually felt such a thing," she persisted.

"*Mademoiselle!*" the little man's annoyance cut through the habitual courtesy with which he treated members of the gentler sex as a flame cuts through wax. "We do waste time. We are discussing you and your case, not the other physicians or their methods. They have failed. We shall give them none of our valuable time. *Bien.* You were saying—"

"That I felt a long, cold hand grasp me about the arm, and a moment later, before I had a chance to cry out or even shrink away, something began scratching my skin. It was like a long, blunt fingernail—a human nail, not the claw of an animal, you understand. But it had considerable force behind it, and I could see the skin turning white in its wake. Dr. de Grandin"—she leaned forward, staring with wide, frightened eyes into his face—"the welts formed letters!"

"U'm?" he nodded unexcitedly. "You do recall what they spelled?"

"They didn't spell anything. It was like the ramblings of a Ouija board when the little table seems wandering about from letter to letter without spelling any actual words. I made out a crude, printed *D*, then a smaller *r*, then an *a*, and finally a *c* and *u*—Dr-a-c-u. That was all. You see, it wasn't a word at all."

De Grandin was sitting forward on the extreme edge of his chair, his hands grasping its arms as though he were about to leap from his seat. "*Dracu*," he repeated softly to himself, then, still lower, "*Dieu de Dieu!* It is possible; but why?"

"Why, what is it?" the girl demanded, his tense attitude reflecting itself in her widened eyes and apprehensive expression.

He shook himself like a spaniel emerging from the water. "It is nothing, *Mademoiselle*," he assured her with a resumption of his professionally impersonal manner. "I did think I recognized the word, but I fear I must have been mistaken. You are sure there were no other letters?"

"Positive. That was all; just those five, no more."

"Quite yes. And after that?"

"After that all sorts of terrible things began happening to me. Father has told you how chairs and tables rise up when I come near them, and how little objects fly through the air?"

He nodded, smiling. "But of course," he returned, "and I, myself, did see one little thing fly through the air. *Parbleu*, it did fly unpleasantly close to my head! And these so strange sleeps you have?"

"They come on me almost any time, mostly when I'm least expecting them. One time I was seized with one while on the train and"—her face flushed bright coral at the recollection—"and the conductor thought I was drunk!"

"*Bête!*" de Grandin murmured. "And you have not heard the voices—the noises which sometimes accompany you, *Mademoiselle?*"

"No, I've been told of them; but I know nothing of what occurs while I'm in one of these trances. I don't even dream; at least, I have no dreams I can remember when I wake up. I only know that I am apt to fall asleep at any time, and frequently wander about while unconscious, waking up in some totally different place. Once I walked half-way to the city while asleep, and narrowly escaped being run down by a taxicab when I came to in the middle of the street."

"But this is villainous!" he burst out. "This is infamous; this must not be allowed. *Mordieu*, I shall not permit it!"

Something of the girl's weary manner returned as she asked, "How are you going to stop it? The others all said—"

"*Chut!* The others! We shall not discuss them, if you please, *Mademoiselle*. Me, I am not as the others; I am Jules de Grandin!

"First, my friend," he turned to me, "I would that you obtain a competent nurse, one whose discretion is matched only by her ability. You know one such? *Très bien.* Hasten, rush, fly to procure her at once. Bid her come to us with all celerity and be prepared to serve until relieved.

"Next"—he seized a pad and scribbled a prescription—"I would that *Monsieur le Capitaine* has this filled and administers one dose dissolved in hot water at once. It is Somnol, a harmless mixture of drugs, pleasant to the taste and of undoubted efficacy in this case. It will act better than chloral."

"But I don't want to take chloral," the girl protested. "I have enough trouble with sleep as it is; I want something to ward off sleep, not to induce it."

"*Mademoiselle,*" he replied with something like a twinkle in his keen little eyes, "have you never heard of combating the devil with flames? Take the medicine as directed. Dr. Trowbridge and I shall return soon, and we shall not rest until we have produced a cure, never doubt it."

"THIS IS THE STRANGEST case I ever saw," I confided as we drove toward town. "The girl's symptoms all point to hysteria of the most violent sort, but I'm hanged if I can account for those diabolical noises which accompanied her down the stairs, or that laugh we heard when she reached the hall, or—"

"Or the knife which nearly split the head of Jules de Grandin?" he supplied. "No, my friend, I fear medical science can not account for those things. Me, I see part of it, but not all, *parbleu*, not near enough. Do you recall the ancient medical theory concerning icterus?"

"Jaundice?"

"But of course."

"You mean it used to be considered a disease, rather than a symptom?"

"Precisely. One hundred, two hundred years ago the craft knew the yellow color of the patient's skin was due to diffused bile in the system, but what caused the diffusion? Ah, that was a question left long unanswered. So it is with this poor girl's case. Me, I recognize the symptoms, and some of their cause is plain to me, but—ten thousand little red devils!—why? Why should she be the object of this persecution? One does not open a window in the wintertime to bid a non-existent bat or bird enter one's house, only to fall victim to such tricks as have plagued Mademoiselle Loudon since that winter's night. No, *morbleu*, there was a reason for it, the thing which tapped at her pane, being outside that night, Friend Trowbridge, and the writing on her arm, that too, came not without cause!"

I listened in amazement to his tirade, but one of his statements struck a responsive chord in my memory. "You spoke of 'writing' on her arm, de

Grandin," I interposed. "When she described it I thought you seemed to recognize some connection between the incomplete word and her symptoms. Is 'dakboo' a complete word, or the beginning of one?"

"*Dracu*," he corrected shortly. "Yes, my friend, it is a word. It is Rumanian for devil, or, more properly, demon. You begin to see the connection?"

"No, I'm hanged if I do," I retorted.

"So am I," he replied laconically, and lapsed into moody silence from which my best attempts at conversation failed to rouse him.

Lulled into counterfeit rest by the drug de Grandin prescribed, Julia Loudon passed the night comfortably enough, and seemed brighter and happier when we called to interview her next morning.

"*Mademoiselle*," de Grandin announced, after the usual medical mummery of taking temperature and pulse had been completed, "the day is fine. I prescribe that you go for a drive this morning; indeed, I strongly urge that you accompany Dr. Trowbridge and me forthwith. He has a number of calls to make, and I would observe what effect the fresh air has upon you. I venture to say you have had little enough of it lately."

"I haven't," the girl confessed. "You see, since that time when I wandered off in my sleep, I've been afraid to go anywhere by myself, and I've even shrunk from going out with Father or Rob—Lieutenant Proudfit. I've been afraid of embarrassing them by one of my seizures. But it will be all right for me to go if you and Dr. Trowbridge are along, I know," she smiled wistfully at him.

"Of a surety," he agreed, twisting the ends of his trim little blond moustache. "Have no fear, dear lady; I shall see no harm comes to you. Make haste, we would be off."

Miss Loudon turned to mount the stairs, a suggestion of freedom and returning health in the spring of her walk, and de Grandin turned a puzzled countenance to Captain Loudon and me. "Your daughter's case is far simpler than I had supposed, *Monsieur le Capitaine*," he announced. "So much I have been accustomed to encountering what unthinking persons call the supernatural that I fear I have become what you Americans call 'hipped' on the subject. Now, when first *Mademoiselle* detailed her experiences to me, I was led to certain conclusions which, happily, have not seemed justified by what we have since observed. Medicine is helpful in most cases of the kind, but I had feared—"

A perfect pandemonium of cacophonous dissonances, like the braying of half a dozen jazz bands suddenly gone crazy, interrupted his speech. Clattering tin cans, jangling cowbells, the wailings of tortured fiddles and discordant shrieks of wood-wind instruments all seemed mingled with shouts of wild, demoniac laughter as a bizarre figure emerged in view at the turn of the stairs and half leaped, half fell to the hall.

For an instant I failed to recognize patrician Julia Loudon in the grotesque thing before us. Her luxuriant black hair had escaped from the Grecian coronel in which she habitually wore it and hung fantastically about
her breast and shoulders, half veiling, half disclosing a face from which every
vestige of serenity had disappeared and on which a leer—no other word
expresses it—of mingled craft and cunning and idiotic stupidity sat like a
toad enthroned upon a fungus. She was bare-armed and barelegged; indeed,
the only garment covering her supple, white body was a Spanish shawl wound
tightly about bust and torso, its fringed ends dragging over the floor behind
her flying feet as she capered like a female satyr across the hall drugget to the
bedlam accompaniment of infernal noises which seemed to hover over her
like a swarm of poisonous flies above a wounded animal struggling through
the mire of a swamp.

"Ai, ai, ai-ee!" she cried in a raucous voice, bending this way and that in
time to the devilish racket. "Behold my work, foolish man, behold my mastery!
Fool that you are, to try to take mine from me! Today I shall make this woman
a scandal and disgrace, and tonight I shall require her life. Ai, ai, ai-ee!"

For a fleeting instant de Grandin turned an appalled face to me, and I met
his flying glance with one no less surprised, for the voice issuing from the girl's
slender throat was not her own: No tone or inflection of it was reminiscent
of Julia Loudon. Every shrilling syllable spoke of a different individual, a personality instinct with evil vivacity as hers seemed instinct with sweetness and
melancholy.

"Cordieu!" de Grandin exclaimed between set teeth, springing toward the
girl, then halting in horrified amazement as though congealed to ice in his
tracks. From every side of the room, like flickering beams of light, tiny bits
of metal flew toward the girl's swaying body, and in an instant her arms, legs,
throat, even her cheeks, were encrusted with glittering pins and needles buried
point-deep in her creamy skin like the torture-implements driven into the bodies of the pain-defying fakirs of India. Almost it seemed as though the girl had
suddenly become a powerful electro-magnet to which every particle of movable
metal in the apartment had leaped.

For an instant she stood swaying there, the cruel points embedded in her
flesh, yet seemingly causing no pain, then a wild, heart-rending shriek broke
from her lips, and her eyes opened wide in sudden terror and consternation.
Instantly it was apparent she had regained consciousness, realized her position,
her almost complete nudity and the biting, stinging points of the countless
needles all at once.

"Quick, Trowbridge, my friend!" de Grandin urged, leaping forward. "Take
her, my old one. Do not permit her to fall—those pins, they will surely impale
her if she drops."

Even as I seized the fainting girl in my arms, the Frenchman was furiously garnering the pins from her flesh, cursing volubly in mingled French and English as he worked.

"*Parbleu*," he swore, "it is the devil's work, of a surety. By damn, I shall have words to say to this accursed *dracu* who sticks pins in young ladies and throws knives at Jules de Grandin!"

Following him, I bore the swooning girl up the stairs, placed her on her bed and turned furiously in search of the nurse. What could the woman have been thinking of to let her patient leave her room in such a costume? "Miss Stanton," I called angrily. "Where are you?"

A muffled sound, half-way between a scream and an articulate cry, and a faint, ineffectual tap-tap on the door of the closet answered me. Snatching the door of the clothes-press open, I found her lying on the floor, half smothered by fallen dresses, her mouth gagged by a Turkish towel, wrists tied behind her and ankles lashed together with knotted silk stockings.

"A-a-ah, oh!" she gasped as I relieved her of her fetters and helped her, half fainting, to her feet. "It took me, Dr. Trowbridge. I was helpless as a baby in its hands."

De Grandin looked up from his ministrations to Julia Loudon. "What was the 'It' which took you, *Mademoiselle?*" he inquired, folding back the shawl from the girl's injured limbs and deftly shoving her beneath the bedclothes. "Was it Mademoiselle Loudon?"

"No!" the nurse gasped, her hands still trembling with fright and nervousness. "Oh, no, not Miss Loudon, sir. It was—I don't know what. Miss Loudon came upstairs a few moments ago and said you and Dr. Trowbridge were taking her motoring, and she must change her clothes. She began removing her house dress, but kept taking off her garments until she was—she was—" she hesitated a moment, catching her breath in long, laboring gasps.

"*Mordieu*, yes!" de Grandin cut in testily. "We do waste time, Mademoiselle. She did remove her clothing until she was what? Completely nude?"

"Yes," the nurse replied with a shudder. "I was about to ask her if she needed to change all her clothes, when she turned and looked at me, and her face was like the face of a devil, sir. Then something seemed to come down on me like a wet blanket. No, not like a blanket, either. It clung to me and bore me down, and smothered me all at once, but it was transparent, sir. I could feel it, but I couldn't see it. It was like a—like a terrible, big jelly-fish, sir. It was cold and slimy and strong, strong as a hundred giants. I tried to call out, and *it* oozed into my mouth—choked me; ugh!" She shuddered at the recollection. "Then I must have fainted, for the next thing I knew everything was dark, and I heard Dr. Trowbridge calling me, so I tried to call out and kicked as hard as I could, and—"

"And *voilà*—here you are!" de Grandin interrupted. "I marvel not you are *nerveuse, Mademoiselle. Cordieu*, are we not all so!

"Attend me, Trowbridge, my friend," he commanded, "do you remain with Mademoiselle Stanton and the patient. Me, I shall go below and procure three drinks of brandy for us—yes, *morbleu*, four I shall obtain, for one I shall drink myself immediately, right away, at once, before I return. Meantime, watch well Mademoiselle Julie, for I think she will require much watching before all is done."

A moment later the clatter of his heels sounded on the polished boards of the hall floor as he hastened below stairs in search of stimulant.

"IT IS DAMNABLE, DAMNABLE, my friends!" the little Frenchman cried a few moments later as he, Captain Loudon and I conferred in the lower hall. "This *poltergeist*, it has complete possession of the poor Mademoiselle Julie, and it has manifested itself to Mademoiselle Stanton as well. *Pardieu*, if we but knew whence it comes, and why, we might better be able to combat it; but all, all is mystery. It comes, it wreaks havoc, and it remains. *Dieu de Dieu de Dieu de Dieu!*" He strode fiercely back and forth across the rug, twisting first one, then the other end of his diminutive moustache until I thought he would surely drag the hairs from his lip.

"If only we could—" he began again, striding across the hall and bringing up before a buhl cabinet which stood between two low windows. "If only we could—ah! What—who is this, *Monsieur le Capitaine*, if you please?"

His slender, carefully manicured forefinger pointed to an exquisite little miniature which stood in a gold easel-frame on the cabinet's top.

Looking over his shoulder, I saw the picture of a young girl, black-haired, oval-faced, purple-eyed, her red lips showing against the pallor of her face almost like a wound in healthy flesh. There was a subtle something of difference—more in expression than in feature—from the original, nevertheless I recognized the likeness as a well-executed portrait of Julia Loudon, though it had been made, I imagined, several years earlier. "Why," I exclaimed in astonishment at his question, "why, it is Miss Loudon, de Grandin!"

Ignoring my remark, he kept his fixed, unwinking stare upon the captain, repeating, "This lady, *Monsieur*, she is who?"

"It's a picture of my niece, Julia's cousin," Captain Loudon returned shortly; then: "Don't you think we could occupy our time better than with trifles like that? My daughter—"

"Trifles, *Monsieur!*" de Grandin cut in. "There are *no* trifles in a case such as this. All, all is of the importance. Tell me of this young lady, if you please. There is a so remarkable resemblance, yet a look in the eyes which is not the look of your daughter. I would know much of her, if you please."

"She was my niece, Anna Wassilko," the captain replied. "That picture was made in St. Petersburg—Petrograd—or Leningrad, as it is called now—before the World War."

"Ah?" de Grandin stroked his moustache gently, as though making amends for the furious pulling to which he had subjected it a moment before. "You did say 'was,' *Monsieur.* May I take it, then, that she 'is' no more?" He cast a speculative glance at the portrait again, then continued: "And her name, so different from yours, yet her appearance so like your daughter's. Will you not explain?"

Captain Loudon looked as though he would like to wring the inquisitive little Frenchman's neck, but complied with his request instead. "My wife was a Rumanian lady," he began, speaking with evident annoyance. "I was stationed for duty at our legation at Bukharest in 1895, and there I met my wife, who was a Mademoiselle Seracki. I was married before returning to floating service, and my wife's twin sister, Zoë, married Leonidas Wassilko, a young officer attached to the Russian embassy, about the same time.

"Things were beginning to move a little, even in those days. One or two near-quarrels with European nations over the Monroe Doctrine had warned even the lunkheads at Washington that we'd best be getting some sort of navy in the water, and there was no time for a protracted honeymoon after our marriage. I had to leave my bride of two months and report for duty to the flagship of the Mediterranean Squadron. Anna, my wife, stayed on at Bukharest for a time, then moved from one port to another along the European coast so as to be fairly near me when I could get infrequent furloughs. Finally I was moved to the China station, and she went to live with her sister and brother-in-law at St. Petersburg. Our baby Julia and their little girl, Anna, were born on the same day and resembled each other even more than their mothers did.

"Following the Spanish War and my transfer to home service, my wife divided her time between America and Europe, spending almost as much time in Russia as she did in Washington. Julia and Anna were educated together in a French convent and later went to the Smolny Institute in St. Petersburg.

"Anna joined up as a nurse in the Russian Red Cross at the outbreak of the World War, and was in France when the Revolution broke. That probably saved her life. Both her parents were shot by the Bolshevists as reactionaries, and she came to live with us after the Armistice.

"Somehow, she didn't take very well to American ways, and when Robert—Lieutenant Proudfit—came along and began paying court to Julia, Anna seemed to take it as a sort of personal affront. Seems she had some sort of fool idea she and Julia were more than cousins, and ought to remain celibate to devote their lives to each other. To tell the truth, though, I rather fancy she was more than a little taken by Proudfit herself, and when he preferred Julia to her—well, it didn't please her any too much."

"Ah?" de Grandin breathed, a trace of the heat-lightning flash which beto-kened excitement showing in his cool eyes. "And Mademoiselle Anna, she is—"

"She—died, poor child," Loudon responded.

"She did commit suicide?" the Frenchman's words were so low we could scarcely hear them.

"I didn't say that," the captain returned coldly.

"*Pardonnez-moi, Monsieur le Capitaine*," the other shot back, "but you did not say otherwise, and, the pause before you mentioned her death—surely that was something more than a tribute of momentary regret?"

"Humph! Yes, you're right. The poor youngster committed suicide by drowning herself about six months ago."

"Six months, did you say?" the little Frenchman's face was so near his host's that I feared the spike of his waxed mustache would scratch the captain's cheek. "Six months ago she did drown herself. In the ocean? And Mademoiselle Julie's engagement to Lieutenant Proudfit, it was announced—when?"

"It had just been announced—but look here, I say, see here—" Captain Loudon began violent protest, but de Grandin was grinning mirthlessly at him.

"I look there, *Monsieur*," he replied, "and I see there. *Parbleu*, I see far past! Six months, six months, everything, it dates from six months of yore! The death of Mademoiselle Anna, the engagement of Mademoiselle Julie, the tapping at her window, the beginning of these so strange signs and wonders—all are six months old. *Grâce à Dieu*, my friend, I begin to see the light at last. Come, Trowbridge, my friend, first for the information, then the action!"

Turning on his heel, he mounted the stairs, three at a time, beckoning me violently as he did so.

"Mademoiselle—Mademoiselle Julie!" he cried, bursting into the patient's room with hardly a perceptible pause between his knock and the nurse's summons to enter. "You have not told me all, *Mademoiselle*, no, nor near all! This Mademoiselle Anna, who was she; and what relation was there between you and her? Of haste, speak quickly, it is important that I should know all!"

"Why," Miss Loudon looked at him with startled eyes, "she was my cousin."

"But yes, that much I know. What I desire to learn is if there was some close bond, some secret understanding between you."

The girl regarded him fixedly a moment, then: "Yes, there *was*. Both of us were in love with Lieutenant Proudfit; but he seemed to prefer me, for some reason. When Anna saw he was proof against all her wiles—and she was an accomplished coquette—she became very morose, and talked constantly of sui-cide. I tried to laugh her out of the idea, but she persisted. Finally, I began to believe she was serious, and I told her, 'If you kill yourself, so will I, then there'll be two of us dead and nobody any the happier.'"

"Ah?" de Grandin regarded her intently. "And then?"

"She gave me one of those queer, long looks of hers, and said, 'Maybe I hold you to that promise, cousin. *Jizn kopyeka*—life is but a kopeck—maybe we spend him, you and I.' And that was all she said at the time. But two months later, just before Lieutenant Proudfit and I announced our engagement, she left me a note:

Have gone to spend my kopeck. Remember your promise and do likewise.

"Next morning—"

"Yes?" de Grandin prompted.

"Next morning they took her from the bay—drowned."

"A-a-h!" he let the single syllable out slowly through his teeth with a sort of hissing finality. "A-a-ah, at last, Mademoiselle, I do understand."

"You mean—"

"*Parbleu*, I mean nothing less. Tonight, she did say? *Morbleu*, tonight we shall see what we shall see!"

"Stay you here, Friend Trowbridge," he ordered. "Me, I go to procure that which is necessary for our work this night!"

He was through the door like a shot, rushing down the stairs three steps at a stride, banging the front door behind him without a word of farewell or explanation to his astounded host.

D ARKNESS HAD FALLEN WHEN he returned, a small black bag in his hand and an expression of unbridled excitement on his face. "Any change in our patient?" he demanded as he entered the house. "Any further manifestations of that accursed *poltergeist?*"

"No," I reported, "everything has been singularly calm this afternoon."

"Ah, so? Then we shall have the harder fight tonight. The enemy, he does marshal his forces!"

He tiptoed to the sickroom, entered quietly, and took a seat beside the bed, detailing his experiences in the city with lively interest. Once or twice it seemed to me the patient's attention wandered as he continued his recital, but his conversation never faltered. He had seen the beautiful flowers in Fifth Avenue! The furs in the shops were of the exquisiteness! Never was there such a parade of beauty, culture and refinement as could be found in that so wonderful street!

I listened open-mouthed with wonder. Time given to extraneous matters when he was engaged in a case was time wasted according to his ideas, I knew, yet here he sat and chattered like a gossiping magpie to a girl who plainly took small interest in his talk.

Eight o'clock struck on the tall clock in the hall below, still he related humorous incidents in his life, and described the chestnut trees and the whistling blackbirds at St. Cloud or the students' masked balls in the Latin Quarter. "What ails the man?" I muttered to myself. "He rambles on like a wound-up phonograph!"

It must have been about a quarter of nine when the change began to show itself in our patient. From polite inattention her attitude toward the Frenchman became something like open hostility. In another five minutes she seemed to have lost all remembrance of his presence, and lay with her eyes turned toward the ceiling. Then, gradually but surely, there came into her already too thin face a pinched, drawn look, the sure sign of physical and nervous exhaustion.

"Ah-ha, we do begin to commence!" de Grandin exclaimed exultantly, reaching beneath his chair and opening the little black bag he had deposited there.

From the satchel he produced an odd-looking contrivance, something like the toy rotary fans to be bought at novelty shops—the sort of fan which consists of three twisted blades, like reversed propeller wings, and which is made to whirl by the pressure of the thumb against a trigger fitted in the handle. But this fan, instead of having blades of colored metal, was supplied with brightly nickeled arms which shone in the lamplight like a trio of new mirrors.

"Observe, *Mademoiselle*; behold!" de Grandin cried sharply, signing to me to turn the electric bulbs on full strength at the same time.

The girl's languid gaze lowered from the ceiling a moment and rested on the little Frenchman. Instantly he advanced the mirror-fan to within six inches of her face and began spinning it violently with quick, sharp jerks at the rotating loop. "*Regardez, si'l vous plaît*," he ordered, spinning the whirling mirrors faster and faster.

The three bright pieces of metal seemed to merge into a single disk, but from their flying it seemed that countless tiny rays of light fell away, like water scattered from a swiftly turning paddle-wheel. For an instant the girl regarded the bright, whirling mirrors without interest, then her eyes seemed gradually to converge toward the bridge of her nose as they sought to follow the fan's rotations, and a fixed, rapt expression began to steal over her features.

"Sleep, sleep and rest. Sleep and hear no orders from those who wish you ill. Sleep, sleep—*sleep!*" de Grandin. commanded in low, earnest tones.

Slowly, peacefully, her lids lowered over her fascinated eyes, her breast rose and fell convulsively once or twice, then her gentle breathing told us she had obeyed his command and lay fast in quiet sleep.

"What—" I began, but he waved me back impatiently.

"Another time, my friend," he promised with a quick gesture of warning. "At present we must not talk; there is too much at stake."

All through the night he sat beside the bed, raising his whirling mirrors and commanding sleep in tones of suppressed fury each time the girl stirred on her pillow. And each time his order was implicitly obeyed. The patient slept continuously till the first faint streaks of dawn began to show against the eastern sky.

"Now, then," he cried, springing from his chair, reopening his black bag and bringing forth—of all things!—a hyssop of mistletoe bough. Around and around the room he dashed with a sort of skipping step, for all the world like a country woman fanning flies from the house in summertime.

"Anna Wassilko, Anna Wassilko, who has wandered beyond the bounds of the tomb," he ordered as he waved his little brush-broom, "I command that you return whence you came. To Death you have said, 'Thou art my lord and my master,' and to the Grave, 'Thou art my lover and my betrothed.' Your business in this world is done, Anna Wassilko; get you to the world you chose for your dwelling place when you cast your body into the sea!"

Near the window, where the dimming electric bulbs' light mingled with the beams of the waning moon and the flushing rays of the coming morning, he repeated his command three times, waving his brush forward and outward toward the ocean which surged and boomed on the beach a quarter-mile away.

Something seemed to brush by him, something invisible, but tangible enough to stir the white scrim curtains trailing lazily in the still air, and for a moment I thought I caught the faint penumbra of a shadow cast against the ivory wall. A monstrous thing it was, large as a lion, yet like nothing I had ever seen or imagined, for it seemed to resemble both a bat and fox, with long, pointed snout, claw-armed forepaws and great, spike-edged wings extending to each side from close behind the head.

"Get you gone, unfortunate one," de Grandin cried, striking directly at the shadow with his sprigs of mistletoe. "Poor soul who would collect the wager of a thoughtless promise, hie you back to your own place and leave the ordering of other lives to God."

The terrible shadow rested against the pale wall another fraction of a second, then, like smoke borne away in a rising breeze, it was gone.

"Gone," de Grandin repeated softly, closing the window and shutting off the lights. "Call the nurse, I pray you, Friend Trowbridge. Her duties will be simpler hereafter. A little medicine, a little tonic, and much rest and food will see Mademoiselle Julie as well as ever."

Together we tiptoed into the hall, roused the sleeping nurse and turned the patient over to her care.

"AND NOW THE OTHER time you spoke of last night has come, I suppose?" I said, rather huffily, as we drove home. "You were close-mouthed enough about it all while it was happening. Will you explain now?"

"Most certainly," he returned in high good humor, lighting a cigarette, breathing in a great lungful of smoke, then discharging the vapor with a sigh of gusty content. "It was most simple—like everything else—when once I knew the answer.

"To begin: When first Captain Loudon explained his daughter's case, it seemed like one of simple hysteria to me, and one which any capable physician could cure. 'Why, then,' I ask me, 'does *Monsieur le Capitaine* seek the services of Jules de Grandin? I am not a great physician.' I have no answer, and at first I decline the case, as you know.

"But when we go to his house and behold Mademoiselle Julie all unconscious as she wandered about, I was of another mind; and when I hear the noises which accompanied her, I was of still a third mind. But when that evil one hurled a knife at my head, I said to me, '*Parbleu*, it is the challenge! Shall Jules de Grandin fly from such a contest?'

"Now, across the Rhine from France, those *boches* have some words which are most expressive. Among them is *poltergeist*, which signifies a pelting ghost, a ghost which flings things around the house. But more often he is not a ghost at all, he is some evil entity which plagues a man, or more frequently a woman. Not for nothing, my friend, did the ancients refer to Satan as the Prince of the Powers of the Air, for there are many very evil things in the air which we can no more see than we can behold the germs of disease. Yes." He nodded solemn affirmation.

"But when Mademoiselle Julie tells me of the mark which came on her arm, and I recognized the Rumanian word for demon, I think some more. And when she tells me of the bird or bat which fluttered at her window and yet was not there, I recognize many things in common with other cases I have observed.

"Foolish people, my friend, sometimes say, 'Come in,' when they think the wind has blown their door ajar. It is not well to do so. Who knows what invisible terror awaits without, needing only the spoken invitation unthinkingly made to enter? For attend me, my friend, very rarely can the evil ones come in unless they are first invited, and very rarely can they be gotten out once they have been bidden to enter. So all these things fit together in my mind, and I say to me, '*Morbleu*, we have here a *poltergeist*, and nothing else. Certainly.'

"But why should a *poltergeist* attach his evil self to that sweet Mademoiselle Julie? True, she are very pretty, but there are other pretty women in the world of whom the *poltergeister* do not seek shelter.

"Then when the demon tell us he hold her completely in his power and makes her to dance almost nude in her father's house and sticks pins and needles in her, I hear something else. I hear him promise to take her life.

"Why? What have she done that she must die?

"Then I see the picture of Anna Wassilko. Very like Mademoiselle Julie she was, but there was a subtle something in her face which makes me know she was not the same. And what story does *Monsieur le Capitaine* tell when I ask about her? Ah, now we begin to see the light! She were Rumanian by birth and partly by ancestry. Very good. She had gone to school with her cousin, Mademoiselle Julie. Again good. She had lived in the same house here, she had loved the same man, and she had committed suicide; best of all. I need now only a little reassuring as to the reason why—the result I already know.

"You know what Mademoiselle Julie told us; it all fitted in well with the theory I had formed. But there was work to be done that night.

"The demon which made Julie do all kinds of things she knew not of had promised to take her life. How to circumvent her? That were the question.

"I think. 'This young woman goes off into trances, and does all manner of queer things without knowing of them,' I inform me. 'Would she not do much the same in a state of hypnosis!' Assuredly, Very well, then.

"I procure me a set of whirling mirrors, not because there is any magic in them but because they are the easiest thing to focus the subject's attention. Last night I use them, and hypnotize Mademoiselle Julie before the poltergeist has a chance to conquer her consciousness. Hypnotism, when all is said and done, is the rendering of a subject's objective mind passive while the mind of the operator is substituted for that of the subject. The *poltergeist*, which was really the *revenant* of Anna, had substituted *her* mind for Julie's on former occasions; now I get there first, and place my mind in her brain. There is no room for the other, and Mademoiselle Julie can not take suggestions or brain-hints from the ghost and destroy herself. No, Jules de Grandin is already in possession of her brain-house, and he says 'No Admission' to all others who try to come in. Mademoiselle Julie slept peacefully through the night, as you did observe."

"But what was all that monkey business with the mistletoe?" I demanded.

"*Tiens*, my friend, the monkey's business had nothing to do with that," he assured me. "Do you, perhaps, remember what the mistletoe stands for at Noël?"

"You mean a kiss?"

"What else? It is the plant held sacred to lovers in this day, but in the elder times it was the holy bush of the Druids. With it they cast many spells, and with it they cast out many evil-workers. Not by mistake is it the lover's tree today, for it is a powerful charm against evil and will assuredly lay the unhappy ghost of one who dies because of unfortunate love. *Voilà*—you do catch the connection?"

"I never heard that before—" I began, but he cut me short with a chuckle.

"Much you have never heard, Trowbridge, my friend," he accused, "yet all of it is true, none the less."

"And that hideous shadow?"

He sobered instantly. "Who can say? In life Mademoiselle Anna was beautiful, but she went forth from the world uncalled and in an evil way, my friend.

Who knows what evil shape she is doomed to wear in the next life? The less we think on that subject the better for our sleep hereafter.

"Come, we are at your house once more. Let us drink one glass of brandy for luck's sake, then to sleep. *Mordieu*, me, I feel as though I had been stranger to my bed since my fifth birthday!"

The Gods of East and West

"TIENS, FRIEND TROWBRIDGE, YOU work late tonight."

Jules de Grandin, debonair in faultlessly pressed dinner clothes, a white gardenia sharing his lapel buttonhole with the red ribbon of the Légion d'Honneur, paused at the door of my consulting-room, glimpsed the box of coronas lying open on the table, and straightaway entered, seating himself opposite me and selecting a long, black cigar with all the delighted precision of a child choosing a bonbon from a box of sweets.

I laid aside the copy of Baring's *Diagnosis in Diseases of the Blood* I had been studying and helped myself to a fresh cigar. "Have a pleasant time at the Medical Society dinner?" I asked, somewhat sourly.

"But yes," he agreed, nodding vigorously while his little blue eyes shone with enthusiasm. "They are a delectable crowd of fellows, those New York physicians. I regret you would not accompany me. There was one gentleman in particular, a full-blooded Indian, who—but you do not listen, my friend; you are *distrait*. What is the trouble?"

"Trouble enough," I returned ungraciously. "A patient's dying for no earthly reason that I can see except that she is."

"Ah! You interest me. Have you made a tentative diagnosis?"

"Half a dozen, and none of 'em checks up. I've examined her and re-examined her, and the only thing I'm absolutely certain of is that she's fading away right before my eyes, and nothing I can do seems an earthly bit of good."

"U'm. Phthisis, perhaps?"

"Not a bit of it. I've tested her sputum numerous times; every result is negative. There isn't a thing wrong with her organically, and her temperature is almost always normal, fluctuating slightly at times one way or the other, but hardly ever more than one or two degrees. I've made several blood counts, and while she runs slightly under the million mark, the deficiency isn't enough to cause alarm. About the only objective symptoms she displays are a steady falling off in weight and a progressive pallor, while subjectively she complains of loss of appetite, slight headaches and profound lassitude in the morning."

"U'm," he repeated thoughtfully, expelling a twin cloud of smoke from his narrow nostrils and regarding the ash of his cigar as though it were something of intense interest, "and how long has this condition of affairs obtained?"

"About three months. She's a Mrs. Chetwynde, wife of a likable young chap who's superintending a piece of railway construction for an English company in Burma. He's been away about six months or so, and while she would naturally be expected to pine for him to some extent—they've been married only a couple of years—this illness has been going on only since about the middle of August."

"U'm!" He knocked the ash from his cigar with a deft motion of his little finger and inhaled a great lungful of strong, fragrant smoke with careful deliberation. "This case interests me, Friend Trowbridge. These diseases which defy diagnosis are the things which make the doctor's trade exciting. With your permission I will accompany you when next you visit Madame Chetwynde. Who knows? Together we may find the doormat under which the key of her so mysterious malady lies hidden. Meantime, I famish for sleep."

"I'm with you," I agreed as I closed my book, shut off the light and accompanied him upstairs to bed.

THE CHETWYNDE COTTAGE WAS one of the smallest and newest of the lovely little dwellings in the Rookwood section of town. Although it contained but seven rooms, it was as completely a piece of art as any miniature painted on ivory, and the appointments and furnishings comported perfectly with the exquisite architectural artistry of the house. Jules de Grandin's round little eyes danced delightedly as he took in the perfect harmony existing inside and out when we parked my car before the rose-trellised porch and entered the charming reception hall. "*Eh bien*, my friend," he whispered as we followed the black-and-white-uniformed maid toward the stairs, "whatever her disease may be, she has the *bon goût*—how do you say? good taste?—this Madame Chetwynde."

Lovely as a piece of Chinese porcelain—and as frail—Idoline Chetwynde lay on the scented pillows of her Louis Treize bed, a negligée of knife-plaited crêpe de chine trimmed with fluffy black marabou shrouding her lissom form from slender neck to slenderer ankles, but permitting occasional high-lights of ivory body to be glimpsed through its sable folds. Little French-heeled mules of scarlet satin trimmed with black fur were on her stocking-less feet, and the network of veins showed pale violet against the dead-white of her high-arched insteps. Her long, sharp-chinned face was a rich olive hue in the days of her health, but now her cheeks had faded to the color of old ivory, and her fine, high forehead was as pale and well-nigh as translucent as candle-wax. The long, beautifully molded lips of her expressive mouth were more an old rose than a coral red, and her large gray eyes, lifted toward the temples like those of an Oriental, shone with a sort of patient resignation beneath the "flying gull" curve of her intensely black brows. Her hair, cut short as a boy's at the back, had been combed across her forehead from right to left and plastered down with some perfumed unguent so that it surmounted her white face like a close-wrapped turban of gleaming ebon silk. Diamond studs, small, but very brilliant, flickered lambently in the lobes of her low-set ears. Some women cast the aura of their feminine allure about them as a bouquet of roses exudes its perfume. Idoline Chetwynde was one of these.

"Not so well this morning, thank you, Doctor," she replied to my inquiry. "The weakness seems greater than usual, and I had a dreadful nightmare last night."

"H'umph, nightmare, eh?" I answered gruffly. "We'll soon attend to that. What did you dream?"

"I—I don't know," she replied languidly, as though the effort of speaking were almost too much for her. "I just remember that I dreamed something awful, but what it was I haven't the slightest notion. It really doesn't matter, anyway."

"*Pardonnez-moi, Madame*, but it matters extremely much," de Grandin contradicted. "These things we call dreams, they are sometimes the expression of our most secret thoughts; through them we sometimes learn things concerning ourselves which we should not otherwise suspect. Will you try to recall this unpleasant dream for us?"

As he spoke he busied himself with a minute examination of the patient, tapping her patellar tendons, feeling along her wrists and forearms with quick, practiced fingers, lifting her lids and examining the pupils of both her luminous eyes, searching on her throat, neck and cardiac region for signs of abrasions. "*Eh bien*," and "*morbleu, c'est étrange!*" I heard him mutter to himself once or twice, but no further comment did he make until he had completed his examination.

"Do you know, Dr. Trowbridge," Mrs Chetwynde remarked as de Grandin rolled down his cuffs and scribbled a memorandum in his notebook, "I've been gone over so many times I've begun to feel like an entry at the dog show. It's really not a bit of use, either. You might just as well save yourselves and me the trouble and let me die comfortably. I've a feeling I shan't be here much longer, anyway, and it might be better for all concerned if—"

"*Zut!*" de Grandin snapped the elastic about his pocketbook with a sharp report and leveled a shrewd, unwinking stare at her. "Say not so, *Madame*. It is your duty to live. *Parbleu*, the garden of the world is full to suffocation with weeds; flowers like yourself should be most sedulously cultivated for the joying of all mankind."

"Thank you, Doctor," Mrs. Chetwynde smiled slowly in acknowledgment of the compliment and pressed the ebony-and-silver bell which hung over the ornamental head of her bed.

"*Madame* has called?" The swart-visaged maid servant appeared at the door of the chamber with a promptitude which led me to suspect her ear had never been far from the keyhole.

"Yes, Dr. Trowbridge and Dr. de Grandin are leaving," her mistress replied in a tired voice.

"*Adieu, Madame*," de Grandin murmured in farewell, leaning forward and possessing himself of the slender hand our hostess had not troubled to lift as we turned to go.

"We go, but we shall return anon, and with us, unless I greatly mistake, we shall bring you a message of good cheer. No case is hopeless until—"

"Until the undertaker's been called?" Mrs. Chetwynde interrupted with another of her slow, tired smiles as the little Frenchman pressed his lips to her pale fingers and turned to accompany the maid and me from the room.

"Be careful—sir," the maid cautioned, with just enough space between the command and the title of courtesy to rob her utterance of all semblance of respect. De Grandin, turning from the stairs into the hall, had almost collided with a statuette which stood on a pedestal in a niche between the staircase and the wall. To me it seemed the woman bent a look of almost venomous hate on him as he regained his footing on the highly polished floor and wheeled about to stare meditatively at the figurine into which he had nearly stumbled.

"This way—if you please, sir," the servant admonished, standing by the front door and offering his hat in a most suggestive manner.

"Ah, yes, just so," he agreed, turning from the statue to her, then back again. "And do you suffer from the mosquitoes here at this time of year, *Mademoiselle?*"

"Mosquitoes?" the woman's reply was half word, half scornful sniff at the little foreigner's irrelevant remark.

"Precisely, the mosquito, the gnat, the *mousquite*," he rejoined with a humorous lift of his brows. "The little, buzzing pests, you know."

"No, sir!" The answer served notice there was no more to be said on the subject.

"Ah? Perhaps it is then that *Madame* your mistress delights in the incense which annoys the moths, yes?"

"No, sir!"

"*Parbleu, ma vierge*, there are many strange things in the world, are there not?" he returned with one of his impish grins. "But the strangest of all are those who attempt to hold information from me."

The servant's only reply was a look which indicated clearly that murder was the least favor she cared to bestow on him.

"*Lá, lá,*" he chuckled as we descended the steps to my car. "I did her in the eye, as the Englishmen say, that time, did I not, my friend?"

"You certainly had the last word," I admitted wonderingly, "but you'll have to grant her the last look, and it was no very pleasant one, either."

"*Ah bah,*" he returned with another grin, "who cares how old pickle-face looks so long as her looks reveal that which I seek? Did not you notice how she stiffened when I hinted at the odor of incense in the house? There is no reason why they should not burn incense there, but, for some cause, the scent is a matter of utmost privacy—with the maid, at least."

"U'm?" I commented.

"Quite right; my friend, your objection is well taken," he responded with a chuckle. "Now tell me something of our fair patient. Who is she, who were her forebears, how long has she resided here?"

"She's the wife of Richard Chetwynde, a naturalized Englishman, who's been working on an engineering job in India, as I told you last night," I replied. "As to her family, she was a Miss Millatone before her marriage, and the Millatones have been here since the Indians—in fact, some of them have been here quite as long, since an ancestress of hers was a member of one of the aboriginal tribes—but that was in the days when the Swedes and Dutch were contending for this part of the country. Her family are rather more than well to do, and—"

"No more, my friend; you have told me enough, I think," he interrupted. "That strain of Indian ancestry may account for something which has caused me much wonderment. Madame Chetwynde is a rarely beautiful woman; my friend, but there is that indefinable something about her which tells the careful observer her blood is not entirely Caucasian. No disgrace, that; *parbleu*, a mixture of strain is often an improvement of the breed, but there was a certain—how shall I say it?—foreignness about her which told me she might be descended from Orientals, perhaps; perhaps from the Turk, the Hindoo, the—"

"No," I cut in with a chuckle, "she's what you might call a hundred and ten per cent American."

"U'm," he commented dryly, "and therefore ten per cent nearer the bare verities of nature than the thinner-blooded European. Yes. I think we may win this case, my friend, but I also think we shall have much study to do."

"Oh"—I looked at him in surprise—"so you've arrived at a hypothesis?"

"Hardly that, my friend. There are certain possibilities but as yet Jules de Grandin has not the courage to call them probabilities. Let us say no more for the time being. I would think, I would cogitate, I would meditate upon the matter." Nor could all my urging extract a single hint concerning the theory which I knew was humming like a gyroscope inside his active little brain as we drove home through the rows of brilliant maple trees lining the wide streets of our pretty little city.

A SPIRITED ALTERCATION WAS UNDERWAY when we arrived at my house. Taking advantage of the fact that office hours were over and no patients within earshot, Nora McGinnis, my household factotum, was engaged in the pleasing pastime of expressing her unvarnished opinion with all the native eloquence of a born Irishwoman. "Take shame to yerself, Katy Rooney," she was advising her niece as de Grandin and I opened the front door, "sure, 'tis yerself as ought to be ashamed to set foot in me kitchen an' tell me such nonsense! Afther all th' doctor's been afther doin' fer yez, too! Desertin' th' pore lady while she's sick an' in distriss, ye are, an' widout so much as sayin' by yer lave to th' doctor. Wurra, 'tis Nora McGinnis that's strainin' ivery nerve in her body to kape from takin' her hand off th' side o' yer face!"

"Take shame ter meself, indade!" an equally belligerent voice responded. "'Tis little enough ye know of th' goin's on in that there house! S'posin' 'twas you as had ter live under th' same roof wid a haythen statchoo, an' see th' misthress ye wuz takin' yer wages from a-crawlin' on her hands-an' knees before th' thing as if she was a haythen or a Protestant or sumpin, instid of a Christian woman! When first I come to Missis Chetwynde's house th' thing was no larger nor th' span o' me hand, an' ivery day it's growed an' growed until it's as long as me arm this minit, so it is, an' no longer ago than yestiddy it wunk it's haythen eye at me as I was passin' through th' hall. I tell ye, Nora darlin', what wid that black statchoo a-standin' in th' hall an' gittin' bigger an' bigger day be day, an' th' missis a-crawlin' to it on her all-fours, an' that slinky, sneaky English maid o' her 'n actin' as if I, whose ancistors wuz kings in Ireland, wuz no better than th' dirt benathe her feet, an' belike not as good, I'd not be answerable for me actions another day—th' saints hear me when I say it!"

I was striding toward the kitchen with intent to bring the argument to an abrupt close when de Grandin's fingers suddenly bit into my arm so sharply, that I winced from the pressure. "No, no, Friend Trowbridge," he whispered fiercely in my ear, "let us hear what else she has to say. This information is a gift from heaven no less!" Next moment he was in the kitchen, smiling ingratiatingly at the two angry women.

"Dr. de Grandin, sor," began Nora, anxious to refer the dispute to his arbitration, "'tis meself that's ashamed to have to own this gurrul as kin o' mine. When Mrs. Chetwynde waz taken sick, Dr. Trowbridge got her to go over an' cook fer th' pore lady, fer all our family's good cooks, though I do say it as shouldn't. An' now, bad cess to her, she fer up an' lavin' th' pore lady in th' midst of her trouble, like as if she were a Scandinavian or Eyetalian, or some kind o' stinkin' furriner, beggin' yer pardon, sor."

"Faith, Doctor," the accused Kathleen answered in defense, "I'm niver th' one to run out from a good situation widout warnin', but that Chetwynde house is no Christian place at all, at all. 'Tis some kind o' haythen madhouse, no less."

De Grandin regarded her narrowly a moment, then broke into one of his quick smiles. "What was it you did say concerning a certain statue and Madame Chetwynde?" he asked.

"Sure, an' there's enough ter say," she replied, "but th' best part of it's better left unsaid, I'm thinkin'. Mrs. Chetwynde's husband, as belike you know, sor, is an engineer in India, an' he's forever sendin' home all sorts o' furrin knick-knacks fer souvenirs. Some o' th' things is reel pretty an' some of 'em ain't so good. It were about three months ago, just before I came wid her, he sent home th' statchoo of some old haythen goddess from th' furrin land. She set it up on a pedistal like as if it were th' image of some blessed saint, an' there it stands to this day, a-poisonin' th' pure air o' th' entire house.

"I niver liked th' looks o' th' thing from th' first moment I clapped me two eyes on it, but I didn't have ter pass through th' front end o' th' house much, an' when I did I turned me eyes away, but one day as I was passin' through th' hall I looked at it, an' ye can belave me or not, Doctor, but th' thing had growed half a foot since last time I seen it!"

"Indeed?" de Grandin responded politely. "And then—"

"Then I sez to meself, sez I, 'I'll jist fix *you*, me beauty, that I will,' an' th' next evenin', when no one wuz lookin', I sneaked into th' hall an' doused th' thing 'wid howly wather from th' church font!"

"Ah? And then—" de Grandin prompted gently, his little eyes gleaming with interest.

"Ouch, Doctor darlin', if I hadn't seen it I wouldn't a' belaved it! May I niver move off'n this spot if th' blessed wather' didn't boil an' stew as if I'd poured it onto a red-hot stove!"

"Parbleu!" the Frenchman murmured.

"Th' next time I went past th' think, so help me hivin, if it didn't grin at me!"

"*Mordieu*, do you say so! And then—?"

"An' no longer ago than yestiddy it wunk its eye at me as I went by!"

"And you did say something concerning Madame Chetwynde praying to this—"

"Doctor"—the woman sidled nearer and took his lapel between her thumb and forefinger—"Doctor, 'tis meself as knows better than to bear tales concernin' me betters, but I seen sumpin last week that give me th' cowld shivers from me big toes to me eye-teeth. I'd been shlapin' as paceful as a lamb that hadn't been born yet, when all of a suddent I heard sumpin downstairs that sounded like burgulars. 'Bad cess ter th' murtherin' scoundrils,' says I, 'comin' here to kill pore definseless women in their beds!' an' wid that I picks up a piece o' iron pipe I found handy-like beside me door an' shtarts ter crape downstairs ter lane it agin th' side o' their heads.

"Dr. de Grandin, sor, 'tis th' blessed truth an' no lie I'm tellin' ye. When I come to th' head o' th' stheps, there was Mrs. Chetwynde, all barefooty, wid some sort o' funny-lookin' thing on her head, a-lightin' haythen punk-sthicks before that black haythen image an' a-goin' down on her two knees to it!

"'Katy Rooney,' sez I to meself, 'this is no fit an' proper house fer you, a Christian woman an' a good Catholic, to be livin' in, so it's not,' an' as soon as iver I could I give me notice to Mrs. Chetwynde, an' all th' money in th' mint couldn't hire me to go back to that place agin, sor."

"Just so," the little Frenchman agreed, nodding his sleek blond head vigorously. "I understand your reluctance to return; but could you not be induced by some consideration greater than money?"

"Sure, an' I'd not go back there fer—" Katy began, but he cut her short with a sudden gesture.

"Attend me, if you please," he commanded. "You are a Christian woman, are you not?"

"To be sure, I am."

"Very good. If I told you your going back to Madame Chetwynde's service until I give you word to leave might be instrumental in saving a Christian soul—a Christian body, certainly—would you undertake the duty?"

"I'd do most annything ye towld me to, sor," the woman replied soberly, "but th' blessed saints know I'm afeared to shlape under th' same roof wid that there black thing another night."

"U'm," de Grandin took his narrow chin in his hand and bowed his head in thought a moment, then turned abruptly toward the door. "Await me here," he commanded. "I shall return."

Less than two minutes later he reentered the kitchen, a tiny package of tissue paper, bound with red ribbon, in his hand. "Have you ever been by the Killarney lakes?" he demanded of Katy, fixing his level, unwinking stare on her.

"Sure, an' I have that," she replied fervently. "More than onct I've sthood beside th' blue wathers an'—"

"And who is it comes out of the lake once each year and rides across the water on a great white horse, attended by—" he began, but she interrupted with a cry that was almost a scream of ecstasy:

"'Tis th' O'Donohue himself! Th' brave O'Donohue, a-ridin' his grrate white harse, an' a-headin' his band o' noble Fayneans, all ridin' an' prancin' ter set owld Ireland free!"

"Precisely," de Grandin replied. "I too, have stood beside the lake, and with me have stood certain good friends who were born and bred in Ireland. One of those once secured a certain souvenir of the O'Donohue's yearly ride. Behold!"

Undoing the tissue paper parcel he exhibited a tiny ring composed of two or three strands of white horsehairs loosely plaited together. "Suppose I told you these were from the tail of the O'Donohue's horse?" he demanded. "Would you take them with you as a safeguard and re-enter Madame Chetwynde's service until I gave you leave to quit?"

"Glory be, I would that, sor!" she replied. "Faith, wid three hairs from th' O'Donohue's horse, I'd take service in th' Divil's own kitchen an' brew him as foine a broth o' brimsthone as iver he drank, that I would. Sure, th' O'Donohue is more than a match fer any murtherin' haythen that iver came out of India, I'm thinkin, sor."

"Quite right," he agreed with a smile. "It is understood, then, that you will return to Madame Chetwynde's this afternoon and remain there until you hear further from me? Very good."

To me, as we returned to the front of the house, he confided: "A pious fraud is its own excuse, Friend Trowbridge. What we believe a thing is, it is, as far as we are concerned. Those hairs, now, I did extract them from the mattress of my bed; but our superstitious Katy is brave as a lion in the belief that they came from the O'Donohue's horse."

"Do you mean to tell me you actually take any stock in that crazy Irishwoman's story, de Grandin?" I demanded incredulously.

"*Eh bien*," he answered with a shrug of his narrow shoulders, "who knows what he believes, my friend? Much she may have imagined, much more she may have made up from the activity of her superstitious mind; but if all she said is truth I shall not be so greatly surprised as I expect to be before we have finished this case."

"Well!" I returned, too amazed to think of any adequate reply.

"TROWBRIDGE, MY FRIEND," HE informed me at breakfast the following morning, "I have thought deeply upon the case of Madame Chetwynde, and it is my suggestion that we call upon the unfortunate lady without further delay. There are several things I should very much like to inspect in her so charming house, for what the estimable Katy told us yesterday has thrown much light on things which before were entirely dark."

"All right," I assented. "It seems to me you're taking a fantastic view of the case, but everything I've done thus far has been useless, so I dare say you'll do no harm by your tricks."

"*Morbleu*, I warrant I shall not!" he agreed with a short nod. "Come, let us go."

The dark-skinned maid who had conducted us to and from her mistress the previous day met us at the door in answer to my ring and favored de Grandin with an even deeper scowl than she had shown before, but she might as well have been a graven image for all the attention he bestowed on her. However—

"*Mon Dieu*, I faint, I am ill, I shall collapse, Friend Trowbridge!" he cried in a choking voice as we approached the stairs. "Water, I pray you; a glass of water, if you please!"

I turned to the domestic and demanded a tumbler of water, and as she left to procure it, de Grandin leaped forward with a quick, catlike movement and pointed to the statuette standing at the foot of the stairs. "Observe it well, Friend Trowbridge," he commanded in a low, excited voice. "Look upon its hideousness, and take particular notice of its height and width. See, place yourself here, and draw a visual line from the top of its head to the woodwork behind, then make a mark on the wood to record its stature. Quick, she will return in a moment, and we have no time to lose!"

Wonderingly, I obeyed his commands, and had scarcely completed my task when the woman came with a goblet of ice-water. De Grandin pretended to swallow a pill and wash it down with copious drafts of the chilled liquid, then followed me up the stairs to Mrs. Chetwynde's room.

"*Madame*," he began without preliminary when the maid had left us, "there are certain things I should like to ask you. Be so good as to reply, if you please. First, do you know anything about the statue which stands in your hallway below?"

A troubled look flitted across our patient's pale face. "No, I can't say I do," she replied slowly. "My husband sent it back to me from India several months ago, together with some other curios. I felt a sort of aversion to it from the moment I first saw it, but somehow it fascinated me, as well. After I'd set it up in the hall I made up my mind to take it down, and I've been on the point of having it taken out half a dozen times, but somehow I've never been able to make up my mind about it. I really wish I had, now, for the thing seems to be growing on me, if you understand what I mean. I find myself thinking about it—it's so adorably ugly, you know—more and more during the day, and, somehow, though I can't quite explain, I think I dream about it at night, too. I wake up every morning with the recollection of having had a terrible nightmare the night before, but I'm never able to recall any of the incidents of my dream except that the statue figures in it somehow."

"U'm," de Grandin murmured noncommittally. "This is of interest, *Madame*. Another question, if you please, and, I pray you, do not be offended if it seems unduly personal. I notice you have a *penchant* for attar of rose. Do you employ any other perfume?"

"No," she said wonderingly.

"No incense, perhaps, to render the air more fragrant?"

"No, I dislike incense, it makes my head ache. And yet"—she wrinkled her smooth brow in a puzzled manner—"and yet I've thought I smelled a faint odor of some sort of incense, almost like Chinese punk, in the house more than once. Strangely enough, the odor seems strongest on the mornings following one of my unremembered nightmares."

"I I'm," de Grandin muttered, "I think, perhaps, we begin to see a fine, small ray of light. Thank you, *Madame*; that is all."

"T HE MOON IS ALMOST at the full, Friend Trowbridge," he remarked apropos of nothing, about eleven o'clock that night. "Would it not be an ideal evening for a little drive?"

"Yes, it would not," I replied. "I'm tired, and I'd a lot rather go to bed than be gallivanting all over town with you, but I suppose you have something up your sleeve, as usual."

"*Mais oui*," he responded with one of his impish smiles, "an elbow in each, my friend—and other things, as well. Suppose we drive to Madame Chetwynde's."

I grumbled, but complied.

"Well, here we are," I growled as we passed the Chetwynde cottage. "What do we do next?"

"Go in, of course," he responded.

"Go in? At this hour of night?"

"But certainly; unless I am more mistaken than I think; there is that to be seen within which we should do well not to miss."

"But it's preposterous," I objected. "Who ever heard of disturbing a sick woman by a call at this hour?"

"We shall not disturb her, my friend," he replied. "See I have here the key to her house. We shall let ourselves in like a pair of wholly disreputable burglars and dispose ourselves as comfortably as may be to see what we shall see, if anything."

"The key to her house!" I echoed in amazement. "How the deuce did you get it?"

"Simply. While the sour-faced maid fetched me the glass of water this morning I took an impression of the key in a cake of soap I had brought for that very purpose. This afternoon I had a locksmith prepare me a duplicate from the stamp I had made. *Parbleu*, my friend, Jules de Grandin has not served these many years with the *Sûreté* and failed to learn more ways than one of entering other peoples' houses!"

Quietly, treading softly, we mounted the veranda steps, slipped the Judas-key into the front door lock and let ourselves into Mrs. Chetwynde's hall. "This way, if you please, Friend Trowbridge," de Grandin ordered, plucking me by the sleeve. "If we seat ourselves in the drawing-room we shall have an uninterrupted view of both stairs and hall, yet remain ourselves in shadow. That is well, for we have come to see, not to be seen."

"I feel like a malefactor—" I began in a nervous whisper, but he cut me off sharply.

"Quiet!" he ordered in a low breath. "Observe the moon, if you please, my friend. Is it not already almost peering through yonder window?"

I glanced toward the hall window before which the black statuette stood and noticed that the edge of the lunar disk was beginning to show through the opening, and long silver beams were commencing to stream across the polished floor, illuminating the figure and surrounding it with a sort of cold effulgence. The statue represented a female figure, gnarled and knotted, and articulated in a manner suggesting horrible deformity. It was of some kind of black stone or composition which glistened as though freshly anointed with oil, and from the shoulder-sockets three arms sprang out to right and left. A sort of pointed cap adorned the thing's head, and about the pendulous breasts and twisting arms serpents twined and writhed, while a girdle of skulls, carved from gleaming white bone, encircled its waist. Otherwise it was nude, and nude with a nakedness which was obscene even to me, a medical practitioner for whom the human body held no secrets. As I watched the slowly growing patch of moonlight on the floor it seemed the black figure grew slowly in size, then shrunk again, and again increased in stature, while its twisting arms and garlands of contorting serpents appeared to squirm with a horrifying suggestion of waking into life.

I blinked my eyes several times, sure I was the victim of some optical illusion due to the moon rays against the silhouette of the statue's blackness, but a sound from the stair-head brought my gaze upward with a quick, startled jerk.

Light and faltering, but unquestionably approaching, a soft step sounded on the uncarpeted stairs, nearer, nearer, until a tall, slow-moving figure came into view at the staircase turn. Swathed from breast to insteps in a diaphanous black silk night-robe, a pair of golden-strapped boudoir sandals on her little naked feet and a veil of black tulle shrouding her face, Idoline Chetwynde slowly descended the stairs, feeling her way carefully, as though the covering on her face obscured her vision. One hand was outstretched before her, palm up, fingers close together; in the other she bore a cluster of seven sticks of glowing, smoking Chinese punk spread fanwise between her fingers, and the heavy, cloyingly sweet fumes from the joss-sticks spiraled slowly upward, surrounding her veiled head in a sort of nimbus and trailing behind her like an evil-omened cloud.

Straight for the black image of the Indian goddess she trod, feeling each slow, careful step with faltering deliberation, halted a moment and inclined her head, then thrust the punk-sticks into a tiny bowl of sand which stood on the floor at the statue's feet. This done, she stepped back five slow paces, slipped the gilded sandals off and placed her bared feet parallel and close together, then with a sudden forward movement dropped to her knees. Oddly, with that sense for noting trifles in the midst of more important sights which we all have, I noticed that when she knelt, instead of straightening her feet out behind her with her insteps to the floor, she bent her toes forward beneath her weight.

For an instant she remained kneeling upright before the black image, which was already surrounded by a heavy cloud of pink-smoke; then, with a convulsive gesture, she tore the veil from before her face and rent the robe from her bosom, raised her hands and crossed them, palms forward, in front of her brow and bent forward and downward till crossed hands and forehead rested on the waxed boards of the floor. For a moment she remained thus in utter self-abasement, then rose upright, flinging her hands high above her head, re-crossed them before her face and dropped forward in complete prostration once more. Again and again she repeated this genuflection, faster and faster, until it seemed her body swayed forward and back thirty or forty times a minute, and the soft pat-pat of her hands against the floor assumed a rhythmic, drum-like cadence as she began a faltering chant in eager, short-breathed syllables:

Ho, Devi, consort of Siva and daughter of Himavat!
Ho, Sakti, fructifying principle of the Universe!
Ho, Devi, the Goddess;
Ho, Gauri, the Yellow;
Ho, Uma, the Bright;
Ho, Durga, the Inaccessible;
Ho, Chandi, the Fierce;
    Listen Thou to my Mantra!
Ho, Kali, the Black,
Ho, Kali, the Six-armed One of Horrid Form,
Ho, Thou about whose waist hangs a girdle of human skulls as if it were a
    precious pendant;
Ho, Malign Image of Destructiveness—

She paused an instant, seeming to swallow rising trepidation, gasped for breath a moment, like a timid but determined bather about to plunge into a pool of icy water, then:

Take Thou the soul and the body of this
    woman prostrate before Thee,
Take Thou her body and her spirit, freely
    and voluntarily offered,
Incorporate her body, soul and spirit into
    Thy godhead to strengthen Thee in
    Thine undertakings.

Freely is she given Thee, Divine Destroyer,
Freely, of her own accord, and without reservation,
Asking naught but to become a part of
    Thee and of Thy supreme wickedness.
Ho, Kali of Horrid Form,
Ho, Malign Image of Destructiveness,
He, eater-up of all that is good,
Ho, disseminator of all which is wicked
    Listen Thou to my Mantra!

"*Grand Dieu*, forgive her invincible ignorance; she knows not what she says!" de Grandin muttered beside me, but made no movement to stop her in her sacrilegious rite.

I half rose from my chair to seize the frenzied woman and drag her from her knees, but he grasped my elbow in a viselike grip and drew me back savagely. "Not now, foolish one!" he commanded in a sibilant whisper. And so we watched the horrid ceremony to its close.

For upward of a quarter-hour, Idoline Chetwynde continued her prostrations before the heathen idol, and, either because the clouds drifting across the moon's face played tricks with the light streaming through the hall window, or because my eyes grew undependable from the strain of watching the spectacle before me, it seemed as though some hovering, shifting pall of darkness took form in the corners of the room and wavered forward like a sheet of wind-blown sable cloth until it almost enveloped the crouching woman, then fluttered back again. Three or four times I noted this phenomenon, then, as I was almost sure it was no trick of lighting or imagination, the moon, sailing serenely in the autumn sky, passed beyond the line of the window, an even tone of shadow once more filled the hall, and Mrs. Chetwynde sank forward on her face for the final time, uttered a weak, protesting little sound, half-way between a moan and a whimper, and lay there, a lifeless, huddled heap at the foot of the graven image, her white arms and feet protruding from the black folds of her robe and showing like spots of pale light against the darkness of the floor.

Once more I made to rise and take her up, but again de Grandin restrained me. "Not yet, my friend," he whispered. "We must see the tragic farce played to its conclusion."

For a few minutes we sat there in absolute silence; then, with a shuddering movement, Mrs. Chetwynde regained consciousness, rose slowly and dazedly to her feet, resumed her sandals, and walked falteringly toward the stairs.

Quick and silent as a cat, de Grandin leaped across the room, passed within three feet of her and seized a light chair, thrusting it forward so that one of its spindle legs barred her path.

Never altering her course, neither quickening nor reducing her shuffling walk, the young woman proceeded, collided with the obstruction, and would have stumbled had not de Grandin snatched away the chair as quickly as he had thrust it forward. With never a backward look, with no exclamation of pain—although the contact must have hurt her cruelly—without even a glance at the little Frenchman who stood half an arm's length from her, she walked to the stairs, felt for the bottommost tread a second, then began a slow ascent.

"*Très bon!*" de Grandin muttered as he restored the chair to its place and took my elbow in a firm grip, guiding me down the hall and through the front door.

"What in heaven's name does it all mean?" I demanded as we regained my car. "From what I've just seen I'd have no hesitancy in signing commitment papers to incarcerate Mrs. Chetwynde in an institution for the insane—the woman's suffering from a masochistic mania, no doubt of it—but why the deuce did you try to trip her up with a chair?"

"Softly, my friend," he replied, touching fire to a vile-smelling French cigarette and puffing furiously at it. "Did you help commit that poor girl to an insane asylum you would be committing a terrible crime, no less. Normal she is not, but her abnormality is entirely subjective. As for the chair, it was the test of her condition. Like you, I had a faint fear her actions were due to some mental breakdown, but did you notice her walk? *Parbleu*, was it the walk of a person in possession of his faculties? I say no! And the chair proved it. When she did stumble against it, though it must have caused her tender body much pain, she neither faltered nor cried out. The machinery which telegraphed the sensation of hurt from her leg to her brain did suffer a short-circuit. My friend, she was in a state of complete anesthesia as regarded the outward world. She was, how do you say—"

"Hypnotized?" I suggested.

"U'm, perhaps. Something like that; although the controlling agent was one far, far different from any you have seen in the psychological laboratory, my friend."

"Then—"

"Then we would do well not to speculate too deeply until we have more pieces of evidence to fit into the picture-puzzle of this case. Tomorrow morning we shall call on Madame Chetwynde, if you please."

We did. The patient was markedly worse. Great lavender circles showed under her eyes, and her face, which I had thought as pale as any countenance could be in life, was even a shade paler than theretofore. She was so weak she could hardly lift her hand in greeting, and her voice was barely more than a whisper. On her left leg, immediately over the fibula, a great patch of violet bruise showed plainly the effects of her collision with the chair. Throughout the pretty, cozy little cottage there hung the faint aroma of burnt joss-sticks.

"Look well, my friend," de Grandin ordered in a whisper as we descended the stairs; "observe the mark you made behind the statue's head no later than yesterday."

I paused before the horrid thing, closed one eye and sighted from the tip of its pointed cap to the scratch I had made on the woodwork behind it. Then I turned in amazement to my companion. Either my eye was inaccurate or I had made incorrect measurements the previous day. According to yesterday's marks on the woodwork the statue had grown fully two inches in height.

De Grandin met my puzzled look with an unwavering stare, as he replied to my unspoken question: "Your eye does not deceive you, my friend; the hell-hag's effigy has enhanced."

"But—but," I stammered, "that can't be!"

"Nevertheless, it is."

"But, good heavens, man; if this keeps up—"

"This will not keep up, my friend. Either the devil's dam takes her prey or Jules de Grandin triumphs. The first may come to pass; but my wager is that the second occurs."

"But, for the Lord's sake! What can we do?"

"We can do much for the Lord's sake, my friend, and He can do much for ours, if it be His will. What we can do, we will; no more and certainly no less. Do you make your rounds of mercy, Friend Trowbridge, and beseech the so excellent Nora to prepare an extra large apple tart for dinner, as I shall undoubtlessly bring home a guest. Me, I hasten, I rush, I fly to New York to consult a gentleman I met at the Medical Society dinner the other night. I shall get back when I return, but, if that be not in time for an early dinner, it will be no fault of Jules de Grandin's. *Adieu*, my friend, and may good luck attend me in my errand. *Cordieu*, but I shall need it!"

"DR. TROWBRIDGE, MAY I present Dr. Wolf?" de Grandin requested that evening, standing aside to permit a tall, magnificently built young man to precede him through the doorway of my consulting-room. "I have brought him from New York to take dinner with us, and—perhaps—to aid us in that which we must do tonight without fail."

"How do you do, Dr. Wolf?" I responded formally, taking the visitor's hand in mine, but staring curiously at him the while. Somehow the name given by de Grandin did not seem at all appropriate. He was tall, several inches over six feet, with an enormous breadth of shoulder and extraordinary depth of chest. His face, disproportionately large for even his great body, was high-cheeked and unusually broad, with a jaw of implacable squareness, and the deep-set, burning eyes beneath his overhanging brows were of a peculiarly piercing quality. There was something in the impassive nobility and steadfastness of purpose in that face which reminded me of the features of the central allegorical figure in Franz Stuck's masterpiece, *War*.

Something of my thought must have been expressed in my glance, for the young man noticed it and a smile passed swiftly across his rugged countenance, leaving it calm again in an instant. "The name is a concession to civilization, Doctor," he informed me. "I began life under the somewhat unconventional sobriquet of 'Johnny Curly Wolf,' but that hardly seemed appropriate to my manhood's environment, so I have shortened the name to its greatest common divisor—I'm a full-blooded Dakotah, you know."

"Indeed?" I replied lamely.

"Yes. I've been a citizen for a number of years, for there are certain limitations on the men of my people who retain their tribal allegiance which would hamper me greatly in my lifework. My father became wealthy by grace of the white man's bounty and the demands of a growing civilization for fuel-oil, and he had the good judgment to have me educated in an Eastern university instead of one of the Indian training schools. An uncle of mine was a tribal medicine man and I was slated to follow in his footsteps, but I determined to graft the white man's scientific medicine onto my primitive instruction. Medical work has appealed to me ever since I was a little shaver and was permitted to help the post surgeon at the agency office. I received my license to practice in '14, and was settling down to a study of pulmonary diseases when the big unpleasantness broke out in Europe."

He smiled again, somewhat grimly this time. "My people have been noted for rather bloody work in the old days, you know, and I suppose the call of my lineage was too strong for me. At any rate, I was inside a Canadian uniform and overseas within two months of the call for Dominion troops, and for three solid years I was in the thick of it with the British. When we came in I was transferred to the A.E.F., and finished my military career in a burst of shrapnel in the Argonne. I've three silver bones in each leg now and am drawing half-compensation from the government every month. I indorse the check over to the fund to relieve invalid Indian veterans of the army who aren't as well provided with worldly goods by Standard Oil as I am."

"But are you practising in New York now, Doctor?" I asked.

"Only as a student. I've been taking some special post-graduate work in diseases of the lungs and posterior poliomyelitis. As soon as my studies are completed I'm going west to devote my life and fortune to fighting those twin scourges of my people."

"Just so," de Grandin cut in, unable longer to refrain from taking part in the conversation. "Dr. Wolf and I have had many interesting things to speak of during our trip from New York, Friend Trowbridge, and now, if all is prepared, shall we eat?"

The young Indian proved a charming dinner companion. Finely educated and highly cultured, he was indued with extraordinary skill as a raconteur, and his matter-of-fact stories of the "old contemps'" titanic struggle from the Marne and back, night raids in the trenches and desperate hand-to-hand fights in the blackness of No Man's Land, of the mud and blood and silent heroism of the dressing-stations and of the phantom armies which rallied to the assistance of the British at Mons were colorful as the scenes of some old Spanish tapestry. Dinner was long since over and eleven o'clock had struck, still we lingered over our cigars, liqueurs and coffee in the drawing-room. It was de Grandin who dragged us back from the days of '15 with a hasty glance at the watch strapped to his wrist.

"*Parbleu*, my friends," he exclaimed, "it grows late and we have a desperate experiment to try before the moon passes the meridian. Come, let us be about our work."

I looked at him in amazement, but the young Indian evidently understood his meaning, for he rose with a shrug of his broad shoulders and followed my diminutive companion out into the hall where a great leather kit bag which bore evidence of having accompanied its owner through Flanders and Picardy rested beside the hall rack. "What's on the program?" I demanded, trailing in the wake of the other two, but de Grandin thrust hat and coat into my hands, exclaiming:

"We go to Madame Chetwynde's again, my friend. Remember what you saw about this time last night? *Cordieu*, you shall see that which has been vouch-safed to few men before another hour has passed, or Jules de Grandin is wretch-edly mistaken!"

Piling my companions into the back seat, I took the wheel and drove through the still, moonlit night toward the Chetwynde cottage. Half an hour later we let ourselves quietly into the house with de Grandin's duplicate key and took our station in the darkened parlor once more.

A quick word from de Grandin gave Dr. Wolf his cue, and taking up his travel-beaten bag the young Indian let himself out of the house and paused on the porch. For a moment I saw his silhouette against the glass panel of the door, then a sudden movement carried him out of my line of vision, and I turned to watch the stairs down which I knew Idoline Chetwynde would presently come to perform her unholy rites of secret worship.

The ticking pulse-beats of the little ormolu clock on the mantelpiece sounded thunderous in the absolute quiet of the house; here and there a board squeaked and cracked in the gradually lowering temperature; somewhere out-side, a motor horn tooted with a dismal, wailing note. I felt my nerves gradually

tightening like the strings of a violin as the musician keys them up before playing, and tiny shivers of horripilation pursued each other down my spine and up
my forearms as I sat waiting in the shadowy room.

THE LITTLE FRENCH CLOCK struck twelve sharp, silvery chimes. It had arrived,
that hideous hour which belongs neither to the day which is dead nor to the
new day stirring in the womb of Time, and which we call midnight for want of a
better term. The moon's pale visage slipped slowly into view through the panes
of the window behind the Indian statue and a light, faltering step sounded on
the stairs above us.

"*Mon Dieu*," de Grandin whispered fervently, "grant that I shall not have
made a mistake in my calculations!" He half rose from his chair, gazing fixedly
at the lovely, unconscious woman walking her tranced march toward the repel-
lent idol, then stepped softly to the front window and tapped lightly on its pane
with his fingertips.

Once again we saw Idoline Chetwynde prostrate herself at the feet of the
black statue; once more her fluttering, breathless voice besought the evil thing
to take her soul and destroy her body; then, so faint I scarcely heard it through
the droning of the praying woman's words, the front door gave a soft click as it
swung open on its hinges.

Young Dr. Wolf, once Johnny Curly Wolf, medicine man of the Dakotahs,
stepped into the moonlit hall.

Now I understood why he had hidden himself in the shadows of the porch
when he left the house. Gone were his stylishly cut American clothes, gone was
his air of well-bred sophistication. It was not the highly educated, cultured physician and student who entered the Chetwynde home, but a medicine man of
America's primeval race in all the panoply of his traditional office. Naked to the
waist he was, his bronze torso gleaming like newly molded metal from the furnace. Long, tight-fitting trousers of beaded buckskin encased his legs, and on his
feet were the moccasins of his forefathers. Upon his head was the war-bonnet of
eagle feathers, and his face was smeared with alternate streaks of white, yellow
and black paint. In one hand he bore a bullhide tom-tom, and in his deep-set,
smoldering eyes there burned the awful, deadly earnestness of his people.

Majestically he strode down the hall, paused some three or four paces
behind the prostrate woman, then, raising his tom-tom above his head, struck
it sharply with his knuckles.

Toom, toom, toom, toom! the mellow, booming notes sounded, again and
still again. Bending slightly at the knees, he straightened himself, repeated the
movement, quickened the cadence until he was rising and sinking a distance of
six inches or so in a sort of stationary, bobbing dance. "Manitou, Great Spirit
of my fathers!" he called in a strong, resonant voice. "Great Spirit of the forest

dwellers and of the people of the plains, hear the call of the last of Thy worshipers:

> Hear my prayer, O Mighty Spirit,
> As I do the dance before Thee,
> Do the dance my fathers taught me,
> Dance it as they danced before me,
> As they danced it in their lodges,
> As they danced it at their councils
> When of old they sought Thy succor.

> Look upon this prostrate woman,
> See her bow in supplication
> To an alien, wicked spirit.
> Thine she is by right of lineage,
> Thine by right of blood and forebears.
> In the cleanly air of heaven
> She should make her supplication,
> Not before the obscene statue
> Of god of alien people.

> Hear my prayer, O Mighty Spirit,
> Hear, Great Spirit of my fathers,
> Save this woman of Thy people,
> Smite and strike and make impotent
> Demons from across the water,
> Demons vile and wholly filthy,
> And not seemly for devotion
> From a woman of Thy people.

The solemn, monotonous intoning ceased, but the dance continued. But
now it was no longer a stationary dance, for, with shuffling tread and half-bent
body, Johnny Curly Wolf was circling slowly about the Hindoo idol and its lone
worshiper.

Something—a cloud, perhaps—drifted slowly across the moon's face,
obscuring the light which streamed into the hall. An oddly shaped cloud it was,
something like a giant man astride a giant horse, and on his brow there seemed
to be the feathered war-bonnet of the Dakotahs. The cloud grew in density. The
moon rays became fainter and fainter, and finally the hall was in total darkness.

In the west there sounded the whistling bellow of a rising wind, shaking the
casements of the house and making the very walls tremble. Deep and rumbling,

growing louder and louder as it seemed to roll across the heavens on iron wheels, a distant peal of thunder sounded, increased in volume, finally burst in a mighty clap directly over our heads, and a fork of blinding, jagged lightning shot out of the angry sky. A shivering ring of shattered glass and of some heavy object toppling to a fall, a woman's wild, despairing shriek, and another rumbling, crashing peal of thunder deafened me.

By the momentary glare of a second lightning-flash I beheld a scene stranger than any painted by Dante in his vision of the underworld. Seemingly, a great female figure crouched with all the ferocity of a tigress above the prostrate form of Idoline Chetwynde, its writhing, sextuple arms grasping at the woman's prone body or raised as though to ward off a blow, while from the window looking toward the west there leaped the mighty figure of an Indian brave armed with shield and war-club.

Johnny Curly Wolf? No! For Johnny Curly Wolf circled and gyrated in the measures of his tribal ghost-dance, and in one hand he held his tom-tom, while with the other he beat out the rhythm of his dance-music.

It was but an instant that the lightning showed me this fantastic tableau, then all was darkness blacker than before, and a crashing of some stone thing shattered into half a thousand fragments broke through the rumble of the thunder.

"Lights! *Grand Dieu*, lights, Friend Trowbridge!" de Grandin screamed in a voice gone high and thin with hysteria.

I pressed the electric switch in the hall and beheld Johnny Curly Wolf, still in tribal costume, great beads of sweat dewing his brow, standing over the body of Idoline Chetwynde, the hall window-panes blown from their frame and scattered over the floor like tiny slivers of frozen moonlight, and, toppled from its pedestal and broken into bits almost as fine as powder, the black statue of Kali, Goddess of the East.

"Take her up, my friend," de Grandin ordered me, pointing to Mrs. Chetwynde's lifeless body. "Pick her up and restore her to her bed. *Morbleu*, but we shall have to attend her like a new-born infant this night, for I fear me her nerves have had a shock from which they will not soon recover!"

All night and far past daylight we sat beside Idoline Chetwynde's bed, watching the faint color ebb and flow in her sunken checks, taking heedful count of her feebly beating pulse, administering stimulants when the tiny spark of waning life seemed about to flicker to extinction.

About ten o'clock in the morning de Grandin rose from his seat beside the bed and stretched himself like a cat rising from prolonged sleep. "*Bon, très bon!*" he exclaimed. "She sleeps. Her pulse, it is normal; her temperature, it is right. We can safely leave her now, my friends. Anon we shall call on her; but I doubt me if we shall have more to do than wish her felicitations on her so miraculous cure. Meantime, let us go. My poor, forgotten stomach cries aloud reproaches on my so neglected mouth. I starve, I famish, I faint of inanition. Behold, I am already become but a wraith and a shadow!"

J ULES DE GRANDIN DRAINED his third cup of coffee at a gulp and passed the empty vessel back for replenishment. "*Parbleu*, my friends," he exclaimed, turning his quick, elfin smile from Dr. Wolf to me, "it was the beautiful adventure, was it not?"

"It might have been a beautiful adventure," I agreed grudgingly, "but just what the deuce *was* it? The whole thing's a mystery to me from beginning to end. What caused Mrs. Chetwynde's illness in the first place, what was the cause of her insane actions, and what was it I saw last night? Was there really a thunderstorm that broke the black image, and did I really see—"

"But certainly, my excellent one," he cut in with a smile as he emptied his cup and lighted a cigarette, "you did behold all that you thought you saw; no less."

"But—"

"No buts, if you please, good friend. I well know you will tease for an explanation as a pussy-cat begs for food while the family dines, and so I shall enlighten you as best I can. To begin:

"When first you told me of Madame Chetwynde's illness I knew not what to think, nor did I think anything in particular. Some of her symptoms made me fear she might have been the victim of a *revenant*, but there were no signs of blood-letting upon her, and so I dismissed that diagnosis. But as we descended the stairs after our first visit, I did behold the abominable statue in the hall. 'Ah ha,' I say to me, 'what does this evil thing do here? Perhaps it makes the trouble with Madame Idoline?' And so I look at it most carefully.

"My friends, Jules de Grandin has covered much land with his little feet. In the arctic snows and in the equatorial heat he has seen the sins and follies and superstitions of men, and learned to know the gods they worship. So he recognized that image for what it was. It is of the goddess Kali, tutelary deity of the *Thags* of India, whose worship is murder and whose service is bloodshed. She goes by many names, my friends: sometimes she is known as Devi, consort of Siva and daughter of Himavat, the Himalaya Mountains. She is the Sakti, or female energy of Siva, and is worshiped in a variety of forms under two main classes, according as she is conceived as a mild and beneficent or as a malignant deity. In her milder shapes besides Devi, 'the goddess,' she is called also Gauri, 'the yellow,' or Uma, 'the bright.' In her malignant forms she is Durga, 'the inaccessible,' represented, as a yellow woman mounted on a tiger, Chandi, 'the fierce,' and, worst of all, Kali, 'the black,' in which guise she is portrayed as dripping with blood, encircled with snakes and adorned with human skulls.

In the latter form she is worshiped with obscene and bloody rites, oftener than not with human sacrifice. Her special votaries are the *Thags*, and at her dreadful name all India trembles, for the law of the English has not yet wiped out the horrid practice of *thaggee*.

"Now, when I beheld this filthy image standing in Madame Chetwynde's home I wondered much. Still, I little suspected what we later came to know for truth, for it is a strange thing that the gods of the East have little power over the people of the West. Behold, three hundred thousand Englishmen hold in complete subjection as many million Hindoos, though the subject people curse their masters daily by all the gods whom they hold sacred. It seems, I think, that only those who stand closer to the bare verities of nature are liable to be affected by gods and goddesses which are personifications of nature's forces. I know not whether this be so, it is but a theory of mine. At any rate, I saw but small connection between the idol and our sick lady's illness until Friend Trowbridge told me of her strain of Indian ancestry. Then I say to me: 'Might not she, who holds a mixture of aboriginal blood in her veins, become affected by the strength of this heathen goddess? Or perhaps it is that fused blood is weaker than the pure strain, and the evil influence, of the Black One may have found some loophole in her defense.' One thing was most sure, in Madame Chetwynde's house there was clearly the odor of Eastern incense, yet nowhere was there visible evidence of perfume save such as a dainty woman of the West might use. Me, I sniffed like a hound while examining her, and kissed her fingers twice in farewell to make sure. This incense which were so all unaccounted for did puzzle me.

"You recall, Friend Trowbridge, how I questioned her maid about the punk smell, and how little satisfaction I got of her. 'There is going on here the business of monkeys,' I tell me as we leave the house. And so I make a print of the front door key that we may enter again at our convenience and see what is what.

"*Eh bien*, my friends, did we not see a sufficiency the following night when we beheld Madame Idoline fall forward on her face and make a voluntary offer of her soul and body to the Black One? I shall say so.

"'How to overcome this Eastern fury?' I ask me. 'The excellent Katy Rooney have bathed her in holy water, and the blessed fluid have burned and sizzled on her so infamous head. Clearly, the force of Western churches is of little value in this case. Ah, perhaps she *have* attacked Madame Chetwynde through her strain of primitive blood. Then what?'

"*Mort d'un chat*, all suddenly I have it! At the dinner in New York I have met the young Dr. Wolf. He is a full-blood Indian and, he have told me, a medicine man of his people, as well. Now, if this woman's weakness is her Indian blood, may not that same blood be her strength and her protection as well? I hope so.

"So I persuade Monsieur Wolf to come with me and pit the strength of his Great Spirit against the evil force of Kali of the *Thags*. Who will win? *Le bon Dieu* alone knows, but I have hopes."

For a moment he regarded us with a quizzical smile, then resumed:

"The Indian of America, my friends, was truly *un sauvage noble*. The Spaniard saw in him only something like a beast to be enslaved and despoiled; the Englishman saw in him only a barrier to possession of the new country, and as such to be swept back or exterminated; but to the Frenchman he was a noble character. Ha, did not my illustrious countrymen, the Sieurs La Salle and Frontenac, accord him his just dues? Certainly. His friendship was true, his courage undoubted, his religion a clean one. Why, then, could we not invoke the Indians' Great Spirit?

"We know, my friends, or at least we think we know, that there is but one true God, almighty and everlasting, without body, parts or passions; but does that same God appear in the same manner to all peoples? *Mais non*. To the Arab he is Allah; to many so-called Christians He is but a sort of celestial Santa Claus; I greatly fear, Friend Trowbridge, that to many of your most earnest preachers He is little more than a disagreeable old man with the words 'Thou Shalt Not!' engraved upon His forehead. But, for all these different conceptions, He is still God.

"And what are these deities of heathendom?" He paused, looking expectantly from one of us to the other, but as we made no reply, proceeded to answer his own question: "They are nothing, and yet they are something, too. They are the concentrated power of thought, of mistaken belief, of misconception. Yet, because thoughts are truly things, they have a certain power—*parbleu*, I think a power which is not to be sneezed upon. For, years, for centuries, perhaps, that evil statue of Kali has been invoked in bloody and unseemly rites, and before her misshapen feet has been poured out the concentrated hate and wickedness of countless monkey-faced heathens. That did indue her with an evil power which might easily overcome the resistance of a sensitive nature, and all primitive peoples are more sensitive to such influences than are those whose ancestors have long been agnostic, however much and loudly they have prated of their piety.

"Very good. The Great Spirit of the Indian of America, on the other hand, being a clean and noble conception, is one of the manifestations of God Himself. For countless generations the noble Red Man had clothed him with all the attributes of nobility. Shall this pure conception of the godhead go to waste? No, my friends, ten thousand times no! You can not kill a noble thought any more than you can slay a noble soul; both are immortal.

"And so I did prevail upon the good Wolf to come with us and summon the massed thought and belief of his great people to combat the massed thought of those despicable ones who have made them a goddess in the image of their own uncleanness of mind. *Nom d'une anguille*, but the struggle was magnificent!

"You, mean to tell me that I actually saw the Great Spirit, then?" I demanded incredulously.

"*Ah bah*, my friend," he replied, "have I not been at pains to tell you it was the massed, the concentrated thought and belief of all the Indians, of today and for countless generations before today, which our good Wolf invoked? *Mordieu*, can I never convince you that thought, though it be immaterial, is as much a thing as—as for example, the skull in your so thick head?"

"But what about Mrs. Chetwynde's maid?" I asked, for deep in my mind there lurked a suspicion that the woman might know more of the unholy sights we had seen than she cared to tell.

"Quite right," he replied, nodding gravely. "I, too, suspected her once. It was because of that I induced the excellent Katy to return to Madame Idoline's service and spy upon her. I discovered much, for Katy, like all her race, is shrewd, and when she knows what is wanted she knows how to get it. It appears the maid was fully aware of her mistress' subjection to the Black One, but, though she understood it not, so deep was her devotion to *Madame* her mistress that she took it on herself to cast obstacles in our way lest we prevent a continuance of *Madame's* secret worship. Loyalty is a great, a wonderful thing, my friends. That poor woman was shocked by the spectacle of her beloved mistress casting herself before the thing of stone, but the bare fact that her mistress did it was justification enough for her. Had she been asked to do so by Madame Chetwynde, I firmly believe she would have joined in the obscene devotions and given her own body and soul to the Black One along with that of her deluded mistress whom she adored."

"Well—I'll be—But look here—" I began again, but:

"No more, Friend Trowbridge," de Grandin commanded, rising and motioning to Dr. Wolf and me. "It is long since we have slept. Come let us retire. Me, *parbleu*, I shall sleep until your learned societies shall issue profound treatises on the discovery of a twin brother to that Monsieur Rip Van Winkle!"

Mephistopheles and Company, Ltd.

1

"MESSIEURS LES AMERICAINS DEAD on the field of honor, I salute you!" Jules de Grandin drew himself rigidly to attention and raised his cupped hand to his right temple in a smart military salute before the Victory Monument in our city park.

The act was so typical of the little Frenchman that I could not forbear a smile as I glanced covertly at him. Ten thousand times a day friends and neighbors—even relatives—of the gold-starred names on the honor roll of that monument passed through the park, yet of all the passers-by Jules de Grandin was the only one who habitually rendered military honors to the cenotaph each time his steps led past it.

His sharp little blue eyes caught the flicker of my smile as we turned from the memorial, and the heat-lightning flash of resentment rose in them. "Ha, do you laugh at my face, Friend Trowbridge?" he demanded sharply. "*Cordieu*, I tell you, it would be well for your country if more persons paid honor to the brave lads who watered the fields of France with their blood that Freedom might survive! So busy you are in this peaceful land that you have no time to remember the wounds and blood and broken bodies which bought that peace; no time to remember how the *sale boche*—

"*Misère de Dieu*, what have we here?" One of his white, womanish hands grasped me so sharply by the arm that I winced under the pressure. His free hand pointed dramatically down the curving, shrub-bordered path before us.

"Eh?" I demanded. "What the deuce—?" I swallowed the remainder of my question as my gaze followed the line of his pointing finger.

A young woman in evening dress, tear-stains on her cheeks and stark, abject terror in her eyes, was running stumblingly toward us.

"*Lieber Gott!*" she cried in a horrified whisper, shrill and thin-edged as a scream, then struggled for breath in a paroxysm of sobs and glanced frightenedly behind her. "*Ach, lieber Himmel!*"

"*Favoris d'un rat,*" murmured de Grandin wonderingly, "a woman of the *boche?*"

"*Enschuldige mich, Fräulein,*" he began, making a wry face, as though the German words were quinine on his tongue, "*bitte—*"

The result of his salutation was as forceful as it was unexpected. Throwing her hands before her eyes, as though to shut out a vision too terrible for mortal sight, the girl uttered a terrified, despairing shriek, swerved sharply away and dashed past him with a bound like that of a rabbit startled by a hound. Half a dozen fear-spurred steps farther down the path her knees seemed to melt under her, she wavered uncertainly a moment, then collapsed to the pavement with a pitiful little moan, huddled in a lovely heap of disordered dark hair and disarranged costume, shuddered tremblingly, then lay still.

"*Pardonnez-moi, Mademoiselle*"—de Grandin flung the girl's native tongue aside—"you seem in trouble. Is there anything—?" He felt her wrists for a feebly fluttering pulse, then laid a tentative hand on her left breast. "*Morbleu* Trowbridge, my friend," he exclaimed, "she has fainted unconscious! Assist me, we must take her home for treatment. I think—"

"Exguse me, zur," a thick-toned voice cut through his words as a big young man in dinner clothes emerged from behind a clump of shrubs with the suddenness of a Jack-in-the-box popping from its case, "exguse me, zur, but I know the young lady, und I zhall be ver-ee gladt her to dake home if you will so kind be as to call me a cab. I—"

"*Ha,* do you say so?" The little Frenchman dropped the swooning girl's wrist and bounded to his feet, glaring up into the other's face with a fierce, unwinking stare. "Perhaps, then, *Monsieur,* you can tell us why Mademoiselle is running through the park at this hour of night, and why she becomes unconscious on our hands. *N'est-ce-pas?*"

The stranger drew himself up with an air of sudden hauteur. "I am not obliged to you exblanations make," he began. "I dell you I know the young lady, und vill—"

"*Nom, d'un chat,* this is too much!" de Grandin blazed. "I make no doubt you know her entirely too well for her comfort, *Monsieur,* and that you should demand that we turn her over to you—*parbleu,* it is the insult to our intelligence; it is—"

"Look out, de Grandin!" I cried, springing forward to intercept the sudden thrust the other aimed at my friend's face with a queer-looking, shining instrument. My move was a split-second too late, but my warning shout came in time. Even as I called, the little Frenchman wrenched himself back as though preparing to turn a reversed handspring, both his feet flew upward, and his assailant collapsed to the grass with an agonized grunt as de Grandin's right heel caught him a devastating blow in the solar plexus.

"Trowbridge, *mon vieux*," he remarked matter-of-factly as he regarded his fallen foeman, "behold the advantage of *la savate*. At handgrips I should have been as nothing against this miscreant. In the foot-boxing"—he paused, and his little round eyes shone with a momentary flash of amusement—"there he lies. Come, let us convey *Mademoiselle* to your office. I doubt not she can tell us something of much interest."

TOGETHER WE ASSISTED THE still fainting girl to the cross street and signaled a passing taxicab. As the vehicle started toward my house I demanded: "Why in the world did you knock that fellow out, de Grandin? He really might have been a friend of this young lady's, and—"

"The good God protect us from such friends," the little Frenchman cut in. "Attend me, if you please. As we turned away from the monument in the park I did first see this woman. She was running in a zigzag course, like a hare seeking to elude the pack, and I greatly wondered at her antics. All Americans are a little mad, I think, but"—he gave a short chuckle—"there is usually method behind their madness. That a young lady of fashionable appearance should run thus through the public park at a quarter to midnight seemed to be beyond the bounds of reason, but what I saw next gave me to think violently. Before she had gone a dozen steps, a man appeared from behind a patch of bushes and took off his hat to her, speaking words which seemed to cause her fright. She turned and ran toward the other side of the park, and another man arose from behind a bench, removed his hat and said something, whereat she flung up her hands and turned again, running toward us, and going faster with each step. A moment before I invited your attention to her, a third man—*morbleu*, it was the same one I later caressed with my heel!—addressed her. It was immediately afterward, as she came toward us with a great fear upon her, that I called your attention."

"H'm," I muttered, "he—flirts?"

"*Non*," he negatived. "I do not think they were making the—how do you say it? mash?—on her. No, it was something more serious, my friend. Listen: I did behold the faces of the men who accosted her, *and each face was as it had been aflame with fire!*"

"Wha—*what?*" I shot back. "Aflame with—whatever are you talking about?"

"I tell you no more than what I saw," he returned equably. "Each man's face glowed with a light like that of a long-dead carcass which shines and stinks in the swamps at night. Also, my friend, I did perceive that each man reached out and touched her with a wand like that with which the so detestable rogue would have struck me, had I not spoiled his plan with my boot."

"My dear chap, you're surely dreaming!" I scoffed. "Men with fiery faces accosting young women in the public park, and touching them with magic wands! This is the State of New Jersey in the Twentieth Century, not Baghdad in the days of the Calif Haroun!"

"U'm," he returned noncommittally. The flame of his match flared lambently as he set a cigarette alight. "Perhaps, my friend. Let us see what the young lady has to say when we have restored her to consciousness. *Pardieu*, I shall be greatly surprised if we are not astounded at her story!"

2

" A LITTLE ETHER, IF YOU please, Friend Trowbridge," de Grandin ordered when we had carried the swooning girl into my surgery and laid her on the examination table. "Her heart action is very slow, and the ether will stimulate—"

A deep-drawn, shuddering moan from our patient interrupted him. "*Ach, lieber Himmel!*" she exclaimed feebly, throwing out her arms with a convulsive movement as her lids fluttered a moment before unveiling a pair of cornflower-blue eyes. "Oh, God of Heaven, I am lost—destroyed—hopelessly damned! Have mercy, Mary!" Her lovely eyes, wide and shining with terror, gazed wildly about the room a moment, came to rest on de Grandin as he bent over her, and closed in sharp nictitation. "*Ach—*" she began again hysterically, but the Frenchman broke in, speaking slowly and mouthing the German words as though they had been morsels of overheated food on his tongue.

"*Fräulein*, you are with friends. We found you in trouble in the park a short time ago, and when you fainted we brought you here. If you will tell us where you live, or where you wish to go, we shall be very glad—"

"*Ach, ja, ja*, take me"—the girl burst out wildly—"take me away; take me where *he* can not get me. Almighty God, what do I say? How can I, the hopelessly damned, escape him, either in life or death? Oh, woe me; woe me!" She knit her slender, nervous fingers together with a wringing, hopeless movement, turning her face to the wall and weeping bitterly.

De Grandin regarded her speculatively a moment, twisting first one, then the other end of his little blond mustache. "I think you would best be securing the restorative, Friend Trowbridge," he remarked; "she seems in great distress.

"Now, *Mademoiselle*," he held the tumbler of chilled water and ether to the sobbing girl's lips and patted her shoulder reassuringly, "you will have the kindness to drink this and compose yourself. Undoubtlessly you have had many troubles, but here you are safe—"

"Safe, *safe*?" she echoed with a hysterical laugh. "*I* safe? There is no safety for me—no spot on earth or in hell where *he* can not find me, and since heaven is forever barred against me, how can I find safety anywhere?"

"*Morbleu, Mademoiselle*, I fear you distress yourself needlessly," the Frenchman exclaimed. "Who is this so mysterious 'he' who pursues you?"

"*Mephistopheles!*" So softly did she breathe the name that we could scarcely recognize the syllables.

"Eh? What is it you say?" de Grandin demanded.

"Mephistopheles—the Devil—Satan! I am possessed by him, sold and bound to him irrevocably through time and all eternity. Oh, miserable me! Alas, that ever I was born!"

She sobbed hysterically a moment, then regarded him with wide, piteous eyes. "You don't believe me," she wailed. "No one believes me, they think I'm crazy, but—"

"*Mademoiselle*," de Grandin interrupted, speaking with the sharp, incisive enunciation of a physician addressing a patient who refuses to control her nerves, "we have not said so. Only fools refuse to believe that which they do not understand, and Jules de Grandin is no fool. I have said it. If there is anything you would have us know, speak on, for we listen." He drew a chair up to the couch where the girl lay, and leaned toward her. "Proceed, *Mademoiselle*."

"My name is Mueller, Bertha Mueller," the girl answered, dabbing at her eyes with a wisp of lace and cambric. "I am from Vienna. A year ago I came here to accept a post as instructress to the children of Herr Andreas Hopfer, who represents the *Deutsche-Rotofabrik Verein*."

"U'm," de Grandin commented.

"This new country was so strange to me," she continued, growing calmer with her recital; "nowhere, outside the house of my employer and a few of his friends, could I find anyone who spoke my mother tongue. I was lonesome. For comfort I used to sit in the park and watch the pigeons while I thought of Vienna—the old Vienna of the empire, not the poverty-stricken city of the mongrel republic. An old lady, a beautiful, white-haired lady, came to sit on a bench near mine. She seemed sad and thoughtful, too, and one day when she addressed me, my heart nearly burst with joy. She was a Frau Stoeger, and like me she came from Vienna; like me, she had lost her nearest ones in the war our envious foes forced upon us."

De Grandin twisted fiercely at the waxed ends of his little mustache and something very like a snort of contempt escaped him, but he controlled himself with a visible effort and nodded for her to proceed.

"One afternoon, when I had told her how my noble brothers died gloriously at the Piave," the girl went on, "she suggested that we go to a spiritualistic friend of hers and see if it were possible for us to converse with the beloved dead. I shrank from the suggestion at first, for Holy Church frowns on such attempts to pierce the veil heaven hangs between us and the blessed ones who sleep in the Lord, but she finally persuaded me, and we went to see the medium."

"Ah?" de Grandin nodded understandingly. "I suppose this Madame Medium told you most remarkable things?"

"*Nein, mein Herr*," the girl negatived eagerly. "That she did not. Me she would have no intercourse with. 'Out of my sight and out of my house!' she cried the moment I entered the room where she sat. 'Begone, accursed woman, you are possessed of devils!' she told me, and moaned and screamed until I had left the building."

"*Parbleu*, this is of the strange unusualness!" de Grandin muttered. "Proceed, *Mademoiselle*, I listen."

"Frau Stoeger was almost as embarrassed as I at the strange reception," the girl replied, "but she told me not to lose hope. Too late she confided that when she first went to the medium's she, too, was bidden to depart because a minor imp had fastened on her; yet she went to a learned man who could cast out devils and had the spirit exorcized without trouble or expense, for the Herr Doktor Martulus will take no fees for his work. Now she is one of the most intimate members of the circle over which Laïla, the Medium, presides."

"Yes? And then?" the Frenchman prompted.

"That very night we drove into the country and met the professor. He listened sympathetically to my case and gave me a little box of pills which I was to take. I followed his directions to the letter, but the pills made me very sick, so I stopped them.

"Next time I met Frau Stoeger she questioned me concerning the medicine, and when she learned it had made me ill, she said it was a very evil sign, and begged me with tears to go for another consultation.

"The moment Professor Martulus saw me he seemed greatly alarmed and called a council of his associates, telling them he was certain I was possessed by one of the major fiends, since the medicine he had given me had never before failed to drive the lesser demons from their victims. But they all assured me there was no need to fear, since Belial, Mammon and even dread Milchim could be thrown from their possession by their spells. Only one demon was proof against them, and that one was Mephistopheles, the Fiend of Fiends, Satan's other self. If *he* claimed me for his own, my case was well-nigh hopeless.

"They took me to an inner chamber where the mystic rites began, and by their magic they sought the name of the fiend possessing me. All efforts were vain, and no response came to their questions until, in fear and trembling, the professor called upon the archfiend himself.

"The dreadful name had hardly passed his lips before the whole building shook with a terrible explosion, blinding flames shot to the ceiling, and I was half smothered by the fumes of sulfur and brimstone. Something hit me on the head, and I lost consciousness. The next thing I knew I was being rushed back to town in a speeding automobile with Frau Stoeger. When I tried to snuggle up to her for comfort, she drew away from me and bade me never touch her, or even look at her again. I was marked by the Devil for his own, and even my breath or glance brought misfortune to those they touched.

"My good, kind sir,"—she regarded de Grandin with a steadfast, pleading stare, like a child striving desperately to convince a skeptical adult of the truth of a preposterous story—"I did not then believe. Much talk I had heard of devils in my childhood, for my nurse was a Hungarian woman, a peasant of the old Magyar stock, and as full of stories of vampires, demons and hobgoblins as a chestnut shell is of prickles, but never had I thought the tales of devils were more than fairy lore. Alas! I was soon to learn the Devil is as real today as when he bought Faustus' soul from him.

"The very next day as I went for my regular walk in the park a little child   a pretty little girl playing with her colored nurse by the goldfish fountain—ran to me with outstretched arms, and as I stooped to clasp her to my bosom she halted, looked at me in terror, then ran screaming to her nurse, crying out that the Devil stood behind me and reached over my shoulder for her. The Negro nurse took one look at me, then made the sign of the evil eye, thus." She bent her thumb transversely across the palm of her hand, encircling it with the second and third fingers, permitting the fore- and little fingers to stand out like a pair of horns, and thrust them toward us. "And as the woman made the sign," the girl sobbed, "she bade me begone to hell, where Satan, my master, awaited me; then hurried from the square with the little girl."

De Grandin pinched his little, pointed chin between a thoughtful thumb and forefinger. "More than a thousand damns!" he exclaimed softly. "There is the monkey's business here, of a surety. Proceed, *Mademoiselle*."

"I became a marked woman," she obeyed. "People turned to stare at me in the street, and all made the sign of the horns at me, Once, as I hurried through the park after sunset, *I saw the Devil grinning at me from behind a bunch of rhododendrons!*

"Finally, I was ready to sell my soul for a moment's peace. Then, by chance, I met Frau Stoeger again in the park. She blessed herself at sight of me, but did not run away, and when I spoke to her, she listened. I begged her on my bended knees to take me to Professor Martulus once more to see if he could break Satan's hold from off my wretched soul.

"That night I went to see the professor once more, and he told me there was one chance in a thousand of my regaining my freedom, but only at the cost of the most terrible sacrifice of humiliation and suffering. When he told me what I should have to do—oh, do not ask me to repeat it!—I was so horrified that I fainted, but there was no help for it. Either I must go through the ordeal he proposed or be forever devil-ridden. At last they said I might hire a substitute, but that I must pay her two thousand dollars. Where was I, a poor governess, almost a beggar, to obtain such a sum? It might as well have been a million!

"Frau Stoeger suggested that I borrow it from my employer. He is wealthy, and she knew I had the combination to his safe and access to a book of signed checks which he keeps in his library desk. When I refused she laughed and said, 'You'll be glad to do worse things than forge a check or steal some paltry jewelry before you're free, my dear.'

"That was a week ago. Since then my life has been an earthly hell. Everywhere I have seen reminders of my dreadful fate. Children scream at the sight of me, women cross the street to avoid me, men turn and sneer as I pass by. Tonight I attended a party at my employer's house, though I felt little enough like dancing. Finally, when I knew I must be alone or go mad, I went for a walk in the park.

"*Mein Herr*—believe me; oh, please believe what I say!—as I entered the square the Devil stepped from behind a patch of bushes and raised his hat to me, saying, 'When are you coming to dwell in hell with me?' As he finished speaking he stretched out his hand and touched me, and *it burned like a white-hot iron!*

"I was terrified at the apparition, but thought my nerves had played a trick on me, so I began to run. Fifty feet farther on, the Devil rose up again, doffed his hat as before, and asked me the same question. And again he touched me with his fiery claw. I screamed and ran like a frightened cat from a pursuing hound, and just before I met you the Devil appeared to me a third time, asked me the same question, and added, 'I have put my mark on you three times tonight, so all who see you shall know you for mine.' At that I went quite mad, *mein Herr*, and ran as I had never run before. When you stepped forward with your offer of help, I thought you were the fiend accosting me for a fourth time, and I must have fainted, for I know nothing more until I found myself here."

"And how did the Devil appear, *Mademoiselle?*" asked de Grandin, edging slightly forward on his chair, his slender hands twitching with excitement.

"Very like a man, *mein Herr*. His body was like that of a man in evening dress, but his face was the face of the foul fiend and the horns which grew from his brows and the beard and mustache on his face were all aglow with the fires of hell. When he spoke, he spoke in German."

"I doubt it not!" de Grandin acquiesced, *sotto voce*, then aloud: "And you say he touched you with his claw? Where?"

"Here!" the girl returned in a stifled whisper, laying a trembling hand on one bare shoulder. "Here and here and here!" In quick succession her pointed finger touched her shoulder, her upper arm and the white half-moon of her bosom where the top of her bodice curved below her slender throat.

"*Sang d'un poisson!*—one thousand pale blue roosters!" de Grandin exclaimed between gasps of incredulity. At each place the girl indicated on her white skin there showed, red and angry, the seared, scorched soreness of a newly made burn; the crude design of a countenance of incomparable evil—a horned, bearded face, surmounted by the device of an inverted passion-cross.

Jules de Grandin regarded the brands on the girl's tender flesh with a wondering, speculative gaze, his lips pursed in a soundless whistle beneath the up-rearing ends of his waxed mustache; his little, round blue eyes seemed to snap and sparkle with flashes of light.

At length: "Name of an old and very immoral cockroach, this is abominable!" he flared. "Who and where is this medium of spirits?"

"They call her Laïla the Seeress," the girl replied with a shudder. "Her atelier is in Tecumseh Street; she—"

"*Très bien*," de Grandin broke in, "you will return to her and tell her—"

"I couldn't—*I couldn't!*" the denial was a wail of mingled terror and repulsion.

"Nevertheless, *Mademoiselle*," de Grandin continued as though she had not interrupted, "you will go to her tomorrow afternoon and tell her you have decided to hire a substitute to undergo the ordeal for you.

"*Parbleu*, but you will," he insisted as she made a half-frantic gesture of dissent. "You will visit her tomorrow, and Dr. Trowbridge and I will go with you. We shall pose as new-found friends who have agreed to finance your employment of an agent, and you shall suffer no harm, for we shall be with you. Meantime"—he consulted the tiny gold watch strapped to his wrist—"it grows late. Come; Dr. Trowbridge and I will take you to Monsieur Hopfer's house and see you safely within doors."

"But," she protested, snatching at his jacket sleeve as a drowning person might clutch a rope, "but, *mein Herr*, what of the Devil? I am afraid. Suppose he—"

A tiny network of wrinkles deepened suddenly about the outer corners of de Grandin's small, round eyes. From the side pocket of his dinner coat he produced a long-barreled French army revolver and patted its walnut stock affectionately. "*Mademoiselle*," he assured her, "should *Monsieur le Diable* manifest himself to us, I think we have here the fire necessary to fight him. Come—*allons* let us go."

"Just what is your idea of mixing up in this nonsense?" I demanded somewhat coolly as we drove home from returning Fräulein Mueller to her employer's house. "This looks like a plain case of hysteria to me, and what you expect to accomplish is more than I—"

"Indeed?" he answered sarcastically. "The brands on Mademoiselle Mueller's flesh, they, too, were perhaps marks of hysteria?"

"Well," I temporized, "I can't exactly account for them, but—"

"But you are like all other good, kind souls who see no farther than the points of their noses and declare all outside that distance to be non-existent," he interrupted with a grin. "*Non, non,* Trowbridge, my friend, I fear you are unable to recognize the beans, even when the sack has been opened for you. Consider, *mon ami,* think, cogitate and reflect on what we have witnessed this night. Recall the details of the young lady's story, if you please.

"Does not her experience point to a great, a marvelously organized criminal band as plainly as a road map indicates the motorist's route? I think yes. Alone and friendless in a strange city, she meets a woman who claims to come from her own country—after she has been told first what that country is. Is that only happen-so? I think no. The girl must have let slip the information that she has access to her master's safe and checkbook, and so she was deemed fitting prey for this criminal gang. Does not every step of her path of misfortune mark the trail these wicked ones followed to bring her to a state of desperation where she would be ready to commit larceny?

"What of the supposed demon who accosted her in the park tonight? She thought he was one, but I saw three men rise up from behind shrubbery and address her. I, too, saw their faces shine with fire, but it was not the fire of flame, as she believed. *Mais non,* did I not say it was like the light given off by rotting carcasses? What then? The answer is simple. Me, I believe these three men who seemed but one to her, wore false beards and eyebrows—masks, perhaps—which were smeared with some sort of luminous paint, the better to simulate the popular conception of the Devil and terrify a girl already half insane with terror.

"Very well, let us proceed another step. The big young man who came upon us so suddenly, the man who claimed to know her and would have borne her off had I not argued with him with the heel of the boot—did he, too, not speak with the accent of the German tongue, even as she does? Surely. Beyond doubt, my friend, he was one of the three men with fiery faces who had addressed her a moment before, and who sought to take her from us when he thought we would rescue her.

"Another thing: I have noted the manners and customs of many men in many places, and I know the charms they employ against evil. 'What of that?' you ask. 'This,' I reply: 'Never does the American or Englishman make the sign of the horns to ward off the evil eye. That is distinctly a continental European custom.' Therefore, when I hear the Negro nurse made the horns at Mademoiselle Mueller in the park I smell a fish in her story. Wherever that black woman—undoubtlessly herself an American—learned that sign, she did not learn it from an American. An American seeing her make that sign would have understood nothing from it; but Mademoiselle Mueller is no American. She is fresh from Europe, where that sign means something, and she understood what the Negress meant when she made the horns at her—as it was intended she should."

"Well," I replied, "what's your theory, then?"

"Simply this: The child who fled from Mademoiselle Mueller, the Negro nurse who made the evil sign at her, the people who passed her in the street and turned away—all had been planted in her path for the purpose of wearing down her resistance, of obtaining her goat, as you Americans say. But listen: They demanded of her only two thousand dollars. Why? Because they thought she could get no more. Yet so elaborate a system as theirs surely would not have been organized for the tiny sum they demanded. No, men do not take elephant guns into the fields to hunt butterflies. This poor girl is but one of many victims these rogues have preyed upon. The Stoeger woman is one of their scouts who happened to fall upon her, but they must have imposed on many other foolish women—men, too, undoubtlessly, and therefore—" He paused, his lips parted in an expectant grin, his little eyes gleaming with excitement and elation.

"All right; I'll bite," I replied. "Therefore—"

"Attend me, my friend," he replied irrelevantly; "have you ever been in India?"

"No!"

"Very good. I will tell you things. In that land the natives are much plagued by tigers, is it not so?"

"So I've heard."

"*Parfaitement.* When the white man comes to rid a community of the striped devil of the jungle, what does he do?"

"Do?"

"But of course! He climbs into a convenient tree and waits, does he not, and beneath the tree, for bait, he tethers a luckless goat, is it not so?"

"Why—"

"Very good, my friend. You and I are the hunters. This gang of miscreants are the tigers. The unfortunate Mademoiselle Mueller is—"

"Good heavens, man!" I exclaimed, the full purport of his scheme dawning on me. "You don't mean—"

"But certainly," he nodded with perfect aplomb, "she is the goat who lures the tigers within range of our guns."

His small, even teeth came together with a sharp, decided click. "Come, my friend," he bade as we drew up before my house, "let us to bed. We shall have need of a good night's sleep, for tomorrow—*parbleu*, I damn think we shall have much good sport before we take the pelts from off these two-legged tigers!"

3

A Negro dwarf, whose excessively ugly features were rendered still less prepossessing by deep smallpox pits, opened the stained-glass-and-walnut

door of the big house in Tecumseh Street where we called with Fräulein Mueller about four o'clock the following afternoon.

"Have you an appointment with the Sibyl?" he asked arrogantly as he ushered us into the rug-strewn hall and paused before a heavily curtained doorway.

"*La, la,*" de Grandin murmured wonderingly, "is she then a dentist or physician that one must arrange beforehand to consult her? We have no appointment, my friend; nevertheless, you will inform her that we desire to see her, and
without unnecessary delay."

The undersized servitor blinked in amazement. Callers on Madame Laïla
were wont to arrive in humble mien, apparently, and the little Frenchman's
high-handed manner was a distinct novelty.

"Perhaps the Seeress will consent to see you, even though it's usual to
arrange for a sitting beforehand," he replied in a slightly more cordial tone,
presenting de Grandin with a pencil and pad of paper. "Kindly write your name
on this tablet," he requested, then, as the Frenchman complied: "Tear the sheet
off and put it in your pocket. It is not necessary for the Sibyl to see it in order to
know your name; we only ask that you write it as a guaranty of good faith. Await
me here; I will see if you can be admitted."

We had not long to wait, for the attendant returned almost before the curtains through which he had vanished had ceased to sway, and bowed formally
to us. "The Sibyl will see you, Dr. de Grandin," he announced, holding the
draperies aside.

I gave a slight start as my companion was addressed by name, for I had seen
him stow the folded sheet of paper on which he had scribbled his signature in
his waistcoat pocket.

"Laïla the Seeress sees all and knows all," the black dwarf informed me,
as though reading my mind. "There are no secrets from her. This way, if you
please."

The room we entered was hung with unrelieved black and lighted only by a
lamp with three burners suspended from the ceiling by a bronze chain. Slightly
beyond the center of the apartment sat a young woman garbed in a long loose
robe of some clinging black stuff with a headdress resembling a nun's wimple of
the same sable hue. Her face denoted she was about twenty-five or twenty-six
years old, though, contrary to the usual feminine custom, she appeared anxious
to seem older. Her long, excessively thin arms were bare, as were her neck and
feet, and the contrast of her pale flesh and black draperies in the room was an
eery one. About her waist was a wide belt of shining black leather clasped with
a garnet fastening which flashed fitfully in the chamber's half-light. In one hand
she held a three-foot wand tipped with an ivory hand with outspread fingers,
and she was seated on a sort of three-legged stool roughly resembling an ancient
Greek tripod. From a brazen censer standing on the floor before her emanated

penetrating, acrid odors, while the charcoal fire in the incense pot glowed and sank to dullness alternately as though blown upon by a bellows, though no instrument from which a draft could come was visible.

"What seek ye here, oh man?" she demanded in a hollow, sepulchral voice, fixing her deep-set eyes on de Grandin.

The little Frenchman bowed with continental courtesy. "*Madame*," he explained, "we have learned this unfortunate young lady's plight and have determined to aid her. The sum of two thousand dollars is required in order to save her the pain and humiliation of a most terrifying ordeal, and this sum we are prepared to advance, provided, of course, you can offer proper guaranty—"

"Thy money perish with thee!" rejoined the Seeress furiously, half rising from her tripod; then, as though relenting: "Stay, power over the spirits have I none, but I can direct thee to one whose power is infinite.

"Woman," her glowing, cavernous orbs bored into the frightened blue eyes of the little Austrian girl, "if thou wouldst be freed from the demon who dominates thee, be at this house at precisely seven o'clock this evening. Come alone and bring the money with thee, and—perhaps—Martulus the Mighty will consent to have thee exorcised by proxy. I can promise thee naught, but what I can do, I will. Wilt thou come?"

"*Ach, ja, ja!*" Fräulein Mueller sobbed hysterically, clutching at the Sibyl's black raiment. But the Seeress had risen from her stool and stalked majestically from the room, leaving us bewildered and alone.

"*Mort d'une sèche*," de Grandin chuckled as we re-entered my study and regarded each other across the table, "but the entertainment they furnish at Madame Laïla's is worthy of the Odéon! Behold how they assault the superstitions of the caller at the very front door with their trick of name-reading. *Parbleu*, but it is droll!"

"It seemed mysterious enough to me," I admitted. "Do you know how it was done?"

"*Tiens*, my friend, am I a little, wondering boy to be mystified by the trickery of a fire-eater?" he returned with a grin. "But certainly, it was the simplest of tricks. The top sheet of the tablet whereon I wrote my name was almost as thin as tissue paper and the pencil was so hard I had to bear down heavily in order to leave any mark at all. The second sheet of paper was coated with a thin layer of wax, and when the colored man took the tablet inside with him they simply dusted lampblack over it, then blew it off and read what I had written where the blacking remained in the pencil's impression in the wax. It is very simple."

"Well!" I exclaimed in astonishment. "What made the charcoal brazier glow and subside—"

"Enough!" he interrupted. "We have more to do than explain the cheap wonders of a cheap fortune-teller's establishment this afternoon, my friend. Do you go for a walk, a nap or a game of solitaire. Me, I have much to do between now and seven o'clock. Be sure to have your car ready and waiting at the corner of Tecumseh and Irvine Streets at fifty minutes after six, if you please. I go to perform important duties." And, lighting a cigarette, he picked up his hat and cane and set off for the corner pharmacy humming a snatch of sentimental tune:

> Le souvenir, présent céleste,
> Ombre des biens que l'on n'a plus,
> Est encore un plaisir qui reste,
> Après tons ceux qu'on a perdus.

4

FROM THE SHELTER OF a convenient areaway de Grandin and I watched the door of Laïla's house as the city hall clock boomed out the hour of seven.

Falteringly, plainly in a state bordering on collapse, but more afraid of turning back than of unknown dangers before her, Fräulein Mueller mounted the mansion's wide stone steps and rang the doorbell timidly.

As soon as the black dwarf had admitted her, de Grandin leaped up the area steps and hastened across the street to the big, black limousine parked before Laïla's door. For a moment he fumbled about the car's gas tank, then sped back to where I waited and riveted his gaze on the portal through which Fräulein Mueller had vanished.

We had not long to wait. Almost before the Frenchman had regained his ambush, the big door swung open and Laïla and the little Austrian girl emerged, descended the curving stairs and entered the waiting limousine. There was a buzzing, irritable hum of the self-starter, the spiteful swish of the powerful motor going into action; then, with a low, steady hum, the car glided from the curb and shot down the street with surprising speed.

"Quick, Friend Trowbridge," de Grandin urged, seizing me by the hand and dragging me to the street, "to your car. Haste! We must follow them!"

I gazed after the fleeing motor and shook my head. "Not a chance," I declared. "They're doing better than thirty miles an hour now, and gathering speed all the time. We'd never be able to keep their trail with my little rattletrap."

"My friend," he replied, piloting me across the street and fairly shoving me into my car, "Jules de Grandin is no fool. Think you he slept away his time this afternoon? *Regardez-vous!*" With a dramatic gesture he pointed to the roadway before us.

I blinked my eyes in astonishment, then grinned in appreciation of his strategy. In the wake of the speeding limousine there shone a faint but unmistakable trail of luminous dots against the cement pavement. Now I understood what he had been doing at the other car's tail during the interval between Fräulein Mueller's entrance and Laïla's exit. Firmly attached to the limousine's gas tank was a small can of luminous paint, a small hole pierced in its bottom permitting its telltale contents to leak out, a drop at a time, at intervals which spattered the roadway with glowing trail-markers every thirty or forty feet.

Through the city, over country roads, up hill and down, over viaducts, across stretches of low-lying marshes, through wide, wooded areas and between long, undulating stretches of fields ripe for harvesting, the chase continued. The mileage dial on my dashboard registered forty-five, sixty, sixty-five miles before the car ahead swerved sharply from the highway, shot down a private lane, and entered the high, iron-grilled gateway of a walled estate.

"Eh bien," remarked de Grandin, "here we are, of a surety, but where is it we are?" Parking our car behind a convenient copse of second-growth pines, we stole forward to reconnoiter the enemy's position. Our progress was barred by the tall iron gates which had been securely locked behind our quarry. Through the grille work of the barrier we could descry tall evergreens bowing and whispering with cemetery-like somberness on each side of a wide, curving driveway, and between their ranks we caught momentary glimpses of the ivy-covered walls and white porch pillars of a large Colonial-type residence.

De Grandin gave the gate-handle a tentative shake, confirming our suspicion that it was firmly secured. "It would be wiser not to attempt scaling these bars, Friend Trowbridge," he decided after an inspection of the iron uprights composing the grille; "the visibility would be too high, and I have no wish to stop, or even to impede, a bullet. Let us see what opportunities the walls afford." We drew back from the entrance and walked softly along the strip of grass bordering the wall's base, seeking a favorable location for swarming up.

"Why not here?" the Frenchman suggested, halting at a spot where the ivy grew thicker than elsewhere. "I will go first, do you keep a sharp lookout to the rear." Pulling his jacket sleeves upward with a quick, nervous jerk, he laid hold of the clinging vines, braced his feet against the bricks and prepared to swing himself upward, then paused abruptly, casting a hasty glance over his shoulder.

"Quick, Friend Trowbridge, to cover!" he urged, suiting action to his warning and dragging me to the shelter of a nearby bush. "We are observed!"

Hand on pistol, he crouched alertly while the light, barely audible step of someone advancing through the thicket sounded nearer and nearer on the carpet of early fall leaves lying on the ground about the tree-roots.

"Dieu de Dieu!" he exclaimed with a noiseless chuckle as the stranger emerged from the thicket. "A pussy!" A big, black-and-white tomcat, returning from an evening's hunting or love-making, strode forth from the undergrowth, tail waving proudly in air, inquisitive green eyes looking now here, now there. The creature paused a moment at the wall's base, gathered itself for a spring, then leaped upward with feline grace, catching the clustering ivy strands with gripping, claw-spiked feet, and lifted itself daintily to the wall-top, poising momentarily before making the downward jump to the yard beyond.

De Grandin stepped from his hiding-place and prepared to follow the cat's lead, but started back with an exclamation of dismay as the brute suddenly emitted an ear-piercing yowl of fear and agony, rose like a bouncing ball, every hair on its body stiffly erect, then catapulted like a hurled missile to the earth at our feet, where it lay twitching and quivering.

"*Sacré sang d'un païen!*" the Frenchman murmured, creeping forward and examining the rigid feline by the light of his electric torch. It was stone-dead, yet nowhere was there sign or trace of any wound or violence. "U'm," he commented, reaching out a tentative hand to stroke the dead animal's fur, then: "*Par la barbe d'un petit bonhomme!*" The hair was still bristling from the creature's hide, and as the Frenchman's fingers slipped over it a sharp, crackling sound, accompanied by tiny sparkling flashes, followed them.

"Ah? I wonder? Probably it is," he declared. Turning on his heel he hastened to the place where our car lay hidden, rummaged under the seat a moment, and dragged out the rubber storm-curtains. "*Mordieu*, my friend," he informed me with one of his elfish grins as he dragged the curtains through the underbrush, "never could I work one of those tops of the one man, but I think me these curtains come in handy for this, if for nothing else."

Once more bracing his feet against the wall, he drew himself up by the strong ivy, hung a moment by one hand while with the other he tossed the rubberized cloth across the top of the wall, then hoisted himself slowly, taking care to let his fingers come in contact with nothing not covered by the auto curtains.

"Up, Friend Trowbridge!" he extended his hand to me and drew me beside him, but: "Have a care, keep upon the curtains, for your life!" he commanded as I gained the wall's top, then played the beam of his pocket flash along the bricks beside us. Running along the wall-top were four parallel wires, each supported at intervals of twenty feet or so by little porcelain insulators. But for the warning we received when the cat was killed, and de Grandin's forethought in fetching the rubber curtains, we should surely have been electrocuted the moment we scaled the wall, for the wires were so spaced that contact with at least one of them could not possibly be avoided by anyone attempting to scramble across the top.

Taking advantage of the ample shelter afforded by the great trees, we stole across the wide lawn and brought up at the house without incident. Nowhere was there any trace of occupancy, for all the windows were darkened, and, save for the night wind soughing through the towering evergreens, the place lay wrapped in graveyard silence. By a side door we found the big black car which had brought Laïla and Fräulein Mueller. Working rapidly, de Grandin unfastened the twisted wires with which the can of luminous paint was attached to the gas tank and tossed the nearly empty tin into an adjacent flower bed. This done, he considered the big machine speculatively a moment, then grinned like a mischievous boy about to perpetrate a prank. "Why not, *pour l'amour de Dieu?*" he demanded with a chuckle as he drew a wicked-looking case knife from his pocket and made four or five incisions in each of the vehicle's balloon tires close to the rims. As the air fled hissing from the punctured tubes he turned away with a satisfied laugh. "*Nom d'un canard*, but they shall blaspheme most horribly when they discover what I have done," he assured me as we continued our circuit of the house.

The tenants evidently placed implicit faith in their electrified wall, for there seemed no attempt to bar ingress, once the intruder had managed to pass the silent sentries on the wall-top. An unlatched window at the front of the building invited us to push our explorations farther, and a moment later we had let ourselves in, and, guided by cautious flashes from de Grandin's pocket light, were creeping down a wide central hall.

"Now, my friend," de Grandin whispered, "I wonder much which way leads to—s-s-sh!" he paused abruptly as a quick, nervous step sounded at the hall's farther end.

There was no time to reconnoiter the position, for the beam of our flashlight would surely betray our presence. Some four paces back we had passed a doorway, and, shutting off his light, de Grandin wheeled in his tracks, grasped my arm and dragged me toward it with all speed.

Fortunately the lock was unfastened and the knob turned soundlessly in his hand. Grasping his revolver, he took a deep breath, motioned me to silence, swung the door back and stepped softly into the room.

5

DARKNESS, BLACK AND IMPENETRABLE as a curtain of sable velvet, closed about us as we crossed the threshold. Dared we flash our light? Was there anyone hidden behind that veil of gloom, ready to pounce on us the moment we disclosed our position? We rested a moment, silently debating our next move, when:

"Doctor—Dr. Martulus"—a weak feminine voice quavered from the room's farther end—"I'll sign the paper. I'll go through the ordeal, only, for pity's sake, let me out. Don't let *him* visit me again. Oh, o-o-o-oh, I'll go insane if he comes again. Truly, I will!"

"Eh, what is this?" de Grandin demanded sharply, taking a hasty step forward in the dark, then pressing the switch of his flashlight. "*Cordieu—pardonnez-moi, Madame!*" He shut the light off abruptly, but in its momentary beam we had beheld a sight which brought a gasp of astonishment to our lips. Tethered to the wall by a heavy chain and metal collar locked round her scrawny neck, nude save for a pair of broken felt house-slippers and a tattered and much soiled chemise, thin to the point of emaciation, a woman crouched sobbing and whimpering on the floor. She was no longer young, and almost certainly she had never been lovely, but her voice, for all its burden of misery and terror, was low-pitched and cultured, and her pronunciation that of a person of refinement.

"Your pardon, *Madame!*" de Grandin repeated, taking another step toward the wretched captive. "We did not know you were here. We—"

"*Who are you?*"

"Eh?"

"Aren't—aren't you Dr. Martulus? Oh, if you aren't, please, please take me away from this dreadful place! They've chained me to the wall here like a mad dog, and—"

"Pardon me, *Madame*," de Grandin interrupted, "but who are *you?*"

"Amelia Mytinger."

"Teeth of the Devil! Not the Mademoiselle Mytinger who disappeared from her home a month ago, and—"

"Yes; I am she. A woman called Laïla the Seeress brought me here one night—I don't know how long ago it was. She told me I was possessed of a devil, and Dr. Martulus could cure me—I'd been suffering terribly from rheumatism and the doctors hadn't been able to help me much—and she said it was an evil spirit which plagued me. When they got me here they told me it was Mephistopheles himself who possessed me, and that I'd have to undergo a terrible ordeal by fire if I were ever to be rid of him. I could have hired a substitute, but she wanted ten thousand dollars, and I refused to pay it. I told them I'd undergo the ordeal myself, and they said I must sign a paper releasing them from all legal liability for possible injury I might suffer before they'd permit me to do it. When they brought the paper they wouldn't let me read it or even see any part of it except the space reserved for my signature, so—"

"Ah, ha," de Grandin muttered aside to me, "do you, too, not begin to sniff the odor of deceased fish in this business, Friend Trowbridge?"

"But they wouldn't let me go," the woman hurried on, ignoring his comment. "They said I was possessed of a devil and would bring terrible misfortune to everyone I met, so they took away my clothes and chained me here in this terrible place. I've never seen anyone from that night to this except Dr. Martulus, who comes once a day to feed me and ask if I've changed my mind about signing the paper, and—"

"'And'," de Grandin quoted irritably, "and what, if you please, *Mademoiselle?*"

"And the Devil!"

"*Queue d'un sacré singe!* The *which?*" he demanded.

"The Devil, I tell you. I never believed in a personal Devil before, but I do, now. Every night he comes to torture me. I see his horrible face shining through the dark and feel his awful claw touch me, and it burns like a white-hot iron. Oh, I'll go mad, if I haven't done so already!" She gasped laboringly for breath, then, as if a thought had suddenly struck her: "You mentioned my having disappeared—I didn't tell anybody I was going to Laïla's that night, I was ashamed to have it known I'd consulted a fortune-teller—but you said I'd been missed. Do the police know about me? Are you from headquarters, by any chance. Will you save me? Oh, please, please take me away. I'm wealthy, I'll pay you anything you ask if only—"

"One moment, *Mademoiselle*," de Grandin cut off her torrential speech. "I desire to think."

He remained immersed in thought a moment, then murmured softly, as though meditating aloud: "*Parbleu*, I see it all, now! As usual, Jules de Grandin was right. This is a gigantic conspiracy—a sort of Mephistopheles and Company, Limited. Yes, *pardieu*, limited only by these villains' capacity to invent devilish tricks to defraud defenseless women. *Mordieu*, this is infamous, this is monstrous, this must not be permitted! Me, I shall —"

His voice shut off abruptly, like a suddenly tuned-out radio, for a sharp *click* sounded from the doorway and something faintly luminous was shining face-high through the dark.

Nearer, nearer the fiery thing floated, and we were able to make out the lineaments of a long, thin, evil face; a face with spiked beard and pointed mustaches, with up-rearing pointed eyebrows and crooked goat's horns growing from its forehead. That was all—no body, no neck—just the leering, demoniacal face floating forward through the blackness, its hideous, fire-outlined eyes gleaming with diabolical amusement as it neared the whimpering, cowering woman in the corner.

"O-o-o-h!" wailed the terrified spinster as she cringed against the wall and the grinning, satanic face bent above her.

"*Ugh!*" A short, surprised grunt answered her outcry, and the fiery face dropped downward through the dark like a burnt-out rocket falling to earth.

"Behold Satan's assistant, *mon ami*," de Grandin commanded, a note of fierce elation in his whisper as he switched the beam of his pocket flash on the prostrate form at our feet.

A tall, broad-shouldered man, his face made up in imitation of the popular conception of the Devil, lay sprawled on the floor within the circle of the flashlight's glow. A long gash, bleeding freely, told where the blue steel barrel of de Grandin's heavy service revolver had struck as the Frenchman lashed the weapon downward through the dark with unerring aim and devastating force.

"*Eh bien*, my friend, we have met again, it seems," de Grandin remarked as he snatched away the makeup from the fellow's face and surveyed his features in the electric light. I started with surprise as I gazed into the unconscious one's countenance. He was the man who had demanded he be allowed to take Fräulein Mueller from us when we rescued her in the park.

As the flashlight switched off momentarily, the mock devil's beard and mustache became alive with glowing, smoking fire. Instantly I realized de Grandin's surmise had been correct. Phosphorus, or some kind of luminous paint, had been employed to make the faces of the men accosting the little Austrian girl glow as though aflame when they met her in the dark, and the same device had been used here to torture Miss Mytinger.

A further explanation lay at our feet, too, for beside the unconscious man's hand we found a queer-looking instrument. A moment's examination proved it to be something like an oversized flashlight, only, instead of a lamp, its tip was fitted with a metal plate on which the design of a devil's face surmounted by a reversed crucifix was soldered. As de Grandin pressed the switch actuating the contrivance we saw the design suddenly glow red-hot. To all intents the thing was a branding-iron which would burn its device on the flesh of anyone with whom it came in contact. The mystery of Fräulein Mueller's disfigurement was solved. This, too, explained what Miss Mytinger meant when she spoke of Satan's "awful claw which burned like a white-hot iron" touching her during the diabolical visitations.

"*Bête—cochon!*" de Grandin muttered, turning the man over with a none too gentle foot. "Let us see what we can find upon his so filthy carcass." A hasty examination of the fellow's pockets disclosed a short-bladed dirk knife, a neat, businesslike blackjack and a bunch of small keys. One of these fitted the lock of Miss Mytinger's iron collar, and de Grandin forthwith transferred the fetter from her neck to that of her late tormentor.

"Let us go," he admonished, as he stowed the loot from his fallen foeman's pockets in his own. "Thus far the luck has been with us, but he who tries heaven's patience too far ofttimes comes to grief." Stepping carefully, we crept from the darkened room into the dimly lighted hall.

6

"HAVE THE CARE, FRIEND Trowbridge," de Grandin warned as we started cautiously down the corridor, "a loose board may betray us, for—*ha?*"

Not fifteen feet ahead of us a door swung suddenly open and the menacing figure of a tall, black-bearded man stepped toward us. He was clad in a flame-colored robe on which was printed in black the figure of a prancing devil. A sort of diadem from which curving horns rose above his forehead gave his lean, cadaverous countenance a look of supernatural evil, and the wicked, sneering smile on his bony features completed the unpleasant picture.

Miss Mytinger gave a high-pitched squeal of terror. "Dr. Martulus!" she cried. "Oh, we're lost; he'll never let us go!"

De Grandin faced the other defiantly, his teeth bared in a grimace which was more a snarl than a grin. "We take this lady from out your damned, execrable house, *Monsieur le Diable*," he announced truculently. "Have the goodness to stand aside, or—"

"*Nelzyá!*" the other retorted, raising a small Mauser automatic from the folds of his red robe.

"Ha! 'It can not be done,' do you say?" the Frenchman inquired sarcastically, and let drive with his heavy revolver, firing from the hip.

Too late he discovered his error. A crash of tinkling, shivering glass sounded, and the vision of the man in red dissolved before our eyes like a scene on a motion-picture screen when the film is melted in an overheated projector. A full-length mirror had been moved into the hall since we came through, and the man we had supposed before us was really at our back. De Grandin had been parleying with the fellow's reflection and—irony of ironies!—fired point blank into the mirror, smashing it into a hundred fragments, but injuring his opponent not at all.

Like the echo of de Grandin's shot sounded the spiteful, whiplike report of the other's weapon. Jules de Grandin clapped his left hand to his right shoulder and dropped like an overturned sack of meal to the polished floor.

Two more figures joined the red-robed man. One of them burst into a roar of laughter. "*Ach*, dot vas a goot vun!" he chuckled. "He vas daking der lady from der house oudt vas he? Now, perhabs, ve dake her back und giff her some more dime to dink ofer vedder she vill der baber sign or not. No?"

"No!—*Nom d'un porc*—NO!" de Grandin echoed, rolling over and rising on his elbow. The chuckling German swayed drunkenly in his tracks a moment, then crashed face downward to the floor, and his red-robed companion fell across him in a heap of crumpled crimson draperies a split-second later as de Grandin's revolver bellowed a second time. The third man turned with a squeal of dismay and leaped half-way through the open door, then stumbled over nothing and slid forward on his face as a soft-nosed bullet cut his spinal cord in two six inches below his collar.

"See to Mademoiselle Mytinger, Friend Trowbridge!" de Grandin flung over his shoulder as, pistol in hand, he charged toward the doorway where his late antagonists lay. "Take her outside, I will join you anon!"

"Where are you going!" I objected. The thought of being separated in this uncanny house terrified me.

"Outside—*cornes et peau du diable!*—outside with you!" he shouted in answer. "Me, I go to find Mademoiselle Mueller and a certain souvenir."

7

THE BIG FRONT DOOR was barred and double-locked. I swung to the right, traversed the room through which we had entered and hoisted the unlatched window a few inches higher. "This way, please," I told Miss Mytinger, pointing to the opening, "it's only a few feet to the ground."

She clambered over the sill and dropped to the soft turf below, and, after a futile look around for my friend, I lowered myself beside her.

"Quick, Friend Trowbridge," de Grandin's sharp whisper commanded even as my feet touched the grass. "This way—they come!"

His warning was none too early. Even as he grasped my arm and swung me into the shadow of a towering cedar, six men charged around the corner of the house, weapons in their hands and looks of fierce malignancy on their faces.

"Sa-ha!" de Grandin raised his revolver and fired, and the foremost of our assailants clapped his hand to his side, whirled half-way round, like a pirouetting ballet-dancer, reeled suddenly to the left and slumped to the ground in an awkward heap. The man immediately behind stumbled over the fallen one's legs and fell forward with a guttural curse. De Grandin pressed the trigger again, but only a harmless click responded. The cylinder was empty, and five armed men faced us across a stretch of turf less than twenty feet wide.

Half turning, the Frenchman hurled his empty weapon with terrific force into the face of the nearest ruffian, who dropped with a scream, blood spurting from his nose and mouth, and grasped my elbow again. "This way, my friend!" he cried, seizing the Mytinger woman's arm with his free hand and rushing across the shaded lawn toward the narrow beach where the waters of Barnegat Bay lapped softly against the sand.

"Where's Fräulein Mueller?" I panted, striving to keep pace with him.

"Yonder!" he answered, and as he spoke a dark form detached itself from the shadow of a towering tree and joined us in flight.

Shouts and shots echoed among the evergreens behind us, but the short start we secured when the second man fell under the impact of de Grandin's hurled weapon enabled us to keep our lead, and, dodging among the shadows, we made steadily and swiftly toward the water.

"It's no use," Miss Mytinger informed us as the cool edges of the little wavelets moistened our feet and we swung toward the south, intent on rounding the edge of the walls surrounding the grounds on the landward side and doubling back to my car. "It's no use. The beach is full of quicksand. I heard them talking about it the night I came here. One of their cows wandered down to eat the sea-grass and was sucked under before they could save her."

"On, my friend!" de Grandin answered through clenched teeth, for the strain was beginning to tell on him. "Better to perish in the quicksands than fall prey to those assassins."

We dashed along the waterline, heading for the beach beyond the wall, and a chorus of triumphant shouts followed us. Our pursuers had noted our course and made certain we rushed to our doom.

"*Parbleu*, what a chase!" de Grandin laughed pantingly, suddenly dropping to the sands and unfastening the lacings of his shoes.

"Yes, and it's not over yet," I reminded him. "They'll be on us in a moment. What's the idea—going paddling?"

"Observe me, my friend," he replied as he drew off his pale mauve socks and took shoes and stockings in hand, running barefoot ahead of us across the sands. "Follow where I lead." He advanced along the beach with long, swinging strides like those of a Canadian voyageur sweeping over a winter drift on his snow-shoes. "Jules de Grandin has been in many places," he flung back over his shoulder, "and one of them was the coast of Japan, where quicksands are thick as pickpockets at a fair. There it was I learned the ways of quicksand from the peasant fishermen. Like all other sand it looks, nor does it quake or tremble until it has its victim fast in its hold, but always it is colder than the sands about it, and the knowing one walking barefoot on the beach can feel its death-chilled borders before it is too late to draw back.

"Careful—to the right, my friends!" Gracefully, sliding one foot behind the other, like a dancer crossing a stage, he swerved inward from the water's edge, finally pausing a moment to feel the ground before him with a tentative toe. "*Très bon*—proceed. The quicksands reach no farther here," he announced, stepping forward with a confident stride.

Following his careful lead we proceeded the better part of a hundred yards when a sudden outcry behind us made me look round apprehensively. Infuriated by the sight of our escape, and assuming that because we had not perished the beach was safe for them, four of our enemies were rushing pell-mell after us, the starlight glinting evilly on the weapons brandished over their heads.

"Hurry, de Grandin!" I urged. "They'll be up with us in a moment!"

"Will they, indeed?" he replied with cool indifference, seating himself on the soft sand and beginning to don his socks and shoes in a leisurely manner. "When they reach us, my friend, I shall be ready for them, I assure you."

"But," I remonstrated, "but—good Lord, man!—here they come!"

"Yes!" he answered, lighting a cigarette. "If you will trouble to look round, I think you will say 'there they go'."

Looking down the beach I saw the four pursuers hurrying forward, running four abreast, like a squad of soldiers going into action.

Suddenly the man to the left stumbled awkwardly, like a person descending a flight of stairs and coming to the end before he was aware of it. He faltered, raised his forward foot, as though feeling for support where there was none, and grasped the man next him.

The second man staggered drunkenly in the frenzied hold of his companion, floundered bewilderedly a moment—all four of them were doing a clumsy, grotesque dance, reeling from side to side, swaying back and forth, raising their arms spasmodically as though grasping at non-existent ropes dangling before them. But oddly, they seemed shrinking in stature, growing shorter and shorter, like inflated manikins from which the air is slowly escaping. They were melting, melting like bits of grease thrown into a heated frying-pan.

I shuddered in spite of myself. Even though they were conscienceless minions of a conscienceless master, stealers and torturers of defenseless women, I could not repress a feeling of nausea as the last of the four heads sank like a corkless bottle flung into a stream. A jet of sandy spray shot up from the level beach, a hand, opening and closing in a paroxysm of terror and despair, rose above the rippling sands, then all was still. The pale stars blinked unconcernedly down upon the bare stretch of smooth, unruffled beach and lapping, whispering water.

"*Tiens*, my friends," de Grandin flung away his cigarette and rose; "that appears to be that. Come, let us go."

I CAN UNDERSTAND YOUR WANTING to rescue Fräulein Mueller, de Grandin," I remarked as we started on our homeward journey with the two women snugly stowed in the rear seat of my car, "but what was that remark you made about getting a souvenir when you left me in the hall?"

The little Frenchman's small white teeth gleamed under the line of his sharply waxed mustache as an elfish smile spread across his face. "Friend Trowbridge," he confided, "I have visited many interesting places in your so interesting country, but never yet have I lodged in a jail, nor am I wishful to do so. Think you I risked good money when I entrusted Mademoiselle Mueller to those villains' care? Not I. I did procure two thousand dollars in counterfeit bills with which she was to pay the wretches, and faithfully did I promise to return those notes to the police museum when I should have finished with them. It was to make good that promise that I left you in the hall."

"And Fräulein Mueller—had they released her when you found her?" I asked.

He suppressed a yawn. "Not quite," he returned. "They had her bound in a chair, and the lady called Laïla was standing guard over her with a wicked-looking knife when I entered. My friend, I greatly dislike manhandling a woman, but ladies who wish not to be mauled should not attempt to stick knives in Jules de Grandin. I fear I was forced to be less than entirely gentlemanly before I succeeded in releasing Mademoiselle Mueller and binding Laïla in the chair in her place. *Eh bien*, I tied her no tighter than was necessary to keep her in place until the police call for her."

"And—?"

"More speed and less conversation, if you please, my friend," he interrupted. "Your house is yet a long distance away, and there is nothing to drink this side of your so adorable cellar. Come, as you Americans say, stand hard upon the gas."

The Jewel of Seven Stones

1. The Coffins from Alexandria

"HELLO, DR. TROWBRIDGE," a cheerful hail accosted me as I turned the corner, hastening on my round of afternoon calls, "I've been meaning to look you up for the last two months, but never got 'round to it. Good thing I met you now; I'm figuring on pulling off a show this evening, and maybe you'd like a ringside seat."

"Oh? How do you do?" I responded somewhat doubtfully, for the grinning young man in the shabby little red roadster at the curb was unknown to me. "I'm afraid you've the advantage of me; I—"

"Oh, yes, you do," he replied with an infectious smile. "I'm Ellsworth Bennett you know. You used to come out to our house a lot when Father was living, and—"

"Why," I broke in, "Ellsworth, boy, I never would have known you. You've grown so—"

"Quite right," he agreed. "It's a habit we all have during early life. Now, what do you say to coming out to my little diggings tonight? I'm parked in the old Van Drub cottage for the season, and I've really got something worth looking at."

"Well," I temporized, "I'd be delighted to have you in to my place to dinner, but I'm so tied up with night calls these times that I fear I'll not be able to accept your invitation."

"Oh rats!" he returned. "Try to come, won't you? You know, I've been connected with the Museum of Ethnology ever since I got my degree, and this spring I ran across the trail of something really big while traveling in Egypt. I think I can show you something brand-new if you'll drop out my way tonight or tomorrow. I seem to recall that you and Father used to spend no end of time talking about Rameses and Ptolemy and the rest of those antique gentlemen when I was too small to know what it was all about."

I regarded the lad speculatively. He was his father's own son, no mistake about it. Those honest, humorous blue eyes beneath the sandy brows, that wide, mobile mouth and square chin cleft with the slightest suggestion of a dimple, even the flecks of russet freckles across the bridge of his aquiline nose reminded me of my dear old classmate whose house had been a second home to me in the days before the influenza pandemic took him off. "I'll come," I decided, clasping the youngster's hand in mine. "You may expect me sometime after eight this evening—office hours have to be observed, you know—and, if you don't mind, I'll bring a friend with me, a Dr. de Grandin, from Paris, who's stopping with me."

"Not Jules de Grandin?" he demanded incredulously.

"Yes; do you know him?"

"No, but I'd like to. Jules de Grandin! Why, Dr. Trowbridge, I'd no idea you traveled in such highbrow company."

"I'd hardly call him highbrow," I replied, smiling at his enthusiasm.

"Oh, Lord!" he threw up his hands in mock despair. "You fellows who have all the luck never do appreciate it. Why, man, de Grandin's one of the foremost ethnologists of the age; his studies in evolution and anthropometry are classics. I'll say you can bring him. I'll be hanging out the window waiting for you tonight. G'bye." With a warning double toot of his horn he set his decrepit motor going and dashed down the street at a speed bound to bring him afoul of the first crossing policeman who spied him.

THE VAN DRUB COTTAGE where young Bennett had his "diggings" was a relic of the days when Swede and Dutchman contended for mastery of the country between the Delaware and the Hudson. Like all houses of its day, it was of the story-and-a-half type, built of stone to the edge of the overhanging roof and of hand-split chestnut shingles above. The ground floor was entirely occupied by a single large combination living-room and kitchen paved with brick and walled with roughly split planks, and small cubby-holes of storerooms flanked it at each end. Bennett's living arrangements were as typical of himself as a photograph. Bookshelves lined the walls and displayed a most improbable array of volumes— de Morgan's *Les Premières Civilisations* and Munzinger's *Ostafrikanische Studien* huddled cheek by jowl with a much-worn copy of Thomas à Kempis' *Imitation of Christ*. A once fine but now badly worn Sarouk rug covered the major portion of the brick floor, and the furniture was a hodgepodge of second-hand mahogany and new, cheap pine. In the middle of the room, as though on exhibition, were two long covered objects, roughly resembling a pair of mummy-cases, raised some three feet above the floor on rough saw-horses. Two kerosene-burning student lamps of the sort used in the late nineties, their green shades removed for greater radiation of light, illuminated the room's center with an almost theatric glare, leaving the corners in shadow all the deeper from the contrast.

"Welcome to the humble student's cave, gentlemen," Bennett greeted as we stepped through the wide, low doorway. "Tonight's the fateful hour; I either uncover something to set 'em all talking for the next ten years, or get myself a free ticket to the booby-hatch."

With sudden soberness he turned directly to de Grandin and added: "I'm on special leave from the Museum to work out a theory that's been haunting me for the last year or so. It'll be an important contribution to science, if I'm right. Here"—he waved his hand toward the sheeted objects on the trestles—"is the evidence. Shall we begin?"

"U'm." Jules de Grandin gave his little blond mustache a vicious tweak as he regarded our host with his direct, challenging stare. "What is it that you wish to prove by the evidence, *mon brave?*"

"Just this"—Bennett's frank, boyish eyes lost something of their humorous gleam and took on the earnest enthusiastic expression of the fanatic's—"that not all the traces of the Greek civilization were obliterated when the Moslems sacked and burned Alexandria."

"Ah? And you will prove it by—?" De Grandin's delicately arched brows lifted slightly as he glanced significantly at the sheeted things.

"By these," Bennett returned. "This spring, while I was over in Africa, I got in with a scoundrelly old Arab who rejoiced in the name of Abd-el-Berkr, and, in return for several liberal applications of *bakshish*, he agreed to turn over two ancient Greek coffins he had found in an old native cemetery in the desert. The old villain knew enough to distinguish between Christian coffins and Egyptian mummy-cases—there aren't any of the latter left in the neighborhood of Alexandria, anyhow—and he was too good a Moslem to disturb the tombs of his co-religionists, even if they had used substantial coffins for burial, which they hadn't.

"I took the old beggar on, for if he were telling the truth his find was worth a lot more than it cost me, and if he were lying—which he probably was—I'd not be so very much out of pocket. As you know, the Mohammedans took about everything that wasn't nailed down when they captured the city, and their descendants have been keeping the good work up. The few Christian cemeteries which survived the first onslaught of Islam were gradually uprooted and their inmates, ruthlessly ripped from their tombs and despoiled of such trifling ornaments as happened to be buried with them. So, even if we don't find anything of great importance in these two cases, the chances are we may recover a few old coins or some antique jewelry—enough to take back to the Museum and prove my time hasn't been entirely wasted."

He paused, eyes shining, lips parted as he surveyed us each in turn, almost pathetically anxious for a word of encouragement.

"I fear we have come on a chase of the wild goose, my friend," de Grandin replied a trifle wearily. "Me, I have unearthed coffins of the olden days from the vicinity of Alexandria, of Tunis and of Sidon, but nothing save the most abominable evidence that all flesh is subject to decay have I ever found. For your sake I hope your hopes are justified. Speaking from experience, I should say the Arab gentleman has driven a most advantageous bargain, for himself. Undoubtlessly he first despoiled the tombs of such trifles as they contained, then sold you the empty boxes for as much as he could. I fear you are—how do you say it?—holding the sack, *mon enfant.*"

"Well, anyway, here goes," responded Bennett with a shamefaced grin as he whipped the threadbare table-cover from the nearest case and took up mallet and cold-chisel. "We may as well begin on this one, eh?"

The coffin was roughly like a bathtub in shape, perhaps six feet long by two and a half high, and composed of some sort of hard, brittle pottery, evidently baked in a brick-kiln, and apparently shaped by hand, for traces of the makers' thumb-marks still showed on its exterior. About its upper portion, an inch or so below the junction of lid and body, ran an ornamental molding of the familiar Greek egg-and-dart design, crudely impressed on the clay with a modeling mold before baking. There was no other attempt at decoration and no trace of inscription on the lid.

"Here we are!" Bennett exclaimed as he finished chipping away the scaling of the casket. "Give me a lift with this lid, Dr Trowbridge?"

I leaned forward to assist him, tugged at the long, convex curved slab of terra-cotta, and craned my neck to glimpse the coffin's interior.

What I had expected to see I do not quite know. A skeleton, perhaps; possibly a handful of fetid mold; more likely nothing at all. The sight which met my eyes made them fairly start from their sockets, and but for Bennett's warning cry, I should have let my end of the casket cover clatter to the brick floor.

Cushioned on a mattress of royal purple cloth, a diminutive pillow beneath her head and another supporting her feet, lay a woman—a girl, rather—of such surpassing beauty as might have formed the theme of an Oriental romance. Slender she was, yet possessing the softly rounded curves of budding womanhood, not the angular, boyish thinness of our modern girls. Her skin, a deep, sun-kissed olive, showed every violet vein through its veil of lustrous, velvet tan. Across her breast, folded reposefully, lay hands as softly dimpled as a child's, their long, pointed nails overlaid with gold leaf or bright gilt paint, so that they shone like ten tiny almond-shaped mirrors in the rays of the hissing student lamps. Her little bare feet, as they dimpled the purple cushion on which they lay, were pinked about sole and toe like those of a baby, and so soft, so free from callouses or roughening of any sort, that it seemed they must have trodden nothing harder than velvet carpets in life, even as they rested on pillows of velvet in death. About ankles, wrists and arms hung bangles of beaten rose-gold studded with topaz, garnet and lapis-lazuli, while a diadem of the same precious composition encircled her brow, binding back the curling black locks which lay about her small face in thick clusters. A robe or shroud of thinnest gauze enveloped her from throat to knees, and about her lower limbs from knee to ankle was wrapped a shawl of brilliant orange silk embroidered with wreaths of shells and roses. Black antimony had been rubbed on her lids to give added size and depth to her eyes, and her full, voluptuous lips, half parted, as though in the gentle respiration of peaceful sleep, were stained vivid vermilion with powdered cinnabar. There was nothing of death, nothing of the charnel-house, about the vision. Indeed, it required a conscious effort to convince me her bosom did not rise and fall with the softly-drawn breath of slumber, and the faint, subtle perfume of violets and orange blossoms which wafted to us from her raiment and hair was no delusion, but a veritable scent imprisoned in the baked-clay tomb for fifteen centuries.

"Ah!" I exclaimed in mingled surprise and admiration.

"Good Lord!" Ellsworth Bennett murmured, staring incredulously at the lovely corpse, his breath rasping sharply between his teeth.

"*Nom d'un chat de nom d'un chat!*" Jules de Grandin almost shouted, standing on tiptoe to gaze over my shoulder. "It is the Sleeping Beauty *en personne!*"

With a quick movement he turned to young Bennett, and before the other was aware of his intention had kissed him soundly on each cheek.

"*Embrasse moi, mon vieux!*" he cried. "Me, I am one great fool of a doubly-damned doubting Thomas! In all my head there is not the sense with which the good God had endowed a goose! *Parbleu*, we have here the find of the age; our reputation is assured; we shall have fame comparable to that of Boussard, *Mordieu*, but we are already famous!"

Characteristically, he had assumed charge of the entire proceeding. "We shall take her to the Museum!" he continued, elatedly; "she shall display her so marvelous beauty for all to see our handiwork. She shall—*misère de Dieu*, behold, my friends, she vanishes!"

It was true. Before our eyes, like a shadowgraph fading on the screen, the lovely being in the ancient coffin was dissolving. Where the full-rounded beauty of feminine perfection had lain a moment before, there stretched a withering, shriveling thing, puckering and wrinkling like a body long immersed in chilled water. The eyeballs had already fallen in, leaving cavernous, unfilled sockets in a face from which every semblance of the bloom of youth had vanished and which showed pinched and desiccated like that of a mummy. The symmetrical, full-fleshed limbs were no more than skin-covered bones as we bent our gaze on the rapidly spreading desolation, and within a space of ten minutes even the skeleton lost its articulation, and nothing but a pile of dust, gray-white and fine as the ashes of cremation, lay upon the purple fabric. While we stared, horrified, even the pillows and mattress which had supported that once-beautiful body, the ethereal, transparent gauze and the heavy, broidered silk of the shawl crumbled like a gaslight filament crushed between thumb and forefinger. Sealed away from contact with the atmosphere for centuries, every vestige of perishable matter, both animal and vegetable, had shuddered into ashes in our oxygen-laden air almost as quickly as if brought in contact with living flame. Only the hard, glittering facets of the gems and the duller gleam of the gold composing her ornaments assured us that the body of a lovely girl had lain before us a short quarter hour ago.

Ellsworth Bennett was the first to recover his self-possession. "Sic transit gloria mundi!" he remarked with a half-hysterical laugh. "Shall we open the other one?"

De Grandin was shaking like a leaf with emotion. Like all his countrymen, he was as susceptible to the appeal of beauty as a sensitive-plant's fronds are to the touch, and the spectacle he had witnessed had shocked him almost past endurance. Taking his narrow chin between his forefinger and thumb, he gazed abstractedly at the floor a moment, then turned to our host with a shrug and one of his big quick, elfin smiles. "Regard not my foolishness, I beseech you," he implored. "Me, I would not suffer such another sight for the wealth of the Indies, but—so great is my curiosity—I would not forego the experience of beholding the contents of that other casket for ten times the Indies' wealth!"

Together he and Bennett broke the clay scaling of the coffin, and within five minutes, the lid was loosened and ready to be lifted from its place.

"Careful, careful, Trowbridge, my friend!" de Grandin besought as the three of us gently raised the slab of brittle clay. "Who knows what we may discover this time? Beneath this cover there may be—quoi diable!"

Instead of the open coffin we had expected to find beneath the earthen lid, a second covering, curved and molded to conform to the outer lid's shape, met our gaze.

Bennett, intent on seeing what lay beneath, was about to strike the opaque white substance with his hammer, but a quick cry from de Grandin halted him. "Non, non!" the Frenchman warned. "Can not you see there is an inscription on it? Stand back, my friends"—his sharp, contradictory orders rang out in quick succession like military commands. "Lights, lights for the love of heaven! Bring forward the lamps that I may decipher these words before I die from curiosity!"

Bennett and I each seized a lamp and we held them above the coffin's inner sealing while the little Frenchman leaned forward, eagerly scanning the inscription.

The curving cover seemed to be made of some softer, less brittle substance than the outer lid—wax, I decided after a hasty inspection—and on it, from top to bottom, in small Greek uncials some sort of message had been etched with a stylus.

De Grandin studied the legend through intently narrowed eyes a few moments, then turned to Bennett with a gesture of impatience. "It is no good," he announced petulantly. "My brain, he has too such burden on him this night; I cannot translate the Greek into English with the readiness I should. Paper, paper and pencil, if you please.

"I shall make a copy of this writing and translate him at my leisure this evening. Tomorrow we shall read him aloud and see what we shall see. Meantime, swear as you hope for heaven, that you will make no move to open this coffin until I shall return. You agree? *Bon!* To work, then; the writing is long and of an unfamiliar hand. It will take much time to transcribe it on my tablets."

2. A Portent from the Past

GOLDEN WAFFLES AND RICH, steaming coffee were waiting on the table when I descended the stairs next morning, for Nora McGinnis, my household factotum, maintained a soft spot in her Celtic heart for de Grandin and his gallant manners, and delays which would have made her nearly snap my head off brought only an indulgent smile when occasioned by the little Frenchman's tardiness. "Sure, Doctor darlin'," she greeted as I seated myself and looked about for my companion, "Dr. de Grandin wuz doin' th' divil's own bit o' studyin' last night, an' 'twould be unfair ter call 'um from his rist, so ut would."

"Fear not, my excellent one," a cheerful voice hailed from the stairs, "already I am here," and de Grandin stepped quickly into the sunlit dining-room, his face glowing from the recent application of razor-blade and cold water, his little blond mustache waxed to twin needle-points at the corners of his small, sensitive mouth, and every blond hair on his head lying as perfectly in place as though numbered and arranged according to plan.

"*Mordieu*, what a night!" he exclaimed with a sigh as he drained a preliminary draft of well-creamed coffee and passed the cup back for replenishment. "*Cordieu*, even yet I doubt me that I saw what I beheld at Monsieur Bennett's cottage last night, and I am yet in doubt that I translated what I did from the notes I made from the second coffin!"

"Was it so remarkable?" I began, but he cut me short with an upraised hand.

"Remarkable?" he echoed. "*Parbleu*, my friend, it is amazing, nothing less. Come, let us first discuss this so excellent food, then discuss the message from the past.

"Attend me, if you please," he ordered, picking up a sheaf of manuscript from the study table when we had finished breakfast. "Give careful ear to what

I read, my friend, for I shall show you that which makes even our vision of yesternight fade to insignificance by comparison. Listen:

Kaku, servant and priest of Sebek, dread God of Nilus, son of Amathel the son of Kepher, servants and priests of Sebek, to who so looks hereon, greeting and admonition:

Not of the creed and belief of Christians am I, neither of the bastard cult of the Greek usurpers. Flesh of the flesh and blood of the mighty blood of the race which ruled Upper and Lower Egypt in the days when Ra held sway is Kaku, servant and priest of Sebek. Learned in the laws and magic of the olden priesthood am I, and by the lore and cunning of my forebears have I sealed the virgin Peligia in unwaking sleep beneath this shield of time-defying cerus, even the wax which sets at naught but the father of acids.

Greek and Christian though she be, and daughter of the race which trod upon my ancestors, my heart inclined to her and I would have taken her to wife, but she would not. Wherefore, I, being minded that she should take no other man to husband, devised a plan to slay her and bury her with the ancient rites and ceremonies of my people, that her body should not know corruption, but lie in the tomb until the Seven Ages were passed, and I might take her to myself and dwell with her in Aalu. Nathless, when I had taken her beyond the city gates, and all was ready for her death, my heart turned water within me, and I could not strike the blow. Therefore, by my magic, and by the magic of my priesthood, have I caused a deep sleep to fall on her, even a sleep which knows no waking until the Seven Ages be past and she and I shall dwell together in Amenaand.

For the Seven Ages shall she sleep within this coffin, obedient to the mystic spell I have put on her, and if no man openeth the tomb and waken her before the Seven Ages be past, then she shall become as the dust of Egypt, and be mine forever and forever in the land beyond the setting sun. But if a man of later days shall lift the covering from off this coffin and take her hand in his and call on her by name, and in the name of love, then shall my magic be valueless, and she shall waken and cleave unto her deliverer, and be his own in that land and generation yet unborn. This is the sum of all my spells and learning unable to withstand.

Yet, ye who look hereon, be warned in time or ever ye seek to open this tomb of the living-in-death. I, Kaku, priest and servant of Mighty Sebek, have sealed this virgin within this tomb that she may be mine and not another's. My shadow, and the shadow of Sebek which is my god, is upon her. Yea, were it seventy times seventy ages instead of seven, and were the earth to perish under our feet, yet would I pursue her until her heart inclines to me.

I, Kaku, servant and priest of Sebek, have sealed this tomb with clay and wax and with my curse, and with the curse of Sebek, my god and master, and the curse of Kaku, and of Kaku's god, shall smite with terror him who openeth this tomb. And on him in ages yet to come who looks upon this coffin with presumptuous eyes and makes bold to open it, I do pronounce my curse and the curse of Sebek, and I do set myself against him in wager of battle, that his days be not long in the land; neither his nor hers to whom life returns and youth and love for the duration of the seven stones upon the jewel, according to the obedience of the eternal gods of Egypt whose kingdom shall have no end.

I have said.

De Grandin laid the manuscript on the desk and looked at me, his little blue eyes round and shining with excitement.

"Well?" I asked.

"Well?" he mimicked. "*Parbleu*, I shall say it is well! Many remarkable things have I beheld, my friend, but never such as this. Come, let us hasten, let us fly to the cottage of Monsieur Bennett and see what lies beneath that shield of wax. *Mort d'un Chinois*, though she subsist but for five little minutes, I must gaze, I must feast my eyes upon that paragon of womanhood whose beauty was so great that even the hand of jealousy forbore to strike!"

3. The Jewel of Seven Stones

DIFFERING FROM HER COMPANION in death as dawn light differs from midnight, the virgin Peligia lay in her terra-cotta coffin when Bennett, de Grandin, and I had lifted off the curving shield of wax. She was some five and twenty years of age, apparently; slightly above middle height, golden-haired and fair-skinned as any Nordic blonde, and as exquisitely proportioned as a Grecian statue of Aphrodite. From tapering white throat to blue-veined, high-arched insteps she was draped in a simple Ionic robe of snowy linen cut in that austerely modest and graceful fashion of ancient Attica in which the upper part of the dress falls downward again from neck to waist in a sort or cape, hiding the outline of the breast while leaving the entire arms and the point of the shoulders bare. Except for two tiny studs of hand-beaten gold which held the robe together over the shoulders and the narrow double border of horizontal purple lines at the bottom of the cape, marking her status as a Roman citizen, her gown was without ornament of any sort, and no jewelry adorned her chaste loveliness save the golden threads with which her white-kid sandals were embroidered and a single strand of small gold disks, joined by minute links and having seven tiny pendants of polished carnelians, which encircled her throat and lay lightly against the gentle swell of her white bosom.

To me there seemed something of the cold finality of death about her pose and figure. After the glowing beauty and barbaric splendor of her unnamed companion, she seemed almost meanly dressed, but de Grandin and Bennett were mute with admiration as they gazed on her.

"*Mordieu*, she is the spirit of Greece, undebased by evil times, brought down to us within a shell of clay," the little Frenchman murmured, bending over her and studying her calm, finely molded features like a connoisseur inspecting a bit of priceless statuary.

Young Bennett was almost speechless with mingled excitement and homage. "What—what did you say her name was!" he asked thickly, swallowing between words, as though the pressure of his breath forced them back into his throat.

"Peligia," de Grandin returned, bending closer to study the texture of her robe.

"Peligia," Bennett, repeated softly. "Peligia—" Scarce aware of what he did, he reached downward and took one of the shapely hands crossed above her quiet breast in his.

Jules de Grandin and I stood fascinated, scarce daring to breathe, for at the whispered name and the pressure of the boy's fingers on hers, the woman in the coffin stirred, the slender, girlish bosom heaved as if with respiration, and the smooth, wax-white lids fluttered upward from a pair of long gray eyes as gentle as the summer and as glowing as the stars. A wave of upward-rising color flooded her throat, her cheeks; the hue of healthy, buoyant youth showed in her face, and her calmly set lips parted in the faintest suggestion of a smile.

"My lord," she murmured softly, meeting young Bennett's gaze with a look of gentle trust. "My lord and my love, at last you have come for me."

And she spoke in English.

"*Morbleu*, Friend Trowbridge, look to me, assist me hence to some asylum for lunatics," de Grandin implored. "I am *caduc*—mad like a hare of March. I see that which is not and hear words unspoken!"

"Then I'm crazy too," I rejoined, leaning forward to assist Bennett in his task of lifting the girl from her coffin-bed. "We're all mad—mad as hatters, but—"

"Yes, *parbleu*," he agreed, fairly dancing before us to toss back the covers of the camp bed and ease the girl upon it, "mad we are, of a surety, but who would own sanity if madness brings visions such as this?"

In another moment the blankets had been drawn about the girl's shoulders, and with Bennett seated at her left, de Grandin at her right, and me standing at the bedstead's foot, she held her little levee like some spoiled beauty of the Louis' court at her salon.

"How comes it you speak English, *Mademoiselle?*" de Grandin demanded, putting in blunt words the question which burned in all our brains.

The girl turned her agate eyes on him with a puzzled little frown. "English?" she repeated. "What is English?"

"*Nom d'un nom!* What is"—de Grandin gasped, looking as if he were in momentary danger of exploding—"'What is it?' You do ask. It is the language we use. The barbarous tongue of the Saxon savages!"

"Why"—still her smooth brow wrinkled with non-comprehension—"is not the tongue we use that of the Empire? Are we not in Alexandria?"

"In Alexandria!" Again the little Frenchman seemed on the point of bursting; then, with a mighty effort, he restrained himself and demanded, "*Parlez vous Français?*"

She shook her head in silent negation.

"But—but," he began; then he stopped short with a look of bewilderment, almost of dismay.

"I understand," she broke in while he waited her explanation. "A moment ago I ceased to hold my lord's hand, and the words you used seemed suddenly meaningless, though before I understood perfectly. See, while his hand is clasped in mine I talk as you do and understand your speech, but the moment I release his fingers my mind becomes a blank, and all about me seems strange. I know the answer to your question. He"—she cast another melting glance on the boy sitting beside her—"he is my love through all the ages, the man who waked me into life from death. While he touches me or I touch him I speak with his tongue and hear with his ears; the moment our contact is broken I am an alien and a stranger in a strange land and time."

"*Cordieu*, yes, it is possible," de Grandin agreed with a short nod. "I have known such cases where patients suffered with amentia, but—"

"Scat!" The interruption came with dramatic suddenness as he chanced to glance toward the open door. Upon the threshold, one forefoot raised tentatively, its big, green eyes fixed on the reclining girl with a baleful gleam, stood a huge black cat.

"Out, beast of evil omen!" the little Frenchman cried, striding toward the brute with upraised hand.

"Ss-s-sh!" Venomous as the hiss of a poisonous reptile, the thing's furious spit greeted his advance, and every sable hair along its spine reared upward belligerently.

"Out, I say!" de Grandin repeated, aiming a devastating kick at the brute.

It did not dodge. Rather, it seemed to writhe from under his foot, evading the blow with perfect ease. With a lithe, bounding spring it launched itself into the air, landed fairly on the covers protecting the girl's bosom and bent forward savagely, worrying at her throat.

Bennett leaped to his feet, flailing at the thing with ineffectual blows, fearing to strike directly downward lest he hit the girl, and missing the writhing brute each time he swung his impotent fists at it.

Then, suddenly as it had appeared, the creature vanished. Snarling once, defiantly, it turned and leaped to the window-sill. As it paused for a final baleful glare at us, we, saw a tiny red fleck against its lips. Was it blood? I wondered. Had the beast fleshed its fangs in the girl's throat? De Grandin had seized a piece of crockery from the dresser and raised his hand to hurl it at the beast, but the missile was never thrown. Abruptly, like a light snuffed out in a gust of wind, the thing was gone. None of us saw it leap from the sill; there was no sound of its feet against the heaped-up dry leaves outside. It was gone, nor could we say how or where.

On the bed, Peligia wept despairingly, drawing her breath with deep, laboring sobs and expelling it with low, quavering moans. "My lord," she cried, seizing Bennett's hand in hers that she might express herself, "I understand it all. That was no cat, but the *ka* of Kaku, the priest of Sebek. Long years ago he put me in a magic sleep with his unclean sorceries, but before he did so he told me that if ever I awakened and loved another man his double would pursue me from the dungeons of Amenti and ravish me from out my lover's arms. And in token of his threat, he hung this about my neck"—she pointed hysterically to the chaplet of golden disks and ruddy beads—"and warned me that my life in the days to be would last only so long as the seven pendants of this jewel. One at a time, he vowed, his *ka* would take the stones from me, and as each one fell, so would my stay in the land of my new-found lover be shortened. Behold, my darling, already he has wrested one of the stones from me!"

Baring her breast of the shrouding blankets, she indicated the necklace.

One of the tiny carnelian pendants was gone. The jewel of seven stones retained but six.

4. The Accident

TWO MONTHS HAD PASSED. Peligia's naive assumption that the man whose voice and touch wakened her from her sesqui-millennial trance was her foreordained mate found ready echo in Ellsworth Bennett's heart. Three days after her release from the Alexandrian coffin he and she were wed at the sole Greek Catholic church our little city boasted, Bennett's innate thoughtfulness dictating the choice, since the service and language of the liturgy employed by the modern *papa* were essentially the same as those to which his bride was accustomed in the days of the Patriarch Cyril.

De Grandin and I attended them at the ceremony and helped them procure their license, and the little Frenchman was near to bursting with laughter when the solemn-visaged clerk of court demanded of Bennett whether his bride was of full age. "*Par la barbe de Saint Gris*," he chuckled delightedly in my ear, "Friend Trowbridge, I am half minded to tell him her true age!" and he stepped forward as though to carry out his threat.

"Come back, you little fool," I admonished, seizing his elbow and dragging him away; "he'll have us all committed to an asylum!" At which he laughed all the harder, to the very evident scandal of the serious-minded attachés of the clerk's office.

The earthenware coffin in which the dead girl had lain, together with her splendidly barbaric ornaments, had been taken to the Museum as trophies of Bennett's researches, and, backed by de Grandin's statement, his story of the find was duly accredited. Of the manner of Peligia's coming nothing had been said, and since Ellsworth was an orphan without near relatives, there was little curiosity shown in his charming wife's antecedents. Their brief honeymoon had been a dream of happiness, and their life together in the cheerful little suburban villa bade fair to continue their joy uninterruptedly. Since the first sinister manifestation on the afternoon of her awakening, Peligia and her husband had received no further visitations, and I, for one, had become convinced that the black cat was really a feline rogue which happened into the cottage by uncanny coincidence, rather than a visitant from beyond the grave.

De Grandin and I faced each other across my study table. In the dining-room the candlelight gleamed on china and silver and cut glass, and from the kitchen emanated odors of gumbo soup, roast chicken and fresh-baked apple pies. Also imprecations as Nora McGinnis strode to and fro across her domain, breathing uncomplimentary remarks about "folks who kape a body's dinner waitin' an' sp'ilin' on th' sthove half an hour afther ut's due ter be served."

The Frenchman consulted the silver dial of the tiny watch strapped to the under side of his wrist for the tenth time in as many minutes. "They are late, Trowbridge, my friend," he announced unnecessarily. "I do not like it. It is not well."

"Nonsense!" I scoffed. "Ellsworth's probably had a blowout or something of the sort, and is holding us up while he puts on a new tire."

"Perhaps possibly," de Grandin admitted, "but I have the *malaise*, notwithstanding. Go to the telephone, I beseech, and assure yourself they are on the way."

"Stuff!" I retorted, but reached for the receiver as I spoke, for it was plain my friend's apprehension was mounting like a thermometer's mercury on an August afternoon.

"Give me—" I began, preparing to name Bennett's number, but the voice of central cut me off.

"Here's your party," she announced, speaking to someone on the other end of the line.

"Is this Dr. Trowbridge?" the cool, impersonal voice of one used to discussing tragedies over the telephone demanded.

"Yes," I admitted, "but I was just attempting to get another party on the wire—"

"I think this is important," the other interrupted. "Do you know a Mr. Ellsworth Bennett?"

"Yes! What about him?"

"This is the Casualty Hospital. Mr. and Mrs. Bennett and their taxi-driver were brought here twenty minutes ago. He regained consciousness for only a moment, and begged us to call you, then fainted again, and—"

"I'll be right over!" I shouted, clashing the receiver back into its hook and springing from my chair.

"Trowbridge, *mon vieux*—it is the bad news?" de Grandin asked, leaping to his feet and regarding me with a wide-eyed stare.

"They've just had an accident—motor collision—at the Casualty Hospital now—unconscious," I jerked out as I ran through the dining-room, notified Nora of the cause of delay, and rushed into the hall for my hat and topcoat.

De Grandin was ahead of me, already seated in the car when I ran down the front steps. "Stand on it; hasten, fly!" he urged as I shot the self-starter and turned toward the hospital at furious speed. "*Sang du diable*, I knew it; in each bone of my body I felt it coming! Oh, hurry, hurry, my friend, or we may be too late!"

"Too late? For what?" I asked crossly. "The nurse didn't say they were seriously hurt."

"Haste, more haste!" was his only reply as he leaned forward like a jockey bending across the neck of his mount to urge it to greater speed.

Rounding corners on two wheels, even cutting across sidewalks in our effort to clip a few feet from our course, our siren shrilling continuously, we dashed through the winter night, finally drew up beneath the hospital's porte-cochère, our motor panting like a winded polo pony after a furious chukker.

"Where are they—*plumes d'un canard!*—where are Monsieur and Madame Bennett, if you please?" cried de Grandin, fairly bouncing through the hospital door.

"Mrs. Bennett's in the operating-room, now," the night supervisor replied, not at all impressed with his urgency. "She was rather badly—"

"And that operating-room, it is where?" he demanded impatiently. "Be quick, if you please. It is of the importance, and I am Dr. de Grandin. "

"The operating-room's on the fourth floor, but no one is permitted there while the surgeons are—"

"*Ah bah!*" he interrupted, for once forgetting his customary courtesy, and starting down the corridor at a run. "Come with me, Friend Trowbridge!" He flung back over his shoulder, pressing his finger to the elevator bell button and continuing the pressure uninterruptedly. "We may not be too late, though I greatly fear—"

"Say, whatsa big idea!" demanded the elevator conductor, slamming-open his door and glowering at the little Frenchman.

"The idea, my friend, is that I shall give you one five-dollar bill in case you take us to the fourth floor immediately," returned de Grandin, extracting a crisp green Treasury note from his wallet.

The car shot upward like a captive balloon suddenly released from its cable and came to a stop at the top floor with a suddenness which set the circuit breakers in the basement to clattering like a battery of field guns. "First door to your right at the end o' the corridor," directed the conductor with a wave of his left hand while with his right he stowed de Grandin's gratuity in his trousers pocket.

WE RAN AT BREAKNECK speed down the wide, solemn hall, paused not a moment at the ominous green-painted door with its gold-lettered sign of "Silence" and "No Admission," but rushed into the brilliantly lighted room where two nurses and a young and plainly worried surgeon stood above the sheeted form of Peligia Bennett.

"Ah—*hèlas*—it is as I thought!" de Grandin almost shrieked as he bounded forward. Even as we entered the room one of the nurses leaned over and grasped some shining object from the unconscious patient's throat, detaching it with a quick jerk. It was the necklace from which a pendant had been lost the day we raised Peligia from the coffin.

"Quick, replace it—put it back! *Barbe de Saint Pierre*—PUT IT BACK!" the Frenchman cried, leaping across the white-tiled floor and snatching at the jewel dangling from the nurse's fingers.

The girl turned on him with an exclamation of surprise, clutched frantically at the golden strand he reached for, and let it fall to the terrazzo floor.

There was a miniature explosion, like that of an electric light bulb bursting, only softer, and two of the carnelian pendants winked out like suddenly extinguished lights. Contact with the floor's hard tiles had cracked them, and each seemed in need of only so slight a concussion to dissolve into a little pile of garnet dust which quickly turned to vapor and disappeared, leaving no trace.

Fairly shoving the nurse from his path, de Grandin seized the mutilated necklace and laid it against the unconscious girl's throat.

"Sir, this is an outrage! What do you mean by forcing yourself in here?" demanded the astonished young surgeon. "This patient is in a desperate condition, and—"

"Desperate? *You* tell *me* that?" de Grandin rasped. "*Parbleu*, you know not how desperate her plight is, *Monsieur!*" As he spoke he flung aside his dinner coat and rolled back his cuffs.

"I am Dr. Jules de Grandin, of Paris," he continued, reaching methodically for an operating-smock. "I hold degrees from Vienna and the Sorbonne, as my friend, Dr. Trowbridge, whom you doubtless know, can certify. With your permission—or without it—I shall assume charge here." He turned imperiously to the nurses, motioning them to bring a pair of sterile rubber gloves.

"I'm afraid you're too late," the other responded coldly. "If you'll trouble to look, you'll see—"

"*Grand ciel*, I do!" the Frenchman gasped, staring with horrified eyes at the pallid form on the table.

Peligia Bennett's face had gone a sickly, deathlike gray, her eyeballs seemed fallen in their sockets and her nostrils had the chilled, pinched look of one in extremity. From between her parted lips sounded the harsh irregularity of Cheyne-Stokes breathing.

"*Mordieu*, she is passing!" he exclaimed; then: "Ah? So?" Bending quickly, he retrieved the necklace from the floor, where it had fallen during his altercation with the surgeon, and placed it about Peligia's throat. This done, he bent two of the tiny gold links together and fastened the strand where it had broken when the nurse snatched it from her bosom. As the jewel shone once more against the fainting girl's white skin I noticed, with a start, that another of the garnet pendants was missing.

The replacement of the necklace acted like a powerful stimulant on the patient. Scarcely had gold and stone touched her flesh again than her respiration became more normal and the bluish, deathlike pallor gave way to the slight flush of strengthening circulation.

"Now, *Mesdemoiselles*, if you please, we shall begin," de Grandin announced, signing to the nurses, and seizing scalpel and forceps he set to work with a speed and deftness which brought a gasp of admiring amazement from the offended young doctor and the attendants alike.

"Not again; not again for fifty thousand francs would I perform such an operation," he murmured as he turned his gloves inside out and shrugged out of his gown. To the nurse he ordered: "Attend her constantly, *Mademoiselle*; on your life, see that the necklace is kept constantly in place. Already you have observed the effect of its loss on her; it is not necessary to say more, *hein?*"

"Yes, Sir," responded the nurse, gazing at him with mingled wonder and respect. Surgical nurses soon recognize a master craftsman, and the exhibition he had given that night would remain history forever in the operating-room of Casualty Hospital.

"I feared something like this," he confided as we walked slowly down the corridor. "All evening I have been ill at ease; the moment I heard of the accident I made sure the hospital authorities in their ignorance would remove the jewel from *Madame's* throat—*grâce à Dieu* we were in time to replace it before the worst occurred. As it is—" He broke off with a shrug of his narrow shoulders. "Come," he added, "let us interview Monsieur Bennett. I doubt not he has something of interest to tell."

5. The Shadow of Sebek

"MR. BENNETT IS STILL under the anesthetic," the nurse informed us when we inquired at my friend's room. "He had a Colles' fracture of the lower right epiphysis, and Dr. Grosnal gave him a whiff of ether while he was repositioning the fragments."

"U'm," commented de Grandin. "The treatment was correct, *Mademoiselle*. The chauffeur who drove them, where is he? I am told he, also, was hurt."

"Yes, you'll find him in Ward D," the girl replied. "He wasn't hurt much, but he was taking on quite a bit when I came through."

"U'm" de Grandin remarked again, and turned toward the room where the Bennetts' taxi-driver lay.

"*Mon vieux*," the Frenchman bent above the patient's cot and laid a friendly hand on his shoulder, "we are come to interview you. You will please tell us what occurred?"

"If you're from th' insurance comp'ny," the chauffeur answered, "I want you to git me, and git me right; I wasn't drunk, no matter what these here folks tell you. I'm off'n that stuff, an' have been ever since th' kid wuz born."

"But of course," de Grandin agreed with a nod. "That much is understood, and you will please describe the accident."

"Well you can take it or leave it," the other replied truculently. "I wuz drivin' south through Minot Avenoo, makin' pretty good time, 'cause th' young gentleman told me he had a dinner date, an' just as I was turnin' into Tecumseh Street I seen what I thought wuz a piece o' timber or sumpin layin' across th' road, an' turned out to avoid it. Blow me if th' thing didn't move right across th' pa'ment ahead o' me, keepin' in me path all th' time. You can believe me or not—I'm tellin' you the gospel truth, though—it wuz a alligator. I know a alligator when I see one, too, for I drove a taxi down to Miami durin' th' boom, an' I seen plenty o' them animated satchels down there in th' 'gator farms. Yes, sir, it was a 'gator an' nothin' else, an' th' biggest 'gator I ever seen, too. Must a' been sixteen or eighteen foot long, if it wuz a inch, an' a lot sprier on its feet than any 'gator I ever seen before, for I wuz goin' at a right fair clip, as I told you, an' Minot Avenoo ain' more'n fifty foot wide from curb to curb, but fast as I wuz goin', I couldn't turn out fast enough to keep that cussed thing fr'm crawlin' right smack in front o' me. I ain't partic'lar 'bout runnin' over a lizard, d'ye see, an' if this here thing hadn't been th' granddaddy of all th' 'gators that ever got turned into suitcases an' pocketbooks, I'd a' run 'im down an' gone on me way; but runnin' over a thing like that wuz as much as me axles wuz worth—he wuzn't a inch less'n three foot high fr'm belly to back, not countin' th' extra height o' his legs—an' me cab ain't paid for yet, so I turns out like there wuz a ten-foot hole in th' pa'ment ahead o' me, an' dam' if that thing didn't keep right ahead o' me till I lost control o' me wheel, an' th' nex' thing I knowed—zowie! I wuz parked up agin a tree wid me radiator leakin' like a cake o' ice lef' out in th' sun on Fourt' o' July, an' me wid me head half-way t'rough th' windshield, an' me two fares knocked right outa th' cab where th' door'd give way in th' smash-up. That's th' Gawd's truth, an' you can take it or leave it."

"*Cordieu*, my excellent one," de Grandin assured him, "we do take it, nor do we require salt upon it, either. This alligator, now, this so abominable saurian who did cause you to collide with the roadside tree, was he in the locality when the ambulance arrived."

"Sa-ay, you tryin' to kid me?" demanded the injured man.

"By no means. We believe all you have told us. Can you not be equally frank with us and reply to our queries?"

"Well," returned the patient, mollified by de Grandin's evident credence, "that's th' funny part o' th' joke, sir. When th' ding-dong came for me an' me fares, I told th' sawbones about th' 'gator, an' he ups an' says to th' murderer 'at runs, th' business end o' th' rattler, 'This here guy's been drinkin' more hootch 'an Ol' Man Volstead ever prohibited.' That's what he says, sir, an' me as sober as a court-house full o' judges, too!"

"Infamous!" de Grandin pronounced, "But the *sine qua non* of your accident, this monster alligator, where was he?"

"Say," the driver confided, "you know what? He wuzn't no place. If I hadn't seen 'im wid me own eyes I'd a' believed th' sawbones when he said I had th' heebie-jeebies; but I tell you I hadn't had nuttin' to drink, an' I ain't so nutty as to mistake a shadder for a real, live 'gator, 'specially a baby th' size o' that one. It'd be different if I wuz a bozo 'at hadn't been around much; but I been to Florida, an' I knows a 'gator when I sees one—git me?"

"*Mais oui*, my friend," the Frenchman nodded, "your story has the veritable ring of verisimilitude."

"It *has*, has it? It's th' truth, an' nuttin' else but!" the offended chauffeur exclaimed as de Grandin rose and with another friendly nod tip-toed from the room.

"That explains it," I jubilated as we walked slowly down the corridor. The uncanniness of the night's happenings had gotten on my nerves, and I had been on the point of believing my friend's mishap might be traceable to the ancient curse, but here was a perfectly natural explanation of the whole affair. "If that man wasn't drunk or half insane with cocaine I'm much mistaken. Of course, he imagined he saw an alligator crossing his path! I'm only surprised that he didn't insist it was pink or baby blue instead of the conventional shade. These taxi-drivers—"

"This particular one told the truth," de Grandin cut in, speaking softly, as though more to himself than to me. "When he assured me he was no longer drinking there was the indubitable ring of truth in his words. Moreover—"

"Yes? Moreover?" I prompted, as he strode a dozen or so paces in thoughtful silence.

"*Tiens*, it is most strange, but not impossible," he replied. "This Sebek, I know him."

"You know him? Sebek? What in the world—" I stammered incredulously.

"Perfectly, my friend. Sebek, the god whom the priest Kaku worshiped, was the typification of the sun's harmful powers. To him the waters of the Nile, when at their lowest ebb, were parceled off as his particular domain. He was represented as a crocodile-headed deity, even as Anubis possessed the head of a jackal, and in all his phases he was evil—very evil, indeed. Granted that the priest's powers were effective—and did he not so hypnotize Madame Bennett that she slept like one dead for more than a thousand years?—what would be more natural than that this god should appear in his traditional form to aid his votary? Bethink you of the wording of the curse, my friend: '*My shadow, and the shadow of Sebek which is my god, is upon her.*'"

"Nonsense!" I scoffed.

"Perhaps," he conceded, as though the point were scarcely worth debating. "You may be right, but then, again—"

"Right? Of course I'm right! The old priest might have been able to suspend Peligia's vital processes by some sort of super-hypnosis unknown to us, but how could he call down on her the curse of a god that never existed? You'll scarcely assert that the heathen gods of ancient Egypt had actual existence, I suppose?"

"There is a difference between an individual entity and an abstract force, whether it be for good or evil," he began, but ceased abruptly at the sudden sound which tore the hospital's sepulchral quiet into shreds.

It was not the wail of tortured flesh giving tongue to insupportable pain as the blessed unconsciousness of the anesthetic waned. No surgeon whose apprenticeship was served at the rear end of an ambulance can fail to recognize the cry of returning consciousness from an etherized patient. This was the horrified, piercing scream of a woman in deadly terror long-drawn, breathless, the reflex outcry of normal nerves suddenly strained past their limit of endurance. And it came from the room where Peligia Bennett lay, still immersed in anesthesia.

"*Mon Dieu*," de Grandin gasped, "the *garde-malade!*" Grasping my arm, he rushed pell-mell down the hall.

The buxom young woman to whose care Peligia had been entrusted when de Grandin finished mending her broken body crouched at the far corner of the room, and her normally florid face was chalky-white under the shaded bedside lamp. "It came out of the wall!" she gasped as we swung the door back. "Out of the wall, I tell you, and there was no body to it!"

"Eh, what do you say?" de Grandin snapped. "What came out of the wall, *Mademoiselle?* What had no body, if you please?"

"The hand—the hand that snatched at her throat!" The nurse groveled closer in the angle of the wall, as though to shield herself from attack from side and rear.

"The hand? Her throat? *Grand Dieu!*" de Grandin leaped across the little room like a cat pouncing on a luckless sparrow and turned back the chaste white sheet enshrouding Peligia's supine body.

"Trowbridge, Trowbridge, my friend," he commanded, and his voice was hoarse as a croaking frog's, "behold!"

I joined him at the bedside and cast my glance where his shaking forefinger pointed.

A fifth pendant had disappeared from the necklace round Peligia's throat. Of the seven stones there remained but two.

6. Catastrophe

A FLURRY OF SNOWFLAKES, WIND-DRIVEN by the January tempest, assaulted de Grandin and me as we alighted from the late New York train. "*Cordieu*," the Frenchman laughed as he snuggled into the farther corner of the station taxicab, "to attend the play in the metropolis is good, Friend Trowbridge, but we pay a heavy price in chilled feet and frosted noses when we return in such a storm as this!"

"Yes, getting chilblains is one of the favorite winter sports among us sub-urbanites," I replied, lighting a cigar and puffing mingled smoke and vaporized breath from my nostrils.

"U'm," he remarked thoughtfully, "your mention of winter sports reminds me that our friends the Bennetts are at Lake Placid. I wonder much how it is with them?"

"They're not there now," I answered. "Ellsworth wrote me that both he and Peligia are completely recovered and he expects to reopen his home this week. We'll have to look in on them later. I wonder if they've had any more visitations from—what was his name?—the old Egyptian priest, you know." I could not forbear the sly dig at my friend, for his stubborn insistence that the series of mishaps befalling Ellsworth Bennett and his wife were due to the malign influence of a man dead and buried more than a thousand years struck me as droll.

"*Prie Dieu* they have not," he responded seriously. "As you have been at great pains to assure me many times, my friend, all has seemed well with them since the night of their motor accident, but"—he paused a moment—"as yet I am unconvinced we have heard the last of that so wicked Kaku and his abominable god."

"We certainly have not, if you insist on raving about them," I returned rather testily as the taxi swung into our block. "If I were you, I'd—"

Clang! Clang! clang-clang-a-lang! Rushing like the wind, its siren shrieking like the tempest, and its bells sounding clamorous warning, a fire-engine swept past us, its uproar cutting short my utterance.

"*Mordieu*, what a night for a fire!" the Frenchman murmured as we ascended my front steps.

The office telephone was shrilling wildly as I fitted my latchkey to the door.

"Hello—hello, Dr. Trowbridge?" an agonized voice hailed as I lifted the receiver.

"Yes."

"Bennett, Ellsworth Bennett, talking. Our house is on fire, and Peligia is—I'm bringing her right over to your place." The sharp click of his receiver smashed into its hook and closed his announcement like an exclamation point.

"The Bennetts are still pursued by Kaku, it seems," I remarked sarcastically, turning to de Grandin. "That was Ellsworth on the 'phone. It was his house the engines were going to. He wasn't very coherent, but I gathered that Peligia is injured, and he's bringing her here."

"Eh, do you say so?" the little Frenchman replied, his small eyes widening with sudden concern. "Perhaps, my friend, you will now believe—" He lapsed into silence, striding nervously up and down the office, lighting one cigarette from the glowing stump of another, answering my attempts at conversation with short, monosyllabic grunts.

Ten minutes later when I answered the insistent clatter of the front doorbell, Ellsworth Bennett stood in the vestibule, a long bundle, swathed in rugs and blankets, in his arms. A wave of sudden pity swept over me as I noted his appearance.

The light-hearted, easy-going boy who had taken his strange bride's hand in his before the altar of the Greek Orthodox church a short four months ago was gone, and in his place stood a man prematurely aged. Lines, deep-etched by care and trouble, showed about his mouth and at the corners of his eyes, and his long, loosely articulated frame bent beneath something more than the weight of the object he clasped to his breast.

"Ellsworth, boy, whatever is the matter?" I exclaimed sympathetically as I seized his shoulder and fairly dragged him across the threshold.

"God knows," he answered wearily, laying his inert burden on the surgery table and turning a miserable countenance to us. "I brought her here because"—he seemed to struggle with himself a moment, then continued—"I brought her here because I didn't know where else to take her. I thought she'd be safer here—with you, sir," he turned directly to de Grandin with an imploring look.

"Ohé la pauvre—" the Frenchman leaned forward and put back the coverings from Peligia's pale face tenderly. "Tell me, mon enfant," he glanced up at the distracted husband, "what was it this time?"

"God knows," the wretched youngster repeated. "We got back from the lake on Tuesday, and Peligia seemed so well and so"—a sob choked him, but he went bravely on—"and so happy, and we thought we'd managed to escape from the nemesis which pursues us.

"We went to bed early this evening, and I don't know how long we'd slept when we awakened together, smelling smoke in the room.

"Flames were darting and creeping under the door like so many serpents when we realized what was happening, and I grabbed the bedside 'phone to call the fire department, but the wires must have burned already, for I couldn't get any response from central.

"When I opened the door the whole hallway was a mass of flames, and there was no possibility of anything human going through; so I made a rope by tearing the bed sheets in strips and prepared to escape by the window. After I'd knotted the sheets together I tossed the other bedclothes out to act as a cushion when we landed, and slid down, then stood waiting to catch Peligia in my arms. I'd managed to slip on some clothes, but her things had been lying on a chair near the door, and had caught fire before she could put 'em on, so there was nothing for her to do but brave the storm in her nightclothes.

"I was standing, waiting to catch her in my arms, and she had already begun to slide down the knotted sheets when—" He paused, and a shudder ran through him, as though the chill of his midnight escape still clung to him, despite my surgery's warmth.

"Yes, what then?" de Grandin prompted.

"I saw him! I tell you, I saw him!" the boy blazed out, as though we had already denied his word.

"Dieu de tous les poissons!" de Grandin almost screamed. "Proceed. What, or whom, did you see?"

"I don't know who it was, but I suspect," the other responded. "Just as Peligia was slipping down the sheets, a man looked out of the window, above her and tried to choke her!

"Mind you, not forty seconds before, we'd been driven from that bedroom by the fire which was raging in the hall, and there was no chance for anything living to pass through that flaming hell, and no one in the room when we quit it, but there was a man at our window as my wife began her descent. He leaned over the sill and snatched at her throat, as if trying to strangle her. I heard her scream above the hiss of the fire as he missed his clutch at her throat and drew back a moment; then he whipped out a knife and slashed the sheet in two, six inches below the level of the sill.

"I couldn't have been mistaken, gentlemen," he turned a challenging glance from one of us to the other. "I tell you, *I saw him*; saw him as plainly as I see you now. The fire was at his back and he stood out like a silhouette against its light.

"God!" he shuddered. "I'll never forget the look of hellish hate and triumph on his face as he hacked that sheet in two and my poor darling came crashing down—he was a tall, cadaverous fellow, dressed in a sort of smock of gray-green linen, and his head was shaven—not bald, but shaven—and so was his entire face, except for a narrow, six-inch beard on his chin. That was waxed to a point and turned up like a fish-hook."

"*A-a-ah?*" de Grandin remarked on a rising note. His level, unwinking gaze caught and held Bennett's, and horrified understanding and agreement showed in the eyes of each.

De Grandin shook his narrow shoulders in a quick, impatient shrug. "We must not let him terrify us, or all is lost," he declared. "Meantime, let us look to *Madame*, your wife." He cast back the covers from Peligia and ran deft, skillful fingers over her form from neck to feet.

"Here it is," he announced, pausing in his examination to finger her rounded left ankle. "A dislocation; no more, let us give thanks. It will be painful, but not serious, I think.

"Come, Friend Trowbridge, the bandages, if you please," he turned peremptorily to me, raising the girl's small, uncovered foot in his hand and gently kneading the displaced bones back into position. "Ah, that is better," he announced, as he completed fastening the gauze about the injured member.

"Now, Bennett, my friend, if you will bear *Madame* your lady upstairs and put her in my bed, I think we can promise—*nom de Dieu de nom de Dieu*—look!" he broke off, pointing a trembling finger at the open throat of Peligia's flimsy muslin night-dress.

Against the white bosom where the ancient necklace reposed, a single ruddy pendant glowed. Six of the seven stones were missing.

7. Wager of Battle

J ULES DE GRANDIN STARED at Ellsworth Bennett, and Ellsworth Bennett stared at Jules de Grandin, and in the eyes of each was gathering terror, hopelessness, defeat.

"What to do—*Mon Dieu!*—what to do?" muttered the little Frenchman, and his voice was almost a wail.

"My friend," he stared fixedly at Ellsworth, "did you do as I suggested?"

"Go to the priest?" the other replied. "Yes. He gave us some sort of little charm—I suppose you'd call it an *ikon*. See, here it is." Reaching inside his wife's gown he drew out a fine silken cord to the end of which was attached a tiny scapular of painted silk showing the device of a mailed champion encountering a dragon. "It's supposed to be a relic of St. George," he explained, "and Father Demitri assured us no harm could come to her while she wore it. God in heaven—if there is one!" he burst into a peal of chattering laughter. "He told us it would protect her! See how it worked!" With another laugh he pointed to the necklace and at its single remaining stone which seemed to wink sardonically at us as it rose and fell with the regular movement of Peligia's breast.

"*Non, non,*" the Frenchman muttered, "new charms are valueless against ancient evils. We must combat that which is old and bad by that which is equally old, but good. But how—*nom d'un canard!*—how?

"Take her upstairs, my friend," he motioned almost frantically to Bennett. "Take her upstairs and lay her in my bed. Watch beside her, and, if you have not forgotten how, pray; pray as you did when a lad beside your mother's knee. Meanwhile I—*Grand Dieu*, I shall do what I can!"

As Bennett bore his swooning bride up the stairs the little Frenchman seated himself beside the surgery desk, put both elbows down upon its polished surface and cupped his pointed chin in his palms, staring straight before him with a fixed, unseeing stare of utter abstraction.

At last: "*Parbleu*, it is desperate but so are we. We shall try it!" he announced. For a moment his gaze wandered wildly about the room, passing rapidly over the floor, walls and ceiling. At last it came to rest on a sepia print of Rembrandt's *Study in Anatomy*.

"I know not whether it will serve," he muttered, rising quickly and detaching the picture from its hook, "but, *parbleu*, it *must!*

"Go, Friend Trowbridge," he ordered over his shoulder while he worked feverishly at the screw-eyes to which the picture's wire was attached. "Do you go upstairs and see how it is with our friends. Me, I shall follow anon."

"Everything all right?" I asked as cheerfully as I could as I entered the room where Peligia lay as silent as though in a trance.

"I—don't know," Bennett faltered. "I put her to bed, as you ordered, and before I could even begin to pray I fell asleep. I just woke up a moment ago. I don't think she's—oh; *o-o-oh!*" The exclamation was wrung from him as a scream might come from a culprit undergoing the torture. His wife's head, pillowed against the bed linen, was white as the snowy cloth itself, and already there was a look of impending death upon her features. Too often I had seen that look on a patient's face as the clock hands neared the hour of two. Unless I was much mistaken, Peligia Bennett would never see the morning's sun.

"*Ha*, it seems I come none too soon," de Grandin's voice came in a strident whisper from the door behind us.

"My friends," he announced, facing each of us in turn, his little eyes dilated with excitement, "this night I enter the lists against a foe whose strength I know not, and I do greatly fear my own weapons are but feeble things. Trowbridge, dear old friend"—his slender, strong hand clasped mine in a quick pressure—"should it so happen that I return no more, see that they write upon my tomb: 'He died serving his friends.'"

"But, my dear chap, surely you're not going to leave us now," I began, only to have my protest drowned by his shout:

"Priest Kaku, server of false gods, persecutor of women, I charge thee, come forth; manifest thyself, if thou darest. I, Jules de Grandin, challenge thee!"

I shook my head, and rubbed my eyes in amazement. Was it the swirl of snowflakes, driven through the partly opened window by the howling January blast, or the fluttering of the scrim curtain, that patch of white at the farther end of the room? Again I looked, and amazement gave way to something akin to incredulity, and that, in turn, to horror. In the empty air beside the window-place there was taking form, like a motion-picture projected on a darkened screen, *the shadowy form of a man*. Tall, cadaverous, as though long dead and buried, he was clothed in a straight-hanging one-piece garment of grayish-green linen, with shaven head and face, protruding, curling beard, and eyes the like of which I had never seen in human face, eyes which glowed and smoldered with a fiery glint like the red reflection of the glory-hole of lowest hell.

For an instant he seemed to waver, half-way between floor and ceiling, regarding the little Frenchman with a look of incomparable fury, then his burning, glowing orbs fixed themselves intently on the sleeping woman on the bed.

Peligia gave a short, stifled gasp, her lids fluttered open, but her eyes stared straight before her sightlessly. Her slender, blue-veined hands rose slowly from the counterpane, stretched out, toward the hovering phantom in the corner of the room, and slowly, laboriously, like a woman in a hypnotic trance, she rose, put forth one foot from the bed, and made as if to walk to the beckoning, compelling eyes burning in the livid face of the—there was no doubt about it—*priest of Sebek* who stood, now fully materialized, beside the window of my bedroom.

"Back!" de Grandin screamed, thrusting out one hand and forcing her once more into the bed.

He wheeled about, facing the green-robed priest of Egypt with a smile more fierce than any frown. "*Monsieur* from hell," he challenged, "long years ago you did make wager of battle against him who should lift thy spell, and the spell of Sebek, thy unclean god, from off this woman. He who submits to ordeal by battle may fight for himself or engage a champion. Behold in me the champion of this man and this woman. Say, wilt thou battle against me for their lives and happiness, or art thou the filthy coward which I do believe thee?"

It was monstrous, it was impossible; it could not be; my reason told me that flesh and blood could not enter the lists against intangible phantoms and hope to win; yet there, in the quiet of my bedroom, Jules de Grandin flung aside jacket and waistcoat, bent his supple body nearly double, and charged headlong into the twining embrace of a thing which had materialized out of the air.

As he leaped across the room the Frenchman snatched something from his pocket and whirled it about his head like a whiplash. With a gasp of amazement I recognized it for a four foot strand of soft-iron picture wire—the wire he had taken from the print in my surgery.

The phantom arms swept forward to engulf my little friend, the phantom face lit up with a smile as diabolical as that of Satan at the arrival of a newly damned soul, yet it was but a moment ere I realized the battle was not hopelessly to the ghost-thing and against his mortal opponent.

De Grandin seemed to make no attempt to grapple with the priest of Sebek or to snare him in the loop of wire. Rather his sole attention seemed directed to avoiding the long-bladed copper knife with which the priest was armed.

Again and again the wraith stabbed savagely at de Grandin's face, throat or chest. Each time the Frenchman avoided the lunging knife and brought his loop of woven iron down upon the ghost-thing's arms, shoulders or shaven pate, and I noticed with elation that the specter writhed at each contact with the iron as though it had been white-hot.

How long the struggle lasted I do not know. De Grandin was panting like a spent runner, and great streams of perspiration ran down his pale face. The other made no sound of breathing, nor did his sandaled feet scuff against the carpet as he struggled with the Frenchman. Bennett and I stood as silent as two graven images, and only the short, labored breathing of the little Frenchman broke the stillness of the room as the combat waxed and waned.

At last it seemed the phantom foeman was growing lighter, thinner, less solid. Where formerly he had seemed as much a thing of flesh and bone as his antagonist, I could now distinctly descry the outlines of pieces of furniture when he stood between them and me. He was once more assuming his ghostly transparency.

Time and again he sought to strike through de Grandin's guard. Time and again the Frenchman flailed him with the iron scourge, avoiding his knife by the barest fraction of an inch.

At length: "*In nomine Domini!*" de Grandin shrieked, leaping forward and showering a perfect hailstorm of whip-lashes on his opponent.

The green-clad priest of Sebek seemed to wilt like a wisp of grass thrown into the fire, to trail upward like a puff of smoke, to vanish and dissolve in the encircling air. "*Triomphe*, it is finished!" sobbed de Grandin, stumbling across the room and half falling across the bed where Peligia Bennett lay. "It is finished, and—*mon Dieu*—I am broken!" Burying his face in the coverlet, he fell to sobbing like a child tired past the point of endurance.

"IT WAS MAGNIFICENT," I told him as we sat in my study, a box of cigars and one of my few remaining bottles of cognac between us. "You fought that ghost bare-handed, and conquered him, but I don't understand any of it. Do you feel up to explaining?"

He stretched luxuriously, lighted a fresh cigar and flashed one of his quick, impish smiles at me through the smoke wreaths. "Have you studied much of ancient Egypt?" he asked, irrelevantly.

"Mighty little," I confessed.

"Then you are, perhaps, not aware of the absence of iron in their ruins? You do not know their mummy-cases are put together with glue and wooden dowels, and such instruments of metal as are found in their temples are of copper or bronze, never of iron or steel?"

"I've heard something like that," I replied, "but I don't quite get the significance of it. It's a fact that they didn't understand the art of making steel, isn't it, and used tempered copper instead?"

"I doubt it," he answered. "The arts of old Egypt were highly developed, and they most assuredly had means of acquiring iron, or even steel, had they so desired. No, my friend, the absence of iron is due to a cause other than ignorance. Iron, you must know, is the most earthly of all metals. Spirits, even of the good, find it repugnant, and as for the evil ones, they abhor it. Do you begin to see?"

"No, I can't say I do. You mean—"

"I mean that, more than any other country, Egypt was absorbed with the spiritual side of life. Men's days there were passed in communing with the souls of the departed or spirits of another sort, elemental spirits, which had never worn the clothing of the flesh.

"The mummification of their dead was not due to any horror of putrefaction, but to their belief that a physical resurrection would take place at the end of seven ages—roughly, seven thousand years. During that time, according to their religion, the body would lie in its tomb, and at the end of the period the soul, or *ka*, would return and reanimate it. Meantime, the *ka* kept watch beside the mummy. Do you now see why no iron entered into their coffins?"

"Because the spirit, watching beside the body, would find the iron's proximity uncomfortable?"

"Precisely, my friend, you have said it. There have been authenticated instances of ghosts being barred from haunted houses by no greater barrier than an iron wire stretched across the door. In Ireland the little people are ofttimes kept from a cottage by nothing more than a pair of steel shears opened with their points toward the entrance. So it was that I determined to put it to a test and attack that shade of Kaku with naught but a scourge of iron. *Eh bien*, it was a desperate chance, but it was successful."

The flame of his match flared flickeringly as he set fire to a fresh cigar and continued: "Now, as to that jewel of seven stones with which Madame Bennett's fate is interwoven. That, my friend, is a talisman—an outward and visible sign of an invisible and spiritual force. In his hypnotic command to her to sleep until awakened by someone in a later age, or else to die completely at the end of seven thousand years, Kaku the priest had firmly planted in her mind the thought that if the seven stones of that jewel were destroyed, her second life should also wane. The seven stones were to her a constant reminder of the fate which overshadowed her like—like, by example, the string you tie about your finger to remind you to buy fresh razor-blades or tooth-powder next time you go past the drug store." He grinned delightedly at his homely example.

"But how could Kaku know when Peligia had been awakened, and how could he come back to fight for her?" I demanded.

"Kaku, my friend, is dead," he replied seriously, "but like your own Monsieur John Brown, his soul goes—or, at least, went—marching on. And because it was not a good soul, but one which dwelt within its body in constant companionship with the ugly thought of jealousy, it was not permitted to continue its journey toward perfection, but was chained to the earth it had aforetime walked. Always in Kaku's consciousness, even after he had ceased to possess a body, was the thought of his unrequited love for Peligia and the fear that she should be awakened from her trance by a man whom she would love. Not more swiftly does the fireman respond to the alarm than did the restless, earthbound spirit of Kaku answer the knowledge that Peligia had returned to consciousness. In the guise of a cat he came at first, for cats were familiar things in old Egypt. Again, in the form of a crocodile he did all but kill the young Bennett and his bride as they motored to dine with us. Once more—and how he did it we do not know—he appeared and set fire to their house, and all but encompassed her death when he caused the rope to part as Peligia escaped the flames.

"This night he came to call her by strength of will from out her fleshly body to join his wandering spirit, but—thanks be to God!—we thwarted him by the use of so simple a thing as a length of iron wire, from which his spirit, earthbound as it was, did shrink."

"But see here," I persisted, "do you mean to tell me Kaku will never return to plague Peligia, and Ellsworth again?"

"Yes," he said, with an elfish grin, "I think I may truthfully say that Kaku will never again return. *Parbleu*, this night the iron literally entered into his soul!

"You saw me contend with him; you saw him vanish like the shadows of night before the rising sun. Draw your own happy conclusions. Meantime"—he reached for the shining green bottle in which the cognac glowed with a ruby iridescence—"to your very good health, my friend, and the equally good health of Monsieur and Madame Bennett."

The Serpent Woman

"**G**RAND *DIEU*, FRIEND TROWBRIDGE, have a care!" Jules de Grandin clutched excitedly at my elbow with his left hand, while with the other he pointed dramatically toward the figure which suddenly emerged from the shadowy evergreens bordering the road and flitted like a windblown leaf through the zone of luminance cast by my headlights. "*Pardieu*, but she will succeed in destroying herself if she does that once too—" he continued; then interrupted himself with a shout as he flung both feet over the side of the car and dashed down the highway to grapple with the woman whose sudden appearance had almost sent us skidding into the wayside ditch.

Nor was his intervention a second too soon, for even as he reached her side the mysterious woman had run to the center of the highway bridge, and was drawing herself up, preparatory to leaping over the parapet into the rushing stream fifty feet below.

"Stop it, *Mademoiselle!* Desist!" he commanded sharply, seizing her shoulders in his small, strong hands and dragging her backward to the dusty planks of the bridge by main force.

She fought like a cornered wildcat. "Let me go!" she raged, struggling in the little Frenchman's embrace; then, finding her efforts unavailing, twisting suddenly round to face him and clawing at his cheeks with desperate, fear-stiffened fingers. "Let me go; I want to die; I must die; I *will* die, I tell you!" she screamed. "Let me go!"

De Grandin shifted his grasp from her shoulders to her wrists and shook her roughly, as a terrier might shake a rat. "Be still, *Mademoiselle!*" he ordered curtly. "Cease this business of the fool, or, *parbleu*"—he administered another shake—"I shall be forced to tie you!"

I added my efforts to his, grasping the raging woman by the elbows and forcing her into the twin shafts of light thrown by the car's driving-lamps.

Leaning forward, de Grandin retrieved her hat and placed it on her dark head at a decidedly rakish angle; then regarded her meditatively in the headlights' glare. "Will you restrain yourself, if we loose you, *Mademoiselle?*" he asked after a few seconds' silent inspection.

The young woman regarded him sullenly a moment, then broke into a sharp, cachinnating laugh. "You've only postponed the inevitable," she announced with a fatalistic shrug of her shoulders. "I'll kill myself as soon as you leave me, anyway. You might as well have saved yourself the trouble."

"U'm?" the Frenchman murmured. "Precisely, exactly, quite so, *Mademoiselle*; and for that reason we shall take pains not to abandon you. *Nom d'un parapluie*, are we murderers? We shall not leave you to your fate. Tell us where you live, and we shall take you there."

She faced us with quivering nostrils and heaving, tumultuous breast, anger flashing from her eyes, a diatribe of invective seemingly ready to spill from her lips. She had a rather pretty, high-bred face; unnaturally large, dark eyes, seeming larger still because of the deep violet circles under them; death-pale skin contrasting strongly with the little tendrils of dark, curling hair which hung about her cheeks beneath the rim of her wide leghorn hat.

"*Mademoiselle*," de Grandin announced with a bow, "you are beautiful. There is no reason for you to wish to die. Come with us; Dr. Trowbridge and I shall do ourselves the honor of escorting you to your home."

"I'm Mrs. Candace," she replied simply, as though the name would explain everything.

"*Madame*," de Grandin assured her, bowing formally from the hips, as though acknowledging an introduction, "the very great honor is ours. I am Jules de Grandin, and this is Dr. Samuel Trowbridge. May we have the honor of your company—"

"But—but," the girl broke in, half-believingly, "you mean you don't know who I am?"

"Until a moment ago we have been denied the happiness of your acquaintance, *Madame*," rejoined the Frenchman with another bow. "You are now ready to accompany us!" he added, glancing toward the car.

Something like gratitude shone in the young woman's eyes as she answered: "I live in College Grove Park; you may take me there, if you wish, but—"

"*Tiens, Madame*," he interrupted, "let us but no buts, if you please."

Taking her hand in his he led her to the waiting car and assisted her to a seat.

"IT'S KIND OF YOU to do this for me," our passenger murmured as I turned the motor eastward. "I didn't think there was anyone who'd trouble to keep me from dying."

De Grandin shot her a glance of swift inquiry. "Why?" he demanded with Gallic directness.

"Because everyone—everyone but Iring—wants to see me hanged, and sometimes he looks at me so strangely. I think perhaps he's turning against me, too!"

"Ah?" de Grandin responded. "And why should that be?"

"Because of Baby!" she sobbed. "Everyone thinks I killed him—I, his mother! The neighbors all look at me as though I were a monster—call their children away when they see me coming—and never speak to me when I pass them. Even Iring, my husband, is beginning to suspect, I'm afraid, and so I wanted to die—would have done it, too, if you hadn't stopped me."

Utter, hopeless misery was in her tones as she spoke, and de Grandin bent forward with quick impulsiveness, taking her hand in his. "Tell us the story, *Madame*," he begged. "It will relieve your nerves to talk, and it may easily be that Friend Trowbridge and I can be of help—"

"No, you can't," she negatived sharply. "Nobody can help me. There isn't any help for me this side of the grave, but—"

It was a long, heart-rending story the young mother retailed as we sped over the dusty summer road to the pretty little suburb where she lived. Ten days before, she and her husband had been to a party in New York and it was nearly two o'clock in the morning when they returned to College Grove. Iring Junior, their ten-months-old baby, had been left in charge of the Negro maid of all work, and both he and his nurse were fast asleep when his parents gently unlatched the front door and tiptoed down the bungalow hall. Dismissing the maid, Mrs. Candace had crept into the little blue-and-white room where the baby slept, raised the window a few inches—for the maid steadfastly refused to accept the virtues of fresh air—bent down and kissed the sleeping child, then stepped softly to her own room across the hall.

Tired to the point of exhaustion, both parents were soon in bed, but some evil premonition seemed to keep the mother's eyelids open. Sitting up in bed suddenly, she heard a tiny whimper in the nursery, the half-articulate sound of a little boy-baby turning restlessly in his sleep, and without waiting to don either house-robe or slippers, she ran barefooted across the hall, pushed open the nursery door and switched on the bedside lamp.

The boy was gone. In the little white pillow of his crib was the dent where his curly head had rested; the shape of his straight little body could be traced by the rise of the light blanket-sheet, but, save for the brown, woolly Teddy bear and the black patent-leather cat mounting guard at the foot of the crib, the nursery was untenanted.

"I called my husband," she went on between deep, heart-racking sobs, "and we searched the house, then looked everywhere outside, but our little son was nowhere to be found. The nursery door was latched, though not locked, but his baby fingers could not have unfastened it, even if he had managed to crawl that far. The nursery window was open about ten inches, and there was no screen in it, but Baby could not have crept through it, for I had the blanket fastened down at the head and foot with clamps to keep him from kicking it off during the night, and he couldn't have gotten out of bed by himself. Yet our baby was nowhere.

"We looked for him all night, and kept our search up most of next day; but there isn't any clue to his whereabouts, no sign to show how he left us, unless—"

She shuddered convulsively.

"Yes?" de Grandin prompted.

"And the rumor got about that I killed him! They say I did away with my own little baby, and they won't come near me, nor let me come near them, and when I walk down the street the mothers run and snatch their children into the house as though I carried plague germs!"

"*Mordieu*, but this is infamous, this is intolerable, this is not to be borne!" de Grandin exploded. "You have undoubtlessly advised the police of the case, *Madame*?"

"The police?" her voice was thin, high-pitched, like the muted scream of one in pain past bodily endurance. "*It was the police who started the rumor!*"

"*Nom d'un coq!*" de Grandin demanded in incredulous amazement. "You would have us to understand that—"

"I would have you to understand just that!" she mocked. "There is no clue to the manner in which my baby disappeared. No footprints, no fingerprints"—for a moment she hesitated, breathing deeply, then continued—"nothing. When the police could find nothing to go on, no person who would wish us misfortune or have a reason for stealing our baby, they said I must have done it. The only reason I'm not locked up this moment, waiting trial for murder, is that they have not been able to find Baby's body—though they've had our cellar floor up and knocked down half the partitions in the house—and our maid's testimony shows that Baby was alive and well fifteen minutes before my screams woke her. They can't figure how I'd had time to kill him and hide his little body in that time—that's the only reason they haven't arrested me! Now you know why I wanted to die, and why I fought you when you saved me," she concluded. "And"—defiantly—"why I'm going to kill myself the first chance I have. There won't *always* be someone to stop me!"

De Grandin's little round eyes were shining like those of a cat in the dark, and on his small, pointed-chinned face was a half-thoughtful, half-dreamy expression, like that worn by a person trying to recall the notes of a long-forgotten tune. Suddenly he leaned forward, staring straight into the tear-stained face of the young mother.

"*Madame*," he spoke with slow insistence, "there is something you have not told us. Twice did I notice your speech halt and falter like a poorly trained horse before the hurdle. At the back of your brain lies another thought, a thought you have not clothed in words. What is it you have not yet told anyone, *Madame?*"

The girl's large, dark eyes widened suddenly, as though a light had been flashed before them. "No, no!" she almost screamed.

"*Madame*," de Grandin's tone was low, but his voice was inexorable, "you will please tell me the thing you have not yet spoken of."

"You'd think me crazy!"

"Madame Candace, you will tell me!" Again the low, even tone of command.

"I—I was brought up in the country," the girl stammered, fighting for breath between syllables like a runner nearly spent, or an exhausted swimmer battling with the surf. "I was brought up in the country, and the day after Baby disappeared I noticed something down at the lower end of our garden—something I hadn't seen since we lived on the farm and I used to walk barefoot on the dirt roads."

De Grandin's features contracted sharply, as though a presentiment of what she would say had come to him, but he persisted. "Yes? You saw—"

"A snake track—the track of a snake, fresh and unmistakable in the soft earth of the rose beds—but not the track of any snake I've ever seen, for it was wide as the mark of an automobile tire!"

"Ah?" the little Frenchman's voice was lower than a whisper, but swift understanding shone in his small blue eyes. "You think, perhaps—"

"God in heaven, don't say it!" she screamed. "It's bad enough to live with the thought; but if you put it into words—"

"Trowbridge, my friend," de Grandin whispered sharply, "yonder is her home. Help me carry her there. She has swooned."

A YOUNG MAN WHOSE FACE showed the deep etchings of sleepless nights and tormented days answered our ring at the cottage door. "Stella!" he exclaimed as he caught sight of his wife's white, drawn face; then, to us: "I've been looking all over for her. This terrible trouble has"—he paused as a sob choked back the words—"her mind, you know, gentlemen."

"U'm?" responded de Grandin noncommittally as we bore her to the couch.

"I've been terribly worried about you, dear," her husband told Mrs. Candace as a slow wave of returning color suffused her face. "When I couldn't find you in the house I went outside, and called and called, but—"

"I know, dear," the young wife interrupted wearily. "It was so hot and stuffy here, I thought I'd take a little walk, but it was too much for me, and these kind gentlemen brought me home."

Young Candace looked doubtfully at us a moment, as though debating whether it was safe to speak before us; then, abruptly deciding we were to be trusted, he blurted: "We've news at last, dear. Part of the mystery is cleared up. Baby's alive—if this is to be believed—and we've a chance of finding him."

"Oh!" Mrs. Candace sprang from the couch as though suddenly shocked by an electric current. "What is it, Iring? What is it?"

For answer he extended a sheet of yellow paper, the sort schoolchildren use to figure their sums upon. "I found this tucked under the screen door when I came back from looking for you," he replied.

Without pausing for permission, de Grandin gazed over the mother's shoulder as she perused the missive her husband had handed her. As she finished reading, he took the paper gently from her and passed it to me.

The words were formed of letters cut from a newspaper and pasted irregularly together, making a sort of crazy-quilt of small characters and large. Many words were grotesquely misspelled, but the message as a whole was easily decipherable:

Mr. & Mrs. Candace, Esq., yUr kid is al right anD well anough and i aM takin gooD care of it but i aint go ing to wait foreVr I'm a poor man an I got to live and you better get me some money mighty dam quik or Ill quit makiNG a bOarding House of myseLf and forgET to feed him but i will hold him in good shape for one week more If you wAnt to see him agan have two thousand $ in cash mOney redy next Tuesday nite at midnite tweLve oclock and throw it from Yur automobil as YOu ride down the piKE between harrisonville an Rupleyville Throw the moneys out where You see a light in the Woods an dont try no triks on me or have the poLice with you or yull never see yur kid no more on account of i bein a desprit man an dont intend no foolin an if they do catch me I wont never tell where he is no matter how much they beat me so yur Kid wIll starv to deth. Have the mony redy when I say an no foolin or you wont never see him agan
    Yurs trulie

By way of signature the note was subscribed with a long, serpentine flourish, like an inverted capital S.

"*Eh bien*, Friend Trowbridge," de Grandin remarked judicially as he took the note back into his hand, "I should say—"

A thunderous knock at the door interrupted his opinion, and a moment later a heavy-set, sandy-haired man in high, mud-spattered boots, corduroy pantaloons and a far from clean blue sweater stalked into the room. "Evenin', Mr. Candace," he greeted, removing his battered felt hat. "Evenin'," he nodded curtly to Mrs. Candace. Of de Grandin and me he took no more notice than if we had not existed. "Did you say you'd had a note from th' kidnaper? Lemme see it.

"Hum," he commented, inspecting the patchwork piece of blackmail under the glare of the living-room electrolier. "Hum-m. When did you git this?"

"I found it tucked under the screen door a few minutes before I 'phoned you," Candace replied. "Mrs. Candace had gone out without letting me know, and I was looking for her. When I couldn't find her in the house I started out into the garden, and found this note folded under the door when I came back. I—"

"Hum." The big man cleared his throat portentously. "Mis' Candace wuz out, wuz she? An' you found this here note in th' door when you come back from lookin' for her, did you? Hum; hum-m. Yeah. I see."

"This is Mr. Perkinson, the assistant county detective," Candace offered a belated introduction, as he indicated de Grandin and me with a wave of his hand. "He's been working on the case, and when I found this ransom letter, I thought it best to get in immediate touch with him."

"Ah," de Grandin murmured softly; then, turning to the detective: "It seems, *Monsieur*, that whoever sent this letter was a cunning miscreant. He has taken most excellent precautions to disguise his handwriting, and the fact that he chose such people as Monsieur and Madame Candace for his victims argues more cleverness. They are neither rich nor poor, but comfortable *bourgeois*. A rich man would have scoured the country with his hired detectives. A poor man could not have paid a ransom. This villain has stolen a child of the middle class and demanded a ransom which the parents can afford to pay. What does it mean? *Parbleu*, I think it indicates he has intimate knowledge of the family's affairs, and—"

"You're damn tootin', Doc," Assistant County Detective Perkinson's agreement interrupted. "I'll say she knows th' family's affairs. Stella Candace," he put a large, freckle-flecked hand on the mother's bowed shoulder, "I arrest ye for the abduction of Iring Candace, Junior, an' it's me duty to warn ye that anything said now may be used agin ye."

"See here—" Iring Candace stepped forward angrily, his face flushed, his eyes flashing dangerously.

"You ignorant, blundering fool!" I exclaimed, thrusting myself between the officer and his prey.

To my amazement, Jules de Grandin remained perfectly calm. "Your perspicacity does you utmost credit, *Monsieur*," he assured the officer with an ironical bow. "By all means, take Madame Candace before the judge. I make me no doubt—"

"I'll be damned if he will!" protested the husband, but Mrs. Candace interposed.

"Don't resist him, Iring" she begged. "He's been aching to arrest me ever since Baby disappeared, and you'll only make matters worse if you try to interfere. Let him take me peaceably, and—"

"And tomorrow, *parbleu*, we shall seek your release on writ of *habeas corpus!*" de Grandin interjected. "After that we shall be free from interference, and may give attention to important matters."

"Good night, dear," Stella Candace turned her lips up to her husband's. "I'll be brave, and you can see a lawyer in the morning, as Dr. de Grandin says. Don't worry."

"Very well, Mr. Perkinson," she said. "I'm ready."

"OH, MY GOD!" *IRING* Candace dropped into a chair, propped his elbows on his knees, cupped his face in his hands and shook with retching sobs. "What shall I do; what *shall* I do? I can't think Stella would do such a thing; but Perkinson—there *might* be something in his suspicions, after all. It's strange I should have found that note after she'd gone out, and yet—"

"*Mordieu*, my friend, there is no yet," de Grandin cut in. "That Perkinson, he is one great zany. *Nom d'un nom*, were all his brains secreted in the hollow of a gnat's tooth they would rattle about like a dried pea in a bass drum!"

"But if Stella's not guilty, how are we going to recover our boy? The police are convinced she did it; we can get no help from them, and the kidnaper will—"

"*Monsieur!*" de Grandin interrupted, offended dignity in his voice. "Have I not said I would undertake the case? *Parbleu*, this kidnaper shall meet his just deserts, be he human or be he—never mind; if I do not apprehend this stealer of little children I am more mistaken than I think I am."

"How will you manage it?" the bereaved father asked with hopeless matter-of-factness. "What can you do that the police haven't already done? The kidnaper will surely suspect if you try to trap him; then our little boy is lost. Oh!"—a fresh burst of sobs broke his words to fragments—"oh, my little son; my little baby boy!"

"*Monsieur*," the Frenchman assured him, "I am Jules de Grandin. What I undertake, that I accomplish.

"*Allons*, Friend Trowbridge," he turned to me; "there remains much to be done and little time in which to do it before we have this child-stealer by the heels."

"NOM D'UN MOUCHERON, BUT it is strange!" Jules de Grandin muttered to himself the following morning as he finished his after-breakfast perusal of the *Journal*. "It is unusual, it is extraordinary, it is ghastly, yet I make no doubt it has some connection with the vanished little one."

"Eh, what's that?" I demanded.

"Read, my friend," he thrust the newspaper into my hand. "Read, and tell me what it is you see."

JERSEY DEVIL IN NEW GUISE?

queried the headline to which his neatly manicured forefinger directed my attention. Below, couched in facetious journalese, was a short article:

Has the well-known and justly celebrated Jersey Devil assumed a new form this summer? William Johannes, a farmer living near Rupleyville, thinks so. Little has been heard of this elusive specter this season, and tired newspapermen had about decided he had retired on a much-needed vacation when Johannes sent in a hurry call to inform the world at large and the *Journal's* city room in particular that he had seen the Devil, and he didn't mean perhaps, either.

Shortly after eight o'clock last night William, who vows he hadn't had a thing stronger than his customary cup of Java with his dinner, was startled to hear an unearthly concert of squeals emanating from the direction of his pig-pen. Armed with his trusty bird gun, William set out hot-foot to see who was disturbing the repose of his prize porkers. As he neared the odoriferous confines of the porcine domicile, he was astonished to hear a final despairing squeal invoke high heaven for assistance, and to see a great, brownish-green snake, at least forty feet in length, go sliding through the bars of the pig-coop. He fired at the monster, but apparently his shot had no effect, for it wriggled away among the bushes and was quickly lost to sight.

Arriving at the pig-sty, William was desolated to discover that three of a litter of six prize Cochin China sucking pigs had completely disappeared, leaving their mother, Madam Hog, in a state bordering on nervous collapse.

In proof of his story William showed your correspondent the tracks of the marauding monster in the soft loam of the woodland adjoining his pig-pen. There were two well-defined trails, one coming, the other going, serpentine in course, and about the width of an automobile—not a Ford—tire. Both were plainly visible for a distance of some twenty feet, after which they were lost in the leaf-strewn ground of the woods.

William says he doesn't mind good clean fun, but when it comes to stealing three valuable piglets the matter ceases to be a joke, and he's going to have the legislature pass a law or something about it.

"Humph!" I grunted, passing the paper back to him. "Some smart-Alec reporter's practicing his imagination again. That 'Jersey Devil' is a standing joke in this state, de Grandin, like the annual sea-serpent fable at Cannes, you know. There's always a stack of fool stories like this in the newspapers about this time of year."

"Indeed?" he raised narrow, black eyebrows. "Do you say so? Nevertheless, my friend, I shall interview the so excellent Monsieur Johannes. It is probable that the journalist is a facile liar, but we did not beat back the *boche* by leaving anything to chance. Me, I shall prove each step of this business."

"What business?" I asked as he pushed back his chair and sought his hat and walking-stick.

"*Ah bah*, my friend," he replied, "you do ask too many questions for the sake of listening to your own voice. Expect me when I return."

"TROWBRIDGE, MON VIEUX, BEHOLD what it is I have discovered," he ordered, bursting into my study some four hours later. "*Parbleu*, but the young man of the press did us an inestimable favor, though he knows it not, when he wrote his tale of the Devil of New Jersey. Observe, if you please!" With a hand that trembled with excitement he extended a bit of folded paper to me.

Opening the slip I beheld what might have been the paring from a horse's hoof made by a blacksmith when preparing to fit a new shoe to the beast.

"Well?" I asked, turning the thing over curiously. "What is it, and what of it?"

"As to what it is, I did not expect recognition from you," he admitted with one of his quick, elfin smiles. "As to its significance—who shall say? That, my friend, is a chip from the belly-armor of a great snake. I did find it after two hours' search upon my hands and knees beside the tracks left by the serpent which raided the sty of Monsieur Johannes' pigs last night. At present I am not prepared to say definitely what sort of reptile shed it, but my guess is in favor of a Burmese python or an African boa. Also, from this scale's size, I should say that terror and astonishment lent magnifying lenses to Monsieur Johannes' eyes when he beheld the snake, for the thing is more likely twenty than forty feet in length, but the good God knows he would be sufficiently formidable to meet, even so."

"Well?" I queried again.

"Well?" he mocked. "Well, what? What does it mean?"

"As far as I can see, it doesn't mean anything, except—"

"*Dieu de Dieu*," he interrupted impatiently "except that Madame Candace was stating only the literal truth when she said she recognized snake tracks in her garden, and that there is actually such a monster abroad in the countryside."

"Why," I stammered as the enormity of his statement struck me, "why, you mean the little Candace boy might have been devoured by this monster? That would account for his disappearance without clues; but what about the ransom letter we saw last night? A snake might eat a child, though I've always under-stood the process of ingestion is rather slow, and I can't quite see how he could have swallowed the little boy before Mrs. Candace reached the nursery; but even you will admit a snake would hardly have been likely to prepare and send that letter demanding two thousand dollars for the child's return."

"Sometimes, Friend Trowbridge," he assured me, solemnly, "I think you a fool. At others I believe you only dull-witted. Can you not reconcile the possi-bility of a great serpent's having made off with the little one and a ransom letter being sent?"

"No, I'm hanged if I can," I admitted.

"*Morbleu*—" he began furiously, then paused, one of his quick smiles driving the annoyed frown from his face. "Forgive me, good, kind friend," he implored. "I do forget you have not had the benefit of my experience at the *Sûreté*. Attend me: Ten days ago the little lad did vanish. The police have been notified, the news of his disappearance has become public. There is no clue to the manner of his going; as yet the pig-ignorant police have no theory worthy of the name. The snake might well be responsible for all this, *n'est-ce-pas?*"

"I suppose so," I admitted.

"*Très bien*. Now suppose some miscreant desired to trade upon the misery of those bereaved parents; what then? Granting that he knew their circumstances, which I strongly suspect he does, what would be easier than for him to concoct such a letter as the dastardly thing we read last night and transmit it stealthily to Monsieur and Madame Candace, knowing full well they would jump at any chance, and pay any sum within their means, to see their baby boy once more?"

"You mean some fiend would trade on their heartbreak to swindle them out of two thousand dollars—knowing all the time he was unable to keep his wretched bargain and return their child?" I asked, horrified.

His small, sensitive mouth set in a grim, straight line beneath the trimly waxed ends of his little blond mustache. "*Précisément*," he nodded. "Such things have been done many times. We of the Paris *Sûreté* are familiar with many such cases."

"But, for the Lord's sake—" I began.

"Exactly," he responded. "For the Lord's sake, and for the sake or those two poor ones whose little man has been stolen away, and for the sake of all other parents who may suffer a similar fate, I shall make it my sworn duty to appre-hend this villain, and, by the horns of the Devil, if it turns out he knows not the whereabouts of the little boy, he will pray lustily for death before I have done with him."

"But—"

"*Ah bah*, let us bother with no buts at this time, my friend. Tomorrow night is the appointed time. Me, I hasten, I rush, I fly to New York, where I would consult with certain expert artificers. By the belly of Jonah's whale, but I shall give this kidnaper such a surprise as he does not suspect! *Adieu*, Friend Trowbridge. I return when my business in New York is completed."

"HAVE A CARE, MY friend," de Grandin ordered the following night as I relieved him of a small black satchel while he climbed into the tonneau of the Candace motor car. "Treat the bag with respect; coddle it like an infant, and, whatever you do, touch not its handles, but hold it by the sides."

Consulting the diminutive watch strapped to the under side of his wrist, he nodded shortly to Candace, who sat at the wheel in a perfect fever of excitement and impatience. "Let us go, *Monsieur*," he ordered, and the powerful motor-car turned southward toward the little Italian settlement of Rupleyville, its engine gaining speed with each revolution of the wheels.

"Do you keep sharp watch on your side of the road, Friend Trowbridge," he directed, driving a sharp elbow into my ribs. "Me, I shall glue my eyes to mine.

"More speed, Monsieur Candace," he urged as the car entered a long, narrow stretch of roadway between two segments of dense pine woods. "Never will our fish rise to the bait if we loiter along the highway. Tread on the gas, I beseech you!"

His face set in grim lines, eyes narrowed as he peered intently before him, Iring Candace advanced his spark and pressed his foot on the accelerator. The car shot ahead like a projectile and darted down the tunnel between the ranks of black-boughed pines with a roar like that of an infuriated beast.

"Good, most excellently good," the Frenchman commended. "At this rate we should—*grand Dieu*, there is the light!"

As the car roared round the bend of the road the sudden yellow gleam of a stable lantern suspended from a tree-bough shone out against the black background of the woods. "Continue—carry on—keep going, *pour l'amour de Dieu!*" de Grandin gritted in the driver's ear as Candace involuntarily slackened speed. Next instant he leaned far out of the rushing car, seized the small black satchel from my lap and hurled it toward the flickering lantern like a football player making a lateral pass.

"Gently—gently, my friend," he counseled, nudging Candace between the shoulder blades as the car rounded the bend, "do but slow down sufficiently to permit us to alight, but keep your *moteur* running and your muffler out. We must persuade the despicable one we are still on our way." Next instant he flung open the tonneau door, dropped silently to the hard-surfaced roadway, and motioning me to follow, crept toward the underbrush bordering the highway.

"Have you your gun ready?" I whispered as I crouched beside him in the long weeds fringing the road.

"S-s-sh!" he cautioned sibilantly, reaching under his jacket and bringing out a small, cloth-covered package resembling a folded sheet-music stand. Feverishly he tore the flannel wrappings from the slender steel bars and began jointing the rods together. In a moment's time he held an odd-looking contrivance, something like an eel-spear, except that it possessed only two tines, in his left hand, while from an inside pocket he produced a skein of strong, braided horsehair rope terminating in a slip-noose, and swung it loosely, lasso-wise, from his right fist.

"*Allez vous en!*" he rasped, crawling farther into the undergrowth.

Cautiously, moving so slowly it seemed to us we scarcely moved at all, we approached the swinging lantern. Nothing indicative of human presence showed in the tiny circle of light cast by the swinging lamp; neither form nor shadow stirred among the tall black pines.

"The Devil!" I exclaimed in furious disappointment. "He's got away."

"Quiet!" warned the Frenchman angrily. "Be still; he does but wait to make sure we were not followed by the police. Lie low, my friend, and be ready—*nom d'un bête*, behold him!"

Like the shadow of a shadow, moving furtively as a weasel between the tree trunks, a man, slender as a youth, stoop-shouldered and narrow-chested, but incredibly quick-footed, had slipped forward, seized the black bag de Grandin flung from the car, and darted back among the sheltering pines, even as the Frenchman gave his warning cry.

Next moment the midnight quiet of the woods was broken by a sudden retching sneeze, another and yet another, and a rushing, stumbling figure emerged from the darkness, blundering blindly into bush and shrub and heavy tree bole, clawing frantically at his face and stopping every now and again in his crazy course to emit a tortured, hacking cough or sternutative sneeze.

"Ha, Monsieur Child-stealer, you expected coin of another sort, *n'est-ce-pas?*" de Grandin fairly shrieked leaping forward to trip the blinded, sneezing fellow with a deft movement of his foot. "On him, Friend Trowbridge!" he shouted. "Sit upon him, grind his face into the earth, seize him, bind him—off to the bastille!"

I rushed forward to comply, then started back, cold horror grasping at my throat. "Look out, de Grandin!" I screamed. "Look out, for God's sake—"

"*Ha?*" The Frenchman's sharp interrogative exclamation was more an expression of satisfied expectancy than of surprise. Almost, it seemed, the monstrous snake which had risen up from the pine needles at our feet was something he had awaited.

"Is it indeed thou, *Monsieur le Serpent?*" he demanded, skipping backward between the trees, advancing his two-pronged fork before him as a practiced swordsman might swing his foil. "It would seem we are met, after all," he added, dancing back another step, then, with the speed of forked lightning, stabbing downward with his prong.

"*Sa-ha, Monsieur*, how do you care for that?" he demanded, his voice high and thin with hysterical triumph as the sharp steel tines sank into the soft earth each side of the great snake's neck, pinning his wicked, wedge-shaped head fast to the ground.

"*Eh bien*, it seems I am one too many for you, *mon ami*," de Grandin remarked calmly as he slipped the noose of his hair rope beneath the squirming head, drew it taut and nonchalantly flung the rope's free end over a low-hanging tree bough. "Up we go," he announced cheerfully, drawing sharply on the rope and hoisting the monster reptile from the earth until it hung suspended from the branch, the tip of its pointed tail and some four feet of brown-mottled body lashing furiously at the scrub pines which grew rank underfoot.

The noisome thing beat the earth futilely with its tail a moment, then drew its glistening body, thick as a man's thigh, upward, wrapping it about the bough to which its neck was pinioned, knotted there a moment in agony, then slid in long, horrifying waves again toward the earth.

"Squirm, my friend," de Grandin ordered, surveying the struggling serpent with a smile of grim amusement. "*Parbleu*, wriggle, writhe and twist, it will do you small good. 'Twas Jules de Grandin tied those knots, and he knows how to deal with your sort, whether they travel on their bellies or their feet. Which reminds me"—he turned toward the struggling man on the ground—"it seems we have you, also, Monsieur. Will you be pleased to rise when I can induce my good Friend Trowbridge to cease kneeling on your biceps?"

"Did you get him?" Candace crashed through the undergrowth, brushed me aside and seized the prisoner's shoulder in an iron grip. "Where's my son, you devil? Tell me, or, by God, I'll—"

"Meestair, let me go!" the captive screamed, writhing in Candace's clutch. "I ver' good man, me. I was passing through the woods, and saw where someone had left a lantern—a good, new lantern—out here, and come over to get him. As I try and take him from the tree, somebody come by and throw a satchel at me, and I think maybe it have money in him, so I pick him up, and then my eyes go all—"

"You lie!" Candace was almost frothing at the mouth as he shook the fellow again. But de Grandin drew him away with a word of caution.

"Softly, my friend," he whispered. "Remember, it is your son we wish to recover. Perhaps we may succeed only in frightening him into silence if we attempt intimidating here. At Harrisonville is a barracks of the state *gendarmerie*. Let us take him there. Undoubtlessly the officers will force a confession from him, and Madame Candace will be cleared before all the world thereby. Let us go."

"All right," Candace agreed grudgingly. "Let's get going. We can get there in half an hour, if we hurry."

T HE LIGHTS OF THE troopers' barracks streamed out into the moonless summer night as Candace brought his car to a halt before the building and fairly dragged the prisoner from the vehicle.

"*Bon soir, Messieurs les Gendarmes*," de Grandin greeted, removing his soft felt hat with a ceremonious flourish as he led the way into the guard-room. "We are this minute arrived from Rupleyville and"—he paused a moment, then motioned toward the undersized prisoner writhing in Candace's grip—"we have brought with us the kidnaper of the little Candace boy. No less."

"Oh, have you?" the duty sergeant responded unenthusiastically. "Another one? We've been getting all sorts of tips on that case—got a stack o' letters a foot high—and we have about a dozen 'phone calls a day, offering us the lowdown on the—"

"*Monsieur le Sergent*"—de Grandin's amiability vanished like the night's frost before the morning sun—"if you are of opinion that we rush about the countryside at midnight for our own amusement, you are greatly mistaken. Look upon this!" He thrust the ransom letter under the astonished policeman's nose, and as the other concluded his perusal of the missive, launched on a succinct account of the evening's adventures.

"Huh, looks as if you've got something we can sink our teeth in, for a fact," the sergeant complimented.

"Where's the kid?" he turned bruskly to the prisoner. "Speak up, you; it'll be worse for you if you don't."

"Meestair," the captive returned with an expressive elevation of his narrow shoulders, "I not know what you talk of. Me, I am hones' man; ver' poor, but hones'. I not know nothing about this keed you ask for. Tonight I walk through the woods on my way home, and I see where someone have left a good, new lantern hanging up. I go to get him, for I need him at my house, and these gentlemens you see here come by in a fast automobile, and—*whizz!*—they throw something into the woods. I think maybe they are bootleggers running from police, so I go to see what's in the bag, and right away something go off right in my face—*pouf!*—like that. It make me all blind, and while I run around like a fish out of water, these gentlemens here, they come up and say, 'You—you steala da keed; we kill you pretty dam' quick if you no tell us where he is!' I not know why they say so, Meestair. Me poor, hones' man. Not steal no keed, not steal nothing. No, not me!"

"Humph!" the sergeant turned to de Grandin with a shrug. "He's probably a damn liar, most of 'em are; but his story's straight enough. We'll just lock him up for a couple of days and give him time to think the matter over. He'll be ready to admit something by the time we have him arraigned, I hope."

"But, Monsieur?" de Grandin protested, "can not you see how absurd that is? While you have this so villainous miscreant in a cell, the little boy whom we seek may starve to death. Your delay may mean his death!"

"Can't help it," the young officer replied resignedly. "I've had more experience with these fellows than you have, and if we try mauling him he'll call on all the saints in the calendar to witness his innocence and yell bloody murder, but we'll never get an admission from him. Give him time to think it over in a nice, solitary cell—that's the way to crack these wops' shells."

"Morbleu"—I thought the little Frenchman would explode with amazed anger—"you have more experience than I—I, Jules de Grandin of le Sûreté? Blood of the Devil; blood of a most ignoble cat! We shall see what we shall see. You admit your inability to force a confession from this one. May I try? Parbleu, if I fail to make him talk within ten little minutes I shall turn monk and live upon prayers and detestable turnips for the rest of my life!"

"U'm?" the sergeant regarded the angry little Frenchman speculatively. "Promise not to hurt him?"

De Grandin tiptoed across the room and whispered something in the policeman's ear, waving his slender hands like a windmill in a hurricane the while.

"Okeh," the officer agreed, a broad grin spreading over his features. "I've heard a lot about the way you fellows work. Let's see you strut your stuff."

"Merci," de Grandin acknowledged, crossing the guard-room and pausing before the tall cast-iron stove which heated the place in winter.

Accumulated paper and a few sticks of light wood lay in the heater's cylinder, and de Grandin set them alight with a match, thrusting the long, steel poker into the midst of the leaping flames. "Will you help, Friend Trowbridge?" he asked as he took a skein of stout cord from his pocket and began making the captive fast to his chair with skillful knots.

"What do you want me to do?" I asked wonderingly.

"Stand ready to hand me a bit of ice from the cooler," he whispered softly in my ear; then, as the poker slowly glowed from gray to red, and from red to pale orange in the fire, he seized its handle and advanced with a slow, menacing stride toward the bound and helpless prisoner, his little, round blue eyes hardening to a merciless glare as the eyes of a kindly house-cat flash with fury at sight of a mongrel street dog.

"Kidnaper of little children," he announced in a voice so low as to he hardly audible, but hard and merciless as a scalpel's edge, "I am about to give you one last chance to speak the truth. Say, where is the little one you stole away?"

"*Signor*," replied the prisoner, twisting and straining at the cords, "me, I have told you only the truth. *Per l'amore della Madonna*—"

"*Ah bah!*" the Frenchman advanced the glowing steel to within an inch of the fellow's face. "You have told only the truth! What does a child-stealer know of true words? *Nom d'un chat*, what does a duck know of the taste of cognac?"

Advancing another step, he suddenly snatched a towel from above the washstand, looped it into a loose knot and flung it over the prisoner's face, drawing it tightly about his eyes. "Observe him well, my friends," he commanded, reaching out to snatch the bit of ice I had abstracted from the water-cooler at his nod of silent command, then ripping the bound man's collar open.

Fascinated, we watched the tableau before us. De Grandin seemed as savage and implacable as the allegorical figure of Nemesis in a classic Greek play. Facing him, trembling and shaking as though with a chill, despite the warmth of the night, his swarthy visage gone corpse-pale, sat the fettered prisoner. He was an undersized man, scarcely more than a boy, apparently, and his small, regular features and finely modeled, tiny hands and feet gave him an almost feminine appearance. His terror was so obvious that I was almost moved to protest, but the Frenchman waited no further word.

"Speak, child-stealer, or take the consequences!" he exclaimed sharply, bringing the scorching poker to within a half-inch of the prisoner's quivering throat, then snatching it back and thrusting the bit of ice against the shrinking white skin.

A shriek of hopeless anguish and pain burst from the captive's lips. He writhed and twisted against his bonds like a scotched snake in the flame, biting his lips till bloody froth circled his mouth, digging his long, pointed nails into the palms of his hands. "*Santissima Madonna—caro Dio!*" he screamed as the ice met his flesh.

"Make answer, villain!" de Grandin commanded, boring the ice farther into the prisoner's neck. "Answer me, or, *pardieu*, I shall burn your lying tongue from your throat!"

The bound man twisted again, but only hoarse, inarticulate sounds of fright and pain escaped his bloody lips.

"*Nom d'un sacré singe*—but he is stubborn, this one," de Grandin muttered. "It seems I must yet burn his heart from his breast."

Dropping the poker into the fire again, he snatched at the prisoner's soiled white shirt with his free hand, ripping the fabric apart and exposing the bosom.

"*Mon dieu!*" he ejaculated as the garment parted in his grasp.

"Good heavens!" I exclaimed in amazement.

"For Gawd's sake—a woman!" the constabulary sergeant gasped.

"*Santa Madonna, Santissima Madre!*" the prisoner gave a choking, gurgling cry and slumped against her restraining cords, head hanging, bleeding lips parted, her bared white bosom heaving convulsively.

"Quick, Friend Trowbridge," de Grandin commanded sharply. "Some water, if you please. She is unconscious."

THE WOMAN'S EYELIDS FLUTTERED upward, even as I hastened to obey de Grandin's command. "*Si, si, signori*," she answered. "I am a woman, and—I took the little one from the Candace house."

For a moment she paused, swallowing convulsively, raising one of her slender hands, from which de Grandin had cut the bonds, to her throat, feeling tentatively at the spot where the Frenchman had pressed the ice, then shuddering with mystified relief as she discovered no brand from what she had thought the red-hot poker.

"I"—she gulped back a sob—"I am Gioconda Vitale. I live in Rupleyville, down by the railroad tracks. The people of College Grove know me as one who works by the day, who scrubs, who tends fires, washes. You, Signor Candace, have seen me in your house more than once, but never have you noticed me more than if I had been a chair or table.

"Last year my man, my Antonio, he die. It was the influenza, the doctor say, and he went ver' quick, like falling asleep after a hard day's work. In life he had been—how you call it? snake-charmer?—with circuses in Italy, then at Coney Island. We make plenty money while he was living, for he ver' good man with the snakes—they call him 'King of the Serpents' on the billboards. But I not like them. All but Beppo, he was ver' good, kind snake. Him I like. That Beppo, the python, my man like best of all, and I like him, too. He has a good, kind heart, like a dog. I not have the heart to sell him like I sell all the others when my 'Tonio die. I keep him, but he ver' hard for to feed, for he eat much every month—chicken, rabbit, anything he can get his hand on. When I not have money for get him what he want, he go out and get it himself.

"'Beppo,' I tell him, 'you get us in plenty trouble if you keep on,' but he not pay me no 'tention. No.

"*Signori*"—she swept us with her large, dark eyes—"when my man die I was left all alone, yet not alone, for there was another with me, the answer to my man's love and my prayers to *la Madonna*. Yes.

"Without my man, all heavy as I was, I go out and work, work, work till I think the bone come through my finger-ends, and at night I sit up and sew, that the *bambino* who is to come should have everything all nice. Yes.

"Presently he come, that beautiful little boy. His eyes are blue like my man's who are in heaven with the blessed saints, for Antonio was of Florence, and not dark like us Sicilians. *Santo Dio*, how I love him, how I worship him, for he was not only the child of my body; he was my man come back to me again! I christen him Antonio, for his father who is gone to God, and every night when I come home from work he smile on me and seem to say, '*Madre mia*, my father up in heaven with the blessed ones, he see all you do, and love you still as when he held you in his arms on earth. Yes, *signori*, it is so.

"The good God knows His ways, but they are ver' hard for women to understand. My little one, my token of love, he were taken from me. The doctor say it is something he have eat, but me, I know it were because he were too beautiful to stay on earth away from the holy angels and the blessed innocents who died that our Lord might live in the days of King Herod.

"Then I have only Beppo. He were a good snake; but no snake, not even the favorite of my dear man, can take the place of the little one who has gone to God. Beppo, he follow me out the door sometimes when I go out to walk at night—mostly when he are hungry, for it cost so much to feed him—but I say, 'Beppo, go back. What the people say if they see me walking with a snake? They tell me I have the Evil Eye!'

"*Signor*"—she turned directly to Candace—"you know what it mean to have empty arms. Me, I was that way. I was one crazed woman. Each time I see a happy mother with her child something inside me seem to say, 'Gioconda, but for the curse of God, there goes you!'

"Pretty soon I can not stand it no more. In Signor Candace's house is a little boy about the size of my lost one if he had lived till now. I watch him all day when I go there to work. All the time my empty heart cry out for the feel of a baby's head against it. Finally, a week—maybe two—ago, I go clear mad. All night I stand outside the window where the little one sleeps and watch the light. Late, ver' late, his mother come in and lean over and kiss him good-night. My heart burst with the nothing which is inside. I can not stand it. *Santa Madre*, I can not stand it! When she put out the light and raise the window, I take a stepladder from the kitchen porch and climb up the house, take the little one from his bed all quiet, replace the ladder, and run to my house.

"Ah, how sweet it are to have a child once more in my arm, to feel the little head against my breast, to kiss back the cries he makes when he wakes up at night! I am wild for joy.

"But how am I, a poor woman, whose husband is with the blessed saints, to bring up this child? I can sell Beppo, but how much money will they give me for him? Not much. A hundred dollar, perhaps. That will not do. No, I can not get enough that way. Then I remember Signor Candace is rich. His wife not have to scrub floors or wash clothes. She is young, too; more children will come to gladden their home, but for me there is only the little *bambino* which I have stole. I shall make the rich father support his child, though he knows it not.

"So I make the letter which ask for money, and threaten to kill the little one if he does not pay. I kill him? *Dio mio*, sooner would I starve myself than have him go without the good red wine, the goat's milk and the fine white bread every day!"

"Good Lord!" exclaimed the horrified father. "Is she feeding *my* child that?"

The woman paid no heed, but hurried on: "*Signori*, I am a wicked woman. I see it now. If I suffer because the good God, who own him, take my little boy to heaven, how much more shall this other poor mother suffer because a mortal, sinful woman, who have no right, steal away her little son from her? Yes.

"You come with me"—she cast big, tear-dimmed eyes pleadingly on each of us in turn—"I take you to my house and show you how nice I keep the little man and how he hold out his baby hands and smile when he see me come in."

Jules de Grandin twisted his mustache furiously and strove manfully to look fierce, but the voice which he tried to make stern had a surprisingly tender tone as he replied: "Take us to your house; we shall get the little one, and if all is as you say, it may be you shall not suffer too greatly for your crime."

"And now, my friends," de Grandin began when the little boy had been restored to his hysterically happy mother's arms, "you are due an explanation of my cleverness.

"When first I heard of the marks Madame Candace saw in the earth of her garden I knew not what to think. Snakes of the size the marks seemed to indicate are not native to this soil; I thought perchance she might be mistaken, even"—he made a quick, apologetic bow to Mrs. Candace—"that she might be stating something with no greater foundation than her imagination.

"When I did behold the letter asking for ransom I thought, 'Surely, this is the explanation of it all. We shall take this miscreant red-handed, perhaps recover the stolen child, as well; but at any rate, we shall take the kidnaper.

"Next morning I read where the excellent Monsieur Johannes lost a pig to a great snake. '*Parbleu*,' I say to me, 'this must be investigated. It may be the snake whose track Madame Candace saw did thrust his so hideous head into the room where her little one slept as lesser snakes thrust their heads into birds' nests, and made off with the baby.' It was not a pleasant thought, my friends; but we must see what we should see.

"So I interviewed Monsieur Johannes, and sure enough, I found the evidence of a real snake, a large one. 'Now, what to do?' I ask me.

"It may easily be someone who knows nothing of the little man's whereabouts was trying to cheat Monsieur and Madame Candace of two thousand dollars, I know. I have seen such cases. He has asked in his letter that we throw the money from an automobile. 'Ah-ha, Monsieur the kidnaper,' I say, 'Jules de Grandin shall throw you something you do not expect.'

I go to New York and have an artizan make me a satchel which is only one great tear-gas bomb disguised. In its top are many tiny holes, and inside its metal interior is much tear-gas, pumped in at great pressure. The handle is like a trigger, and the minute anyone grasps it the holes in the bag's top are opened and the gas rushes out, blinding the person who holds the handles. Remember, Friend Trowbridge, how I warned you not to touch those handles?

"Very good. 'But what connection have the snake with the stealing of the child?' I want to know. Not much, I believe, yet one thing make me stop and think. Was it only coincidence that those tracks appear in Madame Candace's garden the night her little boy was stolen? Perhaps so; perhaps not. At any rate, Jules de Grandin does not sleep when wakefulness is necessary. I have made also a fork something like the notched sticks the Burmese use to catch the great snakes of their country—the snakes which later make shoes for the pretty ladies. Now, I am ready for human kidnapers or reptile devourers of children.

"We go to the woods as the note directs, we fling out the bag, and the little woman who stole to refill her aching, empty heart, is caught by the success of my so clever bomb-satchel.

"So far all is well, but it was as well I had my snake-stick with me, for the excellent Beppo, who doubtless was a most affectionate snake, was also there, and I, not being aware of his good qualities, was obliged to exterminate him in self-defense. *Eh bien*, Beppo is not the first to die because of evil appearances.

"Friend Trowbridge, I think our work is done. We have restored the little boy to his parents; we have made one great fool of that so odious Perkinson person who suspected Madame Candace of killing her son; we have apprehended the kidnapper. Let us go."

He bowed to the company, strode to the door, then paused abruptly, a half-diffident, ingratiating smile on his face. "Monsieur Candace," he asked, "as a favor to me, if you feel at all obligated for the little I have done, I would ask that you be merciful to the poor, bereaved mother when her trial comes up. Remember, though she sinned against you greatly by stealing your child, her temptation was also great."

"Trial, hell!" Candace retorted. "There isn't going to be any trial. D'ye think I'd have the heart to prosecute her after what she told us at the barracks? Not much! As far as I'm concerned, she can go free now."

"*Eh bien*, Trowbridge, my friend," de Grandin confided as we walked down the garden path, "I do admire that Monsieur Candace immensely. Truly, the great heart of America is reflected in the great hearts of her citizens."

As we reached the waiting car he paused with a chuckle. "And the great thirst of the great desert is reflected in Jules de Grandin," he confided. "Come, make haste, my friend, I pray. I would imbibe one of your so glorious gin rickies before I bid myself good night."

Body and Soul

I HAD HAD A STRENUOUS day, for the mild epidemic of summer grippe had lasted over into September, and my round of calls had been double the usual number. "Thank heaven, I can relax for seven or eight hours," I murmured piously as I pulled the single blanket up around my chin and settled myself for the night. The hall clock had just struck twelve, and I had no appointments earlier than nine the following morning. "If only nobody is so inconsiderate as to break a leg or get the bellyache," I mumbled drowsily, "I'll not stir from this bed until—"

As if to demonstrate the futility of self-congratulation, there came a sudden thunderous clamor at the front door. Someone was beating the panels with both his fists, raining frenzied blows on the wood with his feet and shrieking at the top of his voice, "Let me in! Doctor—Dr. Trowbridge, let me in! For God's sake, let me in!"

"The devil!" I ejaculated, rising resentfully and feeling for my slippers and dressing-gown. "Couldn't he have had the decency to ring the bell?"

"Let me in, let me in, Dr. Trowbridge!" the frantic hail came again as I rounded the bend of the stairs. "Let me in—quick!"

"All right, all right!" I counseled testily, undoing the lock and chain-fastener. "Just a min—"

The caller ceased his battering-ram assault on the door as I swung it back and catapulted past me into the hall, almost carrying me off my feet as he did so. "Quick, shut it—shut the door!" he gasped, wheeling in his tracks to snatch the knob from my hand and force the door to. "It's out there—it's outside there, I tell you!"

"What the mischief—" I began, half puzzled, half angry, as I took quick stock of the intruder.

He was a young man, twenty-five or -six, I judged, dressed somewhat foppishly in a suit of mohair dinner clothes, his jacket and waistcoat badly rumpled, his once stiff evening shirt and collar reduced to a pulpy mass of sweat-soaked linen, and the foamy froth of drool disfiguring the corners of his flaccid mouth. As he turned on me to repeat his hysterical warning, I noticed that he caught his breath with considerable difficulty and that there was a strong hint of liquor in his speech.

"See here, young man, what do you mean?" I demanded sternly. "Haven't you any better sense than to knock a man out of bed at this ungodly hour to tell him that—"

"Ssssh!" he interrupted with the exaggerated caution of the half-tipsy. "Ssssh, Dr. Trowbridge, I think I hear it coming up the steps. Is the door locked? Quick, in here!" Snatching me by the arm he dragged me unceremoniously into the surgery.

"Now see here, confound you!" I remonstrated. "This is going a bit too far. If you expect to get away with this sort of thing, I'll mighty soon show you—"

"Trowbridge, *mon vieux*, what is it? What does the alarm portend?" Jules de Grandin, a delicate mauve-silk dressing-gown drawn over his lilac pajamas, slippers of violet snake-skin on his womanishly small feet, tiptoed into the room, his little blue eyes round with wonder and curiosity. "I thought I heard someone in extremity calling," he continued, looking from the visitor to me, then back again with his quick, stock-taking glance. "Is it that someone dies and requires our assistance through the door to the better world, or—"

"It looks as if some drunken young fool is trying to play a practical joke on us," I returned grimly, bending a stern look on the boy who cowered in the chair beside my desk. "I've half a mind to prescribe four ounces of castor oil and stand by while he takes it!"

De Grandin regarded the young man with his steady, unwinking stare a moment, then: "What frightens you, *mon brave*?" he demanded, far too gently, I thought. "*Parbleu*, but, you look as though you had been playing tag with Satan himself!"

"I have—I have!" the youth replied quaveringly. "I tell you, it jumped at me just as I came past the park entrance, and I wasn't a hundred yards ahead when Dr. Trowbridge let me in!"

"U'm?" the Frenchman twisted the ends of his little blond mustache meditatively. "And this 'It' which pursued you, it is what?"

"I don't know," the other responded. "I was walking home from a dance at the Sigma Delta Tau house—been stagging it, you know—and stopped by the Victory Monument to light a cigarette when something—dam' if I know what—jumped out o' the bushes at me and made a grab at my throat. It missed my neck by a couple o' inches, but snatched my hat, and I didn't take any time to see what it would do next. I'd 'a' been going yet if my wind hadn't given out, and I happened to think that Dr. Trowbridge lives in this block and that he'd most likely be up, or within call, anyhow, so I rushed up the steps and hammered on the door till he let me in.

"Will you let me stay here overnight?" he concluded, turning to me appealingly. "I'm Dick Ratliff—Henry Ratliff's nephew, you know—and honest, Doctor, I'm scared stiff to go out in that street again till daylight."

"H'm," I murmured judicially, surveying the young fool reflectively. He was not a bad-looking boy—quite otherwise—and I could well imagine he presented a personable enough appearance when his clothing was in better array and his head less fuddled with bad liquor. "How much have you had to drink tonight, young man?"

"Two drinks, sir," he returned promptly, looking me squarely in the eye, and, though my better judgment told me he was lying like a witness at a Senate investigation, I believed him.

"I think you're a damn fool," I told him with more candor than courtesy. "You were probably so full of rotgut that your own shadow gave you a start back there by the park gate, and you've been trying to outrace it for the last four blocks. You'll be heartily ashamed of yourself in the morning, but I've a spare bed, and you may as well sleep off your debauch here as in some police station, I suppose."

"Thank you, sir," he answered humbly. "I don't blame you for thinking I've got the jim-jams—I know my story sounds crazy—but I'm telling you the truth. Something did jump out at me, and almost succeeded in grabbing me by the throat. It wasn't just imagination, and it wasn't booze, either, but—my God, *look!*"

THE EXCLAMATION ENDED IN a shrill crescendo, and the lad half leaped from his chair, pointing with a shaking forefinger at the little window over the examination table, then slumped back as though black-jacked, his hands falling limply to the floor, his head lolling drunkenly forward on his breast.

Both de Grandin and I wheeled about, facing the window. "Good lord!" I exclaimed as my gaze penetrated the shining, night-backed panes.

"*Grand Dieu—ç'est le diable en personne!*" the little Frenchman cried.

Staring into the dimly lighted room was such a visage as might bring shudders of horripilation to a bronze statue. It was a long, cadaverous face, black with the dusky hue of old and poorly cured rawhide, bony as a death's-head, yet covered with a multitude of tiny horizontal wrinkles. The fleshless, leathery lips were drawn back from a set of broken and discolored teeth which reminded me somehow of the cruel dentition of a shark, and the corded, rugous neck supporting the withered face was scarcely thicker than a man's wrist. From the bare, black scalp there hung a single lock of coarse, straggling hair. But terrible as the features were, terrifying as were the unfleshed lips and cheeks and brow, the tiny, deep-set eyes almost fallen backward from their sockets were even more horrible. Small as the eyes of a rodent, set, unwavering in their stare, they reminded me, as they gleamed with hellish malevolence in their settings of shrunken, wrinkled skin, of twin poisonous spiders awaiting the chance to pounce upon their prey. It might have been a trick of the lamplight, but to me it seemed that the organs shone with a diabolical luminance of their own as they regarded us with a sort of mirthless smile.

"Good heavens, what is it?" I choked, half turning to my companion, yet keeping most of my glance fixed on the baneful, hypnotic orbs glaring at me through the windowpane.

"God knows," returned de Grandin, "but by the belly of Jonah's whale, we shall see if he be proof against shot and powder!" Whipping a tiny Ortgies automatic from his dressing-gown pocket he brought its blunt muzzle in line with the window and pressed the trigger. Seven, eight shots rang out so quickly that the last seemed no more than the echo of the first; the plate glass pane was perforated like a sieve within an area of three square inches; and the sharp, acrid smell of smokeless powder bit the mucous membrane of my nostrils.

"After him, Friend Trowbridge!" de Grandin cried, flinging aside the empty pistol and bolting through the door, down the hallway and across the porch. "*Barbe d'une oie*, but we shall see how he liked the pills I dealt him!"

The September moon rode serenely in the dark-blue sky; a little vagrant breeze, coming from the bay, rustled the boughs of the curbside maple trees; and from the downtown section there came to us, faintly, the muted clangor of the all-night trolley cars and the occasional hoot of a cruising taxicab's horn. After the bedlam of the Frenchman's shots the early autumn night seemed possessed of a stillness which bore in on our eardrums like a tangible sound, and, like visitors in an empty church, we pursued our quest in silence, communicating only in low, breathless whispers. From house to hedge, over lawn and rosebed and tennis court we pushed our search, scanning every square inch of land, peering under rosebushes and rhododendron plants, even turning over the galvanized iron trash-can which stood by my kitchen stoop. No covert large enough to have shielded a rat did we leave unexplored, yet of the awful thing which had gazed through the surgery window we found no sign or trace, though we hunted till the eastern sky began to pale with streaks of rose and pearl and amethyst and the rattling milk carts broke the nighttime quiet with their early-morning clatter.

"Good mornin', Dr. de Grandin." Detective Sergeant Costello rose from his seat in the consulting-room as de Grandin and I entered. "'Tis sorry I am to be disturbin' ye so early in th' mornin', more especially as I know what store ye set by yer breakfast"—he grinned broadly at his sally—"but th' fact is, sor, there's been a tidy little murder committed up th' street, an' I'm wondering if ye'd be discommodin' yerself to th' extent o' comin' up to Professor Kolisko's house and takin' a look around before th' coroner's physician messes everything up an' carts th' remains off to the morgue for an autopsy."

"A murder?" de Grandin's little eyes snapped with sudden excitement. "Do you say a murder? My friend, you delight me!"

"Yes, sor, I knew y'd be pleased to hear about it," the Irishman answered soberly. "Will we be goin' up to th' house at once, sor?"

"But of course, by all means," de Grandin assented. "Trowbridge, my friend, you will have the charity to convey us thither, will you not? Come, let us hasten to this Monsieur Kolisko's house and observe what we can see. And"—his little eyes twinkled as he spoke—"I beseech you, implore the so excellent Nora to reserve sufficient breakfast against the time of our return. *Mordieu*, already I feel my appetite assuming giant proportions!"

Two minutes later the detective, de Grandin and I were speeding uptown toward the isolated cottage where Urban Kolisko, one-time professor of psychology at the University at Warsaw, had passed the declining years of his life as a political refugee.

"Tell me, Friend Costello," the Frenchman demanded; "this Monsieur Kolisko, how did he die?"

"H'm, that's just what's puzzlin' all of us," the detective admitted. "All we know about th' case is that Murphy, who has th' beat where th' old felly lived wuz passin' by there a little after midnight an' heard th' devil's own row goin' on inside. The lights, wuz all goin' in th' lower part o' th' house, which warn't natural, an' when Murphy stopped to hear what it wuz all about, he thought he heard someone shoutin' an' swearin', an' once or twice th' crack o' a whip, then nothin' at all.

"Murphy's a good lad, sor; I've knowed him, man an' boy, these last eighteen years, an' he did just what I'd expected o' him. Went up an' knocked on th' door, an' when he couldn't get no response, broke it in. There was hell broke loose for certain, sor."

"Ah?" returned de Grandin. "What did the excellent Murphy observe?"

"Plenty," Costello replied laconically. "Ye'll be seein' it for yerself in a minute."

Inside the Kolisko house was that peculiar hush which does reverence to the Grim Reaper's visits. Acting on telephoned instructions, Officer Murphy mounted guard before the door, permitting no one to enter the place, and the scene in the small, poorly lighted living-room was exactly as he had come upon it several hours earlier. Like most dyed-in-the-wool students, Kolisko had regarded his home merely as a place to sleep, eat and store books. The room was lined from floor to ceiling on all sides with rough deal shelving which groaned and sagged under the weight of ponderous volumes in every language known to print. Piles of other books, unable to find accommodation on the shelves, were littered about the floor. The rough, bench-like table and the littered, untidy desk which stood between the two small windows were also piled high with books.

Between the desk and table, flat on its back, staring endlessly at the rough whitewashed ceiling with bulging, sightless eyes, lay the relic of Professor Kolisko. Clothed in a tattered bathrobe and soiled pajamas the body lay, and it was not a pretty sight even to a medical man to whom death in its unloveliest phases is no stranger. Kolisko had been thin to the point of emaciation, and his scrawniness was accentuated in death. His white-thatched head was thrown back and bent grotesquely to one side, his straggling white beard thrust upward truculently, and his lower jaw had fallen downward with the flaccidity of death, half an inch or so of tongue protruding beyond the line of his lower teeth. Any doctor, soldier or undertaker—any man whose business has to do habitually with death—could not fail to recognize the signs. The man was dead, and had been so for upward of seven hours.

"Howly Mither!" Costello's brogue came strongly to the surface as he blessed himself involuntarily. "Will ye be lookin' at th' awfulness o' him, sors?"

"U'm," murmured Jules de Grandin, sinking to one knee beside the corpse, raising the lolling head and fingering the back of the neck with quick, practiced hands, then brushing back the bristling beard to examine the scrawny throat attentively, "he had cause to be dead, this one. See, Friend Trowbridge"—taking my hand he guided my fingers slowly down the dead man's neck, then pointed to the throat—"there is a clean fracture of the spine between the third and fourth dorsal vertebræ, probably involving a rupture of the cord, as well. The autopsy will disclose that. And here"—he tapped the throat with a well-manicured forefinger—"are the marks of strangulation. Mordieu, whatever gripped this poor one's neck possessed a hold like Death himself, for he not only choked him, but broke his spine as well! If it were not for one thing, I should say such strength—such ferocity of grip—could only have been exerted by one of the great apes, but—"

He broke off, staring with preoccupied, unseeing eyes at the farther wall.

"But what, sor?" Costello prompted as the little man's silence continued.

"Parbleu, it could not be an ape and leave such a thumb-mark, my friends," de Grandin returned. "The gorilla, the orangutan, the chimpanzee, all have such strength of hand as to accomplish what we see here, but they are not human, no matter how much they parody mankind. Their thumbs are undeveloped; the thumb which closed on this one's neck was long and thin, more like a finger than a thumb. See for yourselves, it closed about the throat, meeting the fingers which clasped it on the other side. Mordieu, if we are to find this murderer we must look for one with twice the length and five times the strength of hand of the average man. Bethink you—this one's grip was great enough to snap Kolisko's spine like a clay-pipe stem by merely squeezing his neck! *Dieu de Dieu*, but he will be an uncomfortable one to meet in the dark!"

"Sergeant Costello," Murphy's hail came sharply from the cottage door, "they're comin'; Coroner Martin an' Dr. Schuester just drove up!"

"All right, Murphy, good lad!" Costello returned, then glanced sharply at de Grandin. "Leave him be, Doc," he ordered. "If the coroner an' Dr. Schuester catch us monkeyin' with their property there'll be hell poppin' at headquarters."

"Very good, my friend," de Grandin rejoined, rising and brushing the dust from his trousers knees, "we have seen as much of the body as we desire. Let them have it and perform their gruesome rites; we shall look elsewhere for what we seek."

Coroner Martin and his physician came bustling in almost as the little Frenchman ceased speaking, glanced casually at Costello and suspiciously at de Grandin and me, then went at their official duties with only a mumbled word of greeting.

"What do you make of it?" I inquired as we drove toward my house.

"*Eh bien*, as yet I make nothing," de Grandin returned. "The man was killed by paralysis resulting from a broken neck, although the pressure on his windpipe would have been sufficient to have slain him, had it but continued long enough. We know his murderer possessed hands of extraordinary strength and size, and is, therefore, in all probability, a man of more than usual height. Thus far we step with assurance. When the coroner has finished with the deceased gentleman's premises, we shall afford ourselves the pleasure of a protracted search; before that we shall request our good friend Costello to inquire into Monsieur Kolisko's antecedents and discover if he possessed any enemies, especially any enemies capable of doing him to death in this manner. Meantime I famish for my breakfast. I am hungry as a cormorant."

The boasted appetite was no mere figure of speech. Three bowls of steaming cereal, two generous helpings of bacon and eggs, half a dozen cups of well-creamed coffee disappeared into his interior before he pushed back his chair and lighted a rank-smelling French cigarette with a sigh of utter content. "*Eh bien*, but it is difficult to think on an empty stomach," he assured me as he blew a column of smoke toward the ceiling. "Me, I am far from my best when there is nothing but flatulence beneath my belt. I require stimu—*Mon Dieu*, what a fool I am!"

Striking his forehead with the heel of his hand, he rose so abruptly that his chair almost capsized behind him. "What's the matter?" I asked, but he waved my question and me aside with an impatient hand.

"*Non, non*, do not stop me, do not hinder me, my friend!" he ordered. "Me, I have important duties to perform, if it be not too late to do them. Go upon your errands of mercy, Friend Trowbridge, and should you chance to return before I quit the surgery, I pray you leave me undisturbed. I have to do that which is needful, and I must do it uninterrupted, if you please."

Having thus served notice on me that I would be unwelcome in my own workshop, he turned and fled toward the front door like a luckless debtor pursued by collectors.

It was nearly four o'clock that afternoon when I returned from my round of calls and tiptoed past the surgery door, only to find my caution unnecessary, for de Grandin sat in the cool, darkened library, smoking a cigar and chuckling over some inane story in *L'Illustration*.

"Finish the important duties?" I asked, regarding him ironically.

"But certainly," he returned. "First, dear friend, I must apologize most humbly for my so abominable rudeness of this morning. It is ever my misfortune, I fear, to show only incivility to those who most deserve my courtesy, but I was all afire with the necessity of haste when I spoke. Great empty-head that I was, I had completely forgotten for the moment that one of the best places to seek clues of a murder is the person of the victim himself, and when I did remember I was almost beside myself until I ascertained to which *entrepreneur des pompes funèbres*—How do you say it? Undertaker?—my God, what a language!—Monsieur Kolisko's body had been entrusted by the coroner. Friend Costello informed me that Monsieur Mitchell was in charge, and to the excellent Mitchell I hurried post-haste, begging that he would permit me one little minute alone with the deceased before he commenced his ministrations."

"H'm, and did you find anything?" I asked.

"*Parbleu*, yes; I found almost too much. From the nails of Monsieur Kolisko's hands I rescued some fragments, and in your surgery I subjected them to microscopic examination. They proved to be—what do you say?"

"Tobacco?" I hazarded.

"Tobacco!" he scoffed. "Friend Trowbridge, sometimes I think you foolish; at others I fear you are merely stupid. Beneath the dead man's finger-nails I found some bits of human skin—and a fragment of human hair."

"Well," I returned unenthusiastically, "what of it? Kolisko was an exceedingly untidy sort of person—the kind who cared so little for social amenities that he was apt to scratch himself vigorously when he chose, and probably he was also addicted to the habit of scrabbling through his beard with his fingers. Most of those European scientists with birds' nests sprouting from their chins are that sort, you know. He was shockingly uncouth, and—"

"And you annoy me most thoroughly, Friend Trowbridge," the little Frenchman broke in. "Listen, attend me, regard that which I am about to tell you: The skin and hair which I did find were black, my friend, black as bitumen,

and subjected to chemical reagents, showed themselves to be strongly impregnated with natron, oil of cedar and myrrh. What have you to say now?"

"Why—"

"And if these things suggest an Egyptian mummy to you, as they may if
you think steadily for the next ten or more years, I make so bold as to ask
what would a professor of psychology be doing in contact with a mummy. *Hein?*
Answer me that, if you please. Had he been an Egyptologist, or even a student
of comparative anatomy, there would be reason for it, but a psychologist—it
does not make sense!"

"Well, then, why bother about it?" I retorted.

"Ah, but I think maybe, perhaps, there is an answer to the riddle, after all,"
he insisted. "Recall the events of last night, if you please. Remember how that
young Monsieur Ratliff came bawling like a frightened calf to our door, begging
to be taken in and protected from something which assaulted him in the public
thoroughfares. Recollect how we suspected him of an overindulgence in alcohol, and how, as we were about to turn him out, there appeared at our window a
most unpleasant-looking thing which made mock of Jules de Grandin's marks-
manship. *Parbleu*, yes, you will recall all that, as well as that the ungrateful Ratliff child did sneak away from the house without so much as saying 'thank you'
for our hospitality while we were out with Sergeant Costello viewing Monsieur
Kolisko's remains."

"Then you'd suggest—" I began incredulously, but he rose with an impatient shrug.

"Ah bah, I think nothing, my friend," he assured me. "He who thinks without knowing is a fool. A connection there may be between that which we saw
last night and that which we viewed this morning. We shall see, perhaps. I have
an engagement to search Kolisko's house with Sergeant Costello this evening,
and I suggest you accompany us. There may be that there which shall cause your
eyes to pop from out your face with wonder. Meantime, I hear visitors in the
reception-room. Go to your duties, my friend. Some neurotic old lady undoubtlessly desires you to sympathize with her latest symptoms."

"WELL, SOR," CONFIDED SERGEANT Costello as he, de Grandin and I set
out for the Kolisko cottage that evening, "this case beats th' Jews, an' th'
Jews beat the devil."

"Indeed?" responded de Grandin politely.

"It sure does. We've been over Kolisko's antecedents, as ye might call 'em,
an' th' devil a thing can we find that might lead us to a clue as to who killed
him. 'Twas little enough they knew about him, at best, for he was a stand-offish
old felly wid never a word for anybody, except when he wanted sumpin, which
warn't often. He had a few Polack cronies, but they wuz few an' far between.

Five months ago a felly broke into his house an' stole some stuff o' triflin' value, an' shot up a State trooper while tryin' to escape to th' next town. Kolisko appeared agin 'im at th' trial, as wuz his dooty, for he wuz subpoenaed, an' later visited 'im in jail, I understand, but this, felly—name o' Heschler, he wuz— didn't take anny too kindly to th' professor's visits, an' he cut 'em out."

"Ah," de Grandin nursed his narrow chin in the cradle of his hand, "perhaps it is that this Heschler harbored malice and wreaked vengeance on Monsieur Kolisko for the part he had in his conviction?"

"P'raps," agreed Costello shortly, "but 'tain't likely."

"And why not?" the Frenchman demanded shortly. Like most men who keep their own counsel, he was easily annoyed by others' reticence.

"Because they burned him at Camden last night, sor."

"Burned? How do you mean—"

"Sure, burned him. Bumped 'im off, rubbed 'im out, gave 'im th' chair— electrocuted 'im. He was a murderer, warn't he?" Costello elucidated.

"U'm," the Frenchman gulped over the information like one trying to clear his mouth of an unpalatable morsel, "you are doubtless right, Sergeant; we may regard this Heschler as eliminated—perhaps."

"P'raps?" echoed the amazed Irishman as I brought the car to a halt before the cottage door. "P'raps me neck! If you'll listen to me, I'll say he's been eliminated altogether entirely by th' State executioner!"

OUR SEARCH WAS STARTLINGLY unproductive. A few letters in envelopes with foreign postmarks, receipts for small bills for groceries and kindred household items, one or two invitations to meetings of learned societies—this was the sum total produced by an hour's rummaging among the dead man's papers.

"*Tiens*, it would seem we have come on the chase of the wild goose," de Grandin admitted disconsolately, wiping the sweat from his forehead with a pale blue silk handkerchief. "*Zut*, it seems impossible that any man should have so much paper of so little importance. Me, I think that—"

"Here's sumpin that might help us, if it's papers ye're after," Costello interrupted, appearing at the kitchen door with a rough wooden box in his hand. "I found it behint th' stove, sor. Most of it seems of little enough account, but you might find sumpin that'd—"

"Aside, stand aside, my friend!" the Frenchman ordered, leaping on the box like a famished cat on a mouse and scattering its contents over the living-room table. "What have we here? *Mordieu*, another receipt from that twenty-times-damned Public Service Company! Name of a rooster, did the man do nothing but contract and pay bills for electric light? Another one—and another! *Grand Dieu*, if I find but one more of these receipts I shall require a strait-waistcoat to restrain myself. What, another—ah, *triomphe!* At last we find something else!"

From the pile of scrambled papers he unearthed a small, black-leather book and began riffling through its pages.

Pausing to read an inscription at random, he regarded the page with upraised brows and pursed lips, seated himself beside the table and brought his eyes to within a few inches of the small, crabbed writing with which the book seemed filled.

Five minutes he sat thus studying the memoranda, his brows gradually rising till I feared they would impinge upon the line of his smoothly combed blond hair. Finally: "My friends, this is of the importance," he assured us, looking quickly from one to the other with his queer, direct glance. "Monsieur Kolisko made these entries in his diary in mingled Polish and French. I shall endeavor to render them into English tonight, and tomorrow morning we shall go over them together. Thus far I have read little, but that little may explain much, or I am much mistaken."

"TROWBRIDGE, MY FRIEND," DE Grandin requested the following morning when my round of calls was finished, "will you please read what I have written? All night I labored over this translation, and this morning my eyes are not sufficient to the task of reading my own script."

He thrust a sheaf of neatly written foolscap into my hands, then lighted a cigarette and leaned back in his chair, his small hands locked behind his head, his eyes half closed, as he surveyed Costello and me lazily.

Glancing from de Grandin to the waiting detective, I set my pince-nez firmly on my nose and began:

April 5—Michel was here again last night, nagging me with his silly talk of the soul and its immortality. To think that one so well educated should entertain such childish ideas! I would have ordered him from the house in anger, as I did once before, had he not been more than usually insulting. After taunting me with the old story about a body's being weighed a few minutes after death and found lighter than before, thereby proving that something of material weight had passed from it, he challenged me to prove the non-existence of any entity separate from the physical being. Fool! It is he who asserts the proposition, not I. Yet I must think of some way to confound him, or he will be everlastingly reminding me that I failed to meet his test.

April 10—Michel is a greater fool than I thought. I hold him and his faith in the hollow of my hand, and by his own act. Last night he proposed the wildest scheme ever broached by man. The burglar who broke into my house last month has been sentenced to death for killing a policeman.

Michel would have me see the fellow in prison, arrange for a transmigration of his soul to a body which he will secure, and await results of the experiment. It is childish folly; I insult my own intelligence by agreeing to it, but I must silence Michel and his everlasting patter of the soul's immortality. I shall undertake the task, if only to prove my cousin a fool.

May 16—Yesterday I saw Heschler in prison. The poor fellow was almost beside himself with joy when I told him of Michel's wild plan. Not dying, but fear of punishment in the world to come seems to terrify the man. If I can provide a tenement for his soul which will enable it to remain away from the seat of judgment a little longer, he will be content, even though he has to live in the body of a child, a cripple or one already bowed with age. Living out the span of life in the second body we provide, he will so conduct himself as to win pardon for misdeeds committed in the frame he now wears, he vows. Poor, hoodwinked fool! Like all Christians, he is bound hand and foot by the old superstitions which have come down to us through the ages. That Heschler, the burglar, should adhere to the *Christus* myth, the God fairy-tale, is not surprising, for he is but an ignorant clod; but that my cousin Michel Kolisko, a learned man, should give credit to beliefs which were outworn and disproved in the nineteenth century is beyond my understanding.

May 30—Today I had another talk with Heschler. He is pitiably anxious to begin the experiment. It was childishly simple. Ordering him to gaze steadfastly into my eyes through the bars of his cell, I soon had him completely hypnotized. "You will hereafter cease to dread your coming execution," I told him. "From this time forth you will think of nothing but the opportunity of living on in another body which is to be afforded you. At the moment of execution you will concentrate all your will upon entering the body which will be waiting at my home to receive your soul." He nodded as I gave each command, and I left him. It will not be necessary to repeat my orders. He was already half insane with the obsession of prolonging his life. My work was more than half done before I gave him the directions. I shall not see him again.

The next page bore a clipping from the *Newark Call:*

Adolph Heschler, confined in the penitentiary at Camden awaiting execution for the murder of State Trooper James Donovan on the night of March 20th last, seems resigned to his fate. When first taken to the state prison he seemed in deadly fear of death and spent most of his time in prayer.

Prison officials say that he began to show signs of resignation following the memorial services on May 30th, and it is said he declares his conscience is cleared by the thought that he shall be allowed the opportunity of atoning for his misdeeds. Curiously enough, Heschler, who has heretofore shown the most devout appreciation of the ministrations of the prison's Catholic chaplain, will have nothing further to do with the spiritual advisor, declaring "atonement for his sins has been arranged." There is talk of having him examined by a lunacy commission before the date set for his execution.

Another translation of the diary followed:

August 30—Michel has come with the body. It is a mummy! When I expressed my astonishment, he told me it was the best possible corpse for the purpose. After hearing him, I realized he has the pseudo-logic of the mildly insane. The body of one who has died from natural causes or by violence would be unfitted for our purposes, he says, since some of its organs must inevitably be unable to function properly. This mummy is not a true mummy, but the body of an Egyptian guilty of sacrilege, who was sealed up alive in a tomb during the Hyksos dynasty. He died of asphyxia, in all probability, and his body is in perfect condition, except for the dehydration due to lying so many thousands of years in a perfectly dry atmosphere. Michel rescued the mummy during his last expedition to Egypt, and tells me there was evidence of the man's having made a terrific struggle before death put an end to his sufferings. Other bodies, properly mummified, were found in the same tomb, and the dying man had overturned many of the cases and spilled their contents about the place. His body was so thoroughly impregnated with the odor of the spices and preservatives, absorbed from the mummies lying in the tomb, that it was not for some time his discoverers realized he had not been eviscerated and embalmed. Michel assures me the dead man will be perfectly able to act as an envelope for Heschler's soul when the electrocution has been performed. Cousin Michel, if this body does but so much as wiggle its fingers or toes after the authorities have killed Heschler, I will believe—I will believe.

I laid down the final page of de Grandin's translation and looked wonderingly at him. "Where's the rest of it?" I demanded. "Couldn't you do any more last night?"

"The rest," he answered ironically, "is for us to find out, my friends. The journal stops with the entry you have just read. There was no more."

"Humph," Sergeant, Costello commented, "crazy as a pair o' fish out o' water, weren't they? Be gorry, gentlemen, I'm thinkin' it's a crazy man we'd best be lookin' for. I can see it all plain, now. This here Cousin Michael o' Professor Kolisko's was a religious fy-nat-ic, as th' felly says, an' th' pair o' 'em got to fightin' among themselves an' th' professor came out second best. That's th' answer, or my name ain't—"

The sudden shrilling of the office telephone interrupted him. "Sergeant Costello, please," a sharp voice demanded as I picked up the receiver.

"Yeah, this is Costello speakin'," the detective announced, taking the instrument from me. "Yep. All right, go ahead. *What?* Just like th' other one? My Gawd!"

"What is it?" de Grandin and I asked in chorus as he put down the receiver and turned a serious face to us.

"Miss Adkinson, an old lady livin' by herself out by th' cemetery, has been found murdered," he replied slowly, "*an' th' marks on her throat tally exactly wid those on Professor Kolisko's!*"

"*Cordieu!*" de Grandin shouted, leaping from his chair as if it had suddenly become white-hot. "We must hasten, we must rush, we must fly to that house, my friends! We must examine the body, we must assure ourselves before some bungling coroner's physician spoils everything!"

Two minutes later we were smashing the speed ordinances in an effort to reach the Adkinson house before Coroner Martin arrived.

Sᴛᴀʀᴋ ᴛʀᴀɢᴇᴅʏ ʀᴇᴘᴇᴀᴛᴇᴅ ɪᴛsᴇʟꜰ in the Adkinson cottage. The old lady, gaunt with the leanness of age to which time has not been over-kind, lay in a crumpled heap on her kitchen floor, and a moment's examination disclosed the same livid marks on her throat and the same horrifying limberness of neck which we had observed when viewing Professor Kolisko's body.

"By Gawd, gentlemen, this is terrible!" Costello swore as he turned from the grisly relic. "Here's an old man kilt at night an' a harmless old woman murdered in broad daylight, an' no one to tell us anything certain about th' murderer!"

"*Ha*, do you say so?" de Grandin responded sharply, his little eyes flashing with excitement. "*Parbleu*, my friend, but you are greatly wrong, as wrong as can be. There *is* one who can tell us, and tell us he shall, if I must wring the truth from him with my bare hands!"

"What d'ye mean—?" Sergeant Costello began, but the little Frenchman had already turned toward the door, dragging frantically at my elbow.

"Clutch everything, *mes amis*," he commanded. "Retain all; me, I go to find him who can tell us what we need to know. *Mordieu*, I shall find him though he takes refuge in the nethermost subcellar of hell! Come, Trowbridge, my friend; I would that you drive me to the station where I can entrain for New York."

SHORTLY AFTER SEVEN O'CLOCK that evening I answered the furious ringing of my telephone to hear de Grandin's excited voice come tumbling out of the receiver. "Come at once, my friend," he ordered, fairly stuttering in his elation. "Rush with all speed to the Carmelite Fathers' retreat in East Thirty-second Street. Bring the excellent Costello with you, too, for there is one here who can shed the light of intelligence on our ignorance."

"Who is it—?" I began, but the sharp click of a receiver smashed into its hook cut short my query, and I turned in disgust from the unresponsive instrument to transmit the Frenchman's message to Sergeant Costello.

Within sight of Bellevue's grim mortuary, enshrouded by the folds of drab East River fog as a body is wrapped in its winding-sheet, the little religious community seemed as incongruously out of place in the heart of New York's poverty-ridden East Side as a nun in a sweatshop. Striding up and down the polished floor of the bare, immaculately clean reception-room was Jules de Grandin, a glowing cigarette between his fingers, his tiny, waxed mustache standing straight out from the corners of his mouth like the whiskers of an excited tomcat. "At last!" he breathed as Costello and I followed the porter from the front door to the public room. "*Morbleu*, I thought you had perished on the way."

"Monsieur," he paused in his restless pacing and stopped before the figure sitting motionless in the hard, straight-backed chair at the farther side of the room, "you will please tell these gentlemen what you have told me and be of haste in doing so. We have small time to waste."

I glanced curiously at the seated man. His strong resemblance to the dead Kolisko was remarkable. He possessed a mop of untidy, iron-gray hair and a rather straggling gray beard; his forehead was high, narrow and startlingly white, almost transparent, and the skin of his face was puckered into hundreds of little, wrinkles as though his skull had shrunk, leaving the epidermis without support. His eyes, however, differed radically from Kolisko's, for even in death the professor's orbs had shown a hard, implacable nature, whereas this man's eyes, though shaded by beetling, overhanging brows, were soft and brown. Somehow, they reminded me of the eyes of an old and very gentle dog begging not to be beaten.

"I am Michel Kolisko," be began, clearing his throat with a soft, deprecating cough. "Urban Kolisko was my cousin, son of my father's brother. We grew up together in Poland, attended the same schools and colleges, and dreamed the same dreams of Polish independence. I was twenty, Urban was twenty-three when the Tsar's officers swooped down on our fathers, carried them off to rot in Siberia, and confiscated most of our family's fortune. Both of us were suspected of complicity in the revolutionary movement, and fled for our lives, Urban to Paris, I to Vienna. He matriculated at the Sorbonne and devoted himself to the study of psychology; I studied medicine in Vienna, then went to Rome, and finally took up Egyptology as my life's work.

"Twenty years passed before I saw my cousin again. The Russian proscription had been raised, and he had gone to Warsaw, where he taught in the university. When I went there to visit him, I was shocked to learn he had abandoned God and taken to the worship of the material world. Kant, Spencer, Richet, Wundt—these were his prophets and his priests; the God of our fathers he disowned and denied. I argued with him, pleaded with him to return to his childhood's belief, and he turned me out of his house.

"Once again he earned the displeasure of the Tsar and escaped arrest only by a matter of moments. Fleeing to this country, he took up residence in your city, and devoted himself to penning revolutionary propaganda and atheistic theses. Broken in health, but with sufficient money to insure me of a quiet old age, I followed him to America and made it the work of my declining years to convert him from his apostasy.

"This spring it seemed I was beginning to succeed, for he showed more patience with me than ever before; but he was a hardened sinner, his heart was steeled against the call of consciousness, even as was Pharaoh's of old. He challenged me to offer evidence of God's truth, and promised he would turn again to religion if I could."

For a moment the speaker paused in his monotonous, almost mumbled recitation, wrung his bloodless hands together in a gesture of despair, pressed his fingers to his forehead, as though to crowd back departing reason, then took up his story, never raising his voice, never stressing one word more than another, keeping his eyes fixed on vacancy. He reminded me of a child reciting a distasteful lesson by rote.

"I see we were both mad, now," he confided drearily. "Mad, mad with the sense of our own importance, for Urban defied divine providence, and I forgot that it is not man's right to attempt to prove God's truth as revealed to us by his ordained ministers. It is ours to believe, and to question not. But I was carried away by the fervor of my mission. 'If I can shake Urban's doubts, I shall surely win a crown of glory,' I told myself, 'for surely there is great joy in heaven over one sinner who repents.' And so I went about the sacrilegious business of the test.

"Among the curios I had brought from Egypt was the body of a man sealed alive in a tomb during the Hyksos rule. It was not really a mummy, for no embalming had been performed, but the superheated atmosphere of the tomb in which he had been incarcerated had shriveled his tissues until it was difficult to tell him from a body mummified by artificial methods. Only three or four such bodies are known; one is the celebrated Flinders mummy, and the others are in French and British museums. I had intended leaving mine to the Metropolitan when I died.

"I brought this body to Urban's house the night before Heschler, the condemned murderer, was to be executed, and we laid it on the library table. Urban viewed it with disgust and skepticism, but I prayed over it, begging God to work a miracle, to permit the body to move, if only very slightly, and so convince my poor, misguided cousin. You know, gentlemen"—he turned his sorrowful, lackluster eyes on us with a melancholy smile—"such things are not entirely unknown. Sudden changes in temperature or in the moisture content of the atmosphere often lead to a movement as the dehydrated tissues take up water from the air. The mummy of Rameses the Great, for instance, moved its arm when first exposed to the outdoor air.

"A few minutes after midnight was the time set for Heschler's electrocution, and as the town clocks began rounding the hour I felt as though the heavens must fall if no sign were manifested to us.

"Urban sat beside the mummy, smoking his pipe and sneering—part of the time reading an impious book by Freud. I bowed my head in silent prayer, asking for a miracle to save him despite his hardness of heart. The city hall clock struck the quarter hour, then the half, and still there was no sound. Urban laid his pipe and book aside and looked at me with his familiar sneer, then turned as though to thrust the body of the Egyptian from the table—*then it sat up!*

"Like a sleeper waking from a dream, like a patient coming forth from the ether it was—the corpse that had been dead four thousand years rose from the table and looked at us. For a moment it seemed to smile with its fleshless lips, then it looked down at itself, and gave a scream of surprise and fury.

"'So!' it shrieked; 'so *this* is the body you've given me to work out my salvation! This is the form in which I must walk the earth until my sins be wiped away, is it? You've tricked me, cheated me; but I'll have vengeance. No one living can harm me, and I'll take my toll of human kind before I finally go forth to stew and burn in Satan's fires!'

"It was stiff and brittle, but somehow it managed to crawl from the table and make at Urban. He seized a heavy whip which hung on the wall and struck the thing on the head with its loaded butt. The blow would have killed an ordinary man—indeed, I saw the mummy's dried-up skull cave in beneath the force of Urban's flailings, but it never faltered in its attack, never missed a step in its pursuit of vengeance.

"Then I went mad. I fled from that accursed house and buried myself in this retreat, where I have spent every moment since, denying myself both food and sleep, deeming every second left me all too short to beg divine forgiveness for the terrible sacrilege I have committed."

"So, my friends, you see?" de Grandin turned to Costello and me as the half-hysterical Pole concluded his preposterous narrative.

"Sure, I do," the detective returned. "Didn't th' felly say he's mad? Be dad, they say crazy folks tell th' truth, an' he ain't stretchin' it none when he says his steeple's full o' bats."

"Ah bah!" de Grandin shot back. "You weary me, my friend."

To Kolisko he said: "Your story supplies the information which we so sorely needed, sir. Whatever the result of your experiment, your motives were good, nor do I think the good God will be too hard upon you. If you do truly wish forgiveness, pray that we shall be successful in destroying the monster before more harm is done. *Cordieu*, but we shall need all your prayers, and a vast deal of luck as well, I think; for killing that which is already dead is no small task."

"Now what?" demanded Costello with a sidelong glance at de Grandin as we emerged from the religious house. "Got some more loonics for us to listen to?"

"*Parbleu*, if you will but give ear to your own prattle, you shall have all that sort of conversation you wish, I think, *cher Sergent*," the little Frenchman jerked back with a smile which took half the acid from his words. Then:

"Friend Trowbridge, convoy our good, unbelieving friend to Harrisonville and await my return. I have one or two things to attend to before I join you; but when I come I think I can promise you a show the like of which you have not before seen. *Au revoir, mes enfants.*"

Ten o'clock sounded on the city's clocks; eleven; half-past. Costello and I consumed innumerable cigars and more than one potion of some excellent cognac I had stored in my cellar since the days before prohibition; still no sign of my little friend. The sergeant was on the point of taking his departure when a light step sounded on the porch and de Grandin came bounding into the consulting-room, his face wreathed in smiles, a heavy-looking parcel gripped under his right arm.

"*Bien*, my friends, I find you in good time," he greeted, poured himself a monstrous stoup of amber liquor, then helped himself to one of my cigars. "I think it high time we were on our way. There is that to do which may take considerable doing this night, but I would not that we delay our expedition because of difficulties in the road."

"Be gorry, he's caught it from th' other nut!" Costello confided to the surrounding atmosphere with a serio-comic grimace. "Which crazy house are we goin' to now, sor?"

"Where but to the house of Monsieur Kolisko?" returned the Frenchman with a grin. "I think there will be another there before long, and it is highly expedient that we be there first."

"Humph, if it's Coroner Martin or his physician, you needn't be worryin' yourself anny," Costello assured him. "They'll be takin' no more interest in th' case till someone else gets kilt, I'm thinkin'."

"*Morbleu*, then their days of interest are ended, or Jules de Grandin is a colossal liar," was the response. "Come; *allons vite!*"

THE LOWEST WORKINGS OF a coal mine were not darker than the Kolisko house when we let ourselves in some fifteen minutes later. Switching on the electric light, de Grandin proceeded to unpack his parcel, taking from it a folded black object which resembled a deflated association football. Next he produced a shining nickel-plated apparatus consisting of a thick upright cylinder and a transverse flat piece which opened in two on hinges, disclosing an interior resembling a waffle-iron with small, close-set knobs. Into a screw-stopped opening in the hollow cylinder of the contrivance he poured several ounces of gray-black powder; then, taking the flat rubber bag, he hurried from the house to my car, attached the valve of the bag to my tire pump and proceeded to inflate the rubber bladder almost to the bursting point. This done, he attached the bag to a valve in the nickeled cylinder by a two-foot length of rubber hose, poured some liquid over the corrugated "waffle-iron" at the top of the cylinder, and, with the inflated bag hugged under his arm, as a Highland piper might hold the bag of his pipes, he strode across the room, snapped off the light, and took his station near the open window.

Several times Costello and I addressed him, but each time he cut us short with a sharp, irritable "Sssh!" continuing his crouching watch beside the window, staring intently into the shaded garden beyond.

It must have been some three-quarters of an hour later that we sensed, rather than heard, the scuffling of light footfalls on the grass outside, heard the door-knob cautiously tested, then the scuttering of more steps, scarcely louder than the sound of wind-blown leaves, as the visitant rounded the cottage wall and made for the window beside which de Grandin mounted guard.

A puff of autumn wind, scented with the last blooms of summer's rosebeds, sent the light clouds drifting from before the moon's pale lantern, and, illuminated in the pallid light of the night's goddess, we saw framed at the window-square the terrifying vision which had followed young Ratliff's story of his escape two nights before.

"My Gawd!" Costello's bass voice was shrill and treble with sudden terror as the thing gazed malevolently in at us. Next instant his heavy service revolver was out, and shot after shot poured straight into the hideous, grinning face at the window.

He might as well have fired boiled beans from a pea-shooter for all the effect his bullets had. Distinctly I saw a portion of the mummy's ear clipped off by a flying slug of lead, saw an indentation sink in the thing's head half an inch above the right eye as a soft-nosed bullet tore through skin and withered flesh and frontal bone; but the emaciated body never paused in its progress.

One withered leg was lifted across the window sill; two long, unfleshed arms, terminating in hands of enormous length, were thrust out toward the Irishman; a grin of such hellish hatred and triumph as I had never conceived possible disfigured the object's visage as it pressed onward, its long, bony fingers opening and closing convulsively, as though they already felt their victim's neck within their grasp.

"*Monsieur*, you do play truant from hell!" De Grandin's announcement was made in the most casual manner as he rose from his half-kneeling posture beside the window and placed himself directly in the mummy's path, but there was a quaver in his voice which betrayed the intensity of his emotion.

A noise—you could hardly call it a snarl nor yet a scream, but a sound midway between the two—emanated from the thing's desiccated throat as it turned on him, threw out one hand and snatched at his throat.

There was a tiny spark of light, as though a match had been struck, then a mighty, bursting blaze, as if time had turned backward in its flight for a second and the midday sun had thrown its beams through the midnight blackness of the room, a swishing, whistling sound, as of air suddenly released from tremendous pressure, and a shriek of mad, insupportable anguish. Then the fierce blazing of some inflammable substance suddenly set alight. My eyes started from my face as I seemed to see the mummy's scraggly limbs and emaciated torso writhe within a very inferno of fire. Then:

"*Cher Sergent*, it might be well to call the fire department; this place will surely burn about our ears unless *les pompiers* hurry with their hose, I fear," remarked Jules de Grandin as calmly as though advising us the night was fine.

"BUT—BUT—HOWLY MITHER O' MOSES!" Sergeant Costello demanded as we turned from watching the firemen salvaging the remnants of Kolisko's cottage. "How did ye manage it, Doctor de Grandin, sor? May I never eat another mess o' corned beef an' cabbage if I didn't shoot th' thing clean through th' head wid me gun, an' it never so much as batted an eye, yet ye burned it up as clean as—"

"Precisely, *mon vieux*," the Frenchman admitted with a chuckle. "Have you never heard the adage that one must fight the Devil with fire? It was something like that which I did.

"No later than night before last a young man came crying and whimpering at Friend Trowbridge's door, begging for shelter from some ghastly thing which pursued him through the streets. Both Trowbridge and I thought he suffered from an overdose of the execrable liquor with which Monsieur Volstead has flooded this unhappy land, but before we could boot him from the door, behold, the same thing which you so unsuccessfully shot tonight did stick its unlovely countenance against our window, and I, who always go armed lest some miscreant do me a mischief, did fire eight shots directly into his face. Believe me, my friend, when Jules de Grandin shoots, he does not miss, and that night I shot exceptionally well. Yet when Friend Trowbridge and I searched the garden, neither hide nor hair of the one who should have been eight times dead did we find. 'There is something here which will take much explaining,' I say to me after we could not find him.

"Next morning you did come and tell us of Professor Kolisko's murder, and when we had viewed his remains, I wondered much what sort of creature could have done this thing. The pressure exerted on his neck were superhuman, but the marks of the hand were not those of an ape, for no ape possesses such a long, thin thumb.

"Then we did find the dead professor's diary and I have the tiny shivers playing tag with each other up and down my back as I read and translate it. It sounds like the dream of one crazed with dope, I know, but there was the possibility of truth in it. Do you know the vampire, my friends?"

"The vampire?" I echoed.

"*Précisément*; the vampire you have said it. He is not always one who can not die because of sin or misfortune in life. No. Sometimes he is a dead body possessed by some demon—perhaps by some unhappy, earthbound spirit. Yes.

"Now, as I read the professor's journal, I see that everything which had transpired were most favorable for the envampirement of that body which his cousin had brought from Egypt so long ago. Yet the idea seemed—how do you say?—ah, yes—to have the smell of the fish on it.

"But when you came and say Miss Adkinson have been erased in the same manner as Professor Kolisko, I begin to wonder if perhaps I have not less nuts in my belfry than I at first thought. In Professor Kolisko's journal there was reference to his cousin. 'How does it come that this cousin have not come forward and told us what, if anything, he knows?' I ask me as we view the poor dead woman's body, and the answer was, 'He has most doubtless seen that which will not be believed, and hides because he fears arrest on a false charge of murder.'

"Right away I rush to New York and inquire at the *Musée Metropolitain* for the address of Monsieur Michel Kolisko, the Egyptologist. I find his living-quarters in East Eighty-sixth Street. Then they tell me he have gone to the Carmelite retreat. *Morbleu*, had he hidden in lost Atlantis, I should have hunted him out, for I desired speech with him!

"At first he would not talk, dreading I intended to drag him to the jail, but after I had spoken with him for a time, he opened his heart, and told me what he later told you.

"Now, what to do? By Monsieur Kolisko's story, it were useless to battle with this enlivened mummy, for the body of him was but the engine moved by an alien spirit—he had no need of brains, hearts and such things as we must use. Also, I knew from experience, bullets were as useless against him as puffs of wind against a fortress wall. 'Very well,' I tell me, 'he may be invulnerable to bullets and blows, but living or dead, he is still a mummy—a dry, desiccated mummy—and we have had no rain lately. It are entirely unlikely that he have gotten greatly moistened in his trips through the streets, and all mummies are as tinder to fire. *Mordieu*, did they not once use them as fuel for locomotives in Egypt when railways were first built there? Yes.'

"And so I prepare the warm reception for him. At one time and another I have taken photographs at night, and to do so I have used magnesium flares—what you call flashlight powder. At a place where they sell such things in New York I procure a flashlight burner—a hollow cylinder for the powder magazine with a benzine wick at its top and a tube through which air can be blown to force the powder through the burning petrol and so give a continuous blaze. I get me also a rubber bag which I can inflate and attach to the windpipe of the apparatus, thus leaving my lips free for swearing and other important things, and also giving a greater force of air.

"I reason: 'Where will this living mummy go most naturally? Why not to the house where he received his new life, for the town in which he goes about committing murder is still new to him.' And so, when *Monsieur la Momie* returns to the place of his second nativity, I am all ready for him. Your shots, they are as ineffectual as were mine two nights ago, but I have my magnesium flare ready, and as he turns on me I blow the fierce flame from it all over him. He are dry like tinder, the fire seized on him like a hungry little boy on a jam-tart, and—*pouf*—he is burn up, incinerated; he is no more!"

"Do you actually mean Heschler's soul entered that dried-up body?" I demanded.

The Frenchman shook his head. "I do not know," he replied. "Perhaps it were Heschler; more likely not. The air is full of strange and terrible things, my friend. Not for nothing did the old divines call Satan the Prince of the Powers of the Air. How do we know some of those elementals who are ever on the watch to do mankind an injury did not hear the mad Kolisko's scheme and take advantage of the opportunity to enter into the mummy's body? Such things have been before; why may they not be again?"

"But—" I commenced.

"But—" expostulated Sergeant Costello.

"But, my friends," the little man cut in "did you behold how dry that so abominable mummy was before I applied the fire?"

"Yes," I answered wonderingly.

"*Cordieu*, he was wet as the broad Atlantic Ocean beside the dryness of Jules de Grandin at this moment! Friend Trowbridge, unless my memory plays me false, I beheld a bottle of cognac upon your office table. Come, I faint, I die, I perish; talk to me no more till I have consumed the remainder of that bottle, I do beseech you!"

Restless Souls

"TEN THOUSAND SMALL GREEN devils! What a night; what an odious night!" Jules de Grandin paused beneath the theater's porte-cochère and scowled ferociously at the pelting rain.

"Well, summer's dead and winter hasn't quite come," I reminded soothingly. "We're bound to have a certain amount of rain in October. The autumnal equinox—"

"May Satan's choicest imps fly off with the autumnal equinox!" the little Frenchman interrupted. "*Morbleu*, it is that I have seen no sun since God alone knows when; besides that, I am most abominably hungry!"

"That condition, at least, we can remedy," I promised, nudging him from the awning's shelter toward my parked car. "Suppose we stop at the Café Bacchanale? They usually have something good to eat."

"Excellent, capital," he agreed enthusiastically, skipping nimbly into the car and rearranging the upturned collar of his raincoat. "You are a true philosopher, *mon vieux*. Always you tell me that which I most wish to hear."

They were having an hilarious time at the cabaret, for it was the evening of October 31, and the management had put on a special Halloween celebration. As we passed the velvet rope that looped across the entrance to the dining room a burst of Phrygian music greeted us, and a dozen agile young women in abbreviated attire were performing intricate gyrations under the leadership of an apparently boneless damsel whose costume was principally composed of strands of jangling hawk-bells threaded round her neck and wrists and ankles.

"Welsh rabbit?" I suggested. "They make a rather tasty one here." He nodded almost absent-mindedly as he surveyed a couple eating at a nearby table.

At last, just as the waiter brought our bubbling-hot refreshment: "Regard them, if you will, Friend Trowbridge," he whispered. "Tell me what, if anything, you make of them."

The girl was, as the saying goes, "a knockout." Tall, lissome, lovely to regard, she wore a dinner dress of simple black without a single hint of ornament except a single strand of small matched pearls about her slim and rather long throat. Her hair was bright chestnut, almost copper-colored, and braided round her small head in a Grecian coronal, and in its ruddy frame her face was like some strange flower on a tall stalk. Her darkened lids and carmined mouth and pale cheeks made an interesting combination.

As I stole a second glance at her it seemed to me she had a vague yet unmis-takable expression of invalidism. Nothing definite, merely the combination of certain factors which pierced the shell of my purely masculine admiration and stock response from my years of experience as a medical practitioner—a certain blueness of complexion which meant "interesting pallor" to the layman but spelled imperfectly oxidized blood to the physician; a slight tightening of the muscles about the mouth which gave her lovely pouting lips a pathetic droop; and a scarcely perceptible retraction at the junction of cheek and nose which meant fatigue of nerves or muscles, possibly both.

Idly mingling admiration and diagnosis, I turned my glance upon her escort, and my lips tightened slightly as I made a mental note: "Gold digger!" The man was big-boned and coarse-featured, bullet-headed and thick-necked, and had the pasty, toad-belly complexion of one who drinks too much and sleeps and exercises far too little. He hardly changed expression as the girl talked eagerly in a hushed whisper. His whole attitude was one of proprietorship, as if she were his thing and chattel, bought and paid for, and constantly his fishy eyes roved round the room and rested covetously on attractive women supping at the other tables.

"I do not like it, me," de Grandin's comment brought my wandering atten-tion back. "It is both strange and queer; it is not right."

"Eh?" I returned. "Quite so; I agree with you. It's shameful for a girl like that to sell—or maybe only rent—herself to such a creature—"

"*Non, non,*" he interrupted testily. "I have no thought of censoring their morals, such are their own affair. It is their treatment of the food that intrigues me."

"Food?" I echoed.

"*Oui-da,* food. On three distinct occasions they have ordered refreshment, yet each time they allowed it to grow cold; let it remain untouched until the *garçon* carried it away. I ask you, is that right?"

"Why—er—" I temporized, but he hurried on.

"Once as I watched I saw the woman make as though to lift a goblet to her lips, but the gesture of her escort halted her; she set the beverage down untasted. What sort of people ignore wine—the living soul of the grape?"

"Well, are you going to investigate?" I asked, grinning. I knew his curiosity was well-nigh as boundless as his self-esteem, and should not have been too greatly surprised if he had marched to the strange couple's table and demanded an explanation.

"Investigate?" he echoed thoughtfully. "Um. Perhaps I shall."

He snapped the pewter lid of his beer-mug back, took a long, pensive draught, then leant forward, small round eyes unwinkingly on mine. "You know what night this is?" he demanded.

"Of course, it's Halloween. All the little devils will be out stealing garden gates and knocking at front doors—"

"Perhaps the larger devils will be abroad, too."

"Oh, come, now," I protested, "you're surely not serious   "

"By blue, I am," he affirmed solemnly. "*Regardez, s'il vous plaît.*" He nodded toward the pair at the adjoining table.

Seated directly opposite the strange couple was a young man occupying a table by himself. He was a good-looking, sleek-haired youngster of the sort to be found by scores on any college campus. Had de Grandin brought the same charge of food wastage against him that he had leveled at the other two he would have been equally justified, for the boy left an elaborate order practically untasted while his infatuated eyes devoured every line of the girl at the next table.

As I turned to look at him I noted from the corner of my eye that the girl's escort nodded once in the same direction, then rose and left the table abruptly. I noticed as he walked toward the door that his walk was more like the rapid amble of an animal than the step of a man.

The girl half turned as she was left alone and under lowered lashes looked at the young man so indifferently that there was no mistaking her intent.

De Grandin watched with what seemed bleak disinterest as the young man rose to join her, and, save for an occasional covert glance, paid no attention as they exchanged the inane amenities customary in such cases, but when they rose to leave a few minutes later he motioned me to do likewise. "It is of importance that we see which way they go," he told me earnestly.

"Oh, for goodness' sake, be sensible!" I chided. "Let them flirt if they want to. I'll warrant she's in better company now than she came in with—"

"*Précisément*, exactly, quite so!" he agreed. "It is of that 'better company' I think when I have the anxiety."

"H'm, that *was* a tough-looking customer she was with," I conceded. "And for all her innocent-looking prettiness she might be the bait in a badger-game—"

"A badger-game? *Mais oui*, my friend. A game-of-the-badger in which the stakes are infinitely high!" Of the ornate doorman he demanded, "That couple, that young man and woman—they did go what way, *Monsieur le Concierge?*"

"Huh?"

"The young man and young woman—you saw them depart? We would know their direction—" a crumpled dollar bill changed hands, and the doorman's memory revived miraculously.

"Oh, them. Yeah, I seen 'em. They went down th' street that-away in a big black taxi. Little English feller drivin' 'em. Looked like th' feller's made a mash. He'll *get* mashed, too, if th' tough bimbo 'at brought th' broad in ketches 'im messin' round with her. That gink's one awful mean-lookin' bozo, an'—"

"Assuredly," de Grandin agreed. "And this *Monsieur le Gink* of whom you speak, he went which way, if you please?"

"He come outer here like a bat outer hell 'bout ten minutes ago. Funny thing 'bout him, too. He was walkin' down th' street, an' I was watchin' him, not special, but just lookin' at him, an' I looked away for just a minute, an' when I looked back he was gone. He wasn't more'n half way down th' block when I last seen him, but when I looked again he wasn't there. Dam' if I see how he managed to get round th' comer in that time."

"I think that your perplexity is justified," de Grandin answered as I brought the car to a stop at the curb, then, to me: "Hasten, Friend Trowbridge. I would that we get them in sight before they are lost in the storm."

I T WAS A MATTER of only a few minutes to pick up the tail light of the big car in which the truants sped toward the outskirts of town. Occasionally we lost them, only to catch them again almost immediately, for their route led straight out Orient Boulevard toward the Old Turnpike. "This is the craziest thing we've ever done," I grumbled. "There isn't any more chance that we'll catch them than—great Scott, they've stopped!"

Improbably, the big car had drawn up at the imposing Canterbury Gate of Shadow Lawn Cemetery.

De Grandin leant forward in his seat like a jockey in the saddle. "Quick, hurry, make all speed, my friend!" he besought. "We must catch them before they alight!"

Try as I would my efforts were futile. Only an empty limousine and a profanely bewildered chauffeur awaited us when we drew up at the burying ground, our engine puffing like a winded horse.

"Which way, my friend—where did they go?" de Grandin vaulted from the car before we had come to a full stop.

"Inside th' graveyard!" answered the driver. "What th' hell d'ye know about that? Bringin' me way out here where th' devil says 'Good Night!' an' leavin' me as flat as a dam' pancake." His voice took on a shrill falsetto in imitation of a woman's. "'You needn't wait for us, driver, we'll not be com' back,' she says. Good God A' mighty, who th' hell but dead corpses goes into th' cemet'ry an' don't come back?"

"Who, indeed?" the Frenchman echoed, then, to me: "Come, Friend Trowbridge, we must hasten, we must find them all soon, or it is too late!"

SOLEMN AS THE PURPOSE to which it was dedicated, the burial park stretched dark and forbidding about us as we stepped through the grille in the imposing stone gateway. The curving ravelled avenues, bordered with double rows of hemlocks, stretched away like labyrinthine mazes, and the black turf with its occasional corrugations of mounded graves or decorations of pallid marble, sloped upward from us, seemingly to infinity.

Like a terrier on the scent de Grandin hurried forward, bending now and then to pass beneath the downward-swaying bough of some rain-laden evergreen, then hurrying still faster.

"You know this place, Friend Trowbridge?" he demanded during one of his brief halts.

"Better than I want to," I admitted. "I've been here to several funerals."

"Good!" he returned. "You can tell me then where is the—how do you call him?—the receiving vault?"

"Over there, almost in the center of the park," I answered, and he nodded understandingly, then took up his course, almost at a run.

Finally we reached the squat grey-stone receiving mausoleum, and he tried one of the heavy doors after another. "A loss!" he announced disappointedly as each of the tomb's great metal doors defied his efforts. "It seems we must search elsewhere."

He trotted to the open space reserved for parking funeral vehicles and cast a quick appraising look about, arrived at a decision and started like a cross-country runner down the winding road that led to a long row of family mausoleums. At each he stopped, trying the strong metal gratings at its entrance, peering into its gloomy interior with the aid of his pocket flashlight.

Tomb after tomb we visited, till both my breath and patience were exhausted. "What's all this nonsense?" I demanded. "What're you looking for—"

"That which I fear to find," he panted, casting the beam of his light about. "If we are balked—ah? Look, my friend, look and tell me what it is you see."

In the narrow cone of light cast by his small electric torch I descried a dark form draped across the steps of a mausoleum. "Wh-why, it's a man!" I exclaimed.

"I hope so," he replied. "It may be we shall find the mere relic of one, but—ah? So. He is still breathing."

Taking the flashlight from him I played its ray on the still form stretched upon the tomb steps. It was the young man we had seen leave the café with the strange woman. On his forehead was a nasty cut, as though from some blunt instrument swung with terrific force—a blackjack, for instance.

Quickly, skillfully, de Grandin ran his supple, practised hands over the youngster's body, pressed his fingers to his pulse, bent to listen at his chest. "He lives," he announced at the end of his inspection, "but his heart, I do not like it. Come; let us take him hence, my friend."

"AND NOW, MON BRAVE," he demanded half an hour later when we had revived the unconscious man with smelling salts and cold applications, "perhaps you will be good enough to tell us why you left the haunts of the living to foregather with the dead?"

The patient made a feeble effort to rise from the examination table, gave it up as too difficult and sank back. "I thought I was dead," he confessed.

"U'm?" the Frenchman regarded him narrowly. "You have not yet answered our question, young Monsieur."

The boy made a second attempt to rise, and an agonized expression spread over his face, his hand shot up to his left breast, and he fell back, half lolling, half writhing on the table.

"Quick, Friend Trowbridge, the amyl nitrite, where is it?" de Grandin asked.

"Over there," I waved my hand toward the medicine cabinet. "You'll find some three-minim capsules in the third bottle."

In a moment he secured the pearly little pellets, crushed one in his hand-kerchief and applied it to the fainting boy's nostrils. "Ah, that is better, n'est-ce-pas, my poor one?" he asked.

"Yes, thanks," the other replied, taking another deep inhalation of the powerful restorative, "much better." Then, "How'd you know what to give me? I didn't think—"

"My friend," the Frenchman interrupted with a smile, "I was practising the treatment of angina pectoris when you were still unthought of. Now, if you are sufficiently restored, you will please tell us why you left the Café Bacchanale, and what occurred thereafter. We wait."

Slowly, assisted by de Grandin on one side and me on the other, the young man descended from the table and seated himself in an easy chair. "I'm Donald Rochester," he introduced himself, "and this was to have been my last night on earth."

"Ah?" Jules de Grandin murmured.

"Six months ago." the young man continued, "Dr. Simmons told me I had angina pectoris. My case was pretty far advanced when he made his diagnosis, and he gave me only a little while to live. Two weeks ago he told me I'd be lucky to see the month out, and the pain was getting more severe and the attacks more frequent; so today I decided to give myself one last party, then go home and make a quick, clean job of it."

"Damn!" I muttered. I knew Simmons, a pompous old ass, but a first-rate diagnostician and a good heart man, though absolutely brutal with his patients.

"I ordered the sort of meal they haven't allowed me in the last half year," Rochester went on, "and was just about to start enjoying it when—when I saw her come in. Did"—he turned from de Grandin to me as if expecting greater understanding from a fellow countryman—"did you see her, too?" An expression of almost religious rapture overspread his face.

"Perfectly, *mon vieux*," de Grandin returned. "We all saw her. Tell us more."

"I always thought this talk of love at first sight was a lot of tripe, but I'm cured now. I even forgot my farewell meal, couldn't see or think of anything but her. If I'd had even two more years to live, I thought, nothing could have kept me from hunting her out and asking her to marry—"

"*Précisément*, assuredly, quite so," the Frenchman interrupted testily. "We do concede that you were fascinated, Monsieur; but, for the love of twenty thousand pale blue monkeys, I entreat you tell us what you did, not what you thought."

"I just sat and goggled at her sir. Couldn't do anything else. When that big brute she was with got up and left and she smiled at me, this poor old heart of mine almost blinked out, I tell you. When she smiled a second time there wasn't enough chain in the country to keep me from her.

"You'd have thought she'd known me all her life, the way she fell in step when we went out of the café. She had a big black car waiting outside and I climbed right in with her. Before I knew it, I was telling her who I was, how long I had to live, and how my only regret was losing her, just when I'd found her. I—"

"*Parbleu*, you told her that?"

"I surely did, and a lot more—blurted out that I loved her before I knew what I was about."

"And she—"

"Gentlemen, I'm not sure whether I ought to have delirium or not with this disease, but I'm pretty sure I've had a touch of something. Now, I want you to know I'm not crazy before I tell you the rest; but I might have had a heart attack or something, then fallen asleep and dreamed it."

"Say on, Monsieur," de Grandin ordered rather grimly. "We listen."

"Very well. When I said I loved her that girl just put her hands up to her eyes—like this—as if to wipe away some unshed tears. I half expected she'd be angry, or maybe giggle, but she didn't. All she said was, 'Too late—oh, too late!'

"'I know it is,' I answered. 'I've already told you I'm as good as dead, but I can't go west without telling you how I feel.'

"Then she said, 'Oh, no, it's not that, my dear. That's not at all what I meant. For I love you, too, though I've no right to say so—I've no right to love anyone—it's too late for me, too.'

"After that I just took her in my arms and held her tight, and she sobbed as if her heart would break. Finally I asked her to make me a promise. 'I'll rest better in my grave if I know you'll never go out with that ugly brute I saw you with tonight,' I told her, and she let out a little scream and cried harder than ever.

"Then I had the awful thought that maybe she was married to him, and that was what she meant when she said it was too late. So I asked her point blank.

"She said something devilish queer then. She told me, 'I must go to him whenever he wants me. Though I hate him as you can never understand; when he calls I have to go. This is the first time I've ever gone with him, but I must go again, and again, and again! She kept screaming the word till I stopped her mouth with kisses.

"Presently the car stopped and we got out. We were at some sort of park, I think, but I was so engrossed in helping her compose herself I didn't notice much of anything.

"She led me through a big gate and down a winding road. At last we stopped before some sort of lodge-house, and I took her in my arms for one last kiss.

"I don't know whether the rest of it really happened or whether I passed out and dreamed it. What I thought happened was this: Instead of putting her lips against mine, she put them around them and seemed to draw the very breath out of my lungs. I could feel myself go faint, like a swimmer caught in the surf and mauled and pounded till the breath's knocked out of him, and my eyes seemed blinded with a sort of mist; then everything went sort o' dark green round me, and I began sagging at the knees. I could still feel her arms round me, and remember being surprised at her strength, but it seemed as if she'd transferred her lips to my throat. I kept getting weaker and weaker with a sort of languorous ecstasy, if that means anything to you. Rather like sinking to sleep in a soft dry bed with a big drink of brandy tucked under your belt after you're dog-tired with cold and exposure. Next thing I knew I'd toppled over and fallen down the steps with no more strength in my knees than a rag doll has. I must have got an awful crack on the head when I went down, for I passed out completely, and the next thing I remember was waking to find you gentlemen working over me. Tell me, did I dream it all? I'm—just—about—played—out."

The sentence trailed off slowly, as if he were falling to sleep, and his head dropped forward while his hands slipped nervelessly from his lap, trailing flaccidly to the floor.

"Has he gone?" I whispered as de Grandin sprang across the room and ripped his collar open.

"Not quite," he answered. "More amyl nitrite, if you please; he will revive in a moment, but go home he shall not unless he promises not to destroy himself. *Mon Dieu*, destroyed he would be, body and soul, were he to put a bullet through his brain before—ah-*ha*? Behold, Friend Trowbridge, it is even as I feared!"

Against the young man's throat there showed two tiny perforated wounds, as though a fine needle had been thrust through a fold of skin.

"H'm," I commented. "If there were four of them I'd say a snake had bitten him."

"She has! Name of a little blue man, she has!" he retorted. "A serpent more virulent and subtle than any which goes on its belly has sunk her fangs in him; he is envenomed surely as if he had been a victim of a cobra's bite; but by the wings of Jacob's Angel we shall thwart her, my friend. We shall show her Jules de Grandin must be reckoned with—her, and that fish-eyed paramour of hers as well, or may I eat stewed turnips for my Christmas dinner and wash them down with ditch-water!"

IT WAS A SERIOUS face he showed at breakfast the next day. "You have perhaps a half hour's liberty this morning?" he asked as he drained his fourth cup of coffee.

"H'm, I suppose so. Anything special you'd like to do?"

"There is, indeed. I should like to go again to Shadow Lawn Cemetery. I would examine it by daylight, if you please."

"Shadow Lawn?" I echoed in amazement. "What in this world—"

"Only partially," he interrupted. "Unless I am much more mistaken than I think our business has as much to do with the next world as this. Come; you have your patients to attend, I have my duties to perform. Let us go."

The rain had vanished with the night and a bright November sun was shining when we reached the graveyard. Making straight for the tomb where we had found young Rochester the night before, de Grandin halted and inspected it carefully. On the lintel of the massive doorway he invited my attention to the single incised word:

HEATHERTON

"U'm?" he nursed his narrow pointed chin between a thoughtful thumb and forefinger. "That name I must remember, Friend Trowbridge."

Inside the tomb, arranged in two superimposed rows, were the crypts containing the remains of deceased Heathertons, each sealed by a white marble slab set with cement in a bronze frame, a two-lined legend telling the name and vital data of the occupant. The withering remains of a wreath clung by a knot of ribbon to the bronze ring-bolt ornamenting the marble panel of the farthest crypt, and behind the desiccating circle of roses and ruscus leaves I made out:

ALICE HEATHERTON
Sept. 28, 1926—*Oct.* 2, 1948

"You see?" he asked.

"I see a girl named Alice Heatherton died a month ago at the age of twenty-two," I admitted, "but what that has to do with last night is more than I can—"

"Of course," he broke in with a chuckle somehow lacking merriment. "But certainly. There are many things you do not see, my old one, and there are many more at which you blink your eyes, like a child passing over the unpleasant pages of a picture book. Now, if you will be so kind as to leave me, I shall interview *Monsieur l'Intendant* of this so lovely park, and several other people as well. If possible I shall return in time for dinner, but"—he raised his shoulders in a fatalistic shrug—"at times we must forego a meal in deference to duty. Yes, it is unfortunately so."

T HE CONSOMMÉ HAD GROWN cold and the roast lamb kiln-dried in the oven when the stutter of my study telephone called me. "Trowbridge, my friend," de Grandin's voice, shrill with excitement, came across the wire, "meet me at Adelphi Mansions quickly as you can. I would have you for witness!"

"Witness?" I echoed. "What—" A sharp click notified me he had hung up and I was left bewildered at the unresponsive instrument.

He was waiting for me at the entrance of the fashionable apartment house when I arrived, and refused to answer my impatient questions as he dragged me through the ornate entrance and down the rug-strewn foyer to the elevators. As the car shot upward he reached in his pocket and produced a shiny thumb-smudged photograph. "This I begged from *Le Journal*," he explained. "They had no further use for it."

"Good heavens!" I exclaimed as I looked at the picture. "Wh—why, it's—"

"Assuredly it is," he answered in a level tone. "It is the girl we saw last night beyond a doubt; the girl whose tomb we visited this morning; the girl who gave the kiss of death to the young Rochester."

"But that's impossible! She—"

His short laugh interrupted. "I was convinced you would say just that, Friend Trowbridge. Come, let us hear what Madame Heatherton can tell us."

A trim Negro maid in black-and-white uniform answered our summons and took our cards to her mistress. As she left the rather sumptuous reception room I glanced covertly about, noting rugs from China and the Near East, early American mahogany and an elaborately wrought medieval tapestry depicting a scene from the *Nibelungenlied* with its legend in formal Gothic text: "*Hic Siegfriedum Aureum Occidunt*—Here They Slay Siegfried the Golden."

"Dr. Trowbridge? Dr. de Grandin?" the soft, cultured voice recalled me from my study of the fabric as an imposing white-haired lady entered.

"Madame, a thousand pardons for this intrusion!" de Grandin clicked his heels together and bowed stiffly from the hips. "Believe me, we have no desire to trespass on your privacy, but a matter of the utmost importance brings us. You will forgive me if I inquire of the circumstances of your daughter's death, for I am of the *Sûreté* of Paris, and make investigation as a scientific research."

Mrs. Heatherton was, to use an overworked expression, a "perfect lady." Nine women out of ten would have frozen at de Grandin's announcement, but she was the tenth. The direct glance the little Frenchman gave her and his evident sincerity, combined with perfect manners and immaculate dress, carried conviction. "Please be seated, gentlemen," she invited. "I cannot see where my poor child's tragedy can interest an officer of the Paris secret police, but I've no objection to telling all I can; you could get a garbled version from the newspapers anyway.

"Alice was my youngest child. She and my son Ralph were two years apart, almost to the day. Ralph graduated from Cornell year before last, majoring in civil engineering, and went to Florida to take charge of some construction work. Alice died while visiting him."

"But—forgive my seeming rudeness, Madame—your son, is not he also deceased?"

"Yes," our hostess assented. "He is dead, also. They died almost together. There was a man down there, a fellow townsman of ours, Joachim Palenzeke— not the sort of person one knows, but Ralph's superior in the work. He had something to do with promoting the land development, I believe. When Alice went to visit Ralph this person presumed on his position and the fact that we were all from Harrisonville, and attempted to force his attentions on her."

"One sees. And then?" de Grandin prompted softly.

"Ralph resented his overtures. Palenzeke made some insulting remarks— some scurrilous allusions to Alice and me, I've been told, and they fought. Ralph was a small man, but a thoroughbred. Palenzeke was almost a giant, but a thoroughgoing coward. When Ralph began to get the better of him he drew a pistol and fired five shots into my poor son's body. Ralph died the next day after hours of terrible suffering.

"His murderer fled to the swamps where it would be difficult to track him with hounds, and according to some Negro squatters he committed suicide, but there must have been some mistake, for—" she broke off, pressing her crumpled handkerchief to her mouth, as if to force back the sobs.

De Grandin reached from his chair and patted her hand gently, as if consoling a child. "Dear lady," he murmured, "I am distressed, believe me, but also please believe me when I say I do not ask these so heart-breaking questions idly. Tell me, if you will, why you believe the story of this vile miscreant's suicide an error."

"Because—because he was seen again! He killed Alice!"

"*Nom d'un nom!* Do you say so?" His comment was a suppressed shout. "Tell me, tell me, Madame, how came this vileness about? This is of the great importance; this explains much which was inexplicable. Say on, *chère Madame*, I implore you!"

"Alice was prostrated at the tragedy of Ralph's murder—somehow, she seemed to think she was responsible for it—but in a few days she recovered enough to make preparations to return home with his body.

"There was no railway nearer than fifteen miles, and she wanted to catch an early train, so she set out by motor the night before her train was due. As she drove through a length of lonely, unlighted road between two stretches of undrained swampland someone emerged from the tall reeds—we have the chauffeur's statement for this—and leaped upon the running-board. He struck the driver senseless with a single blow, but not before he had been recognized. It was Joachim Palenzeke. The car ran into the swamp when the driver lost consciousness, but fortunately for him the mud was deep enough to stall the machine, though not deep enough to engulf it. He recovered in a short time and raised the alarm.

"A sheriff's posse found them both next morning. Palenzeke had apparently slipped in the bog while trying to escape and been drowned. Alice was dead—from shock, the doctors said. Her lips were terribly bruised, and there was a wound on her throat, though not serious enough to have caused death; and she had been—"

"Enough! No more, Madame, I entreat you! *Sang de Saint Denis*, is Jules de Grandin a monster that he should roll a stone upon a mother's breaking heart? *Dieu de Dieu, non!* But tell me, if you can, and then I shall ask you no more—what became of this ten-thousand-times-damned—your pardon, Madame!—this so execrable *cochon* of a Palenzeke?"

"They brought him home for burial," Mrs. Heatherton replied softly. "His family is very wealthy. Some of them were bootleggers during prohibition, some are real estate speculators, some are politicians. He had the most elaborate funeral ever seen in the local Greek Orthodox Church—they say the flowers alone cost more than five thousand dollars—but Father Apostolakos refused to say Mass over him, merely recited a short prayer, and denied him burial in the consecrated part of the church cemetery."

"Ah!" de Grandin looked meaningfully at me, as if to say, "I told you as much!"

"This may interest you, too, though I don't know," Mrs. Heatherton added: "A friend of mine who knows a reporter on the *Journal*—newspapermen know everything," she added with simple naïveté, "told me that the coward really must have tried suicide and failed, for there was a bullet-mark on his temple, though of course it couldn't have been fatal, since they found him drowned in the swamp. Do you suppose he could have wounded himself purposely where those Negro swamp-dwellers could see, so that the story of his suicide would get about and the officers stop looking for him?"

"Quite possibly," de Grandin agreed as he rose. "Madame, we are your debtors more than you suspect, and though you cannot know it, we have saved you at least one pang this night. *Adieu, chère Madame*, and may the good God watch over you—and yours." He laid his lips to her fingers and bowed himself from the room.

As we passed through the outer door we caught the echo of a sob and Mrs. Heatherton's despairing cry: "Me and mine—there are no 'mine.' All, all are gone!"

"*La Pauvre!*" de Grandin murmured as he closed the door softly. "All the more reason for *le bon Dieu's* watchfulness, though she knows it not!"

"Now what?" I demanded, dabbing furtively at my eyes with my handkerchief.

The Frenchman made no effort to conceal his tears. They trickled down his face as if he had been a half-grown schoolboy. "Go home, my friend," he ordered. "Me, I shall consult the priest of that Greek Church. From what I hear of him he must be a capital fellow. I think he will give credence to my story. If not, *parbleu*, we must take matters into our own hands. Meantime, crave humble pardon from the excellent Nora for having neglected her dinner and ask that she prepare some slight refreshment, then be ready to accompany me again when we shall have regaled ourselves. *Nom d'un canard vert*, we have a busy night before us, my old and rare!"

IT WAS NEARLY MIDNIGHT when he returned, but from the sparkle in his eyes I knew he had successfully attended to some of his "offices."

"*Barbe d'une chèvre*," he exclaimed as he disposed of his sixth cold lamb sandwich and emptied his eighth glass of Ponte Canet, "that Father Apostolakos is no man's fool, my friend. He is no empty-headed modern who knows so much that he knows nothing; a man versed in the occult may talk freely with him and be understood. Yes. He will help us."

"U'm?" I commented noncommittally, my mouth half-filled with lamb sandwich.

"Precisely," he agreed, refilling his glass and lifting another sandwich from the tray. "Exactly, my friend. The good *papa* is supreme in matters ecclesiastical, and tomorrow he will give the necessary orders without so much as 'by your leave' from the estimable ex-bootleggers, real estate dealers and politicians who compose the illustrious Palenzeke clan. The sandwiches are all gone, and the bottle empty? Good, then let us be upon our way."

"Where?" I demanded.

"To the young Monsieur Rochester's. Me, I would have further talk with that one."

As we left the house I saw him transfer a small oblong packet from his jacket to his overcoat. "What's that?" I asked.

"A thing the good father lent me. I hope we shall have no occasion to use it, but it will prove convenient if we do."

A LIGHT MIST, DAPPLED HERE and there with chilling rain, was settling in the streets as we set off for Rochester's. Half an hour's cautious driving brought us to the place, and as we drew up at the curb the Frenchman pointed to a lighted window on the seventh floor. "That burns in his suite," he informed me. "Can it be he entertains at this hour?"

The night elevator operator snored in a chair in the lobby, and, guided by de Grandin's cautious gesture, I followed his lead up the stairs. "We need not announce our coming," he whispered as we rounded the landing of the sixth floor. "It is better that we come as a surprise, I think."

Another flight we climbed silently, and paused before the door of Rochester's apartment. De Grandin rapped once softly, repeated the summons more authoritatively, and was about to try the knob when we heard footsteps beyond the panels.

Young Rochester wore a silk robe over his pyjamas, his hair was somewhat disarranged, but he looked neither sleepy nor particularly pleased to see us.

"We are unexpected, it seems," de Grandin announced, "but we are here, nevertheless, Be kind enough to stand aside and let us enter, if you please."

"Not now," the young man refused. "I can't see you now. If you'll come back tomorrow morning—"

"This is tomorrow morning, *mon vieux*," the little Frenchman interrupted. "Midnight struck an hour ago." He brushed past our reluctant host and hurried down the long hall to the living room.

The room was tastefully furnished in typically masculine style, heavy chairs of hickory and maple, Turkish carpets, a table with a shaded lamp, a long couch piled with pillows before the fireplace in which a bed of cannel coal glowed in a brass grate. An after-tang of cigarette smoke hung in the air, but mingled with it was the faint, provocative scent of heliotrope.

De Grandin paused upon the threshold, threw his head back and sniffed like a hound at fault. Directly opposite the entrance was a wide arch closed by two Paisley shawls hung lambrequinwise from a brass rod, and toward this he marched, his right hand in his topcoat pocket, the ebony cane which I knew concealed a sword blade held lightly in his left.

"De Grandin!" I cried in shocked protest, aghast at his air of proprietorship.

"Don't!" Rochester called warningly. "You mustn't—"

The hangings at the archway parted and a girl stepped from between them. The long, close-clinging gown of purple tissue she wore was almost as diaphanous as smoke, and through it we could see the white outlines of her body. Her copper-colored hair flowed in a cloven tide about her face and over smooth bare shoulders. Halted in the act of stepping, one small bare foot showed its blue-veined whiteness in sharp silhouette against the rust-red of the Borkhara rug.

As her eyes met de Grandin she paused with a sibilant intake of breath, and her eyes widened with a look of fright. It was no shamefaced glance she gave him; no expression of confusion at detected guilt or brazen attempt at facing out a hopelessly embarrassing situation. Rather, it was the look of one in dire peril, such a look as she might have given a rattlesnake writhing toward her.

"So!" she breathed, and I could see the thin stuff of her gown grow tight across her breasts. "So you know! I was afraid you would, but—" She broke off as he took another step toward her and swerved until his right-hand coat pocket was within arm's length of her.

"*Mais oui, mais oui, Mademoiselle la Morte*," he returned, bowing ceremoniously, but not removing his hand from his pocket. "I know, as you say. The question now arises, 'What shall we do about it?'"

"See here," Rochester flung himself between them, "what's the meaning of this unpardonable intrusion—"

The little Frenchman turned to him, a look of mild inquiry on his face. "*You* demand an explanation? If explanations are in order—"

"See here, damn you, I'm my own man, and not accountable to anyone. Alice and I love each other. She came to me tonight of her own free will—"

"*En vérité?*" the Frenchman interrupted. "How did she come, Monsieur?"

The young man seemed to catch his breath like a runner struggling to regain his wind at the end of a hard course. "I—I went out for a little while," he faltered, "and when I came back—"

"My poor one!" de Grandin broke in sympathetically. "You do lie like a gentleman, but also you lie very poorly. You are in need of practice. Attend me, I will tell you how she came: This night, I do not know exactly when, but well after sundown, you heard a knock-rap at your window or door, and when you looked out, voilà, there was the so lovely *demoiselle*. You thought you dreamed, but once again the pretty fingers tap-tapped at the windowpane, and the soft, lovely eyes looked love at you, and you opened your door or window and bade her enter, content to entertain the dream of her, since there was no chance of her coming in the flesh. Tell me, young Monsieur, and you, too, lovely Mademoiselle, do I not recite the facts?"

Rochester and the girl stared at him in amazement. Only the quivering of the young man's eyelids and the trembling of the girl's sensitive lips gave testimony he had spoken accurately.

For a moment there was a tense, vibrant silence; then with a little gasping cry the girl lurched forward on soft, soundless feet and dropped to her knees before de Grandin. "Have pity—be merciful!" she begged. "Be merciful to me as you may one day hope for mercy. It's such a little thing I ask. You know what I am; do you also know who I am, and why I am now—now the accursed thing you see?" She buried her face in her hands. "Oh, it's cruel—too cruel!" she sobbed. "I was so young; my whole life lay before me. I'd never known real love until it was too late. You can't be so unkind as to drive me back now; you *can't!*"

"*Ma pauvre!*" de Grandin laid his hand upon the girl's bowed, shining head. "My innocent, poor lamb who met the butcher ere you had the lambkin's right to play! I know all there is to know of you. Your sainted mother told me far more than she dreamed this evening. I am not cruel, my little lovely one; I am all sympathy and sorrow, but life is cruel and death is even crueller. Also, you know what the inevitable end must be if I forebear to do my duty. If I could work a miracle I would roll back the gates of dead, and bid you live and love until your natural time had come to die, but—"

"I don't care what the end must be!" the girl blazed, sinking back until she sat upon the upturned soles of her bare feet. "I only know that I've been cheated out of every woman's birthright. I've found love now, and I want it; I want it! He's mine, I tell you, mine—" She cowered, groveling before him—"Think what a little thing I'm asking!" Inching forward on her knees she took his hand in both of hers and fondled it against her cheek. "I'm asking just a little drop of blood now and then; just a little, tiny drop to keep my body whole and beautiful. If I were like other women and Donald were my lover he'd be glad to give me a transfusion—to give me a whole pint or quart of his blood any time I needed it. Is it so much, then, when I ask only an occasional drop? Just a drop now and then, and once in a while a draft of living breath from his lungs to—"

"To slay his poor sick body, then destroy his young, clean soul!" the Frenchman interrupted softly. "It is not of the living that I think so much, but of the dead. Would you deny him quiet rest in his grave when he shall have lost his life because of you? Would you refuse him peaceful sleep until the dawn of God's Great Tomorrow?"

"O-o-oh!" the cry wrung from her writhing lips was like the wail of a lost spirit. "You're right—it is his soul we must protect. I'd kill that, too, as mine was killed that night in the swamps. Oh, pity, pity me, dear Lord! Thou who didst heal the lepers and despised not the Magdalen, have pity on me, the soiled, the unclean!"

Scalding tears of agony fell between the fingers of her long, almost transparent hands as she held them before her eyes. Then: "I am ready," she announced, seeming to find courage for complete renunciation. "Do what you must to me. If it must be the knife and stake, strike quickly. I shall not scream or cry, if I can help it."

For a long moment he looked in her face as he might have looked in the casket of a dear friend. "*Ma pauvre,*" he murmured compassionately. "My poor, brave, lovely one!"

Abruptly he turned to Rochester. "Monsieur," he announced sharply, "I would examine you. I would determine the state of your health."

We stared at him astounded as he proceeded to strip back the—young man's pyjamas jacket and listen carefully at his chest, testing by percussion, counting the pulse action, then feeling slowly up and down the arm. "U'm" he remarked judicially at the end of the examination, "you are in bad condition, my friend. With medicines, careful nursing, and more luck than the physician generally has, we might keep you alive another month. Again, you might drop over any moment. But in all my life I have never given a patient his death warrant with more happiness."

Two of us looked at him in mute wonder; it was the girl who understood. "You mean," she trilled, laughter and a light the like of which there never was on land or sea breaking in her eyes, "you mean that I can have him till—"

He grinned at her delightedly. There was a positively gleeful chuckle in his voice as he replied: "Precisely, exactly, quite so, Mademoiselle." Turning from her he addressed Rochester.

"You and Mademoiselle Alice are to love each other as much as you please while life holds out. And afterwards"—he stretched his hand out to grasp the girl's fingers—"afterwards I shall do the needful for you both. Ha, *Monsieur Diable,* I have tricked you nicely; Jules de Grandin had made one great fool of hell!" He threw his head back and assumed an attitude of defiance, eyes flashing, lips twitching with excitement and elation.

The girl bent forward, took his hand and covered it with kisses. "Oh, you're kind—kind!" she sobbed brokenly. "No other man in all the world, knowing what you know, would have done what you have done!"

"*Mais non, mais certainement non, Mademoiselle,*" he agreed imperturbably. "You do forget that I am Jules de Grandin.

"Come, Trowbridge, my friend," he admonished, "we obtrude here most unwarrantably. What have we, who drained the purple wine of youth long years ago, to do with those who laugh and love the night away? Let us go."

Hand in hand, the lovers followed us to the hall, but as we paused upon the threshold—

Rat-tat-tat! something struck the fog-glazed window, and as I wheeled in my tracks I felt the breath go hot in my throat. Beyond the window, seemingly adrift in the fog, there was a human form. A second glance told me it was the brutal-faced man we had seen at the café the previous night. But now his ugly, evil face was like the devil's, not merely a wicked man's.

"*Eh bien*, Monsieur, is it you, indeed?" de Grandin asked nonchalantly. "I thought you might appear, so I am ready for you.

"Do not invite him in," he called the sharp command to Rochester. "He cannot come in unbidden. Hold your beloved, place your hand or lips against her mouth, lest she who is his thing and chattel, however unwillingly, give him permission to enter. Remember, he cannot cross the sill without the invitation of someone in this room!"

Flinging up the sash he regarded the apparition sardonically. "What have you to say, *Monsieur le Vampire*, before I send you hence?" he asked.

The thing outside mouthed at us, very fury robbing it of words. At last: "She's mine!" it shrieked. "I made her what she is, and she belongs to me. I'll have her, and that dough-faced, dying thing she holds in her arms, too. All, all of you are mine! I shall be king, I shall be emperor of the dead! Not you nor any mortal can stop me. I am all-powerful, supreme, I am—"

"You are the greatest liar outside burning hell," de Grandin cut in icily. "As for your power and your claims, Monsieur Monkey-Face, tomorrow you shall have nothing, not even so much as a little plot of earth to call a grave. Meanwhile, behold this, devil's spawn; behold and be afraid!"

Whipping his hand from his topcoat pocket he produced a small flat case like the leather containers sometimes used for holding photographs, pressed a concealed spring and snapped back its top. For a moment the thing in the night gazed at the object with stupefied, unbelieving horror; then with a wild cry fell backward, its uncouth motion somehow reminding me of a hooked bass.

"You do not like it, I see," the Frenchman mocked. "*Parbleu*, you stinking truant from the charnel-house, let us see what nearer contact will effect!" He stretched his hand out till the leather-cased object almost touched the phantom face outside the window.

A wild, inhuman screech echoed, and as the demon face retreated we saw a weal of red across its forehead, as if the Frenchman had scored it with a hot iron.

"Close the windows, *mes amis*," he ordered casually as though nothing hideous hovered outside. "Shut them tight and hold each other close until the morning comes and shadows flee away. *Bonne nuit!*"

"For heaven's sake," I besought as we began our homeward drive, "what's it all mean? You and Rochester called that girl Alice, and she's the speaking image of the girl we saw in the café last night. But Alice Heatherton is dead. Her mother told us how she died this evening; we saw her tomb this morning. Are there two Alice Heathertons, or is this girl her double—"

"In a way," he answered. "It was Alice Heatherton we saw back there, my friend, yet not the Alice Heatherton of whom her mother spoke this evening, nor yet the one whose tomb we saw this morning—"

"For God's sake," I burst out, "stop this damned double-talk! Was or was it not Alice Heatherton—"

"Be patient, my old one," he counseled. "At present I can not tell you, but later I will have a complete explanation—I hope."

DAYLIGHT WAS JUST BREAKING when his pounding on my bedroom door roused me from coma-like sleep. "Up, Friend Trowbridge!" he shouted, punctuating his summons with another knock. "Up and dress as quickly as may be. We must be off at once. Tragedy has overtaken them!"

Scarcely knowing what I did I stumbled from the bed, felt my way into my clothes and, sleep still filming my eyes, descended to the lower hall where he waited in a perfect frenzy of excitement.

"What's happened?" I asked as we started for Rochester's.

"The worst," he answered. "Ten minutes ago I was awakened by the telephone. 'It is for Friend Trowbridge,' I told me. 'Some patient with the *mal de l'estamac* desires a little paregoric and much sympathy. I shall not waken him, for he is all tired with the night's exertions.' But still the bell kept ringing, and so I answered it. My friend, it was Alice. *Hélas*, as strong as her love was, her bondage was still stronger. But when the harm was done she had the courage to call us. Remember that when you come to judge her."

I would have paused for explanation, but he waved me on impatiently. "Make haste; oh, hurry, hurry!" he urged. "We must go to him at once. Perhaps it is even now too late."

There was no traffic in the streets, and we made the run to Rochester's apartment in record time. Almost before we realized it we were at his door once more, and this time de Grandin stood upon no ceremony. Flinging the door open he raced down the hall and into the living room, pausing at the threshold with a sharp indrawn breath. "So!" he breathed. "He was most thorough, that one."

The place was a shambles. Chairs were overturned, pictures hung awry, bits of broken bric-à-brac were strewn about, the long throw-cover of the center table had been jerked off, overturning the lamp and scattering ashtrays and cigarette boxes indiscriminately.

Donald Rochester lay on the rug before the dead fire, one leg bent queerly under him, his right arm stretched out flaccidly along the floor and bent at a sharp right angle at the wrist.

The Frenchman crossed the room at a run, unclasping the lock of his kit as he leaped. Dropping to his knees he listened intently at the young man's chest a moment, then stripped back his sleeve, swabbed his arm with alcohol and thrust the needle of his hypodermic through a fold of skin. "It is a desperate chance I take," he muttered as he drove the plunger home, "but the case is urgent; *le bon Dieu* knows how urgent."

Rochester's eyelids fluttered as the powerful stimulant took effect. He moaned and turned his head with great effort, but made no move to rise. As I knelt beside de Grandin and helped him raise the injured man I understood the cause of his lethargy. His spine had been fractured at the fourth dorsal veterbra, paralysis resulting.

"Monsieur," the little Frenchman whispered softly, "you are going fast. Your minutes are now more than numbered on the circle of the watch-face. Tell us, tell us quickly, what occurred." Once more he injected stimulant into Rochester's arm.

The young man wet his blued lips with the tip of his tongue, attempted a deep breath, but found the effort too great. "It was he—the fellow you scared off last night," he whispered hoarsely.

"After you'd gone Alice and I lay on the hearth rug, counting our minutes together as a miser counts his gold. I heaped coals on the fire, for she was chilled, but it didn't seem to do any good. Finally she began to pant and choke, and I let her draw breath from me. That revived her a little, and when she'd sucked some blood from my throat she seemed almost herself again, though I could feel no movement of her heart as she lay against me.

"It must have been just before daybreak—I don't know just when, for I'd fallen asleep in her arms—when I heard a clattering at the window, and someone calling to be let in. I remembered your warning, and tried to hold Alice, but she fought me off. She ran to the window and flung it up as she called, 'Enter, master; there is none to stop you now.'

"He made straight for me, and when she realized what he was about she tried to stop him, but he flung her aside as if she were a rag doll—took her by the hair and dashed her against the wall. I heard her bones crack as she struck it.

"I grappled with him, but I was no more his match than a three-year-old child was mine. He threw me down and broke my arms and legs with his feet. The pain was terrible. Then he grabbed me up and hurled me to the floor again, and after that I felt no pain, except this dreadful headache. I couldn't move, but I was conscious, and the last thing I remember was seeing Alice stepping out the window with him, hand in hand. She didn't even look back."

He paused a moment, fighting desperately for breath, then, still lower, "Oh, Alice—how could you? And I loved you so!"

"Peace, my poor one," bade de Grandin. "She did not do it of her own accord. That fiend holds her in bondage she cannot resist. She is his thing and chattel more completely than ever black slave belonged to his master. Hear me; go with this thought uppermost in your mind: She loved you, she loves you. It is because she called us we are here now, and her last word was one of love for you. Do you hear me? Do you understand? 'Tis sad to die, *mon pauvre*, but surely it is something to die loving and beloved. Many a man lives out his whole life without as much, and many there are who would trade a whole span of four score gladly for five little minutes of the ecstasy that was yours last night.

"Monsieur Rochester—do you hear me?" he spoke sharply, for the young man's face was taking on the greyness of impending death.

"Ye-es. She loves me—she loves me. Alice!" With the name sighing on his lips his facial muscles loosened and his eyes took on the glazed, unwinking stare of eyes that see no more.

De Grandin gently drew the lids across the sightless eyes and raised the fallen jaw, then set about straightening the room with methodical haste. "As a licensed practitioner you will sign the death certificate," he announced matter-of-factly. "Our young friend suffered from angina pectoris. This morning he had an attack, and after calling us fell from the chair on which he stood to reach his medicine, thereby fracturing several bones. He told us this when we arrived to find him dying. You understand?"

"I'm hanged if I do," I denied. "You know as well as I—"

"That the police would have awkward questions to address to us," he reminded me. "We were the last ones to see him alive. Do you conceive that they would credit what we said if we told them the truth?"

Much as I disliked it, I followed his orders to the letter and the poor boy's body was turned over to the ministrations of Mortician Martin within an hour.

As Rochester had been an orphan without known family de Grandin assumed the role of next friend, made all arrangements for the funeral, and gave orders that the remains be cremated without delay, the ashes to be turned over to him for final disposition.

Most of the day was taken up in making these arrangements and in my round of professional calls. I was thoroughly exhausted by four o'clock in the afternoon, but de Grandin, hustling, indefatigable, seemed fresh as he had been at daybreak.

"Not yet, my friend," he denied as I would have sunk into the embrace of an easy chair, "there is yet something to be done. Did not you hear my promise to the never-quite-to-be-sufficiently-anathematized Palenzeke last night?"

"Eh, your promise?"

"*Précisément.* We have one great surprise in store for that one."

Grumbling, but with curiosity that overrode my fatigue, I drove him to the little Greek Orthodox parsonage. Parked at the door was the severely plain black service wagon of a funeral director, its chauffeur yawning audibly at the delay in getting through his errand.

De Grandin ran lightly up the steps, gained admission and returned in a few minutes with the venerable priest arrayed in full canonicals. "*Allons mon enfant*," he told the chauffeur, "be on your way; we follow."

Even when the imposing granite walls of the North Hudson Crematory loomed before us I failed to understand his hardly suppressed glee.

All arrangements had apparently been made. In the little chapel over the retort Father Apostolakos recited the orthodox burial office, and the casket sank slowly from view on the concealed elevator provided for conveying it to the incineration chamber below.

The aged priest bowed courteously to us and left the building, seating himself in my car, and I was about to follow when de Grandin motioned to me imperatively. "Not yet, Friend Trowbridge," he told me. "Come below and I will show you something."

We made our way to the subterranean chamber where incineration took place. The casket rested on a low wheeled track before the yawning cavern of the retort, but de Grandin stopped the attendants as they were about to roll it into place. Tiptoeing across the tiled floor he bent above the casket, motioning me to join him.

As I paused beside him I recognized the heavy, evil features of the man we had first seen with Alice, the same bestial, furious face which had mouthed curses at us from outside Rochester's window the night before. I would have drawn back, but the Frenchman clutched me firmly by the elbow, drawing me still nearer the body.

"*Tiens, Monsieur le Cadavre*," he whispered as he bent above the dead thing, "what think you of this, *hein?* You who would be king and emperor of the dead, you who boasted that no power on earth could balk you—did not Jules de Grandin promise you that you should have nothing, not even one poor plot of earth to call a grave? Pah, murderer and ravisher of women, man-killer, where is now your power? Go—go through the furnace fire to hell-fire, and take this with you!" He pursed his lips and spat full in the cold upturned visage of the corpse.

It might have been a trick of overwrought nerves or an optical illusion produced by the electric lights, but I still believe I saw the dead, long-buried body writhe in its casket and a look of terrible, unutterable hate disfigure the waxen features.

He stepped back, nodding to the attendants, and the casket slid noiselessly into the retort. A whirring sounded as the pressure pump was started, and in a moment came the subdued roar of oil-flames shooting from the burners.

He raised his narrow shoulders in a shrug. "*C'est une affaire finie.*"

IT WAS SOMEWHAT AFTER midnight when we made our way once more to Shadow Lawn Cemetery. Unerringly as though going to an appointment, de Grandin led the way to the Heatherton family mausoleum, let himself through the massive bronze gates with a key he had procured somewhere, and ordered me to stand guard outside.

Lighted by the flash of his electric torch he entered the tomb, a long cloth-covered parcel clasped under his arm. A moment later I heard the clink of metal on metal the sound of some heavy object being drawn across the floor; then, as I grew half hysterical at the long continued silence, there came the short, half-stifled sound of a gasping cry, the sort of cry a patient in the dental chair gives when a tooth is extracted without anaesthetic.

Another period of silence, broken by the rasp of heavy objects being moved, and the Frenchman emerged from the tomb, tears streaming down his face. "Peace," he announced chokingly. "I brought her peace, Friend Trowbridge, but oh! how pitiful it was to hear her moan, and still more pitiful to see the lovely, live-seeming body shudder in the embrace of relentless death. It is not hard to see the living die, my old one, but the dead! *Mordieu*, my soul will be in torment every time I think of what I had to do tonight for mercy's sake!"

JULES DE GRANDIN CHOSE a cigar from the humidor and set it glowing with the precision that distinguished his every movement. "I grant you the events of the last three days have been decidedly queer," he agreed as he sent a cloud of fragrant smoke ceilingward. "But what would you? All that lies outside our everyday experience is queer. To one who has not studied biology the sight of an amoeba beneath the microscope is queer; the Eskimos undoubtlessly thought Monsieur Byrd's airplane queer; we think the sights which we have seen these nights queer. It is our luck—and all mankind's—that they are.

"To begin: Just as there exist today certain protozoa which are probably identical with the earliest forms of life on earth, so there are still, though constantly diminishing in numbers, certain holdovers of ancient evil. Time was when earth swarmed with them—devils and devilkins, imps, satyrs and demons, elementals, werewolves and vampires. All once were numerous; all, perhaps, exist in considerable numbers to this day, though we know them not, and most of us never so much as hear of them. It is with the vampire that we had to deal this time. You know him, no?

"Strictly, he is an earthbound soul, a spirit which because of manifold sins and wickedness is bound to the world wherein it once worked evil and cannot take itself to its proper place. He is in India in considerable numbers, also in Russia, Hungary, Romania and throughout the Balkans—wherever civilization is very old and decadent, there he seems to find a favorable soil. Sometimes he steals the body of one already dead; sometimes he remains in the body which he had in life, and then he is most terrible of all, for he needs nourishment for that body, but not such nourishment as you or I take. No, he subsists on the life force of the living, imbibed through their blood, for the blood is the life. He must suck the breath from those who live, or he cannot breathe; he must drink their blood, or he dies of starvation. And here is where the danger rises: a suicide, one who dies under a curse, *or one who has been inoculated with the vampire virus* by having his blood sucked by a vampire, becomes a vampire after death. Innocent of all wrong he may be, often is, yet he is doomed to tread the earth by night, preying ceaselessly upon the living, ever recruiting the grisly ranks of his tribe. You apprehend?

"Consider this case: This *sacré* Palenzeke, because of his murder and suicide, perhaps partly because of his Slavic ancestry, maybe also because of his many other sins, became a vampire when he killed himself to death. Madame Heatherton's informant was correct, he had destroyed himself; but his evil body and more evil soul remained in partnership, ten thousand times a greater menace to mankind than when they had been partners in their natural life.

"Enjoying the supernatural power of his life-in-death, he rose from the swamplands, waylaid Mademoiselle Alice, assaulted her chauffeur, then dragged her off into the bog to work his evil will on her, gratifying at once his bestial lust, his vampire's thirst for blood and his revenge for her rejection of his wooing. When he had killed her, he had made her such a thing as he was. More, he had gained dominion over her. She was his toy, his plaything, his automaton, without will or volition of her own. What he commanded she must do, however much she hated doing it. You will recall, perhaps, how she told the young Rochester that she must go out with the villain, although she hated him? Also, how she bade him enter the apartment where she and her beloved lay in love's embrace, although his entrance meant her lover's undoing?

"Now, if the vampire added all the powers of living men to his dead powers we should have no defense, but fortunately he is subject to unbreakable laws. He can not independently cross the thread of a running stream, he must be carried; he can not enter any house or dwelling until invited by someone therein; he can fly through the air, enter at keyholes and window-chinks, or through the crack of the door, but he can move about only at night—between sunset and cock-crow. From sunrise to dark he is only a corpse, helpless as any other, and must lie corpse-dead in his tomb. At such times he can easily be slain, but only in certain ways. First, if his heart be pierced by a stake of ash and—his head severed from his body, he is dead in good earnest, and can no more rise to plague us. Second, if he can be completely burned to ashes he is no more, for fire cleanses all things.

"Now, with this information, fit together the puzzle that so mystifies you: the other night at the Café Bacchanale I liked the looks of that one not at all.

He had the face of a dead man and the look of a born villain, as well as the eye of a fish. Of his companion I thoroughly approved, though she, too, had an other-worldly look. Wondering about them, I watched them from my eye's tail, and when I observed that they ate nothing I thought it not only strange, but menacing. Normal people do not do such things; abnormal people usually are dangerous.

"When Palenzeke left the young woman, after indicating she might flirt with the young Rochester, I liked the look of things a little less. My first thought was that it might be a game of decoy and robbery—how do you call him?—the game of the badger? Accordingly, I thought it best to follow them to see what we should see. *Eh bien*, my friend, we saw a plenty, *n'est-ce-pas?*

"You will recall young Rochester's experience in the cemetery. As he related it to us I saw at once what manner of foeman we must grapple with, though at that time I did not know how innocent Mademoiselle Alice was. Our information from Madame Heatherton confirmed my worst fears. What we beheld at Rochester's apartment that night proved all I had imagined, and more.

"But me, I had not been idle meantime. Oh, no. I had seen the good Father Apostolakos and told him what I had learned. He understood at once, and made immediate arrangements to have Palenzeke's foul body exhumed and taken to the crematory for incineration. He also lent me a sacred *ikon*, the blessèd image of a saint whose potency to repel demons had more than once been proved. Perhaps you noticed how Mademoiselle Alice shrank from me when I approached her with the relic in my pocket? And how the restless soul of Palenzeke flinched from it as flesh recoils from white-hot iron?

"Very well. Rochester loved this woman already dead. He himself was moribund. Why not let him taste of love with the shade of the woman who returned his passion for the few days he had yet to live? When he died, as die he must, I was prepared to treat his poor clay so that, though he were already half a vampire from the vampire's kisses on his throat, he could yet do no harm. You know I have done so. The cleansing fire has rendered Palenzeke impotent. Also, I had pledged myself to do as much for the poor, lovely, sinned-against Alice when her brief aftermath of earthly happiness should have expired. You heard me promise her, and I have kept my word.

"I could not bear to hurt her needlessly, so when I went to her with stake and knife tonight I took also a syringe loaded with five grains of morphine and gave her an injection before I began my work. I do not think she suffered greatly. Her moan of dissolution and the portion of her poor body as the stake pierced through her heart, they were but reflex acts, not signs of conscious misery."

"But look here," I objected, "if Alice were a vampire, as you say, and able to float about after dark, how comes it that she lay in her casket when you went there tonight?"

"Oh, my friend," tears welled up in his eyes, "she waited for me.

"We had a definite engagement; the poor one lay in her casket, awaiting the knife and stake which should set her free from bondage. She—she smiled at me and pressed my hand when I had dragged her from the tomb!"

He wiped his eyes and poured an ounce or so of cognac into a bud-shaped inhaler. "To you, young Rochester, and to your lovely lady," he said as he raised the glass in salute. "Though there be neither marrying nor giving in marriage where you are, may your restless souls find peace and rest eternally—together."

The fragile goblet shattered as he tossed it, emptied, into the fireplace.

The Chapel of Mystic Horror

I

T HE WIND WAS BLOWING half a gale and little spits of sudden snow were whirling through the gray November twilight as we alighted from the accommodation train and looked expectantly up and down the uncovered way-station platform. "Seasonable weather for Thanksgiving," I murmured, setting my face against the howling blast and making for the glowing disk of the station-master's light.

"*Barbe d'un pelican*, yes!" assented Jules de Grandin, sinking his chin an inch or so lower in the fur collar of his overcoat. "A polar bear might give thanks for a warm fireside on such a night!"

"Trowbridge—I say there—Trowbridge!" a voice hailed from the lee side of the little red-brick depot as my friend Tandy Van Riper stepped forward, waving a welcoming hand. "This way, old-timer; the car's waiting—so's dinner.

"Glad to meet you, Dr. de Grandin," he acknowledged as I presented the little Frenchman; "it was mighty good of you to come out with Trowbridge and help us light the hearth fires at the Cloisters."

"Ah, then it is a new house that you have, *Monsieur?*" de Grandin asked as he dropped into a seat in Van Riper's luxurious roadster and tucked the bearskin rug snugly about his knees.

"Well, yes and no," our host replied. "The house has been up—in America—for something like eight years, I believe, but it's new to us. We've been in residence just a little over a month, and we're giving a regular old-fashioned Thanksgiving party by way of housewarming."

"U'm," the Frenchman nodded thoughtfully. "Your pardon, *Monsieur*, it is perhaps that I do not speak the American well, but did you not say the new house had been up in this country for only eight years? I fear I do not apprehend. Is it that the house stood elsewhere before being erected here?"

"Precisely," Van Riper agreed with a laugh. "The Cloisters were built or rebuilt, I suppose you'd say—by Miles Batterman shortly after the close of the World War. Batterman made a potful of money during the war, and a lot more in lucky speculations between the Armistice and the Treaty of Versailles. I reckon he didn't know just what to do with it all, so he blew in a couple of hundred thousand on an old Cyprian villa, had it taken down stone by stone, shipped over here, and re-erected. The building was a sort of remodeled monastery, I believe, and took Batterman's eye while he was cruising about the Mediterranean in '20. He went to a lot of trouble having it moved here and put up, and everything about the place is exactly as it was in Cyprus, except the heating and plumbing, which he added as a sort of afterthought. Quaint idea, wasn't it?"

"Decidedly," the Frenchman agreed. "And this Monsieur Batterman, did he so soon tire of his expensive toy?"

"Humph, not exactly. I got it from the administrators. I couldn't have afforded to pay a quarter the price Batterman spent on the place, let alone give him a profit on the transaction, but the fact is the old boy dropped off suddenly a year or so ago—so did his wife and daughter. The doctors said they died from eating toadstools by mistake for mushrooms. Whatever the cause was, the whole family died in a single night and the property would have gone to the State by escheat if the lawyers hadn't dug up some ninety-second cousins in Omaha. We bought the house at public auction for about a tenth its value, and I'm figuring on holding it for a while. It'll be novel, living in a place the Knights Templar once occupied, eh?"

"Very novel—very novel, indeed, Monsieur," de Grandin replied in a queer, flat voice. "You say the Knights of the Temple once occupied this house?"

"So they tell me—some of their old furniture's still in it."

De Grandin made an odd sound in his throat, and I turned quickly to look at him, but his face was as set and expressionless as the features of a Japanese Buddha, and if the half-smothered exclamation had been meant for conversation, he had evidently thought better of it, for he sat in stony silence during the rest of the drive.

The snow squalls had stopped by the time we drew up at the house, but the wind had increased in velocity, and in the zenith we could see the gibbous moon buffeted about in a surf of windblown clouds. Against the background of the winter sky the irregular outline of the Cloisters loomed in a forbidding silhouette. It was a high, rambling pile of gray masonry in which the characteristics of Romanesque, Gothic and Byzantine architecture were oddly blended. The walls were strengthened by a series of buttresses, crenelated with battlements and punctuated here and there with small, cylindrical watch-towers; the windows were mere slits between the great stones, and the massive entrance-way seemed fitted for a portcullis, yet a great, hemispherical dome rose from the center of the building, and a wide, shallow portico with graceful, fluted columns topped by Doric capitals stood before the gateway.

Cocktail hour had just struck as we passed through the wide entrance to the main hall, and a party of sleek-haired gentlemen and ladies in fashionably scanty attire were gathered before the cavernous fireplace, chatting and laughing as they imbibed the appetite-whetting amber drinks.

It was an enormous apartment, that hall, clear fifty feet from tiled floor to vaulted ceiling, and the darkness was scarcely more than stained by the flickering glow of blazing logs in the fireplace and the yellow beams of the tall, ecclesiastical candles which stood, singly, in high, wrought-iron standards at intervals along the walls. Draped down the bare stone sides of the hall hung a pair of prodigious tapestries, companion pieces, I thought, depicting particularly gory battle scenes, and I caught a fugitive glimpse of a black-armored knight with a cross-emblazoned surtout hacking the turbaned head from a Saracen, and the tag end of the Latin legend beneath—"*ad Majorem De Gloriam*." Piloted by our host we mounted the wide, balustraded staircase to the second of three balconies which ran round three sides of the long hall, found the big, barnlike room assigned us, changed quickly to dinner clothes, and joined the other guests in time to file through a high archway to the oak-paneled apartment where dinner was served by candle-light on a long refectory table set with the richest silver and most opulent linen I had ever seen.

Greatly to his chagrin de Grandin drew a kittenish, elderly spinster with gleaming and palpably false dentition. I was paired off with a Miss O'Shane, a tall, tawny-haired girl with tapering, statuesque limbs and long, smooth-jointed fingers, milk-white skin of the pure-bred Celt and smoldering, rebellious eyes of indeterminate color.

During the soup and fish courses she was taciturn to the point of churlishness, responding to my attempts at conversation with curt, unisyllabic replies, but as the claret glasses were filled for the roast, she turned her strange, half-resentful gaze directly on me and demanded: "Dr. Trowbridge, what do you think of this house?"

"Why—er," I temporized, scarcely knowing what to reply, "it seems rather gorgeous, but—"

"Yes," she interrupted as I paused at a loss for an exact expression, "but what?"

"Well, rather depressing—too massive and mediaeval for present-day people, if you get what I mean."

"I do," she nodded almost angrily, "I most certainly do. It's beastly. I'm a painter—a painter of sorts," she hurried on as my eyes opened in astonishment at her vehemence—"and I brought along some gear to work with between times during the party. Van told me this is liberty hall, and I could do exactly as I pleased, and gave me a big room on the north side for a workshop. I've a commission I've simply got to finish in two weeks, and I began some preliminary sketches yesterday, but—" She paused taking a sip of burgundy and looking at me from the corners of her long, brooding eyes as though speculating whether or not to take me further into her confidence.

"Yes?" I prompted, assuming an air of interest.

"It's no go. Do you remember the Red King in *Through the Looking Glass?*"

"The Red King?" I echoed. "I'm afraid I don't quite."

"Don't you remember how Alice took the end of his pencil in her hand when he was attempting to enter a note in his diary and made him write, 'The White Knight is sliding down the poker. He balances very badly'?"

I must have looked my bewilderment, for she laughed aloud, a deep, gurgling laugh in keeping with her rich, contralto speaking voice. "Oh, I'm not a psychopathic case—I hope," she assured me, "but I'm certainly in a position to sympathize with the poor king. It's a Christmas card I'm doing—a nice, frosty, sugar-sweet Christmas card—and I'm supposed to have a Noel scene with oxen and asses and sheep standing around the manager of a chubby little naked boy, you know—quite the conventional sort of thing." She paused again and refreshed herself with a sip of wine, and I noticed that her strong, white-fingered hand trembled as she raised the glass to her lips.

My professional interest was roused. The girl was a splendid, vital animal, lean and strong as Artemis, and the pallor of her pale skin was natural, not unhealthy; yet it required no special training to see she labored under an almost crushing burden of suppressed nervousness.

"Won't it work out?" I asked soothingly.

"No!" her reply was almost explosive. "No, it won't! I can block in the interior, all right, though it doesn't look much like a stable; but when it comes to the figures, something outside me—behind me, like Alice behind the Red King, you know, and just as invisible—seems to snatch the end of my charcoal and guide it. I keep drawing—"

Another pause broke her recital.

"Drawing what, if you please, *Mademoiselle?*" De Grandin turned from his partner who was in the midst of recounting a risqué anecdote and leaned forward, his narrow eyebrows elevated in twin arches, his little, round blue eyes fixed and unwinking in a direct, questioning stare.

The girl started at his query. "Oh, all manner of things," she began, then broke off with a sharp, half-hysterical laugh. "Just what the Red King said when his pencil wouldn't work!" she shrilled.

For a moment I thought the little Frenchman would strike her, so fierce was the uncompromising gaze he bent on her; then: "Ah, *bah,* let us not think too much of fairy tales, pleasant or grim, if you please, *Mademoiselle,*" he returned.

"After dinner, if you will be so good, Dr. Trowbridge and I shall do ourselves the honor of inspecting these so mysterious self-dictated drawings of yours. Until then, let us consider this excellent food which the good Monsieur Van Riper has provided for us." Abruptly he turned to his neglected partner. "Yes, *Mademoiselle*," he murmured in his deferential, flattering manner, "and then the bishop said to the rector—?"

II

DINNER COMPLETED, WE TROOPED into the high, balconied hall for coffee, tobacco and liqueurs. A radio, artfully disguised as a mediaeval Flemish console, squawked jazz with a sputtering obligato of static, and some of the guests danced, while the rest gathered at the rim of the pool of firelight and talked in muted voices. Somehow, the great stone house seemed to discourage frivolity by the sheer weight of its antiquity.

"Trowbridge, my friend," de Grandin whispered almost fiercely in my ear as he plucked me by the sleeve, "Mademoiselle O'Shane awaits our pleasure. Come, let us go to her studio at once before old *Mère l'Oie* tells me another of her so detestable stories of unvirtuous clergymen!"

Grinning as I wondered how the little Frenchman's late dinner partner would have enjoyed hearing herself referred to as Mother Goose, I followed him up the first flight of stairs, crossed the lower balcony and ascended a second stairway, narrow and steeper than the first, to the upper gallery where Miss O'Shane waited before the heavily carved door of a great, cavelike room paneled from flagstone floor to beamed ceiling with age-blackened oak wainscot. Candles seemed the only mode of illumination available in the house, and our hostess had lighted half a dozen tapers which stood so that their luminance fell directly on an oblong of eggshell bristol board anchored to her easel by thumbtacks.

"Now, here's what I started to do," she began, indicating the sketch with a long, beautifully manicured forefinger. "This was supposed to be the inside of the stable at Bethlehem, and—oh?" The short, half-choked exclamation, uttered with a puzzled, questioning rising inflection, cut short her sentence, and she stared at her handiwork as though it were something she had never seen before.

Leaning forward, I examined the embryonic picture curiously. As she had said at dinner, the interior, rough and elementary as it was, did not resemble a stable. Crude and rough it undoubtedly was, but with a rudeness unlike that of a barn. Cubic, rough-hewn stones composed the walls, and the vaulting of the concatenated roof was supported by a series of converging arches with piers based on blocks of oddly carved stone representing wide, naked feet, toes forward, standing on the crowns of hideous, gargoylish heads with half-human, half-reptilian faces which leered hellishly in mingled torment and rage beneath the pressure. In the middle foreground was a raised rectangular object which reminded me of a flat-topped sarcophagus, and beside it, slightly to the rear, there loomed the faint, spectral outline of a sinister, cowled figure with menacing, upraised hand, while in the lower foreground crouched, or rather groveled, a second figure, a long, boldly sketched female form with outstretched supplicating hands and face concealed by a cascade of downward sweeping hair. Back of the hooded, monkish form were faint outlines of what had apparently first been meant to represent domestic animals, but I could see where later, heavier pencil strokes had changed them into human shapes resembling the cowled and hooded figure.

I shuddered involuntarily as I turned from the drawing, for not only in half-completed line and suggestive curve, but also in the intangible spirit of the thing was the suggestion of something bestial and unhallowed. Somehow, the thing seemed to suggest something revolting, something pregnant with the disgusting incongruity of a ribald song bawled in church when the *Kyrie* should be sung, or of rose-water sprinkled on putrefying offal.

De Grandin's slender dark brown eyebrows elevated till they almost met the shoreline of his sleekly combed fair hair, and the waxed points of his diminutive blond mustache reared upward like a pair of horns as he pursed his thin lips, but he made no verbal comment.

Not so Miss O'Shane. As though a sudden draft of air had blown through the room, she shivered, and I could see the horror with which she stared wide-eyed, at her own creation. "It wasn't like that!" she exclaimed in a thin, rasping whisper like the ghost of a scream. "I didn't do that!"

"Eh, how do you say, *Mademoiselle?*" de Grandin challenged, regarding her with his unwinking cat-stare. "You would have us to understand that—"

"Yes!" She still spoke in a sort of awed, wondering whisper. "I didn't draw it that way! I blocked in the interior and made it of stone, for I was pretty sure the Holy Land stables were masonry, but I didn't draw those beastly arch-supports! They were just plain blocks of stone when I made them. I did put in the arches—not that I wanted to, but because I felt compelled to do it, but this— this is all different!" Her words trailed off till we could scarcely catch them, not because of lowered tone, but because they came higher, thinner, with each syllable. Stark, unreasoning terror had her by the throat, and it was with the utmost difficulty that she managed to breathe.

"H'm," de Grandin tweaked the pointed ends of his mustache. "Let us recapitulate, if you please, *Mademoiselle*: Yesterday and today you worked on this sketch? Yes? You drew what you conceived to be a Jewish stable in the days of Caesar Augustus—and what else, if you recall?"

"Just the stable and the bare outlines of the manger, then a half-completed figure which was to have been Joseph, and the faintest outlines of the animals and a kneeling figure before the cradle—I hadn't determined whether it would be male or female, or whether it would be full-draped or not, for I wasn't sure whether I'd have the Magi or the shepherds or just some of the village folk adoring the Infant, you see. I gave up working about four this afternoon, because the light was beginning to fail and because—"

"*Eh bien*, because of what, if you please, *Mademoiselle?*" the Frenchman prompted sharply as the girl dropped her recital.

"Because there seemed to be an actual physical opposition to my work—almost as if an invisible hand were gently but insistently forcing my pencil to draw things I hadn't conceived—things I was afraid to draw! Now, do you think I'm crazy?"

She paused again, breathing audibly through slightly parted lips, and I could see the swelling of her throat as she swallowed convulsively once or twice.

Ignoring her question, the little Frenchman regarded her thoughtfully a moment, then examined the drawing once more. "This who was to have been the good Saint Joseph, now," he asked softly, "was he robed after this fashion when you limned him?"

"No, I'd only roughed out the body. He had no face when I quit work."

"U'm, *Mademoiselle*, he is still without a face," de Grandin replied.

"Yes, but there's a place for his face in the opening of his hood, and if you look closely you can almost see his features—his eyes, especially. I can feel them on me, and they're not good. They're bad, wicked, cruel—like a snake's or a devil's. See, he's robed like a monk; I didn't draw him that way!"

De Grandin took up one of the candelabra and held it close to the picture, scanning the obscene thing with an unhurried, critical stare, then turned to us with a half-impatient shrug. "*Tenez*, my friends," he remarked. "I fear we make ourselves most wretchedly unhappy over a matter of small moment. Let us join the others."

III

MIDNIGHT HAD STRUCK AND de Grandin and I had managed to lose something like thirty dollars at the bridge tables before the company broke up for the evening.

"Do you really think that poor O'Shane girl is a little off her rocker?" I asked as we made ready for bed.

"I doubt it," he replied, as he fastened the sash of his pale lavender pajama jacket with a nervous tug; "indeed, I am inclined to believe all that she told us—and something more."

"You think it possible she could have been in a sort of day-dream while she drew those awful things, thinking all the while she was drawing a Christmas card?" I asked incredulously.

"*Ah bah*," he returned, as he kicked off his purple lizardskin slippers and leaped into bed, "what matters it what we think? Unless I am more mistaken than I think, we shall know with certitude before very long." And turning his back upon me, he dropped off to sleep.

I might have slept an hour, perhaps only a few minutes, when the sharp impact of an elbow against my ribs aroused me. "Eh?" I demanded, sitting up in bed and rubbing my eyes sleepily.

"Trowbridge, my friend," de Grandin's sharp whisper came through the darkness, "Listen! Do you hear it?"

"Huh?" I responded, but:

"*Ps-s-st!*" he shut me off with a minatory hiss, and I held my peace, straining my ears through the chill November night.

At first I heard nothing but the skirling of the wind-fiends racing past the turreted walls, and the occasional creak of a rusty hinge as some door or shutter swung loose from its fastenings; then, very faint and faraway seeming, but growing in clarity as my ears became attuned to it, I caught the subdued notes of a piano played very softly.

"Come!" de Grandin breathed, slipping from the bed and donning a mauve-silk gown.

Obeying his summons, I rose and followed him on tiptoe across the balcony and down the stairs. As we descended, the music became clearer, more distinct. Someone was in the music room, touching the keys of the big grand piano with a delicate harpsichord touch. *Liebestraum* the composition was, and the gently struck notes fell, one after another, like drops of limpid water dripping from a moss-covered ledge into a quiet woodland pool.

"Why, it's exquisite," I began, but de Grandin's upraised hand cut short my commendation as he motioned me forward.

Seated before the piano was Dunroe O'Shane, her long, ivory fingers flitting over the ivory keys, her loosened tawny hair flowing over her uncovered white shoulders like molten bronze. From gently swelling breast to curving instep she was draped in a clinging shift of black-silk tissues which revealed the gracious curves of her pale body.

As we paused at the doorway the dulcet German air came to an abrupt ending, the girl's fingers began weaving sinuous patterns over the keys, as though she would conjure up some nether-world spirit from their pallid smoothness, and the room was suddenly filled with a libidinous, macabre theme in B minor, beautiful and seductive, but at the same time revolting. Swaying gently to the rhythm of the frenetic music, she turned her face toward us, and I saw her eyes were closed, long lashes sweeping against white cheeks, pale fine-veined lids calmly lowered.

"Why," I exclaimed softly, "why, de Grandin, she's asleep, she's—"

A quick movement of his hand stayed my words, as he stole softly across the rug-strewn floor, bent forward till his face was but a few inches from hers, and stared intently into veiled eyes. I could see the small blue veins in his temples swell and throb, and muscles of his throat bunch and contract with the physical effort he made to project his will into her consciousness. His thin, firm lips moved, forming soundless words, and one of his small, white hands rose slowly, finger-tips together, as though reeling thread from an invisible skein, paused a moment before her face, then moved slowly back, with a gliding, stroking motion.

Gradually, with a slow diminuendo, the wicked, salacious tune came to a pause, died to a thin, vibrating echo, ceased. Still with lowered lids and gently parted lips, the girl rose from the piano, wavered uncertainly a moment, then walked from the room with a slow, gliding step, her slim, naked feet passing soundlessly as a drift of air, as slowly she mounted the stairs.

Silently, in a sort of breathless wonder, I watched her disappear around the curve of the stone stairway, and was about to hazard a wandering opinion when a sharp exclamation from the Frenchman silenced me.

"Quick, my friend," he ordered, extinguishing the tall twin candles which burned beside the piano, "let us go up. Unless I am more badly mistaken than I think, there is that up there which is worth seeing!"

I followed him up the stairs, down the first gallery to the second flight and down the upper balcony to the bare, forbidding room Miss O'Shane used as studio. "Ah," he breathed as he struck a wax match and ignited the candles before the drawing-board, "did I not say it? *Parbleu*, Friend Trowbridge, Mademoiselle O'Shane has indulged in more than one unconscious art this night, or Jules de Grandin is a liar!"

As the candle flames leaped to burning points in the still air of the room I started forward, then shrank back from the sketch their radiance revealed. Progress had been made on the picture since we had viewed it earlier in the evening. The hooded figure in the foreground was now clearly drawn, and it was no monk, but a steel-clad warrior with long white surtout worn over his armor and a white hood pulled forward, half concealing his thin, bearded face. But there was a face there, where there had been none before—a thin, vulpine, wicked face with set, cruel eyes which gloated on the prostrate figure before him. The upraised arm which had no hand when Miss O'Shane showed us the drawing after dinner now terminated in a mailed fist, and between the steel-sheathed fingers it held the stem of a chalice, a lovely, tulip-shaped cup of crystal, as though it would scatter its contents to the polished stone with which the picture room was paved. One other thing I noted before my glance shifted to the female figure—the long, red passion cross upon the white surtout was reversed, its long arm pointing upward, its transverse bar lowered, and even as I saw this I remembered vaguely that when knightly orders flourished it was the custom of heraldic courts thus to reverse a sir-knight's coats of arms when he was degraded from his chivalry as unworthy to maintain his traditions.

What had been the rough outlines of the manger were now firmly drawn into the representation of an altar, complete with the crucifix and tabernacle, but veiling the cross, so lightly sketched that, stare as I would, I could not make it out, was an odd-shaped, winged form, somewhat resembling a bat with outstretched wings.

Before the altar's lowest step the female figure, now drawn with the detail of an engraving, groveled starkly, chin and breasts, knees and elbows, instep and wrists pressed tightly to the stones; open, suppliant hands stretched forward, palms upward; rippling masses of hair flowing forward, like a plume of smoke blown in the wind, and obscuring the face.

And what was that upon the second step leading to the sanctuary? At first I thought it an alms-basin, but a second glance showed me it was a wide, shallow dish, and in it rested a long, curve-bladed knife, such as I had seen French butchers wear in their belts while enjoying a noonday smoke and resting for a space from their gory trade before the entrance of an abattoir.

"Good heavens!" I gasped, turning from the grisly scene with a feeling of physical sickness. "This is terrible, de Grandin! What are we going to do—?"

"*Barbe et tête de Saint Denis*, we do this!" he replied in a furious hissing voice. "*Parbleu*, shall Jules de Grandin be made a fool of twice in one night? Not if he knows it!"

Seizing an eraser from the tray, he bent forward, and with half a dozen vigorous strokes reduced the picture to a meaningless smear of black and gray smudges.

"And now," he dusted his hands one against the other, as though to cleanse them of something foul, "let us to bed once more, my friend. I think we shall find something interesting to talk of tomorrow."

Shortly after breakfast next morning he found an excuse for separating Dunroe O'Shane from the rest of the company. "Will you not have pity on our loneliness, *Mademoiselle*?" he asked. "Here we lie, imprisoned in this great jail of a house, without so much as a radio program to cheer us through the morning hours. May we not trespass on your kindness and beg that you play for our delectation?"

"I play?" the girl answered with a half-incredulous smile. "Why, Dr. de Grandin. I don't know one note from another. I never played the piano in my life!"

"U'm?" He looked polite doubt as he twisted the ends of his mustache. "It is perhaps that I do not plead our cause fervently enough, *Mademoiselle?*"

"But truly, I can't play," she persisted.

"That's right, Dr. de Grandin," one of the young men chimed in. "Dunroe's a whiz at drawing, but she's absolutely tone-deaf. Can't carry a tune in a basket. I used to go to school with her, and they always gave her a job passing out programs or selling tickets when the class chorus sang."

De Grandin shot me a quick glance and shook his head warningly.

"What does it mean?" I asked as soon as we were together once more. "She declares she can't play, and her friends corroborate her, but—"

"But stranger things have happened, and *Mordieu*, still stranger ones will happen again, or the presentiment which I have is nothing more than the consequences of a too hearty breakfast!" he broke in with one of his quick, elfin smiles. "Let us play the silly fool, Friend Trowbridge; let us pretend to believe that the moon is composed entirely of green cheese and that mice terrorize the pussy-cat. So doing, we shall learn more than if we attempt to appear filled with wisdom which we do not possess."

IV

"OH, I KNOW WHAT let's do!" Miss Prettybridge, the lady of the scintillating teeth, whom de Grandin had squired to dinner the previous evening, exclaimed shortly after ten o'clock that night. "This is such a romantic old house—I'm sure it's just full of memories. Let's have a séance!"

"Fine, splendid, capital!" chorused a dozen voices. "Who'll be the medium? Anybody got a Ouija board or a planchette table?"

"Order, order, please!" the self-constituted chairwoman rapped peremptorily on a bridge table with her lorgnette. "I know how to do it! We'll go into the dining room and gather about the table. Then, when we've formed the mystic circle, if there are any spirits about we'll make 'em talk to us by rapping. Come on, everybody!"

"I don't think I like this," Miss O'Shane murmured as she laid her hand on my arm. Her usually pale face was paler still, and there was an expression of haunted fear in her eyes as she hesitated at the doorway.

"I don't care much for such nonsense myself," I admitted as we followed the others reluctantly into the refectory.

"Be close to me while this progresses, Friend Trowbridge," de Grandin whispered as he guided me to a seat beside him. "I care not much for this business of the monkey, but it may be the old she-fool yonder will serve our purpose unwittingly. The greatest danger is to Mademoiselle Dunroe. Keep watch on her."

The candles in the dining-room wall sconces were extinguished, and with Miss Prettybridge at the head of the table, the entire company was seated at the board, each one with his hands outspread on the dark, polished oak before him, his thumbs touching lightly, his little fingers in contact with those of his neighbors to right and left.

"Spirits," Miss Prettybridge, in her role of priestess, threw out the customary challenge, "spirits, if you are here tonight, signify your presence by rapping once on the table."

Thirty seconds or so elapsed without an answer to the lady's invitation. A woman half-way down the board tittered in half-hysterical embarrassment, and her neighbor silenced her with an impatient "*sh-s-s-sh!*" Then, distinctly as though thumped with a knuckle, the ancient table gave forth a resounding crack.

"If the spirit is a man, rap once; if a woman, twice," instructed Miss Prettybridge.

Another pause, somewhat longer, this time, then slowly, distinctly, two soft knocks from the very center of the table.

"Oh, a woman!" trilled one of the girls. "How perfectly thrilling!"

"And your name is—what?" demanded the mistress of ceremonies in a voice which trembled slightly in spite of her effort at control.

Thirteen slow, clear strokes sounded on the table, followed by one, then by eighteen, then others in series until nine distinct groups of blows were recorded.

"M-a-r-i-e-a-n-n-e Marie Anne—a French girl!" exclaimed Miss Prettybridge. "Whom do you wish to speak with, Marie Anne? Rap when I come to the name as I call the roll. Dr. Trowbridge?"

No response.

"Dr. de Grandin?"

A sharp, affirmative knock answered her, and the visitant was bidden to spell out her message.

Followed a rapid, telegraphic series of blows on the table, sometimes coming so quickly that it was impossible for us to decode them.

I listened as attentively as I could; so did everyone else, except Jules de Grandin. After a moment, during which his sleek blond head was thrust forward inquiringly, he turned his attention to Dunroe O'Shane.

The logs were burning low in the fireplace, but a shifting, flickering glow soaked through the darkness now and again, its red reflection lighting up the girl's face with a strange, unearthly illumination like the nimbus about the head of a saint in a medieval painting.

I felt the Frenchman's fingers stiffen against mine, and realized the cause of his tenseness as I stole a fleeting glance at Miss O'Shane. Her eyes had closed, and her red, petulant lips were lightly parted, as though in sleep. Over her small, regular features had crept a look of longing ecstasy.

Even my limited experience with psychotherapy was sufficient to tell me she was in a condition verging on hypnosis, if not actually over the borderline of consciousness, and I was about to leap from my seat with an offer of assistance when the insistent pressure of de Grandin's fingers on mine held me back. Turning toward him, I saw his head nod sharply toward the doorway behind the girl, and following his silent bidding, I cast my glance into the passageway in time to see someone slip quickly and noiselessly down the hall.

For a moment I sat in wondering silence, debating whether I had seen one of the servants creep past or whether I was the victim of an optical illusion, when my attention was suddenly compelled to a second figure, then a third, a fourth and a fifth passing the archway's opening like flashes of light against a darkened wall. My reason told me my eyes were playing pranks, for the gliding, soundless figures filing in quick procession past the proscenium of the dining-room door were tall, bearded men encased in gleaming black armor, and shrouded from shoulder to spurs in sable cloaks.

I blinked my eyes and shook my head in bewilderment, wondering if I had fallen into a momentary doze and dreamed the vision, but sharply, with theatrical suddenness, there sounded the raucous, brazen bray of a bugle, the skirling squeal of an unoiled windlass reeling out rope, the thud of a drawbridge falling into place; then, above the whistling November wind there winded another trumpet flourish and the clatter of iron-shod hooves against stone paving-blocks.

"Why, what was that?" Miss Prettybridge forgot the spirit message still being thumped out on the table and threw back her head in momentary alarm.

"Sounds like a troop of scouts out for an evening's lark," put in our host, rising from the table. "Queer they should come out here to toot their bugles, though."

"Ha, *Parbleu*, you say rightly, my friend," de Grandin, broke in, rising so suddenly that his chair tilted back and fell to the floor with a resounding crash. "It is queer, most damnably queer. Boy scouts did you say? Pray they be not scouts of evil in search of some hapless little lad while a company of empty-headed fools sit idly by listening to the chatter of their decoy!

"Did none of you recognize the message the spirit had for me?"

We looked at him in silent astonishment as he lighted the wall-candles one after another and faced us with a countenance gone livid with fury.

"*Ah bah*, it is scarcely worth troubling to tell you," he cried, "but the important message the spirit had for me was a silly little nursery rhyme:

Great A, little a,
Bouncing B.
The cat's in the cupboard,
And can't see me!

"No, the cat might not see that accursed decoy spirit, but Jules de Grandin could see the others as they slunk past the door upon their devil's work! Trowbridge, *mon vieux*, look at Mademoiselle O'Shane, if you will."

Startled by his command, I turned round. Dunroe O'Shane had fallen forward across the table, her long, tawny hair freed from its restraining pins and lying about her head like a pool of liquid bronze. Her eyes were still closed, but the peaceful expression had gone from her face, and in its stead was a look of unutterable fear and loathing.

"Take her up, some of you," de Grandin almost shrieked. "Bear her to her chamber and Dr. Trowbridge and I will attend to her. Then, Monsieur Van Riper, if you will be so good, I shall ask you to lend us one of your swiftest motor cars."

"A motor car—now?" Van Riper's incredulous tone showed he doubted his ears.

"*Précisément, Monsieur*, permit that I compliment you on the excellence of your hearing," the Frenchman replied. "A swift motor car with plenty of fuel, if you please. There are certain medicines needed to attend this sickness of body and soul, and to strike directly at its cause, and we must have them without delay. Dr. Trowbridge will drive; you need not trouble your chauffeur to leave his bed."

Ten minutes later, having no more idea of our destination than I had of the underlying causes of the last half hour's strange events, I sped down the turnpike, Van Riper's powerful motor warming up with every revolution, and gaining speed with every foot we traveled.

"Faster, faster, my friend," the little Frenchman besought as we whirled madly around a banked curve in the road and started down the two-mile straightaway with the speedometer registering sixty-five miles an hour.

Twin disks of lurid flame arose above the crest of the gradient before us, growing larger and brighter every second, and the pounding staccato of high powered motorcycles driven at top speed came to us through the shrieking wind.

I throttled down our engine to a legal speed as the State Troopers neared, but instead of rushing past they came to a halt, one on each side of us. "Where you from?" demanded the one to our left, on whose arm a sergeant's chevrons showed.

"From Mr. Van Riper's house—the Cloisters," I answered. "I'm Dr. Trowbridge, of Harrisonville, and this is Dr. de Grandin. A young lady at the house had been taken ill, and were rushing home for medicine."

"Ump?" the sergeant grunted. "Come from th' Cloisters, do you? Don't suppose you passed anyone on the road?"

"No—" I began, but de Grandin leaned past me.

"For whom do you seek, *mon sergent?*" he demanded.

"Night riders!" the words fairly spat from the policeman's lips. "Lot o' dam' kidnapers, sir. Old lady down th' road about five miles—name o'

Stebbens—was walkin' home from a neighbor's with her grandson, a cute little lad about three years old, when a crowd o' bums came riding hell-bent for election past her, knocked her for a loop an' grabbed up the kid. Masqueraders they was—wore long black gowns, she said, an' rode on black horses. Went away whoopin' an' yellin' to each other in some foreign language, an' laughin' like a pack o' dogs. Be God, they'll laugh outa th' other side o' their dirty mouths if we catch 'em!"

"Come on, Shoup, let's roll," he ordered his companion.

The roar of their motorcycles grew fainter and fainter as they swept down the road, and in another moment we were pursuing our way toward the city, gathering speed with every turn of the wheels.

V

WE HAD GONE SCARCELY another mile before the slate-colored clouds which the wind had been piling together in the upper sky ripped apart and great clouds of soft, feathery snowflakes came tumbling down, blotting out the road ahead and cutting our speed to a snail's pace. It was almost gray light before we arrived at the outskirts of Harrisonville, and the snow was falling harder than ever as we headed up the main thoroughfare.

"*Hélas*, my friend, there is not the chance that we can return to the Cloisters before noon, be our luck of the best," de Grandin muttered disconsolately; "therefore I suggest that we go to your house and obtain a few hours' rest."

"But how about the medicine you wanted?" I objected. "Hadn't we better see about getting that first?"

"*Non*," he returned. "It will keep. The medicine I seek could not be administered before tonight—if that soon—and we can secure it later as well as now."

Rather surprised at our unheralded return, but used to the vagaries of a bachelor physician and his eccentric friend, Nora McGinnis, my housekeeper and general-factotum, prepared a toothsome breakfast for us the next morning, and we had completed the meal, lingering over coffee and cigarettes a little longer than usual, when de Grandin's face suddenly went livid as he thrust the folded newspaper he had been reading into my hand.

"Look, *mon ami*," he whispered raspingly. "Read what is there. They did not wait long to be about their deviltry!"

STATE COP DEAD IN MYSTERY KILLING

announced the headline to which he had directed my attention. Below was a brief dispatch, evidently a bit of last-minute news, sandwiched between the announcement of a sheriff's sale and a patent medicine advertisement:

JOHNSKILL—Sergeant Rosswell of the state constabulary is dead and Private Shoup in a serious condition as the result of a battle with a mysterious band of masked ruffians near this place early this morning. Shortly after ten o'clock last night Matilda Stebbens, of Osmondville, who was returning from a visit to a neighbor's with her three-year-old grandson, George, was attacked by a company of men mounted on black or dark-colored horses and enveloped in long black gowns, according to her story to the troopers. The leader of the gang struck her a heavy blow with a club or blackjack, evidently with the intention of stunning her and seized the little boy, lifting him to his saddle. Had it not been for the fact that Mrs. Stebbens still affects long hair and was wearing a stiff felt hat, the blow would undoubtedly have rendered her unconscious, but as it was she was merely knocked into the roadside ditch without losing consciousness, and as she lay there, half stunned from the blow, she heard the kidnapers exchange several words in some foreign language, Italian, she thought, before they set out at a breakneck pace, giving vent to wild whoops and yells. The direction of their flight was toward this place, and as soon as she was able to walk, Mrs. Stebbens hobbled to the nearest telephone and communicated with the state police.

Sergeant Rosswell and Private Shoup were detailed to the case and started in pursuit of the abductors on their motorcycles, encountering no one along the road who would admit having seen the company of mysterious mounted gangsters. About two miles this side of the Cloisters, palatial country place of Tandy Van Riper, well-known New York financier, according to Trooper Shoup, he and his companion came upon the kidnapers, riding at almost incredible speed. Drawing their pistols, the state policemen, called on the fleeing men to halt, and receiving no reply, opened fire. Their bullets, though fired at almost point-blank range, seemed to take no effect, Trooper Shoup declares, and the leader of the criminal band turned about, and charged him and his companion, deliberately riding Sergeant Rosswell down. According to Shoup, a shot fired by Rosswell, directly at the horse which was about to trample him, took no effect, though the pistol was less than three feet from the beast's breast. Shoup is suffering from a broken arm, three fractured ribs and a severe bruise on the head, which, he alleges, was dealt him when one of the thugs struck him with the flat of a sword.

Physicians at Mercy Hospital, believing Shoup's description of the criminals and the fight to be colored by the beating he received, intimate that he is not wholly responsible for his statements, as he positively declares that every member of the band of criminals was fully arrayed in black armor and armed with a long sword.

Working on the theory that the kidnapers are a band of Italian desperadoes who assumed this fantastic disguise, strong posses of state police are scouring the neighborhood. It is thought the little Stebbens boy was abducted by mistake, as the family are known to be in very moderate circumstances and the chances of obtaining a ransom for the lad are slight.

"You see?" de Grandin asked as I put the paper down with an exclamation of dismay.

"No. I'm hanged if I do," I shot back. "The whole gruesome business is beyond me. Is there any connection between what we saw at the Cloisters last night and—"

"*Mort d'un rat noir*, is there connection between the serpent and his venom—the Devil and the flames of hell?" he cried. "Yes, my friend, there is such a connection as will take all our skill and courage to break, I fear. Meantime, let us hasten, let us fly to the City Hospital. There is that there which shall prove more than a surprise to those vile miscreants, those forsworn servants of the Lord, when next we see them, *mon vieux*."

"What in the world are you talking about?" I demanded. "Whom do you mean by 'forsworn servants of the Lord'?"

"Ha, good friend," he returned, his face working with emotion, "you will know in due time, if what I suspect is true. If not—" He raised his narrow shoulders in a fatalistic shrug as he snatched his overcoat.

For upward of half an hour I cooled my heels in the frosty winter air while de Grandin was closeted in conference with the superintendent of the City Hospital, but when he came out he was wearing such a smile of serene happiness that I had not the heart to berate him for leaving me outside so long.

"And now, kind friend, if you will take me, so far as the procathedral, I shall have done the last of my errands, and we may begin our journey to the Cloisters," he announced as he leaped nimbly into the seat beside me.

The Right Reverend De Motte Gregory, suffragan bishop of our diocese, was seated at his desk in the synod house as de Grandin and I were announced, and graciously consented to see us at once. He had been a more than ordinarily successful railway executive, a licensed legal practitioner and a certified public accountant before he assumed the cloth, and his worldly training had taught him the value of time and words, both his own and others', and rarely did he waste either.

"*Monsieur l'Eveque*," de Grandin began after he had greeted the gray-haired cleric with a rigidly formal European bow, "in the garden of your beautiful church there grows a bush raised from a sprig of the Holy Thorn of Glastonbury—the tree which sprang from the staff of the blessed Joseph of Arimathea when he landed in Britain after his voyage and travail. *Monseigneur*, we are come to beg a so little spray of that shrub from you."

The bishop's eyes opened wide with surprise, but de Grandin gave him no time for reflection.

"Sir," he hurried on, "it is not that we wish to adorn our own gardens, nor yet to put it to a shameful commercial use, but we need it—need it most urgently in a matter of great importance which is toward—"

Leaving his chair he leaned across the bishop's wide rosewood desk and began whispering rapidly in the churchman's ear.

The slightly annoyed frown which mounted to the bishop's face as the little Frenchman took the liberty changed slowly to a look of incredulity, then to an expression of amazement, "You really believe this?" he asked at length.

"More, *Monseigneur*, I almost know it," de Grandin assured him earnestly, "and if I am mistaken, as I hope I am but fear I am not, the holy thorn can do no harm, while it may—" He paused, waving his hand in an expressive gesture.

Bishop Gregory touched one of the row of call-buttons on his desk. "You shall have the cutting from the tree, and be very welcome," he assured my friend, "but I join with you in the hope you are mistaken."

"*Grand merci, Monseigneur!*" de Grandin acknowledged with another bow. "*Mordieu*, but your great heart is equaled only by your massive intellect! Half the clergy would have said I raved had I told them one small quarter of what I related to you."

The bishop smiled a little wearily as he put the sprig of thorn-bush into de Grandin's hand. "Half the clergy, like half the laity, know so much that they know next to nothing," he replied.

"Name of a name," de Grandin swore enthusiastically as we turned toward the Cloisters, "and they say he is a worldly man! *Pardieu*, when will the foolish ones learn that the man who dedicates worldly wisdom to heaven's service is the most valuable servant of all?"

VI

DUNROE O'SHANE WAS ATTIRED in a long, brown-linen smock and hard at work on her drawing when we arrived at the Cloisters shortly before luncheon. She seemed none the worse for her fainting fit of the previous night, and the company were rather inclined to rally de Grandin on the serious diagnosis he had made before rushing away to secure medicine for her.

I was amazed at the good-natured manner in which he took their chaffing, but a hasty whisper in my ear explained his self-control. "Apes' anger and fools' laughter are alike to be treated with scorn, my friend," he told me. "We—you and I—have work to do here, and we must not let the hum of pestilent gnats drive us from our purpose."

Bridge and dancing filled the evening from dinner to midnight, and the party broke up shortly after twelve with the understanding that all were to be ready to attend Thanksgiving services in the near-by parish church at eleven o'clock next morning.

"Ts-s-st, Friend Trowbridge, do not disrobe," de Grandin ordered as I was about to shed my dinner clothes and prepare for bed; "we must be ready for an instant sortie from now until cockcrow tomorrow, I fear."

"What's this all about, anyhow?" I demanded a little irritably, as I dropped on the bed and wrapped myself in a blanket. "There's been more confounded mystery here than I ever saw in a harmless old house, what with Miss O'Shane making funny drawings, throwing fainting-fits, and bugles sounding in the courtyard, and—"

"Ha, harmless, did you say?" he cut in with a grim smile. "My friend, if this house be harmless, then prussic acid is a healthful drink. Attend me with care, if you please. Do you know what this place is?"

"Certainly I do," I responded with some heat. "It's an old Cypriote villa brought to America and—"

"It was once a chapter house of the Knights of the Temple," he interrupted shortly, "and a Cyprian chapter house, at that. Does that mean nothing to you? Do you not know the Knights Templars my friend?"

"I ought to," I replied. "I've been one for the last fifteen years."

"Oh, la, la!" he laughed. "You will surely slay me, my friend. You good, kind American gentlemen who dress in pretty uniforms and carry swords are no more like the old Knights of the Temple of Solomon than are these other good men who wear red tarbooshes and call themselves Nobles of the Mystic Shrine like the woman-stealing, pilgrim-murdering Arabs of the desert.

"Listen: The history of the Templars' order is a long one, but we can touch its high spots in a few words. Formed originally for the purpose of fighting the Infidel in Palestine and aiding poor pilgrims to the Holy City, they did yeoman service in the cause of God; but when Europe forsook its crusades and the Saracens took Jerusalem, the knights, whose work was done, did not disband. Not they. Instead, they clung to their various houses in Europe, and grew fat, lazy and wicked in a life of leisure, supported by the vast wealth they had amassed from gifts from grateful pilgrims and the spoils of battle. In 1191 they bought the Isle of Cyprus from Richard I of England and established several chapter houses there, and it was in those houses that unspeakable things were done. Cyprus is one of the most ancient dwelling places of religion, and of her illegitimate sister, superstition. It was there that the worshipers of Cytherea, goddess of beauty and of love—and other things less pleasant—had their stronghold. Before the Romans held the land it was drenched with unspeakable orgies. The very name of the island has passed into an invidious adjective in your language—do you not say a thing is Cyprian when you would signify it is las-civious? Certainly."

"But—"

"Hear me," he persisted, waving aside my interruption. "This Cytherea was but another form of Aphrodite, and Aphrodite, in turn, was but another name for the Eastern Goddess Astarte or Istar. You begin to comprehend? Her rites were celebrated with obscene debaucheries, but her worshipers became such human swine that only the most revolting inversions of natural things would sat-isfy them. The flaunting and sacrifices of virtue were not enough; they must need sacrifice—literally—those things which impersonated virtue—little, innocent children and chaste young maidens. Their foul altars must run red with the blood of innocence. These things were traditions in Cyprus long before the Knights Templars took up their abode there, and, as one cannot sleep among dogs with-out acquiring fleas, so the knights, grown slothful and lazy, with nothing to do but think up ways of spending their time and wealth, became addicts to the evils of the earlier, heathen ways of their new home. Thoughts are things, my friend, and the evil thoughts of the old Cyprians took root, and flourished in the brains of those unfortunate old warrior-monks whose hands were no longer busy with the sword and whose lips no longer did service to the Most High God.

"You doubt it? Consider: Though Philip IV and Clement V undoubtedly did Jacques de Molay to death for no better reason than that they might cast lots for his raiment, the fact remains that many of the knights confessed to dreadful sacrileges committed in the chapter houses—to children slain on the altars once dedicated to God, all in the name of the heathen goddess Cytherea.

"This very house wherein we sit was once the scene of such terrible things as those. About its stones must linger the presence of the evil men, the renegade priests of God, who once did them. These discarnate intelligences have lain dormant since the fourteenth century, but for some reason, which we will not now discuss, I believe they have wakened into physical beings once more. It was their reincarnated spirits we saw flitting past the door last night while Made-moiselle Dunroe lay in a trance; it was they who took the little boy from his grandmother's arms; it was they who slew the brave policeman; it is they who will soon attempt to perform the hideous inversion of the mass."

"See here, de Grandin," I expostulated, "there have been some deucedly queer goings-on here, I'll admit, but when you try to tell me that a lot of old soldier-monks have come to life again and are traipsing around the countryside stealing children, you're piling it on a bit too thick. Now, if there were any evidence to prove that—"

"Silence!" his sharp whisper brought me up with a start as he rose from his chair and crept, catlike, toward the door, opening it a crack and glancing down the darkened corridor outside. Then:

"Come, my friend," he bade in a low breath, "come and see what I behold."

As he swung the door back I glanced down the long, stone-paved gallery, dark as Erebus save as cancelled bars of moonlight shot obliquely down from the tiny mullioned windows piercing the dome, and made out a gliding, wraith-like figure in trailing white garments.

"Dunroe O'Shane!" I murmured dazedly, watching the retreating form slipping soundlessly down the dark balcony. The wavering light of the candle she bore in her upraised hand cast gigantic shadows against the carved balustrade and the sculptured uprights of the interlaced arches supporting the gallery above, and hobgoblin shades seemed to march along beside her like an escort of unclean genii from the legions of Eblis. I watched openmouthed with amazement as she slipped down the passage, her feet, obscured in a haze of trailing draperies, treading noiselessly, her free hand stretched outward toward the balcony rail. The next moment the gallery was deserted; abruptly as a motion picture fades from the screen when the projecting light winks out, Dunroe O'Shane and her flickering rushlight vanished from our sight.

"Quick, Friend Trowbridge," the Frenchman whispered, "after her—it was through that further door she went!"

Quietly as possible we ran down the gallery, paused before the high, pointed-topped door and wrenched at its wrought-iron handle. The oaken panels held firm, for the door was latched on the farther side.

"Ten thousand little devils!" de Grandin cried in vexation. "We are stalemated!"

For a moment I thought he would hurl himself against the four-inch planks of the door in impotent fury, but he collected himself with an effort, and drawing a flashlight from his jacket pocket, handed it to me with the command, "Hold the light steady on the keyhole, my friend." The next instant he sank to his knees, produced two short lengths of thin steel wire and began methodically picking the lock.

"Ha," he exclaimed, as he rose and dusted the knees of his trousers, "those old ones built for strength, Friend Trowbridge, but they knew little of subtlety. Little did that ancient locksmith dream his handiwork would one day meet with Jules de Grandin."

The unbarred door swung inward beneath his touch, and we stepped across the stone sill of a vast, dungeon-dark apartment.

"*Mademoiselle?*" he called softly. "Mademoiselle Dunroe—are you here?"

He shot the searching beam of his flashlight hither and yon about the big room, disclosing high walls of heavy carved oak, a great canopy bed, several cathedral chairs and one or two massive, iron-bound chests—but found no living thing.

"*Mordieu*, but this is strange!" he muttered, sinking to his knees to flash his light beneath the high-carved bed.

"Into this room she did most certainly come but a few little minutes ago, gliding like a spirit, and now, *pouf*, out of this same room she does vanish like a ghost!"

Though somewhat larger, the room was similar to most other bedchambers in the house, paneled with rather crudely carved, age-blackened wood for the entire height of its walls, ceiled with great beams which still bore the marks of the adz, and floored with octagonal marble tile of alternate black and white. We went over every inch of it, searching for some secret exit, for, save the one by which we had entered, there was no door in the place and the two great windows were of crude, semitransparent glass let into metal frames securely cemented to the surrounding stones. Plainly, nobody had left the room that way.

At the farther end of the apartment stood a stall wardrobe, elaborately decorated with carved scenes of chase and battle. Opening one of the double doors letting into the press, de Grandin inspected the interior, which, like the outside was carved in every available place. "Um?" he said, surveying the walls under his flashlight. "It may be that this is but the anteroom to—ha!"

He broke off, pointing dramatically to a carved group in the center of one of the back panels. It represented a procession of hunters returning from their sport, deer, boar and other animals lashed to long poles which the huntsmen bore shoulder-high. The men were filing through the arched entrance to a castle, the great doors of which swung back to receive them. One of the door-leaves, apparently, had warped loose from the body of the plank from which it was carved.

"*C'est très adroit, n'est-ce-pas?*" my companion asked with a delighted grin. "Had I not seen such things before, it might have imposed on me. As it is—"

Reaching forward, he gave the loosened door a sharp, quick push, and the entire back of the wardrobe slipped upward revealing a narrow opening.

"And what have we here?" de Grandin asked, playing his spotlight through the secret doorway.

Straight ahead for three or four feet ran a flagstone sill, worn, smooth in the center, as though with the shuffling tread of many feet. Beyond that began a flight of narrow, stone stairs which spiraled steeply down a shaft like the flue of a monster chimney.

De Grandin turned to me, and his little, heart-shaped face was graver than I had ever seen it.

"Trowbridge, dear, kind friend," he said in a voice so low and hoarse I could scarcely make out his words, "we have faced many perils together—perils of spirit and perils of flesh—and always we have triumphed. This time we may not. If I do not mistake rightly, there lies below these steps an evil more ancient and potent than any we have hitherto met. I have armed us against it with the weapons of religion and of science, but—I do not know that they will avail. Say, then, will you turn back now and go to your bed? I shall think no less of you, for no man should be compelled to face this thing unknowingly, and there is now no time to explain. If I survive, I shall return and tell you all. If I come not back with daylight, know that I have perished in my failure, and think kindly of me as one who loved you deeply. Will you not now say *adieu*, old friend?" He extended his hand and I saw the long, smooth-jointed fingers were trembling with suppressed nervousness.

"I will not!" I returned hotly, stung to the quick by his suggestion. "I don't know what's down there, but if you go, I go, too!"

Before I realized what he was about, he had flung his arms about my neck and kissed me on both cheeks. "Onward, then, brave comrade!" he cried. "This night we fight such a fight as had not been waged since the sainted George slew the monster!"

VII

ROUND AND ROUND a steadily descending spiral, while I counted a hundred and seventy steps, we went, going deeper into inky blackness. Finally, when I had begun to grow giddy with the endless corkscrew turns, we arrived at a steeply sloping tunnel, floored with smooth black-and-white tiles. Down this we hastened, until we traversed a distance of a hundred feet; then for a similar length we trod a level path, and began an ascent as steep as the first decline.

"Careful—cautiously, my friend," the Frenchman warned in a whisper.

Pausing a moment while he fumbled in the pocket of his jacket, my companion strode toward the barrier and laid his left hand on its heavy, wrought-iron latch.

The portal swung back almost as he touched it, and:

"*Qui va la?*" challenged a voice from the darkness.

De Grandin threw the ray of his torch across the doorway, disclosing a tall, spare form in gleaming black plate-armor over which was drawn the brown-serge habit of a monk. The sentry wore his hair in a sort of bob approximating the haircut affected by children today, and on his sallow immature face sprouted the rudiments of a straggling beard. It was a youthful face and a weak one which de Grandin's light disclosed, but the face of youth already well schooled in viciousness.

"*Qui vive?*" the fellow called doubtfully in a rather high, effeminate voice, laying a hand on the hilt of a heavy broadsword dangling from the wide, brass-studded baldric looped over his cassock.

"Those on the service of the Most High God, *petit bête!*" returned de Grandin, drawing something (a pronged sprig of wood, I thought) from his jacket pocket and thrusting it toward the warder's face.

"*Ohé!*" cried the other sharply, shrinking back. "Touch me not, good *messires*, I pray—I—"

"Ha—so?" de Grandin gritted between his teeth, and drew the branched stick downward across the sentry's face.

Astonishingly, the youth seemed to shrink and shrivel in upon himself. Trembling as though with an ague, he bent forward, buckled at the knees, fell toward the floor, and—was gone! Sword, armor, cassock and the man who wore them dwindled to nothingness before our sight.

A hundred feet or so farther on, our way was barred by another door, wider, higher and heavier than the first. While no tiler guarded it, it was so firmly locked that all our efforts were powerless to budge it.

"Friend Trowbridge," de Grandin announced, "it seems we shall have to pick this lock, even as we did the other. Do you keep watch through yonder grille while I make the way open for us." Reaching up, he moved aside a shutter covering a barred peephole in the door's thick panels; then, dropping to his knees, drew forth his wires and began working at the lock.

Gazing through the tiny wicket, I beheld a chapel-like room of circular formation, cunningly floored with slabs of polished yellow stone, inlaid with occasional plaques of purple.

By the glow of a wavering vigil lamp and the flicker of several guttering ecclesiastical candles, I saw the place was roofed with a vaulted ceiling supported by a number of converging arches, and the pier of each arch was supported by the carved image of a huge human foot which rested on the crown of a hideous, half-human head, crushing it downward and causing it to grimace hellishly with mingled pain and fury.

Beyond the yellow sanctuary lamp loomed the altar, approached by three low steps, and on it was a tall wooden crucifix from which the corpus had been stripped and to which had been nailed, in obscure caricature, a huge black bat. The staples fastening the poor beast to the cross must have hurt unmercifully, for it strove hysterically to free itself.

Almost sickened at the sight, I described the scene to de Grandin as he worked at the lock, speaking in a muted whisper, for, though there was no sign of living thing save the tortured bat, I felt that there were listening ears concealed in the darkness.

"Good!" he grunted as he hastened with his task. "It may be we are yet in time, good friend." Even as he spoke there came a sharp click, and the door's heavy bolts slipped back under the pressure of his improvised picklock.

Slowly, inch by careful inch, we forced the great door back.

B UT EVEN AS WE did so, there came from the rear of th circular chamber the subdued measures of a softly intoned Gregorian chant, and something white moved forward through the shadows.

It was a man arrayed in black-steel armor over which was drawn a white surtout emblazoned with a reversed passion cross, and in his hands he bore a wide-mouthed brazen bowl like an alms-basin. In the tray rested a wicked-looking, curve-bladed knife.

With a mocking genuflection to the altar he strode up the steps and placed his burden on the second tread; then, with a coarse guffaw, he spat upon the pinioned bat and backed downward.

As a signal a double file of armored men came marching out of the gloom, ranged themselves in two ranks, one to right, one to left of the altar, and whipped their long swords from their sheaths, clashing them together, tip to tip, forming an arcade of flashing steel between them.

So softly that I felt rather than heard him, de Grandin sighed in suppressed fury as blade met blade and two more men-at-arms, each bearing a smoking censer, strode forward beneath the roof of steel. The perfume of the incense was strong, acrid, sweet, and it mounted to our brains like the fumes of some accursed drug. But even as we sniffed its seductive scent, our eyes widened at the sight of the form which paced slowly behind the mailed acolytes.

Ceremoniously, step by pausing step, she came, like a bride marching under the arbor of uplifted swords at a military wedding, and my eyes fairly ached at the beauty of her. Milk-white, lissom and pliant as a peeled willow wand, clad only in the jeweled loveliness of her own pearly whiteness, long, bronze hair sweeping in a cloven tide from her pale brow and cataracting over her tapering shoulders, came Dunroe O'Shane. Her eyes were closed, as though in sleep, and on her red, full lips lay the yearning half-smile of the bride who ascends the aisle to meet her bridegroom, or the novice who mounts the altar steps to make her full profession. And as she advanced, her supple, long-fingered hands waved slowly to and fro, weaving fantastic arabesques in the air.

"Hail, Cytherea, Queen and Priestess and Goddess; hail, She Who Confers Life and Being on Her Servants!" came the full-throated salutation of the double row of armored men as they clashed their blades together in martial salute, then dropped to one knee in greeting and adoration.

For a moment the undraped priestess paused below the altar stairs; then, as though forced downward by invincible pressure, she dropped, and we heard the smacking impact of soft flesh against the stone floor as she flung herself prostrate and beat her brow and hands against the floor in utter self-abasement before the marble altar and its defiled calvary.

"Is all prepared?" The question rang out sonorously as a cowled figure advanced from the shadows and strode with a swaggering step to the altar.

"All is prepared!" the congregation answered with one voice.

"Then bring the paschal lamb, even the lamb without fleece!" The deep-voiced command somehow sent shivers through me.

Two armored votaries slipped quietly away, returning in an instant with the struggling body of a little boy between them—a chubby child, naked, who fought and kicked and offered such resistance as his puny strength allowed while he called aloud to "Mamma" and "Grandma" to save him.

Down against the altar steps the butchers flung the little man; then one took his chubby, dimpled hands in relentless grip while the other drew backward at his ankles, suspending him above the wide-mouthed brazen bowl reposing on the second step.

"Take up the knife, Priestess and Queen of goodly Salamis," the hooded master of ceremonies commanded. "Take up the sacrificial knife, that the red blood may flow to our Goddess, and we hold high wassail in Her honor! O'er land and sea, o'er burning desert and heaving billow have we journeyed—"

"Villains—assassins—renegades!" Jules de Grandin bounded from his station in the shadow like a frenzied cat. "By the blood of all the blessed martyrs, you have journeyed altogether too far from hell, your home!"

"Ha? Interlopers?" rasped the hooded man. "So be it. Three hearts shall smoke upon our altar instead of one!"

"*Parbleu*, nothing shall smoke but the fires of your endless torture as your foul carcasses burn ceaselessly in hell!" de Grandin returned, leaping forward and drawing out the forked stick with which he had struck down the porter at the outer gate.

A burst of contemptuous laughter greeted him. "Thinkest thou to overcome me with such a toy?" the cowled one asked between shouts. "My warder at the gate succumbed to your charms—he was a poor weakling. Him you have passed, but not me. Now die!"

From beneath his cassock he snatched a long, two-handed sword, whirled its blade aloft in a triple flourish, and struck directly at de Grandin's head.

Almost by a miracle, it seemed, the Frenchman avoided the blow, dropped his useless spring of thornwood and snatched a tiny, quill-like object from his pocket. Dodging the devastating thrusts of the enemy de Grandin toyed an instant with the capsule in his hand, unscrewed the cap and, suddenly changing his tactics, advanced directly on his foe.

"Ha, Monsieur from the Fires, here is fire you know not of!" he shouted, thrusting forward the queer-looking rod and advancing within reach of the other's sword.

I stared in open-mouthed amazement. Poised for another slashing blow with his great sword, the armed man wavered momentarily, while an expression of astonishment, bewilderment, finally craven fear overspread his lean, predatory features. Lowering his sword, he thrust feebly with the point, but there was no force behind the stab; the deadly steel clattered to the floor before he could drive it into the little Frenchman's breast.

The hooded man seemed growing thinner; his tall, spare form, which had bulked a full head taller than de Grandin a moment before, seemed losing substance—growing gradually transparent, like an early morning fog slowly dissolving before the strengthening rays of the rising sun. Behind him, through him, I could dimly espy the outlines of the violated altar and the prostrate woman before its steps. Now the objects in the background became plainer and plainer. The figure of the armored man was no longer a thing of flesh and blood and cold steel overspread with a monk's habit, but an unsubstantial phantom, like an oddly shaped cloud. It was composed of trailing, rolling clouds of luminous vapor which gradually disintegrated into strands and floating webs of phosphorescence, and these, in turn, gave way to scores of little nebulae of light which glowed like cigarette-ends of intense blue radiance. Then, where the nebulae had been were only dancing, shifting specks of bright blue fire, finally nothing but a few pin-points of light; then—nothing.

Like shadows thrown of forest trees when the moon is at her zenith, the double row of men-at-arms stood at ease while de Grandin battled with their champion; now their leader gone, they turned and scuttled in panic toward the rearward shadows, but Jules de Grandin was after them like a speeding arrow.

"Ha, renegades," he called mockingly, pressing closer and closer, "you who steal away helpless little boy-babies from the arms of their *grand-mères* and then would sacrifice, them on your altar, do you like the feast Jules de Grandin brings? You who would make wassail with the blood of babies—drink the draft I have prepared! Fools, mockers at God, where now is your deity? Call on her—call on Cytherea! *Pardieu*, I fear her not."

As it was with the master, so it was with the underlings: Closer and closer de Grandin pressed against the struggling mass of demoralized men, before his advance like ice when pressed upon by red-hot iron. One moment they milled and struggled, shrieking for aid to some unclean deity; the next they were dissolved into nebulous vapor, drifting aimlessly a moment in the still air, then swept away to nothingness.

"And so, my friend, that is done," announced de Grandin matter-of-factly as he might have mentioned the ending of a meal. "There crouches Mademoiselle O'Shane, Friend Trowbridge; come, let us seek her clothes—they should be somewhere here."

Behind the altar we found Dunroe's nightrobe and negligee lying in a ring, just as she had shrugged out of them before taking up her march between the upraised swords. Gently as a nurse attending a babe, the little Frenchman raised the swooning girl from her groveling posture before the altar, draped her robes about her, and took her in his arms.

A wailing cry, rising gradually to an incensed roar, echoed and reverberated through the vaulted chamber, and de Grandin thrust the unconscious girt into my hands. "*Mon Dieu*," he exclaimed, "I did forget. *Le petit garçon!*"

Crouched as close to the wall as he could get, we found the little lad, tears of surprising size streaming down his fat cheeks as his little mouth opened wide and emitted wail after broken-hearted wail. "*Holà*, my little cabbage, *mon brave soldat!*" de Grandin soothed him, stretching out his hands to the weeping youngster. "Come with me. Come, we shall clothe you warmly against the cold and pop you into a bed of feathers, and tomorrow morning we return you to your mother's arms."

Panting under my burden, for she was no lightweight, I bore Dunroe O'Shane up the long, tortuous flight of steps.

"Morphine is indicated here, if I do not mistake," de Grandin remarked as we laid the girl on her bed.

"But we haven't any—" I began, only to be checked by his grin.

"Oh, but we have," he contradicted. "I foresaw something like this was likely to come about, and abstracted a quantity of the drug, together with a syringe, from your surgery before we left home."

When we had administered the narcotic, we set out for our own chamber, the little boy, warmly bundled in blankets, held tightly in de Grandin's arms. At a nod from the Frenchman we paused at Dunroe's studio, lighted several candles and inspected her work. Fairly spread upon her drawing-board was a pretty little scene—a dimpled little boy crowing and smiling in his mother's lap, a proud and happy father leaning over them, and in the foreground a group of rough bucolics kneeling in smiling adoration. "Why, the influence, whatever it was, seems to have left her before we went down those secret stairs!" I exclaimed, looking admiringly at the drawing.

"Do you say so?" de Grandin asked as he bent closer to inspect the picture. "Look here, if you please, my friend."

Bringing my eyes within a few inches of the board on which the Christmas scene was sketched, I saw, so faint it was hardly to be found unless the beholder looked for it another picture, lightly sketched in jerky, uneven lines, depicting another scene—a vaulted chapel with walls lined by armed men, two of whom held a child's body horizontally before the altar, while a woman, clothed only in her long, trailing hair, plunged a wicked, curve-bladed knife into the little one's body, piercing the heart.

"Good Lord!" I exclaimed, in horror.

"Precisely," agreed Jules de Grandin. "The good Lord inspired talent in the poor girl's hand, but the powers of darkness dictated that sketch. Perhaps—I can not say for sure—she drew both the picture we see here, and the good one was formerly the faint one, but when I overcame the wicked ones, the wicked scene faded to insignificance and the pleasing one became predominant. It is possible, and—*nom d'un nom!*"

"What now?" I demanded as he turned a conscience-smitten face toward me and thrust the sleeping child into my arms.

"*La chauve-souris*—the bat!" he exclaimed. "I did forget the poor one's sufferings in the stress of greater things. Take the little man to our room, and soothe him, my friend. Me, I go down those ten-thousand-times-damned stairs to that never-enough-to-be-cursed chapel and put the poor brute out of its misery!"

"You mean you're actually going into that horrible place again?" I demanded.

"*Eh bien*, why not?" he asked.

"Why—those terrible men—those—" I began, but he stopped me.

"My friend," he asked as he extracted a cigarette from his dressing gown pocket and lighted it nonchalantly, "have you not yet learned that when Jules de Grandin kills a thing—be it man or be it devil—it is dead? There is nothing there which could harm a new-born fly, I do solemnly assure you."

VIII

J ULES DE GRANDIN POURED out a couple of tablespoonfuls of brandy into a wide mouthed glass and passed the goblet under his nose, sniffing appreciatively. "Not at all, *cher ami*. From the first I did suspect there was something not altogether right about that house.

"To begin, you will recall that on the night Monsieur Van Riper took us from the station he told us his progenitor had imported the house, stone by single stone, to this country from Cyprus?"

"Yes," I nodded.

"Very good. The stones of which it is erected were probably quarried from the ruins of some heathen temple, and like sponges soaked in water, they were full to overflowing with evil influences. This evil undoubtedly affected the old warrior knights who dwelt in that house, probably from 1191, when Richard of England sold Cyprus to their order, to 1308, when the French king and the Roman pope suppressed and destroyed the order—and shared its riches between them.

"That the souls of those old monks who had forsaken their vows to the God of Love to serve the Goddess of Lust with unclean rites and ceremonies could not find rest in peaceful graves there is little doubt. But that they were able to materialize and carry on the obscenities they had practiced in life, there is also much doubt. Some ghosts there are who can make themselves visible at will; others can materialize at certain times and in certain places only; others can show themselves only with the aid of a medium.

"When the rich Monsieur Profiteer took up the old house and brought it to America, he doubtless imported all its evil influences intact; but they were latent.

"Then, only one little week ago, that which was needful came to the house. It was nothing less than Mademoiselle O'Shane's so beautiful self. She, my friend, is what the spiritualists call a sensitive, a psychic. She is attuned to the fine vibrations which affect the ordinary person not at all. She was the innocent medium through which the wicked knights were able to effect a reincarnation.

"The air may be filled with the ethereal waves from a thousand broadcasting stations, but if you have not a radio machine to entrap and consolidate those waves into sound, you are helpless to hear so much as a single squeal of static. Is it not so? Very good. Mademoiselle Dunroe was the radio set—the condenser and the amplifying agent needed to release the invisible wickedness which came from Cytherea's wicked altar—the discarnate intelligences which were once bad men. Do you not recall how she was greeted in the chapel of the Black Lodge: 'Hail, Priestess and Queen—She Who Gives Her Servants Life and Being?' Those wicked things which once were men admitted their debt to her in that salutation, my friend.

"Remember how Mademoiselle Dunroe told you of her inability to draw what she wished? The evil influences were already beginning to steal her brain and make her pliable to their base desires. They were beginning to lay plans to feed upon her vitality to clothe themselves in the semblance of humanity, and as they possessed her, she saw with her inward eye the scenes so many times heretofore enacted in that chapel.

"From the first I liked not the house, and when the poor Mademoiselle Dunroe told us of her troubles with her drawings, I liked it still less. How long it would have taken those old secret worshippers of evil to make themselves visible by the use of Mademoiselle Dunroe's vitality, I do not know. Perhaps they might never have succeeded. Perhaps she would have gone away and nothing more would have been heard of them, but that flap-eared she-ass of a Mademoiselle Prettybridge played the precise game the long-dead villains desired. When she held her so absurd séance in the dining-room that night, she furnished them just the atmosphere they needed to place their silent command in Mademoiselle O'Shane's mind. Her attention was fixed on ghostly things; 'Ah-ha,' says the master of the Black Lodge, 'now we shall steal her mind. Now we shall make her go into a trance like a medium, and she shall materialize us, and *la, la*, what deviltry we shall do!' And so they did. While they sent one of their number to thump upon the table and hold us spellbound listening to his nonsense rimes, the rest of them became material and rode forth upon their phantom steeds to steal them a little child. Oh, my friend, I dare not think what would have been had they carried through that dreadful blood-sacrifice. Warm blood acts upon the wicked spirits as tonic acts on humans. They might have become so strong, no power on earth could have stayed them! As it was, the ancient evil could be killed, but it died very, very hard."

"Was Dunroe under their influence when we saw her at the piano that night?" I asked.

"Undoubtedly. Already they had made her draw things she did not consciously understand; then, when they had roused her from her bed and guided her to the instrument, she played first a composition of beauty, for she is a good girl at heart, but they wished her to play something evil. No doubt the wicked, lecherous tune she played under their guidance that night helped mightily to make good, Godfearing Dunroe O'Shane forget herself and serve as heathen priestess before the heathen altar of a band of forsworn renegade priests."

"H'm," I murmured dubiously. "Granting your premises, I can see the logic of your conclusions, but how was it you put those terrible ghosts to flight so easily?"

"I waited for that question," he answered. "Have you not yet learned Jules de Grandin is a very clever fellow?

"Attend me, for what I say is worth hearing. When those evil men went forth in search of prey and killed the poor policeman, I said to me, 'Jules de Grandin, you have here a tough nut, indeed!'

"'I know it,' I reply.

"'Very well, then,' I ask me, 'who are these goblin child-stealers?'

"'Ghosts—or the evil representations of wicked men who died long years ago in mortal sin,' I return.

"'Now,' I say, 'you are sure these men are materialized by Mademoiselle O'Shane—her strange playing, her unwitting drawings. What, then, is such a materialization composed of?'

"'Of what some call ectoplasm, others psychoplasm,' I reply.

"'But certainly'—I will not give myself peace till I have talked this matter over completely—'but what is that psychoplasm, or ectoplasm? Tell me that?'

"And then, as I think, and think some more, I come to the conclusion it is but a very fine form of vibration given off by the medium, just as the ether-waves are given off by the broadcasting station. When it combines with the thin, unpowerful vibration set up by the evil entity to be materialized, it makes the outward seeming of a man—what we call a ghost.

"I decided to try a desperate experiment. A sprig of the Holy Thorn of Glastonbury may be efficacious as a charm, but charms are of no avail against an evil which is very old and very powerful. Nevertheless, I will try the Holy Thorn-bush. If it fail, I must have a second line of defense. What shall it be?

"Why not radium salt? Radium does wonderful things. In its presence non-conductors of electricity become conductors; Leyden jars cannot retain their charges of electricity in its presence. For why? Because of its tremendous vibration. If I uncover a bit of radium bromide from its lead box in that small, enclosed chapel, the terrific bombardment of the Alpha, Tau and Gamma rays it gives off as its atoms disintegrate will shiver those thin-vibration ghosts to nothingness even as the *Boche* shells crushed the forts of Liege!

"I think I have an idea—but I am not sure it will work. At any rate, it is worth trying. So, while Mademoiselle O'Shane lies unconscious under the influence of evil, I rush here with you, borrow a tiny little tube of radium bromide from the City Hospital, and make ready to fight the evil ones. Then, when we follow Mademoiselle Dunroe into that accursed chapel under the earth, I am ready to make the experiment.

"At the first door stands the boy, who was not so steeped in evil as his elders, and he succumbed to the Holy Thorn sprig. But once inside the chapel, I see we need something which will batter those evil spirits to shreds, so I unseal my tube of radium, and—*pouf!* I shake them to nothing in no time!"

"But won't they ever haunt the Cloisters again?" I persisted.

"*Ah bah*, have I not said I have destroyed them—utterly?" he demanded. "Let us speak of them no more."

And with a single prodigious gulp he emptied his goblet of brandy.